Penny Gillman
The Author

Penny is a Counsellor and Inner Child Therapist, as well as a Healer Member and Tutor with The Healing Trust. She lives happily in Essex with husband Michael and is the proud Mum of two wonderful adult sons and their growing families.

She has always written stories and poems and wrote her first novel with Wigapom as the central character when she was fourteen. He, like her, has grown up since then!

As an ex-primary and nursery teacher she was always aware of the power of storytelling in delivering a message and wanted to incorporate her spiritual and psychological understanding in this way, with the aim of appealing to the Child in every Adult and the Adult in every Child. She hopes she has achieved this in *The Wigapom Quest.*

She has a great love of all the creative arts, and in her spare time writes, sings, directs and performs in local musical theatre shows. She is at present writing her second novel.

For news and spiritual articles, plus a FREE Inner Child Meditation download, please visit:

www.pennygillman.com

the Wigapom
Quest

Penny Gillman

To Deborah

"So much of life isn't about having
the right answer; it's about
knowing the right question"

Duane Hewitt.

I hope this helps a bit in answering yours
about me!

Penny.

Matador
5 Weir Road
Kibworth Beauchamp
Leicester LE8 0LQ, UK
Tel: 0116 279 2277
Email: books@troubador.co.uk
Web: www.troubador.co.uk/matador

Cover design by Russell Gillman www.russellgillman.co.uk

All quotations are reproduced with their original spelling
and are correct to the best of the author's knowledge.

ISBN 978 184876 531 3

British Library Cataloguing in Publication Data.
A catalogue record for this book is available from the British Library.

Printed in the UK by MPG Biddles Kings Lynn

Matador is an imprint of Troubador Publishing Ltd

Acknowledgements and Dedication

Thanks to all at Matador for their help in making my dream a reality, and for being such a professional and helpful bunch of people.

Thanks to Tom Lucas and Valerie Hall for agreeing to read the manuscript and saying such complimentary things. Additional thanks go to Valerie for being my spiritual mentor for many years.

Thanks to my son Russell who, as well as designing the front cover, creating my web site and taking the mug shot of me, was the first person to read it and has been such a wonderful support throughout the whole process of writing by giving me constant encouragement, constructive criticism, advice and endless time and patience.

Thanks to my son, Lawrence, and to Lisa, and countless friends for their love, encouragement and interest throughout the process. I hope I have done you proud!

Thanks to my long-suffering husband, Michael, for putting up with years of me tapping away at the computer, lost in my own little world. He knows I won't ever stop writing, but at least knows the process now! I have always felt cherished by his quiet support and unwavering love.

Thanks to my inspirational Mum, whose love, support and connection with Wigapom go back to my childhood. I know she is proud of me and I am so glad that she will see both Wigapom and myself in print at last.

Thanks to Wigapom, who has grown and matured with me, and to the Universe for putting him there in the first place, and nurturing his progress.

Thanks to my dear Dad who, with his passing, was unwittingly instrumental in setting me firmly on my spiritual path and who is thus initially responsible for this book coming into being. I dedicate this book to his memory.

Finally, thank you for reading it.

"To conquer fear is the beginning of wisdom."
Bertrand Russell

PROLOGUE
'Evenio'

She was telling him things he did not want to hear, showing him things he did not want to see, changing her beautiful shape into something black and monstrous. Legs everywhere, eyes everywhere. He tried to avert his own eyes, both to block out the horrific images before him, and also escape her penetrating gaze but even with his eyes tightly closed the images trampled over his mind like a relentless army. Her long legs trampled over him, wrapping him in a fine silk thread that streamed from her body and imprisoned his own in a silken cocoon. He could not escape. Could never escape.

In his mind he asked her, 'Why does it have to be like this?' yet he couldn't bear to hear the answer, even from her. Especially from her. His mother. The Spider. He had trusted her to love him, protect him, yet the words and images she wove into his mind, and the web she was weaving around him, were destroying him. She was betraying him! No. He could see in her eyes she was not, but he wanted it all to stop. To go away. He had his own destiny, he knew that now but it was one he didn't want, and refused to acknowledge, he tried to fight against it, fight her. How could this happen to him, to them? He sobbed; he ranted; he pleaded; he screamed; yet the silk blocked out the sound and no one heard him, and no one came. Finally he succumbed to the inevitable: to her all-encompassing embrace that had wrapped itself around him like a shroud. He felt alone and frightened. Yet he wasn't alone. She was with him. She understood. She soothed him, telling him there was no other way and that this way had always been the way. To trust the process.

Part *1*

Self-Awareness

"We are made wise not by the recollection of our past, but by the responsibility for our future."
George Bernard Shaw

CHAPTER 1

Before The Beginning

"All souls must undergo transmigration . . . by being born into another body."
Jean Paul Richter

The soul was waiting to be born. He stood in the circle, along with the elders, and knew that it would soon be his time. He was keen to get started, having already chosen from amongst the higher selves around him, all those who would assist him on the journey to come. He acknowledged them all: those from his soul group who had agreed to be his birth parents, and who would give him so much of themselves; those who would raise him and provide him with necessary, early experiences from which the rest of his personality would come – he knew they cared for his progress too, each in their own way. Then there were those who would be the constants in his life, providing true friendship and love; or those who would come in, and out of his life, at various times, to help him on his way – he felt their love and compassion too. Then, lastly, there were those who would give him the greatest challenges in the life to come, the hardest lessons – his enemies – who would test him to the limit of his endurance. He knew that they loved him best of all, wanting him to be more than he had ever dreamed he could be. He was grateful to each of them for allowing him to grow even nearer to being the highest vision of himself and the source of all things.

'Look below you, and begin to understand,' said the elder closest to him. He looked down, and saw a scene unfolding: a fortified castle on an island, joined by a wind-whipped walkway to the shore, where powerful dark waves lashed at its base, and weary-eyed soldiers peered from battlements above, looking for any enemies threatening attack under cover of the approaching night.

'This is to be my place of birth?' he asked. The elder nodded, and allowed him to look inside one of the dimly lit upper rooms of the castle, where anxious, female faces surrounded a woman in a richly canopied bed.

3

'And here is the one soon to be your mother,' said a soft voice from his soul group.

The woman in the bed clutched tightly at the bedclothes as the painful pangs of childbirth increasingly took their hold; her perspiring brow soothed and cooled by a concerned, capable midwife.

'Nearly there, Your Majesty,' he heard the midwife intone kindly. 'Nearly there, just relax and breathe deeply now, it'll soon be time, you've just got to be patient.'

He saw her gently stroke a sweet-smelling compress across her mistress's brow: such a compassionate gesture, he thought, and his energy went out towards her. His future mother was now speaking: he could sense the distressed panic in her voice, and wondered why this should be.

'Where is my husband? Where is the King? Is he safe?' she was saying.

He noted that her long, chestnut hair was damp with sweat; that her brows were furrowing again.

'She is in pain!' he said to the elders, as he watched another contraction sweep over her. 'My birth is causing her pain!'

'Giving birth is a painful process,' was the reply.

'But a joyous one, also,' said the soft voice from his soul group. 'She will soon forget the agony, and remember only the ecstasy, when she holds you in her arms.'

The midwife below was looking concerned, but continued to offer placating words.

'Don't worry, Your Majesty,' he heard her say. 'He will be here soon, I'm sure.'

'Whom do they speak of?' he asked, unsure, yet, of the whole story unfolding below.

'Your father-to-be,' said another elder.

He watched the woman sink back on the sheets in fatigue and despair.

'She is very unhappy,' he said, and his energy and compassion poured towards her, keen to be with her.

'She has a beautiful soul,' replied the voice from his soul group.

His future mother *was* beautiful, even in the agonising throes of giving birth to him: he admired her rich, chestnut hair, curling in tendrils across the silk pillow, and the firm gaze of the clearest, purest, greenest eyes he had ever seen. He felt another sharp pull to be with her, but was told 'not yet,' and his attention was drawn to another scene unfolding below him.

He was back viewing the exterior of the fortified castle, which seemed to grow from the very rock on which it sat, towering and majestic, silhouetted against the dark of the sky, and emitting a penetrating feeling of gloom, as merciless ocean waves licked hungrily around it. Mournful, seagull cries were tossed, forlornly, on the air currents, like the sounds of those who had fallen on the blood-soaked battlefield that he was now being shown.

'What a terrible place! So much fear! Is my father–to-be here?' he asked, scanning the scene below him.

The elder drew his attention to the thick of the battlefield.

'Behold, the one you seek.'

He looked, and saw a tall, muscular man, astride a mud-spattered, yet magnificent, white horse. The figure wore no helmet to protect his head from the elements, or the missiles that flew around him – just a circlet of plain gold that shone defiantly in the fading light. His eyes were steely as he rallied his soldiers with encouraging cries to fight the dark oppressors.

'He is a brave and valiant man, but it seems the battle is lost to him,' he observed from above.

'There is your future adversary,' said a voice from those who loved him most. 'His soul has battled with many demons, in many lifetimes, but has chosen to assist your progress this time, rather than his own.'

'His soul must love me a great deal,' he mused, looking at the dark figure being pointed out to him, who, in contrast, was not an active participant in the bloody battle, but, instead, sat erect and aloof astride a huge, nightmare of a horse that, like every part of his army, was born from his necromancy.

'What cold eyes: black and without emotion,' he noted, 'and his army look terrifying – yet lost.'

'They are the Living Dead. Their souls are unable to return to us as yet. Their strength comes only from the Dark One for now.'

'My quest will not be easy then, but I am keen to begin,' he said, more aware now of what he had agreed to take on in this coming life.

He looked again at the Living Dead: their very presence oozing terror and coldness into the already chill day; featureless and expressionless, they were doing their master's bidding without question. It was clear that the Dark One was the true source of power in the land below, and there was no mistaking the evil that reigned there. It permeated everything with a black, poisonous fog, putrefying and deathly in its noxiousness.

'There is something else you must see before we continue,' said the elder at his side, as time slid backwards. He was being drawn through the walls of a beautiful building in the centre of a city, into a space of considerable size and grandeur, where he saw a white-haired wizard and black-clad sorcerer, locked in magical combat.

'That is the Dark One!' he said, pointing to the sorcerer. 'The one I have just seen on the battlefield! What are they fighting over?'

'*The Book of True Magic*,' came the reply, 'which holds the power of all wisdom. Both are struggling for supremacy of their way of life – the dark versus the light.'

'Who is the white-haired one?'

'Magus, the last wizard: he prepares your path to become the first Wizard of the New Age.'

'I don't understand…'

'Then watch, and learn.'

The wizard was lifting his crystal-tipped staff, from which shot beams of shimmering light that arched towards the streaks of lightning shooting from the sorcerer's fingertips. Some of the streaks seared the wizard's gown, yet his own arc of light knocked the book from the sorcerer's grasp. It fell open with a thud – its creamy pages spread-eagled on the floor, exposing the book's green spine, sparkling with seven coloured crystals. In an instant the wizard summoned the crystals with his staff, and they shot out of the spine like balls of light, and into the safety of the wizard's hand. More lightning strikes erupted from the sorcerer's fingers to surround the book. It singed at the edges, but did not burn, as it was drawn back, instantly, into his grasp.

'I have the book, Magus!' the sorcerer yelled. 'Your stones are nothing without it. You will never retrieve it, and neither will her unborn child – I will kill him first!'

The wizard opened his mouth to respond, but time had shot forward again and there, instead, was the beautiful woman with the chestnut hair, her face and body straining with the continued effort of giving birth.

'It is almost time for you to leave us,' said the elder. 'Are you ready for the journey?'

'I am,' came the straightforward reply, and his energy leapt to the scene below, keen to begin.

'So be it.'

He could hear the midwife speaking, more urgently now.

'The baby's coming! The baby's coming! Push, Your Majesty, push hard!'

At last it was time to go on his next big adventure: he was ready, and prepared for it. He felt himself pulled forward: first into a quiet, dark, yet comforting space, then, almost immediately, squeezed down into a narrow, slippery tunnel, with just a glimmer of light ahead, until, with a final push, he was swept out into a world of incomprehensible noise, dazzling bright light, and constant bustle.

He felt a short slap on his back, which made him cry out in surprise as he gulped his first breath of air, before experiencing kindly hands holding him aloft. Strange textures touched his new skin as he was wrapped against the cold of the day; blinding light hit his eyes, and he felt small, helpless and confused. Then, like a welcome homing beacon, he recognised the warm, sweet fragrance of his mother, as the bliss of her milk nursed him. He felt safe again, forgetting immediately and completely all that had gone before. He was now brand new again.

CHAPTER 2

Gone To Earth

". . . a small evil becomes a big one through being disregarded and repressed."
Carl Jung

'It's a boy, Your Majesty – a fine, healthy boy,' said the midwife, as she expertly delivered the tiny form, and wrapped him in a blanket against the cold of that dark, late February day. A lusty cry echoed around the room, a sound of hope, which allowed those few in attendance to momentarily lift their feelings of gloom, and smile at each other.

'A new Prince, Lord bless us,' said the midwife, as she laid the small bundle in the waiting arms of the weary new mother.

The woman in the bed sighed with happy exhaustion: her eyes soft and tender, as she looked at her son for the first time, nestling him to her breast, her green eyes shining with the sense of achievement common to all first-time mothers, but they also contained a sadness and resignation that those close to her understood.

'My son, our future – what a world in which to be born, my love. What a time to choose,' and she kissed him, gently, on his head.

She continued to suckle him, naturally responding to her maternal instincts, and wanting to experience, however briefly, the closeness and bonding that she craved, but which she knew she would soon have to relinquish. As his eager mouth sucked at her milk, such bitter-sweet feelings filled her: pleasure at feeding her child, yet devastation at knowing she had to give him up if she were to give him a chance of life, and the old kingdom of Arcanum any future hope of survival. She knew she would never see his smile, or hear his voice, or watch him grow; she would never feel the touch of his hand in hers as he rushed to show her something he had found; she would never tell him stories, or feel him cuddling up on her lap; never wipe his tears, or sooth a grazed knee. A warm tear slid down her cheek and landed on the baby's brow, trickling down the side of his face, now gazing up at her with wide-open eyes.

'There, there, Your Majesty! No tears on such a happy occasion!' jollied the midwife as best she could, knowing only too well what must be going on inside the Queen's mind. The Queen smiled a wan smile.

'You're right, Maya, but my joy is inevitably tinged with sadness,' and she tenderly wiped the tear away with her finger, making a sacred sign on his head as she did so, before softly whispering the special birth-name she had chosen for him under her breath. A name, she knew, he would never answer to with her, but which, in time, would help him understand who he was, and its relevance to his life, and the life of others.

Pushing back another tear from her eye, she held him, closer than ever, in a protective embrace; the delicate smell of his new skin mixing with the traditional aroma of silver fir needles, burned by the midwife, to bless and protect both mother and child. She wanted to hold onto this sensory moment forever, but knew that it was as transient as earthly life itself. As she suckled him she prayed, fervently, that there would be enough magic left to keep him safe from the countless, unknown harms that awaited him outside the sanctuary of this room, whilst trying to cram a lifetime of memories of her son into these few, precious moments: a vain hope! Her time with him was numbered. Another tear escaped from her eyes onto her new son, as she clung onto him in those last, precious moments of motherhood. How had it all gone so wrong? How, indeed? This question was in the minds of many that watched, and waited anxiously, for news of the King.

Maya, the midwife, was doing what she did best, grateful to be so busy: it helped, in times such as these, to deal with practical issues to block out painful emotions.

'Some lavender water and a few drops of neroli oil on the compress, Aimee, to relax Her Majesty. Come on, girl, don't dither!' she instructed, as her wide-eyed niece jumped to her bidding. Maya was a kind woman, skilled in her profession, and doing her best to focus on her beloved mistress. Yet try as she might, she could not blot out her wistful recollections of the old days of Arcanum: it had always been so peaceful, governed as it was, with care and kindness, by the Magi: the magicians and wizards of the True Magic, under the benevolent stewardship of the ancient lineage of kings – ah, such days! She refocused her thoughts as Aimee added the neroli oil.

'That's it, not too much. Now, stay with her Majesty while I wash his young Highness.'

With practised dexterity, she took the child from the Queen, and held him in the crook of her left arm, as she washed away the afterbirth, before wrapping him warmly in a fine woollen shawl. Then, satisfied that he was now properly presentable, she placed him, once more, into the waiting arms of the Queen, and allowed her thoughts to drift again: yes, the magical old kingdom, under King Orryen and Elvira, his Queen, had been a very wonderful place; there may have been a few minor disagreements on occasions, but, on the whole, life had been peaceful. Many different races living in harmony with each other and Mother Nature: Faerie folk, like herself, with their natural healing abilities, and deep understanding of the medicinal use of plants, lived, and worked, alongside dwarves, gnomes, trolls, elves, and the native Arcanese; each race sharing their talents for the benefit of all: the mining and metallurgy skills of the dwarves; the green-fingered skill and animal husbandry of the gnomes; the intelligence and creativity of the Arcanese; the physical strength and kind nature of the trolls, and the gentleness and wisdom of the elves – all had their place in the greater scheme of things, all brought their unique, mystical or mainstream characteristics to blend, in harmony, together. They were good times indeed, until the Shadow overtook them! She shuddered, and brought her thoughts back to the present.

'There you are, Your Majesty,' she soothed, her voice as gentle as her hands. 'Just rest now with your son. Let us do the work for the moment – you've done enough!'

What love she had for this beautiful woman with the heart of gold! She remembered the arrival of the elven princess, and her court, as if it were yesterday! There was such excitement at the visit – such colour and spectacle to behold! Such radiance and spiritual grace shining from the princess's lovely face! Such promise of a gloriously happy future! If only they had known, then, what monster this visit would unleash, they would have been better prepared, but then, nothing could have prepared them for the terror now riding, rampant, across the land. She shuddered involuntarily, and dipped a piece of fresh cloth into the mix of lavender and neroli, before carefully wringing it out, and replacing it, tenderly, on the new mother's brow: lavender for relaxation; neroli for soothing the nervous system – in these troubled, stressful times these essences would have to work so much harder. Maya sighed. How different it had once been: then it had been a magical place in every way.

Asgar, the young apprentice, working with the last High Wizard, Magus, in the South tower of the castle, was thinking about magic too, as he cleared phials of coloured liquid from the scrubbed-oak table in his master's workroom. Not about sorcery and necromancy, which were now contaminating the land, but real magic, that benefited all, and which he had been studiously learning to use before the troubles arose. Now, they were more than troubles; indeed the old ways of life were fighting for survival, and his lessons had to make way for more urgent matters; but he was still learning, albeit in different ways, and his devotion to Magus and the sovereign's family was without question, yet he needed to keep reminding himself of what he already knew about magic, in preparation for the longed-for day when the newly-born young Prince would grow to fulfil his destiny, and rid the land of the evil that reigned here now.

As Asgar replaced the phials back on the carefully ordered shelves, full of powders, potions, and other magical paraphernalia, he reminded himself, again, of the definitions of magic, taught to him by his revered teacher, Magus. He could almost hear his Master testing him.

'Magic is there to benefit every part of life, Asgar – it is the light that illuminates all. There are three main types,' he would say, 'now, let me see if you have learned well. Tell me about Low Magic first, as this is the most common and familiar.'

Asgar was indeed familiar with this form of magic, having been brought up, like his parents and their parents before them, as a student of the magic 'Schola'. Here they studied magic words, philosophies, formulae and spells, which together formed the foundation stones of the Arcanum civilisation. How delighted and proud they were when he was chosen as apprentice to the great Magus himself, to further his understanding and education! He did not know if he would ever attain the elevated status of Wizard, for this took great wisdom to achieve, but he would be proud to become a Magician, and he was now pleased to demonstrate his growing knowledge to Magus.

'Low Magic, Master, is the use of potions, powders and positive spells to benefit everyone. It can be used to heal a cut finger, or maybe move a heavy object, or … create a magnificent firework display!' he finished, his eyes shining meaningfully.

Magus had laughed then, at his student's youthful enthusiasm.

'I see you have a good memory!' he said.

'How could I ever forget your most wonderful firework display in celebration of Princess Elvira's arrival! It was the most marvellous event from my childhood!' came the bright reply.

His master had beamed with delight.

'Yes, I believe I excelled even myself on that occasion!' he acknowledged.

Magus had had such a twinkle in his blue eyes then: now they were worried and anxious. Asgar hated to see the change the troubles had made to him. He wanted him back the way he was.

'Don't forget,' Magus had said, 'Low Magic can also be used to take a person from one place to another, sometimes by flying, or even by thought alone!'

'Both in sleep or waking,' had been Asgar's quick reply.

Asgar had been in the middle of learning about such astral travel when the troubles began, and his formal education had ceased. He was fortunate enough to still be working with Magus, learning all he could, by watching and listening. Magus was a good teacher, and Asgar a quick learner.

'And what of High Magic, my keen student,' Magus would then ask.

Asgar knew this answer well, and was always keen to demonstrate his knowledge.

'High Magic is the study of the zodiacal year, the positions of the stars and planets and how they affect lives and events,' he said with pride.

'Quite right! And don't forget alchemy, where we experiment with the blending of elements to create the magic and science of change and transformation. That too, is part of High Magic.'

'I will remember,' Asgar had said, earnestly.

'But now, what do you understand of the True Magic?' Magus had said, in a reverential voice, testing Asgar to the full.

Here, Asgar had floundered a little. He knew that True Magic was the most important one of them all, mastery of which created Wizards, as opposed to the lower order of Magicians, but he was still very much a novice, as it took much longer to master; it was something that had to be understood at a much deeper level. He was working hard at it but some aspects still eluded him. One day, maybe he would be as wise as his revered teacher: however, he had answered with what he knew.

'True Magic has the ability to turn the power of knowledge into the grace of wisdom,' he said, pleased with his definition, and Magus' positive response. 'It allows us to truly know ourselves.'

'You're doing well, Asgar; we'll make a Magician of you yet – maybe even a Wizard! Remember Asgar, all forms of magic are valuable in their own way and can be learned and used by anyone who chooses to understand them. Magic means hidden wisdom; hence the root of wizard, and this wisdom has been handed down, to those ready to receive it, through generations, to use, always, for the highest good. It is the essence of Oneness.'

Ah yes, the concept of Oneness – the understanding that everything and everyone is connected, like the facets on a cut diamond. Asgar knew that the True Magic of Oneness was an esoteric code to live by, achieved not only by gaining knowledge, but transforming that knowledge into true wisdom, which Magus told him was the ability to understand one's own true self and acknowledge it as part of the greater One; this he was just beginning to understand.

The wisdom of transcending the Self, however, Asgar found more difficult to understand, but liked to think that one day, he too would have mastery of it, so he could spread the message of unconditional love, forgiveness and compassion to others. He would have to overcome his negative feelings towards the Dark One to achieve this. This thought brought him back to the present, for his path to wisdom had been blocked by this same Dark One, a former High Magician, who had used his extensive knowledge of Low and High Magic and abused them by creating evil necromancy and sorcery, thus blocking out True Magic, and weakening the others. A climate of fear now permeated every level of society – every race, every creature – which the newborn Prince would one day have to challenge for the benefit of all. Asgar hoped to be able to help him in some way in the future, but that seemed a long way off right now.

Dugard, the sentry at the castle gate, watched the wooden walkway connecting the castle to the mainland vigilantly, but with increasingly tired eyes, for any sign of the King. He too was thinking hard about the Dark One, as he was referred to now: folk fearing that the use of his real name would bring even more bad energy onto them. Superstition, it seemed, had arisen as an ugly bedfellow to suspicion and fear!

The weary guard shifted his weight from one aching foot to another, remembering those days before the troubles began, when the King and his white knights would give displays of various chivalric skills for the pleasure and entertainment of the populace: chivalry, but never war; entertainment and skill, never aggression. Such wonderful days! Such camaraderie! It was hard to believe that the Dark One had once been one of those white knights. Now, many of the white knights had been slain, but were refused the peace of death by him. They now formed the Haideez – evil fighters and bodyguards of the Dark One and part of his army of the Living Dead. Dugard shivered in the cold air as he thought of them. Their role was to not only protect the Dark One, but supervise the skeleton, ghoul and zombie battalions, all created from those poor civilians or soldiers, many of them Dugard's friends, whose lives had been brutally taken in battle, and were now condemned to roam the earth forever in the service of evil. He prayed, inwardly, that he would never become a member of that dead army: that one day he would be able to retire to a life as a fisherman, and live out his life in peace.

Dugard had been in the service of the King since boyhood, and witnessed much, but he could still barely believe that the Dark One, who had once found such favour with the King, could have betrayed him, and all of Arcanum, so terribly. He had once been a bright and shining star of knighthood, a possessor of great intellectual gifts, personal charm, and true magical potential – a fact spotted early by Magus and the other Magi, who had invited him, at an unusually young age, to join their magical elite. Dugard had been present at his induction ceremony, and remembered it well. He racked his brain for when things had begun to change: it had been so subtle, no one had noticed it happening until it was too late, but now, with the benefit of hindsight, Dugard could see that it had started when the elven princess had visited with her court.

Femina, as lady-in-waiting to the Queen, always did the best she could to keep her hands and fingers occupied these days, in a futile attempt to quell her fearful thoughts. Today, her fingers flew over the cloth she was embroidering with a skill that came from a lifetime's experience of such delicate work. She may have given the appearance of diligent calmness as she sat at her embroidery by the side of the Queen, but her thoughts were not on her work, and they were anything but calm. They raced between her immediate concerns for her mistress, and the new Prince, to her increasing fears about the future. Even now, she could barely understand how it had all happened in the first place, and under their very noses!

It was hard enough these days not to feel laden down with thoughts of 'what if' and 'if only' and these were articulated silently in her mind on this day of great magnitude: 'What if the elven princess had never visited Arcanum?' or 'If only she had not fallen in love with the King.' What would their lives be like now?

Her fingers worked faster as she reflected deeply on this. Would they still be living in peaceful harmony, going about their daily lives as they had for aeons? Or would this state of affairs have happened in some other way? What would become of them all? There were never any answers, only more questions, but she could not, and would not, place any blame on the Queen or King: to fall in love is a wonderful thing, and deserves a lifetime of happiness, not misery – she blamed everything on the Dark One, or Darqu'on, as she had once known him. Her mouth pursed at the thought of him, and furrows crept across her brow – she may be anxious for the future, but she was brave enough to name him in her mind.

When she had travelled with Princess Elvira from the elven land of Immortalia, they had all been full of such excitement. The visit was an opportunity to share knowledge, wisdom, and magical ideas – but amongst the young ladies-in-waiting, the talk had all been about the dashing young King!

'I hear he is very handsome.'

'And very gallant.'

'With a truly masculine figure.'

'Ladies! We are here to forge bonds between our races, not discuss the physical attributes of the King,' laughed Elvira.

'But how much more pleasant to forge bonds with someone who is young, good looking… and single!' giggled Femina.

If only they had all known then what penalty they would pay for those forged bonds!

Femina hoped no one else noticed the wet stain of a teardrop on her embroidery, but it was hard, especially now, with the birth of the much-awaited Prince, not to succumb to tears. She admitted to herself that she was prone to sentimentality, yet, at first, the tears had been of joy. It had been evident from their first meeting, how attracted King Orryen had been to Princess Elvira; how their eyes had shone when they met each others gaze; how they took such pleasure in each other's company, like two parts of a whole coming together in perfect symmetry. It had been a fairytale, with the whole court wrapped up in the love story playing out before them. So wrapped up in fact that no notice was paid to the King's friend and newest Magi, Darqu'on, and his feelings for Elvira: at least not until it was too late. He had become infatuated with Elvira's beauty and grace, and believed himself in love with her, yet it was a possessive, jealous love to trap her in, rather than one to liberate her spirit, and it was unreturned. Although she was never unkind to him, Elvira had eyes for no one but King Orryen.

For Darqu'on, this rejection had touched deep, dark places inside him, bringing pain and hurt up from his past: a pain he could never forget, or forgive. Femina did not know the full reason for this – not even the King knew about Darqu'on's life before he arrived suddenly in Arcanum, as a young boy. Whatever secrets lay behind his behaviour, Darqu'on had begun to seek revenge for his perceived rejection, to take everything that belonged to the King, especially his wife, Elvira, and his power. To do this he began to misuse his magical abilities; to hurt, harm and attack. Fed by jealousy and envy, which quickly turned to hate and revenge for all, he created the dark arts of sorcery and necromancy.

15

By the time of the royal marriage, emotions never before experienced in Arcanum were slowly being given life, spreading and multiplying into the kingdom, like cancer cells through a body, and when Elvira become pregnant with her husband's child, the situation had worsened to the extent that no one could ignore it any longer, and only then realised how their previously luminous way of life had been so overtaken by the darkness of Darqu'on's Shadow.

'And we were all so blind to this!' muttered Femina under her breath, losing her concentration momentarily, and pricking her finger on the needle. A tiny spot of blood stained the work she was doing: she noted the symbolism of bloodshed on a thing of beauty, and how synonymous it was with what was happening in Arcanum, yet she tried to quell her fear and lift her hopes, praying that it only referred to the past and present and not the future. Yet she, like many others, could not see the part they had played in this sorry tale, and continued to blame Darqu'on for it all. It was easier to make him responsible for everything than admit any personal culpability.

Aimee, the young wet nurse, hovered anxiously, close to the bed, pretending to watch Maya but, in truth, she had eyes only for the child: she was aching to nurse him in her own arms. Since the recent, tragic loss of her own baby, she had a chasm in her maternal heart that nothing but another child to cherish could fill. She didn't have the confidence to take him too soon, even though she knew she would eventually be his temporary carer.

She felt sorry for the young Queen, knowing only too well the pain of losing a child. The circumstances of her own loss brought hot tears stabbing like burning needles into her eyes. She fought them back as best she could, but it made her determined not to let another new life be snuffed out, if she could help it. The baby had to be got to safety – away from the clutches of Darqu'on, who, in his twisted mind, had sworn to kill him. The nursemaid could barely comprehend such evil. How could anyone want to willingly kill an innocent child? Her own child had been stillborn, but this child had a sacrificial price already on his head, and he was barely an hour old. He was so beautiful, lying there peacefully in his mother's arms. Oh, how she wished they were her arms! She longed to wrap them around him, to hold him, and protect him, at least for as long as it took to take him to the place of safety that she knew had been arranged. She was not party to that information, however: too many spies around, maybe even in the Castle on the Crag! What sort of world was it, with neighbour suspicious of neighbour? The world had truly gone mad!

The old kingdom of Arcanum had become unrecognisable, wherever she went; even in her home village of Nepton-by-Sea, just across the bay from the castle: Suspicion, fear, anger, and any number of negative emotions had arisen, as her mother had said 'like leviathans', emerging from the turgid, emotional waters created by the Dark One's evilness, and bitten deep into the lives and souls of them all.

Aimee had seen the tragic effects of this in her own family. Her impressionable younger brother had allowed his head to be turned by the dark side. Small things at first: cursing; stealing; getting into bad company; then dabbling in sorcery himself, to commit terrible deeds, fuelled by increasing anger, resentment and greed. Their father had tried to remonstrate with him, but his youngest son had lashed out in such blind rage and bitterness that he had fatally wounded his father in his frenzied attack. Aimee's husband had jumped in to defend his father-in-law, and a terrible fight ensued. Aimee, ignoring her own safety and that of her unborn child, had struggled to separate them and become caught in the crossfire of blows herself, one of which mortally wounded her husband and sent her sprawling. The fall, coupled with the shock of losing those she loved, had brought on the stillbirth, so close to term.

Her child had never drawn breath, dying there, in her womb, as though declaring it wanted no part in this world of hate and revenge. She still had to go through the agony of birth: but without the joy of a living child at the end. With the loss of her father and husband at the hand of her brother it might have seemed a small casualty out of so many, but it was to have an everlasting impact.

As she mentally re-lived her own tragedy, her breasts strained under the surge of unused milk, as though equally desperate to nurture the baby before her: she was meant to be a mother. She hoped that the King would return soon so that she could begin the task she felt she had been born to fulfil.

The coachman, Swift by name and swift by nature, paced impatiently up and down in the stables; his short, squat stature indicating his proud gnomic lineage, but belying amazing physical strength, as well as mental resolve. He was keen to get going: the carriage was ready, his fastest horse harnessed to it – he just awaited the call.

As he paced, he thought of how many of his own gentle race had changed for the worse under the shadow of the Dark One's sorcery; how many had morphed into evil goblins under the influence of his Shadow, and even now were waging vicious battles against their one time cousins, the dwarves, tragically besmirching the once noble name of the gnomic race.

Swift stopped pacing, momentarily, to stroke the horse's muzzle with his caring hand. He loved all animals: they were less complicated souls than their two legged companions – always loving and loyal – that was why he loved them, he supposed. All his life he had looked after them. He was the first on the scene if an animal was in need. His powers of animal healing were beyond reproach, yet the race of gnomes was now forever sullied by the renegade goblins springing from them! The coachman did his best not to be bitter and twisted: he did not want to become like them! He did his best to channel any anger he might feel into positive ways: hence his volunteering for the job of taking the young Prince to safety. He knew he could get the best speed from the horse because it would be given with love by the animal, and received similarly by him. Like the horse, he could outrun anyone; now it seemed he might have to out-fight, too, if he was to get the child to safety. His jaw strengthened with resolve: he would do it if he had to.

The King was coming home! Battle wearied and scarred, yes, but Orryen found an inner reserve of strength and hope as he rode his mud-spattered horse back towards the Castle on the Crag, along with the few knights he had left. The loss of so many of his friends and colleagues brought such a weight of sadness to his already burdened heart that he felt he would drown in sorrow: each knight lost had been a fine example of all that was honourable and good, in a world now increasingly bereft of this quality. How ironic that those brave souls who had given their lives for the power of good were now trapped in enforced membership of Darqu'on's army. But the knight he still mourned most of all was Darqu'on himself: they had been such friends; like brothers. From the moment his father, the King, had found the poor, sickly boy lying hungry and ragged by the palace walls and taken him in, he had been accepted as a member of the family. How Darqu'on had flourished in this environment! He had been such a good companion: intelligent, witty, amusing, and bright. He had everything, until everything changed. Even before he stole *The Book of True Magic* he had become totally unrecognisable; he thrived on the fear and chaos he created and used every evil act to spread it further and further afield. He had forced Orryen and his court into exile, and by using his malevolent powers of sorcery and the other dark arts, had cast the Shadow over the land that was still increasing, day-by-day. Then later, without *The Book of*

True Magic to guide his hand, Orryen had begun to lose support from all but those closest to him, and was forced to fight instead, with whatever weapons and troops he could muster, in an effort to fight like with like. Yet the sorcery became even more powerful, and Orryen knew, in his heart, that it was a battle that could never be won by force: the very act of defensive fighting seemed to create more fear, and thus more evil, for it to feed from.

As he and his remaining knights turned into the forest, all of which had once been called enchanted, but now looked increasingly dark and forbidding, a shape loomed towards them. Orryen's horse reared as he raised his sword in defence.

'My Lord,' gasped the shape before him. 'I bring good news! You have a son!' It was Tomas, the outrider, hot with sweat, but with his eyes shining at the tidings he delivered.

'A son! I have a son!' exclaimed Orryen as his knights congratulated him, and together they and Tomas galloped back to the castle with hope in their hearts for the future.

Magus, the last Wizard, and chief Magi, pushed back his long, white hair with sensitive fingers before scrying into his divination bowl for what seemed the thousandth time that day: still nothing, no sign, but there would have to be soon, or the child would have to be taken to safety without his father's personal blessing: not a good portent for the future. Both the King and Magus knew that the only hope lay in the young Prince surviving to manhood to fulfil his destiny by restoring *The Book of True Magic* to its rightful place and thus ridding the land of Darqu'on's Shadow. With some of what remained of the fading magic, Magus had created a 'hidden village' beyond the reach of Darqu'on, and it was here that the baby must now be taken until he was old enough to leave its safety and fulfil his destiny.

In the sanctity of his wizard's cell, Magus had transformed the crystals he had salvaged from the book into coloured stones, each one containing one the seven elements of the True Magic – the wisdom of self awareness. These would only reveal themselves to the young Prince when he showed, by his thoughts, feelings and actions, his readiness to receive them. Magus knew this was a major task to undertake, with no certainty of success. So much depended on the character and personality of the young Prince. He knew that if the boy turned out to be a sluggard, or weak-willed, or even too burdened by what he had to endure in life, then none of this would happen, and Darqu'on would reign supreme. The consequences of this were unthinkable, and Magus refused to even contemplate them, trusting the higher process as much as his concern would allow. Yet there was still no word from the King: would he not return to bless his only son and heir? These were anxious times indeed. No one knew if the King had even survived to be able to greet his infant son, and time, precious time, was passing fast.

Magus found it hard to quell his concern as he wrapped his cloak around his bony frame, against the increasing chill of the castle, and once more peered into his divination bowl for news of the King's whereabouts. Had the outrider's message of the birth reached him? Was he safe? Again he saw just thick, grey mist swirling haphazardly around the bowl, obscuring all else from his vision.

'Anything yet, my Lord?' questioned Asgar, hopefully.

'Nothing, nothing at all,' replied Magus, his white eyebrows furrowing together in concern. 'There is much stronger sorcery at work here than we have previously known – our own magic is weakening beyond endurance. Who knows whether we can ever dissolve the forces of the Dark One? Time will tell, as always, but with no news of the King it seems increasingly desperate.'

'But we must have hope, my Lord,' replied Asgar, his eyes shining like beacons in the darkened room.

'Indeed we must, Asgar, for hope may be all we have left,' said Magus, as he turned to cast a glimmer of a smile at his pupil. 'And if one day I am unable to play my part in the young Prince's destiny, you will be my hope to do so.'

Asgar held himself erect.

'It will be an honour, my Lord,' he said.

Magus acknowledged his apprentice's dedication, but still felt concern over the future. Yet he must have the hope he spoke of: they were nothing without it. He turned to the divination bowl once more, but his heart was elsewhere. Hope. He had been hoping for so long, as had they all, and he had seen each hope dashed on the rocks of despair: hope that Darqu'on could be defeated, hope that he might even see the error of his ways: all had proved futile. Magus believed the weight of responsibility was his for much of what had happened, no matter what others said to the contrary. He blamed himself, blinkered as he had been, by pride in his most promising protégé, Darqu'on: he had loved him as the son he never had. But more than that, he had bathed in his glory – allowing his ego to overcome his wisdom. Such foolishness – especially from a wizard! How stupid he had been in trusting Darqu'on. How full of his own importance, not to see what was happening in front of his eyes. He berated himself over and over again for this. How could he not have seen the signs? Too blinded by the genius of his student; too sucked into the limitations of his own ego and pride to notice, or want to notice, what was happening, until it was too late?

He had taught Darqu'on all he knew, and had refused completely to acknowledge how his student had been misusing the powers and knowledge bestowed upon him with such dedication. He had seen his growing obsession with the Queen, yet had ignored it, not believing that Darqu'on could turn from the light to the dark. How fatuous! How blind! Darqu'on had betrayed Magus' love and fellowship and Magus felt that by ignoring the problem, he had betrayed his calling, and the other magicians and wizards of the Magi, who, all but he, were now trapped in the living death of Darqu'on's army. This was the bitterest blow of all, and one which he believed he would never totally overcome. Others told him not to blame himself, that they were all, in some way, responsible for Darqu'on's terrible rise to power.

'Our complacency and pride let the darkness of the Shadow in, Magus. None of us are without fault in this,' the King had said.

Magus had tried to see it that way as best he could, but he knew he would carry the burden of the guilt with him forever. But no matter now: what was done was done. The dark energy created by Darqu'on's jealousy, anger and hatred, crept like a noxious poison into the very fabric of society, and had to be vanquished before the ways of light, encapsulated in this tiny child, could return. Magus' chosen duty was to see that he arrived safely, and secretly, at the already prepared hidden village. It was the only way he felt he could begin to make amends for his behaviour.

'Is all ready for the journey, Asgar?' he asked, anxiety beginning to colour his tone.

'Yes, Master, all is in place,' said Asgar, tapping the important red cloth package lying on top of the bench, as if waiting for its moment.

'Good,' he replied, yet he felt increasingly uneasy. 'Where is the King? Will he not return in time?' he asked rhetorically, refusing to acknowledge the possibility that he might not return at all.

Magus had an even deeper question to wrestle with, however, which he kept to himself: would the dark energy always remain more powerful than the light? If that were so then, no matter what happened, they were doomed. This thought had snapped at Magus' heels like a sharp-toothed dragon on many occasions, refusing to go away. He didn't want to believe it; he couldn't: Light had to be stronger than the dark, it just had to be – yet why had this all happened? Was it a lesson for them all to learn? If so, it was proving to be a very hard one. A deeply philosophical part of him wondered, at times, whether the Shadow was part of the light in a way that he, as a mere humble being, could never fully understand. Perhaps it was present to give challenges, and opportunities for growth? Maybe Darqu'on's arrival and prominence had a higher purpose than Magus could understand? He wanted to believe it so, to believe that under all this chaos, there *was* a higher order working for the good of all, and that it was all part of the process of life. He sighed, not for the first time, as these thoughts came, and went, like the relentless tide ebbing and flowing around the Castle on the Crag.

As Magus continued to look for the King's whereabouts in the shiny black bowl, made of the protective crystal, haematite he did his best to remember the lesson the crystal taught – that all perceived limitations are of our own making – but instead it just reminded him, again, how truly dazzled he had been by Darqu'on's brilliant mind, and his amazing ability to see possibilities that no other trainee magician or wizard of the Magi had ever seen. How sad that he had used that brilliance to create such means of death and terror. Magus began to list them in his head: first, the spectral Roth-Riders on their fiendish nightmare steeds, bringing dread, terror, and often death, to any innocent being who had the misfortune to come upon them. Then the Wulverines, the hounds of hell, whose fangs dripped with poison and whose glowing, red eyes stupefied their prey as they howled and prowled their way through the forests in large, vicious packs. Then the Ghouls – savage creatures with sharp teeth and nails, and sickly green skin that dripped from their bodies like slimy mucous, who, with the Skeletons and Zombies, were all part of the Living Dead army. If this were not enough Darqu'on had also raised from the pages of mythology such ancient creatures as the Basilisk who, with one look, would turn the observer to stone; he had reincarnated the female night-demon Lilitu, who brought pestilence and disease on the wind and thrived on the blood of innocents, and, with his devilish sorcery, brought to life one he termed the 'Hybrid', a monstrous, three-headed mix of reptile and bird that scavenged for unsuspecting travellers.

Darqu'on could also use his sorcery to shape-shift into any of these creatures at will, even elements, such as wind, and fire: causing destruction, terror and chaos to an already troubled and fearful land, for no one knew when he was in their midst. Magus knew that much of Darqu'on's twisted pleasure came from creating fear and uncertainty, and he fed on the power it brought. Darqu'on's creations challenged the world of light's own magical creatures, such as the fabled white hart, the sacred phoenix and mystical unicorn, to the point of extinction. It would take an infusion of pure light energy to redress the balance: a Lightbearer. This was the weight of responsibility now invested in the baby that lay contentedly, and unsuspectingly, in his mother's arms.

Magus drew his mind back from reflecting on the past, and endeavoured, at least, to see the present, if not the future, through the still-impenetrable mist in his divination bowl. Still nothing. He sighed, and made a sacred symbol in the air with his crystal-tipped staff, before affirming with all his strength and resolve that the King was safe and would return soon.

'The King is safe, all is well, the King is safe, all is well.'

He chanted with an urgency that he had never experienced before, and with such pure intent that the energy of the words vibrated in the air around him with a golden glow for those that could see.

Perhaps it was the intensity of the moment that caused the mist in the bowl to clear and hazy images to be observed, or perhaps it was because the King was already riding across the walkway joining the mainland to the castle, but suddenly there were images of knights slain on the battlefield, their torn and trampled tabards bearing the entwined emblems of both the phoenix of the King and the unicorn of the Queen. Above them the black and gold serpent and lightning ensigns of Darqu'on waved victoriously against the torrid sky. Finally he saw an image of an exhausted, but still determined King, defiantly galloping at speed across the now open drawbridge into the castle courtyard. Magus breathed a sigh of relief.

'He's here at last, Asgar! Go and greet him. Tell him I will meet him at the birthing chamber, but hurry,' and he sent Asgar scurrying down the tower steps as he looked deeper into the bowl. His prayers had been answered: for now, at least. He watched carefully as the mist formed, and then cleared again, giving him a glimpse of the compact village of Brakendor, part of Arcanum, but because of the invisible shield Magus had created around it in preparation for this day, a world away from the troubles. The Prince could safely grow to manhood here. It was not perfect, but it was full of good, ordinary folk determined to maintain that goodness and decency with a true sense of community and care for each other. Parochial? Perhaps, but all to the good. He saw the image of the still unsuspecting baker and his wife, in their snug white-washed bakery, near a brook sparkling from reflected light; he saw the deep forest that created a natural barrier between the village and the rest of the kingdom, and knew that he had chosen well. Now it must receive its newest and most important inhabitant, and a final input of protective energy to seal it from prying eyes. No one there, apart from the baker and his wife, would ever know any of this had ever happened.

23

There was no time to waste: carefully picking up the cloth package containing the seven differently coloured stones from the bench, Magus placed the package purposefully in the deep pocket of his gown and, retrieving his staff from the chair, went at last to meet the King.

There was the sound of voices outside the birthing room: male voices, urgent and concerned – one specifically, giving orders and directions in a tired, yet resolute way.

'Call all members of the court here who can be spared, and see that Swift is ready. Come Magus, it is time.'

The door opened, and in walked the King, followed by Magus and Asgar. All in the room bowed low, but the King urged them to rise.

'We are all equal here,' he said, his sweat-streaked face, fresh wounds and stained garments showing signs of the severity of his recent unsuccessful battle.

He walked, however, with purposeful strides into the room and, as he knelt by the bedside of his beloved wife, tenderly laid a loving hand on her forehead, and kissed her softly.

'Well done, my love, well done,' he murmured, as he took a long look at his infant son and heir, knowing only too well that this moment would have to last for a lifetime in his memory.

The perfect features of his son's face temporarily gladdened his battle-weary heart: the child's eyes were open and curious already it seemed; tiny, soft fingers curling around his battle-hardened ones; a crop of unruly brown hair already crowning his perfectly-shaped head. The King could not help but smile tenderly at the child: despite all that he had just experienced in the battle, such innocence and purity enshrined in this new and precious child washed away those devastating scenes. Gently he lifted him from his mother's delicate arms and cradled him in his own strong ones before addressing the assembled company, some of whom were quietly weeping at the emotion and pathos of the moment.

'This is my beloved son. I present him to you now as my rightful heir. New hope has been born today. He will always be our joy. He is the future of our land, which is suffering such trials at this time, and I thus ask a blessing on his life that he may grow in strength, honour and courage, and one day, through his own choice, restore the True Magic to the land that we love, and hold so dear. It is our deep sorrow that he has to leave us now, and not know his heritage until the time is right, but we put our trust in a higher authority for his safety and his progress. Swear now, all of you, trusted friends, to speak no more of this, but hold it silently in your hearts and minds until the silence is safe to be broken again.'

There was a soft murmur of assent around the room as, with a final tender kiss on the child's head, King Orryen and Queen Elvira said goodbye to their only son and passed him, at last, into the trusted care of Aimee, who, with Magus leading the way, hurried out of the castle towards the stables, where Swift was waiting, and all began to play their vital part in the next stage of the Prince's life.

And so began his first dangerous journey, wrapped in Aimee's arms against the cold of the moonless night, leaving his mother weeping silently into her pillow.

CHAPTER 3

The Journey Begins

"The shadow is very much a part of human nature,
and it is only at night that no shadows exist."
Carl Jung

Cold night air; the darkness and warmth of a soft cloak; the sound of feet on gravel, of wheels creaking, and a horse whinnying; warm breath spiralling into the air; the jolt of a carriage as wheels rolled over gravel, moving at speed, yet silently as possible. Thankful for the good fortune of a moonless night to hide them, and praying for safe passage across the land, the travelling party journeyed far away from the harsh, majestic scenery of the northerly castle, towards the softer, gentler hills and valleys of the south, where the hidden village lay. Here Magus could leave the child with peaceful folk living peaceful lives. Magus' crystal staff was the only point of light in the carriage and gave some comfort to Aimee, who gazed with reverential tenderness as the baby nursed in her arms.

The carriage, expertly driven by Swift, passed at speed along the rugged coastal route, through inhospitable wasteland and into mountains, where narrow tracks weaved precariously around and through still snow-encrusted peaks.

Nights turned into days, and back into nights. They left the mountains and swept through open valleys of moorland and scrub, into woods and copses of bare trees. Each day brought a new challenge: freezing snow, drenching, icy rain, hard, bitter frost, the carriage enduring ice and mud in equal measure, as the season threw everything it had at them: they endured it all as each day brought them closer to the longed for end of their journey.

Gradually, softer hills became their terrain, with wide rivers meandering through fields. The wind dropped; the temperature felt milder, and even hazy sunshine peeked occasionally from behind grey clouds, as though unsure of the welcome it might receive so early in the year. Although they tended to avoid any route that would take them too near a town, or even a village, the south of the Kingdom opened her arms to greet them, and Swift and Aimee at least felt heartened that their journey was drawing to a close with no physical sign of Darqu'on or any of his creations being seen. He may have been in the harsh elements, but they had braved those, and Aimee at least, began to relax and truly enjoy her young charge. But whilst she enveloped herself in surrogate motherhood, Magus remained tense: he had learned to be wary of the unexpected. He insisted Aimee and the baby keep inside the carriage, hidden from view, and advised Swift to stick to the less travelled roads, where possible. He continued to look frequently into his divination bowl, watching for any sign of Darqu'on's presence, or evidence that he was following their progress, but there had been nothing appearing at all, apart from swirling, opaque mist, yet, tired as he was, he refused to relax: he knew better than to underestimate his former pupil, and the feeling that they were being allowed to travel without major problems niggled at him. He found this more unsettling than if he had been face to face with an actual threat. But the further they travelled, the more tired he became and, against his better judgement, but in response to his travel weariness and constant, exhausting state of alertness, he began to unknowingly relax his guard.

They were drawing close to their destination and, apart from rare rests for food and water, the hard-working horse had been moving almost non-stop; now he needed to rest more frequently and Swift indicated a suitable spot ahead of them that could provide what they needed. A wide river glistened in the early morning, close to grass sparkling with dew. There was good tree cover, and even some weak sunshine trying to break through the clouds at times. It looked safe enough, almost peaceful; they would have to take a chance, however risky it might be. They all needed to stretch their legs and rest from the constant motion of the carriage. Magus, his sharp eyes darting like a hawk for any danger, helped Aimee, who was carrying the baby, alight from the carriage. He would fight if he had to, but he could still use some of the remaining reserve of magic in the crystal staff, as long as he left enough to reseal Brakendor.

Swift unharnessed the horse from the carriage, leading him to the river to drink, just as the sky began to darken. A strong wind whipped through the trees and across the water from nowhere, noisily shaking the branches. An accompanying low rumble echoed throatily around them, like an impatient growl. They had experienced storms already on their journey – it was that time of year – but it had seemed calm enough just a moment ago. Magus glanced apprehensively at the sky, a glimmer of unease registering in his eyes. Perhaps they should have remained in the carriage in case this was more than seasonal weather. Heavy, low-lying cloud scudded overhead. Was it Darqu'on disguised as the destructive Shivastrom wind? Or could it be the demon, Lilitu that whipped at their clothes and clawed their faces? Magus feared the worst, but at the same time, hoped for the best; the horse had to rest – they had no choice but to stop, although Magus asked Swift to re-harness the horse to the carriage, just in case.

The dark clouds had already swallowed the wintry sunshine, and an ominous change descended, like a shadow of menace, around their shoulders. The wind screamed like a banshee, as clouds scudded, ever changing and threatening, across the sky. Swift sensed the change as, harness in hand, he hesitated, with concern in his eyes.

'Is it him, my Lord?' he asked, not wishing to even name him, but ready to strike out in strength, or run with speed, depending on the need.

'Let us hope not –' began Magus, but before he could complete his words, or Swift finish hitching the horse, heavy steps thudded along the ground, shaking the earth with their vibration, and huge creatures hurtled at speed towards them, blood-curdling cries issuing from cavernous mouths. Soon they were surrounded. Magus recognised them as ogres, monstrous parodies of human form, clearly with murder and mayhem on their minds. They might not be Roth Riders or Wulverines, but they still meant trouble: exactly what kind, they soon found out.

'Make no move, or we kill you!' grunted a rough voice, his face in darkness under a hood, but exuding an atmosphere that chilled the observers to the very core.

'Give us your valuables or we'll take your lives!' growled another.

Magus steadied his nerves, trying to recall how ogres had once been gentle giants, placid and inoffensive, despite their size – in an effort to dispel the fear that was threatening to rise up in him. It was not easy: they no longer looked or acted placid or inoffensive, but were huge, strong, creatures who, since the emergence of Darqu'on, had allowed their baser instincts to rise to the fore. Although not directly connected to Darqu'on's dark forces they nevertheless lived in his Shadow and fed now upon the fear of others and, occasionally, their flesh. There were many such groups of previously harmless creatures that had become opportune thieves, brigands and murderers. The former suited the ogres especially, who, with their huge size, thick skin and limited intelligence, had seemed to take to the role of aggressor as a duck takes to water.

'We have nothing,' Magus said, keeping as steady a voice as he could, and ever mindful of the malevolent-looking clouds. 'We are but poor travellers.'

He hoped that the disguise of their simple clothes would testify to this. The sky continued to darken, although the wind had dropped.

'Poor travellers or not, you're bound to 'ave somethin', old man, that we want or need, even if it's just your 'ead on a roastin' spit!' cried the first ogre, his own head and face still partially obscured by the hood, but with a long, sharp dagger in his hairy hand.

'We have nothing worth taking,' asserted Magus again, but the ogres ignored him.

'Search the wagon!' commanded the second ogre of the others. 'Take anythin' they 'ave!'

'Will you leave us with nothing!' exclaimed Magus, trying to buy time, whilst concealing his staff in his gown. 'We are travelling to relatives in the next village. Would you leave us helpless and with nothing?'

'We don't care for you, or your family, but if you want to live you'll be silent,' spat out the first ogre, thrusting his dagger under Magus' chin.

Magus felt the cold tip of the blade on his skin, and smelt the deadly breath escaping from the ogre's mouth, and even as he involuntarily recoiled, knew he had to keep quiet – if they lost a few pots and pans, so what? Better to lose these than their lives. As long as they did not find his staff, or the all-important package in his pocket, then they would not suspect that anything was untrue about the story he had given, and hopefully leave them alone.

He was sure that the disguising spell he always cast over his divination bowl would stop it from being discovered. If only his magic still had the power it once had and could have made them all invisible, they would not be in this predicament now! But then, if the magic were still as strong as it once was they would not need to be travelling at all, and the ogres would still be the gentle giants of the past! The irony of this made its impact on Magus, and once more he silently berated himself for his failure to stop the events that had brought them to this point.

He clutched his staff tighter, and stood protectively in front of Aimee, who, despite shaking with fear, would defend the child she held close to her to the end. Swift, who had instinctively resisted the attack by the ogres by striking out with his fist, was now being forcibly held by one of them, whilst the remainder ransacked the carriage. Objects flew out, rejected as worthless, and tempers rose amongst the marauders.

'There's nothin' 'ere worth 'avin'!' yelled a disgusted voice from inside the coach. 'They're either so poor they're not worth spittin' at…'

'Or they're hidin' stuff on 'em!' said another, turning his hulking frame towards Magus, and glaring at him as though trying to see through him.

'Search 'em!' said the hooded ogre, slavering at the mouth in his ferocity, as the other ogres lumbered towards the travellers, looking as though searching them could translate as tearing them apart.

Being searched was what Magus had feared. He would have to act to stop them now. He could not risk them finding the package or the staff as that would clearly indicate he was no poor traveller, but a High Wizard of the Court that, even now, Darqu'on was seeking to exterminate. They would all have a price on their head, especially if they realised who the baby was. The thought of what might happen to the child was too terrible to consider. His hand gripped the staff inside his cloak. He could feel his fingers tightening, his knuckles tense and hard; he was ready to summon up more of the precious and fast diminishing magic if need be, but he was ready to strike a hard blow first. He had temporarily forgotten the ominous sky, but a sudden sharp gust of wind whipped up again to remind them all. Momentarily the ogres were distracted; even they could sense that Darqu'on's Shadow was now too close for comfort, and all watched as the dark clouds formed into the shape of a hag-like creature, from whose mouth came a shaft of sickly yellow lightning, shooting across the sky like septic pus bursting from an open wound. A deafening screech echoed around them as Lilitu made her presence known! The vibrational force of the sound, and severity of the flash, sent tremors into the earth, startling both ogres and travellers alike, as the creature now coalesced into hundreds of bestial shapes, writhing around them, before re-forming again into Lilitu. Her fork lightning fingers streaked towards the ground, where Aimee stood holding the precious baby tightly in her arms. Aimee screamed; Swift yelled, and the ogres stared open-mouthed at the sky, their concentration temporarily broken. Only Magus seemed to grow in resolve, rising to the challenge that both of these threats presented. The apparition might be Lilitu but he knew Darqu'on was in his midst – he recognised the energy of his former pupil and somehow, up close, he was not afraid of him. There was no point in trying to pretend any more – Darqu'on had known all along what their moves were. No doubt he had been watching them since they left the castle. Magus just didn't understand why he had made no real attempt on them before. He withdraw his staff from concealment in his cloak, and raised it high to the violent force of Lilitu, as if in challenge to its creator, but to his surprise, even though the hag swirled closer, the creature was restrained, as though by an unseen barrier. Magus heard a frustrated scream over-ridden by a maniacal laugh, as though Darqu'on was purposefully holding her back. Not for the first time did Magus feel that he was part of Darqu'on's entertainment, yet with the temporary retreat of Lilitu's presence, it was to the ogres that he now directed his attention, uttering a spell to immobilise them as much as possible, as well as casting further protection around Aimee and the child, hoping that it would all be enough. He had no choice but to use his magical knowledge and whatever power he could muster.

'*Bhlendh, Feohtan!*' he cried, as out from the crystal staff came a flash of bright light that streaked towards the ogres.

The ogres thought he was attacking them, and their own reflex action was to attack back, but the light had blinded them temporarily. They floundered, with fists and daggers flying. Magus couldn't risk using magic again. He had to conserve what little he had left: he might still have to use it against Darqu'on. He would have to use good old-fashioned force, intelligence, and muscle power to stop them.

An ogre lurched at him from the carriage.

'Keep back!' he cried, swinging his staff round to trip the marauder up, then using it to lash out at another who was grappling with Swift, who, although small in stature was using every ounce of his considerable strength to overcome the sightless attacker.

Despite their size, or maybe because of it, the ogres had been caught unawares by the force of Magus' retaliation and Swift's attack. Now, without the benefit of sight, they stumbled heavily, their clumsy bodies crashing into each other as they tottered under the unexpected strength of Magus and Swift's blows. They hit the ground howling at each other. The air was filled with rolls of thunder, like a deep-throated laugh. They could not, of course, see the yellow streaking-shape of Lilitu or her pus-coloured fingers extending towards them, but they felt the chill of her encircling touch and taste of her poisonous breath. Magus was baffled – it was as though Darqu'on was helping in the ogres' defeat! What was he playing at? Whatever the reason, this action gave Magus and Swift more time to collect themselves.

Swift, freed now from the ogre's grip, put his own nimble strength to good use and hit out again with a well-thrown punch that caught the falling ogre on the temple, stunning him.

Lilitu's lightning fingers and poisonous breath continued to wrap themselves around an ogre's throat, and he let out a long gurgle as the last breath before death expired from his body. Lilitu's yellow fingers were momentarily freed and began to turn towards Aimee and the baby, just as another unseeing ogre, hearing the death rattle of his companion, turned towards the sound, and lumbered in front of them. Swift used this moment to dive at the ogre's feet, and pull him into Lilitu's path, allowing Aimee to escape, as Swift reversed his arm movement to wind another ogre with his quick elbow.

Magus swung his staff in front of him, spearing another ogre under the chin, which sent the brute grunting and reeling with the sudden sharp pain of it. The ogre lost his grip on the dagger as it flew from his hand, making an arc in the air, before streaking to earth and imbedding itself in the ground between Magus' feet, where it vibrated, back and forth, like a needle on a dial. The ogre fell sideways from Magus' blow, cracking his head on the hard ground as the chilling rumble of Darqu'on's laughter, intermixed with the screeching of Lilitu, filled the air. With a further anguished groan, the ogre slithered into unconsciousness. The hag's lightning fingers reached towards the figure, drilling into its sightless eyes, and the ogre shot back into consciousness, giving such a scream of pain that it shook branches from the trees. Magus held his ears against the sound, and felt his stomach retch at the gratuitous violence inflicted by Lilitu and Darqu'on on this creature. Compassion for his enemies filled his heart, despite knowing that they could have killed him and his companions. Even bullies, such as the ogres were now, did not merit this treatment. Involuntarily he cried out to Darqu'on.

'For pity's sake stop! Enough of this violence!'

There was the laugh again, and a feeling of uselessness swept over him – did he really think Darqu'on would listen to him? Foolish stupidity! He felt the immediate closeness of Darqu'on's presence breathing on his face, and feared for the safety of the child.

'Get into the carriage!' he cried to Aimee, as Lilitu's fingers curled towards them, wrapping around him like a boa constrictor, intent on squeezing out his life.

Aimee responded quickly to the command, the baby crying at the sudden movement, as she jumped back with him into the carriage. Magus vaguely heard Swift yell something about the horse, but then the air around him went bitterly cold as Lilitu began to deepen her hold. He could hear words, whisperings, taunting – all incomprehensible. He strained to hear what they said but felt, instead, something inside him, urging him to pick up the dagger on the ground in front of him. This suddenly seemed the most important action in the world. As if in a trance he scooped it up, with little thought for why, and immediately felt the weight comfortable in his hand: a sense of total power flooded through him such as he had never felt before; he was invincible. One of the ogres began to stir. The hag's putrid fingers extended deeper into Magus. He could not see Swift, but felt the overwhelming need to focus only on the ogres. He felt pure hatred towards them. He couldn't let them live to tell the tale, he had to kill them each one; had to tear their flesh to threads; had to spill their blood over the earth, and then spill that of the child! A sacrifice! A sacrifice! The voice in his head was shouting, 'Kill! Kill! Kill!' He barely heard another that quietly told him that he was not a violent man. He lifted the knife. The blade glistened yellow in his hand as he made to bring it down onto the nearest ogre with a murderous thrust!

The voice in his head was louder now, 'Kill, Kill, Kill' it repeated, with blood lust, and he knew he could so easily do it – a couple of quick thrusts with the knife and it would be over – it would be so easy!

Magus raised the dagger higher, and would have struck if it had not been for the triumphant voice clear in his own head, saying, 'Do it! Yes! Do it – join me!' – a voice he recognised only too well. Darqu'on was inside his head! Immediately he knew that he was allowing himself to be used by the dark forces; that the dagger in his hand was now Darqu'on, as was the voice inside his head, and the thoughts urging him to kill. All were Darqu'on, and Magus had so nearly allowed himself to be used by him – and against the Prince too. He was filled with horror at what could have been, and immediately threw the dagger into the river, where it briefly sliced the water before disappearing into its depths. He jammed his hands hard against his ears once more to block out the murderous voice, trembling with shock, but he would not succumb again!

'You will not take me over to the dark side, Darqu'on! I am a being of light, as you were once, yet unlike you, I will only respond to the light. Get away from me!'

There was another sound of deranged laughter borne on the screeching wind, and a sharp flash of putrid yellow lightning as it swallowed up the hag-shape of Lilitu into a cavernous black hole of negative energy. Another crack of thunder erupted, followed by the whirl of a further gust of violent wind that swirled and sucked with an all-consuming power that enveloped them all in its blackness. It upended the heavy carriage, as if it were no more than a toy being cast aside by a petulant child.

Aimee screamed from inside the carriage as she fell against the sides like a rag doll, dropping the precious child as she lost her balance. Magus, however found himself rooted to the spot as the carriage tumbled over and over, faster and faster, spinning towards him like a ball towards a wicket. Somehow he managed to roll out of its way, using all the strength he could muster, and instead the carriage smashed straight into the remaining ogres still in its path. Roars of pain followed sharp cries of surprise and terror before a deafening silence told Magus that his physical adversaries were no more. The Dark One had taken them, as though they were nothing. Yet the carriage was continuing to roll, over and over, like a hoop bowled along by a whip. The ear-splitting noise of splintering wood and objects smashing against objects was as deafening as the noise and force of the wind, which threw Magus into the air like a dog might toss a rabbit. He felt his arm wrenched back from his shoulder and involuntarily cried out with pain. The carriage hit a tree, and stopped rolling as Magus heard the cry of a baby coming from far away. Magus' pain dissolved into concern. The child! Had he really heard him cry? Or was it yet another piece of deceptive sorcery by Darqu'on to confuse him? He could only castigate himself again, and pray the baby was all right, which he did with every ounce of energy left in his shattered body. He was somehow aware of Aimee, at the corner of his vision, attempting to struggle to her feet, and he saw the bodies of the ogres crushed, lifeless, in front of him, but of Swift there was no sight or sound, nor was there a further cry from the baby. Magus had to find the child. He cursed himself for letting his guard relax; for his weakness in nearly letting himself be hijacked for such destructive ends. He had so nearly succumbed to the evil of those dark thoughts implanted in him by Darqu'on's sorcery. Even when he'd fought Darqu'on for the crystals in *The Book of True Magic* he had never experienced such destructive energy. Darqu'on's power was increasing! Magus had only ever done things for the greater good – and in that he had found his strength. Was it now, like so much else in the land, in danger of being turned to the worst evil? He felt his body sting from the sudden onslaught of sharp, icy stones, and realised that fierce hail was now smashing into him and the ground, like shards of breaking glass. Lightning streaked across the blackened sky, thunderbolt after thunderbolt crashed around them like unseen missiles, thrown by a giant hand playing a violent game. But this was no game; this was real and venomous.

He pulled himself painfully to his feet, and with this simple act of constructive intent his energy returned and strengthened him with inner resolve until another deafening thunderbolt felled him physically again. Darqu'on's power was very real and very present. Magus felt his head splitting open with the intensity and vibration of the sound. Now he cried out in real pain, but he took it gladly, knowing that by embracing the pain himself he was somehow deflecting it, and the dark forces, from harming the baby – as long as the child still lived.

The pain shot through every fibre and cell of his body like a thousand volts of electricity, and he jerked as a thing possessed. The tree beside him began to combust, the flames crackling and belching out thick, black smoke, blotting out everything for Magus except the pain. It was as though he was being sucked into some heavy, black hole where only the weight of darkness existed. He could feel himself falling into its imploding depths. He almost willed it to embrace him, and take away the pain. He could fight no more...

From somewhere far away he heard a child cry again; a lusty cry, a hungry cry! The crying grew stronger, and more insistent by the minute. It seemed to be pulling him back from whatever dark place was trying to annihilate him and the acrid smoke from his eyes, nostrils and throat began to clear. He fought to return. He would not leave. He would not give in, not now. He had to take the child out of Arcanum. He felt himself rushing back from this deep, dark and forbidding place, until suddenly he could see the pale blue of sky again, feel the ground, smell the cold air, hear the powerful crying. The dark force of the storm had blown away, driven off, Magus wanted to believe, by the strength of his intentions: and he, Magus was still alive, as was the baby.

Pulling himself to his feet with the aid of his staff, he followed the sound of crying to a nearby clump of tall grass. A shape was bending over it, with arm outstretched. Magus involuntarily raised his staff to strike at the shape, but stopped in time to see that it was the figure of Aimee, bruised and shaken, but intent on doing what she could for the precious child, who was crying hungrily, yet safely, amongst the tussock of grass in which he had fallen, and been hidden.

'The Prince is safe, sir,' she said, turning to look at Magus with relief lighting her eyes, as she tenderly picked the child up to check for injury. 'Not even a scratch. He has been blessed!'

'He has indeed,' replied Magus, thankfully. 'As have we. This is a good sign for the future.'

Magus lowered his staff with a relieved sigh, and as he did, felt his stomach turn, as he saw the broken, shattered body of Swift, partially submerged in the river, a sheen of dark, red liquid spreading out across the flowing surface of the water. The horse stood over him, whinnying forlornly and nudging the lifeless body, as though trying to wake his much-loved master. Not all had been blessed then. Not all saved. A sacrifice had been made after all.

'Don't look, Aimee,' he said, but she already had, and gasped at the bloody sight of Swift before her, but it was not the first time she had seen death, and no doubt not the last, and she remained strong.

Magus admired her resolve, yet sadness and compassion flowed over them both for all those lost, mixed in almost equal measure with relief: so much death around them in the midst of so much life. What magic Magus had used had thankfully stopped any of the dead joining Darqu'on's army, for which both he and Aimee were grateful.

'We must give them a burial, sir,' said Aimee.

'There's no time, Aimee, to do anything but mourn,' explained Magus, 'Mother Nature will claim them as her own, and their souls will be allowed to soar. Swift's sacrifice saved the horse for our continued journey, for we surely cannot use the carriage any longer,' and he lightly touched her arm. 'Come, we must continue.'

Aimee picked up a broken branch and tossed it into the water like a remembrance posy. There was nothing else to use, but her loving gesture did not go unnoticed by Magus. He walked quietly over to the horse in the river, whispering soothing words of comfort, as he softly took the bridle in his hands. The horse turned and looked at Magus with sad eyes, but seemed to know that he had a duty to complete, and let himself be led back to the bank, where Aimee and the child were waiting. Magus knew they would be more vulnerable on horseback, without the carriage to hide them, and the journey would be hard, but the entry point to the hidden village of Brakendor was not far off, and a little discomfort was a small price to pay for their lives. He just had to hope that there was enough strength in all of them, and in his crystal staff, to do what was required of them.

'Hurry,' he said urgently to Aimee, taking the child from her as she mounted the horse, 'time is precious.'

He had to get the child to safety: now, in case Darqu'on changed his mind.

Magus gently passed the child back to Aimee. It was only then he remembered his divination bowl, and the important package wrapped in the cloth.

His eyes scanned around quickly, and there, close to where the baby had landed, was the bowl, looking like an ordinary, simple piece of cooking equipment, as he had intended. He picked it up thankfully, but did he still have the package?

Hurriedly, he felt in his gown for the package containing the seven important stones imbued with True Magic, and his heart sank when he found his pocket empty. He panicked momentarily, and then calmed himself. The package must have fallen out when he was being tumbled over by the storm. Likely it had split open, and the precious stones would be lying scattered amongst the grass. He knew that they would appear as he wanted them to, as ordinary stones to others, but to him he would see them as the crystals they really were. He just had to look for them, and all would be well, but where were they? They could have fallen over a very large area. It could be like looking for needles in haystacks!

He ran his long fingers through the grass, searching for the familiar and comforting feel of the stones. Did he see a glint of something over there? Yes, a flash of bright orange glistening for his eyes only. Fortune smiled upon him! He pocketed it swiftly – now to find the others. There, muddied in the grass, was the cloth they had been wrapped in, but he could see no more stones. He could not stay around here too long: that would be too dangerous. He would need to consult the divination bowl to find them. As he looked into the bowl, he was horrified to see, coming from it, a cloud of black smoke, heavy with a sense of burning evil that seemed to move into his throat with choking fingers. He held his resolve, looking deeper into the bowl, hearing as he did so, the familiar and once-loved voice of Darqu'on rising from it, and seeing the dark outline of his face rise within it.

'Magus, my old friend, how good to see you again.' The voice was sickly-sweet.

'I wish I could say the same of you, Darqu'on,' answered Magus, concerned that Darqu'on somehow knew about the loss of the stones.

'Come, come Magus, are you still so defensive with your old pupil?'

'Your concern is not convincing, Darqu'on. You tried to use me before – you will not do so again, so do not insult my intelligence by continuing.'

'Such coldness now, from an old friend and colleague whom I admired so much. Do you remember those times, Magus?' Darqu'on's voice was silky-soft again.

Magus did not allow himself to reply directly to the question, but said instead:

'If you think that you can turn my mind, Darqu'on, with supposed flattery and reminiscence, then think again. I know you too well, and I can see what you have become. All that you once were to me is now lost, forever. There is no point in returning to the past, or to what might have been.'

'You seem troubled, old friend. Have you lost something?' the voice mocked. 'Oh dear, where can they be!'

Magus froze. He knew about the stones. Did he have them?

Darqu'on seemed to read his mind.

'You will never know, will you Magus? If I have them, then nothing you can do will restore the magic. If I don't, well then, the child will never be safe from me. Either way I win and you lose.'

Magus knew this to be the truth, yet the sound of the once-loved voice, despite its now mocking tone, brought back such memories to him, that they were all that inhabited his mind for a few moments. They were good memories, of times when they read together, teacher and student, from the multitude of magic books; how the young Darqu'on had devoured them! Despite everything that had happened, he still carried love for him in his heart, a love that, if he was not careful, could be used against him by Darqu'on's brilliant, and cold-hearted cunning.

No! He would not weaken. He knew what Darqu'on was doing, getting into his mind again, but he would not let him succeed, not this time. He had to keep focused, for the sake of the child, for the sake of them all.

'I will always trust in the power of the highest good, Darqu'on,' he answered firmly, and in his head cast a spell, entrusting the missing stones to the safe keeping of Mother Earth, where Darqu'on, at least for now, had no power. He must hope that she would be their only custodian.

He knew he could not let fear overtake him again. He had to remain strong. So much depended upon it. The tone of Darqu'on's voice changed, immediately, inside his head, to one of sarcasm and venom.

'Such fighting talk from my old teacher! Admirable, but misguided. You think you can win, Magus – that you can magic this child away to a place where I can't find him, but he is only safe if I choose for him to be, remember that. I could have killed him, and you, many times since you left the castle. Indeed, I had to stop Lilitu from taking events into her own hands just now, and do you really think that it was all your own strength that stopped those pathetic ogres? Such naivety, Magus, is not worthy of you. I would have stopped you too, although that became unnecessary. You have seen for yourself how easy it would be to kill him now, but where is the challenge, the pleasure, or the power in that? The time will come, but his life, or death, is my choice, and mine alone. He will never be safe whilst I have power, although you, and he, may sense the illusion of safety. You are my toys, my playthings, and always will be, and I *will* have my way as and when I choose. His chances of restoring what you so pitiably call 'The Magic' are nil. There is no magic any longer. All magic died for me when his mother made her choice. And I made sure it died for everyone else. Now there is only the power of sorcery, and I control that. You cannot win, old teacher, and neither will their son. He is damned, as surely as he lies in that young girl's arms over there. Pretty little thing, isn't she? I could enjoy taking her. But that can come later.'

'Don't harm Aimee, Darqu'on! Leave her alone, she has suffered enough,' blurted out Magus, in spite of himself.

'Suffer? You don't know the meaning of the word, old man, and I will do what I choose with anyone. I will be watching, always, and I will destroy him, and you, and your precious magic when I decide to finish using you all, including her, for my pleasure. However long I decide to wait for these enjoyable moments, and however many others I choose to destroy before I take him as the final prize, you will never know. But be assured, the power of my Shadow will inevitably swallow the light and neither you, their son, nor your magic, will even be a distant memory.'

38

If Magus felt his heart sink at these words, he did not show it. Instead he thought quickly. Darqu'on was saying he had chosen not to kill the child now. That it hadn't been the Magic that saved him. Was he really that powerful? Was everything that Magus was doing going to amount to nothing in the end? No! He would not let that thought take root in his mind: that would bring in fear, and the fear would kill them both, with, or without Darqu'on having to wield another blow. He would not succumb to any more such thoughts. Neither would he allow past memories of better times to sway him from his course. He transmitted his reply by thought alone.

'You may wish me to believe that you are more powerful than the light, but light will eventually extinguish darkness, no matter how much darkness is created, or for how long it is allowed to remain. The Magic cannot be destroyed, only hidden away. It is always waiting to be found by one who has light in his heart, mind and soul. You had that once, Darqu'on, until you let jealousy and hatred capture them all. Such things are corrosive Darqu'on. They will eventually weaken and defeat you, of that I have no doubt. Yet even you cannot hide your true self forever. Even you must have a spark of light still at your core, and that may yet still dissolve your sorcery, and allow you to attain salvation.'

Magus' tone of such firm confidence caused the black smoke to curl up from the bowl with a hiss of annoyance, and through it Magus was able to see, briefly, but more clearly, the features on the familiar face, before they disappeared. Magus' spine tingled with shock. So this is how he looked now! The golden haired youth with so much promise, and life, now replaced by this grey-skinned, sunken-cheeked creature! Magus was suddenly overcome with sadness and compassion again, towards this lost soul, and the destructive transformation that the Shadow of his sorcery had wreaked upon him. Compassionate, yet detached: at that moment Magus fully separated from what had been, and knew only that light would triumph eventually, and bring blessed relief, not only to the land, but also to the essence of the real Darqu'on. He knew any success would not be by force, as that only made the Shadow stronger, but by resilience, and refusal to be drawn into the illusions and fear games that Darqu'on played – then, there was real hope of victory. There was another way, of this Magus was now certain. For the first time in the journey he allowed himself to smile, and felt his heart lightening. This was the way to vanquish the darkness: to lift the Shadow of sorcery. It was compassion and love. This gave him so much hope.

'I pray for your release, Darq'uon,' he said, quietly.

Darqu'on's face appeared again, momentarily, and looked surprised and lost. He had not expected compassion, and it caught him temporarily off-guard. The harshness with which he surrounded himself seemed to blur slightly, at the edges. This was the chink in his armour, and Magus had found it. Neither would forget.

'I do not want your prayers! I do not need compassion!' spat out Darqu'on's hardened voice, 'I want power and control and I have that. I have it NOW!' and a flash of putrid yellow spewed from the bowl towards Magus, who doubled over with pain, as though he had been kicked. As he did so, his eyes caught sight of something bright and shiny, glimmering red in the grass. It was one of the missing crystals! Darqu'on did not know it, but that act of pain had helped Magus find part of what he needed to restore the magic. There was a strange sense of pleasurable irony in this, which Magus did not fail to notice. He scooped the red stone secretly into his sensitive fingers, as he stood straight, without pain. The divination bowl was clear once more. Darqu'on had gone, but there was no time to waste. Magus had two of the stones but five were still missing. He had no idea if any of them were with Darqu'on. He had to hope that Mother Earth, with the help from the nature sprites and elementals, had heard his plea to keep them safe. Whilst in the ground they would be safe enough, and only surface when the grown Prince showed himself ready to receive them . He made sure the baby and Aimee were secure behind him as he urged the horse forward with renewed hope, and trust in his heart.

As the horse moved away from the clearing tiny, sharp-eyed creatures appeared from out of the earth to retrieve the five lost stones, taking them back into the depths from whence they had come and into safekeeping, hardly disturbing a blade of grass as they did so.

CHAPTER 4

Brakendor

"It takes a whole village to raise a child."
African Proverb

Magus knew Brakendor was close, although they could not see it – the invisibility spell worked well, yet he saw the ancient hollow tree just ahead – the portal by which it could be accessed.

'Hold tight Aimee,' he said as he urged the horse straight towards the trunk, extending his crystal staff like a lance ahead of him.

'*Ouvret Visio Tondala!*' he cried. Aimee stifled a scream as the tree loomed closer, gnarled bark and branches racing towards them. She was sure they would crash into it. Instead there was a powerful rush of air and a feeling of suction drawing them in and the horse and its riders found themselves inside the hidden village, clattering over the cobbled streets under cover of a cloud-filled, night sky. Together, they moved as quietly as they could, past silent, stone cottages, and thickly thatched roofs. The sign on the inn said The Ram and Ewe, and it swung creakily back and forth in the night breeze, as though ushering them further in to the parochial safety of this little backwater.

At the top of the street they stopped outside the red door and proudly polished knocker of a whitewashed cottage, where bold letters painted across the large window informed visitors this was Sawyers – Bakers & Confectioners – for all your baking needs.

The streets were deserted at this time of night, villagers tucked up around their own warm hearths after a long working day. It was a comfortable place, which drew Aimee to it, but she felt bereft as she held the baby close to her, realising she would have to give him up very soon. She had grown to love him in the short time she had spent with him, and hoped that his new mother would love him as much as she and his real mother did.

Magus helped her down from the horse, and looking quickly about him with all-seeing eyes, ignored the bright knocker, and tapped lightly on the shop door with his crystal staff. There was a long pause before a bemused middle-aged man with prematurely greying hair opened the door wide, wondering who could be calling at this time of night.

'Samuel Sawyer?' clarified Magus quietly.

'That's right, can I help you?' said Samuel puzzled at the strange-looking party at his door.

'Indeed you can,' smiled Magus kindly, and held Samuel's gaze with his own hypnotic one as he spoke, 'This is the longed for Prince, whom I need to leave in your care until he is old enough to leave you. You will raise him as your own, always keep him safe, and never mention this day to anyone. Do you understand?' Samuel nodded, mesmerised.

'Best come in from the cold,' he said in a hushed voice, already affected by the need for secrecy as Magus continued to weave his magic. He ushered Magus, and Aimee, with the child in her arms, into a small, narrow hallway. Behind him, his wife Sarah, her plump face etched with curiosity, greeted them. Already mother to two grown-up daughters, Magus knew he had chosen well. He shifted his steady gaze to her with a smile, and worked his magic yet again.

'Here is your new son,' said Magus, and Sarah immediately understood her role and never questioned it for a moment as Aimee, somewhat reluctantly, passed the sleeping baby into her experienced arms.

'We will call him Willerby,' she said, 'I'll guard him with my life, Sir,' and she looked, for the first time, into her new son's face, and then into that of her husband. 'We both will.'

Through the magic worked by Magus they knew, without words being spoken, how important this child was; that caring for him carried a huge weight of responsibility, and that by keeping him safe they were also ensuring the continued safety of Brakendor. Sarah made a silent promise to herself at that moment that this child would be kept protected and cocooned. It was some years now since she had cared for a baby, and she was unsure how she would cope with the disturbed nights, the teething, and the tantrums, and all the other paraphernalia and challenges that raising a child brings, but she felt her maternal sense rise within her as she looked at him. This small child, so dependent on her, would be safe; no harm would ever come to him whilst she watched over him. She would remain vigilant: never take her eyes from him for one second. It would not be easy at her time of life, but it was a price worth paying, and a burden she was prepared to carry for as long as was needed. As Sarah held the child, Magus passed a small package to Samuel.

'Keep this safe, along with the child,' said Magus. 'No one, not even he, must know his true identity. He will discover it himself in time. Tell no one of what has happened tonight, or what I have given you. You must wait until the hired man calls before you release the package into his care. Do you understand?'

'No word will pass our lips, you can depend upon us,' replied Samuel, placing the package in his pocket.

'I know I can trust you both,' acknowledged Magus. 'You will give him what he needs for as long as he needs it. Know that one day he will leave, but Brakendor is his home until then.'

Samuel nodded. They would not let him down.

'May peace and good fortune be with you,' said Magus, as he took one last look at the child in which so much hope was invested.

'And with you too, Sir,' came back the reply. Nothing further was said: just looks exchanged between husband and wife that spoke more eloquently than words. The baby and the package would be safe here with them. They closed the door and thus severed all connection of the child with his heritage, and indeed much of the memory of what had just occurred, until the time came for them to reclaim it.

Aimee let out a barely audible sigh as she and Magus turned and retreated once more under cover of the night. Their job done, the young nurse and elderly Magi mounted the horse once more and, with another small sigh from one, and a cautionary look over his shoulder from the other, they rode away into the velvety blackness, towards the hollow tree. Their exit was gentler, as though the power contained within the tree was ready to release them into the troubled land once more. Here Magus raised his staff and re-sealed the village. For those who had eyes to see, there shone a powerful, protective bubble of shimmering, golden energy around the invisible village and surrounding fields, which extended out beyond the brook to the outer edges of the forest. No enemy would invade this space, and Magus allowed himself a sense of satisfaction that at least here, all was as safe as he could make it. Time had already begun to stand still as far as progress was concerned there, but progress had done nothing so far for Arcanum, so the villagers would lose nothing, and no doubt gain much from a quiet, non-progressive, protected life.

Magus was thankful that he was instrumental in providing the child with the chance of a trouble-free upbringing, as well as a means to connect with his heritage in time. Somehow that seemed to make up for his past transgressions. He thought of the remaining stone he would now teleport to Asgar to give to the young Prince one day in the future, knowing that he would not see either again in this life. He thought of the other five stones now in the care of the nature sprites, just waiting to be unearthed: It would be up to the young Prince to earn them and restore them to *The Book of True Magic*. Only then could Arcanum return to the light. He sighed long and deep, knowing he had done his best, and would continue to do so up to and beyond the time when death finally called him home. He already had some idea of how close that moment was.

The baker and his wife heard the hooves fade over the cobbles and silence settle once more, like an enveloping blanket, around Brakendor and the bakery. With Magus' magic still affecting them they carried the child into the front parlour, any link between them and Magus and what he represented now firmly in the past: the true identity of the child hidden before it had a chance to be revealed. Their role was to keep him safe: An important responsibility, which they would fulfil till their dying breath.

Held inside this protected, and potentially constricting environment of the small, warm bakery, and over-responsible parents, the baby awoke and looked up into his new mother's eyes, as if he knew instinctively what his coming life would entail. As she held him more tightly to her, as though reluctant to ever let him go, he let out a loud and complaining cry that filled the bakery and echoed hauntingly around the empty streets.

Aimee sat in front of Magus on the horse. She missed the feel of the baby in her arms, and in her thoughts imagined she was nursing him still, but then she would find her thoughts going back to the baker's house, and re-living those painful moments when she had had to give him up. Her arms ached to hold him again. She had grown to love him in that short, but emotionally charged journey, investing in him all her maternal feelings that he had given her the opportunity to experience again. When her own child had been stillborn the pain of that loss imprisoned itself deep into the pit of her being, tossing and turning like a tortured soul with no reprieve – until this child had been laid in her arms, then all pain flew away. She would have given her life for the little one who had looked up at her with such trust and innocence in his eyes, yet now he too, was gone, this time to another, and the pain was back, gnawing at her insides like a ravenous wolf. It was a cruel thing to lose two children. How she yearned for a child of her own to love, and nurture, and keep. Yet there would always be a special place in her heart for the one she lost, and the one that she had to give up. One she had borne, the other, suckled – they were both part of her and their memories intertwined and became one. She would always feel umbilically connected to them both, she would ask Magus if one day she could return through the hidden portal to watch as her surrogate son grew.

She sighed, and brought herself back from her reverie. The night was drawing out, and the glow of a blood-red dawn flooding in when her eyes caught sight of something ominous ahead: a large, dark and familiar shape on the horizon. Her heart plummeted to her toes, and involuntarily she pulled her cloak deeper around her.

'Look sir,' she said, nodding her head towards the shape silhouetted against the horizon. 'Look ahead.'

But Magus had already seen it and felt its ominous presence, and knew it was his nemesis. A hideous apparition stretched upwards from the horizon. It could only be Darqu'on, ready to wreak his vengeance on them at last. Magus shuddered, not with fear, but with revulsion at what horror had been created. That his own star pupil, now devoid of any humanity, would kill, without a second thought, the one who had taught him lovingly, brought such sadness. That it had come to this. Yet Magus was strangely calm. Since fulfilling his own destiny of delivering the child safely to Samuel and Sarah he had found a place within his deepest soul that breathed acceptance of the inevitability of his own death. Magus had seen his demise reflected in the black gaze of those soulless eyes peering at him from the divination bowl earlier. He had felt it in that black hole in which he had temporarily found himself, and heard it whispered on the wind as he left the protected space of Brakendor. It had padded like a hungry wolf silently behind him, just waiting for the opportunity to strike. He knew it was his time now. He almost welcomed it. But he was concerned for Aimee at his side, and his heart went out to her. She had played an important role in the deliverance of the child, and the future of Arcanum. Magus hoped that his inevitable fate would not befall her. She was so young, with too much still to offer life. He prayed she would survive. He would do his best to keep her from death. He winced at the images in his head of what lay ahead for her at Darqu'on's hand. Yet he prayed that from her suffering good would be born. Yes. He could still do this perhaps. She would suffer, but she would not die, and from her pain, a pureness of spirit would find expression. He saw her destiny now as clearly as he had seen his own. Her role in this story had not been played out; there was something she still had to do for the greater good.

He felt Aimee tensing against him as the nebulous, surging shape morphed into Lilitu once more: malevolent, evil, without compassion or pity. He could hear Darqu'on's voice inside his head again.

'Don't think I don't know what you have done, Magus. And in the greater scheme of things it will make no difference. He will return one day and I will kill him. It is only a matter of time. Now, Magus, I claim *your* life, but before your demise, behold what your resistance has resulted in!'

There was a tumultuous clap of thunder, which echoed all around them as the hag-shape split in two and pouring from the centre came hundreds of shadowy children, writhing, as if in agony. Any previous innocence in their eyes now replaced with the haunted look of the living dead. Darqu'on's heinous creation, Lilitu, the child-killing witch, had claimed her prize after all, wreaking vengeance on other young innocents!

Magus felt horror fill his eyes, followed by tears of compassion at the sight before him. There was nothing he could do to save these poor young souls! They were doomed to exist like this forever, or at least until *The Book of True Magic* was re-activated by the one for whom they were sacrificed. Darqu'on had made his point very clearly. He was the power from which there would be no escape until the child, now spared, embraced his destiny.

The split, black shape began to re-form, taking the image of the she-witch, Lilitu once more. She sucked the images of the children inside her, growing even denser, even larger, until her bloated form blotted out the landscape entirely. Magus felt the terrified grip of Aimee's hand on his arm, but neither she, nor he could escape the inevitable. From out of the she-witch came such shrieking and wailing that it penetrated to the marrow in their bones and vibrated every sinew of their bodies, as though plucked and played by a malevolent hand in a sinister symphony. Erupting from her centre came the powerful, very physical maleness of a virile figure in the prime of manhood: Darqu'on, as Magus remembered him. The figure straddled the roadway in front of them, but no matter how Darqu'on chose to present himself from moment to moment, there could never be any disguising the soullessness of his being.

From Darqu'on's right hand spurted a serpent, its blood red gaping mouth, reminiscent of the pit of hell from which it came. It spat venom as its body writhed and expanded to fill the roadway. Slanted, yellow eyes fixed themselves onto Magus, drawing him into their centre. Aimee screamed as the creature wrapped itself around the Last Wizard, pulling him from the horse with one swift flick of its enormous, muscular body and began to squeeze the life out of him. Yet Magus no longer struggled. This life was over. He gave himself up to the process of death willingly, and any pain was removed before it had time to register. It was a good day to die. The serpent gave a final squeeze before flipping its prey expertly into its mouth and swallowing Magus whole, its flexible body expanding to the

46

shape before its teeth, powerful muscles and gastric juices reduced the Last Wizard to nothing.

Aimee did not see this final horrific act. She had horror of her own to face as the powerful figure of Darqu'on, eyes leering, pinned her to the ground with brutish sexual force. The sound of her screams went unheard, but echoed in the emptiness long after Darqu'on had used her for his bestial pleasure, and continued to reverberate as the silent herald of a New Age.

Part 2

Self-Worth

"When you please others in hopes of being accepted,
you lose your self-worth in the process."
Dave Pelzer

CHAPTER 5

Gateway of the Moon

"The day the child realizes that all adults are imperfect,
he becomes an adolescent; the day he forgives them, he becomes an adult;
the day he forgives himself, he becomes wise."
Alden Nowlan

If Willerby Sawyer had been asked to highlight what he most remembered about his childhood up to the age of thirteen, it would likely have been the phrases 'No you can't', and 'Be careful', for he heard these, and felt their impact, every day of his young life. He was smothered with restrictions, 'for your own good', as his mother constantly affirmed.

'No Willerby, you can't go to the brook/the forest/down the road – it's too far/not safe/dangerous', or 'Be careful, you might fall/get lost/be ill/get hurt.'

They might just as well have told him not to have a life, because he was suffocated by these injunctions delivered by his anxious mother and reinforced by his unemotional, strait-laced father, and he suffered frustration, lack of self-esteem and self-confidence because of them.

It didn't help that he was a gawky kind of child either, with tufts of brown hair sticking out in all directions and gangly legs like those of a newborn faun. He had few friends, except for Fynn, who was slightly older and seemed to take him under his wing, as he did all the waifs and strays of the village. There was also a girl called Sophie, who seemed kind and caring, but she and her mother kept themselves to themselves. The other children, however, delighted in ridiculing him.

'Cowardy-cowardy custard! Who's a Mummy's boy then!' they would taunt.

The truth of this hurt Willerby more than anyone knew.

His peers had always seen him as a bit of an oddball: pitying him at best, despising him at worst, and he got used to being laughed at, bullied and ignored. He was never quite sure which of these was worse, although at least when people laughed or were rude to him, he knew he existed! But he never had the courage to stand up to them: this task fell to Fynn many times as they were growing up.

'Leave him alone won't you, he's done nothing to you,' Fynn would say, taking on the role of protector and champion.

Willerby was always grateful for this, but often wondered why Fynn bothered with him; yet Fynn seemed to detect something in Willerby that was worth knowing. As children they would play games of make-believe together, prompted by the stories of mythical heroes they both loved so much. They imagined fighting monsters in the forest, or rescuing damsels (for in his imagination, at least, Willerby was fearless), but even then his mother had intervened.

'Be careful, Willerby, you'll hurt yourself! Why can't you play nice, quiet indoor games?' she remonstrated once when she found six year old Willerby and slightly older Fynn in the yard behind the bakery, both wielding string-tied wooden swords that were barely holding together, let alone capable of smiting ferocious beasts!

'But it's boring playing quiet games. We want adventure!' Willerby had replied, thrusting at imaginary foes, which might well have had his mother's face on them.

'Adventure, you say,' mocked his mother 'And this from the boy who is scared of his own shadow! Poppycock! Now, let me have those nasty-looking weapons you two, before you get splinters or hurt yourselves! Go inside and read a book, so I know where you are, and what you're doing!' And she watched as they stomped reluctantly upstairs.

So Willerby never got a chance to test his capabilities, and grew up doubting his abilities.

'She never lets me do anything I want,' he moaned to Fynn when he was nearly ten. 'She says adventure's dangerous and I couldn't cope. Is she right, Fynn?'

'Do you think you could cope?' asked Fynn, very diplomatically for a ten year old.

'I don't know, how can I if I don't get the chance?' sighed Willerby. 'She's always fussing over me, always with me, always interfering, always wanting to know where I am, and who I'm with. It drives me mad! It's like being in a prison with padded walls that are closing in on me more and more every day: I can hardly breathe!'

Fynn laughed at his dramatic language.

'Oh Will! I know your parents don't let you do as much as mine, but they aren't that bad, you exaggerate. C'mon, let's read the book about the forest monsters. I like that one'

Monsters of the Forbidden Forest was one of their favourite books, found, amidst other such books, years ago at the back of the hall cupboard in the bakery. They had managed to get them up to Willerby's room without detection. They all had a mystical quality about them, with their faded watercolour illustrations of a strange land of myth and magic; of monsters supposedly found in the forest, if anyone dared to go there, and, like all children, Fynn and Willerby loved to be frightened, as long as it was only a story!

'Do you think these stories are true, Fynn?' asked Willerby.

'No idea,' laughed Fynn 'and I'm not sure I want to find out – pretending to fight monsters is a bit different to meeting them face to face.'

'I suppose so,' replied Willerby ruefully, 'but it would be great to be an adventurer.'

'Wouldn't you just be the teeniest bit scared if you came face to face with the huge Bogus worm!' asked Fynn, jokingly, reminding Willerby of one of the creatures which Willerby's father threatened would eat him, or any child that ventured into the forest.

'Of course not,' bluffed Willerby, ignoring the sensation of butterflies fluttering unbidden into his stomach. But Fynn understood the fear behind the bravado, and played along.

'Then I'll come with you.' He said. 'We'll go on a quest or something, like the heroes in the stories. Adventurers into the unknown.'

Willerby smiled at his friend, thankful that Fynn indulged his fantasies and made it all sound possible, somehow.

'It does and we will,' he agreed, 'one day, when we're older: you and me, together!'

'That's a deal then,' said Fynn.

'Absolutely!' replied Willerby, and they shook hands on it before dropping the subject like a hot potato, as if to face any more details of any future challenge was too much for either of them to handle just yet.

Fynn didn't really believe that Willerby would ever have the courage to leave, or do anything even vaguely heroic, any more than he would: they were Brakendor boys and would both live the lives mapped out for them – the baker for Willerby, farm labourer for Fynn – that was how it was; but he didn't mind humouring him. Fynn knew that all these shows of bravado gave Willerby hope, and that was fine: everyone needed hope, and Willerby was pretty smothered by his over-cautious and intractable family. As the years passed, he never for one minute thought it would come to anything.

Willerby had always had dreams, which his mother put down to a nervous stomach caused by an excitable nature, and she offered camomile or peppermint tea but little interest or understanding. Willerby didn't mind too much. He could get lost in the dreams, especially if they were of heroic acts, but sometimes they were more like nightmares – of being almost suffocated by a huge soft cloud, or of almost transparent hands grabbing at him through a crack in a hollow tree and trying to pull him through. But when he was almost thirteen he began having dreams that were different to his previous ones. These took place in quiet, mystical places where he would meet with amazing people or animals who all had kind eyes and soft voices, and taught him things that were very important during the dreams but which, on waking, were as nebulous as air and just as untraceable, leaving just a vague sense of peace and stillness, which lasted until he woke fully to the cold light of day. He often likened the feeling in these dreams to one of 'going home,' yet he shared these with no one and certainly not his parents – he told them very little anyway! He didn't even tell Fynn – not that Fynn wouldn't have listened – he was kindness itself, even if he did think Willerby exaggerated events at times, but Willerby felt awkward about speaking about them. He couldn't remember much about them anyway, but he was scared that if he spoke of them openly they would disappear entirely from his life, and that special feeling of 'homecoming' would vanish. Sometimes this was all he could cling onto, especially when it came to his difficulties with other children from the village.

He wanted to be accepted by his peers, and amazingly, he had been invited to Ewan Bostock's party in the summer – a real chance to prove his worth– but his mother was now jeopardising this by telling him he couldn't go.

'No Willerby, out of the question! Sleeping outside? – In tents? – Cooking on an open fire? – Without adults around? That's far too dangerous and you're far too young,' she said, anxiety as well as criticism colouring her voice.

'But I'm thirteen tomorrow!' complained Willerby 'How can that be too young? Everyone else will be going and I'll look stupid if I don't.'

'I don't care what other parents are letting their children do. I'm not letting you go. That's all that matters,' she said, in a voice that meant business.

'But you never let me do anything exciting,' moaned Willerby again.

'You're having a birthday party here tomorrow, with a conjurer. That should be excitement enough for someone of your age.'

'Corrin, the conjurer is boring, compared to Ewan's party!' he argued.

'Well, there's gratitude for you; after all we do for you! The trouble is, Willerby, you're never satisfied,' shot back his mother with the martyred look he knew so well.

'But Ewan's father is going to set up a rope ladder and assault course. It'll be great – a real adventure.'

'Assault course! Then you definitely won't be going, my boy. Whatever is Farmer Bostock thinking of?' replied his mother, aghast at the potential danger.

'But you promised I could do grown-up things when I was thirteen!' wailed Willerby. 'You promised.'

Being thirteen was special in Brakendor: the beginning of the years, which marked the first stage on the journey towards adulthood, so he wanted to feel grown up. His friend, Fynn, thirteen last summer, was already being treated as responsible but this was not the case for Willerby.

'I said you could help your father and me in the bakery, not go gallivanting in tents and over assault courses,' retorted his mother. 'That's far too dangerous for someone your age.'

'Dangerous! Cooking on an open fire and sleeping in a tent? What's dangerous about that?'

'It's dangerous because I say so,' retorted his mother, 'and your father will agree,' and of course his father did.

'Whatever your mother says, goes, Willerby,' said Samuel.

'But didn't you ever do exciting things when you were young?' Willerby asked.

'No. Can't say I did. I like the quiet life and the comforts of home, which should be good enough for you too, Willerby.'

But it wasn't good enough for Willerby because he didn't have much of a life in Brakendor, being so held back by the anxieties and limitations of his parents. Perhaps if they had been a little more relaxed he would never have wanted to break free, but breaking free was his dream. In his imagination and dreams he was still an invincible hero, a white knight to whom nothing was impossible, yet in the cold light of day Willerby didn't feel a hero. He had become his mother's fear, and he hated what it did to him even more than he hated his mother's intransigence.

'You didn't let me go to Fynn's party, either,' he persisted. 'Everyone will laugh at me and think I'm a baby if I don't go.'

'You can still play around the bakery, within sight of us, we're not stopping that,' said his mother, in that "look at what we are doing for you" sort of voice she employed at times like this.

'But there will be no one to play with, they'll all be at Ewan's – and what's the point of me working in the bakery if you won't let me deliver the orders around the village – you let my sisters do this when they were young, 'cos they told me! Why not me?' and his voice turned into a squeak the more frustrated he became, then dropped into his boots when he least expected it!

His mother just turned her back in a huff, and refused to answer. He knew that tears of martyrdom would be welling in her eyes, and Willerby felt her rejection, and his guilt lodged in his chest like two heavy boulders, yet how could he test himself if he was wrapped in cotton wool by parents intent on stopping him growing up into a responsible and independent person? In his frustration he threw out another barbed comment.

'What's the point of me being thirteen tomorrow if you still treat me like a child!' he retorted angrily.

'Maybe it's because you still act like a child,' snapped back his mother, 'and for that little outburst you'd best go to your room without supper, and give that temper of yours a well-earned rest, or you may find yourself with no party to enjoy tomorrow at all.'

Willerby wanted to shout and kick out in frustration, but he knew it was no good, so instead he stumped off to his room. He didn't really want to risk losing out on his party tomorrow, even one with a conjurer, as it was a chance to be, perhaps, finally accepted by his peers. Everyone was coming, and with his father being the village baker and confectioner the food, at least, would be good!

He pushed back his frustration until he closed the door to his room resenting with every breath the limitations and constraints he felt himself shackled to here in Brakendor.

Sarah saw her son's pain but shut it out. All his life she had watched over him, and done her best, more than her best, to keep him safe, as she knew she had to.

'I don't know what more we can do Samuel' she said. 'We try our hardest and all we get are tantrums. You'd think he'd be more grateful.'

'Yes, my dear,' was Samuel's non-committal reply. He left most of the bringing up of Willerby to his wife, having long ago decided he didn't understand children, especially this errant and complex lad.

'We only have his best interests at heart after all. We have to keep him safe,' his wife continued and Samuel looked over his glasses at her in silent understanding.

Neither of them ever mentioned that night when Willerby arrived, because time had blurred the memory. They had even begun to believe their own stories as to how Willerby came to be in Brakendor.

'He was such a surprise,' she told her neighbours. 'I thought it was the 'change', not a baby! But what a blessing to have a child at my time of life! He'll want for nothing!'

And she had been true to her word – Willerby had everything a child could want, except a carefree childhood, and knowledge of his real identity.

Yet there was more to Sarah's over-protectiveness, for in her heart of hearts she didn't want him to grow up: she wanted to keep him as he was, young and dependent on her, to stop time! Sarah buried her head in the sands of avoidance over the fact that one day he would grow up and leave home. She loved this child as her own, convincing herself he really was hers and she never wanted to lose him: no, she couldn't relax; couldn't let him go, she had to do everything she could not to put Willerby at risk, he was hers now. She and Samuel had taken him into their home and their lives willingly and with good intent, but now he was in her heart and loosing him would break it.

In the sanctuary of his bedroom Willerby let his frustrations out and they came in long, heaving sobs, fists banging the pillows on his bed. He wanted to run away from here – but where could he go? He was too young to leave home. He had only ever known Brackendor and there was no escape from the kind but cloying attentions of his parents, nor the small community of which they were a part.

'One day, I'll leave here, and I won't be scared,' Willerby shouted at himself in the mirror, but the eyes that looked back told a different story.

He looked at his desperate expression, wincing at the red-rimmed eyes and tear-stained cheeks, hating the pathetic creature that was Willerby – where was the brave and daring superhero he dreamed himself to be? Why was he such a wimp in reality?

'I HATE you,' he shouted at his reflection, 'you're a coward and I HATE you! I HATE YOU! I wish I'd NEVER BEEN BORN!' and he flung himself once more onto the bed and sobbed himself into an uneasy, dream-filled sleep.

He was in a clearing, in the middle of a forest, in the moonlight. It was familiar. There were trees all around him, standing, straight and tall, like pillars holding up the star-studded roof of the night sky. A sense of secret expectancy hung in the air as, standing in a luminous shaft of ethereal moonlight was a woman whose long thick chestnut curls cascaded down her back. He felt he knew her.

On her head she wore a silvery white circlet surmounted with a shining crescent moon. She had eyes of the most amazing clear green and was so beautiful that Willerby involuntarily drew breath. When she smiled at him and held out her arms he just knew he had to run into them, and here he could sob for all the unknown losses in his life. She held him close to her in an embrace that seemed to fulfil all his childhood needs at once.

She did not speak, but he heard a voice in his head, soft and gentle, that he knew was hers.

'My son, my son, all is well!'

Her words gave him peace, even bliss. There was a deeper connection with her than he had ever felt for anyone in all his young life, even Fynn, or sweet Sophie. As he enjoyed the sensation of being nurtured she drew from her shimmering gown seven stones, each a different colour of the rainbow, and each containing a letter of the alphabet: they reminded him of the reading cubes he'd had as a young child that helped him spell simple words.

She was placing the coloured stones in a special order so that they too spelled out a word, but it was a strange word that meant nothing to him. It read 'Wigapom'. Still no sound came from her lips but Willerby could hear the word intoned inside his head.

'Remember, "Wigapom", my beloved child,' the voice continued, 'this is given to you in love and recognition of who you really are. It will soon be time to use it again; use it well and wisely, and be patient, precious child, soon you will understand why you are here and what you must do.'

In the dream Willerby reached out a hand to collect the stones from her but just as he touched them he was falling, falling, falling, with the stones tumbling around him. He thrust out a hand and thought he caught just one, and then all was still and he was back in his room, clutching the bedclothes tightly in one hand, and with the word 'Wigapom' imprinted on his very soul.

The moonlight shimmered through his window, casting strange shadows by its silver light. It was eerily quiet and still, and Willerby was feeling very cold as he realised he had fallen asleep on top of the covers. Shivering, he crawled under them, drawing the blankets high up around his shoulders and curled into a small tight ball in his effort to get warm and recreate the feeling of the dream. Unlike previous dreams he could remember everything about this one. He ran it through in his mind as clearly as if it had just taken place that second. It was so clear that he began to doubt whether it was a dream at all, half expecting to see the lady with the chestnut hair beside him, and him still in the forest – but he was definitely in his bedroom. If it was a dream, why did it seem so real? This had never happened before. It wasn't one of his usual dreams, nor was it one of his increasingly frequent nightmares, which left him waking in a sweat in an effort to escape some overpowering monster! He closed his eyes again and saw the beautiful lady with the flowing chestnut hair, felt the softness of her skin and the incredible feeling of peace and contentment that flowed through him. He wanted to sink into the feeling once more, but although the memory was still clear, the feeling was receding like the tide and he was empty and lost again, but he did not forgot her, nor the memory of how wonderful the feeling had been, nor the stones she showed him, nor the strange word that continued to roll around in his mind for the rest of the night and beyond.

As he drifted this time into a deep, yet dreamless sleep, that word was like a lullaby, singing itself softly inside his head. He didn't know what it meant, but it brought that same sense of peace he remembered, which he had never thought possible before: Wigapom…Wigapom…

When he awoke the following morning, the dream was still real but made no sense to Willerby's now logical and awake mind, as dreams rarely do in the cold light of day. As he lay in bed Willerby continued to toss the word around in his mind, even writing it down several times on a piece of paper, as though by seeing its shape in print he could get the full essence of the word there on the page before him. It made the whole experience of the dream more tangible, and brought him closer to it, and its association with the beautiful lady. He was so engrossed in this activity that he forgot temporarily that it was his birthday, or that he had had such an argument with his mother last night. It was a surprise, therefore, to hear his father's rather clipped voice outside the door.

'Happy Birthday Willerby,' the voice said. 'I hope you're in a better temper today.'

The door opened and his father entered, along with the unmistakeable smell of fermented yeast that always seemed to accompany him. Willerby had little time to sort his thoughts, so to cover his confusion he pretended to be still asleep, hiding the piece of paper with Wigapom scrawled all over it under his pillow: instinctively he felt the need to keep it secret – one of the few things he could call completely his own and that his parents could not involve themselves in. This made him feel powerful for the first time in his life.

'Are you awake, Willerby?' asked his father, 'Time to get up. We have a busy day ahead.'

Willerby made a good display of waking, giving a wide yawn and huge stretch as he blinked his eyes open.

'Good morning, father,' he said, as sleepily as he could, slipping automatically into his usual formal way of addressing his parent: theirs was a civil, but distant, relationship.

'Happy Birthday, Willerby,' said his father again, and just as Willerby expected, extended his hand towards him, as though Willerby was already an adult and not just thirteen. Unfortunately this grown-up treatment extended no further than the outstretched arm.

Willerby took the offered hand and sitting up, shook it solemnly, as though greeting a stranger. Samuel, although a kind man, was not an expressive one and found his highly emotional and volatile son strange and difficult to understand. This reserved attitude saddened Willerby: although he'd always wanted to be treated as mature and responsible, just for once he would have loved his father to hug him, or even just ruffle his hair, but that had never really been Samuel's way and he was unlikely to change now.

'Your mother says you are forgiven for your outburst yesterday, *if* you behave yourself today, so we'll let bygones be bygones. Breakfast is ready and presents are waiting for you to open. We can open them together while I wait for the bread to bake, if you like. I have just enough time.'

'Thanks, said Willerby in a resigned, yet relieved sort of way: resigned to his father's stiffness, yet grateful that his outburst from yesterday had been forgiven if not forgotten.

The thought of forgiveness and presents didn't resolve his underlying frustration, but somehow the dream and the peaceful feeling it created, along with the word Wigapom, tucked secretly under the pillow, seemed to make things less hopeless than before. It also meant the party was still on – and even a boring conjurer was better than nothing at all! He dressed hurriedly, slipping the crumpled slip of paper with the word on it into his pocket and bounded downstairs to the warmth of the kitchen. By the time breakfast was over and it was present opening time he had all but forgotten it, lying in his pocket, and had stored the dream somewhere in the back of his mind, allowing himself, instead, to become swept into the special moments of his milestone birthday and all that it entailed.

CHAPTER 6

Could It Be Magic?

"Magic is believing in yourself, if you can do that, you can make anything happen."
Johann Wolfgang von Goethe

The birthday tea, despite the problems of yesterday, showed him that his parents did care about him – they had made such an effort; the table was laden with delicious food, the living room decorated so colourfully with streamers and balloons, and a 'Happy Birthday' banner was strung jauntily across the chimneybreast – these gladdened his heart and made him feel special, as well as guilty at his treatment of them. They did want the best for him, in their own way, and he allowed himself to appreciate this, and enjoy the occasion along with those he now hoped to truly call his friends.

'Pass the sweets around to your guests,' said his mother, determined he would be on his best behaviour today. Willerby did as he was told, approaching Sophie shyly first.

'Thank you, but I don't like sweets,' she said, 'but Happy Birthday, anyway,' and she smiled at him so beautifully that his face beamed as much as hers.

The birthday tea was nearly over: thirteen candles successfully blown out; the last few cakes and pastries munched; lemonade gradually drained from glasses and the delicious birthday cake sliced into equal portions for the number of guests, and all thoughts turning to the highlight of the afternoon.

Uncle Corrin, the conjurer, was familiar to them all, with his bright green hat with a flower on top. Normally he was Mr Chumbley, the undertaker, with sombre silk topper, polished to a shine, who, along with his wife Betsy – who 'did the remembrance flowers' – made sure that the necessary dispatches were sent off with as much pomp and circumstance as Brakendor could muster before being laid to rest in the quiet cemetery. He was a much-liked individual who could turn on solemnity as well as chuckles at the drop of whatever hat he happened to be wearing at the time. Today it would be the green one with the flower, so chuckles were expected!

Uncle Corrin and his unchanging act had been at many childhood parties over the years and Willerby feared that the choice might bore his growing guests. So when the knock came on the door, announcing his arrival, Willerby was nervous as to how they would respond to the all too familiar conjurer, in his striped trousers and funny hat, and the same routine of making coins appear from behind ears, and dice disappear from under cups. It was a great surprise, therefore, for Willerby to see a strange and much more exotically attired creature glide through the open door of the living room and cast a mysterious gaze around the room. Willerby wondered for a moment just what had got into his parents to invite someone so outlandish. He certainly didn't recognise him as any costumed villager.

The stranger was tall and lean, with sharp features and a confident smile that showed dazzling white teeth. His shining deep brown eyes swept over the assembled party, captivating everyone in a gaze that held both mystery and danger. Willerby felt fascinated and unsettled at the same time, unable to pull his eyes from him and taking in every astonishing detail.

As the stranger moved, sinewy snakes appeared to slither their way between dazzling suns and silvery moons emblazoned across his deep blue-green cloak. In his right hand he held a staff tipped with a glistening crystal and on his head a deep bluey-green pointed hat, studded with multi-coloured shining stars that reflected the light and sparkled as they seemed to change position, creating different constellations every few moments. Willerby's logical side of the brain told him that this was just a trick of the light but his imaginative side wistfully hoped it was true.

'The blessings of the four winds to you,' the stranger said, in a voice that ran up and down the musical scale like deft fingers across harp strings. The singsong quality quite mesmerised Willerby as it rose and fell in equal measure, and he listened, spellbound, as the stranger continued.

'Today, I am Marvo, the Magician,' he announced, sweeping his hat off with a deep bow to the assembled audience, 'although, one day *you* will know me as Asgar,' he whispered to Willerby, in a conspiratorial way, and his eyes twinkled like the stars on his gown. 'I am here, on this auspicious day, to mystify you all with such magic, the like of which you will never have experienced before!' and he scattered shimmering golden dust in the air.

The audience gasped, and gasped again, as he swept his hat once more to the floor with his amazingly long, tapered fingers, revealing a snow-white dove, which settled on the Happy Birthday banner, with a loud 'croo-croo'. Everyone laughed and clapped as the bird fixed each one with a quizzical gaze.

The Magician winked at Willerby as he produced yet another shower of iridescent dust from inside his cloak, which formed zodiacal shapes and star patterns in the air, before settling on the heads of each one of the audience. Everyone gasped and laughed again, eyes wide with excitement! Uncle Corrin this was not!

Marvo replaced his hat again with another flourish, whisking his hand inside his cloak, this time withdrawing a small box, from which he began to lift an enormous array of items in quick succession: books that were reading themselves; musical instruments already playing a tune; flowers bursting into bloom and then folding back into buds again and multi-coloured streamers that swirled and jigged in the air, tying and untying themselves into complex knots and bows, before forming the words 'Happy Birthday' in the air! The partygoers gasped at the wonder and magic of it all. There was no time to ask how these items all managed to be inside the box, let alone do all these amazing things because out flew a stream of multi-coloured lights from the box, which darted and exploded in the air like frenzied fireworks. There were squeals of delight as the lights dipped and dived between the spectators,

'And here is a treat for everyone!' Marvo said as, quick as a flash, out shot a blaze of brilliant-coloured tiny dots of light – brighter even than the lights before – from the end of his long crystal tipped staff. They ricocheted around the room in all directions, accompanied by a cacophony of bangs, whirrs, high-pitched whistles and tinkling bells before changing into a shower of exotically shaped sweets, wrapped in gaily-coloured paper which began to fall noisily amongst the partygoers, who all began scrabbling for them before popping them greedily into their waiting mouths. For one mad, timeless moment, there were excited shouts and cries of 'ooh' and 'wow' and 'yummy' from the party guests so that only Willerby was aware of Marvo's cloak enveloping him, and he felt a vibratory tingle, as the softness of the cloak brushed against his arm. The snakes were still slithering up and down between the suns and moons, and the stars were still changing their constellations, and Willerby was caught up in an altogether different world to his guests: as though just he and Marvo were sharing this magical space. Willerby heard the cadence of Marvo's voice rise and fall again, like a snake charmer's melody, and he succumbed completely to the spell it cast: he could not help but listen.

'And for the birthday boy only, a special gift,' said Marvo and his hand proffered a small glistening package towards Willerby.

'Here is a special present, just for you, Wigapom – not to be eaten, but inwardly digested, and kept safe.' Willerby felt Marvo's long slender fingers lightly drop the package into his hand, whereupon the bright wrapping paper opened of its own accord, revealing a shiny stone of the most joyful orange. It had strange markings etched on one side and, although it seemed fanciful, it appeared to be vibrating in his hand!

The blaze of bright, noisy lights and fast-descending sweets had ended as timelessly as they began, but the guests continued happily munching their way through the carpet of sweets left on the floor, oblivious now to Marvo's presence. Willerby was still very aware, however, unable to drag his eyes away. He saw the Magician sweep the white dove from her perch with his hat; heard him announce his departure in the hypnotic singsong voice.

'Farewell, young Prince, and greetings from those who love you. Guard your gift well, and your new name – all is well, and as it should be,' and with a final smile at Willerby and a flourish of his amazing cloak, Marvo the Magician dissolved into the air with a faint shimmer of dappled light!

Willerby felt as though he had suddenly travelled back from a deep, distant place and found himself just staring at the space that Marvo had just inhabited. Where had he gone? He had not gone out of the door, of that Willerby was certain. He just was no longer there. If this were not perplexing enough it also seemed that only Willerby had noticed Marvo's disappearance: indeed, as he heard the excited chatter around him, it seemed to Willerby that they were not even aware that Marvo had even been there! Instead they were swapping comments with each other, as they cleared the floor of sweets, about how wonderful Uncle Corrin had been this time!

'But didn't you see him,' Willerby cried, trying to make himself heard above the excited voices and crackle of opening sweet papers, 'didn't you see what he did? All that magic and then he just disappeared!'

But they were too busy enthusing about Uncle Corrin.

'He was amazing!' said Ewan.

'Best he's ever been!' agreed Bryony.

'Fantastic, yummy sweets!' said Rhys, stuffing several into his mouth at once. It was as though Marvo had never existed!

'What are you talking about? It wasn't Corrin!' he said, but they just didn't hear him – too busy eating the sweets that Willerby knew had materialised from the tiny lights that shot from Marvo's crystal staff! How could they not remember such an amazing character, especially when they were eating the sweets that he had created?

Realisation slowly spread across Willerby's face: the sweets! It must be something in the sweets that had blotted out all memory of Marvo!

Willerby hadn't eaten any because Marvo was talking to him at the time and giving him that strangely beautiful orange stone. He'd thought it was a shame not to have tried one but perhaps he had not been meant to. He was meant to remember Marvo instead! But why should he have been singled out for this? Things like this just didn't happen in sleepy Brakendor!

The excitement and bustle of the party carried on around him, yet he felt strangely separated from it all. He looked down at the unusual orange stone with its etched pattern and remembered Marvo telling him to keep it safe. Suddenly he got the very strong feeling that he was to talk to no one else about this stone for the moment. He knew that somehow there had been real magic here today, such as he had only read about in storybooks before, and a delicious shiver curled up his spine: he was thrilled yet confused; he had never experienced magic before, conjuring tricks yes, but not real magic – he hadn't believed it really existed! Yet there could be no doubt in his mind that this is what he had witnessed today. What was going on? There were stories in the books he and Fynn had found in the cupboard of how magic had once been used in the Kingdom of Arcanum, an apparently mythical land of knights and their ladies, where magicians and wizards helped people to live well and honourably. These same stories told also of a magician, who had destroyed the good magic and become an evil sorcerer! Willerby had thrilled to these stories but never believed them to be true – now suddenly he didn't know what was real anymore. It was unsettling, confusing, but unbelievably exciting! He felt as though a door in his head, which had been firmly shut and bolted for so long, had suddenly swung open onto a brilliant and magical world of possibility! Yet the partygoers were oblivious. As they prepared to leave, chattering and smiling, they each told him what a great time they'd had.

'Marvellous party, Will, thanks for inviting us!' they said.

Willerby was confused. He seemed stuck between two worlds, the real and the unreal, yet the friendliness of his guests was intoxicating and he soon found himself beaming. He could hardly believe how friendly they were towards him! It was as if he was the most popular boy in the village! He had never felt so welcomed!

'Great party!' said Fynn, as he got ready to leave. 'That Corrin! What a guy, eh? Same old tricks but I still can't work out how he does them, especially the dice disappearing bit. Amazing! Great time! Bye Will, see you tomorrow.'

Willerby's euphoria bubble popped: even Fynn didn't remember Marvo! What was the point of having friends if they couldn't share in the most amazing event of his young life? Suddenly he was alone again: still separate from everyone because their memory of his party, his special party, would always now be so different to his own: no one else would remember Marvo's strange, dangerously fascinating eyes, or the hypnotic tone of his voice, or the books that read themselves or the fireworks that flew from his crystal staff, or the lights that changed into sweets and littered the room – they would only recall Uncle Corrin and the disappearing dice!

Had he got it wrong? Had he so desperately wanted his party to be a success that he had imagined Marvo – imagined everything? He looked across at his parents who were beginning to clear away the party debris and they too were talking about how reasonably priced Corrin was, and didn't he do well for his age, even after all these years, and that they never got bored with watching him. Willerby sighed. He must have imagined it after all. But no, it had happened, for there, in his hand, was the shiny orange stone with the strange markings: proof that everything he remembered was real, but this awareness created more questions than answers. Willerby needed time to think. He put the orange stone in his pocket and it came into contact with the piece of paper on which he had written the word from his dream. Suddenly, with a jolt he remembered what Marvo had called him: Wigapom! Not Willerby, but Wigapom! It was the same word the beautiful lady had spelled out from the coloured stones in his dream, except Marvo had used it as a name. He could hardly believe that this was just a coincidence, this was magical! How else could Marvo, even with all his wonderful magic, be able to know what Willerby had dreamed? If it had not been for the very real presence of the orange stone Willerby would have thought he was going well and truly mad! From the back of his mind he thought Marvo had called him something else too. What was it? He racked his brain but he couldn't remember. He had to be on his own to think what this could all mean! Then everything changed.

Another whoosh of tingling energy shot up his spine and into his head, exploding all his senses with new and potent experiences. The rest of the room was a noisy blur except, he realised, for the clear presence of Sophie who was looking at him very intently, and he returned her gaze with equal intensity, as though they were really *seeing* each other for the first time. As their eyes locked the room began to spin in a kaleidoscope of colour and light and suddenly they were flying! He, on the back of the fabled Phoenix with Sophie astride a Unicorn with wings like Pegasus, looking down on the dazzling world of his dreams spread out below them! Rivers winding through green fields studded with colourful flowers, tall turrets towering over stunning castles, shining silver cities, a ring of dazzling standing stones, and throngs of happy, joyful people. It was exhilaratingly liberating and as Willerby and Sophie talked and laughed, their voices blended as one. Willerby wanted this moment to last forever, but everything began to spin again and suddenly he was back in the room, with Sophie standing in front of him, her hand resting lightly on his.

'I saw it all, Willerby. I won't forget. It was wonderful,' she said, her blue eyes dancing with light. 'You're not alone, after all,' and then she left, her golden hair bouncing around her shoulders.

Willerby stared after her, excitement bubbling like an underground spring. She knew! But how? Then he recalled she didn't eat sweets.

Later, in the peace and solitude of his room, he held the stone in his hand again, and felt the same vibrating pulse from it he had felt before, yet stronger this time. It was a pleasant feeling, making him want to smile – yes – it was a smiley sort of stone! He was curious about the etched markings on one side of it – if he had expected them to be a recognisable letter, such as he had seen in his dream the night before, he was disappointed because whatever the symbol meant or represented was unknown to him. It was an attractive pattern though and became very familiar to him, as he always kept the stone about him, finding that it helped to lift his spirits whenever he was feeling down or cross. The word on the paper however, took some time to get used to. He liked the sound it made when he spoke it although it seemed a strange name. Over the next few weeks he began to spend time saying it out loud into his mirror on the dresser, as though introducing himself to it. He pulled strange faces as he let the word roll around his tongue and laughed at the sounds he made and at his reflection: somehow he didn't mind too much looking at his reflection as Wigapom. But he never told anyone else. The ones who needed to know already did and that was enough for now.

CHAPTER 7

Growing Into Being

"We grow neither better nor worse as we get old, but more like ourselves."
May Lamberton Becker

Time passed, and such memories and events remained special but slipped somewhere into the deeper recesses of Willerby's mind whilst life carried on. In many ways it was better than before. He had acceptance from his peers at last and by his fifteenth birthday, although in the throes of adolescence, when spots seemed to sprout like self-sown seeds across his face, he was more at ease with himself: his voice had stayed lower, his head higher, he was less lanky and self-conscious than before, his teeth were straighter and legs less gangly and his mother had slowly begun to relax a little from her smothering of the past. Willerby had also begun to realise that girls were more fascinating than he had ever imagined and was shyly paying them more interest, Sophie particularly. She had grown into a real beauty, with delicately pretty, cornflower-blue eyes, honey-blonde hair and a slender frame. She also had a quiet maturity that belied her youth and seeming fragility. He felt protective towards her nonetheless, and she increasingly filled his imagination and dreams as the typical 'princess' from the stories he knew and loved so well. She seemed to like him too, but their attraction to each other was lived out mainly from afar. There was always a connection, because of the party experience, but, apart from the occasional 'hello', or 'goodbye' it was expressed mostly silently: he would look at her, and smile shyly whilst she would glance at him from under her long lashes and smile back. The birthday party incident was never mentioned again, but Willerby didn't mind, because knowing that it had happened was enough and their glances communicated more than words. So this quiet 'relationship' continued just between the two of them. For the adolescent Willerby this made it even more special. Only once did they ever really have a meaningful conversation together, if it could be called that: Sophie was on her way home from school later than normal, carrying a pile of books, and Willerby was delivering a specially-commissioned cake to the schoolmistress. Both were deep in their own worlds until they literally bumped into each other in the middle of the street. Willerby managed to stop the cake from splattering on the ground but Sophie was not so lucky with the books.

'OH!' they both said at the same time.

'I'm so sorry. Can I...' they both asked together, eyes meeting in consternation, then they both laughed awkwardly, again at the same time, which made them both blush, together.

'You first...' they said in unison, and laughed again, eyes meeting in embarrassment and amusement. Then both took a deep breath and Willerby spoke first.

'Can I help you with your books?' he said, in his most chivalrous manner.

'Thank you,' Sophie replied graciously, adding, 'I'm glad your cake is alright.'

'So am I,' said Willerby, as he helped pick up the books. He hoped this unexpected, but very pleasurable chance encounter would continue: suddenly he wanted to ask her about their shared memories of his thirteenth birthday party, but didn't know how to start.

'You're very kind,' said Sophie again, as the last book was placed back in her arms.

'You looked wonderful on the Unicorn!' blurted out Willerby before he could stop himself. He then blushed with acute embarrassment at his forwardness, trying to cover his confusion by picking up the cake, and hiding behind it!

'And so did you on the Phoenix,' said Sophie, so very quietly, that it was almost a whisper, but Willerby heard it, loud and clear, and his heart sang as his confidence grew.

'That day, at my party, 'he began. 'We really flew, didn't we?' Sophie lifted her eyes to his and held his gaze, and it was as though the continuation of the whole world was dependent on her reply.

'Yes,' she said quietly, 'it was wonderful. It felt like going home.' Willerby's heart pounded, hearing her describe it so, but then her face saddened inexplicably and she dropped her eyes to the ground.

'I've got to go now,' she said, 'Mother's expecting me,' and she started to walk away but stopped and turned back, saying something, which Willerby didn't really understand at the time, although came to reflect upon much later. It left him with a sense of something good, even though he wasn't quite sure why.

'You can't judge a book by its cover, you know,' she said, filling his vision with blue, as she looked him straight in the eyes, 'but you have to look inside to find out what it's really about. That's like us really: we have to look deep inside ourselves to be who we really are, no matter what has happened. In difficult moments I do my best to remember that.'

Willerby nodded automatically, not really understanding what she meant. It seemed very philosophical, wise and grown up – characteristics which Willerby did not feel he had, and then she was off, and apart from a few glances and the odd 'hello' they rarely spoke again – but the feeling remained. Strange as it may seem, this one encounter had a great deal of positive effect on Willerby's confidence and how he viewed himself.

One effect was he became more interested in his appearance, and identity. Until he had that strangely wonderful conversation with Sophie he'd never thought he was much to look at really. Shaggy, thick brown hair that refused all attempts to lie down, as though trying to reach higher places, a nose too long, a mouth too big, eyes? They were OK, he supposed, a sort of greenish colour or something similar: but now he seemed to be able to see beyond those physical limitations to the person beneath.

Today he was looking at himself in the mirror, straight in the eyes this time, ignoring the hair and spots as he mouthed the secret, but by now familiar name of 'Wigapom'. He'd not thought of it as a name until the magician used it as one but had since begun to embrace it as an identity. It still had that special ring about it and left him feeling calm and at peace with himself, despite the spots! As he said the name he noticed that his eyes were actually *all* green – quite a dark green in fact. They reminded him of the eyes of the beautiful lady in his dream of long ago.

He said the name again, out loud, adding 'I am,' at the beginning and this felt very natural and right somehow: he could really identify with it. He absentmindedly fingered the orange stone in his pocket, which he always carried and which now vibrated slightly as he said it again.

'I am Wigapom!'

His stomach seemed to flutter with recognition.

'I AM WIGAPOM!' he announced loudly to the mirror, smiling at himself, and the reflection said it too, smiling back at him. In that moment he really began to like himself.

The character of Willerby began to recede like the hair on his father's balding head and Wigapom was born. All the turmoil he had experienced before as Willerby seemed to fall away, as though it had happened to another person, and he embraced being Wigapom with a passion that he never fully understood logically but only knew now 'felt right', and this was good enough for him. Now it would have to be good enough for others too! It was time for secrecy to end and for Wigapom to declare his presence: to be who he had always wanted to be. He addressed himself in the mirror, light-heartedly.

'After all, at your age, Wigapom, you can make your own decisions as to what you want to be called.'

'Absolutely,' he answered back, 'and I want to be called Wigapom! I AM Wigapom!'

He grinned appreciatively at himself: he'd never been happy as Willerby – Willerby was the restricted past and Wigapom a brighter future. With a different name he could begin to live the life he chose for himself. He stood tall and straight, almost a man now, and felt empowered with this revelation, striding purposefully downstairs to introduce his new self to his parents.

Perhaps unsurprisingly, his announcement went down like a lead balloon. His father, once the first look of shock had subsided, just looked at him over the corner of his spectacles, and said condescendingly.

'What a very foolish name,' and allowed the corner of his mouth to curl slightly in the look of amused restraint often employed for such occasions, and which had always been such a spirit-crusher for Willerby for as long as he could remember. But it had now reached the ears and eyes of Wigapom and he was proud of himself when he let it roll over him.

His mother, too, who had always taken things much more to heart than her husband, looked both hurt and cross at the same time: a look that had left Willerby guilt-racked in the past, but which now required a new response from Wigapom.

'Always wanting to be someone different,' complained his mother. 'Always wanting to call attention to yourself! What's wrong with the name we gave you? Not good enough for you I suppose? Nothing we ever do for you seems good enough. I don't know where we've gone wrong with you, Willerby; we've always done our best to raise you properly and give you a good home, and now you want to throw that in our faces and change the name we gave you for some foolish one that means nothing! Well, young man, let me tell you, Willerby you are and Willerby you will always be whilst under our roof, and don't forget it!' and his mother's eyes misted with martyred tears as he knew they would.

'Mother's right, as always,' replied his father and, true to form, said no more about it.

This would have been a setback for the old Willerby, but as Wigapom it seemed less of a problem.

'It's not meant as a criticism, you have always done your best by me. It's just it feels right. I don't mind what you call me at home because it doesn't change who I am inside, and that is Wigapom.'

Neither of his parents responded to this comment and he found it surprisingly easy to accept that he would never be called Wigapom at home, but it didn't matter. His friends seemed to like it anyway and it was soon abbreviated affectionately to 'Wiggy,' perhaps as a reference to his unruly hair, which had a mind of its own, as much as his new name. Whatever the reason, in his eyes Wigapom was born.

He never told anyone about the dream, nor did he show anyone the stone – these were still hidden: part of the fragile magic he felt was forming inside him – as if, by sharing them he would risk losing them.

And then his father died.

Samuel had been old in mind and body for a long time and had gradually been leaving more of the day to day work to his son, spending more time sitting by the fire, or out in the sun, depending on the season. Wigapom didn't mind, he even relished the responsibility at first, never thinking that change was just around the corner. It came one afternoon as the last glancing beams of the autumn sun warmed the brick wall of the bakery, and Samuel finally slipped away, sitting in his rocking chair, overlooking the street where he had lived and worked all his life, leaving the now nineteen-year-old Wigapom with the sole duty of providing the village with its cakes and daily bread.

Through the tears of her widow's grief, Sarah said to her grown up son,

'It's up to you now Willerby, to carry on the family business, as your father would have wished. Brakendor relies on you. This is your place now.'

And, like a sapling felled before its time, those words severed the magic developing inside Wigapom, its energy faded, as the patterned curtains in the living room had done many years before. The golden autumn flung itself mercilessly into the worst winter for many years and Wigapom's future seemed as bleak as the view from the window across to the forbidden forest. Like a thief in the night Willerby had returned, unbidden and unwelcome, and there seemed no escape.

Part 3

Self-Confidence

"Self-confidence is the first requisite to great undertakings."
Samuel Johnson

CHAPTER 8

The Sun Stone

"No man is free who is not a master of himself."
Epictetus

The smell of freshly baking bread wafted aromatically around the bakery and, as if delighting in its new found freedom, made an easy exit through the half open door that led onto the small, tidy backyard. It continued on its journey, turning the corner of the building and sending its mouth-watering message out onto the cobbled streets, lined with cosy houses and quaint shops, that made life comfortable, if unchanging, in this close-knit community. It was one of the everyday smells that gave a sense of peace and security to the inhabitants of the sleepy village of Brakendor, slowly awakening their drowsy senses to a new day of the tried and tested rituals of their lives – work, rest, play, and sleep, until the day came when they too, would sleep forever, resting eternally in peace in the shade of the oak tree in the quaint cemetery at the far end of the village.

For these folk, this was all they would ever ask of life, all they thought they wanted. It was true that some moaned and groaned at times, but this was often part of their pleasure and they were content with their lot, undemanding, placid, accepting, neighbourly and, for the most part, cheerful. They wanted nothing more than a good gossip, a soft chair after a hard day's work, enough food on the table to fill their bellies and to slip comfortably into an uneventful old age. All except the baker, that is.

Wigapom, just twenty years old but feeling more like forty, with the full weight of family and community responsibility burdening his young shoulders, had already been at work from the early hours, as he had been, six days out of every seven, since his father had passed away and taken up permanent residence under the oak tree in the cemetery last autumn.

'Have I really suffered this life for nearly half a year?' thought Wigapom to himself desperately, as he withdrew another batch of crusty loaves from the deep, hot oven.

He set them aside to cool before replacing them with yet another tray full of uncooked white dollops of dough. Six months of mixing, kneading, pounding, shaping, baking, cooling and selling to the same old faces, who made the same old comments with the same old smiles or frowns as was their personality, on the same old days of every week! How had he stuck it for so long? His life was more limiting than ever, no room for dreams, no time for future plans, now it was work, work, work and he was surely going mad with the sameness of it all!

'Morning Wiggy,' Mr Sams, the shoe smith, would say every Tuesday, his rotund stature reminding Wigapom of a doughnut without the jam. 'I'll have my usual loaf, not too done on top, if you please.' Wigapom wanted to burn it!

'Ah! Warm bread, fresh from t'oven, just the way he likes it!' quipped Mrs Merriweather, the apple-cheeked wife of the greengrocer. 'His one pleasure in his old age, or so he tells me!' Wigapom wanted to spit on it!

'A nice crusty loaf, Wiggy if you please,' said Helda Farthing, invariably gossiping to her friend Cressida Dewer every Thursday about some poor villager: 'I saw Molly Finch shopping in her slippers again, she's getting more forgetful every day!'

'As long as she didn't forget to put her clothes on!' answered Cressida, and they would chuckle at their little joke. 'Just three soft rolls today Wiggy.' Wigapom would feel like banging their heads together, not caring if his bad temper became the object of their gossip later.

Mondays, Fridays and Saturdays were equally predictable and Sunday was worse, as he had family duties, parochial gossip and the criticism of his mother and sisters to contend with.

'I hope you've remembered to clean the ovens thoroughly, young man, your father would never bake in a dirty oven,' his mother would chide, ensuring her son was keeping up the high standards of her dear-departed husband. He wanted to shut her inside it!

As time had gone on Sarah had become more dependent on her son, as she had her husband, and saw him as the son she should have had. She did her best to block from her mind how he had come into her life, the visit by the stranger, the package or the hired man who was supposed to collect it. The latter had never come, although the package was still hidden away. Secretly she hoped she would never need to reveal it, never need to lose her adopted son and replacement provider. Wigapom was very aware of her dependence and it was suffocating him.

Wigapom's nephew Dylan had just become Wigapom's young apprentice, just as Wigapom had been for Samuel.

'Nice to keep it in the family' said his sister Eunice, Dylan's mother, who was, like her sister Martha, a younger version of Sarah.

'Ready for when I'm pushing up daisies in the shade of the tree!' thought Wigapom morosely.

No wonder he was beginning to feel his life was over before it had a chance to begin! He despised such an existence: he could hardly call it a life, something he confided to Fynn on the rare occasions they socialised together at The Ram and Ewe.

'I feel I'm just biding my time before I end up in the cemetery! Sometimes that seems to be the better life! If I don't get out of this place soon I'll be as good as dead anyway!'

Fynn had nodded sympathetically, doing his best to understand what it must be like for his friend.

'What does my life consist of?' Wigapom had continued, 'More to the point, where's it going? I'll tell you – nowhere, that's where.'

'It can't be that bad, surely,' said Fynn.

'It's not bad, it's terrible!' Wigapom replied. 'Look at me. I feel so stuck. What's happened to those years since I changed my name to Wigapom? I felt I'd found myself then, and life held such promise. But it's all just drifted away somehow, like flour when the bakery door's open. A door means access to somewhere else, Fynn, but mine just keeps me trapped. I've let myself be thumped and kneaded into submission like the lumps of dough I handle every day. I've lost Wigapom somewhere and Willerby's back in harness and doing what's expected of him by carrying on the family tradition. No one asked me if I wanted it – that's never even come into the equation – it's just expected. I've never been so unhappy, frustrated or angry in my life before.'

Fynn saw Wigapom's turmoil, and had begun to wonder about his own situation – his life had followed a similar pattern of family expectations: as a farm hand like his father and grandfather before him. He knew no different and had never challenged it before now, but the passion and despair in Wigapom's voice caused him to reflect on his life in a way he had never done before.

This didn't make Wigapom's any better though and here he was, on this unusually bright and clear spring morning, brown hair flopping irritatingly into his clear green eyes and up to his scrubbed elbows in floury dough, arguing with himself loudly whilst taking out his pent-up frustration on the last batch of dough waiting to be made into rolls, loaves and fancy twists.

'What am I doing here?' he quizzed himself again, as he once more threw the dough violently onto the floured table 'I don't want this! What's the point of being Wigapom if I only live the life of Willerby? I hate Willerby and everything he stands for, but that's who I've become again.

Things have to change: I have to reclaim *me* before it's too late. I need to get out of Brakendor, do something different with my life.'

'How can you even think of leaving your home and your family,' retorted the voice that always sounded so like his mother's, only it was now living permanently inside his head. 'Where's your gratitude, your sense of duty? This is where you should be, where you've always been, have you forgotten that?'

Then the real Wigapom's voice took over.

'What's the point of life if it only consists of drudgery and sameness every day? I've got to leave!'

The Willerby voice chimed in guiltily, 'how can I leave all this, what will people say? And, anyway, what other life do I know? There's nothing else I can do, but stay here and be a baker.'

The Wigapom voice rose to the surface like a great whale breaking the surface of the waves.

'What do you mean? There's always something more than this! There's a world out there that I know nothing about, apart from the scary tales people tell me, and how do I know if they're true or not if I don't find out for myself?'

His mother's voice butted in again, 'There might be more out there but it's not your place to find it; you should be here, doing what's expected of you. What would your father think if you abandoned his business? What will the villagers do if there's no one to bake their bread? You belong here now, and what makes you think you could manage anywhere else anyway? You only know about baking – you only know about Brakendor – you could never leave and survive – think yourself lucky you have what you have.'

He waited hopefully for the Wigapom voice to answer back but it had given up trying and abandoned him in silence and despair, leaving only smothered Willerby in its place – and he wasn't talking either – what was the point?

This increasingly desperate argument had been going on inside his head every day for months now and left Wigapom more and more depressed, unsettled and frustrated with himself than he could remember being since childhood, before he changed his name. But the name and what it represented was based on a dream, and had no bearing on the reality of the moment. Even though he still carried the stone in his pocket the memory of how it came to be was gathering dust.

He threw the last batch of dough into the waiting floured tins with considerable venom, sweat pouring off him, as much from frustration as from the heat of the oven, and thrust the last loaves inside.

'Thank goodness that's done!' he said to himself. 'I need some air.'

He had to get away, even if only for as long as it took the bread to bake: half an hour to call his own, then the village would have woken up and be demanding his attention once more, as well as his mother, checking up on him – as if he didn't know what he was doing by now and couldn't be trusted! Oh! If he didn't get out he would just snap with frustration and rage! He took his chance, threw off his floury apron, and without stopping to wash the flour from his hands or face, strode out of the door into the shimmering early morning light.

He headed for the brook that meandered gently along the edge of the village, providing a natural boundary between the fields that led eventually to the forest, beyond which no one in Brakendor ever ventured. He often used the brook as a refuge from the restrictions of his life, finding peace amidst its clear waters and cheerful chatter as it bubbled over the stones and pebbles. He needed that peace more than ever today: just plunging his hands into the brook or sipping its delicious coolness would allow him to make connection with an outside world that was otherwise so far out of reach.

As he hurried towards the brook he found it a sad testament to his character that even today, despite his mood, he was still only going to the edge of the brook, not attempting to break free and cross it.

The dew was still wet and shining on the ground as he walked through the village. It was quiet and peaceful – luckily few other inhabitants stirred this early. He would probably have snapped or scowled at any greeting! For a while at least he had the place to himself, and how he needed this space! Yet he was blind to the natural beauty all around him, blind to the world's newness, and promise of re-birth: so stuck in his own misery he didn't see or feel anything: not the fresh spring flowers or the fledgling warmth of the sun, not the song of the birds overhead, not the fresh green leaves budding on the branches. He couldn't see that everything was waking up from its long dark winter sleep; that springtime was arriving in all her glory and with such promise of what was to come. He did, however, recognise the playful sound of the water bubbling over the smooth stones on its way to the sea, and his heart lifted. The sea! Sometimes in his dreams he thought he could hear it and smell it, but he'd never seen it, so how could he know? This last realisation hit him hard, compounding his frustration even more.

'I know nowhere apart from here,' he said, despair colouring his voice. 'I don't even know where the water from the brook comes from, or goes to, yet I use it every day of my life!'

Despair switched to rage as he kicked at a stone viciously with the toe of his shoe, sending it flying into the brook with a loud plop. It was all too much for him at that point and despair flooded back as he slumped dejectedly down on the wet ground of the bank, wincing with the sudden sharp pain this caused him. His trousers soaked up the dew from the grass as he dipped his floury hands into the cold water, lifting it to his face and lips, and drinking deeply of the clear droplets that cascaded down his tight throat.

Perhaps it was the physical sensation of making contact with the water and the earth that drew him back into his body, allowing him to re-connect with everything around him, but suddenly all seemed crisper, more defined, more real and immediate than ever before: he noticed the colours of the flowers, the freshness of the leaves, and the rainbows in the water as the droplets caught the sunlight. He saw more clearly than he had for a very long time as his gaze was drawn to a bright yellow something caught between grey pebbles, bobbing backwards and forwards with the motion of the water. It was a stone. A memory stirred.

Curious, he dipped his hand into the brook again to lift it into view. Despite the coldness of the water, the stone, round and bright like the sun, and with an etched pattern on one side, was oddly warm and inviting to Wigapom's touch, and very familiar.

He felt deep inside his pocket and touched the orange carved stone, bringing it out to compare with the new one. He held them both up, allowing the water droplets to fade from the yellow stone as the air began to dry it. The brilliance of its colour did not diminish with the drying and Wigapom was able to compare the intricacy of the carving on its surface with that of the first stone. It was different in design but similar in style: there were the same strange lines, skilfully carved, but the meaning, if indeed there was one, was still lost on him. He knew he had made an important find: he was sure of that – in fact he felt he had been meant to find it. This wasn't coincidence; it was a sign – but a sign of what? Despite his hopes, the presence of the orange stone had not led to any great permanent change in his life, why should the yellow stone be any different? All he knew was, that like the orange stone, it felt comfortable, as it, too, gently vibrated in his hand, in time with his own pulse. The carvings on both stones fascinated him, and placing them together in the safety of his pocket he made a promise to himself that he would find out their meaning somehow. As they both slid down into the darkness and secrecy of his pocket they made a satisfying clunking sound .

'Almost as though they're saying hello!' said Wigapom fancifully, out loud. He smiled, recognising that his anger and frustration had abated and, looking around again, marvelled at the brilliance and beauty of the world he now felt part of at last, as though any moment something would happen to change his life.

At that precise moment something did.

In front of him, rising out of the water, was the woman he recognised from a dream a long time ago. Yet this was no dream: Wigapom felt more awake than he had ever felt in his life as the woman who had given him his name opened her arms wide to him, as if to embrace him. She was still as beautiful as he remembered, hair the colour of chestnuts fresh from their casings, eyes as clear and green as before, shining with the clarity and depth of the water from which she had risen, the folds of her translucent gown clearly evident, although he could see through them to the fields beyond. In one outstretched hand she held a staff capped with a pointed quartz crystal from which was pouring crystal-clear water that tumbled into the brook below, the soft pure sounds becoming words, a poem, that flowed in a steady stream into his mind, transfixing him with their fluidity and clarity.

> *It is time, dear Wigapom, to nurture your dream,*
> *And wake up to your destiny.*
> *To acknowledge the truth of who you are,*
> *And become who you must be.*
> *You have, in your hand, the start of your journey:*
> *Two keys from the seven are here.*
> *One other is close, the others are far,*
> *Gain them, and all will seem clear.*
> *When you dig down deep inside yourself,*
> *They will come to you.*
> *All will find their way back home,*
> *If, to your heart, you are true.*
> *Seek out the Book, to set them in,*
> *From the Sorcerer's hidden place.*
> *Keeping your wits about you*
> *Will reveal the secret space.*
> *Then, like the Phoenix, you will rise again,*
> *And when you find The Magic Book,*
> *Place them in its open spine –*
> *Remember to closely look.*
> *Do not judge a book by its cover,*
> *But only by what you feel,*
> *Then all the doors will open for you,*
> *And your life will be more real.*

In times of darkness, remember the light,
That will always lead you home:
In times of despair and loneliness,
Know you are never alone.

Wigapom absorbed this extraordinary message in the time it took for sunlight to sparkle on a dew drop, and in that special moment he had instant understanding as his mind seemed to fill his whole body – every cell and fibre of his being, from the tips of his toes to the top of his head, buzzed with life and potential.

The beautiful woman smiled and her face lit up with a golden brilliance that spread out, enveloping and illuminating everything it touched with a radiance brighter than the sun. Wigapom saw everything with great clarity as he soaked up the intense rays, letting them percolate deep inside him whilst he also took in what he had just heard. He had been given a Quest, like the heroes in the stories. He was meant to find some stones and place them in a magic book. He had another purpose to his life after all as well as a feeling that he had touched something very special within him.

He looked into the light again, but she had gone, and with her that moment of clarity and understanding, but it didn't matter, she was with him already, at least her essence was, and he knew that she would be true to her word, and never leave him. He could feel her warmth, peace and beauty even now, and he breathed a sigh that released tension in his body, so that in that moment it, too, felt as peaceful as his soul.

He would return to the bakery with a lighter heart because he knew that his time in Brakendor was finally coming to an end. It was time to leave this safe, sleepy place that had been his home – or his prison – for so long. It could and would continue without him, for Wigapom was on the brink of a new life. Fingering the two carved stones in his pocket, and nurturing all that had been felt in his heart, and spoken into his soul, he turned for the penultimate time, to the bakery to face his customers.

CHAPTER 9

Off With the Old and On With the New

"No matter where you go, there you are."
Confucius

He was late in returning, and already customers were queuing at the door. His calmness receded as he returned to the old and familiar, and his mind raced.

'Sorry! Sorry I'm late, bit of a walk,' he explained.

'Thought you'd had a lie in!' joked Pepperell Armitage, winking at the other customers.

'All right for those that can,' moaned Cressida Dewer, 'some of us have work to do.'

Wigapom opened the door to let his customers in and the smell and fog of overcooked bread hit them. Wigapom quickly removed the bread from the oven and faced the criticism of his customers

'Look at these loaves, Wiggy, they're burnt!' admonished Cressida, 'Your father would never have let that happen.'

'I said I'm sorry, Mrs Dewer – just an accident, that's all.'

He apologised for the burnt loaves all morning, and how he got through listening to the moans, groans and gossip of his customers he would never know. The coloured stones seemed to be burning a hole in his pocket, and he was desperate to get them out again. Two out of seven! Five more to get! From where? How? One close and the others far, and what about the Book to put them in, the Magic Book, from the Sorcerer – where would he find them and why had he been entrusted with this Quest? He was so excited at the prospect he could hardly concentrate on anything else. He fingered the stones whenever he could, as if to reassure himself they were both still there, and by the time the last customers had left, clutching their warm, if considerably overdone, bread, the midday sun was now fully overhead, casting short shadows on the ground.

Wigapom breathed a sigh of relief as he removed his apron again. Apart from his nephew, Dylan, cleaning out the ovens, he was alone. Wigapom knew he now had the time he needed to make his plans.

'Just going for a walk Dylan,' he said lightly, 'can I leave you to finish off?'

'Yes Uncle, I know what to do, I'm almost thirteen, remember?' said his nephew solemnly, looking up from wiping the sink.

'Almost thirteen!' replied Wigapom. 'Quite grown up then!'

That was the age he'd been when he'd received the first stone, and begun the process of booting pathetic Willerby from his life to become Wigapom. It had taken a long time to happen, and he'd lost his way, but he was Wigapom again now and the Willerby years were well and truly banished. He would never lose sight of Wigapom again; never let Willerby back into his life, and this time any change would be permanent.

He stepped out of the door and began to walk back towards the brook: it seemed to draw him towards it, but there was no doubt about the reality of what he had been asked to do: he had the proof literally in his hands: The yellow stone, now safe with the orange. He would not fail in this Quest, no matter what it took. At last all his past yearning was making sense: this was what he was meant to do! He had a purpose, and he knew it was real. He just had to do it.

He was therefore somewhat disturbed to find his friend, Fynn, descending on him at speed, with a wide smile reaching Wigapom before the warmth of the physical greeting he knew only too well to expect.

'Wiggy, my friend! You look... different. Fancy a drink at The Ram before it gets too crowded?' Fynn's eyes danced in his face like two bright fireflies.

Fynn, as a man of the soil, seemed content with his lot, blessed with a sunny disposition that could blow away the blues from even the most determined depressive! Wigapom could feel the cheery 'Fynn effect' even before the firm handshake and affectionate slap on the back came and his cheery smile was returned.

'Hello Fynn – I was going for a walk actually, got some thinking to do.'

'Thinking, on a lovely day like this?' joked Fynn. 'Well, if you must think it's always more pleasant with a glass of barley brew in your hand, and someone to share your thoughts with, that's what I say.' His voice was light and Wigapom almost refused the offer, but he was positively bursting to tell someone what had happened and who better than his dearest and oldest friend?

'Alright,' he replied, 'I need someone to talk to,' and together they turned towards The Ram and Ewe.

84

The inn was busy, as it always was at this time of day, but they managed to find a quiet corner near a window, where the sun cast warm shafts of light over them. Wigapom wasn't sure how to start the conversation. How do you just tell someone that you've seen a vision and are leaving Brakendor to go on a Quest to find some coloured stones to put in a Magic Book? Not exactly an everyday conversation opener!

Fynn, however, began the conversation, sensing that something special had happened.

'OK, Wiggy, what's up? Something's happened to you today. You've been a misery for months and now you look like the cat whose got the cream! Come on, what's changed? Spill the beans. You can tell me, that's what friends are for, aren't they?'

Wigapom looked into the kindly, no-nonsense face of his friend and was suddenly so grateful that he had such a person in his life, but at the same time wondered how his friend would cope with hearing all he had to tell him – and did he tell him everything? He really didn't know what was going to come from his mouth at that point, but words just seemed to flow of their own accord, so he let them come.

'Oh Fynn, I don't know whether you'll believe this, but I've just seen a vision, a beautiful woman. I've seen her before, in a dream ages ago, and she gave me my name, but this time she was real, although I could see right through her! She gave me a yellow stone, to go with the orange one Marvo gave me all those years ago at my party, only you won't remember him because you thought he was Corrin but he wasn't, he was a real Magician, who enchanted you with the sweets – oh well, never mind that now. This beautiful woman at the brook told me I had to find five more stones, get the Magic Book from a Sorcerer and put them in it, so I've got to leave Brakendor... to, er... find them,' he finished lamely, catching sight of Fynn's increasingly bemused face.

'What?' said Fynn. 'You've met a sweet woman you can see through like a saucer and she was stoned?'

Wigapom laughed, in spite of himself, at Fynn's face and misinterpretation of what he'd heard.

'No, no, nothing like that. I've had a vision of a woman who told me I have to find five more special stones, keys, she called them. I've already got two of the seven I need. They unlock a special Magic Book held by a Sorcerer and will help people wake up to who they really are...'

'Have you already been drinking today?' said Fynn, 'Sorcerers? Stones in magic books? Waking up? Who's the one who sounds as though he's dreaming?'

Wigapom sighed. Oh dear, it had come out all wrong again. He tried another approach.

'Listen Fynn, I'm not drunk and I'm not dreaming, I'm serious: something important has happened to me today and whether you believe it or not, I've got to leave Brakendor to find these stones, I know I have to. I've wanted to leave here for ages anyway, you know that. I've never been happy living here and certainly not being the village baker, and I never will, it's just not who I am. I've always felt I had something different to do with my life, and now I've been given a Quest! I have to do it. More than that, I *want* to do it. I know it sounds crazy to you, but I've been chosen to do this. I don't know why, but I have to do it. At the very least it will be an adventure, like we always dreamed of, and it might help people too, so I can't lose either way. Do you understand, dear Fynn, or do you think I've lost the plot completely?'

Fynn faced Wigapom squarely and there was a pause in which he looked as though he was thinking more deeply than he'd ever had to before: somewhere, in the dark and dusty corners of his mind, a light of awareness was beginning to glow that he had not realised existed.

'Seems to me that you haven't lost the plot, Wiggy,' he said eventually, 'it's just that you seem to be re-writing it.'

'Yes Fynn, I am,' Wigapom replied, so pleased that Fynn seemed to understand after all. Had Wigapom been able to read Fynn's mind at that point, he would have known he was struggling with the unfamiliar light in his head. It had shone a few times before when he listened to Wigapom but now it was a bit too bright, a bit too quickly, and having experienced the intensity of the glow, he snuffed it out for now, with some relief, and settled back into the cosy shadows of what he knew.

'Well, I do think we need to do what's right for us, but visions and magic and strange Quests to find coloured stones? I don't understand that. I'm a simple chap, Wiggy and it all sounds too weird to me. Perhaps you just need time off or something, you work too hard you know!'

Wigapom smiled sadly. How could he ever have expected his friend to really understand? He sighed.

'Maybe, Fynn,' he said. 'Maybe all I need is a break, even though there aren't too many places for that around Brakendor. Thanks for the advice anyway.'

'No problem, Wiggy, that's what friends are for,' said Fynn, settling back into his chair and comfort zone, and putting all thoughts of visions and Quests from his mind to focus on the more mundane, but easier to understand beer in his hand.

Wigapom, too, leant back: it was hopeless expecting Fynn to be what he wasn't: he couldn't expect him to understand, but he wished he did.

'You've always been a good friend, Fynn. I'll always value what we had.'

'What we *still* have, Wiggy,' corrected Fynn, 'I'm not going anywhere.'

Wigapom smiled, and thought to himself, 'You may not be, but I am.'

He would really miss Fynn: pity he couldn't come too, but he could never see him leaving Brakendor, could he? – No – he'd never leave his home and family to go on some hair-brained Quest like his mad friend! It had only ever been make-believe for Fynn. This was the parting of the ways for them now.

They drained the last of the beer from their glasses, savouring every drop, but for entirely different reasons: Fynn, because he loved the taste and Wigapom because he knew it was the last he would ever drink in Brakendor, and that made it special somehow! They shook hands and separated outside The Ram and Ewe – Fynn going back to work and Wigapom…? Only time would tell where he was going.

The stones in his trouser pocket seemed to grow warm and pulse again. He hadn't even shown them to Fynn! Perhaps that was for the best. Wigapom took them out and gazed at them, turning them over and over in his hand, mystified by the carvings, strangely affected by the touch of them, but seeming to connect with them. He felt they were trying to communicate with him, but as yet he didn't think he spoke their language. But then, perhaps he did, without consciously being aware of it, because as he walked through the door of the bakery, the first thing he saw was the picture he had placed on the wall when he took over as baker, which he'd found in a dusty cupboard after his father died. It was of a Phoenix, rising from the ashes. He'd always loved the stories about the mythical bird that burnt itself, only to be reborn from the flames, and wondered why this picture should be hidden away in his father's possession. His mother had not liked it being moved but Wigapom was insistent on placing it on the wall for all to see. He'd flown on its back once and the vision of the woman had spoken of a Phoenix. Now, right below the picture, was a fresh loaf he'd baked that morning, just sitting on the table, seeming to say, 'Take me with you,' and by the side of it, a neat pile of coins just waiting to be spent on whatever he would need on his journey. As if simultaneously, he noticed by the sink a flask of fresh water, as though just waiting to quench his thirst on the journey ahead; and across the back of the chair, what should he see but his thick winter coat, waiting to keep him warm on dark and unfamiliar nights; and hanging on the hook at the back of the door, a knapsack, just biding its time patiently before it contained all these possessions, allowing him free and easy movement as he strode out into the unknown. They were signs telling him to leave.

He picked each article up and heard what they were saying to him, putting the bread, water and coat carefully in the bag, and the coins in his other pocket – the one without the stones. It was as simple as that; it always had been; only now the time was right! He looked around at the bakery:

familiar, full of memories: some good, some not. All in the past now. The future beckoned him. He thought of his mother and what his leaving would do to her, and old feelings of guilt began to surge again, but he replaced them with a new-found resolve: he wouldn't let guilt or fear stop him this time; he had a greater duty now – one that excited him like nothing ever had before.

'I am Wigapom,' he said loudly to the familiar items in the bakery. The Phoenix stared down at him from the wall as if in approval, and this confirmed his newly discovered confidence.

He quickly wrote three letters of explanation:

'Dear Mum,

Forgive me for letting you down, but I've had to do it. I've left Brackendor for good and I won't be coming back for a long time. Sorry, I've tried my best to be who you want me to be here but it's making me unhappy and angry inside and I can't live like that any more. I've been asked to do something very important by someone very special, that I hope will help others, so don't feel too badly.

I'm sorry to let you know like this but it's the best way – easier for all of us. No tears or goodbyes. Thank you, Mum for what you have done for me. We haven't always seen eye to eye but you have done your best by me and loved me, and I will always be grateful for that.

Love W.'

And to Fynn he wrote:

'Thanks, Fynn, for listening today, even if you didn't really understand.

It's a pity our friendship has to end, I've always valued it so much. It would have been good to share this with you but as you said, everyone has to be true to themselves. Have a good life.

Your friend Wiggy.

PS: If you see Sophie, please tell her I said goodbye, and that I'll always remember her.'

And to his customers:

'Thanks, everyone, for doing your best, and for putting up with my moods. I haven't always been easy to live with, I know. But now I have a chance to be me, whoever that is. I've never been a baker, or wanted to be one, but Dylan will make a fine one, in time. Don't think too badly of me. Sorry.

Wiggy.'

Then, with a last look at the picture of the Phoenix, which seemed to be smiling at him now, he left the notes clearly visible in the shop window amongst the cakes and buns and walked out of the bakery, closing the door firmly behind him and hearing the bell jangle for one last time before setting out towards the brook again, knowing that this time he was going to cross it and move out to where he had never ventured before. The yellow stone bounced reassuringly against the orange stone in his pocket.

CHAPTER 10

The Forbidden Forest

"The hero's main feat is to overcome the monster of darkness... "
Carl Jung

He actually found himself whistling as he walked along, something he thought he had forgotten the art of doing, so long was it since he had heard the sound come through his lips. It was a cheery, chirpy tune that he made now, and each step was light on the pathway. He had no painful knees either, which had been bothering him of late, as though his decision to leave had freed up any prematurely ageing joints and allowed him to move forward with ease. With his knapsack on his back he felt like one of the heroes in the myths he read as a child, setting out on his Quest to find himself, and make the world his own. He spent some pleasant moments deciding which one he most resembled and decided that he had a bit of each one of them: their bravery, and quick thinking – these were his abilities too now and he felt refreshingly alive and purposeful, both spirited and childlike, whilst at the same time commanding and powerful. It was an exhilarating feeling!

He walked at a frantic pace, as though making up for all those lost years, and refused to give another thought to his rather hasty departure, or the likely repercussions. He justified his actions by assuring himself that going on a Quest of such magnitude needed a quick response, and thus there was no time for procrastination, or sentimental farewells. He had taken a leap of faith into the dark, yet it felt more like a leap into the light!

Soon he was once more at the brook. There was still no one around and the water was pure and sparkling in the afternoon light. In no time at all Wigapom was negotiating a crossing amongst the flat rocks that dotted the water like stepping-stones. He'd never even noticed these before, and laughed to himself that a means of escape had been there all along, if only he had seen it! He made a game of judging which stone would support him and keep his feet dry and which wouldn't. This was both a source of laughter and a test of skill – a first challenge that he thought he fulfilled well! And then he was clear of the brook and on his way across the fields that led to the Forbidden Forest, his shoes immersed in the long grass as he strode out with purpose across the ground. One minute he had to negotiate low hillocks and tufts, and the next it was flat and smooth and easy to walk. He made a game of this too, seeing each different terrain as a challenge or reward, small but significant milestones on his Quest to the stones, and self-fulfilment. He felt so alive that he gave no thought to the fact that the forest had always been declared 'off-limits' to those in Brakendor. The scary stories of his childhood and the dangers reputed to lurk in the Forbidden Forest and beyond held no fear anymore. He thought only of the excitement of his Quest, of the stones to be located, and the Magic Book to be found and opened with them. What exciting places would he discover; what interesting people would he meet? He could hardly wait for it all to happen!

He threw back his head and held his face to the gentle warmth of the sun and never once looked back, never once turned his head to catch a fading glimpse of where he'd come from, but just focused his firm and resolute gaze on the wonders of the present moment, and the potential of the future. He jangled the stones in his pocket as he walked, and positively swaggered towards the forest. In time he saw the forest edges approaching and remembered the stories about trees that walked there, but all looked still and immobile to him! He looked at the tall dark, firmly-rooted trees stretching up the hillside ahead and marvelled that he, Wigapom, who used to be plain, pathetic Willerby, was about to ascend to the top of this peak, when so many others had not even got to its base! He quickened his step to reach the trees that marked the Brakendor boundary.

'Not moving today then!' he said to one of them, a wide hollow oak, and put out his hand to touch it, but came up against a resistance he had not expected. Surprised, he pushed against the invisible barrier, fancying that he saw a faint shimmering as he pushed really hard. It felt as though he was trying to break into, or maybe out of, a very strong bubble! How fanciful was that! He told himself he was daft to even imagine it and pushed again, hard. He hadn't got this far to be forced back by something he couldn't even see! It was tough though, whatever it was, He made another valiant effort and this time the invisible barrier seemed to 'pop' and dissolve as though, having tested his determination, it chose to hold him back no longer. Surprisingly it felt as though he fell through the tree, for he found himself on the other side of it, hearing as he fell forward another sound, like a popping in reverse, along with a sensation of something reforming behind him, but he dismissed it all as fanciful –

jumping jeepers, he might end up believing in walking trees, and large worms! The fact that he was only on this journey at all as a result of a strange magician, a mystical vision and some pulsating stones seemed to have temporarily escaped him!

The sun had disappeared behind a heavy cloud and the air became chill, the thickness of the trees blotting out what little light there was, making the day appear darker than before, and the forest more forbidding, but he could still hear the scuffle of what he assumed were animals scurrying out of sight into the undergrowth, and he decided to view this as comforting rather than concerning.

He smelled the richness of the damp earth beneath his feet, mixed with the woody smell of the ancient forest and felt the rough touch of a sudden breeze whipping across his face. It stung rather, but he paid it scant attention. He felt free for the first time in his life! Here he was, right inside the Forbidden Forest, but the trees were not walking, nor were their roots waiting to take him down into the earth with them! There were no monster worms either, nor red-eyed beasts! All he could hear was the occasional squirrel, rabbit, badger or maybe deer, scuttling amongst the trees and undergrowth! This was an ordinary forest, not a forbidden one. If there were enemies or monsters out there surely their names were Limitation and Fear? Wigapom made a vow right there and then that he would never let this happen again.

It was a new, resourceful Wigapom who slung his knapsack firmly back on his shoulders and prepared to conquer this new world. It was perhaps fortuitous that this new found bravado seemed to have dulled his senses temporarily, for had it not he might have heard the more insistent rustle of dry leaves dogging his steps, and seen a hunched shape and moving shadows making their way expertly through the undergrowth behind him, keeping their distance but always watching. He may also have sensed the increasingly heavy atmosphere building around him as he went deeper into the Forbidden Forest, and he might have lost his nerve and returned to what he knew. Then he would never have had the opportunity to fulfil his destiny: at this point at least, ignorance truly was bliss.

Somewhere, nearer than he would have liked to think, a dark figure looked into one of the many mirrors before him that had long since stopped reflecting his own image but instead spied on Arcanum. He watched silently as a glowing, moving shape made its route haphazardly through the trees. He was able to chart the course well, despite its erratic nature, but there were other moving shapes getting closer to the first and their presence seemed to create a smudging of the image, making it less clear at times. The dark figure made the image larger by twisting the black ring on his almost translucent hand. The face of the image became clear and defined: dark green eyes; thick, unruly, brown hair; strong chin; long nose. The dark figure unconsciously traced the face with his long, pale finger and quelled the strange feeling in the pit of his stomach as he saw for the first time what he knew to be *her* son: so this was what he looked like now? – hmm – he had her eyes.

He had often wondered how he would feel when he actually saw him as a young man, rather than the infant from all those years before. He was right to have waited: revenge would be sweeter now. Yes, The Brat had her eyes, but he also had his father's jaw and shape of face; he was his son too; their son; they had made him together. He swallowed back the feeling that had first arisen and turned them to stone inside himself: hard and uncompromising stone.

'Will you kill him now, Master?' said the slimy voice at his side, slavering at the thought of what was to come. Darqu'on looked down at the reptile and silently asked himself that question: would he kill him now, and end it all so quickly, or would he wait? He pushed down every emotion he felt: hurt; jealousy; envy; anger; rage, covering them expertly with controlled disdain, hardness and false amusement.

'No, I want his demise to be slow and painful, Scabtail, I want him to suffer and I want to enjoy witnessing it.'

The reptilian creature looked disappointed, but his feelings were of no interest to Darqu'on, who was relishing the thought of the entertainment ahead. The beginning of the final act in the drama of ensuring his revenge was complete, and ultimate power achieved. He would not fail, but neither would he rush. He'd waited a long time for this. He did not know his adversary yet, other than his identity, or any power that his heritage may have conferred upon him, but as he looked at him he felt again the rush of hatred surge through his body. He hated him with a passion, and this hatred provided the energy and power he needed to keep his grip firm, and resolve strong: to replace all he felt he had lost. The black hole, where once his heart had been, needed filling and this would only happen when The Brat, their son, was dead, and ultimate power belonged to him, and him alone! The end would be slow and painful, very painful, and his final revenge would be all the sweeter! A frisson of anticipation moved through him like an electrical current. This was payback – how thoroughly delightful!

As Wigapom watched what light there was gradually diminish, it turned the dark branches into gnarled fingers that seemed to want to snuff out the fading daylight and make everything darker, quieter and more sinister. The only sound remaining was the soft and regular crunch of his feet on the undergrowth of a previous summer's ferns and brambles, now brown and brittle, and the occasional swish and shuffle of unknown creatures. With no bird song and little breeze, a strange stillness swept over the forest as the deepening dusk-chill began to pervade the air and his body. He stopped for a moment to listen to the silence and felt an extra chill sweep over him, as though someone had walked on his grave. He pulled his coat from the bag and snuggled into its comforting warmth and familiarity, glad that he had brought it. In the coldness of the gathering dusk all was not quite so appealing as it had first seemed, and not for the first time did he wish he had brought a lantern to help guide his way and offer a friendly glow. He was also beginning to think ruefully that his rather headstrong departure had perhaps not been very well thought through after all. Strange how in the daylight things can be inviting, but as dusk falls, and night quickens, things can seem so different. Where was he heading? The forest seemed so much bigger than he had ever anticipated. How did he know where to find these stones; how would he know where to locate the Sorcerer or the Magic Book they were meant to unlock – was he really cut out for this sort of adventure after all? Behind him, the trees swept their branches towards him, edging up to him as if blocking any return to Brakendor: their roots rippled through the earth towards him, creeping silently closer, closer all the time; eyes peered through the darkness, watching and waiting; the chill breeze reappeared and encased Wigapom in its freezing fingers. There was a sudden sound. He started, involuntarily: was it just rabbits or something more sinister? Had he caught a flash of something bright moving over there? Suddenly, all the stories of giant underground worms, spectral riders and shape shifting creatures seemed more probable than when the sun was full and bright. He peered into the gloom, half expecting to see his fears realised, but there was nothing, just dark, tall, shadowy trees moving in the breeze.

Wigapom tried to convince himself that the sudden involuntary shudder that shook his body, was because of the strengthening chill of the air, but he knew in his heart of hearts it was an increasing tug of fear, coming up from the pit of his stomach, fed, no doubt, by his fertile imagination, but feeling very real. He did his best to push these feelings away as unbecoming in a hero on a Quest, deciding he needed to eat to stop the gnawing sensation in his stomach: he felt very empty inside and realised he had not eaten since breakfast that morning.

There was a tree just in front of him, wide and old, which looked as though it could offer some protection from whatever it was that Wigapom feared, and he settled his back as comfortably and securely as he could against it and took out the loaf. It was cold now of course, still burnt, and somewhat squashed from being rammed into his knapsack. It seemed much less appetising than before, but it would satisfy his hunger pangs – pity that he hadn't thought to bring some cheese, or a pie, or cake. His mouth watered at the thought, but he had to make do with what he had. Strange how excitement can keep hunger at bay for so long, he thought, biting ravenously into the loaf and trying to imagine that it was spread with thick butter, and maybe jam. It wasn't: it was dry and burnt. No matter, it would fill his stomach – he hoped it would quell his fear too, but his stomach stubbornly refused to stop rumbling and grumbling alarmingly in the all-encompassing silence of the forest, no matter how much of the loaf he consumed. Fear was enlarging the space inside him. He looked around, wide-eyed, in the gloom: who knew what or who was in the forest? Myths and legends were often based on fact, weren't they? It was all too easy to believe them now that he was here. His vivid imagination, now working overtime, flew back to the stories of his childhood: of the forest Wulverines with their red eyes, said to be the spirits of those killed by the Roth Riders, those ghostly creatures of terror who tore their victims apart and scattered the pieces to the winds! He recalled more descriptions of the shining red eyes and sharp teeth of the huge and fearsome Wulverines that hunted in packs, preying on unsuspecting travellers: they sucked blood so he had been told, as a bargaining tool to be reborn again. He tried to think of the gentler creatures – like his favourite, the Phoenix. The dreamlike experience with Sophie at his party flashed momentarily before his eyes, but somehow the presence of the Wulverines seemed far closer than that of the fabled bird. He shivered at the thought of being eaten by a red-eyed Wulverine, and tried to block it from his mind. Instead he recalled tales of the evil Sorcerer shape-shifting into the Shivastrom wind – destructive and violent in the extreme, sucking unsuspecting travellers into a vortex of dark energy! Was this real after all? Was it the same Sorcerer who had the Book? He brought to mind the grisly details of Bogus, the giant worm said to swallow unsuspecting travellers whole, and spend a lifetime masticating them in his enormous jaws before squeezing them down into his endless belly! He recalled the tales of the Basilisk, turning victims to stone with one glance, or the Hybrid, part vulture, part serpent, whose talons tore travellers to pieces! Or the poisonous breath of the hag, Lilitu! He tried to remember the gentler White Hart, or the Unicorn, but they stayed firmly absent as his fear pushed them away. He tried to swallow more of the bread but found himself gagging on its dryness; his eyes became increasingly wide, as imagination and fear took hold – and were those trees really moving over there? He folded himself tightly into the tree trunk, trying to shrink into its protection, yet at the same time checking to see that its roots were not wrapping themselves around his legs and arms, and all the time despising himself for feeling this way – this was more scaredy-cat Willerby than hero Wigapom! But the fear was too strong to ignore – Willerby had returned and he was sure those trees were not in the same position as before but nearer, bigger, taller! He began to hyperventilate, his palms becoming greasy with cold sweat, as panic and fear rose like internal beasts to swallow him down. He was too far away to contemplate turning back, and, looking back, couldn't recognise the pathway he had just taken. Was it the dark making it seem different or had the trees really moved after all?

If his sense of sight had altered momentarily his sense of hearing seemed heightened to every slight crackle, shuffle or thud around him. He was on red alert, waiting for something to jump out at him from any direction. Somewhere, amongst the noise and clamouring of his irrational fear, internal chastising voices were yelling at him mercilessly.

'I told you so! You shouldn't have come! You should have stayed in Brakendor!' shrilled the critical voice of his mother.

'Don't listen to her!' retorted another, 'You're letting yourself be scared. There's nothing to be frightened of but fear itself.'

'But he is stupid to have left the safety of Brakendor. And irresponsible. It will only lead to trouble!' retaliated his mother's voice.

'Take no notice!' continued the other voice, 'If you collapse with fear when there's nothing to be frightened of, how will you cope when there is? You're jumping at shadows – like Willerby the wimp! Pull yourself together Wigapom and don't be such a fool.' With both voices now ganging up inside his head, the pressure became too much. But there was more.

'I'm so scared' cried the young Willerby voice. Wigapom stiffened – what was Willerby doing back in his life? – He thought he'd got rid of him for good! That was the final straw.

'SHUT UP, ALL OF YOU, AND LEAVE ME ALONE!' Wigapom yelled inside his head, doing his best to remain in control, but he was pushed back as frightened Willerby engulfed him with a huge tidal wave of fear. Primed for action, like a cocked gun, his automatic response to flee kicked in at that moment, just as he heard a sharp crack close by. The trees amplified the sound, and he was sure he saw the glow of a large, penetrating red eye peering at him. Years of anxiety programming took over, blotting out Wigapom the Hero and sending instead frightened Willerby the Wimp into panic mode. He pushed himself onto his feet, adrenalin kicking in from somewhere, and ran, full throttle. He kept on running, as fast as his legs would take him: ducking and diving through the trees; slipping and sliding down banks; darting under branches; jumping over thick sinewy roots and fallen tree trunks, all of which seemed to purposefully be blocking his path. He battled with them all and did whatever he could to put as much distance between himself and whatever his fear told him was chasing him. He had become so wholly focused on escaping the original sound that disturbed him that he seemed oblivious to a softer but more constant crackle and swish that followed him doggedly as he sped through the dark night. He ran for a very long time, out-running the sound behind him. Finally he could run no longer: his heart pounded; his ears rang with exertion and his lungs were near bursting for want of breath. He threw himself against the trunk of an ancient elm and tried to shrink into its darkness, wanting it to envelop and hide him from whoever or whatever was chasing him, whilst desperately trying to stop the palpitating of his heart, which was making so much noise within his chest, it was like a clarion call to every unwelcome creature – surely a perfect indicator of his whereabouts!

He needed water to moisten his dry mouth but found it hard to swallow. His hands were still cold and clammy and his whole body pounded with pain. His hand touched a root of the tree, which moved under his touch. He jumped again in fear and staggered away, tripping over another large root erupting from the ground and blocking his path. He went sprawling, sliding into an oak, which, to his relief was hollow and unmoving: here was a hiding place of sorts. He tucked his bruised and frightened body inside it, desperate for the comfort of the bark around him and hoping against hope that it was not a short cut to a wormhole! Here, at least, he was away from the penetrating wind that had blown up suddenly and was intent on accompanying his first night in the forest, and the roots of this tree were comfortingly stationery! He hoped that the space might protect him from whatever had been following him.

In truth, he was so tired and exhausted that he gave himself up to whatever would befall him: he could fight no more. His eyes began to close, in spite of his fear. Frightening blackness! He shot them open again: more blackness: no moon wanted to penetrate the forest, no friendly stars peeked through the branches: just the blackness of night and uncertainty of the forest were his companions and he had to surrender to them completely. He drifted fitfully in and out of sleep, no matter how much he tried to keep awake. When he closed his eyes he hallucinated, his brain confused as to what was real and what was imagination: sinewy roots touched his body, growing around his arms and legs, pulling him down and down and down … Yet when he sprung his eyes open everything was as it had been … He entered a black hole and felt and heard the pressure of something fat and slippery swallowing him down in a regular rhythm... Down, down, down, but his eyes flung open and he heard only his heart pounding... He saw the glowing eyes of a Wulverine, which changed into a Hybrid, then a Basilisk, which turned his rigid body to stone! Again he forced open his eyes and saw only the darkness of the night. He forced his eyes to stay open this time and with muscles frozen with fear as well as cold he remained still and hidden, not daring to move. There were still crackles and rustles but no red eyes peered through the darkness at him and he could no longer keep his eyes from closing. The only thing that gave him any comfort at all, and which he clutched all night long like a security blanket, were the two carved stones in his pocket. Finally he allowed himself to succumb to the dark in an uneasy, nightmare-filled sleep. As he slept fitfully, the hollow tree held him secure inside its ancient trunk; its branches sweeping down to cover him; thick, gnarled roots wrapped themselves around him, taking him deeper and deeper into their embrace as he disappeared into the camouflaging blackness.

CHAPTER 11

Face-To-Face

*"To remain a child too long is childish, but it is just as childish to move away
and then assume that childhood no longer exists because we do not see it."*
Carl Jung

He was trying to run towards the lady with the chestnut hair and beautiful green eyes, but huge arm-like roots held his legs as he was being sucked through an enormous wormhole. The beast with the red eyes was bearing down on him and no matter how much he tried to get away it kept moving and blocking his path. All the while a cold cloying something clung to his legs like icy fingers, with a grip as strong as a vice, pulling him further and further down. The more he struggled, the harder it was and the lady with the beautiful eyes was moving further and further away – he couldn't reach her! Panic rose in his throat, and he wanted to scream, but his mouth was full of strange coloured stones that were choking him! He couldn't be heard; couldn't run and was being sucked into the earth as help faded away! The hot breath of the red-eyed beast was on his neck – it was only a matter of time before its vampire-like fangs bit deep into his flesh – unless the masticating jaws of the Bogus Worm got him first and squeezed out his life. They were taunting him, calling his name, loud and insistent…

'Wiggy, Wiggy, WIGGY!'

Wigapom made a last valiant effort to defend himself and flung out an arm, hearing the thud as his flailing fist thumped against a strong body.

'OOff!' said the voice, 'for goodness sake, Wiggy, it's me! – Mind what you're doing! Wake up, will you!'

Wigapom's eyes shot open in confusion, coming face to face with two exasperated and very familiar blue eyes peering at him from a mud-spattered face.

'Fynn?' cried Wigapom in utter disbelief as his senses returned, thrusting him back into the present and forcing him into painful awareness of the numbness in his body; the cold stiffness of his legs wedged amongst the roots; the hard bark jammed against his spine; and the spiral of warm air coming from his mouth as it hit the cold morning air, joining with that of the most welcome but unexpected presence of his dearest friend.

'Course it's me. Who else?' snorted Fynn. 'Did you think I'd let you do something as crazy as this on your own? After all the promises we made to each other as children? What sort of a friend would I be?'

Wigapom was extricating himself from his cramped space and pulling himself awkwardly into a more upright position, feeling the uncomfortable jabbing of pins and needles in his feet and legs as they struggled to come back to life.

'How did you know where to find me?' Wigapom said, eyes now wide but still unable to get over seeing Fynn in front of him, and feeling foolish all over again.

'Followed you of course, and jolly difficult it was too, make no mistake,' said Fynn, rubbing his arm and picking off chunks of dried mud from his jacket.

'The more I thought about what you said when we were at The Ram the more I realised you really were going to leave, and no doubt straight away, and the more I thought, the more I realised I didn't want you to go alone: so I ran after you, but by the time I got to the bakery you'd already gone and there was a crowd round the window reading the letters, all in a proper state of panic, including your mother, and so I said, not to worry, that I would find you, so I grabbed some stuff and left. I had no idea which way you'd gone but I got a feeling I had to cross the brook and then I managed to pick up your trail after a bit, but when I got to the edge of the forest you seemed to have disappeared completely as though something had swallowed you up. I thought I saw you by a hollow tree at one point but when I got nearer and went to look inside everything began to spin and I had to push my way out of something I couldn't see.'

'That happened to me. It was like breaking out of a bubble' said Wigapom, remembering his own experience of this.

'Yes, just like that! It was so strong I fell over! Well, once I got through that I was in the forest and I couldn't find your trail at first: nothing looked the same from one minute to the next. I almost began to believe those stories of walking trees! I completely lost my sense of direction and I went all over the place until I picked up your trail again. I heard you call out and I almost reached you, but I fell over a root that just appeared out of nowhere and let out a yell. Then you charged off like a bat out of hell and I had to chase you to keep up! I fell into a pile of mud in the process too, look at the state of me! But then, look at the state of you – you're no better! What a to do! Taken me all night to find you again – thank goodness I had my lamp,' and Fynn held up a lamp with a flashing red light on the top.

Wigapom felt suddenly ashamed and childish as he saw Fynn's lamp – so that was what the red 'eye' was that he thought he had seen, and the flashes of light, and dark shape and the noises in the forest? Just Fynn no doubt, trying to find him! No wild beasts, no strange creatures – well unless you counted the both of them! He felt an overwhelming sense of relief pouring over him and just wanted to laugh with the release of it all. The comical sight of both of them, covered in mud, twigs and old leaves left them both laughing, grateful to be together again in safety and companionship.

They shared their stories, and the food and drink that Fynn had left, Wigapom having lost his in his panic. Wigapom felt another pang of guilt at the thought of his mother worrying, but there was no going back now, so he pushed it deep down inside him. He told Fynn more about the vision of the woman at the brook and what she had said to him and showed Fynn the yellow stone, then the orange one, and when he realised that Fynn wasn't going to laugh at him, told him everything there was to know that he had for so long kept secret. Fynn was baffled by some of it but knew more than Wigapom had ever dreamed he would.

'Don't know about the beautiful woman – pretty strange that, and what she said to you,' he said, scratching his head hard, as though trying to dig deeper into his understanding, 'but these markings on the stones look like elven runes to me,' and he inspected the markings closely.

Wigapom looked at Fynn in amazement. 'What? How do you know that? And what are elven runes, anyway?' he asked.

'A sort of alphabet, I think,' said Fynn, 'my grandmother told me about them, but said I had to keep it secret or I'd get in trouble because the runes have magic powers, if you understand them, and no one practised magic anymore. I didn't really take her seriously and always thought she was just telling me more stories – she was a bit strange, my grandmother, and got stranger as she got older. She used to do weird things on the night of the full moon and talk to the gravestones in the cemetery.'

'Did she? You never said.'

'Would you, if your grandmother did that?' retorted Fynn. Wigapom agreed he wouldn't.

'What do you mean by magic powers?' said Wigapom, 'making things appear or disappear, that sort of thing?'

'I don't know. Maybe. She didn't say. My father said she was doo-lally but harmless and to take no notice, but Granny told me strange things before she died. I was a bit frightened of her really I suppose. One day she cornered me on my way home from school and told me she had Befind blood in her, whatever that is, and said she knew about sprites, faeries and their ways – that's who she talked to in the cemetery, apparently. She drew some runes for me once, that's how I recognised them. Don't know what they mean though – she never told me that.'

Wigapom didn't know what to be more amazed at: Fynn knowing about elven runes or him not telling Wigapom anything about it, after all these years of friendship! Wigapom was obviously not the only one to keep secrets and there was more to Fynn than he had ever suspected. Fynn was turning the stones over in his hand and Wigapom was brought back into the present.

'Nice looking things, aren't they?' said Fynn.

'Mmm. Have you noticed how they both seem to pulse, like a heart beat, when you're holding them, and they feel warm when you'd expect them to be cold, being stone?' replied Wigapom.

'Really? No. Don't feel anything like that myself,' replied Fynn, 'they're just stones with markings on them, as far as I can tell.'

'Oh,' said Wigapom, surprised and disappointed that Fynn's heritage did not extend to feeling what Wigapom felt, and suddenly aware that it was, perhaps just him that could feel life in the stones.

Fynn passed them back to Wigapom, who took a long look at them before putting them safely back in his pocket.

'Well, I guess we'll wait till sunrise and find our way back home then,' said Fynn, casually, 'I said I'd have you back before supper.'

Wigapom's jaw dropped in disbelief: was Fynn suggesting that after all that had happened he wanted to take Wigapom back to Brakendor?

'Go home?' said Wigapom, incredulous, 'I'm not going home, Fynn, I thought you understood? I know I let Willerby back in last night and got scared, but I'm not going back. I'm going to see this through, wherever it leads.'

Fynn's blue eyes twinkled as he slapped his thigh, chuckling.

'Had you worried then, didn't I?' he laughed.

Wigapom reddened. Why did he always fall for Fynn's teasing? He would have to take things less seriously! He chuckled back at his friend.

'Pest! You were pulling my leg again, weren't you! I never learn! So you'll come with me after all? Share this adventure, like we always planned?'

'Of course I'm coming too! Just you try and stop me! Can't let you have all the fun. Anyway, how would you manage without me?' and Fynn gave a cheeky wink to Wigapom. Wigapom beamed. It was just what he wanted to hear.

'To tell the truth, Wiggy, you've been a bit of an inspiration to me, leaving like that, I just thought to myself, I won't ever do anything different in my life if I don't do it with you. Don't get me wrong, I'm not following you blindly. I keep asking myself why I want to do it all the time, but asking questions doesn't always give us answers does it – we've got to make those happen, and that's exciting!'

'I didn't realise you were such a philosopher, Fynn, in fact there seem to be lots of things that I don't know about you, and I've known you all these years.'

'Just goes to show that we all have hidden depths!' replied Fynn.

'Never judge a book by its cover, as the vision said. By the way, did you see Sophie?'

'No time, Wiggy, I had to follow you.'

'Oh… Well, never mind,' said Wiggy, disappointed, 'sad to think I might never see her again though.'

'You've got me, Wiggy,' said Fynn, his tongue very firmly in cheek.

'You're not as pretty as Sophie though!' said Wigapom, responding in a similar way, 'But you'll have to do!' although at that moment he really couldn't think of anyone else he would rather share this adventure with.

'One for all and all for one,' Fynn said 'as it says in the stories. Seems to fit us doesn't it? Now – let's find a way out of here.'

They looked around to get their bearings. It was true what Fynn had said about the trees seeming to have moved, and backed up what Wigapom had previously thought. But then, everything looked different in the morning light. They could have been in a totally different forest. The only thing that seemed normal was the dawn light beginning to break through the trees, but even this had a more ethereal glow to it than they'd ever noticed in Brakendor, with its pale white and gold shafts of light shining through the trees and spotlighting the ground. A mist rose up from the earth, swirling into soft, mysterious tendrils around them, and birds at last sang their chorus to the morning: the silken sound weaving its way enticingly around the two travellers. It didn't matter that everything looked different; the forest was just beautiful and held no threat at that moment.

The scaly creature with a stumpy, scarred tail looked into the mirror alongside his Master.

'There is another with him, my Lord,' he said, obsequiously.

'I can see that, Scabtail,' said Darqu'on with some irritation. 'Go back and watch them both, but keep your distance: I don't want him to know he is being followed yet. I want to enjoy the chase: always more enjoyable than the capture I find, and now I have two playthings to toy with! How delicious! I must create some exciting games to tease them with before I go in for the final kill.'

'Indeed my Lord, excellent idea. If there is anything I can do to serve you more then you only have to ask...'

'Yes, yes Scabtail, I know,' interrupted Darqu'on tetchily, 'you constantly tell me to the point of boredom.'

'I do not mean to bore you, my Lord, just prove my loyalty. Forgive my transgression, I beg you,' and the creature prostrated himself at his master's feet.

'Get up, Scabtail, or I'll have you hung inside out!' snapped back Darqu'on, moving closer to the reptile, and wondering quite why he had created this creature. He irritated him so, yet he was useful. At times.

'A truly creative suggestion, my Lord, for torture – but for someone else I trust?' said Scabtail, strategically moving away, 'I am your ever-willing servant.'

'You are my slave, Scabtail, remember that: I created you and I own you, as I own everyone here – all do my bidding; all are dependant on me for their continued existence, even you.'

'Yes, my Lord, of course,' came Scabtail's fawning reply, '... although there are some who still reject you...'

Too late, Scabtail, realised he had said too much and held his scaly limb in defence of an expected attack from Darqu'on. He was not disappointed: a fierce tongue of flame shot from his master's fingertips and leapt around his tail. He winced with familiar pain as Darqu'on spat back his reply.

'Idiot! I need no reminding of those that still endeavour to resist me, but I am always in control – never forget that. I allow it, Scabtail – for my pleasure. I could wipe them out whenever I choose, as I can wipe you out,' and from his fingers more tongues of bright red and orange flame spurted, singeing the scaly creature's stumpy tail again, which now smouldered alarmingly.

'My Lord, forgive me!' cried the creature, wincing with pain. 'I seek only to serve!'

But Darqu'on was focused intently on the mirror once more.

'What's this I see? A different figure, or the same as before? No, a third one! How fascinating, especially as this one is a creature formed from fear and anger! The Brat has more in common with me than I first thought,' and he snarled, thin lips curling like a jagged scar across his pale face. 'Let's see what happens when they meet face to face. I could not have planned this better had I tried, Scabtail, I'm going to enjoy this; I always relish seeing someone hating another and I think we are in for some real entertainment here. Follow them, Scabtail, watch them closely, but do not let them know you are there, not yet.'

'Consider it done, my Lord,' replied Scabtail, relieved to be dismissed from his master, whom he feared as well as admired. Nursing his still smouldering tail, he slithered away into the gloom.

Wigapom and Fynn gathered their few belongings together and began to walk eastwards towards the rising sun.

'How did people react when they knew I'd left?' asked Wigapom, guilty still that he had gone so quickly and in such a headstrong way, without saying a proper goodbye.

'Shocked, especially your mother, she kept crying and wringing her hands and saying she'd let you down and where was the hired man?'

'Let who down? Me? What hired man?' said Wigapom.

'Don't know. It didn't make any sense to me at all, but I don't think she meant you somehow.'

'I wonder if she meant you? You used to be a hired man on the farm, didn't you?'

'That wouldn't make any sense either, I was there, standing by her side,' said Fynn, 'I think she was just so upset and shocked she didn't know what she was saying at the time.'

'We didn't always see eye to eye but I never meant to hurt her.'

'It's too late now. I'm sure she'll get over it in time, and everyone else will be living off the gossip for years to come – you'll go down in Brakendor history as the one that got away!'

'And you, Fynn – you got away too!'

'Mmm, suppose I did.'

'Was it really difficult to find me?' said Wigapom.

'It was once I got into the forest – the paths seemed to change and I couldn't always work out which track to follow.'

'What do you mean?' said Wigapom, 'how many tracks were there?'

'More than one, that's for sure,' said Fynn, 'and they were all fresh. Lucky for both of us I found the right one.'

Wigapom nodded. Just rabbits or deer tracks he thought, but his senses became acute again to all the sounds and sights around them, and a feeling they were being followed became very real. He could sense yesterday's fear threatening to become today's unless he took control. A twig cracked close by, followed by an intake of breath. Wigapom turned sharply. A branch swished back into place in an otherwise still forest.

'Who's there?' he whispered to Fynn.

Before Fynn had a chance to answer the sound came again – this time like soft feet following them over the fallen leaves. They both turned: was that a small shape quickly disappearing behind that tree to the right? A flash of orange amongst the grey of the trunks? All was still and quiet again.

They walked on, as if daring whatever it was to identify its position once more, and it did: another crackle; another footfall; another flash of orange behind the tree as they turned.

'There's something there alright,' said Fynn, quietly gripping a large stick that he had been swinging just in case he might be called upon to use it, although, in truth, he had never raised a weapon against anyone or anything before.

They walked a few more steps and, at the next footfall, Wigapom swung round and managed this time to see a small shape in a dark orange jerkin disappear behind a tree. This was not Wigapom's idea of a scary monster – it reminded him more of a child, although why a child should be following them, or even be in the forest was unclear. Whatever it was did not look frightening, and this helped Wigapom take control over his feelings and his confidence to return, stronger than before, as the daylight increased. Having got through his first night outside Brakendor it was as though he'd wiped out the fact that the Forbidden Forest was reputed to be dangerous and was instead in a blissful, if somewhat naïve, state of mind, imagining there was nothing with which he could not deal, especially as he had Fynn to back him up. He stood squarely, facing the path they had just walked and spoke out boldly and commandingly.

'Who are you?' he challenged, 'What do you want?'

There was no sign of any movement, no flash of orange, but there was the quiet sound of breathing coming from behind the tree. Again Wigapom showed no fear or concern, where perhaps he could have expressed caution.

'We know you're there,' he said, 'come out so we can see you.'

More shuffling, more breathing, then slowly and uncertainly a shape appeared from behind the tree. A boy, about twelve perhaps, with thick untidy hair, and defensive green eyes blazing in a pale face, wearing an orange jerkin at least one size too big and a pair of brown trousers far too short for his gangly legs. He wore sturdy, if scuffed, boots on his feet and a look on his face that contained both anxiety and hope mixed in equal measure with resentment and defensiveness. A complex mix! The sight of him stirred vague memories in Wigapom, leaving him feeling decidedly uncomfortable, but he couldn't work out why. Whenever he tried to grasp the memory it floated away from him, just out of reach.

'Who are you?' said Wigapom again, some of that feeling expressing itself in his over-harsh voice.

'What's it to you?' replied the boy defensively.

Wigapom was somewhat taken aback by this response at first – he'd not expected such arrogance, or was it fear? But then, he was not really sure what he'd expected at all – although he felt it safe to assume that it had not been this child in front of him! His tone reflected this as he responded to the boy.

'Because I want to know,' he replied, equally arrogantly, annoyed that this child should question him in this manner. They looked squarely into each other's eyes, as though trying to score points off each other, seeing who would capitulate first. There was a long silence while they weighed each other up. This could have gone on indefinitely if Fynn had not stepped in.

'So who are you?' he said, thinking how much he reminded him of Wigapom.

'I'm Will,' said the youngster, not once removing his gaze from Wigapom, and throwing the name down like a gauntlet, daring Wigapom to accept the challenge.

Wigapom continued to stare at him, affronted and strangely disturbed – his insides churning alarmingly with what he could only describe as resentment and condemnation. Where had he seen this boy before?

Fynn sensed the atmosphere brewing between them and whilst not understanding it, felt he had to break it again.

'Well, hello Will, why are you following us?' he said, quite jovially.

'I'm not following you, I'm following him,' said the boy, still looking intently at Wigapom as he jerked his grubby thumb towards him.

Both Wigapom and Fynn were taken back with this further statement. Fynn thought it quite amusing but Wigapom felt hackles rising along his spine. What a cheek this child had! He disliked him already and he barely knew him.

'Why are you following me?' he demanded, expressing this thought with an angry, defensive edge to his voice that defied logic.

'Why not?' came the equally defensive reply, 'free country.'

This retort did make Fynn laugh.

'Well, I'm not so sure that Arcanum is as free as it used to be, not if all the stories we heard are to be believed, but you're a cheeky customer and no mistake!' he said, 'reminds me of you, Wiggy, when you were his age – you had a chip on your shoulder at times and a great line in backchat, especially with your mum and dad! Always got you into trouble too. He even looks like you, and he's got your old name, before you changed it to Wiggy.'

'My name was Willerby, and I changed it to Wigapom, not Wiggy,' snapped Wigapom petulantly, 'and I was never this rude!'

'All right, keep your hair on,' said Fynn, in mock dismay, laughing at his unintentional pun on Wigapom's nickname, 'I'm only making an observation, Wiggy! Anyhow, I wouldn't call you rude exactly, but stroppy, definitely stroppy, quite a lot of the time,' and he laughed again at Wigapom's reddening face, which matched that of Will.

Wigapom collected himself together. He was over-reacting, he knew that. Why did he feel so angry? What was making him feel this way? He had to calm down, be more adult.

Wigapom looked at his friend and then at Will. He did his best to apologise.

'Well, maybe I just felt I had to stand up for myself,' he said grudgingly, admitting to Fynn's description of him. There was no denying how hurt he felt though.

He looked at Will again, more closely, but refused to see any other similarities between them, even though they seemed clear to Fynn, and struggled to assert himself again.

'Well, young Will, if that's your name, it might or might not be a free country but my friend Fynn and I don't want to be followed by you, or anyone for that matter, so kindly go home to where you belong and leave us alone,' and he shooed him away patronisingly.

'Don't have no home no more, nor no family, neither' came the unexpected, and ungrammatical reply. There was such sadness in the gruffness of his tone that, despite himself, Wigapom's heart made a small lurch in the boy's direction. He tried to cover this up though, as the last thing he wanted was to be seen as sympathetic to him – this could be manipulation on the young lad's part – a sob story to lure them into compassion and then, when their guard was down – the boy could run off with all they had! Oh yes, he had to be careful, or they could lose everything! That they had nothing worth taking was conveniently ignored.

'Well lad,' said Fynn, 'as from today we're travellers. We don't have a home either and we don't even know where we're going, so we've got nothing to offer you.'

'You could let me travel with you,' said Will, still directing all his attention to Wigapom. He said, almost pleadingly, 'we could talk and get to know one another, and help each other. I could be useful.'

Wigapom's attempt to get a grip on his emotions failed miserably as he found himself repeating words he had heard himself, and hated, as a child. He regretted it the minute it was out of his mouth, but there was no going back.

'You foolish boy! What makes you think you can do things to help us? You're far too young to be responsible, or trusted, you'd just be in the way!'

Will looked at him with daggers for eyes, exhibiting an emotion Wigapom had experienced himself. He knew he had hurt him but pure, stubborn pride would not allow him to apologise.

'I *am* responsible,' came the reply. 'You just give me responsibility and I'll prove it to you. I won't get in the way – I might even be able to help you find what you're looking for, and as for trust – well, that works both ways, doesn't it? If I'm willing to trust *you* then the least you can do is trust *me!*' Will's arms folded defiantly across his chest. Wigapom was loath to admit his grudging admiration at this speech.

'Fine words do not make fine actions,' he replied haughtily.

He turned to Fynn then, not wanting to take the full responsibility for any decisions. 'What do you think, Fynn?'

Fynn's reply was measured and thoughtful.

'I'm not sure that my opinion really matters here,' he said, looking from Will to Wigapom and back again, 'but if it did, I'd say "yes".'

This approval from Fynn seemed to spur Will on and his eyes shone with a passion.

'I can help you … I can be another pair of eyes… I can run fast… I can carry things… I can be and do whatever you want… I'll prove myself to you, just wait and see. I won't let you down if you promise not to let me down.' There was real desperation in this last statement – almost like a bargaining tool, and Fynn at least sensed the real need behind it. The boy wanted to be accepted and valued. Wigapom knew what that felt like. He also had a feeling that this decision would have a major impact on his future, but despite himself he grudgingly admired the spirited nature of this young boy, and detected hope mingled with frustration, which was very akin to his own feelings at times: was it this closeness that he was still fighting inside?

'Alright,' he said, 'you can join us, but I'll be watching out for light-weights, just remember that.'

'I won't forget,' said Will, sheer delight dancing in his green eyes, 'I'll be watching out for you too. We can watch out for each other!' and suddenly the child's defensiveness had gone and he looked happy and light-hearted.

He moved away from the tree and came within arms length of Wigapom. For a moment Wigapom felt he wanted to ruffle Will's hair playfully, but he stopped himself in time – he was not ready for such familiarity yet. Instead he extended his hand to him, man and boy, and they sealed the deal with a handshake.

'Welcome, Will,' said Fynn, 'I think we'll all be firm friends.'

For the first time Will looked at Fynn and smiled, before looking back once more at Wigapom.

'We already are,' he said and began to lead them through the forest as dawn finally broke.

Darqu'on looked pensively into the mirror that reflected back the images of the three travellers. He had been taken by surprise at the presence of the young boy and was increasingly intrigued by what he saw. He felt he could use him in time, but first he wanted to test them all, to get a measure of how they would react together in a situation.

He touched the black ring on his index finger, twisting the stone sharply, as though strangling a chicken. There was a small hiss as something jerked into life.

'Scabtail,' he said into the ring. Immediately before him a wavering image of the reptilian servant appeared, plucked from wherever he had been hiding from the travellers. He looked shocked and wary to be called back so soon but his voice was as oily as ever.

'Yes Master?'

'A testing time is required, Scabtail. I want to see how they handle the Roth Riders. Watch and wait: The Riders will hunt them but not kill them. The Brat and his companions must taste real fear.'

'An excellent suggestion Master – fear is a valuable weapon, it brings out the very worst in people.'

'Don't tell me what I already know, you foolish creature, just do it!' ordered Darqu'on, and he again twisted the ring back into position as Scabtail's image shivered out of view.

Darqu'on took a phial of dark purple liquid from a shelf and stirred the contents into some yellow powder he had placed into a bowl: the mixture began to bubble and change colour from yellow, to purple to grey to black As the colours changed, so he spoke words under his breath, incanting them slowly and deliberately.

"Out of the light and into the dark,
INVENI TIMAYO
The purpose now to quell the spark
INVENI OCCIDERE!"

He threw the bubbling liquid into the fire, where it spattered like hot fat, shooting out vicious tongues of foul-smelling flames, which filled the room. Darqu'on breathed in the fumes deeply with an exultant expression on his face.

'Let's see how they deal with the Roth Riders!' he said, out loud to the wall of mirrors around him.

CHAPTER 12

Worms and White Harts

*"You are led through your lifetime by the inner learning creature,
the playful spiritual being that is your real self."*
Richard Bach

The three of them began to climb upwards towards a brilliantly lit clearing amongst the trees – as though a doorway to another world had mysteriously opened, letting light transfuse the previously dark forest. It certainly felt more enchanted now than forbidden and they felt as though they were waiting for something amazing to happen. As if to prove them right a white hart appeared out of the mist. Its smooth, curved, bleached antlers dipping towards the ground as it grazed. Its thick white coat almost luminous in the early morning light. They all stood and watched, as if to move would disturb the magic of the moment. The white hart gently lifted his head to face them, but suddenly the atmosphere changed. Whilst the white hart was still bathed in the almost spectral glow of the dawn light, the rest of the forest darkened, as if a heavy, threatening black cloud had just obliterated the sun. The temperature plummeted as a vicious wind whipped through the trees, violently flinging the branches into turmoil, as though something inherently evil had entered the space. Everything began to shake, including the travellers. Instinctively, Wigapom and Fynn crouched down amongst the undergrowth, Fynn pulling Will down with him urgently. Even with the majesty of the white hart nearby they knew a darker, more powerful force was present and the three huddled together, hoping to find courage and strength in each other.

The oppressive atmosphere overpowered them, permeating their bones with cold as the air itself began to vibrate with the sound of distant drumming, sending a primitive message of doom thundering ever closer. They held their breath. The white hart pricked up his ears, lifting his face to sniff the scent of evil on the morning air. To their surprise he seemed strangely unperturbed, standing his ground, when they thought he would run at the first disturbance. The white hart was looking keenly behind them at dark shapes hurtling through the trees. The travellers turned to face the noise as a posse of spectral horsemen swept down upon them, phantasmal cloaks spreading out around their ghostly shapes like vulture wings, their unseen faces hidden beneath cavernous hoods; their skeletal fingers gripping wisp-like reins that flapped against the spectral outline of their nightmare mounts, announcing with their frightening presence the arrival of the wraith-like Roth Riders.

The forest was stung into silence by their presence; no bird song, no rustling of leaves, just the deafening pounding of hooves that never touched the ground but bore down relentlessly upon the travellers huddled together in the undergrowth, right in their path. Hearts were in mouths at the thought of what was to come. Wigapom, without realising it, was clutching the stones in his pocket. He clutched them so tightly the runes made marks on his palms. There was no doubt now that the stories in the books they had read as children were true.

Their hands were clammy with sweat as the colour drained from their faces. The landscape around them became grey, apart from the mound where the white hart still stood – this, by contrast, was still eerily and beautifully bathed in sunlight.

The Roth Riders were almost on top of the travellers, moving through every solid object in their path. It was clear now that the apparitions were faceless – just black gaping holes where flesh should have been and they emanated an aura of such evil that it left an indelible fear in the pit of the travellers' stomachs. The trio couldn't move – frozen in terror to the spot. The rawness of their fear told them they were about to die. It swept over them like a tidal wave. Wigapom gripped his stones even tighter, expecting the worst, but they had not allowed for the majestic creature on the mound, who suddenly leapt into action, spreading a flash of pure white amongst the dark gloom of the trees. The white hart glided out, with graceful ease, in front of the Roth Riders, eyes bright, ears erect and, as the travellers watched in wonder, he turned skilfully on strong yet slender legs, and galloped away, as though encouraging the Roth Riders to change course and follow him instead! The spectral nightmare horses snorted and reared, turning round in circles, nostrils flaring wide as the Roth Riders, momentarily confused by the appearance of the white hart, turned in the direction he had gone and, as if with one mind, followed him as he disappeared through the undergrowth, leading them away from where the travellers were crouching.

From deafening noise to sudden peace in an instant. For a moment no one spoke, until at last Fynn broke the silence.

'I thought we'd had it then,' he said, letting out a long relieved sigh through chattering teeth.

'So did I,' agreed Wigapom, struggling to his feet, still shaking from the experience. 'They came from nowhere, and headed straight for us. If it hadn't been for the white hart turning up and then running off we could be dead, or worse. We were really lucky.'

'It wasn't luck. He led them away,' said Will, 'the white hart. He saved us by leading them away.'

Wigapom and Fynn stopped and looked at Will as realisation, like the day, slowly dawned. It was only when the obvious was stated that Wigapom and Fynn appreciated the simple truth of Will's statement. The white hart had indeed led the Roth Riders away from them. He had risked his life to save their own. They couldn't begin to guess why, but they were grateful. They moved carefully through the forest now, much more mindful of keeping hidden, whilst listening for every sound. They hurried on, silently, eyes and ears alert, on the lookout for any sign of the Roth Riders return. It was exhausting, being so vigilant, but they wouldn't relax. This was the first real experience of anything connected to the terror of the Sorcerer's Shadow they had read about in the stories. Now face-to-face with the reality, it was sobering to realise they were all now in more danger than they had ever been in their lives before.

Will, who was being as good as his word and acting as lookout in front, suddenly crouched down again and held his fingers to his lips in a sign that said clearly, 'Be quiet'.

Wigapom and Fynn dropped down too, and crawled to reach Will, who was by now pointing, wide-eyed, to something behind a tree.

'What is it?' whispered Wigapom as soon as he was close enough to Will.

'Look,' whispered back Will, pointing to the ground just in front of them. As they followed his shaking finger they saw that the ground was moving, as though a giant mole was disturbing the earth underneath with its digger paws. Large clods of earth were being dislodged, flying through the air and rolling towards them.

'Is it an earthquake?' said Will, eyes wide.

'I don't think it can be, it's only moving in one spot,' said Fynn.

'What is it then?' said Will, barely taking his eyes from it.

'The Bogus worm?' suggested Wigapom, with dread in his voice. 'We've had the Roth Riders, we know they're real – everything we've read about could be real too.'

'What do we do?' asked Will, his voice shaking almost as much as the earth.

'Move fast I think,' said Wigapom. But before any of them could move another muscle, something started to appear from under the earth that transfixed them to the spot. A huge, brown, tube-like creature with a pointed end was erupting slowly through the earth. Large in circumference, it had shiny, ring-like markings around it that gave it considerable flexibility. More earth fell away as the hole grew bigger and the most enormous worm they had ever seen or imagined emerged from the ground.

'It *is* the Bogus worm!' Wigapom uttered in a hushed voice, too amazed now to be frightened, 'I can hardly believe what I'm seeing!'

'Don't look then,' said a deeply sorrowful voice coming from somewhere on the worm, 'we have to manage without sight, why shouldn't you?' and the pinkish pointed tip of the huge worm waggled in the air, looking strangely comical.

'It's a *talking* worm!' exclaimed Fynn, hardly able to believe his ears.

Wigapom knew then that this worm was no monster, despite its enormous size, but had received a rather bad press in terms of its behaviour. It was strange to feel sorry for an earthworm but he couldn't help that emotion flowing over him, along with a great deal of relief.

'I didn't mean to offend you,' said Wigapom, 'it's just, where I come from you've been portrayed as something quite scary.'

The worm was further out now and filling quite a bit of the space in front of them.

'That's life, I suppose,' it said in a glum way, 'folk think the worst of things they don't understand and then start rumours, and before you know it we are bogey men to all the children.'

'Perhaps that's why they called you the Bogus worm,' said Wigapom.

'Perhaps. We're really Megadrills, earthworms, to you. We have other names, but I'd prefer to be called Ollie.'

'And I like Annalid best,' said a quicker, higher, more feminine voice coming from the other end of the worm, which had also appeared out of the ground.

'Ooh! You two are part of each other then?' said Will, excited at the prospect of two in one.

'Yes,' said the deep, slow voice of Ollie 'I'm the Animus, the male, and she is the Anima, the female, both separate but forever joined.'

'You have lots of names' said Fynn, recovering from his shock at a talking worm.

'Oh yes, even Hermes and Aphrodite would you believe – no matter, we answer to pretty much anything. We dig tunnels you know.'

'I'm the long and slender part that smoothes out the tunnel,' said Annalid, preening herself.

'And I am the strong muscular part that digs it,' said Ollie's deep, slow voice, and he swelled to double his size with pride.

'We work together very well. A perfect team,' said Annalid, 'and those that know about us think we are very useful.'

'What do you mean?' said Fynn, tickled pink that he was actually having a conversation with a giant worm!

'Well, our tunnels make it easy for people to move about from place to place without the Dark One seeing them,' said Annalid, who seemed to be the end that spoke the most.

'Who's the Dark One? Why can't he see what goes on underground?' asked Wigapom, intrigued.

'He has the power these days above ground, but he still can't control the underground as it's far too deep for him. He won't look that far down, in himself, let alone anywhere else. Besides, the earth has too many treasures that it would never give up to him,' explained Annalid, 'although he has tried to get them before.'

'But I thought you said he was all-powerful!' exclaimed Fynn.

'He is to those who want to fear him in that way but there are many that refuse to and we help them in their resistance,' continued Annalid.

'By digging tunnels? said Wigapom, fascinated at the idea of an underground resistance movement.

'Yes, that's right,' said Ollie ponderously, 'it helps them get about unseen when they need to.'

'Of course, not everyone knows this – we're only telling you because we know we can trust you,' added Annalid.

'How do you know that?' said Will.

'We sensed your light, and the light of the white hart of course, so we know you are friends,' explained Annalid.

'So you don't gobble up people and masticate them in your belly and spew them out at the other end after all,' said Will, sounding perhaps a little disappointed now that his fear had gone.

'Certainly not, don't believe everything you read,' said Annalid outraged that their reputation had been so besmirched. 'How positively disgusting even to think it! Anything that comes out of us is just nutrient rich soil if you please! We *help* people, not harm them. How do you think crops would grow if we did not aerate the soil? Tell me that.'

'No offence meant,' apologised Fynn, trying to placate her, 'It's just that you're so large. Where we come from we've not been used to such huge worms before, they're only very small in Brakendor.'

'Not all worms are this big, only us,' explained Annalid waving her own Megadrill end expressively as she spoke, 'and for that you can blame, or praise, the Dark One, depending on your point of view. In his very early years of magic training, before he sold his soul to sorcery, he concocted a spell that made us this size and we've been so ever since. It was partly because he couldn't change us back that he lost control over creatures and materials in the earth, although of course he exerts his power on everything he chooses above the ground.'

'So the Dark One is the evil sorcerer of the stories?' said Wigapom, thoughtfully.

'Unfortunately, yes,' replied Annalid.

'Would you like to be smaller?' said Fynn, wondering what it really must be like to be so amazingly huge all the time and thinking that it must certainly have considerable limitations.

'Yes,' said Ollie, sadly, 'because then we could have a family without causing the earth to collapse!'

'Ollie would like to be a father,' said Annalid wistfully, 'but Megadrills give birth to hundreds of babies at one time. You can imagine the problem, I expect.'

'Not enough space for you all and too many tunnels waiting to collapse and carry everything down with them!' said Fynn.

'Exactly,' said Annalid, 'it could be nothing short of disastrous. So we go without children for the good of all. Luckily we live a very long time! But one day, when the True Magic returns, we can be made small again. Until then we use our size to do what we can to help those who resist the Dark One. We're content enough with that for now.'

'As long as no unpleasant stories are told about us,' said Ollie, pointedly in his ponderous voice.

'We promise that we will never do that again,' said Wigapom, determined never to think badly about another creature.

'We're very kind and big-hearted you know,' said Ollie, as though pressing home his point, 'we have five of them, not just one!'

'Jumping Jeepers!' said Wigapom, not really knowing what else to say about that last amazing piece of information, coming as it was on top of so much more.

'Well Ollie,' said Annalid, 'we must get back into the earth again, we're drying out too much here and it makes it more difficult to tunnel like that. It has been nice meeting you.'

'Before you go – do you know anything about missing stones and a Book of Magic?' asked Wigapom.

Annalid and Ollie waggled their ends in the air, like periscopes coming up from the ocean.

'Why?' they asked together.

'I've just been asked to find them, that's all. Just wondered if you could point us in the right direction,' replied Wigapom, not sure whether he had now said too much.

'Then you must be…' began Annalid excitedly, but Ollie interrupted,

'We can't tell you, but speak to Cassie; she'll know what to do. She lives in the cottage on the edge of the forest. Got to go now. Things to do.'

'Of course,' said Wigapom, thankful for their help but wondering what Annalid had meant and who Cassie might be.

'I *know* we will meet again,' said Annalid, barely able to suppress her excitement.

'We hope so,' said Fynn.

The Ollie end of the Megadrill began to burrow once more down into the soil and Annalid, of course, followed him, waving her end as if in farewell. Soon all that was left was a freshly churned large mound of earth.

'So this is how they get the hills and mounds around here,' said Fynn. Somehow they felt a little safer to think that the underground at least was free of this Dark One. If they ever needed to escape all they needed to do was find a wormhole!

'Talking about mounds,' said Wigapom, 'I wonder how the white hart got on?'

'I think we're just about to find out,' said Fynn, 'look.'

Standing just ahead of them, head erect and proud, and bathed in the same ethereal light as before was the white hart. There was no sign of the Roth Riders.

'He escaped the Roth Riders,' whispered Fynn, 'That's some animal!'

Will suddenly jumped up and ran impulsively towards the white hart, before Wigapom could restrain him.

'Stupid child,' hissed Wigapom, through his teeth, angry that this boy should do something so thoughtless that might have put them all in danger again – after all, this could be a trick: the Roth Riders could be waiting to catch them off guard, using the white hart to lure them.

Will was close to the white hart now but the creature seemed undisturbed, grazing as though nothing had happened. Will held his hand out to stroke his neck. The white hart raised his head, and let him run his hands down his pure white flank, while he looked straight into Wigapom's eyes. Wigapom felt he was being challenged to reflect on his reactions to Will and was suddenly ashamed of his fear, and of his anger towards the young lad. Will was just a child who was grateful to the white hart for saving them. What was wrong with that? He felt he'd let the white hart down in a way he couldn't fully understand, but he seemed to be drawn into those eyes. They penetrated his being and he was unable to look away.

It didn't even seem surprising when young Will carefully and gently got onto the white hart's back and lay with his face nestled in his neck. It seemed the most natural thing in the world. The moment seemed to be suspended in time. Nothing moved: not Will, not the white hart, not Fynn, not a blade of grass or a leaf. Only Wigapom could move but he was also hearing a voice – and he was sure it was coming from the white hart. It was calm, strong and gentle and he felt enveloped in its peace.

'Wigapom,' said the voice, 'you have tasted fear, both imagined and real, and felt and seen what it can do. Remember there is nothing to fear but fear itself. The more you give it focus, the more you give it power. You have also experienced bravery, which vanquishes fear. You have a choice always as to which one you follow. Choose wisely. Now you have come face to face with your old emotions of anger, distrust, and judgement. You will need to battle with these even more than you will battle with the Roth Riders. Again you have choice: do not allow yourself to be misled. There are those who wish to trap you. Be vigilant. Above all, learn to trust your finer instincts, and recognise yourself in others, for we can learn much from them and much from our own shadow. Trust also in that which is greater than you and which will uphold you when you choose to allow it.'

Wigapom had been drawing closer to the white hart as he heard these words, and as he reached him everything was kick-started again, becoming as it was before: Will lying contentedly on his back as the breeze moved the branches of the trees; Fynn walking a little way behind, looking about him stealthily. The white hart lowered his soft muzzle into Wigapom's outstretched hand and he felt the warmth of its breath spread through his fingers. The white hart turned and began to walk away, with Will still on his back, as if encouraging them all to follow. Wigapom walked by his side, his hand lightly on the hart's front flank; Fynn drew up the rear as they followed the hart up a gentle incline. At the top, they stopped and Will slid to the ground. Below them lay a river valley. The forest had thinned out leaving just occasional trees and bushes, and they could see a curl of smoke spiralling from a cottage chimney in the valley below. Cassie's cottage. They knew they'd been led here on purpose. Wigapom turned back to where the hart had been but there was no sign of him.

'Where did he go?' said Fynn, looking about him with surprise.

It was as though the magnificent creature had never been there at all.

'He comes and goes when he chooses, I suppose,' said Will, with the easy acceptance of a child.

'I've never known that kind of freedom before,' said Wigapom with a sigh.

Will said quietly, 'Me neither.'

'Well,' exclaimed Fynn, endeavouring to lift the mood, 'Roth Riders and white harts, Bogus worms, sorry, Megadrills – whatever next? I always thought they were just stories – just goes to show that truth is stranger than fiction, eh, not to mention this Dark One. Where do you think the white hart went? How did he escape those Riders, and, more to the point, where are they now?'

'Does it matter?' said Will, 'They've all gone and we're still here.'

Such straightforward common sense from one so young, thought Fynn, with a smile to himself, and said no more about it.

'Did you hear the voice, Fynn?' said Wigapom, ignoring Will's last comment 'Was it the white hart speaking, do you think, before he disappeared?'

'I heard a talking worm, Wiggy, and I'm still getting used to that,' said Fynn, 'but a talking white hart as well? No, I didn't hear that. That would be too much for me to take in on one day.'

Again Wigapom realised that Fynn couldn't experience all that he was experiencing – the vibrating stones, the voice of the white hart. He didn't know why he seemed to be singled out. He was thus somewhat surprised and confused to hear Will, say quietly,

'I heard him.'

Wigapom looked at this strange, young companion, and not for the first or last time wondered just who he was, and why he had come into his life at this time.

Before he could reply Fynn clapped an arm around Wigapom's shoulders.

'See that smoke down there?' he said, 'In my experience where there's smoke, there's a nice warm fire and where there's a nice warm fire, there could be a nice hot breakfast just waiting for us, and a mug of tansy tea, and that sounds like just what we need right now. I reckon it's this Cassie's cottage Ollie told us about, and the white hart did seem to lead us here, but we'll never know if we don't find out. We've got to take a chance – otherwise we won't need the Roth Riders to finish us off – we'll just die of starvation! Shall we chance it?'

Wigapom smiled at Fynn's down to earth nature. 'Let's get going then!' he said. 'Come on Will – move yourself!'

Wigapom and Fynn strode companionably down the slope into the valley below with Will following closely behind, looking intently at both of them.

'So the white hart came in to save them! How gallant,' spat Darqu'on as he turned away from the mirror, which darkened as soon as his eyes left it. He ignored the worm, as this was too much of a reminder of things that had gone wrong for him in the past. He only chose to focus on things that he controlled, and the worm was not one of them, to his eternal annoyance. So his thoughts and plans were only of the white hart.

'He must be destroyed,' he said to himself, 'I have done it before, and it's now time to do it again!'

He recalled, in clear, gruesome detail, how he had personally shot the arrow that killed the last white hart he had come into contact with – so many moons ago now but still fresh in his memory. An accident, or so he had said, but pride, arrogance and the desire to be the best had gripped him even then: an archery contest; a flash of white amongst the trees as he took aim, a quick eye and eager hand on the arrow along with a desire to impress his companions, especially her, had resulted in the death of the white hart. They were creatures of legend. The King had been angry at the loss of the beautiful creature, even afraid, believing the travelling soothsayer who said the death of a white hart would foretell the death of the king – well the old hag had been right, thought Darqu'on, but it had been the King's fear that led to his death, not the white hart, so Darqu'on believed, even though his own hand had finally stilled the King's last breath. It was the cold realisation that the king could be affected by fear that had planted the seed of dominance in his mind – that, and his own lust for her. His final descent into depravity had been born then, and just grew and grew.

He did not want to remember any more, he just wanted to get even: to unleash all his hatred towards those who made his memories so terrible to endure. It would be a pleasure to kill another white hart and purge himself again.

CHAPTER 13

Cassie's Cottage

"There is no trouble so great or grave that cannot
be much diminished by a nice cup of tea."
Bernard-Paul Heroux

The smoke was closer now, coming from the single chimney of a compact cottage, set in a verdant garden. Here chickens ran free; two goats munched a pile of turnip leaves; a cat slept on a cushion perfectly placed for feline comfort, and a cow and donkey stood companionably, side by side in a small paddock. A little oasis of peace and great charm on the outskirts of the forest, where they knew immediately they would receive a safe and warm welcome. As they approached the white gate the goats looked up from their turnip tops in mild interest but continued to chew, slowly and carefully. A comfortably proportioned woman, brightly attired in a yellow dress and crisp white apron, stood by the well, drawing up a huge bucket of water. She waved at them with a fresh, white handkerchief, her beaming smile lighting up her rosy apple-cheeked face, like a shaft of sunshine on a gloomy day. She steadied the bucket with one hand on the side of the well, and waved again, and they waved back, automatically – it would have seemed churlish not to somehow. It was as though they were expected.

'At last,' she said in a cheerful voice that reminded Wigapom of the sound of the brook bubbling in Brakendor, 'all this time and now you're here at last, especially escaping those Roth Riders, thanks to the white hart, bless him. He made sure of your safety. What times we live in! Anyway, come in, come in, kettle's on, eggs are cooking, and there're fresh clothes for you all laid out inside. Come in, and make yourselves at home' And without more ado she hoisted the bucket onto one hip and strode into the cottage.

Wigapom and Fynn exchanged bemused glances. How on earth did she know about their escape from the Roth Riders, or about the white hart, or even that they were arriving? Would Annalid and Ollie have had time to tell her? Why would they want to tell her?

So many questions it seemed, and not many answers yet. Young Will didn't concern himself on these matters: he'd already leapt over the gate and gone inside, so they, rather more sedately, unfastened the latch and followed him, not without taking a cautionary glance behind them first, just in case; but all seemed clear.

The rosy-cheeked woman was already pouring out steaming mugs of tea for them as they entered the spotless kitchen. Will was curled up, fingers wrapped around the comforting warmth of the mug, toasting his toes by the inviting fire crackling cheerfully in the grate, whilst listening to her chatter away as though she had known him all her life.

'Ah, there you are,' she said, stopping mid–way in a sentence that seemed to be exploring the delights of toasted crumpets or some such, and passed Wigapom and Fynn their mugs of tea.

'Sit down and drink your tea. There's nothing like a cup of tea to take your troubles away, I say. Make yourself right at home.'

'Where are we exactly?' asked Wigapom.

'Love your sweet soul my dear, you're in Arcanum, in the Enchanted Forest. And you are from the village of the Inbetween. Will and me's been getting acquainted. I'm Cassie, by the way. I'll just get your breakfasts while you warm up.'

'The village of the Inbetween?' said Wigapom. He did not understanding why it was called something different. 'But we come from Brakendor.'

'Yes, dear, you lived there, and now you're here, where you belong, at last.' replied Cassie.

'But why is it the village of the Inbetween?' persisted Wigapom, confused.

'Because it's the hidden village: the village in-between' said Cassie. 'Now, would you like a wash first? You all look a might grubby, I do declare.'

'I don't understand…' said Wigapom again, exchanging glances with an equally bemused Fynn.

'No matter!' smiled Cassie, brushing off their confusion as one would a fleck of dust, 'A good wash and brush up always makes you feel better, that's what I always say!' Instantly, or so it seemed, three bowls of hot soapy water were placed in front of them, along with soft, yellow towels, and as they washed hands and faces under the beaming gaze of her rosy smile they had to admit that they enjoyed the feeling of cleanliness and calm again after recent events.

Cassie, meanwhile, began piling eggs, mushrooms, fried potato and tomatoes, as well as thick slabs of brown bread spread with creamy yellow butter, onto warm plates. They were soon tucking into this delicious fare, hardly able to believe their situation, and unable to get a word in edgewise, even had they wanted to, for Cassie kept up a constant chatter, as though they were already great friends, continually filling their mugs with copious amounts of strong, sweet tansy tea.

Apart from discovering Cassie was short for Cassandra, and that she knew their names already, they found out that she had a long faerie lineage; sold healing potions from the herbs she grew, as well as vegetables and home-made cheese, all of which she sold at market. She lived alone, apart from her animals, who all had names – from the donkey right down to each chicken; she'd been living at this spot, on the edge of the forest (which she insisted was called 'Enchanted' rather than 'Forbidden') for many years and had never been troubled by the Roth Riders, or any of 'that there sorcery', as she so quaintly termed it.

'There's good magic in this forest,' she said, 'always has been and no doubt always will be, no matter how much the Dark One tries to destroy it. He doesn't hold dominion over everything, no matter what he thinks.'Course, the magic is not as strong as it used to be, but I live in hope that it will be enough to keep him at bay a bit longer,' and here she fastened her bright eyes momentarily onto Wigapom before continuing with her chatter. 'Some folks didn't feel safe here however, and that's why they moved to the towns and cities out there beyond the Enchanted Forest, but it seems to me they're worse off than I am these days. Terrible places those towns and cities. I only go there to sell my produce at the market. I wouldn't stay there. All smoking chimneys and dark, narrow alleyways, not like here, where there's fresh air to breathe and plants to grow! I wouldn't live anywhere else! That there sorcery doesn't bother me if I don't bother it, and I'm happy here, with my animals and plants and simple life. It's only going beyond the forest that the real troubles lie, if you want my opinion, and then you have to have your wits about you. There's some not very nice folk around these days who want to make trouble for others. I've friends in Lampadia, the nearest town, and what a change I've seen there in the last twenty years or more, a different sort of sorcery there to my mind; machines that do things that people or animals have always done! Cutting into beautiful natural trees and putting ugly buildings in their place, taking the greenness away and making it all grey, losing contact with the rhythms of the earth and the inspiration of the sky and being ruled by greed and fear – a terrible place full of unhappiness and frightened people who are more likely to pull a knife on you than share a smile! I don't go there more than I can help, and so far the good magic has lasted here for me.'

'Tell us more about the Dark One,' asked Wigapom. 'I think he has the book I need to find.'

'Oh we don't want to talk about him, not now – plenty of time later – let me tell you about my healing herbs ...' and she regaled them again with her many skills and interests including her vegetable growing, her cake baking and speciality teas, of her love and understanding of the stars, and even the finer points of cheese making! She was prone to a boast or two about her skills, but she was so charming with it that they all warmed to her immediately. It was such happy, inconsequential chatter for much of the time that it pushed the dark memories and experiences further away from their minds, allowing them to relax for the first time since beginning their journey.

'Thanks for the delicious breakfast,' said Wigapom, full and content now as he wiped his plate clean with his last piece of buttered bread, and dabbed his mouth on the checked napkin.

'My pleasure, my pleasure,' beamed Cassie, busily clearing the dishes into another frothy bowl of hot water, 'we've been waiting for you for a very long time – I was so excited when the Megadrill told me but it was when I saw the hart again that I knew you were here at last.'

'You knew we were here because of the white hart?' repeated Will.

'Well, in truth dear, I didn't know *you* were, at least not to begin with, but I did know these two were here,' she said, indicating both Wigapom and Fynn, 'especially Master Wigapom,' and she looked with shining eyes at Wigapom as though he was the answer to a long held prayer. 'Your coming has given me hope for the future,' she said, 'things can get moving at last, and not before time, I do declare! Oh I don't mean that to sound like a criticism dear – you had to come of your own free will, I know that, but I can't tell you how happy I am to think that the dark days will soon be behind us after all these difficult years.'

'I don't understand,' said Wigapom, 'how did you know we were coming, and why is it so important that I'm here? I thought I was going into places where no one would know me, but it seems that you've been expecting me all along, yet I only decided to come yesterday! Do you know about the Quest I've been given? Do you know about the stones, or The Book? And where do Will and the white hart fit into all this, and the Roth Riders and everything?'

'Oh my, what a lot of questions!' said Cassie beaming another one of her sunshine smiles, and trying to make light of what she'd said. 'Me and my mouth, I've gone and done it again! Blathering on about things that I really should keep quiet about: but that's me – take me or leave me I say!' and she threw up her soapy arms in mock horror, sending rainbow filled bubbles scattering in all directions.

Wigapom was not going to be so easily put off, however, and repeated his question again.

'Cassie, how did you know I would come one day, how could you know? Who told you and why am I expected?'

'There, there, now!' she flustered, realising that she couldn't ignore the questions forever, but unsure of what to say that would be enough, but not too much. Oh she really would have to watch her tongue in future, it always seemed to get her into a pickle! 'All these questions! It would take a month of Sundays to explain them all. You'll understand in good time – sooner than you'd like I don't doubt, what with those Roth Riders on your trail, but that's then and this is now – and you all need fresh clothes – so up you go and get into them – everything's laid out for you – even you, Master Will, I managed to find something for you too – take it all – and I'll clear up here,' and with that she ushered them up the narrow staircase before they had an opportunity to ask anything more.

They found themselves in a cosy, narrow room with a sloping ceiling and small window looking towards the forest. On the bed, laid out neatly, were three sets of clothes and new boots for them all. Wigapom and Fynn liked the idea of having fresh clothes, as the ones they were wearing were very tattered after yesterday's exploits. Will didn't mind what he wore but no doubt would feel better too, having clothes that actually fitted him at last, but the whole thing was nevertheless baffling and unexpected.

They put their new clothes on as they talked about all Cassie had said, and even more about what she had not, and ended up more confused than before. Wigapom was very careful to transfer the two coloured stones from his old pocket to his new, deeper one, and as he held the stones in his hand again they vibrated, as though trying to communicate with him once more.

'Can I hold them?' asked Will.

Wigapom hesitated: he wasn't sure he wanted Will to touch them.

'Go on Wiggy, let him see them,' urged Fynn.

'Alright,' said Wigapom reluctantly, 'but be careful with them.'

Will held them in his palm and giggled.

'Ooh! They tickle,' he said, 'they feel as though they're jiggling in my hand.'

Wigapom was surprised: Will could feel them vibrating too! He didn't like the idea of Will sharing this with him, but then remembered he'd also heard the white hart speak. He found this rather disturbing.

'I'll have them back now,' he said, more sharply than he needed, and hurriedly put them in his pocket again. Just as he did so an ominous shadow passed across the window, darkening the room, which seemed suddenly smaller and more oppressive. There was a low rumble of what could have been thunder and the atmosphere hung heavy and malevolent, whilst the temperature plummeted. There was an unearthly howling like the baying of wolves and also the sound of ghostly hooves pounding! The three of them froze. The Roth Riders were back, and it sounded as though the Wulverines were with them!

Wigapom felt himself tighten his grip on the stones, as if knowing instinctively what was about to happen next, and at that exact moment they heard the violent rage of a windstorm beating at the cottage walls like hundreds of angry fists demanding entry. This was followed by the sound of the door being wrenched from its hinges by a monstrous force.

'They're inside!' said Fynn as the sound of chairs, tables and china being sent crashing to the floor, rose up the staircase amid the howling of the Wulverines, and the screeching wind, like manic laughter, mixed in with Cassie's piercing screams.

'We've got to help her!' they cried in unison and made a rush to open the door, but it would not budge an inch.

They could feel the force of the tempest as it shot up the stairs, banging on the other side of the door, as though trying to break through. They could feel the presence of the terrifying Roth Riders and hear the baying of the Wulverines outside the room but nothing entered and the door refused to budge. No matter how heavy the banging became, it stayed firmly shut and even the Roth Riders, despite their previously demonstrated ability of moving through any solid object, were unable to get to them. Being trapped and unable to help Cassie was horrifying, as were the sounds of destruction beneath them as the cottage's very foundations shook, but they could do nothing, until everything stopped as suddenly as it had begun: the coldness evaporated, and there was silence once more, save for gentle sobbing coming from downstairs.

All three were shaking behind the door, hardly able to believe they were still alive. They had heard the sounds of the creatures, knew the Roth Riders had been outside the door; knew that they had the ability to pass through anything, so why had they been unable to get to them when they entered easily enough into the cottage itself? It didn't make any sense, until Wigapom looked down at his hands and realised he had been holding the stones all this time. Were these, with their strange elven runes, anything to do with it? Had they somehow prevented the Wulverines and Roth Riders from passing through the door and reaching them? Fynn's grandmother had said the runes carried magical powers, and he knew the stones did, else how would they activate the magic book? It seemed they all owed a lot to those stones, and their secret symbology. But they had to get to Cassie.

Wigapom, his hand still trembling, released the stones into his pocket and tried the door again. It opened with ease and they fell against each other in surprise, before sprinting down the stairs, two at a time. Utter devastation met their eyes: the table where they had eaten their meal lay cleft in two; chairs and plates lay smashed into a thousand fragments; food was splattered everywhere; whilst curtains lay ripped and shredded amongst the glass from shattered windows. Cassie's treasured possessions lay strewn around the room, as if flung with a great, angry force, and there was Cassie in the middle of it all, sobbing on the floor, legs crumpled beneath her, her rosy cheeks now pale and streaked with tears.

'Cassie! Are you all right? Did they hurt you?' they chorused in unison, for a moment not knowing what to do for the best.

Cassie was too distraught to speak so they gently lifted her to her feet, set what remained of the sofa upright and sat her down as gently as they could, wrapping her shawl about her shivering shoulders to help assuage the shock and fright of it all. She blurted out words that were as much a shock to them as the attack had been.

'It's you they wanted, not me!' she stuttered, turning her tear-stained face to Wigapom. 'They've never bothered me before. They knew you were here, that's why they came, but something stopped them getting to you. I don't know why they didn't kill me, but you're not safe here. You must go before they return, as I'm sure they will. He wants you dead!' and she dissolved into tears again.

'Who wants us dead, Cassie?' asked Wigapom, but Cassie was too upset to speak any more, so Wigapom and Will, confused and disturbed by her words and the recent events, did their best to comfort her and clear up the debris indoors, whilst Fynn went to see what damage had been wreaked outside.

The garden was unrecognisable, as though hit by a tornado. Everything above ground ripped from the soil and flung about by brutal force. Fynn picked his way over the wreckage, horrified, angered, and fearful of the results of the venom he witnessed, being something totally outside his experience. But there were worse things to see in the horrific sight of the slaughtered animals strewn around the once peaceful homestead: goats, chickens, the milk cow, even the poor cat, lay mangled and lifeless amongst the desecration. How would he tell Cassie this terrible news? But worse was to come for, as he turned the corner an even more horrific sight faced him. One that turned his stomach over and brought the full reality of the evilness of the terror of the Sorcerer's Shadow home to him more forcefully than anything could ever have done. A noble head, severed from its body, lay in a large pool of blood, which stained the pure white skin of the creature, a bright and hideous pink. Fynn needed every iota of strength to gather both his emotions and his retching stomach before re-entering the cottage, grim faced.

'Don't tell Cassie just yet, 'he whispered quietly to Wigapom on his return, 'but they've butchered all her animals and beheaded the white hart.'

CHAPTER 14

A Bit of a Problem

"Temper gets you into trouble. Pride keeps you there."
Unknown

When they were eventually able to calm Cassie enough to break the terrible news, they discovered there had been one small miracle to give some consolation: the donkey had somehow escaped the massacre. At first they thought he had been annihilated, as there had been no sign of him, but when they searched a wider area Fynn found him sheltering in a small copse some way from the cottage, chewing grass as though nothing had happened. Cassie was so overjoyed to see him she hugged his neck, tears streaming into his stumpy mane.

'Oh, what a blessing, what a blessing!' she repeated.

Wigapom and Fynn wanted to stay, to help her deal with the practical and emotional loss, but Cassie would hear none of it.

'No, you're not safe here, they'll come back for you and next time you might not be so lucky. Who knows what his plan is! You must leave. Now. Go to the town, that's closest, there are more places and more people to hide you safely there: some nice and others not so but that's the way things are these days. If he sends the Roth Riders back, there's nothing to keep you safe here anymore.'

'Who's the "he" you keep talking about Cassie?' asked Wigapom, frowning with concern.

'The Dark One, my dear, he wants you dead!'

'The Dark One again. Why does he want us dead?' replied Wigapom.

'There's no time to explain: you must get to Lampadia first.'

'But what about you, Cassie, you won't be safe here any more,' said Fynn.

'He doesn't want me, I've been left alone here all these years and I'll be so again. It's you they're after, not me,' Cassie assured them.

'I don't understand, Cassie,' said Wigapom, 'are you saying that this

Dark One sent the Wulverines and Roth Riders looking for us especially – that we were the intended target of all this?' He swept his hand around the room. 'Are you saying it wasn't just a chance encounter?'

'They were and you are,' insisted Cassie. 'That was no chance meeting in the forest earlier either, they've never bothered me before you came, and so it was no coincidence that they came here. They're looking for you, to hunt you down; he wants you dead, and he always has. You must understand that you are always in danger from him, wherever you are. He won't rest until he has you!'

'But why us – he doesn't know us. Is it to do with the Book and the stones? You must tell us Cassie, please,' Wigapom pleaded.

'It's *you* they want Master Wigapom – Fynn is in danger only if he is with you – and Will: well I don't know about that, time will tell.'

'What's Will got to do with this, and why are they only after me?' insisted Wigapom, pressing Cassie for an answer.

'I can't tell you that either, it's not my place. You'll know soon enough. Just be careful, that's all. The Dark One is devious and will stoop to anything, trickery as well as aggression, to get what he wants.'

'Cassie,' said Wigapom firmly, 'you're holding something back – I need to know. I've only just met Will and only just arrived here – no one knows me here apart from Fynn, the Megadrill, and now you. Yet you're telling me that I'm public enemy number one. I don't understand!'

Cassie took a long look at Wigapom's concerned face and compassion filled her eyes. With a sigh she spoke as though the information were being reluctantly pulled from her, like teeth.

'I can't tell you all, it's not my place, and I only know some things, but it's no accident that you came here – no accident that you met young Will neither, I should say, but that's another tale, I reckon. All is not what it seems, especially you, you might not know that yet – but the dark forces do – your energy is sending strong vibrations rippling across Arcanum – the like of which we've not experienced for many years – many of us folk welcome you with open arms – your arrival has been our one hope for these twenty years, but for others…' And here she looked anxiously over her shoulder before she continued, 'well, you're not wanted – a threat to the Dark One and the power he wields over this land. That's why you will be hunted down, and I don't know what you can do to defend yourself. Although if I were you I'd make sure those stones, as you call them, stay close at hand.'

Wigapom looked as though he wanted to ask about this, but she held up her hand as if to stop him.

'I can't tell you more;' she said resolutely, 'I've said enough already. I've put my foot in things before with what I've said, and I won't do it again. Now you must go, as fast as you can, to Lampadia town, just a few miles away in the hills. You can take the donkey and the cart, he was obviously saved for a reason, bless him, even though the others…' And her lips began to tremble again, until she pulled herself together. 'Never mind that, it's over and done with, no going back. You must find my friend, Aldebaran; he's expecting you, too. You'll find him in the house in Arcadia Lane, with the bull-shaped knocker. Tell him: "Lightbearer" and he'll let you in. You can leave the cart in the market square, near the old Bull Lamp and I'll collect it later. Arcadia Lane, that's what you want. You'll be safe there for a while and get some answers to your questions, no doubt – and don't worry about me, I've faced hardship before and come out smiling, and I'll do it again. I won't let anything that Dark One does bother me. They can kill my animals, and they can damage my home but they can't defeat my spirit unless I let them. And I ain't about to do that, no sir.' And with that Cassie wiped her hands on her apron, as though wiping away the problems that she and all those in Arcanum had suffered for a very long time, with a courage that Wigapom found inspiring.

They did as Cassie insisted and prepared to leave, but as Will and Fynn busily readied the donkey cart for their journey, Wigapom's mind was full of other things. In fact his head was positively whirring with all that had happened since he left Brakendor, all of which either didn't make any sense or seemed too far-fetched to be real. The 'Dark One' (whoever he really was) wanted to kill him, though he had no idea why, but it seemed there was further reason, other than the Quest. He was special in some way, which somehow seemed to link with Will – yet he had never felt special in his life before, and Will was only a stroppy boy who had followed him, and demanded to be taken with them, as he had no one of his own. What possible connection could there be between them? Wigapom then reflected on his own self: despite his early childhood dreams he was just ordinary, a baker's son from Brakendor. (Now why had Cassie called it the hidden village? Another mystery!) Yet here he was, in a place that until yesterday he had never thought he'd see, having some very extraordinary things happen to him. There must be a connecting thread somewhere. But if there was he couldn't see it. Everything felt so different now to those first few euphoric moments when he'd set out on his Quest, barely a day ago. Wigapom knew he would have no peace until he received answers, and he had to find them soon.

'Ready, Wiggy?' said Fynn, as he finished hitching the donkey to the cart. 'We're all set. Cassie says the donkey knows the way. He's been there often enough! We should get a move on.'

There was urgency in Fynn's voice, but empathy and compassion too. He didn't seem to be at all concerned that by choosing to be with Wigapom he had put his own life in danger. Not for the first time did Wigapom appreciate the true friendship that Fynn demonstrated, and he valued him more than ever.

'Best you hide in the cart, Master Wigapom,' explained Cassie, 'just in case the Roth Riders, or anyone else for that matter, should spot you. You should find it easy enough to blend in in the town, there are enough people there, for sure, but those roads can be lonely and troublesome and you don't want to draw attention to yourself if you can help it – and they'll be looking out for three people now, not two.'

Wigapom gave her a heartfelt thank-you hug as he crawled under the tarpaulin that she lifted up for him on the cart.

He wedged himself amongst the turnips, cabbages and slabs of cheese they had salvaged and were to serve as camouflage. He was rather reluctant to hide here, not only because the cabbages and cheese smelled rather strong and the turnips were heavy, but also because Will was already on the front of the cart, looking as though he owned it, legs dangling, eyes bright and sharp – keeping a lookout for anything that might be trying to stop their progress. Wigapom didn't know why, but he felt uncomfortable again, being so close to Will.

'What harm can he do?' Fynn said, instinctively picking up on his discomfort. 'He's just a boy.'

'Is that *all* he is?' replied Wigapom, unsure. 'How do we know we can trust him – that he isn't part of these dark forces?'

'I'm going to speak frankly here, Wiggy. I think your attitude to him is more the problem here, not him,' replied Fynn. 'Now duck down and keep quiet until we get to the town.'

This sharp response from his friend surprised Wigapom, but he reluctantly did as he was told. He didn't want to create more problems, but he was very wary still.

'If anyone asks why you're driving the cart,' Cassie instructed Fynn, 'say you're my nephew, helping me out,' and she waved her handkerchief in farewell as, with a flick of the reins and a click of his tongue, Fynn expertly turned the donkey and cart towards the town and, with a final encouraging smile to Cassie, they left the cottage behind.

Will waved to Cassie for as long as he could and Cassie waved back with her brightest smile shining on her face and the handkerchief fluttering in the breeze, but Wigapom, peering from under the tarpaulin, noticed that the smile didn't quite reach her anxious eyes this time.

The donkey trotted out of the clearing, the cart wobbling from side to side as it trundled over the rough ground. Soon the path smoothed out into a wider cart track and the donkey picked up speed, as though used to the journey, and they made their way towards the town.

It was uncomfortable and stuffy under the tarpaulin amongst the cheese and vegetables and Wigapom kept it slightly lifted just to get some air. This also allowed him to keep some sort of eye on Will, who kept up an easy conversation with Fynn, as though he had known him all his life. Why did that also make Wigapom feel agitated?

It was clear, as they travelled along, that the road this side of the Forbidden Forest was much as Cassie had said it would be: a place of greyness, and neglect, mixed with an ominous feeling of tension and surveillance

Flocks of vulture-like black birds, whose hooded, yellow eyes watched the travellers' every move, compounded the whole sense of decay, fear and corruption. The birds sat hunched on branches, or peered down from fences like guards around a prison, or strutted and squawked at each other as though passing messages in an unknown tongue. The natural world had never seemed so unnatural or menacing.

They were leaving the valley now, the road climbing upwards. Here there were more carts and wagons on the road. All off to market it seemed. Life still had to go on. A fortified town in the hills lay ahead, looking as though it had been hacked out of the craggy rock formations and jutting peaks. Grey, stone walls, ancient towers and turrets, and steeply sloping grey slate roofs reflected a higgledy-piggledy mass of styles that broadcast a sense of forbidding neglect and desperate despair so strong that it was hard to quell. Billowing clouds of grey smoke rose from unseen chimneys more indicative of depressed living and pollution than warmth and cosy fires. There was noise though, plenty of it, and a sentry at the town gate. But, thankfully, being market day, they were waived through as just another market trader struggling to eke out an existence in these difficult times.

Soon the donkey was pulling them diligently into narrow, cobbled streets strewn with rubbish and broken glass. What once must have been beautiful, even in its grey austerity, now exuded an air of neglect and decay from each piece of crumbling plaster and broken stonework. Yet despite the depressive feel of the town it was thronged with all kinds of folk busily going about their day to day affairs, distrust and fear etched into their down-turned faces, suspicion hovering in each wary eye, mouths turned down and tightly shut, unless openly abusive. It was easy to see why, as threading amongst ordinary townsfolk roamed many of the 'undesirables' that Cassie had spoken of: goblins with shifty eyes and quick fingers, ready to pinch your purse at the slightest opportunity, or flick out a knife in antagonism; a handful of ogres lumbering aimlessly, or lying collapsed in alleyways, often the worse for drink, or other noxious substances; gangs of hooded, feral-looking snotleys loitering suspiciously on street corners, with nothing better to do than create trouble without provocation, and other equally unsettling characters that no one would want to cross or come up against in a dark alley. It was not a happy place.

There was plenty of noise and bustle, but no good-natured banter as one would expect to find in a community such as this: No friendly 'hello's or 'how are you?' or passing the time of day, as had been the case in Brakendor. Here it was sombre, functional, suspicious and repressed: rage and fear bubbling together as if in a pressure pot, waiting to explode. For the townsfolk it was as ordinary a day as they got in these unpleasant and difficult times, where it paid to be nameless and faceless. People doing their best to scratch out a living, yet with a sense of constantly needing to watch their backs, and living, sometimes literally it seemed, on a knife edge of fear. The travellers set about losing themselves amongst the crowds whilst attempting to identify the landmarks Cassie had told them about. Wigapom did not question that this would happen – so many strange and unexpected things had already happened since he began his Quest that he was quite prepared, he thought, to expect anything. As long as it led to him receiving the stones and finding *The Book of True Magic* to place them in, he would be happy. It was important to him to fulfil the request from the lady in his vision at the brook, and he was becoming aware that it was also important to a lot of others too.

'There's the square!' said Will's voice from above.

'And that lamp with the round glass must be the Bull's Eye lantern, just as Cassie said,' added Fynn

Wigapom, since entering the town, had thought it best to keep completely hidden, so he could see nothing of this, but it was stuffier and smellier under the heavy tarpaulin than ever, and he was anxious to get out.

The cart stopped with a jolt and Wigapom could hear clearly the bustle around them, people selling, shouting, and shopping. He so wanted to see for himself, but quelled his impetuousness until Fynn gave him the all clear.

Fynn was taking in the scene himself. They were now in a spacious square that must once have been very grand and gracious, with tall, elegantly carved and heavily timbered buildings, and fine, long windows facing onto the square. Here people were already setting out their stalls and shouting out their wares to any who would listen.

In the centre of the square was a very tall, extravagantly carved column topped by an enormous round lantern with six round lenses, each pointing to different parts of the square. It was easy to imagine how powerful the light must have been when it was lit, but it was quite obvious that this had not been the case for a very long time. The glass was broken on all sides, the framework bent, and more of the noisy black vultures were using it as a look out perch, streaking it with their grey droppings, which ran down and solidified into the fine carving, creating a sinister parody of a sculpture of its own. A heavy sense of being under surveillance was evident.

Fynn tethered the donkey to an old hitching post close to the lantern, as Cassie had told them to, along with other such carts. Fynn walked to the back of the cart, as if to unload the goods. Now was a good time for Wigapom to sneak out.

'OK Wiggy,' hissed Fynn, and he lifted the tarpaulin slightly.

Wigapom quickly began to emerge from amongst the vegetables and cheeses, pleased to be free at last. There was so much going on around him that it would be easy to get out before anyone noticed. At least it would have been a smooth action if Will, who had also jumped down from the cart, had not tried to help him. Wigapom, who still felt inexplicable antagonism to this lad, threw off his outstretched helping hand, with some force, as he leapt from the cart, which accidentally ended up as a hefty blow in a passing gnome's face.

'Oi! Watch where yer goin,' said the unfortunate recipient with a rough, angry voice. 'You nearly 'ad me eye out!'

'Sorry!' said Will. 'Not looking where I was going.'

'And where *are* you goin' – or more to the point, where've you come from?' added a suspicious goblin close by, who had caught a glimpse of Wigapom appearing from under the tarpaulin.

The gnome rubbed his reddening eye and glared with the other.

'That's a point. You're not from these parts, I know. Yet I recognise the cart and the donkey.'

'What's your business here?' continued the goblin. 'And why were you hiding?'

A crowd suddenly seemed to be forming, attracted by the altercation, yet mindful of their own security with these strangers. Some of them however, looked ready for any excuse for a fight.

Wigapom and Fynn exchanged glances.. It seemed they might have a problem here. They'd done the one thing they had set out to avoid and drawn attention to themselves, all because Wigapom had refused Will's help, again. Wigapom was angry, but not with himself. He instinctively placed that blame onto Will. 'Stupid boy,' he thought, 'if only he'd let me get out by myself.' Now they had to get out of a tricky situation without causing any more trouble.

'Just delivering these to market,' said Fynn as casually as he could, 'I'm just helping my aunt Cassie out as she can't get to market today.'

'Haven't seen you before,' said the aggrieved gnome still rubbing his increasingly reddening face.

'We're just visiting my aunt, and seeing if we can get a good price for her goods, you know how it is these days. We all have to do what we can to make ends meet,' said Fynn again, taking charge of the situation in the calm, relaxed way that Wigapom had always so admired.

There were murmurings of 'We don't trust strangers' and 'Stay in your own town' and even 'They're trouble waiting to happen,' which Wigapom would have thought amusing had the situation not been so potentially explosive.

'All right,' said another aggressive-looking goblin from the crowd, lairy with liquor and with a volatile tongue and extra suspicious mind to boot. 'If that's the case, what you got in there?' and he jabbed a finger towards the cart. He obviously didn't trust their explanation. Or else he was looking for easy pickings. Or trouble.

This took Fynn a little off guard at first.

'What do you mean, what have I got? Oh, what have I got to *sell?*... Er ... turnips and cabbages and cheeses. Lots of em,' replied Fynn, trying not to recoil at the smell of the intoxicated breath coming his way, 'my aunt's been busy lately.'

Wigapom, spurred on by Fynn's seeming confidence, felt he too could enter into the pretence. He should have been more cautious.

'Want to buy some?' he said, rather too eagerly 'We can give you a good price.'

'No, I blooming don't,' came the retort, 'I hate turnips and cabbages, and these look damaged to me, and I don't like the smell of your cheese either.' His huge nostrils flared as he sniffed the air close to them, 'nor the smell of you three, you're trouble, I can tell!'

There were mumblings of agreement from the ever-increasing crowd at this comment, which seemed to encourage their protagonist even more.

'We've got more than enough trouble already, without you comin' to rob us!' he said, slurring his words together in spittle. There was more loud general agreement from the crowd.

'We're not robbing you at all!' replied Wigapom, all repressed anxieties and anger rising in his voice, and reflecting the criticism he felt he was being given. He was demonstrating clearly that he was not listening to an insistent voice inside him telling him to be quiet and lie low.

Wigapom's annoyed retort incensed their swaying opponent even more and Fynn tried to placate the situation by offering him free vegetables, but by then things were declining rapidly.

'I just told yer I don't like cabbage and turnips!' yelled the goblin, knocking the vegetables out of Fynn's hand and thrusting a bristly, puce face so close that Fynn could smell the foul stench of rotting teeth as well as liquor on his breath. 'Ain't yer listenin? Don't try to fob me off with what I don't want! You're just trouble and I ain't having it!' and there were more loud mumblings of agreement from the gathered crowd, which now included a whole gang of goblins, who were making swift work of people's pockets. Snotleys, also attracted by the aggression and keen to start a fight, swaggered into view, and a group of mean-faced trolls appeared, who were always ready for trouble these days.

Fynn thought it best to back off at this point, not wanting to inflame the situation any more. He did his best to hold back Wigapom, who was becoming more and more angry and red-faced himself, but no one had remembered Will, until this little chap drew himself up to his full height, with eyes blazing,

'You're the trouble!' he shouted, already reeling from the rejection he had had from Wigapom, and unable to stop himself from making matters worse. 'Not us. *And* you're drunk!'

This was the final straw for the aggrieved goblin, who now towered over an immediately cowed Will, plunging him into his shadow.

'You're accusing *me* of bein' trouble!' he sputtered, spit flying from the corners of his mouth and landing on Will's jerkin, 'You're sayin' I can't hold my booze? You cocky little beggar! There's enough of your kind causing trouble already round here. I've just about had enough of you,' and he swiftly lashed out at Will with a heavy, ill-aimed fist, urged on with shouts of, 'Go on, hit him hard!' and other such inflammatory encouragement from the blood-thirsty crowd.

Will ducked the blow easily, and the punch landed instead on a snotley standing behind him. That was the spark that finally lit the touch-paper of this explosive situation and within seconds punches were flying in all directions: all over something as innocuous as a cabbage! A quick exit was required.

Grabbing Will with one hand and Wigapom with the other, Fynn hauled them away from the fight; Wigapom, as a final angry response, spilling the cabbages, turnips and cheeses from the cart where they spread out in all directions. At least it made a delaying tactic as the produce rolled amongst the crowd, like bowling balls on a green, tripping some, hitting others.

The three travellers made a run for it, ducking and diving under the crowd, hoping that in the chaos their departure would not be noticed and they would be swifter on their feet than anyone who might try to follow them.

'Down here,' said Fynn, darting down a dark alleyway, which fortuitously bore the name 'Arcadia Alley', bolted to the grimy stonework. What luck! This was where Aldebaran lived. Something seemed to be on their side at last!

The alley was thankfully devoid of townsfolk by now, its normal inhabitants either in the main square brawling and shouting at each other or hiding, in fear, behind closed, locked doors, The sound of three pairs of feet pounding on the cobbles echoed around the alley, and the thump of three heartbeats were loud in their chests in this otherwise silent place.

'Stop running,' hissed Fynn, 'act naturally for goodness' sake and calm down!'

Fynn seemed to have taken on the role of leader during all this, and Wigapom, calmer now, was grateful if rather ashamed, realising what an idiot his hot-headedness had made of him. He saw the sense in not drawing any more attention to themselves than they needed and, to hide his own shame, snapped at Will to do as Fynn said, as though Will, and Will alone, had been responsible for what happened. Will looked sharply at him, biting his lip in resentment.

Wigapom had convinced himself that none of the debacle had been his fault at all and instead laid it squarely at Will's small feet! He would have such strong words with this troublesome lad when they were safe, indeed he would!

The alley took a sharp turn to the right, moving further and further away from the trouble in the market square. They passed a bakery, the smell of fresh bread wafting into the street, and for a brief moment Wigapom felt a small pang of nostalgia, mixed with guilt, as it reminded him of the shop, family, customers and quieter life he had left behind so suddenly yesterday. Were they angry? Worried? Confused? Would his young nephew, his apprentice, be the butt of his sudden departure? Wigapom had never intended to hurt anyone with his actions but felt compelled to go with his need for adventure: but this was not quite what he had imagined his adventure would be, even though it seemed it might all have been pre-ordained anyway!

Wigapom grimaced wryly to himself. He still didn't understand that aspect fully. He didn't want to regret his decision about leaving Brakendor, but there was just a fleeting second, when he smelt the bread, when he half wished himself back into his old life and its familiar routine! Fynn was beginning to think the same, had Wigapom but guessed; he'd given up as much as Wigapom, and for very different reasons. He hadn't realised it was going to be like this, especially not the trouble between Wigapom and Will. He wondered what the future would hold.

Wigapom, however, felt very small and foolish all of a sudden and was surprised to feel Will's soft hand touch his arm for just a moment.

'Sorry for the trouble I caused.' said Will. 'I was upset and angry, that's all. We'll be alright, won't we?' as though he knew exactly what Wigapom was thinking. 'At least we've got each other, if you'll have me?'

This unexpected kindness, especially coming after his rough treatment of Will in the market square, on top of making him completely responsible for everything that occurred, unsettled Wigapom again and he felt flustered and angry with himself, but yet again he took it out on Will. Before he could stop himself, he had torn his arm away again, as though Will had delivered a massive electric shock through his palm, and instead turned angry eyes upon the lad.

'What do you mean – I've got you? It's because of you that we got set on out there, you and your angry ways! And what makes you think I should want you! I don't even *know* you and I certainly don't want you! I don't want you at all! Fynn and I would be much better off on our own!'

Will's small face visibly crumbled at these harsh words, and tears began to prick his eyes, but he threw them off and became angrily defensive again.

'I only wanted to help, but you won't let me. You've NEVER wanted me!'

'Hey!' said Fynn. 'Stop it, the two of you. Have you forgotten where we are? What on earth is wrong with you both?'

'Sorry,' said Wigapom grudgingly 'but he started it.'

'I didn't!' yelled Will.

'Well, it wasn't me!' retorted Wigapom.

'Stop it, both of you,' said Fynn, doing his best to separate them and exasperated at their behaviour. He wondered to himself briefly whether the aggression exhibited at the market place could possibly have been contagious! 'You should know better Wigapom. You're acting like a child.'

It was Wigapom then who felt hurt. He hated to feel criticised by his best friend. But he knew Fynn was right, and facing this uncomfortable fact made him angry with himself all over again, which made him even angrier with Will! He was stuck in a vicious circle that he couldn't understand, let alone stop. The anger seemed to go right into the pit of his stomach and he winced momentarily with the physical pain of it. They all walked on in silence, each one nursing their own wounded thoughts and feelings, until they came to the end of the alleyway and found the green door with the bull's head knocker.

'We're here,' said Fynn brusquely, 'at last.'

CHAPTER 15

The Keeper of Stories

"It takes a thousand voices to tell a single story."
Native American Proverb

The house with the bull's head knocker stood apart from the other buildings they had seen, not only in the fact that it was detached, but that it was generally in a better state of repair than any of the others. Someone obviously cared for this property enough to polish the knocker to a bright and gleaming shine.

Fynn gave three knocks on it and the sound echoed in the quiet street. First there was just a deathly silence and they began to wonder what they would do if Aldebaran wasn't there, but then, from behind the door, came the sound of slippered feet shuffling towards them and a crusty, almost falsetto voice saying:

'Who is it? What do you want?'

'Cassie sent us,' said Wigapom in a whisper, mindful to keep this information as quiet as possible. 'She said to give you the word, "Lightbearer".'

There was a muffled gasp that turned into a raspy cough, as the sound of a great bolt slid back from behind the door, revealing in the dimly-lit passageway, a wizened old dwarf whose pale, ice-blue eyes peered over small round spectacles, and a long straggly beard hung below a shiny bald head framed by wispy tufts of white hair either side of a pair of over-large ears.

The travellers exchanged glances with each other, differences temporarily forgotten: was this Aldebaran? He was not what they had expected, and again they realised their vulnerability and lack of knowledge could get them into unforeseen dangers far too easily.

'Come in, and be quick about it,' said the voice behind the beard, and a gnarled hand like the roots of an ancient tree shot out to pull them all hurriedly inside.

It was so gloomy in the narrow passageway that it took them all some time to adjust to it, even from the dark alleyway they had just left behind, but they had little opportunity to notice much, even as their eyes became accustomed to the gloom, because the shrivelled little dwarf was speeding them down an interminably winding corridor. They were perhaps just aware of some dark and dingy pictures in ancient frames hanging on the walls, and candles in sconces casting looming shadows and eerie shapes on the walls between pockets of complete darkness. Here they had to hope there was nothing in front to trip them and just as they were all beginning to wonder if this corridor would ever end – it did – in a dead end. What now?

The dwarf ran his knobbled hands quickly over the solid wall in front of them, which began to slide open, slowly accompanied by a grinding noise that set their teeth on edge. The opening revealed steep steps to negotiate, with just a wooden handrail on one side to help them avoid falling headlong down into the blackness.

'Quickly, quickly,' urged the dwarf, speeding them down the staircase.

When they reached the bottom there was another solid wall, but this time the travellers were less surprised when it creaked open to reveal yet another corridor. However, this corridor could not have been more different from the first: The walls, bathed in a warm, golden light, were highly decorated with red and gold symbols that looked familiar to Wigapom, although he couldn't think from where at that moment.

The corridor sloped downwards fairly gently for a while before another shorter series of steps came into view, this time made of the finest marble. The corridor continued, with more steps, more symbols and pictures, all illuminated by the golden light.

It seemed to Wigapom that the decoration on the walls became more ornate and refined as they progressed, with multi-coloured shining spheres set into arched niches in the wall, and then yet another solid wall, highly decorated with swirls, spirals and lines in intricate patterns. Here their somewhat flustered guide once more touched a portion of the wall, which divided into two and created a wider opening through which they were hastily ushered.

'In here, wait in here,' he said impatiently in his falsetto voice, ushering them inside the room with his ancient fingers before disappearing as the door sealed behind them. All they heard was the distant sound of his footsteps scurrying at speed back down the corridor from whence they had come.

The travellers, each in their own way, suddenly realised their situation. They were in a strange, if beautiful place, many feet below ground, with no visible means of exit. They felt very vulnerable.

'Where are we?' said Will, quite in awe of the place in which they found themselves.

'Deep underground, that's for certain,' replied Fynn.

'But where are the exit doors, and where has the funny little man gone? Is he Aldebaran do you think? Can we trust him?' asked Wigapom, voicing the questions they were all thinking.

'I have no idea, but have you seen anything like this place before?' said Fynn, awe struck by their surroundings.

It was the most incredible space imaginable: A place that took their breath away. A huge circular chamber faced them, of the most magnificent opulence and scale that could be imagined. In the centre was a mid-height, finely-carved column, reminiscent of the carving on the Bull's Eye's lantern in the market square, but finer, cleaner and more dazzling in its execution. It supported a circular bronze dish, set sideways on a tripod made of the shiniest yellow metal, with knobs and dials all around it and encircled by an open orb of silver. It was impressive, but its function was a mystery. Above this was a domed ceiling decorated with paintings of the planets, astrological symbols and star constellations. The floor was highly polished marble with inlaid designs of animals, fish and birds. Four life-size mosaics of contrasting seasons decorated the centre, encircling the column. Most wonderfully, around the walls, were life-size images of different everyday scenes, trees and people, animals and buildings, which were constantly changing. This was the most fascinating aspect of a fantastic place and it was all such a contrast to the barren greyness and dilapidation of the town through which they had just come they could hardly take it all in. The only thing they noticed to spoil its perfection was a slight crack running across the ceiling.

It was Will who first noticed the relevance of the changing images around the walls.

'Wow! Look at this!' he said, pointing to one of them. 'This is just like Cassie's cottage. It's even got the donkey and cart outside!'

Wigapom and Fynn looked and saw the picturesque cottage where only a few hours earlier they had been made so welcome.

'Would you believe it,' said Fynn, as the scene changed slightly, 'but here are the Roth Riders preparing to attack it. How horrible they look!'

'That's strange,' said Wigapom, 'Cassie said she had never been attacked before today. So how can it be recorded here?'

'Don't know but look, here's the Megadrill, just coming up from underground,' added Fynn. 'It's Ollie's end I think.'

'Oh look, Fynn,' chimed in Wigapom 'there's the hollow tree where I spent last night. Jeepers, if I didn't know better I'd say that was me asleep there under the roots and branches.'

'It *is* you!' said Fynn, 'because here's me falling over in the mud when I was chasing you, Wiggy!'

'What?' said Wigapom, incredulous that both of them should be depicted in this place.

'You're not the only ones shown,' piped up Will proudly, 'look, here's me on the white hart, with you two standing beside me.'

Sure enough, on one section there were the three figures of Wigapom, Fynn, and Will with a regal-looking white hart, just as they remembered from earlier that day. It seemed as though everything that had happened to them since entering the forest was indeed depicted on the walls of this amazing place, like a visual storyboard.

'I don't understand this,' said Fynn.

Wigapom would, under normal circumstances, have been similarly amazed but he was beginning to realise that the impossible was possible in this place. He had also noticed more of those familiar symbols running around the base of the circular room. and he knew now what they were.

'Look Fynn, aren't these runes, like on my stones? Elven runes?' he said excitedly.

'They certainly look like them,' replied Fynn.

'Let's check,' said Wigapom as he drew the stones from his pocket. One look confirmed they had the same symbolic link, but then there was immediate frustration because the meanings were still unknown.

'Some of these are identical to those on the stones,' said Fynn.

'Exactly! So we might be able to work out what they say,' said Wigapom excitedly.

Just at that moment the hairs on the back of his neck began to stand to attention and he had the strangest feeling he was being invaded in some way. It was an uncomfortable feeling and he turned round, only to find Will looking at him with piercing eyes.

Before Wigapom could stop himself he snapped harshly at him.

'What are you looking at?'

'Only you!' snapped back Will. 'And those marks. What's wrong with that?'

'I don't like being stared at, that's all,' said Wigapom defensively.

Will ignored this but said instead:

'You won't understand those stones until you find someone who can read them in the first place.'

'I know that, I'm not stupid!' retorted Wigapom as he moved away to another part of the chamber, leaving Will scowling at him from the other end.

'Don't start that again!' said Fynn, irritated by their animosity to each other, 'For goodness sake, get on you two, won't you?'

Wigapom scowled a little more, rattled yet again by his own instinctive and none too pleasant reactions to Will. Why was he behaving so horribly towards him? Why couldn't he be civil? He'd not felt like this since he was a boy struggling against those who didn't seem to want to understand him. He didn't like being like this but he just didn't seem able to stop it.

There was no more opportunity for soul searching or rune deciphering at that point as they heard the hidden door opening again and all eyes turned towards it, wondering who or what they would see behind it.

The first person to enter was the dwarf, looking less harassed than before and now carrying a crystal topped staff as though it was the most precious object in the world. A memory stirred for Wigapom of Marvo the Magician. He'd had one of those. The dwarf stood to one side of the opening and announced in his falsetto voice.

'The Lightbearer, Sir,' then bowed, and stood back against the wall.

Again the travellers didn't understand: Was he referring to them, or one of them? Or to the powerfully built man who entered behind him? It seemed they would have to wait for any answer as the second figure filled the room with his presence and big booming voice.

'Welcome, welcome, to you all! To you Fynn, a true friend and companion, I offer my hand in comradeship. To you young Will, child of the past and future, I give you the compassion of my heart, and to you, Master Wigapom, the hope of us all, I give my allegiance and my pledge of service and duty. I am Aldebaran, Keeper of the Stories. Here, I trust, some of your questions will be answered, and no doubt new ones created – but first, some refreshment perhaps, and rest? I beg your forgiveness for the stealth and secrecy of your admittance here, but my doorkeeper, Lucas, was taken by surprise at the speed of your arrival.'

'But you must have known we were coming – everything we've done is depicted here on the walls,' blurted out Wigapom.

Aldebaran looked kindly at him.

'Indeed, yes, as you have noticed, your path through the forest has been well charted, although you may have also noticed that there is no record of anything that happened to you en route to Lampadia, or in the town itself.'

None of the three had noticed this, they had been too taken up with the fact that they were depicted at all! Aldebaran explained:

'We had known to expect your imminent arrival since yesterday, and anticipated it, of course, for many years. Yet, such is the state of things here since the Shadow of Sorcery blotted out the Light of Magic that we do not get information all the time. We do our best, but our magic is intermittent and fades more than we would wish.'

Wigapom opened his mouth to ask another question, but Aldebaran continued.

'Enough for now, refreshment and rest first. Time enough for questions after, when the head is clearer and the body restored,' and he turned to Lucas who was standing close by, peering at the three intently in a somewhat unnerving way.

'Lucas, instruct the others that they are here. We will meet together tonight after dinner, for the ceremony.'

'I will see to it at once,' replied the dwarf and he shuffled away at speed in his soft velvet slippers through yet another concealed door.

Aldebaran watched him go and then crossed to the other side of the chamber in front of them and began to tap another part of the wall with his fingers. Yet another doorway slid open.

'Follow me,' he said, leading the way with striding steps so that the travellers had to almost run to catch up with him.

They were in yet another corridor: this time of red granite walls, which glistened as they made their way down a small flight of stairs leading to a smaller, equally beautiful but more intimate chamber. Again circular, with a pointed domed ceiling of patterned coloured glass, the walls had softly lit alcoves, each bearing the face of a person. Wigapom was surprised to find that some of them seemed familiar. Especially a woman with chestnut hair. He had to pull his gaze away from her though, as they were being ushered to comfortable chairs of amber silk set round a table where simple, yet appetising food was laid out in highly polished crystal bowls, while flagons of honey coloured liquid stood waiting to be poured. They again realised how hungry they all were and tucked in with relish. The food restored them and questions began to rise once more to the surface, but Aldebaran pre-empted this with his own words.

'I know that you have many questions,' he began in his deep, resonant voice, 'and are confused at present, but seekers of truth have always been thus. It is part of the soul's journey to work through the confusions and questions of life before attaining illumination of the spirit. Let your eyes be the lamps of your soul – when your eyes are open to all possibilities, and seek only the good, then your soul beams light through your body. When you are full of light then you can truly see. Direct this light to others and they in their turn are illumined – and so it goes on.'

'This all sounds very grand and inspiring but I don't understand a word,' said Wigapom. The others nodded their agreement. It must mean something very profound but not one of them had any idea of what that could be. Wigapom could feel his frustration building again.

'We need simple, straightforward answers, not out of our depth philosophy!'

'Then ask away,' invited Aldebaran.

Now he had the opportunity to ask questions Wigapom was unsure where to start – so many were clamouring for attention! The question that pushed itself ahead was not, therefore, the most relevant, but it was a start.

'What is this place?' Wigapom blurted out, 'And how can there be somewhere so beautiful, when outside everything is so ugly?'

Aldebaran paused for a few moments as though weighing up this young man before him.

'Good questions deserve good answers,' said Aldebaran. 'I will do my best to serve. This place is beautiful, as you so rightly say, because some of us were still intent on upholding the old ways of Arcanum as the Shadow fell over us. We retreated here, into the safety of the earth, and built what we once had above. As above, so below. You are in the Oraclium Temple, the place where we record and value our history, and where hopefully, we learn from it. The first room you saw is called the Story Chamber, where we keep the Astrolabius…'

'Was that the strange dish thing in the middle?' queried Fynn.

'Correct. Both allow us to chart and record the past, and present positions of our citizens, as well as the potential future. For this we use the positions of the stars and planets. In times before the Dark One became powerful we had the ability to see clearly many aeons ahead, had we wished to do so, and with hindsight perhaps we should have done this more, and thus avoided the emergence of the Dark One, from amongst our own magicians. However, we chose to foolishly focus primarily on the memories of the past and the immediate pleasures of the present, paying little mind to the deeper subtleties of the moment or their repercussions on the future. By the time we became aware of the encroaching darkness of the Shadow we had lost the ability to see the future, and it was all too late.'

'Cassie told us that the Dark One wishes to kill Wigapom,' said Will, 'but she didn't tell us why, or who he really is.' If they hoped for an explanation at that moment they were disappointed as Aldebaran continued with his story.

'The Dark One has caused much destruction, and took control under our very gaze. Now the past is too painful to see and the future too terrible to anticipate, so we focus on the present moment again, yet with more regard for its importance. Perhaps it is better this way. We created below ground what used to be above in the hope of stemming the tide of the Dark One's destruction, but despite our best efforts, the power of the

Astrolabius is gradually weakening. Hence the fact we were unable to see your exact arrival. The Temple is slowly reducing in size and function and we fear will inevitably return to the underground cavern it once was if the Shadow is not destroyed. You will no doubt have noticed the first signs of this,' said Aldebaran, indicating a crack in the wall. 'If the Temple succumbs to the darkness of the Shadow completely before the book is found and replenished, then I fear for the return of True Magic.' Aldebaran's face took on a sad and far-away look momentarily, but then he drew himself back to the moment once more.

'This is no doubt difficult for you all to understand as yet. Enough to say that today we have more hope than yesterday,' and here he looked straight at Wigapom. 'I believe one day the Temple will be rebuilt in the open once more where all will benefit from it again.'

'So the Astrolabius is how you knew we were coming? said Fynn.

'Partly,' replied Aldebaran, 'although the messages are not as clear as they used to be. Yesterday, however, we experienced a surge that seemed to indicate that things were beginning,' and again he looked directly at Wigapom.

'Cassie said you'd been expecting us, or rather me, for years,' said Wigapom. 'How did you know I would travel here, when I didn't even know myself until yesterday?'

Aldebaran's deep eyes softened as he smiled with gentle understanding.

'Nothing is ever without planning or agreement on some level and there are no chance happenings, only moments of synchronicity, when two or more travellers on life's journey meet at pre-ordained times. What seems to you a spur of the moment happening has been laid down precisely in many different possibilities of execution. The vision you saw yesterday was but the most recent step on a long pathway of progression to this point. You have created, and now met, your destiny.'

'Destiny?' echoed Wigapom, 'what do you mean? That I have no choice in the matter? I don't know how you know about my vision Aldebaran, but Fynn and I both chose what we wanted to do, no one made us. I followed the request I was given because it was something I'd always wanted to do, and Fynn followed me because he wanted to – all on the spur of the moment!'

'There is always choice on some level. You can always exercise your conscious mind, but there is a mind that is both deeper and higher than that, and it was this that led you both into situations that made conscious choice not so much personal free will, but soul destiny,' replied Aldebaran calmly.

Wigapom was struggling to understand.

'What is my destiny then?' he asked. 'Is it just to find the other stones as the lady in my vision told me, and return them to *The Book of True Magic* when I find it? Is that my destiny or do I have a choice?'

'Firstly, the stones will find you when you prove yourself ready to receive them. So in that way you will choose when you move forward in your Quest. But choice is not always so easy to define. We all have the gift of free will, but a higher choice may have been made long before we were aware of it ourselves.'

More confusion addled Wigapom's brain. He needed clearer answers. He would have to ask clearer questions. He tried again.

'You talk about magic,' he said 'yet it seems to mean several different things here. We didn't have it in Brakendor. Can you explain what you mean by it? It might help me know what I'm looking for.'

'Another good question,' replied Aldebaran. 'There are three types of magic in Arcanum. Low Magic consists of spells to make things happen on a visual, practical level, yet always for the highest reasons, be that to create joy, or offer help…'

'You mean like Marvo did all those years ago at my party when he made all those things appear and disappear? interrupted Wigapom.

'The Marvo I saw as Corrin,' stated Fynn.

'Yes, the same,' replied Aldebaran. 'Marvo, as you call him, was the magician who volunteered to visit you, Wigapom, to start you on your Quest. We know him as Asgar.'

'I remember now, that was the name he told me as well!' replied Wigapom.

'Hang on a minute, Aldebaran,' interrupted Fynn, remembering his grandmother and her strange, secret ways, 'could magic also be the making of potions to help people get better in some way, like Cassie does, and my grandmother did?'

'That is yet another form of the Low Magic, yes.'

'So we did have magic in Brackendor after all,' reflected Fynn quietly. Aldebaran just smiled.

'The white hart was magic too wasn't he?' interrupted Will.

'Indeed,' said Aldebaran, pleased at their understanding. 'Then there is High Magic, which encompasses things in space, such as stars and planets, and the music of the spheres, and their relevance in our lives.'

'I remember the stars moving on Marvo… Asgar's cloak,' mused Wigapom. 'They were mesmerising.'

'What's the third type of magic then?' asked Will.

'Ah!' replied Aldebaran, a look of peace spreading momentarily over his face. 'That is the True Magic. The hidden wisdom of life. True Magic is a code to live by: a way of understanding the world and all that's in it so that harmony and peace both within and without can prevail; a true awareness of self and all creation. An understanding of the Oneness of the All, motivated by unconditional love and acceptance.'

'Oneness,' repeated Wigapom, 'you mean feeling that we're all connected somehow, whether we're plants, or animals, rocks or people?' Aldebaran nodded in agreement.

'That sounds very special,' said Will simply, with the unique understanding that often only a child can have.

'It *is* very special. And it's that which we have lost – which Wigapom is destined to find and return to us so that we all may throw off the Shadow of separation, which results in fear, anger, brutality and despair, and live instead in the knowledge and wisdom of enlightenment, which generates the peace and clarity of Oneness,' replied Aldebaran, smiling kindly at Will.

'Can you explain Oneness a bit more?' asked Fynn, who'd not quite grasped it as well as Wigapom or Will.

'Of course.' said Aldebaran and began his story of the One.

'Long before Darqu'on, the Dark One created the Shadow of separation with his sorcery, we all lived in the understanding that we were all one soul, with many identities. When you know your neighbour, or your colleague or members of your family, your animals, the plants in your garden or trees in the forests, even the ant in the soil, are all part of you, part of the One, then you do not wish to hurt them in any way, because that means you would hurt yourself. This is the way we lived for many, many years – in a blissful state of connection with everything. But when part of that Oneness feels separated, as Darqu'on did, it changes the whole perspective. He saw something that another part of the Oneness had, but rather than feel blessed by this, instead, felt deprived, and so jealousy, envy, greed and lust were born, and the reality of Oneness became fractured and the illusion of separation began. You saw for yourself how living in a state of separation is destructive. Restoring the True Magic, the hidden wisdom, will allow us to live peacefully again as One.'

'So Darqu'on is the Dark One? Who is he and how did the Shadow take over?' said Fynn.

'Darqu'on, or the Dark One, as many now call him, was once a magician here of the highest calibre. He had a brilliant mind but, for reasons as yet unknown, had an unstable heart, which turned to stone when he rejected the reality of Oneness and saw only the illusion of separation. When thwarted in his desire he sought to gain all power for himself, by misusing the magic to oppress others and that power corrupted him and all he touched. The magic, which had only ever been used to

151

spread peace and light, could no longer be sustained, and darkened into sorcery.

'So he is the Sorcerer – he has *The Book of True Magic!*' exclaimed Wigapom.

'Yes, he stole the book from Magus, and the more sorcery was used, the more evil took over from all that was good in life. Evil fed on the fear it created and the Shadow of this gradually spread over Arcanum, penetrating everywhere. With each act of fear, anger or brutality the Shadow increased, and so it is today, with the Dark One still at its core. He will not rest until the old ways way of Arcanum are snuffed out by the Shadow – which is why he seeks to destroy you Wigapom, as you are the one foretold to bring the light of magic back to Arcanum.'

'So *I* am the Lightbearer!' said Wigapom in amazement.

'Yes,' said Aldebaran, 'that is your destiny. If that is also your choice.'

'Back to choice again, I see,' said Wigapom.

'Things always come back to that in the end,' replied Aldebaran, looking carefully at Wigapom, as if attempting to read what his choice would be.

'Did no one else try to stop the Dark One in the past?' said Fynn.

'Oh yes. Our last King,' replied Aldebaran. 'He fought valiantly against the Dark One, his one-time friend, but despite his honourable intentions, he was not powerful enough against the increasing strength of sorcery. Neither he, nor the magicians nor knights who supported him, realised at that time that fighting one negative force with another negative force would only increase the power of the Shadow. The King chose to take the Dark One on in battle – to fight like with like –but with no understanding of the power of evil, he lost the fight.'

'Do you mean he died?' said Will.

'Yes, the King was killed, not long after his only son was born. And the people who had supported him lost not only their leader but also their belief that things could change for the better. They became fractured. More separated. They lost hope, or many of them did, and soon succumbed to the Dark One's evil ways, deceived by their lower appetites and existing then, as now, in a state of fear and separation.'

Aldebaran paused in his narrative and the sudden silence hung heavy in the air. Eventually Fynn broke the silence.

'You talk of people living in fear, and succumbing to their lower appetites, but you, Aldebaran, do not seem one of them. Cassie neither,' he said.

'That's true,' added Wigapom. 'Nor is this place where we sit now a place of darkness and shadows, at least not yet. Some light must remain still – shadows themselves can only be present if there's a light source somewhere.'

'You speak true, Master Wigapom, there are those of us who have done our best to maintain the light of truth as best we can, whilst waiting for the rightful one to free us from the contamination of the dark, and release the True Magic of wisdom once more.'

'And that person is supposed to be me?' said Wigapom, feeling as though he had already guessed the answer and the weight of responsibility that went with it.

'Yes,' said Aldebaran simply.

'You said the 'rightful one,' repeated Wigapom, 'what do you mean by that? I'm only a baker's son from Brakendor! I don't even belong in this place.'

'You were raised in Brakendor by the baker and his wife, but you were born here in a castle, to a King and his Queen,' said Aldebaran quite softly.

'What?' said Wigapom, unsure if he'd heard correctly. 'You mean … You mean … You mean *I* was the son born to the King?' He stuttered in disbelief.

'Yes,' said Aldebaran simply.

'Wow! That makes you a Prince!' cried Fynn, eyes almost popping from his head as he looked at Wigapom with different eyes, 'I'm friends with a Prince!'

'No,' denied Wigapom. 'I can't be a Prince! I'm ordinary! It's not possible! I'm not special.' He was shocked at this revelation.

'Everyone is special, Wigapom' corrected Aldebaran, 'whether born into royalty or not.'

'Well yes, I know, but I'm just me! I'm no different to anyone else!' said Wigapom, barely able to take in that he was not who he thought he was, and Samuel and Sarah had not been his parents after all!

'We are all different, unique, wherever we come from,' said Aldebaran in reply, 'this diversity is the glory of being part of the One. We each experience things in different ways and in different places – and I believe you have felt different from others all your life, Wigapom – is that not true?'

Wigapom sighed with acknowledgement.

'I've always felt that I had something more to do than be a baker in a small village,' he replied, 'not that there's anything wrong with being a baker, it just wasn't me – and I wanted more freedom than my parents and my life were giving me. But I never thought that they weren't my real mother and father, or that I had a secret past.'

'They did their job well then, Master Wigapom, for if they had provided a different life you would perhaps not have wanted to leave Brakendor – and leave it you had to, of your own free will, if you were to fulfil your destiny.'

Wigapom's head was a battleground of questions fighting each other to be answered.

'So how did I get to live in Brakendor? Why did Cassie call it the village of Inbetween? What are the stones for and why was I told to change my name? And what about the dream and the vision? What does all that mean… and supposing I don't want to do this, Aldebaran? Suppose I'm not good enough for the task? What then? And what about Fynn – where does he come in?'

'And me,' piped up Will resentfully, 'you always forget me – but I'm part of this too, and I won't go away anymore.' Wigapom turned to him, in surprise. He'd forgotten Will was even there. He wished he wasn't, but why? What was it about this child that Wigapom found so difficult to accept? As if he didn't have enough confusions already!

Aldebaran spoke again.

'Wigapom is the elven name given you by your real mother, Elvira, the Queen. Only she and the chief magician, Magus knew the relevance of the name and the secret still lies with them, as both are now dead. Magus, the last great Wizard played another vital part in your story by creating a hidden village, which you know as Brakendor and which we here, because we could not see it, called the village Inbetween. Magus lost his life in the process. The name Willerby,' and here he looked both at Wigapom and Will, 'was a pseudonym created to protect you when you were too young to protect yourself. The stones are crystals with specific properties to defeat the dark forces. They are keys to find the True Magic. Four of them were lost here many years ago and the full seven are needed to unlock the book and thus match the Dark One in strength, but not might. Magus cast a spell on the lost stones, instructing them to reveal themselves to you when you had proved yourself worthy of having them. Each stone means something different.'

'So what do the two stones I have mean, and what did I do to receive them?' queried Wigapom, still struggling to take everything in.

'The orange stone was the first to be revealed to you, was it not, on your thirteenth birthday?'

Wigapom nodded, holding the orange stone in his hand where it felt warm and buzzing with vitality. He was not even amazed anymore at how much Aldebaran knew of his past.

'The orange stone represents the natural Child self, often called our Soul Child, which is located in the sacral area of the body. It is a stone of joy, spontaneity and vitality. Creativity itself – the freedom to be who we really are.'

'But I wasn't free to be me when I got this stone. I didn't have much joy either,' argued Wigapom.

'All is potential, Wigapom. By your thoughts and actions you had proved your potential to be your natural self. It is in us all, and recognises either consciously or subconsciously, our purpose in this life – and it was speaking to you. Deep down you knew what your purpose was and the stone came along to reinforce this. An example of synchronicity, which gave you hope.'

'It certainly did that. That's when I changed my name and became the me I felt comfortable with! I did always know there would be more to my life, but I got so angry with myself when I couldn't or wouldn't make it happen,' recalled Wigapom.

'The impatience of the Child! It is only the Adult in us that truly understands patience,' smiled Aldebaran.

'You spoke the words 'Child' and 'Adult' as though they were in capitals!' Wigapom commented, surprised.

'They are,' explained Aldebaran.★ 'The Child within us can be either Natural, or Adapted; whilst the Adult in us is logical and rational. We also have a Parent inside – sometimes loving and encouraging, sometimes critical and limiting.'

'I recognise the Adapted Child and Critical Parent in me,' grimaced Wigapom, 'and I'm just discovering the Natural Child I think, but I struggle to find any Adult at times.'

'He is there – just give him time,' encouraged Aldebaran.

'Can I ask what you mean by synchronicity?' asked Fynn.

'Of course: it means events that seemingly happen by chance but have a higher purpose – a reason for happening,' explained Aldebaran.

'You mean like me just happening to meet Wigapom as he was thinking of leaving Brakendor after he found the yellow stone? I almost didn't walk that way, you know, but felt I had to, and there he was,' said Fynn thoughtfully.

'That's a good example.'

'What about the yellow stone,' asked Wigapom, the one I got just yesterday – jeepers, it seems a lifetime ago already! What does it mean?'

'The yellow stone is indicative of the personality, or ego self, being formed in the solar plexus. Here we find self-confidence. The stone arrived when you proved you had the confidence to be the real you and do what you always said you would; leave Brakendor and strike out on your Quest.'

★ Based on concepts found in 'Transactional Analysis in Psychotherapy' 1961, by Eric Berne, MD.

'And I did!'

'Yes indeed, and now you must prove yourself worthy to have the other stones revealed to you. The last four stones you have to find, however, will be the hardest to earn. Many of us get stuck in the ego, or lower self as it's often called. This is where the sense of separation begins. Many live their lives in only this space. You have to move into your higher self by creating, and crossing the bridge that joins one to the other. This will be part of your Quest.'

'I have to create a bridge as well as find the stones?' cried Wigapom, overwhelmed suddenly by all these tasks that were springing up.

'I don't think Aldebaran means a real bridge, Wiggy,' said Fynn, trying to be helpful. Aldebaran laughed kindly.

'Don't worry, when you're ready, you will understand and it will be easier than you think!' and he placed a relaxed hand on Wigapom's tense shoulder.

'You were born for this task, Wigapom. Only you, it seems, have the right mix of blood in your veins to defeat the Dark One, and when you do you will open out the opportunity for all others to follow and set themselves free, if they choose. But you too have free choice, Wigapom, as I said before, and only you can decide if you are up to the task. Only you can decide whether, when, and how to pursue it. I will not patronise you with compliments about your capability. You must search your own heart for answers.'

Aldebaran then turned to Fynn and Will. 'And as for you two...' he paused with a faint smile on his face. 'Fynn's story is being written by him even now. He has already shown the depth of his friendship and trust in you, Master Wigapom, to leave all that he had to follow you. He also has faerie blood in him, which will help. The faerie race are known for their kindness and compassion, amongst other attributes.'

'What do you mean, faerie blood!' blurted out Fynn, astonished at this news.

'Your grandmother was a Befind, was she not? A Befind is part of the faerie race, they are renowned as healers.'

'Wow!' said Fynn, finding himself unable to express anything more profound at this unexpected news.

'What about me?' said Will.

Aldebaran turned to Will and his smile changed to a quizzical look.

'You, Will, are an unknown at present. Your physical presence was unexpected in this story, although I have my suspicions as to why you're here, which I will keep to myself, in case they're incorrect. There could be more at stake here than we know. It's now in the hands of fate to see what you'll do with all this.'

Will's deep green eyes looked boldly into Aldebaran's without flinching. Whatever he was feeling he was not giving anything away. Wigapom shuddered involuntarily, as though someone had just walked over his grave again.

'You were right about answers leading to more questions,' said Fynn, finding his voice once more and scratching his head, 'You're telling me that my oldest friend is an elven Prince of light and that faerie blood runs in me! Well, grandmother or no grandmother, anything less like a faerie than me would be hard to find, I think! No wonder I'm confused. More confused than I was before! At least, I think I am!' And he looked so puzzled, as he scratched his mop of blond hair, that the others couldn't help laughing, and the intensity of the moment lightened noticeably.

'Come,' said Aldebaran, standing up, 'enough for now, time for rest. Tonight we celebrate a rite of passage. There are others to meet, there is much to enjoy and a future to create. Time enough for serious talk tomorrow.'

He led the way through more corridors in this stunning rabbit warren of a place, and into a spacious room with soft pillows, comfortable beds and warm rugs.

'Rest now all of you,' said Aldebaran, 'there is much to be done but it cannot be accomplished without sleep. Life is nothing without balance. There is time enough for everything.'

CHAPTER 16

The Riddle of the Runes

*"Destiny plans a different route, or turns the dream around, as if it were a riddle,
and fulfills the dream in ways we couldn't have expected."*
Ben Okri

Wigapom didn't think it would be possible to sleep after all that had happened to him, but no sooner had his head touched the soft pillows and he had snuggled down under the warm blankets, than he slipped easily into a deeply peaceful dream-filled slumber:

He was in a huge cavern that continued to expand as he walked through it, as if it had no end, or beginning. The walls were covered with symbols and two enormous stones; one orange and the other yellow stood side by side on the floor. When he touched them they became soft, downy pillows that cushioned him in comfort. It was totally peaceful here and when he awoke some hours later he felt refreshed and clearer-headed than before.

He was beginning slowly to see how everything was fitting together, like the pieces of a giant jigsaw. He'd still only managed to do the corner bits of the puzzle, and some of the straight edges, but a framework was beginning to take shape; he felt less adrift than he had since this craziness began.

He was not yet fully able to appreciate his royal parentage, or his birth connection to the elven folk and all that might entail, although he had read of their wisdom and gentleness in the stories as a child; but to associate himself with them was still difficult – he'd spent too many years as a humble baker's son for that, but he did know, again from stories, that the presence of the white hart had always signified the coming of royalty, as well as a time of trial; thus it seemed it was not chance but Aldebaran's concept of synchronicity that had brought them together when it did. Much of what Aldebaran had said Wigapom had found confusing, but he felt it was important to listen and learn what he could from him.

He wondered whether the woman in his childhood dream, and the recent vision at the brook, were of his mother, the elven Queen. He hoped so. He also remembered the portrait in the alcove in the Temple; he was sure it was of her; it matched his memory of the images and visions he'd had. He remembered how complete he'd felt with her in both of them. If her physical self was dead, and that would likely be the case, she was still very alive to him, and he was aware of her loving presence more and more. It was at these moments he felt calm; even serene.

He didn't know how he'd do the task he'd been born to do, or what implications there were to being Wigapom, the Lightbearer: what would he have to do to earn these stones; where would the Quest take him, what would it involve? He hoped he was up to the task; it was a tremendous responsibility to have to bear. He was so glad he had Fynn for company – imagine Fynn with faerie blood! Wigapom part elf and Fynn part faerie – how about that! How good to have such a friend. But he still struggled when Will came to mind: he resented this boy, and he thought he was beginning to understand why. Will reminded him too much of himself when he was growing up before he received the first stone. He'd hated himself then, with all his insecurities and frustrations battling inside. It was a time when he felt he had no control over his own young life.

Wigapom could feel all the sadness, anger and loneliness inside Will; it was painful because it brought back how he'd felt when he was just plain Willerby. He didn't like being reminded of it and Will did remind him, all the time.

He closed his eyes and sighed, and as if by habit put his hand in his pocket and rattled the familiar stones that always seemed to give him comfort. As he felt their familiar shapes he remembered he had to find the other five, but just a minute, hadn't Aldebaran said that only four had been lost. He was no mathematician, but even he knew that the two he had and the four that were lost only made six, and he had seven to find! Where was the other one?

As he puzzled this over he could clearly feel the rune markings with his fingers. Suddenly he was wide-awake as he remembered the runes illustrated on the wall of the Astrolabius; he felt compelled to see them again.

He left the still sleeping Fynn and Will, snoring happily in their beds, and made his way back as well as he could remember towards the Astrolabius; corridors, steps, secret doors, waiting for the tell tale click, more corridors, more steps, more doors, more clicks, until he was back in the huge circular chamber again, with the pictures of the zodiacal year around him and the storyboard of their adventures in the forest. He noticed some now showed their arrival by donkey cart: it seemed the Astrolabius was still working, if slowly!

He dropped to the floor and hunted around the base for a runic symbol that he recognised: there was one! Wigapom felt a rush of triumph shoot up his body. He matched the symbol with the one on the orange stone; but he was no further forward.

'I still don't know what any of them stand for,' he said to himself, and the triumphant feeling took a nosedive, landing with a thud like a clod of earth inside his belly.

'Are they letters, or does the whole symbol denote a whole word?' he wondered softly to himself.

A small voice inside his head seemed to say, 'They're words,' and he wondered where that thought came from, but the frustration of not knowing for sure was overpowering. If they were words, what did they mean? Until he understood one symbol, at least, they would all remain a mystery. He would have to ask Aldebaran.

'The runes are an ancient language few understand,' said a deep voice at his shoulder. Wigapom nearly jumped out of his skin to find Aldebaran there.

'Oh! Aldebaran! You scared me! I didn't know you were there!' he said, unsure whether he ought to have been here, uninvited – would Aldebaran think he was prying?

'You were engrossed, Master Wigapom. It is not surprising that seemed more real to you.'

'I was trying to make sense of these runes. Trying to understand their meaning but I can't see how I will ever find out. Can you read them at all?'

'A little, although for most it is a skill that has gradually been lost over time: even when they are read they are not always understood.'

More deep philosophy, thought Wigapom, and stored it somewhere for when he could fully understand.

'They appear on the stones I was given,' he explained. 'I think they might be important to restoring the magic. This one matches the one here, on the wall,' said Wigapom pointing to the rune on the orange stone.

Aldebaran looked carefully. The shapes were angular and placed in a square on the stone.

'I do recognise this, it's a joining word that means *is* in our language,' he said.

'*Is*?' said Wigapom, surprised, and a little disappointed that the word was somehow not more exciting. 'That's a very ordinary word. I'd thought it might be something more inspiring.'

Aldebaran however saw the word differently. Wigapom did his best to see it too.

'What could be more inspirational than being something that *is*?' Aldebaran said philosophically.

Wigapom furrowed his brow: more riddles from Aldebaran! He really wished he spoke about things he knew, or at least that he could understand easily – he was harder than the strange runes to comprehend at times!

'Forgive me, Aldebaran. I've never had to think this deeply before and it's not something that comes that easily,' said Wigapom.

Aldebaran saw his confusion and did his best to explain.

'The word *is* is connected to our being in the world, to being in our physical body. It's a statement about who we are, our 'I am-ness' if you like, remember from your school days, Wigapom? He is, you are, I am. This word is more than a word, it is a concept, an idea, a statement of being who you are. Who do you think you are, Wigapom?'

Wigapom sighed. What a question! He used to believe he was the baker's son, but that never felt totally right; now he was told he was a Prince and that felt even weirder. He wasn't sure that he had ever known who he really was, yet he had to give an answer. He spoke, weighing things up as carefully as he could.

'I know who you tell me I am – the only son of the King and Queen; the Lightbearer; potential saviour of Arcanum; potential discoverer of the hidden wisdom and possible restorer of the True Magic, and all of that, but I don't feel like any of those, Aldebaran – but then I never felt like the son of the baker either: I always felt awkward and out of place there. Since I left Brakendor, I think I'm beginning to see that I'm just me – not that special; not always that nice either – certainly not confident enough yet, despite the presence of the yellow stone, to believe I can do all that's expected of me. In fact right now I feel about as small as the word *is*, and no closer to understanding what all this is about!'

'Perhaps you're being invited to be more than you've ever dreamed of being before, Wigapom?' said Aldebaran kindly, placing a fatherly arm around his rather dejected shoulders. 'We never know what we are capable of until we are tested and I am sure that you will be tested to the very depths of your being now you have finally taken up the Quest.'

'I'm not so sure I want to take it now – I'm not sure I'm good enough, I mean,' said Wigapom. He didn't want anyone to assume he was going to do it, not at the moment anyway. It was such a responsibility having the future of Arcanum on his shoulders! Things seemed so much harder now than before.

He produced the second stone from his hand. 'Do you know what the rune on this one is?'

Aldebaran looked at the yellow stone. This too had a basic square shape but the markings were more complex this time.

'I'm not sure. This is a more complicated rune than on the last stone, and one I am not so familiar with. Let's see if we can find the meaning by consulting the grimoire.'

'The what?' said Wigapom, totally unfamiliar with this word.

'A grimoire is a book of grammar, a description of magical symbols, such as these runes, which show you how to combine them properly and translate them into words,' explained Aldebaran, reaching his hand into the air and plucking a book magically from it.

'Wow!' said Wigapom, in awe of the magic he had just witnessed.

'Low Magic can still be used for some important matters,' explained Aldebaran.

They began to hunt for similar shapes to that on the stone. At last they found one contained in a descriptive phrase. Aldebaran reached for another book, in a similar fashion to the first, to translate the elven words into a language they could both understand.

'Now, I understand part of this phrase, which, when translated, means 'when one's word is given it must be acted upon.'

'That means you have to keep your promise?' said Wigapom.

'That's the meaning of the phrase, yes, but the word...' Aldebaran's voice trailed off for a moment as he worked things through in his head. Finally he said with some confidence.

'I believe the word is *given*.'

'*Given?*' said Wigapom, 'what's that supposed to mean? That's as confusing as the first word!'

'I can't tell you the answer,' said Aldebaran, 'but perhaps it suggests that you have received a gift: to be given something is such a gift, although as yet you do not know what that gift is.'

'Aldebaran! Talk so that I can understand! This is not making any sense to me!' cried Wigapom in exasperation. 'I have two words – *is given* yet all they've given me is more confusion than before. What a huge riddle to unravel. I'm not sure that I can do this.'

'If you believe you can't then you won't. Remember that, Wigapom. Do not lose heart. You would not have been given the stones if you were not able to understand their relevance, nor would you have been given this Quest if you were not capable of seeing it through. We are never given things in life that we cannot handle on some level. Everything we are given in life, whether we like what it is or not, is indeed a gift. We just have to recognise what that gift is.'

'I like what you say, but it still sounds like a riddle to me, Aldebaran. I don't see any of this as being a gift at the moment. In fact I almost feel I'd give it all up and settle for a boring life as a baker in Brakendor right now!'

'Is that who you are?'

Wigapom looked into Aldebaran's eyes, which seemed to challenge him, and thought for a moment: was he really a baker? Did he really want to be back in the bakery at Brakendor, kneading the dough, listening to the same old moans and comments, living that same restricted life? His head cleared, as though a refreshing breeze had blown away the clouds in his head. No, of course he didn't; that wasn't who he was! It was the thought of playing that role for the rest of his life that had finally spurred him on to making changes. Maybe Aldebaran was right after all. Everything that had happened to him *was* a gift; he'd been given it for a reason; now it was up to him to find out how to use the gift, whatever it was. Perhaps it was the gift of understanding himself? Maybe. Perhaps these problems were really opportunities for growth. He could choose to believe he wasn't good enough; to worry about it, be frightened of it, run away, or he could choose to think of it as an amazing opportunity to not only help the outer world of Arcanum, but explore his own inner world too: a chance to really discover what he was made of. Wasn't that what he had asked for? What he'd always wanted.? Wasn't this just the gift that he needed?

'You're right, Aldebaran. I don't want to be a boring Brackendor baker, although I realise that for some that's a valuable job. I will see this all as a gift that I've been given. I think I have to trust that I'm being helped by something bigger than me to pursue this Quest. I've been helped so much already, now perhaps it's time to give something back?'

Aldebaran smiled and put his hand once more on Wigapom's shoulder.

'If that is what you want.'

'I think I do – I know it's what's expected of me here, and what my real parents expected of me.'

'Do not do things just because others expect you to do them, but because you feel it is right, inside you. Do not forget your free will, Wigapom, or that every choice carries its own consequences. You have total choice of what to do and how to do it in this life. If you do not choose to accept the challenges then there is nothing we can do to alter that. We only know what's happening at the moment and that can change in the blink of an eye. We laid the foundations, but you are responsible for the main structure: we are only ever responsible for the individual parts we play. Nothing is guaranteed, unless we make it so – all is just potential.'

'So it's not guaranteed that I will be able to restore the True Magic and thus free this place from the dark forces, as everyone hopes?' said Wigapom, thoughtfully.

'There are no guarantees in life,' replied Aldebaran.

'So anything can happen, depending on what I do, or don't do?' clarified Wigapom again.

'Depending on what *everyone* does or doesn't do.' corrected Aldebaran. 'Remember, we are all One, ultimately. But, yes, anything can happen.'

'It's quite daunting really,' said Wigapom, 'yet there is a part of me that's quite excited. Does that seem strange?'

Aldebaran shook his head. 'Not at all. We are comprised of many contradictory parts. What is important is that we manage to integrate them into the whole person.'

Wigapom looked at Aldebaran as though he had just said something that turned a light on, somewhere in his head.

'Do you mean, we have parts of us that we might not like, or that we don't always want to have around? Parts that we might get cross with or find a nuisance?'

'That can happen more often than you think,' replied Aldebaran, looking intently at Wigapom, as if willing him to make a connection with the floating thoughts in his head.

Wigapom went towards the part of the wall now showing him and Fynn with young Will walking up Arcadia Alley.

'I don't understand about… about Will,' he said. 'I get angry with him, yet there's no reason. He's just a child. I expect him to do things but then I don't trust him to be able to do them properly. I didn't really want him here on this journey, I don't even know where he came from, yet I couldn't send him away: it was as though he was meant to be here, somehow. Sometimes he feels like me when I was a child; sometimes I feel like his Parent; and just occasionally I've felt quite Adult; grown up and kind toward him – do you understand?'

Aldebaran nodded kindly as Wigapom continued with his train of thought:

'He seems to empathise with what I feel when I'm unsure or sad, but I reject his kindness, and then I hate myself for behaving like that and take it out on him even more. How crazy is that?'

Wigapom looked at Aldebaran, as though wanting confirmation of his thoughts but Aldebaran remained silent, as though allowing Wigapom mental space to work things through, so he continued:

'Sometimes when I look at Will, it's as though I'm looking at myself: well, a part of myself that I didn't want and thought had gone. Does that sound silly?'

'It sounds possible to you – so it doesn't matter what I think or feel. We all create our own realities, Wigapom – what I do know is that inside each one of us, however old in our physical being, is a magical Child; the Soul Child I spoke of earlier. Whatever happens to that Child in life is reflected in his behaviour. That Child can often be a nuisance and get into trouble; he can feel frightened or angry, sad or lost; yet he can also be joyful, spontaneous and creative. We need this Child to be his natural self so that we can feel his joy and zest for life lived through us – when we have this we have our own brand of magic – but when that Child feels misunderstood or unheard, or worse, invisible, then this magic dims and the Child believes he has no worth. His essential light becomes dull and he either retreats from the world or rebels against it.'

'I used to feel like that,' said Wigapom quietly. 'I used to feel that my parents – foster parents – didn't understand me or want to listen to what I needed from life. They loved me, I knew that, but the restrictions they placed on me left me feeling as though there was an invisible wall separating us, which I couldn't break. I wanted to get them to notice me, the real me, not the person they wanted me to be, so I tried to rebel and this got me into trouble, which got me attention of the wrong kind. I was still so angry and unhappy at times that I'd cry myself to sleep, but still no one heard. I believed that what *I* wanted didn't matter to anyone – that the real me inside didn't matter to anyone – so I had to be someone I didn't want to be. I didn't like being that little boy, especially as I saw him as weak and unable to stand up to authority. Believe me, I was glad to get rid of him.'

'What does it feel like – having a part of you that does not like or accept another part of you?' said Aldebaran.

'I've never looked at it like that before – I've only ever seen myself as me – just one – but I can see now that one part of me *has* disliked and ignored another part – this Child part as you call it. I guess if that were a real person he'd feel very unhappy to be hated so much; he wouldn't think he was worth much.'

'What would he need from the other part to feel better about himself?' asked Aldebaran.

Wigapom shrugged.

'To be recognised, I guess; heard; valued.' Suddenly, like a bolt of lightning, a possibility illuminated Wigapom's mind that seemed to be both fanciful and the most natural thing in the world. He was astonished he'd not seen it before.

'Aldebaran, this sounds crazy, but could Will be that Child part of me, become real?'

'What do you think, Wigapom?'

'Strange as it seems, I think he could be – it feels right. Cassie said the Forbidden Forest was really an Enchanted Forest: perhaps I thought Will into existence. Could that be possible?'

'All things are possible,' said Aldebaran, 'and our thoughts and emotions are very powerful things. It is very possible that he is a thought form you have made real. We were certainly not expecting him. He just seemed to appear, as if from nowhere. But often the unexpected are the greatest gifts of all, Wigapom. I'm sure that you will learn much from him about yourself. Regard him as a gift, much as we were talking about.'

'He's not a gift I'd choose exactly,' said Wigapom wryly. 'That's why I haven't wanted him around – he reminds me too much of how I felt as a Child, and it's hard. But I'm making things worse, aren't I? I need to accept him, and believe in him and listen to him. I need to help him feel good about himself. Myself. Oh how confusing this is… But then, perhaps it's not that confusing: maybe that's why he's appeared as a real boy – because I'd never have recognised he was there if he hadn't. I didn't realise what I was doing before, but now I know that every time I rejected him, I rejected me. I don't want to do that anymore. I want us to grow together and be more than we have ever been apart.'

Aldebaran's voice was gentle and his smile wide.

'Wigapom,' he said, 'you have taken a big step already towards bringing the True Magic back into this land. You've discovered the beginning of the path to self-healing, which is self-awareness. To reclaiming the light of that awareness for all. It takes just one person to create the potential for enormous transforming powers in others: this is True Magic – the hidden wisdom that you now seek. You have done well.'

'Have I?' said Wigapom. 'And all without realising that was what I was doing! Wow! So Will is really part of me! And knowing that will help me get the magic back! I feel lighter already for knowing that! I do feel quite magical inside, although I'm not sure I feel wiser. It's a pretty heady feeling, Aldebaran. I want to tell the world how it feels so they can feel it too – especially I want to share it with Will, to make up for all the times I've been hateful and horrid to him, or rather, me! I want us both to have the chance of the childhood that we wanted,' and Wigapom laughed with real joy.

'Your intentions are honourable, Wigapom, but putting them into practice is harder than you think. It takes time for your wounded emotions to catch up with the logic of your head. It may take time to get the relationship right, to embrace the Natural rather than Adapted Child, jettison the Critical Parent in you, and find the replacement of the Loving Adult. Your Child will test you too, be sure of that. Don't be hard on yourself if you do not always succeed in loving and nurturing your Child self as you now would wish. Remember, small steps lead to big change – so don't seek to run before you can truly walk!'

Wigapom was not listening any more: he was too full of the euphoria of finding another part of himself to think that Aldebaran's wise words related to him, and brushed them off. He didn't really understand about Critical Parents and Loving Adults. He just knew that in Will was his Child self who wanted to be free, and he was going to do everything he could to make that happen by being a free Child too.

'Will and I will be fine,' he said boldly and brightly. 'I need to see him right now, Aldebaran, and make up for lost time,' and with that he seemed to forget all about the stones, and the runes etched on them, and focus only on making amends with his Child self.

'This will all wait,' he said, waving his hand around the room. 'After all, good things are worth waiting for, aren't they Aldebaran, you said so yourself!' And with that he left the Astrolabius and ran to find Will and share the good news.

Aldebaran watched him go, aware that the whole success of the Quest now hinged on this new relationship between Wigapom and his inner child, Will. They would all have to wait and see its outcome.

CHAPTER 17

The Wheel of Life

"The Self is the hub of the wheel of life."
Prashna Upanishad

Lucas was busy. Guests were arriving through the various tunnels cut into the hillside. A few even came through the front door, although disguised, of course. He was quite run off his slippered feet. The guests had all swiftly responded to the joyous news of the arrival of the Lightbearer: their beloved King's only son. Expectations were high and excitement intense.

'What is he like, Lucas: has he the King's tall stature?' asked Langan, one of the gnomes from the glen.

'He seems shorter than one would expect,' replied Lucas.

'Has he his father's firm voice?' asked Tamsan, dwarf of the dale.

'It can still be a trifle shrill.'

'Has he his mother's loving disposition?' said Sybil, the statuesque faerie of the flowers.

'He has not yet demonstrated this.'

'Has he the light of wisdom in his eyes?' asked Gobann, the dwarf and master smith from the Bluestone hills.

'Only time will tell.'

The more questions Lucas was asked, and the more he answered, the more they drew conclusions that Wigapom did not, perhaps, match up to their idealised image of what the longed for Prince should be.

'We should not judge,' said the thoughtful voice of Tamsan, who along with his companion Gobann, was fully prepared to give Wigapom time to settle.

'But if he is not up to the job we are doomed,' interrupted Langan, 'Can we trust him with our very survival?'

'We must give him time,' replied Gobann. 'He needs time to understand us, as much as we need time to understand him.'

'According to Lucas, he is wanting time to understand himself,' said Langan, somewhat critically.

'That is a worthy attribute,' said Gobann, in Wigapom's defence.

'But do we have that time available to us?' intoned Sybil, with real concern.

'We must trust that all is perfect, even in its seeming imperfection,' said Aldebaran, who had come to greet his guests and introduce them to the subject of their conversation, 'and as Tamsan so wisely says, we must not judge.'

Yet it was hard *not* to judge, and it would be true to say that there were several amongst those gathered that evening that had reservations about the Prince, whose arrival they had long anticipated. Time and longing have a way of embellishing reality until what is created or fantasised about becomes something impossible to achieve, and this had happened with hopes and dreams of Wigapom: so much had been invested in him, so much expected of him, that, in truth, nothing and no one could ever be that perfect. They had created an impossible dream and at the sight of this young man, who seemed so wide-eyed about everything he saw and did, they were let down, not by him of course, but by the impossibility of their expectations.

Some, however, like Gobann and Tamsan, were more tolerant of any perceived shortcomings, and prepared to give him the opportunity to prove himself. In reality, of course, they had to, as Wigapom was the only means through which they could reclaim what they had lost. They had to be patient, tolerant, and above all forgiving.

Aldebaran knew that some would be able to do this more than others. Since the rise of Darqu'on and his Shadow of sorcery, tolerance, compassion and understanding, as well as forgiveness, had to be worked on much harder than ever before. Even those souls who refuted the dark forces and formed part of the essential underground resistance in their endeavours to keep the way open to light, were still, to varying degrees, open to contamination by them, and all needed to be vigilant. Some were better able to do this than others: Wigapom, Fynn and Will would find out over time who these were, and indeed, how much they were able to do this themselves, for all were on a personal voyage of self-discovery, whether they realised this or not, and it was part of each one's personal journey to work on their own prejudices and weaknesses.

Wigapom, for his part, enjoyed meeting these new guests, some of whom he took to immediately, and looked forward to seeing again, others with whom he felt more unsure, and some whom he found it hard to relate to at all, but, in truth, he was more keen to have time alone with Will than anyone: the idea that he had created this person from feelings inside himself seemed at the time the most wonderful magic of all. He was keen to start building their relationship, which perhaps meant he did not pay as much attention as he could have to things that were said, done or hinted at. In many ways he had what could safely be called 'information overload' and the rite of passage ceremony that Aldebaran talked about and which eventually took place in the huge circular Story Chamber, whilst amazing and astounding in many ways, tended to carry Wigapom along with it in a dreamlike state, so that he remembered little of the events in the days after. On a level underneath his conscious awareness however, it remained, waiting to surface when the moment was right.

He did his best to listen, as did Fynn and Will, to the tales of how the Shadow of Sorcery had begun and how it had spread; stories of how folk disappeared from their homes without trace; and of the dark and deadly deeds undertaken by the Roth Riders, Wulverines and other messengers of doom, and began to build a picture of what life had been like, and was like, for those outside his own familiar Brakendor environment. He began to realise that in comparison, life there, although restricted, had perhaps been not so bad after all. At least he had been able to sleep safely in his bed at night!

When the time came for the ceremony of the Wheel of Life, Aldebaran called everyone together.

'Friends and custodians of light, we are here this evening to mark a rite of passage for which we have been waiting for many years. The Lightbearer is now amongst us, and we bless his arrival with this ceremony, creating a sacred space of healing energy to help him take up the responsibilities to which he was born.'

There was a buzz of excitement as guests all formed a circle around the walls of the chamber, some faces were solemn, others smiling in encouragement at Wigapom, whilst there were some whose faces gave nothing away.

Wigapom was asked to stand in the centre of the circle, or 'wheel' as it was termed. He hesitated at first.

'Go ahead Wigapom, the centre is yours,' encouraged Aldebaran.

'I was thinking,' said Wigapom, nervous and awkward amongst all these new faces. 'I was thinking that Will ought to stand in the circle with me, as he's part of me. That would feel right for me. Could he do that?'

A low buzz of mixed comments ran around the room: this was not what had been expected! Two of them in the centre meant for one? This had never been known before.

Aldebaran held up his hands for silence, and the mumblings gradually ceased. Aldebaran addressed the gathering.

'My friends, under normal circumstances this would be a strange request, as all would agree.' The mumble began again, seeming to confirm this. Aldebaran raised his hand for silence, and all was quiet once more as his strong voice filled the chamber.

'We would all agree however that these are not normal circumstances, or normal times, and thus we need to release ourselves from the restrictions of old habits and embrace new ways of thinking and being. For some reason, which as yet no one knows, least of all Will or Wigapom, Wigapom's inner self has incarnated: let us trust the process to guide us. Let us truly embody the concept that two are one. Is this not, after all, what the understanding of the One is all about? Please Will, enter the circle with your other self.'

Will looked very small and rather scared: he had somehow been summoned, not only from inside Wigapom but to also play a major part in this enfolding story and was overwhelmed. He hesitated, then he caught sight of Wigapom looking at him and there was real approval shining in Wigapom's eyes: he wanted Will to be there!

'Come on, Will,' Wigapom said, offering his hand, 'you belong here too. You've waited long enough. Let's do this together.'

Will needed no second bidding: he positively bounded into the centre of the circle, like a frisky newborn lamb, beaming with pleasure at his other self.

Together they stood and faced the crowd. As One.

The ceremony could then begin and Aldebaran spoke:

'The circle that surrounds you represents the Wheel of Life. It has seven attributes:

'To the North, we place a turtle shell on a handful of earth to represent your ancestors, and the grounding and stability that comes from them.

'To the East, we place an eagle-owl feather to represent your new birth and the ability to move swiftly towards change and thus a new vision of yourself.

'To the South, we place the orange stone, along with a lit candle to represent the fire of passion and love, and the yellow stone and a crown, to represent the strength and courage of the lion, the king of the beasts: both of which indicate the meaning of your life.

'To the West we place a bowl of water, synonymous with the depth of your unconscious mind, and the healing power within you.'

'In the centre, we place a pure white feather, signifying Father Sky and thus the potential for your spiritual ascendancy and the direction through which to attain this. In contrast, nurturing Mother Earth is represented by your own mother's ring, made of purest elven gold, mined from deep within the Aureate Hills. This symbolises the meaning and interpretation of dreams and visions.' Wigapom noticed that the ring, in the unusual shape of a snake eating its tail, was threaded on a chain.

'The seventh and final aspect is the circle itself, representing the one continuing Creator within everyone. All that we need is already within. Do you understand?'

'Yes,' replied Wigapom and Will together, because it would not have seemed right to say 'no'.

'Please, both of you, now walk to the Southern aspect and collect the lighted candle representing the healing light of love and bring it to the centre of the circle.'

This they did with full solemnity.

'Now we invite you to approach each of the remaining aspects to collect the items you find there and bring them also to the centre.'

Soon there was quite a pile of objects in the middle.

'Place the chain holding your mother's ring around your neck, Wigapom, and keep it safe.'

Wigapom first slipped the chain over Will's neck for a moment before placing it permanently over his own, where it nestled against his heart. He found this a particularly emotional moment.

'Now you have accepted all of these attributes,' Aldebaran continued, 'please walk around the inside of the circle to receive a blessing from each of us gathered here.'

This seventh aspect was the most wonderful to experience: each person hugged them both and gave them individual blessings as well as words of encouragement, advice or kindness. Both Wigapom and Will felt truly honoured and moved by it all, never having had so much positive attention before. Fynn gave them both a strong hug; he was pleased to see them both getting along so well at last!

To finish the ceremony, all those in the circle recited a blessing together.

'To you, the one who came today
To walk the Wheel of Life,
To you we give our hearts and minds
To live a wholesome life,
To garner help from the past;
To gather life anew;
To grow in strength and courage;
To heal yourself and be true.
Let Father Sky point the Way,
Let Mother Earth hold you dear,

*Let all who walk the Wheel with you
Be creators without fear.'*

Then each person broke the wheel by walking across it, to the other side of the circle, before making the sideways-eight infinity shape and disbanding. Wigapom and Will were instructed to collect the items from the centre and place them in what Aldebaran called a Graal: a deep bowl made of burnished metal, which was then placed in an alcove as a reminder of the event.

Both Wigapom and Will had much to talk and think about, and Fynn too. By the time the evening was over and they eventually crept back under the soft covers they all had much to dream about.

Darqu'on sat hunched over the blank mirror and fumed. His target must be underground! He let out a hiss through the slit that now served as his mouth, and the cold air he exhaled frosted in front of him. He needed revenge for this temporary set back: did he release Lilitu and pestilence perhaps, or maybe cause another child murder? Or bring on a flood to wash away homes and livelihoods, or maybe a tornado or two? Should he instil greed and violence into some goblins or trolls, to wreak a catastrophe somewhere? It didn't matter what it was as long as he exacted revenge against Mother Earth for barring his way to her. He decided to send the Roth Riders out again, and flicked his skeletal fingers to summon them. This act would compensate him somewhat for the continued frustration that he still could not see what was happening under the earth. He ignored the part he had played in this, placing all responsibility on the nature sprites or elementals of the Hollow Hills, as they were known, who were guardians of the earth. Their magic, although weakened was still proving too resistant for his sorcery for the moment: and it was all that wretched worms fault! This meant that anything underground was not visible to him – yet. He was frustrated that his power was not absolute, although he did feel their magic slipping away slowly as the strength of his own sorcery increased. That restored his temper somewhat: no matter how hard they tried to claw it back, they could not win. It would not be long before he had full dominion over everything, and everyone. True, he still had to defeat the last small pockets of resistance, as Scabtail annoyingly reminded him, putrid creature that it was, but this was within his grasp, and at last his new adversary – their son – was his for the taking. Evil pleasure throbbed through his veins at the thought. He had waited a long time to enjoy this particular killing. No point in rushing it. Each moment of it would be savoured, as destroying The Brat's parents had been.

A thin smile slit his face as he remembered how he had killed The Brat's father – a slow and agonising death on the battlefield at Dragonmound. What a moment of triumph that had been – such a rush of power! And then, her destruction, for even though she had committed suicide, he knew he had pushed her to it, as good as pushing her physically from the window of the tower: to see her broken body spread out and bloodied on the ground had been a defining moment of his life! She would never betray him again! Now it was their son's turn, and his death would erase the last vestiges of memory of what once had been, and destroy the hurt and pain that still ripped at his innards like sharp, poisoned claws. How he still suffered! He would make The Brat suffer, as he suffered. Make him hurt as he hurt. The sins of the father would be revenged on the son! Oh such pain to inflict! Such pain! He *had* to inflict so much pain to relieve his own! The hatred inside him boiled, white hot. His body convulsed with it, contorting in its vice-like grip, and bringing him to his knees in agony.

Control! He must get back control! With a rasping gulp he swallowed the pain back inside him, where it remained festering and eating away like maggots on putrid flesh.

He grew rigid once more. Controlled. The feelings were now stored within him ready to be unleashed, when the time came, on the object of his venom: The Brat. He would not say his name; would not sully his thoughts with that word: the name she gave him – oh yes, he knew what it was: neither she nor Magus could keep that from him in the end!

Another painful contortion throbbed throughout his body as he thought of her again and he reeled in pain. He had loved her, desired her, but she had rejected him, like all those he had wanted love from had done, and this time his love had turned to hate. Only hate would sustain him and give him power! These moments were the hardest for him, when emotion threatened to disempower him. He would not let emotion rule him again. He grew rigid and controlled once more. He could never show that aspect of himself to anyone. He was Darqu'on, once the greatest Magician there ever was, and now the most powerful Sorcerer and Necromancer there ever would be. He was all-powerful! He would never let anyone forget that, and he knew just what to do next to bring down The Brat: he would use The Brat's own emotional creation, The Squirt and turn it against him. He smiled at the irony of The Brat causing his own self-destruction. Two for the price of one!

Darqu'on turned away from the blank mirror and towards a small phial of dark red liquid standing nearby. He knew what he needed to do and he did not need to see The Brat to do it. The thin smile sliced through his face again: how thoughtful of his enemy to provide a means of causing such trauma and distress – as well as entertainment for him!

He picked the phial up in his pale, thin fingers, holding it high; noting the blood-red colour coat the sides.

'PUER INSANUS!' he incanted, making sorcery symbols in the air, before turning to throw the phial hard at the mirror, where it smashed against the glass, streaking it with its blood-like contents before bubbling into a shape that looked much like the outline of a child.

Part 4

Self-Love

"Until we learn to really love ourselves we cannot truly love another."
Anonymous

CHAPTER 18

Double Trouble

*"But if we return to the 'children's land' we succumb to the fear of becoming childish,
because we do not understand that everything of psychic origin has a double face.
One face looks forward, the other back."*
Carl Jung

At first things went well. Much learning went on over the course of the next few weeks, as Wigapom and Will got to know each other better. Together, they learnt all that Aldebaran could teach them about runic symbology. It was a complex as well as ancient language and they spent hours pouring over the grimoire and other ancient texts, until they were as proficient in it as they could get. Wigapom hoped that some additional inspiration would come when he needed it to understand the deeper meaning of the words. On a more personal level Wigapom and Will also learnt how to create a relationship with each other.

It was not always easy, as Aldebaran had said. Sometimes Wigapom would feel strong dislike for this younger self and criticise him mercilessly, but he soon came to learn that this did not help him feel good about himself at all, and certainly did not help his Child self to feel confident or worthwhile.

So gradually they formed a more affectionate bond: Wigapom encouraging and supporting Will, and Will responding by dropping some of his more objectionable behaviours, and they found, with pleasant surprise, they began to have more fun with each other as a result of changing these patterns of behaviour, even when pouring over the strange shapes and squiggles that made up the runes. Neither had experienced anything quite like this before, not even with Fynn.

Wigapom's friendship with Fynn, whilst strong, could never be as close as the connection now being established between Wigapom and Will – how could it be when they were one and the same person? This did not go unnoticed by Fynn, but being the easy going sort that he was, he did not mind too much at first – he was just pleased that Wigapom and Will were getting along rather than scrapping all the time! He fully believed that the strength of his own friendship with Wigapom could withstand anything; they had known each other all their lives – even if their lives were now very different from the Brakendor days, but he found it hard to comprehend that Will was a part of Wigapom and, slowly but surely, the balance of the friendships began to change, although awareness of this was slow for all of them.

Because Wigapom and Will were quick learners they enjoyed the lessons with Aldebaran. Fynn on the other hand had always been more practically inclined and found academic study difficult, if not to say tedious, so he took to spending more time apart from Wigapom and his new found alter ego, showing a real interest instead in both the workings of the Astrolabius and the maintenance of the Temple and continued construction of the tunnels. Whilst Wigapom and Will increasingly laughed the days away as they studied the runes, Fynn kept busy by helping in the structure of a further escape tunnel through the mountainside, towards the small village of Oakendale. Here he met Ollie and Annalid many times, of course, as the Megadrill actually excavated the tunnels, whilst Fynn helped to shore them up with pit props to make them safe.

'I thought I'd stopped being a hired worker when I left Brakendor!' he joked to Ollie on one of these occasions. 'I was wrong, wasn't I?' And he shifted another large bucket of earth from the tunnel.

'It's a good, honest job,' replied Annalid, encouragingly.

'What's your friend, Wigapom, doing,' asked Ollie. 'He's not around much these days.'

'Oh, he's gone back to school, with Will. I don't see him as much as I did. He doesn't even notice I'm not around,' replied Fynn, trying to make light of it.

'You sound sad about that,' said Annalid, not fooled by Fynn's tone.

'Do I? Well, maybe I am. It wasn't what I expected when I joined him on this Quest. I didn't expect to be shovelling earth, either, but that's alright, I enjoy physical work.'

'But you miss Wigapom's company?' said Annalid, perceptively.

'Yes, I do, I feel a bit left out, I suppose. They will be talking about the events of their day, which I don't know about, or sharing jokes, which I don't understand. It's difficult. But I do my best to understand that this is important to them both, and it can't last forever now, can it? Soon Wigapom will have sorted whatever he needs to sort with Will and we can leave him safely here and get back to our Quest for the stones and *The Book of True Magic*, together. It's certainly no place for a child, I can see that now.'

To Fynn, who was a straightforward rather than a complex thinker, Will had no real part to play in the Quest – he was just a child – and still separate from Wigapom. He was also feeling more and more that two was company but three was most definitely a crowd! However, weeks turned into more weeks and still there was little sign of anything changing for the better: indeed it seemed to be going the other way entirely; Wigapom, far from acting like a responsible twenty-year-old Prince on an important Quest to save his Kingdom from the evil of Darqu'on's sorcery, was, instead, living through another childhood with Will – and, what was worse, having a tremendous amount of fun into the bargain! Fun that did not include locating stones and magic books – or involving Fynn!

As the schoolwork lessened, so the play increased. All of which became a real concern for Fynn, but a wonderful time for Wigapom, to whom it seemed life had never been so good: there were no restrictions on him; no nagging, overprotective parents to curtail his activities or tell him what he could or couldn't do; no tedious jobs he felt obliged to perform; just endless hours to do exactly as he pleased, in exactly the way he wanted to – and with a companion who knew exactly what he was thinking and feeling! Freedom indeed, which had rather gone to his head! In fact, it seemed to those around them, with the exception of Will, who was loving all the attention, that Wigapom had completely forgotten the reason for the Quest at all. All Wigapom would say when the matter was broached, as it was increasingly by Fynn, was:

'Oh, I'll get down to that tomorrow,' but of course, tomorrow never came.

Aldebaran shook his head sadly at this, but seemed prepared to let Wigapom make his own choices, however hurtful to others they may be: his philosophy was that by letting things run their course Wigapom would be more likely to get this immature and somewhat feckless behaviour out of his system and then get back to his real purpose and destiny of his own accord. He knew there was no point in forcing Wigapom to do anything he was not ready to do. He also suspected that Darqu'on's sorcery might be playing a part in what was happening, and that Wigapom would have to fight this in his own way. The fact that the Temple now had deeper cracks in its walls, and the Astrolabius worked only in fits and starts, was a penalty that had to be paid to allow Wigapom the freedom to choose, as well as the opportunity to develop.

Fynn, on the other hand, was not so accommodating of Wigapom's behaviour, finding it increasingly difficult not to show his frustration at what he saw as Wigapom's absurd need for a second childhood with Will. He was becoming increasingly annoyed at his friend, whom he felt he no longer recognised as such anymore. He noticed the cracks in the Temple, and was constantly annoyed at the wonderful time Wigapom seemed to be having. Had he owned up to his deeper feelings he would have recognised that his own jealousy was also at work here, but he chose to ignore this and blame and criticise Wigapom for everything instead.

'For goodness sake, Wiggy,' he said in exasperation one day, after they had been living in the Temple for many weeks, 'when are you going to pull yourself together? We're supposed to be on a Quest to save Arcanum – your Kingdom remember? From this Dark One we hear so much about, but all you seem to want to do is play silly games and mess around! I didn't leave my home to act as a childminder to you and Will, you know – and what about Aldebaran and Cassie, and all those that are relying on you to help them? Don't you think about them at all?'

'Oh, lighten up, Fynn,' came Wigapom's curt reply. 'Why can't I enjoy myself for once? I've not had this much fun in years. In fact I've never had this much fun. Ever. I've spent all my life doing what other people wanted, or rather didn't want me to do, and now I have the freedom to do exactly what I want, when I want, and I'm making the most of it! Time enough for serious things later – I want fun now, and I get it with Will. Unlike you, you've gone all boring on me. Will, on the other hand, knows exactly what I want to do because he *is* me – we're like two peas in a pod and I'm realising what a great person he is after all this time, and I want to make the most of him.'

'That's all very well, Wiggy, but…'

'There are no buts in my life at the moment, Fynn, unless you put them there! Either enjoy life with me and Will, or keep out of it!'

'Wiggy, you are testing my patience! I can't keep out of it, even if I wanted to: look around you at the destruction happening!'

'A few old cracks, that's all' scoffed Wigapom.

'This can't be you speaking! You're not yourself any more,' frowned Fynn in despair.

'For your information, Fynn of the frowning face, I've never been *more* myself than I am at the moment,' replied Wigapom, rather rudely, 'in case you hadn't noticed!'

'You see?' said Fynn, as though Wigapom had just proven everything he had accused him of. 'Listen to yourself! This is not the Wigapom I know: you sound bewitched or something; I feel I have to watch your every move. You're not safe to be left on your own!'

'You sound like my mother, Fynn, for goodness sake. Leave me and Will alone!'

'You heard him,' piped up the increasingly obnoxious Will, his ever-willing accomplice. 'He wants me, not you! You're no fun, not like me. C'mon, Wiggy, let's hang out in town.' And with that the dissolute pair disappeared out into the alleyways they seemed to want to frequent more and more these days, regardless of any risk to themselves.

Fynn frowned deeply, wondering what on earth had come over Wigapom, and increasingly worried for his safety. It really was as though he had some devil inside him, making him behave in this way. Wigapom however, loved the freedom; he loved the danger; he was exhilarated by it all. He was especially drawn to the excitement of the town: the sense of living life on the edge seemed highly intoxicating and addictive – so what if he was bewitched: he was enjoying himself!

Inevitably he and Will began to draw attention to themselves; the wrong sort of attention that would likely get them into trouble before long. There were also mutterings amongst some of the resistance group lodged in the Temple.

'He doesn't seem to have developed any form of responsibility yet to his role.'

'He's too full of himself – along with young Will.'

'He needs to grow up and control some of his more childish impulses.'

'He has no balance of behaviour in his life. If we are not careful he could tip us all over the edge into destruction.'

Fynn heard everything and agreed with all of it. He approached Aldebaran with his concerns.

'Can't you do something, Aldebaran? He's making a fool of himself with that boy. Can't you stop him before he gets totally out of hand and lands himself and us in real trouble?'

'My dear Fynn, you are right that this behaviour is not helping Wigapom or Will, or any of us, but until he is able to see this for himself there is nothing that anyone can do to stop him. This need for a free and unfettered childhood has been held inside him for many years and he believes it now needs to find expression. This is what he is choosing to manifest. It is childhood rebellion. It seems worse because he is not a child to look at: but inside, at this time, he is a young boy and expressing a need to do the crazy things that children do when they have been restricted for so long and now have no boundaries. We can only hope he will recognise this and learn from it soon. Then his Adult self will be able to work with the Child, and together they will find the balance needed, and return to us. We must be patient.'

'But we don't have time to be patient! The Astrolabius is barely working, the light is dimming in the Temple, more cracks are beginning to appear in the walls – something has to happen! Something has to put

Wigapom back on track before he takes us all over the edge with his reckless stupidity and belligerence!' fumed Fynn.

'Speak to him about it if you feel the need, but until Wigapom is ready to see the error of his current behaviour there is nothing we can do. Resistance to him will drive him further away from his logic, and us. Trust in the process of life, Fynn! You need to realise this is as much a test for Wigapom as it is for us, but each test is an opportunity to be more than we were before! Learn to trust.'

'I can't trust him! I really do think he's been bewitched by Darqu'on,' complained Fynn.

'You may well be right. Darqu'on takes pleasure in playing on our weaknesses. That is an additional challenge for Wigapom, and for us all. We just have to hope that Wigapom's own strength of character will wake him to this fact, before it is too late.'

'And if it doesn't?'

Aldebaran merely shrugged.

So Fynn watched, and waited, and worried, in the hope that Wigapom would change, but there seemed little sign of it and Fynn still chose not to hear the small but persistent voice of jealousy in his own head, at the fun the troublesome pair were having, and that he was excluded from. Instead he trailed along behind them like a parent without power.

One evening in early summer Fynn was following them towards the market square, just before the dusk curfew, and was remonstrating with them yet again.

'It's too late to be out, Wiggy, come back for goodness sake.'

'Oh, do stop fussing,' replied Wigapom, feeling irritated. 'I'm my own person here and I can do what I like.'

'Within reason, Wiggy, but nothing you do is reasonable these days. It's just stupid kid stuff,' said Fynn, exasperated by this irrational behaviour.

'Aldebaran said I had free choice and this is it!' retorted Wigapom, like some belligerent adolescent. 'Besides, we've been here now for ages and never felt in the slightest danger. No Roth Riders, no spies knocking on doors in the middle of the night, no goblins or demons marking us out! Even the snotleys have left us alone! Don't worry about us. We've had enough fussing. Go away and leave us alone!'

'If I leave you alone goodness only knows what trouble you'll get into. You're reckless these days – and what about the stones and restoring the True Magic? Have you forgotten what you have to do?'

'That's just it Fynn, I don't *have* to do it – I can choose. Aldebaran has said that all along. I'm fed up with having to do things I *should* – I want to do things I shouldn't for a change.'

'I don't know you these days, Wiggy – you just don't sound like yourself any more.'

'And you sound more like my mother, Fynn! For goodness sake, let go! Will and I are fine – aren't we Will?'

Will grinned and nodded his head enthusiastically: he agreed with everything Wigapom said. Fynn shrugged his shoulders in exasperation but continued to trail after them to the market square – what else could he do?

Darqu'on smiled to himself – the curse had worked well. He really had so little to do at the moment as far as The Brat was concerned: just a whisper here; a thought there, but most of this was down to The Brat himself – not forgetting The Squirt, and of course the jealous friend! He knew only too well what jealousy could do! Now all he had to do was let it run its course, and watch what chaos they caused themselves before any other intervention, but he was always open to possibilities! And if he got bored? Well, there was always pestilence to pass on!

Dusk came and went. Despite the curfew that drew most back to their homes, some undesirables still lurked amongst the darkening shadows. A few snotleys were loitering on a street corner, cursing, sparring and being generally objectionable and intimidating; a drunken ogre lay carousing in the gutter, unaware of having his pocket picked by a stealthy goblin; a fierce and bloody fight had broken out between two opposing gangs of snotleys in another dark alley and Wigapom and Will still showed no sign of wanting to return to the safety of the Temple: there was something exhilarating about being out at night, under the stars and the moon in the dark streets and alleyways, which they did not want to give up, despite Fynn doing his best to discourage them. Adrenalin was pumping and it all felt wickedly exciting!

'We're not coming, Fynn. Don't be such a spoilsport! If you want to go back, then do, but we're staying here,' said Wigapom, sounding like the twelve year old that Will really was!

Fynn was torn. His good sense told him they all ought to be back in the

Temple, and he wanted to be there, but his loyalty and concern for these two idiotically behaving juveniles kept him with them, against his better judgement! Someone had to watch out for them!

It was dark now, apart from the luminous glow of a gloriously full moon and a myriad of stars that shone like beacons against the black of the sky. The city gates were shut and bolted. In the market square; the usual sentry-like vultures had even deserted the Bull's Eye lamp that towered above them, for once. It was a perfect opportunity to do something particularly crazy, which neither Wigapom nor Will could resist, and which caused escalating concern in Fynn.

The Bull's Eye lamp had been expertly hammered out of a mystical metal found in the Hollow Hills by the dwarves many aeons ago, and intricately carved by their own craftsmen at forges in the centre of the earth. It was one of the great artefacts of Arcanum, and despite its sad and sorry state, retained its mystical energy. It was said that whoever could climb to the top, without using his feet to propel him, would see where the dwarves had buried their gold and have untold wealth at their disposal. No one had ever succeeded at the challenge, but Wigapom and Will, that night, were preparing to undertake it.

'Of course we can do it. Our arms are strong, and it only says feet can't be used... So we can shin up using our arms and legs instead!' they laughed, thinking how they would outwit the ancient dwarves.

'I can't believe you are even contemplating doing this!' said Fynn. 'It's absolute madness! Supposing you fall for a start? Or worse, supposing the dwarves don't like you trying to trick them? They're not all as tolerant as Gobann or Tamsan.'

'We're safe enough!' Wigapom said. 'We can look after ourselves, can't we Will? Anyway, it's a challenge!'

'Pity you can't challenge yourself by looking for the stones, instead of gold,' grumbled Fynn under his breath: a comment that, if heard, went totally ignored by Wigapom and Will.

Will just grinned from ear to ear at Wigapom; he looked upon him now as a big brother, a leader of a gang of two, and not only hung on every word that Wigapom said, but also egged him on to more audacious actions. He was enjoying this new Wigapom – they were buddies! Together they were invincible!

So they both began the climb, Wigapom first, then Will. Some of the snotley gang, up to no good, slouched into view, and began egging them on.

'Go on, higher, higher! That's it, get on up there!'

Fynn hopped nervously from one foot to the other, eyes darting left and right, as well as up and down, all the time expecting trouble to come from some quarter or another.

The first stages of the climb were easy; by gripping with arms and legs only they found they could pull themselves up quite well – the intricacy of the patterning on the lamp helping to provide something to hold onto. They were jubilant! Encouraging whistles from the snotleys helped. As they continued, however, their muscles grew more tired and heavy, and the going was slower and more laboured. Soon Will could go no further; being only twelve he did not yet have the strength of muscle control as his older self – he slid down the lamp with a disappointed sigh. The snotleys booed him loudly and he shot them a challenging look. Fynn thought Wigapom would slide down too, now that Will had failed, but he was wrong: Wigapom kept going.

'Come down, Wiggy, please,' urged Fynn.

'Keep going, Wiggy,' countered Will.

'Oooh, Wiggy-wiggle!' mocked the snotleys. 'Come on Wiggy-wiggle! Keep going. Right to the top! UP! UP! UP! UP!' they chanted, louder and louder, laughing mockingly, hoping for disaster.

Wigapom had no intention of giving in: he was over half way now and in the bright light of the huge full moon could see over the city walls to the countryside beyond: it was breathtakingly beautiful, but he was especially drawn to the moon, which seemed to hang suspended in the sky, just out of his reach. Its silvery light shone on him, both soft and radiant. It reminded him of the dream when he was about Will's age, of the moon amongst the trees and the beautiful woman, his mother, coming towards him with her arms outstretched. The memory of this seemed to mesmerise him and draw him into the light. Softly he felt he could hear her voice calling him.

'Come to me, come to me, come to me,' said the voice of the moon. Wigapom forgot he was climbing the lamp, forgot the promise of the dwarves' gold, forgot about how high he was, forgot Will, and Fynn, and the ribald snotleys far below him. He even forgot about the desire to do something outlandish that had propelled him up thus far: he remembered only the peace he had found in the woman's arms, his mother, and wanted to be with her again. Suddenly he felt so powerful that he believed he could fly to her; that he could fly to the moon! That he could just stretch out his arms and legs and fly to where she was waiting for him, somewhere on that shiny, silvery surface. He began to release his hold on the lamp, letting go with his legs and fingers, listening to the hypnotic voice urging him to let go and fly …

Will, far below him, was also looking dreamily at the moon and extending out his arms as if to reach it; the snotleys started a chant of 'FLY, FLY, FLY!' Fynn looked to where Will was pointing, and saw, not a beautiful face, but a hag-like shadow with sneering lips beginning to obliterate the moon, blocking the light, and in that moment he suddenly saw the real danger Wigapom was in, but oblivious to!

'WIGGY!... STOP!... DON'T!' he cried as Wigapom released his hold on the lamp and, instead of flying, began falling to the ground to the sound of the snotleys cheering. Something small and bright seemed to be falling too, away from Wigapom, but Fynn couldn't be bothered about what it was: he had to save Wigapom! He pushed a dazed Will to one side and threw himself as best he could underneath the fast-descending Wigapom, his own arms outstretched; his knees braced; ready to catch his weight. He didn't know if he would be able to break his friend's fall or whether he would suffer in the process, but he had to try.

Wigapom was falling fast, arms and legs flailing in the air, too shocked to cry out, and landed, spread-eagled, into Fynn's outstretched arms. Fynn grabbed him and held on, rolling safely into a ball, ending up on his back with the bulk of Wigapom's weight on his chest, which threatened to crush the life from his body. They were both exhausted and shaking but they were alive! Will ran over, out of breath himself, but he came not in concern but excitement.

'You almost did it!' he cried to Wigapom, ignoring the fact that Wigapom could have died, and that Fynn might be hurt.

Fynn would have remonstrated had he the breath to do so, but he was shocked to hear Wigapom's faint reply.

'I know. It was great!'

What was wrong with the pair of them? Didn't they see how Darqu'on had used them? Hadn't Wigapom nearly killed himself? Hadn't Fynn just saved him in an heroic act of courage? Hadn't Wigapom and Will acted absolutely stupidly, jeopardising everything for some ridiculous prank? Fynn had had enough. He threw Wigapom off his body and struggled to his feet.

'You are just the *end* Wiggy! I don't understand you any more. I've had enough!'

Wigapom's eyes focused slowly on Fynn, but he hadn't heard him. Instead he was feeling in his pocket.

'I've lost one of the stones,' he said unemotionally.

'WHAT!' yelled Fynn, in disbelief. 'You've lost one of the stones? You're supposed to be *finding* them not losing them! But then, you've forgotten all about them, haven't you, you and your buddy here, your partner in idiocy! So why am I surprised? You've lost yourselves, let alone a stone, and if you don't get a grip on yourselves soon, then you'll lose me! I've had it, just about to here!' and Fynn jabbed above the top of his head with his hand, which was now stinging from a nasty graze inflicted by the fall. The snotleys were making various loud and rude comments but Fynn ignored them all, storming away from Wigapom, Will and the market square before he did something he might later regret.

Fynn had done his best to understand this compulsion of Wigapom's to let rip, but now he was really angry. For Fynn this was a new emotion; he had never felt the need to be angry before, always managing to find a smile or a positive thought. But now anger built up inside him like a volcano about to erupt: how dare Wigapom seem to abandon their friendship, and all that they had stood for over the years; how dare he treat people like this; how dare he lose one of the stones! The only things that could restore peace and harmony again, and only if Wigapom found them! No, not found them, *earned* them; well, he was earning nothing but notoriety at present – and losing his friendship with Fynn because of this utterly irrational and childish behaviour, and his obsession with creating a bond with Will – a dangerous bond that was helping no one.

Fynn was angry, too, with Aldebaran, for doing nothing to stop this. Aldebaran just stood back with what he called 'compassionate detachment' – well, Fynn wanted to know how you could be compassionately detached when the beautiful building you had sweated blood over was beginning to fall apart before your very eyes, when each day the magic could be felt to lessen more and more!

Fynn had always found it hard to understand the complex bond between Wigapom and Will, especially when he could still only see them as two different people: it was hard for him to understand that they were really just different aspects of the same person. It was especially hard to hear from Aldebaran that Wigapom's behaviour, and how Wigapom dealt with it, was all part of the process, part of the Quest, part of what Aldebaran called 'The Awakening.' All Fynn saw was Wigapom jeopardising everything they had planned because he wanted to behave like a stupid child again; and it really hurt that Wigapom wanted to share this with someone other than him: not that Fynn wanted to be a child anymore, but he didn't want to lose his friend; yet he had been, more and more every day, and now this silly episode with the stone! His insides were churning to the point of explosion: it could only be a matter of time before this really happened. He stormed back to the Temple.

Aldebaran knew something had occurred the minute Fynn returned, alone.

'What's happened?' he asked, at the sight of Fynn's scratched face scowling at him.

'Ask your precious Prince!' spat Fynn, and took himself off to wash his wounds, and nurse his hurt ego. Aldebaran said nothing, but waited for Wigapom and Will's return, some time later.

'Where's Fynn?' said Wigapom, looking a little worse for wear.

'He's resting his cut head,' replied Aldebaran. 'Is there something you need to tell me?'

'We lost a stone, that's all, it fell out of my pocket. It's alright, Will found it. A snotley had it. We fought him for it. The snotley lost. No harm done. Don't know why there seems to be so much panic.'

'Perhaps you need to search your conscience for answers,' replied Aldebaran quietly, as he left the chamber.

Perhaps Wigapom did as Aldebaran said, or perhaps not, but things did quieten down a little over the next day or so. It was an uneasy silence however, particularly when they heard that the Roth Riders had attacked a nearby town, and that open warfare had been declared between rival snotley gangs in Lampadia and yet another, deeper, crack had appeared in one of the Temple walls.

Fynn avoided Wigapom. Wigapom avoided Fynn. Will sulked. He had lost his playmate temporarily. Aldebaran suggested that perhaps they would benefit from getting out of the Temple, and Lampadia for a while, helping to finish off the tunnels leading to Oakendale.

'Perhaps by working as part of a team on something for the greater good of the community, you might find it in all your hearts to mend the situation,' he said.

They all avoided his eyes but agreed to go, not that they thought they would resolve anything, but because nothing could be worse than being stuck inside together!

Fynn didn't believe for one minute that they would sort their issues out; nor that Wigapom or Will would work hard; nor for that matter, that any important stones would want to gravitate towards two ridiculously behaving infantile beings right now; it was all seeming such a hopeless, useless task. He wished he had never left Brakendor.

CHAPTER 19

An Ill Wind

"But certain winds will make men's temper bad."
George Eliot

The summer was degenerating into stormy skies and heavy outbursts of rain: weather that matched their moods. The Megadrill had virtually finished excavating the tunnel, and proper supports were being inserted before the sides were lined, to complete the job. Ollie and Annalid were pleased to meet Wigapom and Will again, but were quick to pick up on the atmosphere between them and Fynn. They tactfully chose to say nothing, and for a while all worked hard in their teams, getting earth removed and the tunnel lined. It was exhausting work and after a while they took the opportunity to get some air outside, not far from the tunnel entrance.

The rain had stopped and, although the air was muggy, weak sunshine was struggling to appear – the only positive thing about the day as far as Fynn was concerned. He sat on a rock, with a face like thunder, glowering at Will and Wigapom, who had already begun to play silly 'catch me' games amongst the rocks, further and further from the tunnel entrance. He and Wigapom had not talked about that night in the market square since it had happened, so he had no idea what Wigapom had seen or why he had let go of the Bull's Eye lamp so suddenly. He didn't really want to know, if he was honest with himself; he wanted to feel disgruntled and victimised. With Wigapom and Will reverting back to their old childish ways, this was easy. Fynn tried hard to block out their silly, excited cries, wanting to leave them to their idiocy, but yet again, his sense of responsibility kicked in and he felt that he shouldn't leave them alone. Someone had to look out for them, as they seemed incapable of looking out for themselves, but how he hated having to be their minder all the time!

He watched, with growing irritation, as Will ran shouting down a slope, with Wigapom echoing his cries as he chased in hot pursuit. Fynn almost wished that the Dark One would come out from behind a rock and attack them, just to make them realise how ridiculously they were behaving, but there was no sign of anything untoward. Instead Wigapom and Will's excitable, noisy voices disturbed his peace as they drifted on the breeze. Fynn hated it most of all when they were noisy. It was surely foolish to go out of your way to make your presence known, he thought. Supposing this general lack of dark force activity was all a plan, to lull them into a false sense of security and thus leave them open to unexpected attack. Couldn't they see that? Why was he the only one with any sense around here? Here they were, shouting out loudly again in abandoned excitement, like a pair of little kids! All the resentment and anger he had been holding in for days was building into a tidal wave of rage, but still he held it in, just blurting out, in a voice dark and heavy with bitterness, 'Keep the noise down, will you!'

His voice drifted away from Wigapom and Will, and caught on the breeze, so neither seemed to hear him: Fynn thought they had ignored him. Their apparent disregard for him, added to all that had happened lately, broke the dam of his restraint and swept him over the edge into a chasm of emotion, the like of which he had never known existed before, let alone experienced. It poured out of him with a force of such magnitude that it not only rocked him, but also vibrated its way around the mountainside.

'THAT'S IT!' he yelled to the sky, now darkening again with heavy, grey clouds. 'I might just as well not *be* here for all the notice you take of me! What's the point? When are you going to wake up to yourselves?'

His voice got lost on the wind that was strengthening by the moment, whipping across the terrain.

'I might as well leave you to it, you stupid idiots! You deserve whatever happens to you! I'm not going to baby-sit you any more!' and he stood up from the rock forcefully and, spitting venom, yelled, 'I'M GOING HOME!' Not caring whether they heard him or not, he began to stomp his way back towards the tunnel with every intention of getting his things and finding his way back to Brakendor that very moment.

His chest was pounding, his head spinning, his stomach churning with the unfamiliar and frightening emotion of it all; he felt sick and shaking with rage. He was soon out of sight of them, but he could still hear their silly, excitable cries in the distance.

'IDIOTS!' he yelled, angrily, into the air. Hurtful, dark thoughts filled his mind as his whole body churned fiercely like a whirlpool.

The sky darkened even more, which mirrored his mood, and added to his own inner darkness. When the wind suddenly began to whip itself into frenzy, it was true poetic justice, and he enjoyed the sensation as it ripped across the hillside with a force that matched his rage, pushing him further away from them, along the path, as though encouraging him to create distance from them, and send him home. It was incredibly empowering, and for a moment he felt free of any emotion other than one that teetered on madness. He punched the air and yelled support to the spiralling wind, and the oppressive, blackening sky, heavy with dark, thunderous clouds, as though encouraging it. The dense clouds rolled over him, much as his own churning stomach had been rolling over just moments earlier.

'YES!' exulted Fynn, revelling in the tempestuous atmosphere already gaining in strength with every second, as if it were feeding on his anger and rage. Ferocious fork lightning streaked across the sky, followed by the menacing rumble of thunder, and he felt the first few heavy drops of rain beat against his face. He wanted more! He felt at one with this storm: it expressed his mood so perfectly and he wanted it to last, to never stop until Wigapom and Will begged for mercy. He yelled to the rain, now streaking down his own face like angry tears, to lash down on those two idiots whom he had once called friends! He wanted the thunder, deafening his ears, to pound them into submission, and the lightning to split open their stupid heads! He wanted to watch while they suffered, and he tried to turn back, but found he could not move – the force of the wind was too strong! Panic leapt in. Now it was not exhilarating, but terrifying! He felt powerless, and out of control. The whirling wind held him to the spot, pinning him to the ground. As he looked up he saw, in horror, stronger black clouds swirling and belching towards him like thick smoke, as they formed into a powerful, huge vortex of spinning energy, which sped from him towards Wigapom and Will. He watched as the massive vortex of energy expanded, creating a mighty rushing, roaring sound, which almost destroyed his eardrums! Whatever this thing was, it was heading straight for Wigapom and Will, ripping everything up in its path and sucking it down as water is siphoned through a drain!

Fynn stared in horror, all rage replaced now by real fear. This was not just any wind, not just any storm; this was Darqu'on's Shivastrom! And Fynn felt responsible for it! He was sure that somehow he had helped conjure it with his rage! He tried to run towards them, to help them, to save them, to make whatever recompense he could for the tempestuous and destructive element he had helped create out of his fury, but he was now helpless, his legs held fast in that spot by some powerful, invisible force that he couldn't control. He bent double as he tried to push his way through the forceful air spiralling in front of him but he knew he was going nowhere. Something terrible was happening; he knew it, but couldn't reach them! He cried out, but any sound was swallowed by the ferocity of the Shivastrom! Guilt at hating them so much racked his exhausted body; if he was responsible for this, how could he ever forgive himself?

Wigapom had heard Fynn's parting call – he heard more than Fynn gave him credit for, and the sensible part of him had wanted to respond, to make friends again and say he was sorry, but it seemed that this devil-may-care childishness that had control over his mind and body these days had other ideas, taking him further away from Fynn and common sense. He never got a chance to make amends then, as his world imploded.

He barely had time to sense the sky darken, hear the rushing noise of the manic wind, feel its devastating force hit him and sweep him off his feet. It all happened so quickly he had no idea what had hit him or where he was at first. He was being tossed, like a rag doll, in the deafening, twisting air. He could see nothing, just hear the angry roaring of the wind and something that sounded like screaming. He realised then that it was his screams he could hear, but there was another shriller sound than his voice. A small body, with arms and legs whipping passed him. Will!

Will was right in the epicentre of this Shivastrom of terrifying energy – his small frame tossing around mercilessly whilst Wigapom was caught up at its edges, but both were totally at its mercy, being sucked into the gaping black mouth of a featureless creature, with only oblivion awaiting them.

Fynn heard the screams too, and the sound seared itself into his flesh like a vicious branding iron. He watched in horror as Wigapom and Will were whipped away by the Shivastrom, disappearing as quickly and as violently as it had come. Even though he regained the ability to move once the Shivastrom disappeared, he still remained rooted to the spot: his legs refusing to move, in sheer disbelief and horror. He wanted to see his friend, and Will, playing silly games on the hillside again. To turn back time. But the hillside was empty.

Silly games. This had been his judgement of them, borne of his anger, rage and, he now admitted, his jealousy, and look where it had got them! The Shivastrom had appeared at the same time as he had let rip his rage, as if his emotions had created it. Had he really aided the Dark One with his out of control feelings and made him even more powerful? Aldebaran had said this could happen, but Fynn didn't want to acknowledge it, yet he kept recalling how Aldebaran had spoken to them all about the energetic power of emotions and how thoughts create reality, and now this had happened. Guilt and shame flooded in now: He had certainly felt very powerful and destructive, exultantly so; a totally new experience, which he was ashamed to admit he had revelled in, but which he never wanted to feel again. It came fully home to Fynn at that moment how truly frightening Darqu'on's power could be, and how easy it was to be manipulated. The thought also dawned on him that maybe Darqu'on had been manipulating Wigapom and Will into behaving the way they had. This would explain their behaviour – perhaps none of them were to blame after all! He began to relax a little in relief that he could blame Darqu'on for everything that had happened – yet hadn't Aldebaran also talked about free choice? That no one could be made to think anything, or do anything that they didn't, on some level, choose to do? That brought the burden of shared responsibility for what had happened right back again: he couldn't answer for Wigapom or Will, but he felt sick to his stomach once more at his complicity. If only he could turn back time.

Others from the tunnels were now running towards him, horror on their faces, as Fynn began to shake and sob in shock, fear and despair.

'It's my fault!' he sobbed. 'All my fault,' and he truly believed that. Because of him, the hope of Arcanum had literally vanished!

Tamsan and the others tried to soothe him, but Fynn could not be placated. Since he had left the secure cocoon of Brakendor he had been faced by so many new emotions, from himself and others, some positive, but most were not: anger, jealousy, hatred, vengeance, suspicion, guilt, shame and fear. He had experienced them all. The worst were the ones that seemed to wheedle their way in deep, and take root there, like a tick in flesh; they crept up, unannounced, and once attached would not let go. He felt gripped by cold fear right now – its freezing fingers twisting inside his stomach, grappling into his chest, twisting into his throat, winding around his windpipe as though choking the life from him. He had never known so much fear than when he realised Wigapom and Will were gone. Really gone. He didn't know if he would ever see them again! Sheer panic shot through every fibre of his being, mingled, even now, with disbelief and denial. He tore himself away from the others, knowing that Aldebaran had to be told and fast, but more than that, needing to confess his part in it and release his guilt. He took flight then, running across the hillside; through the town gates; down the narrow alleyways, until he returned to the house with the bull's head knocker. He didn't care who heard him as he hammered hard and loud, sobbing and shouting for Aldebaran to come. But even in his haste to tell what happened was the ever-gnawing fear of being blamed for it all!

His one hope was that the Astrolabius might be functioning well enough to show where Wigapom and Will had been blown. He did not dare consider how he might get them back: he just had to know where they were. Most of all he needed their forgiveness, and Aldebaran's. He wasn't yet aware that he also had to forgive himself.

'WILL!' cried Wigapom, but his voice was lost in the strength of the Shivastrom as he was churned, turned and twisted as though he was as inconsequential as a feather. He'd lost sight of Will, he'd lost sight of everything: all was just a mass of swirling black energy. He could only hear a deafening howling sound as his body, cold and clammy from the dampness that seemed to emanate from this powerful force of energy, was buffeted and twisted in the air, upside down, horizontal, vertical, upside down again, spinning every which way, and with no sensation of coming back down: yet he felt he *was* being sucked down somehow – not to the solid ground – but instead into a huge black hole of empty space. His face contorted with the pressure of it, his ears were pinned tight against his head and bursting from the pressure. Pain. Such pain, and all the time spinning down, down, down; faster and faster; spinning, hurtling, descending into a deeper blackness than he could ever imagine possible; swallowing him into total oblivion.

Darqu'on threw back his head and laughed like a thing possessed. He had not had so much pleasure from invoking the Shivastrom for many years! So much better than the ones he had created before, and all thanks to the emotions generated by The Brat's companion!: oh such anger and rage to behold, and harness! What an excellent subject the angry friend had been – he would use him again! It had been like being born into his evilness all over again! That quick flood of adrenalin, that intoxicating surge of power, that addictive feeling of control and dominance – nothing could beat it! The realisation that he could have almost endless pleasure with The Brat, The Squirt and The Other filled him with such a sense of irrepressible malevolence that he thought he would burst with the sheer hellish pleasure of it all! Oh! Revenge was so sweet! – and it was only just beginning! It was time to march again. To show his dominance in person. He turned away from the mirrors on the wall to plan his next move.

CHAPTER 20

The Sea of Emotion

"The sea is emotion incarnate."
Christopher Paolini

The roaring and turning had stopped. His body was blissfully still, yet achingly so. He could still see nothing but complete blackness. From somewhere in the total darkness he could hear a rushing sound. It didn't sound like the Shivastrom, not even a storm. It was thundering from somewhere ahead of him. If only he could see.

Were there other sounds too? Like human cries? He couldn't be sure. His eyes were wide open yet seemingly blind – unless there really was nothing to see. He tentatively extended a hand to sense his surroundings, praying that this lack of vision would somehow increase his sense of touch. His fingers desperately groped for something recognisable: earth, or stone perhaps, yet he grasped only air. He didn't even recognise what he was standing on; it was soft, and seemed to shift with each tentative step he made forward. It was a struggle to stand upright at times. He put his hand down to touch this strange substance with probing fingers; anything to help him feel connected with reality. His fingers came into contact with something fine, dry, and gritty. He had not touched anything quite like this before. It wasn't earth or stone that ran through his fingers like powdered water. He groped deeper into the blackness but there was nothing else – just this fine grit that crunched slightly underfoot, and shifted disconcertingly as he cautiously slipped and dipped forward.

He could smell something too. Tangy, even salty. He thought he might have recognised the smell, but from where? From when? It was getting stronger, as was the rushing, thundering sound, and now he was sure he could hear cries, many cries, unearthly cries.

His heart sank to his belly and he turned, in some panic, to face the sounds. He felt compelled to follow them, although he was scared of them, as there was no other indicator of life around him. Were they creatures in pain, or did they threaten his safety, or both? What about Will? Was he threatened too? Surely he would feel what Will was feeling – there was no pain now, just fear and confusion, and panic at being unable to see. Was Will experiencing all of these things too? He must be, of course, for he and Will were one and the same; like twins, but more than twins – they were each other. Will must be thinking the same thoughts, feeling the same feelings. Wigapom hoped so, but he was suddenly uncertain. If only he knew where he was. Perhaps if he tried very hard to focus his mind, he could make a telepathic connection with Will and find out his location. Aldebaran had been telling them about this only yesterday but they had yet to try it.

'You see,' Wigapom thought sadly, as if in answer to some imagined reproof from Fynn, 'I did listen sometimes.'

'He wouldn't listen to me any more, Aldebaran,' cried Fynn, trying hard to explain what had happened in those last few moments out on the hillside: moments that seemed to last an eternity.

'I was so angry with him, and jealous too. If I'd only had the sense to admit it. He was my friend, but I'd lost him to this boy… Then the sky blackened, and the terrible wind came – the Shivastrom – and just blew them away; and it was all my fault. By the time I realised it I couldn't do anything about it! I lost them Aldebaran, all because of my angry thoughts and temper! I must find them! I must help them. I must bring them back! Can you see where they are on the Astrolabius? Please tell me you can find them. I'll never forgive myself if you can't. Will they ever forgive me?' Fynn's face was contorted with grief. His knuckles were white as he twisted his hands together, as though trying to wring out the memory of it all, and especially his part in it.

He and Aldebaran were already in the huge Story Chamber, looking into a stubbornly blank Astrolabius, when Tamsan, his brother Demeter and Gobann arrived from the tunnels, ushered in by a young woman whom Fynn had not seen before, but he was too distraught to take much notice of any of them.

Aldebaran placed a calming hand on Fynn's shaking shoulder.

'Calm yourself Fynn. Nothing can be achieved by panic. It creates more problems than it solves.'

He turned to the Astrolabius again, twisting another dial, and thankfully it slowly juddered then whirred into action: moving pictures came to life on the walls before Fynn's eyes – scenes from the town this time: another fight over something, or nothing; an angry boundary dispute somewhere; even a fleeting image of Cassie in the cottage, preparing her medicines – a nice image for once, but old images, as Fynn knew only too well.

'The Astrolabius appears to be running behind time again,' said Aldebaran, by way of explanation. 'The energy powering it is becoming weaker. We may have to wait a while for any recent images to filter through.' He turned a few more dials and suddenly, in a rather jerky fashion, a very current image of Fynn running back from the hillside appeared before breaking up and disappearing. Fynn shuddered at the memory, but there was nothing of Wigapom or Will's whereabouts, no sign of what may have happened to them.

'Where *are* they?' said Fynn, in further desperation. 'Anything could have happened by now!'

'What has happened, has happened then,' spoke out the young woman's voice from behind Fynn, 'there is nothing you can do to stop it now. So you must accept and learn to trust.'

Fynn turned and noticed the owner of the voice properly for the first time. She was a little younger than him, with an athletic frame, shiny, dark hair and clear, determined brown eyes, which met his with a firm unwavering gaze. In his new vulnerable state Fynn felt a brand new feeling flush around his body. He felt himself blush, and was embarrassed by this. He had never felt like this before with anyone.

'This is my daughter, Skye,' explained Aldebaran, 'she has just returned from working with the resistance movement in the capital city. It seems the Dark One could be planning to go on the march again.' Tamsan, Demeter and Gobann exchanged glances, aware of what this could mean, but Fynn was confused.

'On the march, what do you mean?' he said.

Skye replied, 'When news filtered through about the arrival of Wigapom and the death of the white hart, by Darqu'on's own hand, we feared it would not be long before he led his army in physical combat again. We believe he could be preparing to do so now and make his actual presence known physically. This is the time to be most feared, as it is the time of battle.'

'So Darqu'on got a personal taste of blood and killed the white hart himself, not the Roth Riders?' asked Fynn, temporarily distracted from his grief by this news. 'I thought at the time that the slaughter of the white hart looked different to that of Cassie's animals.'

'Yes, you can usually tell Darqu'on's direct hand in something,' replied Aldebaran.

'And you believe he wants to taste more blood by going into battle?' established Fynn.

His daughter shifted impatiently from one foot to the other, as though anxious to continue her story.

'Yes, we do. Darqu'on's lackey, the repulsive Scabtail, has reportedly been seen around Dragonmound, site of the last great battle, where the King lost his life.'

'Wiggy's father you mean,' interrupted Fynn.

'Yes,' said Skye, looking earnestly at Fynn, who had to avert his gaze as he felt his face redden alarmingly again. 'We believe that this sudden interest could be connected to Wigapom's disappearance.'

'Disappearance? Do you mean Wigapom isn't dead and this might have nothing to do with me after all?' said Fynn, relief beginning to wash over him like pure, cooling water .

'No. I don't mean that. All things are interconnected,' said Skye, somewhat brusquely, 'we all play our part.'

Guilt surged back again through Fynn's veins and he reddened once more under her penetrating gaze, yet this time he fought to maintain his failing self esteem and turned to meet her eyes with a glare of his own.

'At least it's not only me, then,' he said defensively, hoping she could not tell from his face how sick his stomach was still feeling.

There was a sense of combatancy forming about their meeting which others could not fail to notice: a battle of wills creating a jagged space between them while they both silently struggled for supremacy.

Skye was as unsettled by Fynn as he was by her. Had the energy between them been tangible it would undoubtedly have been sharp! Aldebaran's voice broke through the invisible barrier.

'It's working again! Look! There's Wigapom! He's on the Shifting Sands!'

'That must mean he's …' began Skye, looking at her father, but she got no chance to finish.

'Exactly!' replied Aldebaran.

Wigapom stepped his way blindly through the shifting substance below his feet, reproaching himself with every floundering step. If only he had listened more to Aldebaran and Fynn perhaps then he wouldn't be in this predicament now. Another thought stopped him in his tracks. Where was Fynn? Had he been caught in the Shivastrom too? Was he safe? The thought of something happening to Fynn scared Wigapom most of all. He didn't have a connecting link to Fynn as he did with Will, other than years of friendship, and he valued those so much, although he felt bad now about how he had treated him lately: they had argued so much. He knew it was over his relationship with Will. Guilt crept in like a thief in the night, but he couldn't let that get to him now, he just had to hope Fynn was safe. Wigapom sent out a fervent message for his safety just in case, as Aldebaran had shown them how, but he couldn't keep thinking of Fynn – he had to focus on Will to connect with him again. He moved forward one more step towards the thundering sound.

He and Will would be stronger together than apart, although Wigapom thought ruefully about how foolish their behaviour had been of recent weeks. He had only wanted to make things up to his inner self after all those years of smothering and suppression: just to experience the freedom and acceptance that both had felt deprived of – was that really too much to ask? Wigapom had already answered his own question: he knew it was, especially in the way that he'd done it. He couldn't understand how he had allowed himself to act in that way. How stupid! Will was a Child who needed some sensible Adult common sense (to use Aldebaran's capitalised parlance) as well as encouragement and support. Well, Wigapom hadn't been a sensible Adult at all, and his behaviour hadn't helped either of them. He certainly hadn't helped Aldebaran, or the people of Arcanum – especially those who had been so good to him. He'd abused their kindness, their help, their trust and he'd led Will and himself into danger. What kind of a hero was he?

He was ashamed. If he and Will ever got out of here alive, he'd make sure he changed. Would they be forgiven? Did they deserve forgiveness? Tears of regret, and self-pity, began to run down Wigapom's face. He was desperate to find Will and to start afresh: if only he could see!

'Oh, where are you, Will, where *are* you?' he thought frantically.

'Here,' popped a thought into his mind. 'Here, in here!'

Wigapom stood stock-still. Will's voice, inside his head. It had worked! He'd connected telepathically with Will. He could find him now and they could escape from here: wherever here was.

'Where's here, Will?' thought Wigapom, hard.

'Here, in the dark. I'm frightened,' came the thought back. Wigapom could sense the fear, and began to understand why he could not see.

'Don't be frightened. I'm here and I'll find you and we'll be safe together,' thought Wigapom in his most calming, caring way, 'If you can't see where you are, feel around and let me know.'

Slowly Will's thought came back to him.

'I can hear water all around me, I think. It's very loud. And some cries too. I'm in something that feels like wood, and it's moving up and down, very fast. Help me, Wigapom. Help me!'

Wigapom's brain sprang into action. Will was in the water, in something wooden – a boat? Was he by a river? Surely not, rivers in his experience were never so noisy, nor so tangy in their smell. Could it possibly be the sea – the place he had always wanted to visit? Well if this was the sea he would give anything to be far, far away from it! It sounded frightening and smelled awful! Yet it rang distant bells of recognition. He tried to remember, but the feeling kept slipping out of reach. This didn't matter now – Will was in the water and needed his help. He moved quicker towards the rushing sound, and felt a spray of water pepper his face, then another; it tasted salty. He spat it out, pulling a face. He was desperate to get to Will, and thinking hard, but that seemed to be blocking out Will's thoughts and words: he had to stop thinking to connect again. Just relax and let go, he said to himself. Open your mind and let the feelings in... And they came, in a rush this time.

'I'm in a box.'

Suddenly, in front of him there was a change in the blackness. Shades of grey were visible now: moving; changing. The sound of the water was deafening. He was hit by a rush of salty water and swept off his feet, yet again. As his head went under, he swallowed a mouthful of the stuff and spluttered to spit it out, his arms and legs flailing madly in an effort to stay above the water. It crashed onto him from above, like some sea monster pouncing on its prey, and once more he was swept along by a force of such power and magnitude, which he felt could crush him at any moment.

The cold, salty water filled his mouth and ears again and again, and stung his unseeing eyes as he was hurled from the crest of one wave to the depths of another and back again with such ferocity that he struggled to breathe. He feared he was drowning! He cried out and his cries mingled with the cries around him. Who or what were they? Panic gripped him. He struggled in the water, his sodden clothes weighing him down and making the effort doubly hard, but resistance made things worse so he tried to move with the water, to let it carry him where it would and float on the surface, just as he remembered watching sticks and leaves float when he dropped them into the brook at Brakendor. Once he gave up struggling it was easier to stay on top. It wasn't pleasant but he was alive! He could hear Will's thoughts in his head again. They seemed louder than before. Closer.

'I'm here. In the dark.'

Suddenly Wigapom's body hit a hard solid object that was being buffeted by the strength of the water. He grabbed at it – it felt like wood! Was it the box that Will was in? If only this blackness would lift. He made a grab for the object and felt his hand smash through it with a painful thrust. He touched flesh and cloth and heard Will gasp and light flooded in once more and they could both see.

'WILL!' he managed to say, catching sight of his scared face and taut body now soaked with the water. But they both swallowed a mouthful and neither could speak as they sputtered to eject it.

All they could see, apart from the box, was water, violent grey-green water, rising and falling and roaring in equal measure. Wigapom knew then that he had been right, this was the sea! He had never been to the sea before. Never experienced waves or touched sand. No wonder he could not make sense of anything. And huge grey birds made the cries, but bigger and fiercer, with cruel red-tipped beaks snapping open as they screeched and swooped around them both – seagulls perhaps; he had heard of those. If they were they were nothing like he had ever imagined – these were huge predators, intent on attacking both Will and Wigapom. He had to cling onto Will and what remained of the box, whilst fending of the ferocious birds at the same time. How angry the birds seemed. How sharp their beaks as they viciously attacked arms and legs where bright red blood began to ooze from their wounds into the surging sea. Will was screaming with fear, or was that his own voice raised in distress? It was difficult to tell them apart, as sounds and wounds seemed to be forged together. This excited the birds even more. They came back time and again, savagely gouging at the exposed flesh and screeching even louder with triumph at the obvious exhaustion of their victims.

Both Wigapom and Will were tiring fast. How much longer could they fend these creatures off? – Wigapom didn't think it could be long. They needed some protection. He knew instinctively, with some sense of irony, they had to protect their eyes from the razor-sharp beaks – if only they had something to put over them: could they use the box? The box was long and narrow – more like a coffin! Wigapom had no idea how Will had ended up in it, where it had come from or who or what put him in it. Somehow he didn't think there was a rational answer to any of these questions, but it did look very like a coffin! No! He wasn't going to think that. He had to think positively. Coffin or not, if they could put it over their heads it would help protect them from the scavenging birds. He smashed out the top of the box, leaving just three solid sides.

'We have to turn the box over, to protect us,' he yelled at Will, who understood and nodded.

Together they did their best to overturn it, but it was sodden with seawater and amazingly difficult to shift, especially as the birds continued their attack.

'It's too heavy!' cried Will, ready to give up.

'Don't give up!' encouraged Wigapom. 'Come on, we can do this together! One more heave.'

With every muscle in their tired and saturated bodies they heaved and pushed once more until the box flipped over!

'Get underneath it, Will,' yelled Wigapom above the noise of the waves and birds' cries, 'but keep your head above the water.'

Will took a deep breath before ducking his head down into the waves and then straight up under the box into the trapped air. Wigapom followed him.

They could still see out if they lifted the box slightly but the birds could no longer reach them, and after a few vain stabs at the timber, the scavengers soared, screeching, back into the sky, their savage efforts thwarted.

Wigapom both heard and saw them, their huge wings riding the currents as they flew off to find new prey, their cries echoing across the wind and the waves.

Wigapom and Will breathed a sigh of relief from under the shelter of the box. Now it was safer to come out from under it and use what was remaining as a raft to hold onto, half in and half out of the water. This they did and, whilst it was a relief to be out in the air once more, they were still tossed mercilessly by the waves and getting colder and colder with every moment. Will was already turning blue. How much longer could they last like this before the sea claimed them? There was no sign of dry land or any indication where they were, or if there was anyone to save them.

'That's them!' cried Fynn, wanting to both laugh and cry at the bedraggled sight of Will and Wigapom, underneath a box that looked like a coffin, in the middle of what seemed to Fynn, who had also never seen the sea, a huge and violent lake without end. At least they were alive, if not yet safe: there was hope.

'Where are they? What is that place? Can we help them? Oh I feel so helpless!' he cried out in frantic despair.

'It's the Sea of Emotion,' said Skye, 'beyond the Shifting Sands of Sorrow. We couldn't get there even if we wanted to – at least not that part of it. That is Wigapom's own emotional creation – aided by yourself and the Dark One of course, but still unique to him and Will.'

'The Sea of Emotion! What sort of place is that and where is it?' said Fynn, still not understanding.

'It's inside his head – he has created it, from all the tumultuous feelings he has churning inside him. It isn't a real place, like here, but it is very real to him and only he can get himself out of it,' added Aldebaran. Fynn looked blank – it was all too much for him.

'But there must be something we can do?' he said.

'Perhaps you've done enough already,' retorted Skye, as if to dig at Fynn once more. He understood that – and felt the pain of it.

'So I'm to blame for this too in some way! Thanks for making me feel so good about myself,' said Fynn, ruefully.

'You asked and I told you. The truth hurts sometimes. Just get over it. You feeling guilty won't help them,' snapped back Skye. Fynn didn't like or understand her sharpness and decided he was not going to be made the scapegoat for everything that had happened, and so he snapped back in defence.

'Look, I get the feeling you don't like me for some reason. If it's because all of your hopes for the return of the magic have been dashed suddenly because of Wigapom's disappearance then you need to know that he is equally responsible for what has happened – and to quote your own words – you just have to get on with it! Now I suggest we call a truce from these hostilities between us and get to know each other properly, or we will all as likely find ourselves at sea, in our own emotional ocean, which will do none of us any good.'

He thought he heard Aldebaran chuckle to himself, but his eyes were on Skye alone, whose face registered surprise at his strong response.

'I take your point, Fynn. No need to hammer it in any further!' she said, and he noticed a flushing of her cheeks before she turned away from him to study a seemingly fascinating part of the wall. Something very strange was happening between these two and perhaps only Aldebaran understood it, but he kept his counsel.

'So… That's what a sea looks like,' said Fynn, at length, trying to settle the energy around them again, which felt very jagged still. 'I heard stories as a child, but I never dreamed it was like that! There must be something we can do about Wigapom and Will. I won't just watch them drown! If my thoughts are partly responsible for getting them into this state then surely my thoughts can help get them out?'

'Now that *is* positive thinking, 'said Aldebaran. 'It's certainly worth a try,' and he looked calmly at Fynn, as though willing him to dig deep into his own resources. 'What do you suggest?'

'I'll… think up someone to save them! And I won't try it, Aldebaran – I'll do it!' said Fynn with determination etched indelibly into his face and voice, as he shot a determined glance at Skye.

'That's tough talking,' said Skye, meeting his gaze as if grudgingly acknowledging a strength in Fynn that she hadn't seen before. 'Who had you in mind?' Fynn felt he was being tested, and he rose to the challenge.

'Castor and Pollux: they're twin stars that look after people in trouble on the sea. Wigapom knows about them, we used to create stories about them when we were younger. We can think of them, create them in our minds and direct those thoughts to Wigapom and Will! Perhaps they'll pick up our thoughts and imagine them for themselves. It's worth a chance.'

'Star twins!' said Skye, dismissively again 'I thought you meant something more definite.'

'Have you any better idea?' shot back Fynn, irritated again by her seeming condemnation for him.

'Nothing will be achieved if we do not work as One,' said the placating voice of Aldebaran, 'and star twins could be very helpful.'

'Exactly,' said Fynn, who didn't quite understand what working as 'One' really meant, but at least it seemed that Aldebaran was supporting his idea over his quick-tongued daughter.

'Then let's do it and find out,' said Skye looking at him challengingly, with her deep brown eyes, which brought another flush to Fynn's face, and a not unpleasant vibrancy to his stomach. He hadn't realised how attractive she was before and this recognition unsettled him in a strangely bittersweet way. Whatever was going on between them certainly brought out mixed emotions that Fynn was beginning to rather like. There was no time to focus on that now, however: they had the star twins to recreate.

CHAPTER 21

It's All In the Mind

"What we think determines what happens to us,
so if we want to change our lives, we need to stretch our minds."
Wayne Dyer

Wigapom was almost ready to give up. As he lay, exhausted, clinging onto the box as best he could, he found himself drifting in and out of a muddled, sleepy state, one in which images from his childhood kept appearing and disappearing. He was recalling stories he had loved about the sea, of the wonderful whales, and huge sea monsters, and pirates and ghostly galleons. One story that seemed to keep coming and going from his mind, like the very tide itself, was that of Castor and Pollux, the twin stars who saved people from the waves. He let these thoughts drift in and out a few more times as he and Will continued to be buffeted by the water; but something else, less helpful and pleasant, seemed to be more insistent in his head and began to push the heavenly twins from his mind.

He saw, in his dream-like state, two large heads emerging from the water, which was beginning to boil around them. The heads branched out from one colossal and heavily armoured neck, liquid fire spurted from mouths rimmed with terrifyingly sharp, jagged teeth, smoke billowed from wide, flaring nostrils, red-hot eyes glowed like beacons of flame and the heavily scaled body seemed to stretch forever. It was the dragon of the sea – the fabled Leviathan!

This horrific dream image forced Wigapom to open his eyes again! As he did so, he thought he saw something very large sink below the waves and disappear, but then it could just have been the rise and fall of the water because all he could now see was the ocean again, and Will of course, totally exhausted and draped over the box with half-open eyes.

'Can't... Go... On,' said Will's small voice.

'You can… You… Must,' replied Wigapom, trying desperately to keep his own eyes open, but losing the battle and thus allowing the Leviathan a chance to rise once more.

'Why didn't he accept the star twins?' said Fynn, desperate again as he had seen the huge image of the Leviathan appear in the Astrolabius, 'why is he creating monsters instead of helpers?'

'He is very weak,' said Aldebaran, 'and his mind is drifting as well as his body: he is prey to any thoughts being transmitted to him. I suspect the Leviathan is Darqu'on's influence. We will have to work harder to get the positive thoughts transferred to him rather than let the negative ones take over.'

'Are we really up against Darqu'on again?' Fynn asked. 'Has he taken control of Wigapom's mind?'

'He is influencing him, as we are, but it is Wigapom's ultimate choice which one he responds to,' said Aldebaran, 'he has his own battle between the forces of good and evil.'

'So all we can do is keep sending positive thoughts of help, and hope for the best,' said Fynn.

'That's all anyone can ever do,' agreed Aldebaran.

'Then let's do it.' said Skye impatiently, 'and not just talk about it!'

The images of Castor and Pollux kept returning in Wigapom's head, emerging from the waves on sea-spray horses, undulating towards Wigapom and Will with a promise of salvation, yet the Leviathan too, was rising to the surface; its heads lunging towards Wigapom and Will so that they felt the hot breath erupting from both its mouths, and its great body smashing through the violent surface of the water with a force that took all their attention and maintained their fear. The monster circled them, rising and falling with the swell of the ocean, as though rounding them up in its own watery corale, seeming to push them to the deepest part of the ocean. Wigapom and Will thrashed about in the water, panicked by the monster, which seemed both real and unreal to them. This was a dreamlike state fast becoming a nightmare. The monster loomed over them again, its sinewy necks stretching down towards them, mouths wide, ready to swallow them. There was no escape. Castor and Pollux had disappeared. All help had gone. But Wigapom was not ready to die, and he wouldn't let Will die either.

'SWIM, SWIM!' he yelled, grasping Will's arm and pulling him desperately away from the Leviathan, using every scrap of his failing energy to create distance between the monster and himself. As he did so he saw a ghostly ship in full sail arise from the depths, complete with its deadly crew of cut-throat pirates and, at the helm, the skeletal figure of Death, who turned its eyeless gaze on Wigapom, and grinned, exposing a mouth of decayed teeth. It was a hideous and horrifying sight but better, Wigapom felt, than the Leviathan and he felt himself drawn towards it, as if here they might even find refuge! The figure of Death stretched out its bony arms towards Wigapom and he heard the word 'Come', floating on the air. In his exhausted, almost unconscious state it was tempting: On the ship they would be out of reach of the Leviathan, who remained menacingly close; they would also be dry, and even with the knowledge that once on the ship they would be imprisoned on that floating fortress for ever, this seemed better than the living hell they were in now. He and Will would listen to Death and follow him.

'He's not listening to us!' yelled Fynn in sheer panic, 'He's listening to Death!'

'Don't let your own thoughts be hijacked by negative ones,' warned Aldebaran. 'Keep sending positive thoughts of the heavenly twins: and hope that they finally hear.'

The figure of Death loomed above them from the seaweed-covered bow. It was all that Wigapom could see, and all that he could hear were deep pirate voices singing a sea shanty, the sound of which pulled him closer towards them.

'*Heave ho, twill soon be done.*
Heave ho and Death will come.'

It was hypnotising: Death will come. Death will come: it was just a matter of time…

But the figures of Castor and Pollux had not disappeared entirely and kept appearing on his mental horizon, doggedly refusing to give up. Wigapom could see the starlight shining from them, illuminating the water all around them. They looked magnificent and strong. They were the saviours of sailors, he remembered, as they galloped closer on their fine white wave-horses, at first indistinct, then stronger and more urgent. They were competing with the ghost ship and the figure of Death, and the Leviathan, who rose again to block them from Wigapom's sight, but Wigapom could see through the monster now and the creature lost its magnitude and began to fade. Instead Wigapom was being pulled between the hope of the star twins and the lure of Death, this way, that way, this way, that way. The Leviathan slunk back into the depths and the water boiled momentarily as its shape descended to nothing. The figure of Death, meanwhile, looked directly at Wigapom, beckoning with his bony finger. Suddenly Wigapom felt pain, real pain, as though the finger had pierced his body like a hot knife. He cried out in shock, and the sound of his voice echoed in his head, forcing him back to full consciousness again and the choices were suddenly very real, right there, in the water in front of them: the ghost ship with the figure of Death or the star twins on horseback riding the waves! Adrenalin filled Wigapom's body. This was no dream – this was real. He had to act to save himself and Will! He didn't want to be taken on the ship! He would not be claimed by Death! He was not ready to die. He began to fight mentally, willing the star twins to get to him first: they had to save him and Will. He shouted to Will, trying to rouse him.

'Will! Remember Castor and Pollux from the stories? Think of them saving us, and nothing else. Don't argue, just do it!'

Will, from the depths of his exhaustion and increasing desire to give in to Death, heard the urgency in Wigapom's voice and was pulled back from the very brink of annihilation. He saw white shapes like two horsemen forming and galloping closer across the waves. He remembered them! They both worked together, as one, focusing exhausted eyes and minds more firmly on the horsemen drawing alongside them, ignoring the hovering figure of Death spreading his shadow across the surging water as the deadly pirates threw ropes to wrap around Wigapom and Will – ropes which morphed into octopus tentacles whose strong suckers stretched out towards them, wriggling and writhing, to pull them on board. Yet the star twins were there too in the midst of it all, along with a whole herd of white wave-horses. their watery manes flying out like spray, wide nostrils flaring, and powerful front hooves pawing the air before plunging back into the water, only to rise again as the next wave formed. Side by side on the two leading horses were a pair of identical figures holding trident-topped spears in one hand and seaweed reins in the other. Around their heads were flames of fire, blazing with fiery brilliance in the grim surroundings, and above each head, as though suspended in the air itself, was a glittering star. Their rippling, glistening muscles reflected in the spray and the light from their eyes shone out across the water like golden beacons. With their shining spears they slashed at the tentacles, now with pirates shinning down them, intent on grabbing Wigapom and Will in their deadly grip. The light from the star twins was so intense it blinded the pirates as they fell into the water with loud cries and curses before the wave-horses trampled them into oblivion. The figure of Death hissed and a huge jet of steaming water spewed from his mouth as the wave horses leapt over the prow of the ghost ship and onto him. Death hissed again at the star twins, who now rode either side of the ship, pointing their starlight emitting spears at him. The starlight pierced the air with brilliance and the figure of Death slowly began to disintegrate, letting out a last, long hiss that seemed to say, 'Next time, next time,' as the ghost ship sunk without trace.

Castor and Pollux scattered a path of twinkling stars across the water as they rode back towards Wigapom and Will, who were exhausted but still clinging to the remains of the box. Wigapom felt a deep peace at the sight of these two childhood heroes astride their wave horses. The sea was now flat and tranquil, like the millpond in Brakendor, and Wigapom knew they had been brought back literally from the clutches of Death, but there was still danger whilst they were in the water. It wasn't over yet.

Castor and Pollux held out their spears like lifelines towards Wigapom and Will, their faces etched with determination. Their intent was crystal clear without the need for words.

'Will!' Wigapom called, 'take hold of the spear when I say so, and don't let go!'

The spears were within arms' reach now, so close that Wigapom could see the drops of water spinning off the ends: they looked fragile but somehow he knew they would hold their weight. They just had to make a grab for them. No time for more thought. Just action.

'NOW!' yelled Wigapom and thrust his hand towards the spear nearest to him, grabbing hold and feeling its comforting strength. Will did the same. As they did so the water erupted once more into turmoil, with the heaving bulk of the Leviathan surging upwards, shattering the peace: his cavernous mouth open just inches from where Wigapom and Will were swinging in midair.

'NO!' cried Wigapom, lashing out with his feet and struggling to land somehow behind Castor, on the surprisingly solid back of the wave-horse. The Leviathan snapped his double jaws inches from him.

'NO!' yelled Wigapom again, in challenge to the beast, as he managed to twist his head to see Will landing behind Pollux on the wave-horse.

'HOLD FAST!' The star twins cried in a single voice, sounding like the roar of the waves sprinkled with the whisper of stardust falling to earth. The Leviathan launched his necks towards them, mouths gaping, eyes glaring.

Neither Wigapom nor Will needed a second bidding. The air, filled with the force of the star twins defiant cries, mixed with those of Wigapom and Will and the ear-splitting sound had a power all of its own. So powerful it split the Leviathan in half – the water soaring like a mountain range as the cleft creature collapsed, lifeless, below its depths. The water bubbled then calmed as Wigapom breathed easily again. He cast a triumphant glance at Will, who punched the air in delight. The danger was over and the fun had just begun, for off they went on an amazing journey across the water. Brilliant colours such as they had never seen before surrounded them and a school of dolphins leaped joyfully around them, sending energy to their exhausted minds, bodies and spirits with their infectious play and cheerful sounds.

For a while the dolphins' chatterings, playful whistles and calls were the only sounds they heard, which with the regular movement of the wave-horses began to have a strangely soporific, even meditative effect on both Will and Wigapom. They felt their eyelids becoming heavier and heavier by the moment. They resisted at first by endeavouring to jerk them open, but a great weight seemed to be attached to their eyelids, and they could no more stop them closing than they could tell the stars not to shine. They began to drift to a nirvana-like state of perfect peace: a borderless land of feelings and sensations over which they desired no control. How long they remained in this timeless suspended state they would never know, but as the bliss of healing sleep gradually overtook and surrounded them all the torment of the past few hours drifted away into a far and distant memory.

'Phew, it worked!' sighed Fynn, sweat beading his brow. 'That was a close thing.'

'It's not over yet,' warned Aldebaran, as he saw what was now happening in the Astrolabius.

They were still floating, but no longer on water. When Wigapom eventually opened his eyes the star twins and their watery horses and even the sea had evaporated into the atmosphere. Instead they were drifting upwards, as though attached by invisible wires, held by an unseen, benevolent hand, on gentle currents of air towards soft, fluffy, white clouds, gently moving across a sapphire blue sky.

The sense of weightlessness was a tranquil and blissful experience and Wigapom wondered fleetingly if they had perhaps changed into drops of water themselves and were evaporating into the vapour clouds above; yet, as he looked, he could see quite clearly that he and Will were the same as before, although Will was still asleep in a state of euphoric oblivion. Wigapom wondered what his mother from Brakendor would say if she could see them now, floating in midair: she would no doubt have apoplexy at the very thought – but it didn't feel at all dangerous, or even strange, and as they drifted and floated higher and higher into the atmosphere Wigapom allowed a feeling of wistfulness to waft over him as he thought again of all that he had left behind in Brakendor: his family, his home, Sophie – ah yes, Sophie. He smiled as he recalled her beautiful, gentle face. Would he ever see her again? It was only when he began to recall the recent troubling events with Fynn that he was finally brought back to reality with a bump and he began to drop down, jerkily, until the air current stabilised him once more. Where was he? What was happening to them? How and why were they floating in the clouds? Would they ever get down, ever see Fynn and Aldebaran again?

As these more disturbing present-moment thoughts filled his head he felt himself once more lurch downwards with the weight of them.

'Whoa!' he called, struggling to relax enough to be weightless again.

'What's happening?' yawned Will, rubbing sleep from his own eyes. 'Where are you, Wigapom?'

'Right here,' said his older self, managing to gain the lost height once more and feeling as though he was coming out of one crazy dream straight into another, 'but other than that I have no idea.' Will looked below him and with forethought Wigapom held onto him, as their unexpected location temporarily filled Will with fear and he too began to disappear downwards through the clouds.

'It's Ok, you'll float, as long as you don't feel scared or anxious,' Wigapom reassured Will, and together they took in their surroundings.

All they could see above, below and around them now were clouds, masses of them, forming, merging, blending together, with ever changing shapes and patterns: resembling snow-capped mountain peaks and valleys before morphing into strange and indescribable creatures before transforming back into mountains or valleys again – wonderful, nebulous creations made of nothing but water vapour.

The sapphire sky had disappeared and they were riding on and in the clouds, as part of them. How they carried them along was a mystery, but carried along they were, supported by this weightless water-vapour world of amoebic landscapes and creatures. They had no idea what might be about to happen to them but somehow it just didn't seem to matter. This was a dream world from which they might never want to wake.

As the cloud formations continued to change and evolve Wigapom and Will rolled around inside them, like peas tossing on a never-ending cotton-wool mattress. How long they travelled like this neither could tell, yet gradually they began to sense something was changing.

'Is it getting darker?' said Will, euphoria being invaded by concern.

'It seems so, the clouds aren't light and fluffy any more,' replied Wigapom, noticing how the white clouds were fast being replaced by thick, grey cumulonimbus ones.

These suggested trouble, looked stormy and felt threatening, coloured by an eerie half-light. They no longer provided the same safe, cocooned environment as before. Wigapom had a feeling of being barely suspended between two worlds and feared they were about to be expelled pretty violently.

'Is it the Shivastrom again?' said Will, his voice trembling.

'I don't think so, but these clouds are storm clouds, nonetheless! I have a feeling we could be in for a bit of trouble,' said Wigapom, making what turned out to be a major understatement of their predicament.

A sudden and violent lightning crack, accompanied immediately by a long, threatening roll of thunder, sliced the clouds that held them and they knew that what had gone so peacefully and effortlessly up would soon come down in rather more of a hurry. If the falling rain didn't plunge them to their deaths then maybe the lightning would finish them off. These cloudy saviours had fast turned into enemies.

'Brace yourself, Will! The storm's about to burst. This is going to be a rough ride!' he warned.

As quickly as this thought dawned in his head, the storm cloud burst with a deafening explosion, transforming instantly into trillions of tiny, yet powerful droplets of driving, heavy rain, pattering and pounding to the ground at great speed and intensity, pulling Wigapom and Will with them, plunging them towards the hard earth coming up to meet them.

'Pray for a soft landing!' Wigapom cried out before the force of their descent took his breath away.

Sodden first with seawater and now the subsequent torrential rain, they fell heavily, towards the fast-appearing ground. For a moment they were in free-fall, arms spread wide, spinning round like the seeds of a sycamore, grabbing at the air as gravity took over. Then they hit the earth, sinking into something soft, squelchy, and very smelly.

The softness of the substance in which they landed at least broke their fall – a miracle in itself – but the smell was disgusting: worse than all the rotting food, and bad drains of the world put together! Yet it could have been so much worse, thought Wigapom philosophically as he lay winded, but otherwise unhurt, in the foul-smelling putrid substance that turned their stomachs but saved their lives.

'Quick thinking Fynn!' said Aldebaran admiringly, as they watched the safe landing in the Astrolabius. 'Your thoughts are very powerful when you want them to be!'

'But did you have to think them into that?' said Skye, turning up her nose at the thought of what they had fallen into, but her eyes twinkly with suppressed laughter.

'First soft thing that came to mind,' apologised Fynn, 'comes from working on a farm all those years, I suppose!' and he allowed himself a smile for the first time for days. He was pleased to see the smile returned by Skye, and felt that they too, had landed softly in a more conducive place in their relationship.

'The images are fading once more,' said Aldebaran. 'The Astrolabius' energy supply is exhausted again: we've used it too much today.' As if to prove Aldebaran's words, the Astrolabius made a tired, spluttering sound before going completely blank and deathly quiet.

'You mean we've lost them again!' cried Fynn, as he stared at the Astrolabius, trying to will the images back again.

'They're on their own now until we can replenish the energy source from somewhere,' said Skye, 'and goodness knows when that will be.'

CHAPTER 22

Reality Or Illusion?

"Everything you can imagine is real."
Pablo Picasso

For a while neither of them could move, every drop of energy knocked from them. Even the heavy rain didn't revive them from their shock and they lay still and stunned, aware only of the vile-smelling gunge in which they had fallen, but with no strength to remove themselves from it. It coated every part of them, with a thick and putrid sludge that stuck like glue to their clothes and bodies. It was only by holding their faces upwards to the heavy rain still pouring down that they were at least able to wash it from their faces and hands. Eventually Will could stand it no longer and struggled to right himself.

'Where are we?' he spluttered, spitting bits of rotting, half-masticated objects and other indescribables out of his mouth, 'Cos it smells and tastes like hell!'

'Thankfully, I don't think it's that!' replied Wigapom, with irony in his voice and perhaps a glimmer of what might almost have passed for a smile. 'It's pigswill, – nothing more!'

'It's disgusting gunge!' spat Will, covered as he was with smelly, slimy potato peelings, stinking rotting apples and other foul-smelling decomposing vegetation. He turned his head to look at Wigapom, but instead came face to face with an enormous, dirty and wet pink snout snuffling at him, as though he was something good to eat! Two small, pale eyes peered from under huge, floppy ears and the thing grunted loudly in Will's face. Will fell backwards with the shock, going deeper into the stinking stuff, his eyes wide and terrified.

'Gerrof! Gerrofme you monster!' he shrieked as the creature's huge tongue explored his cheek.

Despite their situation Wigapom was laughing now, all tension released in the craziness of the moment: it was just what he needed after so much trauma.

'It's a pig, Will! Not a monster: just an inquisitive, hungry pig that wants his dinner. We're back in the real world again: at least I think so. We're in a farmyard – somewhere! Normality of sorts.'

'You call this normal?' said Will with a grunt almost as loud as the pig, who was now attempting to lick off a particularly smelly piece of rotting cabbage from Will's shoulder.

Wigapom laughed again as he struggled to remove himself from the gunge and lend Will a helping hand. The pig obviously didn't like the thought of a moving dinner and trotted off to search out something less mobile and they had an opportunity to look around them.

They were definitely in a farmyard, but it didn't look as real on second inspection as it had first time around. True, there were normal things around, like pitchforks and buckets and other farming paraphernalia, but it all looked a little one-dimensional, as though it was part of a picture or painting, yet he and Will were real enough and so was the gunge! It didn't make much sense yet.

There were barns and stables in a rectangle around them; but they looked sadly neglected and forlorn. Under an open-sided barn were a broken wagon and some old farm trucks that looked as though they were beyond fixing. Nearby was a water trough, brimming with slimy green water, and a pitchfork or two with bent or broken prongs standing against it. Apart from a few bedraggled chickens pecking at the ground, and the snuffling hungry pig, there was no other sign of real life, which felt a little disquieting.

The rain had now stopped and Wigapom was attempting to wash the worst of the gunge from his clothes with water from the trough; it was fairly useless but better than nothing.

'Get the worst off with this,' he said to Will, 'then best hide in that barn while I have a look around to see if I can find out where we are. I'll call you when I think it's safe.'

'It's a funny sort of place,' said Will, 'real yet not real, if you know what I mean. Sort of sad and empty.'

'I do,' said Wigapom. 'It's as though it has no, well, heart, I suppose.'

'Don't go far,' said Will, not sure that he wanted to be left here with the pig, who was walking back in Will's direction again, 'and don't be long.'

'I won't', said Wigapom as he set off out of the farmyard, taking care to use the buildings to hide him as much as possible from any unseen, spying eyes. He had no idea whether this was a friendly or dangerous place: but it *was* without heart, empty and sad, and this intrigued Wigapom because he had never seen or felt anything so dead before, which still gave the impression of life: it reminded him of the atmosphere in Lampadia town but this was far sadder even than there. As he walked he thought of everything that had happened since he'd left Brakendor and, not for the first time, did he regret his childish behaviour over the last few weeks. People in Arcanum were living in fear and trepidation as the shadow of Darqu'on's sorcery enveloped the land and he had done nothing so far to help them. He realised now, with hindsight, that what Will had really needed from him was not another child to play with, but loving guidance and acceptance from a caring Adult. Will, as his child self, needed help to grow into a creative, loving Adult and this would not happen if Wigapom didn't behave like one. He didn't want to squash Will's spontaneity or sense of fun, because life without those two characteristics would be a very boring one indeed, but he needed to help him channel this positively; he felt he needed to become his conscience, and thus help them both develop greater awareness and maturity, and above all self-love.

Wigapom remembered asking Aldebaran about unconditional love, which was one of the things needed to restore the True Magic, or hidden wisdom.

'What do you mean by unconditional love, Aldebaran?' Wigapom had asked.

'Accepting and loving another person just as they are, Wigapom. Without trying to change them, or judge them in any way.'

'But supposing that you don't like what they do?' Will had said.

'Not liking someone's behaviour doesn't mean that you can't accept the person: a person is not the behaviour they show – that's just the result of how they feel they have to act in those circumstances. Don't judge a book by its cover: in other words, look past what you first see, to what's inside. Then you can acknowledge everyone's individual specialness and treat that specialness as though it was part of your own self. That leads to everyone valuing each other as part of themselves.'

'It would be wonderful to be able to be like that,' said Wigapom, 'but it would prove hard to do. It was hard to do with Will at first, and of course, me!'

'Practice makes perfect though, eh Wiggy!' Will had said with a cheeky smile. Wigapom had not fully taken Aldebaran's words to heart then but now they flooded back. If Wigapom had learnt anything from this experience it was that he had to be responsible for his thoughts and actions, and to help Will do the same: then Will in turn would help him: they needed to blend their talents and work together. To really be One.

He looked about him. He was outside the farmyard now, standing on a wide path choked with dead, brown weeds. This led to a large, unfinished house, built in two separate sections on either side of the pathway, as though the builder had lost heart part way through its construction and just given up trying to connect the two halves. The more complete part, despite being very run down, looked occupied, but the other part was a mere shell, standing precariously, with no roof, and weeds running amok amongst its unfinished walls.

Wigapom would not have been surprised if it were yet another figment of his imagination as such strange things had occurred since the Shivastrom blew them away that he felt anything was possible. He reflected that he could be in a virtual reality world where everything was just a thought or a dream; but who would want to create this strange place? He felt instinctively there had to be a reason why they had landed here: somehow this place would help them get back on the right path to continue the Quest. He was ready to do this now.

He was closer to the finished part of the house, but was still keeping under cover, just in case. He could see how uncared for it was; the peeling paint, the broken window latches, the cracked and shattered glass. It was a sad place, for sure, and Wigapom felt sorry for it, and any inhabitants.

He was edging forward through the bushes, crouching down in silence, when he saw a female figure coming out of a side door into the neglected garden. Maybe she could help them. She was acting very bizarrely, wringing her hands in despair and pacing backwards and forwards, looking both angry and distressed in equal measure. A few moments later someone else appeared, this time from the front door – an unkempt man with stubble round his chin and clothes in disarray. He too looked agitated and began to argue with the woman in a loud and forceful voice, although Wigapom couldn't understand what they were saying. They were clearly both very angry and unhappy, but quite what had caused these feelings was not evident. Wigapom's curiosity got the better of him and he edged even closer. As he did so another man came from round the side of the more finished part of the house, similarly dishevelled and angry looking with a pitchfork in his hand, and he too began to complain loudly to both the man and woman. The woman shouted back then began to cry in deep heart-wrenching sobs.

At that moment a young girl came running from the back of the less-finished building, followed by a scruffy dog yapping at her heels. The girl looked scared at the shouting and the crying; the woman began to admonish them both very loudly through her own tears; the girl began to cry; the dog began to bark; and the noise created a huge wall of sound that separated them even more from the unfinished part of the house: the distress, anger and fear of each one was disturbing to witness.

Strangely, Wigapom did not feel scared for himself, but his heart filled with compassion for them. He could see they needed help and he wondered if there was anything he could do. Suddenly there was a loud sound from inside the house, as though someone was smashing crockery, and a large china plate whizzed through a broken window, over the pathway and landed as rubble on the unfinished part of the house. The woman threw her hands up in horror at the sound but continued pacing back and forth in a disturbed way; the young girl continued to look fearful and lost, and the men were still agitated and argumentative, but no one made any attempt to do anything constructive about what was going on inside the house. More plates and cups, and even saucepans, were winging their way through the broken window and littering the unfinished building – it was a place in chaos.

Wigapom was drawn to these people's plight: they looked like ordinary folk, just like him, yet they were so disordered and unhappy. He knew what unhappiness was like and could empathise with their despair and distress, even though he had no idea of the cause, but he had never seen people quite so traumatised or so unable, or unwilling perhaps, to change their situation. He felt the urge to help them in someway, although he recognised he still needed to be cautious and he kept being reminded of what a state he was still in himself from the frequent putrid whiffs of the pigswill streaking and now hardening on his clothes and skin: he would not be a very popular visitor like this. However, he edged closer to hear the words being spoken. He managed to hear enough to get an idea of the problem.

'How could the Master just abandon us like this? Leaving our house in such a state?' cried the woman wringing her hands.

'We can't fix it on our own. We need his help to save us,' moaned the first dishevelled madman.

'Save us, save us!' echoed the young girl.

'This part will crumble if he doesn't complete the other!' cried the man with the pitchfork.

'It'll collapse! The whole building will collapse on top of us!' shouted the woman again.

And so it continued. The same cries, by the same people, but no resolution, no change in behaviour, no ability to work things out for themselves. Wigapom's brain was whirring – so their Master had abandoned them and the incomplete building, and now it was threatening to collapse around them! Who was their Master? Where was he? Why had he abandoned them? And why were they so unable to organise themselves properly without him being there? These questions tumbled into Wigapom's mind, but one thing was clear: they were like children without a parent to show them what to do. It reminded Wigapom of his own childish behaviour with Will; they hadn't been unhappy, but their actions had brought about a similar state of chaos – he was sure this was why they were in this mess now, literally! Perhaps if he helped them, he could put to right his own mistakes? Perhaps that was why they were here?

He found himself connecting telepathically to Will and having a dialogue with himself in his head.

'What do I do? Leave these people alone to get on with their disordered and argumentative lives? Or see if I can help in some way?'

'It would be good to help if we can and they might be able to help us find our way back to Lampadia, and Fynn,' came back the reply.

'And if I don't ask them for help, who else might there be? I have to use the opportunities that present themselves and, anyway, I feel we are meant to help them.'

'But how?' said the voice of Will in his head.

'I have no idea!'

'That's a tricky one then!'

'I know, but something will turn up.'

'Supposing they ask questions about us? What then?'

'They're already in such a state I don't think they would. Anyway, we can always make something up.'

'It will have to be a pretty good story to explain why we smell as bad as we do!'

Wigapom looked down at himself. Even these distressed folk might wonder about the smell that was travelling with him at present! He and Will would have to clean up a bit. They needed some other clothes.

As if in answer to his thought, a pile of old clothes, thrown from another window flew, like kites on a breeze. They landed very close to him.

'Now that's what I call luck!' he thought.

'Aldebaran would call it synchronicity,' came Will's reply.

'And he'd probably be right: he does have a habit of being right about most things!'

Wigapom dragged the clothes towards him.

'Right. Time to clean up. I'm on my way back.'

'OK...'

Wigapom yawned: he was feeling pretty tired all of a sudden. Not surprising really, considering all that had happened. Anyone would be tired. It was amazing he was still awake! Holding the clothes away from his smelly body he began to retrace his footsteps carefully back through the bushes, slinking into the farmyard under the cover of the buildings, as before. He was still yawning as he made his way into the makeshift barn, where he had told Will to hide. There was no sign of him. Wigapom tried to make connection telepathically again but there was nothing – his mental screen was totally blank.

'Will? Where are you?' he hissed under his breath, not wanting to make too much noise. 'Will? Answer me!' He called. No response. Wigapom stifled yet another yawn and, as he did so, heard, coming from the inside of the broken cart, a soft snore. Will! Of course! He was tired too and had already fallen asleep!

Wigapom clambered up on the cart via the only unbroken wheel and there was Will, dirty, but almost angelic-looking, fast asleep on top of a pile of old straw. Relief flooded over Wigapom: no wonder his telepathic screen had gone blank – Will was out for the count!

Leaving Will to sleep a little longer, he peeled off his own slurry-hardened clothes and rubbed himself clean as best he could with some of the straw that lay in the cart. Then he dressed himself in a shirt and trousers, remembering first to place the orange and yellow rune stones in his new pocket. It was so lucky he had not lost them in the sea. Seeing them again brought up further feelings of guilt that he had wasted so much time in setting out to find the other five, but it was no good living with regret about the past – he had to forgive himself and make amends now; Aldebaran had said the stones would find him when he proved himself ready to receive them – well, perhaps he could make a start today.

He heard a sound from Will, beginning to stir from his sleep. The more Will had slumbered the more refreshed and awake Wigapom felt: as though one was sleeping for both of them. There were certainly some advantages to having his other self living a separate physical life!

Will stretched out and looked at Wigapom, a big smile spreading across his face. Wigapom smiled back.

'Come on lazybones! Time to get up and dressed in your best,' he said to Will, holding out a shirt and trousers. 'We have a house to complete and runes to find!'

CHAPTER 23

The Master's House

*"The human race is challenged more than ever before to
demonstrate our mastery – not over nature but of ourselves."*
Rachel Carson

They decided it was best to tell the truth as much as possible, but keep it simple: they would pretend to be lost – well they were, of course, so it wouldn't take much pretence! They would start by asking for directions back to Lampadia and see what happened.

They walked more boldly than they felt up the weed-choked path towards the unfinished house, but by now the garden was deserted, and all was quiet. Wigapom assumed the residents had all gone back inside the occupied part of the house. He noticed as they got closer to that part of the house that it appeared an archway, or bridge, had been intended to join the two parts together, but this was being shored up by some very unsteady scaffolding at the moment. It was a miracle the house was still standing!

Wigapom and Will stood by the large front door and knocked loudly. The door shook, the house groaned and creaked under the force of their knocks, and several large pieces of plaster fell from the walls, narrowly missing them both. They jumped at the sound, knees knocking together with shock. Just then the door creaked open on one hinge to reveal the grubby, tear-stained face of the young girl, followed closely by the scruffy dog and a large litter of puppies, who all sniffed and jumped hungrily around their legs.

'Yes?' said the girl, making no attempt to check the dogs, all of whom seemed particularly interested in sniffing their clothes.

'We… seem to have lost our way – can you direct us back to Lampadia town please?' replied Wigapom in his most pleasant voice.

'No, I can't,' said the girl, with no emotion in her voice at all.

'Oh,' said Wigapom, taken aback at the abruptness of her answer, 'Well, is there someone else who could?'

'No,' said the girl again, looking blankly at them.

'No one at all?' said Wigapom, knowing there were at least four other people inside.

'There's the Master,' said the girl unexpectedly, 'He's upstairs. You'd better come in.'

This was something Wigapom had not expected. He had assumed that the Master was not there from what he had heard before, and now he was being told he was upstairs!

'Who is it Martha?' screeched a voice from behind a partially closed door.

'Dunno,' came back the disinterested reply from the girl, as she wiped her nose on her sleeve.

Suddenly the door was flung fully open, revealing the most untidy and chaotic room Wigapom had ever seen, with objects of every description piled high on top of each other, some teetering on the edge of collapse and some already crashing to the floor. The woman, whom Wigapom recognised as previously pacing, now stepped through the door, or rather over the fallen piles, wielding a large, carving knife.

'And who have we here?' she cried in an angry voice, her hair in knotted strands whipping across her face as she moved. Wigapom and Will had to use every bit of their courage to stand their ground and not run; she was quite a fearsome creature with her wild hair, staring eyes and very sharp knife!

'Someone to see the Master,' said the girl sullenly. The woman screeched her reply in a voice that may well have contributed to a pane of glass shattering in the hallway.

'The Master can't see any one, not even us! So he won't see you!' she said, peering at Wigapom with those dark, scary eyes whilst jabbing the knife towards him, rather too close for his comfort.

'I see,' said Wigapom gulping and doing his best not to register any fear or concern, yet unsure what to say or do next, 'we'd better go then.'

'You can't go until you've seen the Master.'

'But you just told me he won't see anyone,' said Wigapom, also confused and wishing he had not started any of this in the first place.

'I said he *can't* see you, not that he won't. He's asleep. His eyes are shut tight and he can't see anyone!' The woman glowered at Wigapom and Will and just as suddenly burst into demonic-sounding sobs which racked her shoulders and led to her wiping the huge tears away with her grubby apron.

'We *want* him to wake up so he can tell us how to finish the house before it falls down around our ears, but he just keeps sleeping. He'd almost finished this half of the house and started the bridge, but then he fell asleep. All we can do is wait until he wakes up. Until then we suffer, every day we suffer! Oh what'll we do, what'll we do?'

There was such immediate and total despair and fear in her voice that Wigapom's heart went out to her, as before.

'I am sorry you're so distressed. Can't you wake him up?' he said, wondering at the same time why no one had done this before.

'Wake up the Master? We daren't! We don't know how to, or even if we should; supposing he doesn't want to be woken? Supposing we *can't* wake him?'

'Well, have you ever tried?' said Will.

'Never. We're too scared,' piped up the young girl.

'Who is your Master?" said Wigapom, deciding to see if he could help whilst wondering what sort of creature these people could possibly be so afraid of.

'How long has he been asleep?' added Will.

'He is Shakta, the Sleeping Dragon and has been asleep for always and ever,' said the woman, her eyes wide and glaring as she suddenly flung the knife to the ground, where it stuck into the floorboards, wobbling backwards and forwards where Wigapom's feet had been moments earlier. He had luckily seen it coming and jumped out of the way in time, tripping over several of the puppies, which were still yapping around them as he did so, and knocking into a shelf, causing a statue of a serpent-like dragon to come crashing to the ground from where it was precariously placed. The young girl and woman screamed as the pieces flew everywhere, but no one did anything about clearing it up: it was as though they were frightened to touch it.

The woman was crying again, wringing her hands and pacing back and forth along the hallway. The girl had moved away and was staring at the puppies with a deadpan look on her face, as though she didn't know what to do with them or herself. Into this melee stormed one of the two men; his hair as wild as his face.

'What are you doing? What are you doing? he yelled, and without waiting for an answer, took one look around the room before storming back from whence he came. What a desperate place!

As the dust and broken fragments from the statue settled around them Wigapom and Will began to think that this was the maddest, strangest and saddest household they had ever come across. Wigapom was also intrigued by it, and wanted to help. Will was especially fascinated by the idea of a sleeping dragon in the house. Whatever viewpoint they had, all thoughts of getting back to Lampadia were temporarily pushed to the back of their minds.

'Could there *be* such a thing as a sleeping dragon?' wondered Wigapom, aloud and somewhat incredulous.

'What do you know about such things?' challenged the woman, angry and defensive again, even through her tears.

'There *are* such things as dragons, Wiggy, we read about them in books!' said Will to Wigapom, and the little girl nodded her head in agreement.

'I remember, but... Well, anything's possible,' said Wigapom, 'I've learned that much – but what do you mean by always and ever?' he added. 'He must have been awake at some time.'

'I can't remember that far back!' said the woman, with an angry snort, tears now stopped and anger very much in their place as she stormed back through the door, slamming it behind her. The walls shook again and a lopsided picture, again of a coiled dragon, fell from the wall, glass and frame shattering to add to the air of chaos.

The girl, who had gone back to staring at the puppies looked up and spoke again.

'He really is a dragon and the longer he sleeps the bigger he gets; that makes it even scarier to think about waking him – so we don't. You can see him if you like. This way,' and the girl disappeared up the long staircase in front of them, picking her way gingerly over the broken glass, and fragments of statue as she did so, and, in the absence of anyone else being around to help, there was nothing for Will and Wigapom to do but follow her.

Once up the staircase the house seemed to take on dimensions of massive proportions: it had never looked this big from the outside and was quite cavernous.

She led them into an enormous room at the end of a very long, dark corridor. Thick, dusty drapes stretched across a tall, single window, blocking out all but a thin glimmer of light, and as Wigapom strained his eyes in the gloom he could see an equally enormous shape, swathed in a mass of heavy covers, virtually filling the otherwise empty room. As his eyes grew more accustomed to the darkness, he could just make out the rise and fall of whatever was under the covers, breathing rhythmically.

'This is the Master,' whispered the girl. 'When he wakes up you can ask him the way,' and before they knew what was happening, she scurried out of the room, closing the heavy door firmly behind her, as though afraid to be in the room with them any longer. The most disquieting thing was, they heard a key turn in the lock.

'Wait a minute!' began Wigapom, realising too late what had happened. But the door was firmly locked from the other side and the door would not budge.

'She's locked the door!' stated Wigapom in amazement at their sudden and unexpected imprisonment.

'This is a crazy house!' said Will, looking at the huge shape with awe, before turning to Wigapom. 'Why don't they just wake him up and stop him growing bigger?

'I don't know, Will, I really don't.'

'Is it *really* a dragon, do you think,' asked Will again, backing away to the corner of the room, 'and will he really be asleep – FOREVER?'

'I don't know that either, but they're scared of waking him, that's true enough,' replied Wigapom with real concern in his voice. 'Whatever it is under there, we seem to be stuck in here with it, and we can't get out!'

There was a long, heavy silence as both fully understood their predicament.

'We have to find out what it is, and wake him, don't we, if we want to get out of here?' said Will.

'Yes,' said Wigapom in a whisper, 'we do. Best keep your voice down though for the moment, while we look.'

Will understood the reason for that only too well, as Wigapom slowly and carefully began to lift a small corner of the cover nearest to him. Will held his breath. The creature sighed and shifted position under the bedclothes. Wigapom dropped them fast, with a gasp.

'It's a dragon, isn't it?' stated Will in a scared whisper.

'It might be. It's too dark to see clearly. And I don't want to risk touching him in case.'

'In case what?' asked Will.

'Well, in case he wakes up!' replied Wigapom, lamely, realising in that moment what the people of the house felt about disturbing this enormous creature. 'No one's ever tried before, but that doesn't mean he couldn't wake up. If the Master, or Shakta or Sleeping Dragon as they call him, has been asleep for so long, how would he feel about being woken up by us?'

'He might get angry, or violent,' said Will.

'Exactly! And anyway, is it our place to wake him?' questioned Wigapom.

'But if we don't wake him up then we might never get out of here!' replied Will, with a very clear grasp of the situation they were in.

Wigapom attempted to take another look at the slumbering occupant under the covers, but even peeking seemed risky, and the covers were pulled up so high he wouldn't have seen any features. The room was so dark anyway that it was difficult to see anything at all.

'Perhaps we could let some light in through the curtains,' he said and went to pull back the drapes from the window. He did so, but the window was boarded up with thick planks on the outside, making escape impossible, but there were enough chinks of light between the boards to see a little clearer. He could also see through the cracks that the window overlooked the scaffolding around the shored-up bridge and unfinished part of the house.

With the better light they gingerly approached the gently breathing shape again and lifted a different edge of the covers. This time the sight of a long, spiked and scaly tail wrapped around a huge coiled body assured them that, unless the Master had fallen asleep in fancy dress, there really was a dragon lying asleep under there! Will gulped; Wigapom felt the colour drain from his face. He dropped the cover quickly.

'It really is a dragon!' they whispered in unison.

Now they wanted to get out, fast; but they were stuck in the room with this increasingly large sleeping dragon, which had now started to snore in a rumbly sort of way that shook not only the bed covers but even the walls and floor of the room! Very carefully they lifted the cover again, as if needing to confirm what they had already seen. Yes: it really was a dragon, with silvery-white scales, reflecting pearlised colours of pale pinks and greens shimmering in the small amount of light in the room. Wigapom wasn't as scared now somehow and could only imagine how beautiful it would look with full daylight shining on it – quite dazzling! It was such a pity that it was slumbering in the dark! But they couldn't stay here for always and ever like the dragon: they would have to do something that had not been tried before.

'We've got to wake him up, got to take a chance,' whispered Wigapom, stating exactly what Will was thinking, 'We'll tell him that his servants need him awake, because they can't manage without him – surely it can't be that difficult? No Master, or dragon, however sleepy, would want to lose his home and his servants through his own slumber. He'd want to know if things were falling apart,' reasoned Wigapom, and things were certainly falling apart without the Master to guide them. Order and sanity were lost and the whole house, as well as its inhabitants, were in real risk of collapse!

'If you say so,' replied Will, standing behind Wigapom for protection, just in case.

'I do. Nothing ventured, nothing gained, as they say.'

Wigapom was resolved; they would wake the Master up no matter what it took or whatever outcome there might be. This was a Quest wasn't it – to bring the hidden wisdom of the True Magic back? Well, this was as good an opportunity to make a start as any, and an impressive one too, which he wouldn't fail in this time: it was a golden opportunity to make up for his stupid and selfish behaviour of recent days. They would release the dragon Master from his sleep state so that the dragon

Master could release his servants from their confusion and misery – it all sounded so simple when put like that – then he and Will could get out of the house and find their way back at last to continue the Quest in earnest.

'I think I'm a bit scared of dragons,' said Will. 'They breathe fire and do terrible things, don't they? Supposing this dragon does the same when we wake him?'

'We have to take that chance,' Wigapom said honestly. 'There's no way of knowing really, but not all dragons are bad, you know, Will. There are plenty of stories about good ones, you must remember some of them surely?'

Will racked his brain to find one and came up smiling.

'D'you mean stories about them being guardians of special treasure – treasure that helps people to be better than they were before?' he said.

'Yes,' encouraged Wigapom, 'the treasure they guard can transform people in powerful ways and bring sparkle back into their lives! These people certainly need that. We just have to hope that this dragon is one of that kind!'

'I don't see any treasure,' said Will, peering around the darkened room.

'Treasure's not always gold and jewels, Will, sometimes it's just seeing things in a different way, so that life can be happier.'

'You mean that happiness is often the hidden treasure waiting to be found?' said Will, beginning to understand.

'Exactly. But to find it, the dragon has to be woken first.'

'OK,' said Will, fingers crossed tightly behind his back, just in case, as if this would be any use against the huge creature under the bedclothes if he wasn't a friendly, happy dragon after all! 'You try first.'

'Here goes then,' said Wigapom, and he gently and then more firmly shook the sleeping dragon Master under the mound of clothes.

Nothing happened: the sleeping shape barely seemed to register the effort that Wigapom had used.

'Help me, Will. He's very big.'

So Will went to the other side of the sleeping mound and together they shook and rocked the dragon as best they could to try and rouse him. No response: not a flicker of wakefulness could be seen or felt – indeed the snoring increased! They were baffled but persistent. They carried on shaking and used their voices to shout, loudly, hoping to be heard above the snoring.

'Wake up, please, wake up – please wake up. WAKE UP, PLEASE!' they yelled.

But there was still no response: this dragon was a very heavy sleeper, and no mistake! They tried again, together, even more loudly, until their voices were hoarse and rasping with the effort.

'WAKE UP! PLEASE WAKE UP! WAKE UP!'

Still no response to this, by now, frantic activity.

They tried everything they could think of to wake the sleeping dragon, throwing all caution to the wind: they shouted, they yelled, they clapped, they shook him, they stamped on the floor around him, Will even clambered up onto him in desperation, jumping up and down on him, but nothing they did made any difference. The shape under the covers was as fast asleep as ever, and snoring even louder, and getting even bigger.

'This is really crazy!' said Will, in despair. 'What do we have to do to get him to wake up?'

'Not what we are doing, obviously,' said Wigapom, collapsing exhausted on the floor with the effort: he thought long and hard until something rose from the depths of his awareness, like a wisp of smoke from a previously dead fire. At first it was almost imperceptible – faint and unclear, a tickling sensation in the base of his spine, that quickly became stronger and clearer as it rose towards his head until he saw everything clearly and was amazed it hadn't come to him before: he sat up with renewed vigour.

'Perhaps *we* shouldn't be waking him up. Perhaps outsiders like us can never wake someone else's Master,' he said to Will as the idea finally dawned bright and bold. He got to his feet, more excited now.

'Perhaps the servants themselves have to wake him. They've never tried because they've always been too scared of him, but perhaps this is the only way to wake him.'

'How do we get them up here?' said Will, 'We're locked in!'

Wigapom had forgotten that momentarily, but he was so certain now that he had the answer, he knew a solution would be found.

'Try the door again, Will. I'm sure that it will open now, because I've found the key!'

'Where?' said Will, who had searched every inch of the room before with Wigapom and hadn't found anything remotely like a key.

'We don't need a real key, don't you see, Will?, we just need the proper solution and this is it! That's the key! Go on, try the door!'

Will did as he was told. He trusted Wigapom to make the right decisions even if he couldn't always understand them. He was only twelve still. He wasn't really surprised when he put his hand on the door handle to find the heavy door that previously had barred their exit now swung open with perfect ease!

'We could just leave now and not worry about waking the sleeping dragon,' he said, and grinned at his older self!

Wigapom grinned back.

'You know we aren't going to do that, don't you? This is not just about us, Will, it's about helping these poor people to be happy and fulfilled again.'

'I know that really, just testing!' said Will cheekily. They grinned at each other again.

'Run downstairs, Will and get as many of the servants up here as you can. It's time they woke their own Master before he grows too big and destroys them, and the house. We can't do it for them. They have to do it themselves. Hurry!'

Will sprang into action, racing along the corridor, down the staircase and into the hall as though he had wings on his feet. He found the young girl first, sitting forlornly on the bottom stair, still staring at the puppies, one of whom was on her lap, trying, but failing to get her proper attention.

'Quick!' said Will, excitedly, 'Come upstairs! Get everyone to come upstairs, right now,' and he was so authorative in his order that she did exactly as he asked without question, scooping up the puppy in her arms as she did so.

Soon all of the servants were following him. It had been easier than he thought to get them all upstairs – it seemed they wanted to take direction from someone who showed such confidence and self-belief, even if that someone was just a twelve-year-old boy! Will began to feel his own confidence growing inside: he suddenly felt taller, older, and more mature, and he began to like himself for the first time in his life!

Soon all of the inhabitants that Wigapom had seen earlier, plus an even larger assortment of maids, footmen, under footmen, cooks, gardeners, and handymen were crowded into the corridor outside the room, arguing with each other as to who would go in first. Wigapom had to shout to be heard above them.

'Quiet, all of you! Quiet! There is no need to be frightened, or angry anymore. I know how you can wake the Master up! In fact you have to, if you want to save yourselves and your home from destruction.'

'How?' asked the man with the pitchfork.

'It's simple! All you have to do is *ask* him, otherwise how does he know he's needed? Only *you* are powerful enough to do this: he won't hear anyone else but you,' enthused Wigapom, with authority.

The servants looked at him, some with amazement, some with excitement, but all of them with a light of something sparkly in their eyes that Wigapom had not seen previously; he thought it must be hope.

He encouraged them again.

'You surely don't want to carry on living in such disorder and disagreement do you? You're living half a life and it can only be full and complete when you take control and wake up your Master.' The servants looked excited and nodded their heads in agreement.

'Well, what are you waiting for? Wake him up!'

It was as though someone had turned the light out again.

'But what do we say?' said the young girl with the dog.

Wigapom opened his mouth as though to tell them. It would have been so easy to give them the answer, but he realised that they had to get used to making their own decisions, so he threw the question back to them.

'What do you think?' he said. For a moment there were blank looks and Wigapom grew concerned, but he still said nothing, just willed them to use their hearts and minds to find the answer.

'How about 'Please wake up, we need your help?" said the man. with the bedraggled clothes and pitchfork. The light in his eyes switched back on.

'That seems as good as anything,' said the hand-wringing woman from the kitchen as her face lit up too, and the others nodded enthusiastically. The space around them began to glow.

'We could all chant it together,' said another. More light. More agreement.

'We could even sing it,' laughed another, enthusiastically. Even more wonderful light!

Wigapom realised this was probably the first time they had ever agreed with each other on anything. He could feel the energy in the corridor lighten even more, as though a hundred thousand fairy lights were twinkling all around. A deep peace began to descend amongst them like the comforting wings of a dove. They smiled at each other in encouragement as, of the same accord, they stepped into the room close to the enormous covered shape of the dragon, and stood, quietly reverential, around it as though still a little unsure about breaking the habits of a lifetime. Then they all took a breath… then hesitated again, temporarily unsure of their power. The little girl spoke.

'Come on, everyone. We can do it!' she encouraged, stroking the puppy in her arms with real love and affection for the first time. Love and encouragement – this was just what they all needed.

Instinctively they held hands, forming a huge unbroken circle around the bed and began to speak their mantra of 'Please wake up,' in unison, tentatively at first then stronger and more determined, before finally raising their voices in glorious song and singing out in perfect harmony. It was a truly magical moment, and sounded wonderful! Wigapom was sure it was the first time they had ever done anything together for a common cause.

There was such strength and beauty in their joined voices; such power in the sound, such depth of meaning, intention and purpose in the confident request to the dragon Master to finally wake up and, most importantly, such love between each of them – and it was working – the shape under the covers moved position and began to uncoil. The servants gasped: this had never happened before! They continued singing, the sound rich and joyous. It rose to the roof top like music from an angelic choir, spreading out around the room and the whole house until cracks that had been in the walls started to close up, the broken glass began to mend and the old drapes and boarding fell from the windows, letting in the full light of the day. The house was restoring itself through the harmonic sound of their raised voices and the covers over the dragon fell away, revealing him in all his opalescent glory. The iridescent pearl colours shone just as Wigapom imagined they would.

A deep and happy sigh came from the dragon as he stretched out, as though pleased to be finally waking. His huge eyelids flickered. The singing continued, stronger and more beautiful than ever, and the dragon opened his eyes completely – big, bold, yet gentle eyes – and looked around at the gathered group. The servants stopped singing although the vibration of their sound resonated for a while on the air until at last a deep hush finally fell around the room. The dragon yawned, breaking the expectant silence, and instead of fire from his mouth, a bright and sparkling pink stream of energy emerged like clouds of vapourised candy floss, swirling around and inside everyone present, even Wigapom and Will, filling their hearts and minds with light and loving thoughts until all were smiling with sheer joy, including the dragon.

'Now that's better,' he said, in a rich, smooth voice, like warm honey. 'Thank you for waking me. I never thought you'd ask,' and he began to get smaller as he spoke. 'So you want my help do you? How nice, after all this time. I will see what I can do. No doubt we can help each other.'

The dragon was changing: not only in size, but his tail was also disappearing, his face was shortening, and the pearl scales were dropping from his body where they dissolved into dazzling light! He was transforming before their eyes into a kindly, venerable sage with sparkling eyes that danced with love and laughter!

'I know who you are!' cried the dishevelled woman, who was now looking quite radiant and happy.

'And I know you too, Serena,' said the man with the dancing eyes, 'I know you all. It's so good to be home.'

Wigapom looked around at all the faces: every one of the servants now looked so different; happier, kinder, alive, more loving and peaceful, each with an inner radiance that shone like sunlight dancing on water. The servants broke into a cheer that brought every blade of grass, every bush and tree in the garden, every flower outside, springing back into bright green and pink abundant life, and he couldn't help but smile as his own heart glowed with warmth.

The Master rose to his feet, tall and strong and ageless. Wigapom and Will felt increasingly buoyant that they had been able to help in this amazing transformation. It was real heart therapy!

'It's all thanks to these two,' said the little girl, indicating Wigapom and Will, her eyes bright and happy.

'We were pleased to help,' said Wigapom. 'It's truly heart-warming to see everyone so happy, but perhaps you can help us too? We have strayed away from home somehow and got very lost. Can you tell us the way back?'

The Master looked at Wigapom and Will with considerate, kindly eyes, but to their dismay he shook his head.

'I am afraid not. I am the Master of *this* house, and this house only. It is not in my power to help you find your way home, however much I might wish to. In the same way that my servants had to wake me, so you have to wake your own Master, and seek his help to put you on the right path.'

'I didn't know we had a Master too,' said Wigapom simply.

'Not many do, and even when they know, they do not always call on him, like my servants here, and remain in their lower state when they could be embracing their higher, but everyone has a Master, who is waiting to be called upon; call on yours and he will serve you for your own Highest Good.'

'How do we know where to find him?' said Will.

'He is always with you, just waiting for you to wake him.'

'He is with us now?' asked Wigapom, looking around, as though expecting to see him walk through the door.

'Of course. He is inside you. But don't take my word for it. Find out for yourself. Call on him. Please excuse us all now. We have much to talk about and do after such a long sleep.'

The Master began to move out of the room with his household as the young girl stepped forward to Wigapom and Will.

'Thank you for helping us,' she said kindly. 'We would never have known what to do if you hadn't shown us.'

'It was nothing really,' answered Wigapom, brushing aside the compliment as though embarrassed that it was given, 'and you did know what to do – you just chose not to do it for a very long time, that's all, but that's OK; we have to do things when the time is right for us and I guess now was the right time! We just helped you see that, and I'm glad to have done it.'

'Maybe someone will do the same for you,' she said, smiling sweetly as she began to follow the others out of the room. Suddenly she ran back.

'Ooops, I nearly forgot. I found this in the garden earlier and didn't know what to do with it, but I want you to have it now, as a thank you for being so kind and compassionate to us all,' and she pressed something small and hard into Wigapom's hand before catching the others up. Wigapom and Will were left alone. This time the door was not locked on them but left wide open.

Wigapom looked down at his hand to find a heart-shaped green stone, etched with familiar patterns in his palm. It was warm, vibrating like a strong heartbeat.

'We've got another stone,' he said.

'I rather thought we might,' Will beamed, looking quite grown up suddenly. 'After you, Mr Sawyer,' he said, using their old surname.

'No, after *you*, Mr Sawyer,' laughed Wigapom.

So they walked through the door together and down the corridor, which was now full of light, towards the staircase; the puppies were playing peacefully at the foot of the stairs, the picture was back on the wall, the dragon statue in pride of place on the shelf, and there was happy singing coming from the kitchen – all was spotless, loved and cared for and the whole place radiated love.

As they stepped out into the sunshine of a beautiful day they walked into the now luxuriant gardens, full of beautiful green trees and bright pink flowers. The house was complete and connected now by the bridge, the paintwork bright and shiny, the windows sparkling in the sunlight. It seemed that waking up the dragon Master had worked wonders on everything.

'Oh, this is a beautiful place!' cried Will.

'It certainly is,' agreed Wigapom, 'and I think we've just helped construct that bridge that Aldebaran talked about when we first arrived in Lampadia. It wasn't hard at all, in the end, just like he said.'

For a moment everything hung suspended in pure light: there was such a sense of love and peace, forgiveness and compassion, harmony and balance everywhere, which they both breathed deep into their chests. As they did so, the gardens, house and all of its inhabitants and contents began to dissolve into sparkling sunbeams and in their place was, instead, a lush green meadow of sweet smelling grass and summer flowers waving in the gentle breeze, as though inviting them to walk into a new reality. Somehow this all seemed perfectly normal, as if disappearing houses, people and gardens were a common occurrence!

'Well, that had a happy ending,' said Will with a smile. 'I like happy endings!'

'Me too,' agreed Wigapom, 'Let's hope we can make one for ourselves.'

'Can I see the stone she gave you?' asked Will, curious to see it again.

Wigapom became aware of the heart-shaped stone pulsating in his hand and opened out his palm. There it was, a brilliant green stone with etched markings on the surface. If there had ever been a tinge of doubt over the reality of what had just happened, here at least was tangible proof.

'I wonder what it says?' said Wigapom.

They could look at it properly now: it was a beautiful colour, a rich vibrant green with flashes of sparkling soft pink when the sunlight caught it. He felt a warm feeling deep in his heart and a smile spread across his face without him being able to stop it, even if he had wanted to. He held it out for Will to see and as he did so felt the familiar vibrations in the other two stones he carried with him.

'The other two seem excited to have a new mate,' he laughed. 'I've got another rune stone without even looking for it,' he mused, 'they've all come to me like that, just as Aldebaran said they would. They find me when I'm ready. I wonder why this one came when it did?'

'Perhaps because we were kind and helped those people, and the Master? We helped them lose their fear of the dragon so they could wake him and put love and happiness back in their lives,' said Will.

'You're right Will, and d'you know, you sound older than twelve,' Wigapom said in surprise, looking at his child self with new eyes, 'In fact you even *look* older than twelve – more like fifteen – goodness, there's stubble appearing on your chin – how did that happen?'

'Perhaps the dragon Master transformed me,' said Will, stroking the soft stubble around his chin thoughtfully.

'Umm, well I said some dragons had good energy didn't I. But I think you've done it yourself, or rather we have, together. Whoever is responsible seems to have transformed the time of year too – look at the flowers, it's more like mid-June now and was barely May when we were swept up into the Shivastrom. We seem to have been lifted forward in time, as though things are speeding up. I hope Fynn and Aldebaran haven't forgotten about us.'

'Course they haven't,' snorted Will, in derision, 'this is us we're talking about – or rather you. We might be one and the same, but it's you who is receiving the stones, not me.'

'Well, maybe one day you'll get a chance to receive one. We are the same person after all, so strictly speaking you could. Anyway, enough of such future speculation. We must translate the inscription on this one first

– that will help us understand more, surely. But first we've got to get back to Lampadia and make things right again with Fynn and Aldebaran. We've had our problems, Will, but we have learnt from them and turned them into opportunities, like Aldebaran said we could. And real good has come out of this experience, because we have another rune stone. Only four more to earn now, and *The Book of True Magic* to find, of course, and then we can release the magic and restore the hidden wisdom once more!'

'You're forgetting, we still don't know where we are, or how to get back home, or indeed what is real and what is not,' replied Will, sounding quite adult in his assessment of the current situation.

'Ummm,' said Wigapom again, this time in deep thought.

'So… what are we going to do?' prompted Will, more urgently.

'Pardon?' Wigapom began absent-mindedly. 'Oh! What are we going to do, did you say? What they told us I suppose: find our own Master to get us home.'

'But how…?' began Will, slipping back once more into adolescent confusion.

'For someone who is growing up fast you don't always pick things up that quickly,' teased Wigapom, affectionately. 'Didn't you hear what the Master said, Will? *Our* Master is inside us, waiting to be awakened; that means we have all the answers inside already, we just need to know how to get at them.'

'Course I heard him, and you too – we know how to get home already, is what you mean,' replied Will, determined that Wigapom saw that he really did have a full grasp of the situation.

'Exactly,' replied Wigapom, pleased with his other self.

'I guess we just have to trust that whatever needs to happen, will happen,' continued Will, with a sudden leap of maturity again.

'Well said, Will,' replied Wigapom, looking closely at his maturing other self. Will *was* older and taller, and his voice lower since leaving the Master's house and that took some getting used to: but he was still Will and Wigapom realised with a rush of warm, heart-felt emotion, that he really liked him, in fact he felt he loved him; he loved his own Self – what a rich sensation this was!

'Come on, Will, let's go. Somehow I think we'll get on the right road to take us just where we need to be,' smiled Wigapom, confidently setting out across the meadow.

Will again put his trust in Wigapom and followed him, continuing to grow into his own Adult Self.

Part

5

Self-Expression

"Speak your truth and know yourself."
Anonymous

CHAPTER 24

The Way Forward

"I took the road less traveled by, and that has made all the difference."
Robert Frost

Darqu'on stood still and erect in the shadows, just a faint glow from the black stone on his finger casting an eerie light onto his face that otherwise remained hidden from view, even from the repulsive reptile, who was again back at his side. The silence was heavy with thought until Darqu'on spoke at last – was there a hint of concern in his voice, thought Scabtail?

'The Brat has crossed the bridge, Scabtail, between the lower self and the higher. I didn't think he would get that far: and he has *another* stone. He is proving to be more worthy of note than I thought. He has strong friends, too, who support him, and much as I am loathe to say it, he has held himself well against his younger self, forming a far too positive relationship with him in spite of all I threw at him: none of which I anticipated. Things are not going to plan.'

'He will tire of him, Sire, eventually,' hissed Scabtail in his slithery, slimy voice, which matched the way he slithered and slid around Darqu'on's feet.

'I am not so sure of that, Scabtail. They've created a strong bond between them, which is dangerous, as he is now doubly strengthened inside. Look how they both survived the emotional energy of the Shivastrom with a fortitude and resilience that I had not expected either of them to exhibit; and how he helped those fools find their Master in the house. And look at The Squirt's growing maturity. If I am to weaken him, I must have those stones: the more he receives of them, the more of an opponent he becomes – they are more important to his personal growth and awareness than I first estimated. If I didn't hate him so much, I could almost respect him, and that thought makes me hate him even more! But he will not win in the end. He cannot. I am more powerful than he... And I shall enjoy killing him, even more than I thought...' announced Darqu'on as the venom shot back into his voice.

'Kill him! Yes Sire!' echoed Scabtail, his wide mouth filling with globules of saliva at the thought. Darqu'on did not hear him, lost in his own musings.

'… And now he looks as though he is on his way to finding the greatest part of himself, that few ever come to know, or are even aware of. No doubt he will wish to use it for the highest good, rather than the maximum gain. Misguided boy. I thought like that once, until I saw the light… Or perhaps I should say the dark!' And his thin lips split into what might have been a smile, had it not resembled a jagged wound, whilst his macabre laugh echoed hollowly around the room, making even Scabtail shudder.

'But still…' Darqu'on continued, 'such mastery in one so young…'

'He is their son…' said Scabtail, by way of explanation, realising too late he had said the wrong thing again and his voice trailed away as a look of pure hatred infused Darqu'on's jet black eyes.

'I need no reminding of that, you diabolical creature,' hissed Darqu'on, holding his body rigid. Scabtail held his breath, wishing he had first held his tongue, knowing that times like these often indicated unpredictable moods, and eventual punishment, for which he was always the fall guy: his scarred tail quivered in fear, but Darqu'on somehow maintained control, his voice coming back to cold precision. Scabtail breathed again.

'Yes, Scabtail, I must give him more credit, as well as find more to challenge him, more to hurt him – not enough to destroy him yet, you understand, just enough to enjoy the chase even more. I am not yet ready to dispose of this source of my entertainment!'

Scabtail looked disappointed, but nodded his scaly head in affirmation, whilst secretly wondering, for the first time, if Darqu'on was less in control than he assumed: but he wouldn't dream of letting this slip out! He valued his tail too much!

'Excellent choice, Master, as always,' he said instead, slithering backwards into a corner, hoping to be forgotten for a while, just in case circumstances changed for the worse.

Darqu'on turned away from the mirror and in the half-light his shadow fell against the wall, towering over the room and all in it. Scabtail felt his tail shake with a further frisson of fear at the presence of his Master and waited for instructions that he knew would come. He did not have to wait long.

'Prepare the troops to march today Scabtail – I must go out amongst my people. I've been distant from them for far too long. It's time they felt again the power of my… embrace and the strength of my … concern. Let's see how he fares amongst my dark forces. Today, Scabtail, *this* Master is claiming his own!'

Wigapom and Will had been walking for some time along a track that wound its stony way through fields, woods, and moorland and then into fields again. It seemed an endless, curving pathway, along which they had both stumbled from time to time before picking themselves up and continuing – ignoring the fact they kept seeing familiar landmarks repeated along the way. Will had put so much faith in Wigapom that he had expected the friendly faces of Fynn, Aldebaran or even Cassie to be waiting around every bend. But he was continually disappointed and became increasingly tired and disillusioned. When he tripped once more and cut his knee on a familiar jagged stone that he had tripped over an hour ago, he could take no more.

'Ouch! Look at my knee, Wiggy! That's it! I can't go any further. We're not going anywhere – just round in circles! This path doesn't lead anywhere except back to where it began! My knee hurts, I want to rest, I want something to eat and drink and a comfortable bed. I want to stop *everything*!' and with that tirade vibrating around the hillside, he flung himself angrily to the ground, refusing to go any further. Wigapom knelt by his side, pulling off a fresh, comfrey leaf from beside the pathway and holding it tightly against the wound, as Sarah used to do back in Brackendor, trying to soothe him as well as stop the blood flowing from the cut knee. The herbal remedy worked but he was still as disillusioned as Will.

'I'm sorry Will – I'm leading you a merry dance. I thought I knew where we were going, but I don't. I don't know what to do. I'm sorry. I'm so sorry.'

It did indeed seem that they were going round in circles – but how to stop it? There was no other pathway but this one.

Will wiped the angry tears from his eyes and looked at Wigapom, with kind understanding.

'It's not your fault, Wigapom. I'm just hurting and tired. You're doing your best.'

'My best is not good enough though, is it?' replied Wigapom dismally. 'I thought we'd have no problems finding the way – finding our own Master – but it and he seem more elusive than ever.' Wigapom's shoulders sagged as though he had the weight of the whole world on them. It was now Will's turn to show compassion. He lightly touched Wigapom's arm.

'Don't let this get you down. Remember what you told me – the answers are out there, we just have to find them.'

'If we know the right questions to ask, that is,' said Wigapom dejectedly.

'We must do!' said Will. 'Here, look, my knee has stopped bleeding:

you sorted that out, so we can sort this out. Come on,' he said, jumping to his feet, the painful cut knee a thing of the past, 'think: how can we find our way back?'

'That's just it!' cried Wigapom, 'I don't know!' He was exasperated that Will didn't seem to understand the gravity of the situation, but Will understood more than Wigapom at that moment and wanted Wigapom to understand too, without any help from him. He prompted him again.

'YES, but how *could* we get back, if we didn't follow this path?'

'What a stupid question!' said Wigapom, exasperated even more, 'If I knew that I wouldn't be sitting here now!'

Will sighed. Now *he* felt the older of the two, having to wait for Wigapom to catch up. He had been inspired by a new and illuminating thought which to him seemed to make total sense and was amazed that Wigapom could not see it himself. It seemed to indicate that, somehow, they were becoming separate people. He began to explain it very slowly, as one would to a child. He did not see the irony of this at the time!

'We could leave this path and make one of our own and see where that takes us – we could make our *own* decisions about our journey rather than follow a path that someone else has set out. Don't you see Wigapom, it has to be our decision – *our* path! Not an old one. We've done that before and it's got us nowhere. We have to be creative, Wigapom, take control and make our own pathway!'

Wigapom suddenly looked as though a light had switched itself on in his own head.

'Make our own path? Of course! How brilliant you are, Will! You're absolutely right! We have to create our *own* way forward – one that's unique to us! Brilliant Will! Absolutely brilliant! We have to trust in *ourselves*, not others! Why didn't I see that myself?'

'You probably did, if I did, only you refused to recognise it,' explained Will, kindly making excuses.

'Jeepers, it's great to have a brain like yours and mine!' laughed Wigapom again, all stress disappeared. 'Come on, brainbox – which way shall we choose to make our own path?'

They looked about them. To their left, it was overgrown and prickly, shaded by dark trees that looked uninviting. But to their right, there was a green valley with glancing beams of sunlight dancing over the grass, as if inviting them forward. The decision was easy.

'This way, don't you think?' said Will, pointing to the right.

'You took the words right out of my mouth!' replied Wigapom, with a smile, as they began to walk purposefully towards the valley, making a smooth new pathway through the rippling grass as they did so.

Skye, Aldebaran and Fynn were looking intently at the flickering Astrolabius. It had suddenly sprung back into some sort of life again after several weeks of total inactivity, which had created a personally difficult time for Fynn, who on the one hand felt he was never going to see his dear friend Wigapom again, or be able to forgive himself, or make amends for what he had done, and on the other, one in which he had been enjoying a strange on-off sort of relationship with Skye, when sometimes they could be really close and other times when they fought like cat and dog. The thing was, he liked her. In a special way. In fact he knew he was growing to love her, but didn't know how to tell her. She in her turn was growing to love him, but was annoyed when he wouldn't express how he felt towards her. With neither of them able to be honest with each other they had a seesaw of a relationship that was proving difficult and stressful at times.

Undoubtedly some of it was to do with the tension over the non-appearance of Wigapom and Will. The uncertainty of where they were or what they were doing, or even if they were still alive, was a strain on them all. Neither was the news good that Darqu'on was going on the march again. Reports from other resistance members had confirmed their previous fears that he would head towards Dragonmound. Fynn knew it was where Wigapom's father had been killed and it was not far from Oakendale, where the tunnels ran, but did not yet know the extent of its true importance. But as the Astrolabius crackled into life once more they all experienced the relief of seeing Wigapom and Will appear again, and Darqu'on's proximity, and the significance of his destination was temporarily put to one side.

'At last! Where on earth have they been all these weeks?' Fynn said with a mix of relief and irritation, as the two familiar and welcome figures appeared once more on the walls of the Story Chamber.

'Who knows,' said Skye, 'but I think I know where they are now – or at least where they might be heading.'

'Yes, I'm afraid I do too,' said Aldebaran, 'they're near Dragonmound.'

'Dragonmound?' said Fynn, 'but you said that was where Darqu'on and his army were heading.'

'Exactly,' replied Aldebaran solemnly, 'they seem to be on a collision course with them!'

'What! Then we must go and get them,' said Fynn, in concern, 'and bring them home!'

'Not so fast, Fynn,' cautioned Aldebaran, 'Dragonmound is a strange place with a long history of enchantments, both good and bad; remember it was here that Wigapom's father lost his life, at Darqu'on's hand. Darqu'on will likely want to make that a double killing, of father and son; to create even more negative energy. It's likely that he already knows Wigapom is heading that way, but if not, and we draw additional attention to the place by our presence, it could be even more dangerous for them, as well as us, not to mention the villagers who live in Oakendale.'

'But ...' began Fynn, unable to accept this reasoning.

'Father's right,' said Skye, 'you can't just go barging in like a knight in shining armour to save them you know – anyway, perhaps it's up to them to save themselves in this situation.'

'What do you mean?' said Fynn, amazed that no one was prepared to help Wigapom and Will this time, now they had finally appeared again. 'We saved them last time.'

'Then you were partly responsible; now you are not. They don't need help from us,' retorted Skye, 'they have to do this themselves.'

'But that's crazy!' argued Fynn. 'They're walking straight into the path of Darqu'on – we know it, they don't, and yet you say we mustn't help them – where's the sense in that?'

'It's destiny,' stated Aldebaran, 'it's unwise to interfere with that.'

'Destiny? His destiny?' cried Fynn, passionately. 'His destiny was supposed to be returning the True Magic, but if we don't help him now his destiny, as you call it, will be destruction at the hands of Darqu'on and his gathering thousands. And what happens about the future of us all then, and especially the True Magic, I ask? Lost forever, that's what. You might be prepared to let that happen but *I'm* not. I prefer the idea of choice, and I choose to not sit by. Wigapom is my friend, and he needs my help, our help. He can't be expected to do this alone. Anyway, my destiny and his are entwined together – ever since I chose to come with him on this Quest. He and I are One. All for one and one for all. Just like we used to read in the stories as children. – and you, Aldebaran tell us that we are all One! Well, that's a pretty good reason for us to all stick together in my opinion! Then we have combined strength and they at least have a fighting chance of survival. Don't forget, Wiggy has to survive. He has to gain the stones and find *The Book of True Magic*. Help me to help him and that can happen.'

Aldebaran was nodding his head.

'An impassioned speech, Fynn, and I do not doubt your sincerity and your sense of kinship, but Dragonmound is a place of great energy and what will happen there may already be written. If that is the case it will happen, with or without our help. However, as you show so much love and care for your friend we will go to Dragonmound. If we are called upon to help we will, or else just bear witness to what is destined.'

Fynn was not sure that this was exactly what he wanted, but at least it meant they would not abandon Wigapom completely. That would have to be enough for the moment.

'We can use the tunnels to take us to Oakendale, and seek the assistance of the underground resistance there. Darqu'on will not see us approaching if we take that route,' said Fynn.

'Indeed,' agreed Aldebaran, 'and in truth, it will be good to be active once more, after much watching and waiting. But you must understand, Fynn, that our involvement could lead to more danger than it seeks to solve.'

'We'll just have to take a chance on that,' said Fynn, glad at least he had the support of Aldebaran at last. 'What about you, Skye? Will you help?'

Skye looked at Fynn in the way that Fynn had been finding so pleasantly disconcerting over these last few weeks. But he didn't redden under it this time and their eyes met tenderly.

'I admire your commitment to your friend and there is always strength in numbers, even against those such as Darqu'on. Yes, Fynn, of course I will help. I see your determination and I admire your courage.'

'Thanks,' said Fynn, involuntarily laying a hand on her am, heartened by her support and acknowledging to himself, at last, how he really felt about this attractive and feisty woman, and ready now to do something more definite about it.

'Then let's get going,' said Aldebaran decisively as the flickering Astrolabius petered out, once more drained of power.

CHAPTER 25

Dragonmound

"Strength does not come from physical capacity. It comes from an indomitable will."
Mahatma Gandhi

They were following a trickling stream that wound its way gently through the valley. The cool, pure water was wonderful to drink and helped to quench their thirst as they walked. The breeze blew softly against their faces and the midsummer sun warmed their bodies and sparkled on the water. The sky was clear and blue, all sign of stormy weather long gone, and they found themselves enjoying the journey. Along the way they found succulent wild strawberries dotted along their path, and their sweetness filled their stomachs, giving them new energy.

So it was that, all things considered, they were both feeling more optimistic about finding their way back than they had since starting out.

But fate, or destiny, had other ideas it seemed.

'What's that sound?' said Will, who was already picking up a dull, rhythmic thud from somewhere ahead of them. 'Can you hear it, Wigapom?'

Wigapom stood still for a moment, all his senses alert.

'Yes I can. I can feel it too, the ground is vibrating. It's like hundreds of feet, marching in unison.'

'Has someone come to find us, do you think, and take us back home?' said Will, a certain innocence in his voice suddenly.

'I don't think so somehow,' said Wigapom as the hairs on the back of his neck began to rise in sharp points, as though magnetised. 'At least, it's no one friendly. Look!'

Wigapom pointed to a large grass-covered mound in the distance, where the valley seemed at its widest. Appearing on the mound, like black ants, were line upon line of marching figures. Hundreds of them. Some of them moving over the ridge of the mound and down into the valley towards Wigapom and Will, as countless others still streamed along the ridge. The army moved as one force, one mind, one body. This inspired not a feeling of joy but of growing fear. Wigapom knew instinctively who or what they were and his heart began to pound in his chest, competing with the beat of the marching feet still thudding ever closer towards them. He dropped instantly to the ground, pulling Will with him.

'It's the army of the Living Dead, Will,' he whispered, 'Darqu'on's army!'

He and Will slithered swiftly and silently into thick undergrowth and rocks nearby, which provided temporary refuge from the menacing swathe of marching figures now moving closer. It was only then that Will realised that another group had suddenly appeared behind them, as though they had erupted from the earth itself! His first thought was that they were surrounded by Darqu'on's forces, yet this group was smaller, less structured, familiar even and, coming from the ground. They couldn't be anything to do with Darqu'on, and they continued to keep close to the ground, as though no more keen to be seen than Wigapom and Will.

'Wigapom!' Will hissed. 'Look, isn't that Aldebaran and Lucas and … isn't that Fynn?'

Wigapom looked and his heart leapt. Yes! The face that stood out for him was Fynn! His dear friend. He also noticed an attractive but unfamiliar female at his side.

'What are they doing here? Surely they're not planning on taking on the dark forces in open combat? That would be total suicide! Unless they've come to help us! Could they really have done this for us? Especially after all the trouble we've caused them! Oh Will, how inspiring it is to have such marvellous friends! Especially wonderful, impetuous, loyal Fynn! Was there ever a better friend and companion?'

'Who's the girl next to him?' said Will.

Wigapom didn't recognise her, but there was no denying she was good looking and he could see by the set of her determined jaw that she was as dedicated to whatever plan of action they had hatched as was Fynn. His heart took a leap of another sort. Yet how could any of them stand up against the army sweeping down on them? Annihilation was surely just moments away.

'I'm not sure if they've seen us, but they've definitely seen the army! Has the army spotted them?'

'Or us?' added Will.

A frightening question. Wigapom knew from Aldebaran that Darqu'on's army consisted of many heinous creatures – bodies of those slain in battles of the past and now trapped as flesh-devouring ghouls, zombies or skeletons, forever in the service of Darqu'on, the Sorcerer, who controlled their every move. They responded only to his commands or thoughts. Darqu'on would never give power to anyone other than himself.

At the front were battalions of Skeletons, the fallen warriors summoned by Darqu'on's necromancy to act without question on his orders. Behind them battalions of green-skinned cannibalistic Ghouls, with their sharp teeth and fingernails and a grisly compulsion to eat their prey. Behind those, battalions of Zombies: grey skin hanging loosely from their bodies and staring out of dead, black-rimmed eyes.

These were the infantry of his army. But there were more dark forces than these. Behind the Zombies came the Shadim, the devilish daemons, corrupted by their own desires and now summoned by Darqu'on's sorcery to do his bidding and create the downfall of others. Amongst them was Lilitu, the she-witch, with such an air of evil darkness exuding from her that it contaminated the air around them like a foul and rancid breath. Behind them on ghostly horseback rode the Haideez, the slain knights, lords and nobles of the deceased King, now trapped in the role of close bodyguard to Darqu'on himself, forced forever into defending their former opponent.

Wigapom felt the terror that the dark forces projected, but there was no doubt in his mind where the real evil was. He could smell it, like a rotting corpse, in the midst of the Haideez. Here was Darqu'on, the real adversary, the powerhouse of evil, the wellspring of all fear, astride his own black mount. The countless troops marching on his orders were nothing without him.

Wigapom felt fear creeping over him like a rash, yet he breathed deeply to keep it at bay. It was at that precise moment that he had a strangely unearthly experience; a sense of slipping out of his body, whilst still feeling attached to it. Everything else around him stayed totally still, as though held suspended in time and Wigapom could observe his bodily self quite clearly, attached to him by a silver cord, but some distance away. It looked real enough, but he was not part of it. He noted, quite dispassionately and with merely the slightest curiosity, that this self looked quite pale, with wide eyes and small beads of perspiration dotting his brow. He saw too that Will, also attached to the silver cord, was just as white and pale. The detached Wigapom felt deeply compassionate to these two aspects of himself. Curiously, he had a similar feeling of compassion towards the Living Dead army and especially Darqu'on; seeing him, in that moment, not as an evil perpetrator of fear and pain but as someone lost to himself, unsure and fearful. It was easy to feel compassion for someone like that – for anyone – and at that moment all seemed to be one being, which he was observing with compassionate detachment.

This strange, rather wonderful feeling lasted but a short time but its impression remained in Wigapom's heart and mind, even as he returned to his body, feeling real again. Everything else was still suspended in a different

time and space; he could feel Will's emotions, and this was nothing new –
the fact that they could do this had been self-evident throughout their time
together – but this time Wigapom was surprised to find that right now he
was not feeling as frightened as Will looked, or felt. It was as though he was
aware of Will's feelings but not experiencing them himself. Indeed
Wigapom was surprisingly calm; quite dispassionate and disassociated, as
though he was viewing it all from his eyes but was not caught up with the
negative emotions.

As Will trembled with understandable fear, Wigapom's heart reached
out towards him as if to hold Will within its loving protection. His heart
felt bigger and more open than ever before and with this openness came a
gentle strength. A state of complete calmness and inner peace filled him
and the scene before him took on a brightly coloured shimmer, like light
reflecting off water, that led him to a place within his soul he had never
been before. He could see through the bluff of Darqu'on's supposed
strength to the real pain and isolation inside. Despite the huge army, the
terrible creatures, the outer expressions of power, Wigapom could clearly
see that Darqu'on felt totally alone and desperately lonely. He had no one
who cared for, or about him. Only Scabtail spoke to him, but even he was
Darqu'on's creation, and made as slimy and reprehensible a creature as it
was possible to be, totally in fear of the one who created him. As this
realisation dawned like a glorious sunrise over Wigapom he felt stronger
and more loved and supported with his small band of friends behind him
than he believed Darqu'on ever could, or would, even with the might of
his army surrounding him. Wigapom knew he wouldn't change places
with Darqu'on for anything. Darqu'on might think he had power and
control and a huge army to order around, but Wigapom had a greater
power: he had friends who loved him, friends like Fynn and Aldebaran,
and peace in his heart, and there was no comparison in his mind. Darqu'on
had sacrificed close friendship and love for isolating power. How soul-
destroying that must be! No wonder he was so cruel and heartless. In that
moment Wigapom really understood him, and most important of all, was
no longer afraid of him.

At that realisation a bright, warm light filled his heart and spread its
rays throughout his body, extending out all round him like a protective,
illuminating shield, as through the brilliance of the light came a beautiful
silver dragon with shining translucent wings, moving gracefully towards
him. It approached him with such a look of peace and love that Wigapom
was humbled and in awe to witness it. It reminded him of the dragon
Master from the strange house, and somehow Wigapom knew this one was
just there for him.

The dragon approached Wigapom and lay at his feet, its enormous silvery white paws almost touching Wigapom's toes. Between the dragon's front paws sprung an ancient olive tree, long associated with love and kindness, and its branches spread over him, as if offering even more protection. Underneath the spreading branches stood the tall figure of a knight with a plain gold circlet around his head and his hands resting lightly on top of his downturned silver sword, which seemed more protective than aggressive.

Wigapom knew with certainty that this was his father. His real father. The King. He, like the tree, had an air of loving protection about him. Both seemed strong and secure. When his father spoke, the voice was as rich as the earth and as expansive as the sky.

'Wigapom, my dear son,' he said, 'receive my love, for you are the guardian of the True Magic, the hidden wisdom, and your greatest challenge is now upon you. Trust your heart and do not allow yourself to fall into the trap that others have done before. You are loved and supported and will be upheld. The future of the hidden wisdom depends on the choices you now make for its continued existence. Choose wisely and well.'

Wigapom drew those words into his heart, yet even then expressed doubt in his ability to be wise.

'Father, I have made so many mistakes and foolish judgements, both now and in the past. How can I trust myself to be wise?' he asked.

'Listen to your heart,' replied his father.

'But isn't wisdom something that only magicians and clever people gain after years of study? I'm neither of these. Do I know how to be wise?'

'Listen to your heart,' repeated his father enigmatically.

'What does that mean...?' began Wigapom, but suddenly a bright, shining green leaf caught his eye as it floated down towards him from the gnarled branches of the olive tree. The leaf reminded him of the colour of the new rune stone, now vibrating powerfully in his pocket. Without being able to stop his hand Wigapom reached up and caught the leaf. He was not surprised to see a word cut into it. He knew instinctively that this was the meaning of the rune carved on the green stone in his pocket, but if he had hoped for something wise and profound he was disappointed: the word was *as*.

'I don't understand!' puzzled Wigapom, wanting his father to help him. The figure remained quietly smiling under the tree.

'What sort of word is this to help me to be wise – it's small, insignificant, meaningless – like me!' he continued. Yet even as he said the words he felt other, calmer thoughts flowing through his head and into his heart. He listened, and then spoke his thoughts out loud.

'All right, it's a connecting word too,' he continued, 'A word that is nothing without another. Yet a word, nonetheless, that language would be much poorer without: there would be no opportunity for description, as in 'strong as an ox', or of comparison, 'as above so below' – perhaps it is more important than I first thought – in relation to others and also to me in my relationship to everything about me. I feel little and insignificant, just like the word, and yet so much rests on my just being here and the role I choose to play. We are all like that, we are all interdependent. We all have a part to play in the great scheme of things. Maybe my role is to be a connecting point for others in the same way that the word connects other words to communicate meaning?'

He put the three words he had so far been given together in his head, and they began to form part of a sentence still waiting to be finished – *is given as...* – but the relevance still eluded him.

'It still doesn't make sense!' he said, confused. 'What is given, and as what?'

The figure of his father was still silent, but an answer of sorts came from his heart – it was beyond words – a feeling, nothing more; a sense of something that he couldn't quite catch hold of, yet that filled his being in a moment of brief but vital clarity: something wise and loving, which he could use to help others, as well as himself. He turned to face the figure of his father again, but time had slipped back into being without him noticing and the vision had gone: there was no dragon, no tree, no figure, no green leaf even; yet the light around him burned bright and the light of growing awareness within him burned brighter still. He felt truly alive and awake in that moment.

He and Will remained hidden between the two armies – if Fynn's band of brave light-workers could be called that – and Wigapom could feel the magnetic energy between them. They were all so close now that he could feel the air stir from their movements. Yet neither they nor the dark forces had seen him or Will yet. He knew he had choices open to him: he could continue to hide with Will and hope that Darqu'on and his army would pass him by – but this was unlikely; he and Will could join Fynn's group – but that would mean putting his friends in more danger. He rejected any idea of running away. That would never be an option. He felt too strong for that and, besides, he could never abandon those he cared about. Yet there was another course open to him that he had sensed under the tree, like a warm breath inspiring him. He could offer an olive branch of peace and love. Others might not think it wise; it was certainly a choice not many would have taken, but to Wigapom it was the perfect way.

He turned to Will.

'Keep hidden Will. I'm sure you know what I'm going to do. Even if you don't really understand it, it's the right thing. I'll be back, don't worry.'

'I trust you,' replied Will, who had sensed instinctively what Wigapom was about to do.

Wigapom cast a kind and understanding look at him, and slowly and steadily stood up from behind the rocks and undergrowth until he was clearly visible to all. Leaving Will safe and still unseen, he began to walk with purposeful, confident steps and a compassionate heart towards the mound on which Darqu'on's army was assembled. All he had to do to maintain this state was to keep compassion uppermost and fear at bay. He felt the powerful strength of the silver dragon around him, along with the loving presence of his father holding out his sword as a protective, unaggressive force, and a glorious tunnel of strong light began to form around him and illuminate his way. He knew that here, at Dragonmound, no matter what happened, a force stronger and more lovingly powerful than anything he had ever known before, was with him.

'That's Wiggy!' whispered Fynn in astonishment and disbelief. Any delight in seeing his friend again immediately erased by the foolhardy action Wigapom was now openly undertaking. Had he left his senses behind him on the hillside when the Shivastrom struck, in what seemed another life and time away?

'What does he think he's doing out there, Aldebaran? It's suicide. We have to stop him.'

'No. Wait,' said Aldebaran, holding Fynn back with one hand, whilst encouraging the others to remain still and hidden.

As if by synchronicity, Darqu'on's army also stopped and remained immobile, as though a greater force had switched off their power for a moment.

Wigapom remained in the middle of the two groups – in a sort of no-mans land dividing them. He could feel powerful, negative energies coming at him from the mound ahead, as well as from the valley in which he stood, and the hills around him, but they bounced off the tunnel of light surrounding him. The positive strength of the silver dragon energy filled his body, encouraging him forward, yet he was still aware of the darker energy spreading towards him like a noxious disease. He had to keep them at bay by focusing on love and not succumbing to fear. Whilst he did this he would stay safe. He moved closer to the dark forces, barely knowing why he was doing this, but filled with a compassionate compulsion and powerful instinct that all was as it should be. Darqu'on's army stared sightless, waiting for an order from their master.

'I've got to save him Aldebaran!' cried Fynn trying to move forward towards Wigapom, but now held back by the additional arms of Skye and Lucas. 'I have to save him from himself!'

'That is just what you must not do,' said Aldebaran firmly, 'only he can save himself. We do not know what is in his mind or his heart, but we must respect what is there.'

'There was always this danger,' said Skye, 'when we set out to rescue him from here. I did warn you.'

'But I didn't understand ... I still don't!' cried Fynn 'Wiggy...!'

Wigapom heard his friend but did not turn to face him. Instead he sent a thought message to Fynn in the hope that he might pick it up and understand.

'I'm all right Fynn. I know what I'm doing. Trust me. Trust what's happening. It's bigger than anything we can know.'

He was now level with the first battalion of the Living Dead – the Skeletons – their bleached bones, picked bare of flesh, jerked into action, re-animated now to live a parody of life, in perpetual pain and half memory of their violent passing on the battlefield. Their hollow eye sockets glared at him as they howled, screamed and lunged at him with their claw-like boney fingers, but they couldn't touch him, not whilst he was receiving the love from those who cared about him and not whilst he saw through the illusion of the skeletal bones to the lost souls beneath. He could feel nothing but empathy for them and he passed safely through.

Next came the green-skinned Ghouls – a further grim parody of humanity that would have chilled Wigapom to the bone in earlier times, but who he saw were now just lost souls, trapped forever against their will, in a living death. He felt overflowing compassion for them too as he walked between them, seeing beyond the ghoulish exteriors to the people they had once been and the souls that they really were. As he did so their terrifying forms jerked into action, as though switched on by an unseen hand; their faces contorted into grotesque expressions as they reached out with deadly fingers to grab at him, threatening to tear the flesh from his bones, Their ear-splitting shrieks rent the air as they battled to reach him through his protective tunnel of light. Their power was stronger and Wigapom had to work harder to hold on, as best he could, to his previous image of them as lost souls. He felt the pull of fear tugging at his heart, and threatening to rip his protection from him. He had to work even harder to keep it at bay and called on the strong energy of love and support from his father, the silver dragon and his friends to mend any gaps. With that protection he knew the Ghouls could not touch him, however much they lunged for him, or tried to break his resolve. This invisible barrier kept them from entering his space: creating a corridor of safety through which he continued to walk, closer and closer towards Darqu'on.

Wigapom's heart was beating fast and loud: he was sure Darqu'on could hear the sound on the crest of the mound. Wigapom held onto the feeling of compassion, seeing the image of Darqu'on's loneliness and sadness in his mind – he pictured him as a lost little boy. He wondered what was going through Darqu'on's mind: Shock? Disbelief? Relief even, that someone cared? Would it be enough to get Darqu'on to change his ways? Wigapom hoped so as he continued to walk unmolested through the ranks of the Living Dead. Darqu'on did nothing to stop him – could not, perhaps?

He now drew parallel to the Zombies, their loose grey skin slapping against them as they, too, fought to reach him. The heavy stench of death was stomach-turningly strong, and polluted the atmosphere as cudgels and axes were wielded with unbelievable venom by these grotesque beings. They were stronger still, but Wigapom was so wrapped in his loving protection that their forceful attack came to nothing as Wigapom walked between them: the invisible corridor of safety forming even stronger protective walls around him, to the frustration of all Darqu'on's creatures. They were desperate to drag him with them into their living hell, to force him to suffer as they suffered, in a torment of perpetual agony.

Wigapom was aware of his body trembling, but it was not with his own fear: He was sensing the fear vibrations from every creature around him. It was terrible to experience, yet worse was to come. As he passed amongst Darqu'on's sorcery-inspired Shadim, the fear and malevolence intensified: here was Lilitu, wild hair flying out behind her as she cast her long deadly shadow on the ground before him, but which could not swallow him up. The other daemons of the Shadim surged towards him, gargoyle-like faces contorted into grotesque masks, replicating every evil imaginable. They leapt at him with such ferocity that the very air shook with their screams and Wigapom had to fight even harder not to buckle under their fear-inducing cries. He breathed steadily and kept his gaze focused only on Darqu'on, remaining firm in his progress and keeping the corridor of protection strong.

He was now approaching the Haideez, those past friends and protectors of the King now forced forever to guard Darqu'on. Their empty eyes stared at him but they made no physical attempt to reach him, instead

Wigapom could feel penetrating cold spreading like contagion from them to him as the blackness of their souls endeavoured to corrupt the space beyond his tunnel of light. He shivered, knowing the barrier was thinner here and that he had to work harder to maintain it. Yet it was at its thinnest as he came before Darqu'on, whose jet-black eyes were such a contrast to his deathly pale, almost translucent skin and whose black-clad body exuded such an aura of evilness that Wigapom, despite his compassion, could feel his stomach physically sickened by it.

He began to shake with real emotion, the negativity beginning to break though the tunnel of light, and he felt he might collapse from the streams of bile issuing from this creature if he let his own resolve fail. Yet amidst the feeling of nausea in his stomach another feeling was pouring into his heart and speaking directly to him.

'See through the mask to the person beneath.'

It reminded him of the words he had heard Sophie say all those years ago, and which he had heard recently in the dragon Master's house – 'don't judge a book by its cover'. With these words the outer casing of evilness was once again stripped away to reveal the vulnerability of what was hidden inside. What he saw, in reality this time, albeit it briefly, was a lost little boy trapped in a life filled with hardship, rejection, abandonment, fear and pain…Wigapom's heart went out to him and, in that instant, any nausea left him; the terror, repulsion; all went and he was left with pure and simple compassion for this lost, tormented soul, along with a deep desire to help him reclaim himself.

'You are Darqu'on, who some say is my enemy,' he said in a soft, gentle voice as he looked up at the mounted figure before him.

Darqu'on stared down at the boldness of the youth before him, unsure at first what to make of him. He was used to people running from him, cowering at his power and malevolence, turning from him with fear. This treatment allowed him to feel strong. To experience The Brat walking towards him openly, with that gentle look in his eyes, so reminiscent of the look The Brat's mother had given him, was something beyond his present comprehension. He didn't know how to respond. To realise the ineffectiveness of his dark forces in the face of such love, courage and composure was destabilising; and to hear him speak with a softness so like hers was more than he could bear. For a moment he wanted to absorb the kindness into his being… He stopped in his tracks. No. He was Darqu'on. No one ever spoke to him, unless he chose, other than the pathetic reptile, Scabtail, and he did not count! Darqu'on pulled himself together – he had to reclaim his power, before he weakened further. He had to call back the hate and loathing.

He gathered these harsh, yet familiar defences about him, as though drawing a suit of rough armour around him and replied scathingly, with hatred inflaming his whole self.

'You speak to me as though you are my equal!' came his reply. 'How can you even begin to think you are on my level? You are the curse of the lowest creature, the dung heap of the masses, the cesspit of life! Yet you approach ME and speak to ME with no reverence, no fear or terror? What is within you, oh offspring of deceit and betrayal?'

'I don't understand your words, Darqu'on, all I feel is your pain, and I come in peace and compassion to offer you the hand of friendship and the chance to change, to lead you out of your hate and bring an end to the fear and terror around you.'

Darqu'on stared in stark disbelief at The Brat before him, pushing away the memory of her eyes and her kindness that he was reminded of so much at this moment. He had been offered compassion! Friendship! Unthinkable! Yet... Yet... No! He could not, would not weaken! He *had* to hate. It flowed in his veins. It gave him strength; it was his reason for being. It allowed him to exist!

'WHAT ARE YOU SAYING?' he roared, 'That I need your pity? It is *you* I pity! You, the pup sprung from creatures of such deceit! You, the weakling who I have chosen as my plaything until I decide to destroy you!'

'I do not pity you, Darqu'on,' replied Wigapom. 'I offer you compassion. I recognise your pain and I come to offer you a release, if you will accept it.'

Darqu'on was now incandescent with blind rage. Hatred and fear he could handle, but love and kindness? Never!

'SAY NO MORE, YOU PATHETIC SNIB, I WILL TOLERATE NO MORE!' he shouted with a voice that reverberated around the mound and valley beyond. A cloud of cloying darkness erupted from his mouth, swirling like choking fumes around Wigapom's body. It formed a dark aura around Darqu'on and began to shape-shift his body and that of his mount, leaving just black, foul-smelling fumes, which entered Wigapom's eyes, nose and throat, choking and stinging him with putrid malevolence.

Wigapom struggled to keep his eyes open and to breathe through the noxious smog that was now Darqu'on, hearing clearly as he did so, poisonous words inside his head: words meant only for him.

'Such bravery, or is it foolishness, in one so young? Only time will tell and there is no more time for you! You do not know and cannot control what now happens. I am your Master now and you will suffer as you have always been meant to suffer. I killed your father on this very spot, like the dog he was, and her too, your mother. She also died because of me and now I will kill you. I will destroy all those that oppose me. Especially you,

Brat of theirs. You and I cannot exist together. I am the King now and you the Pretender. I am not planning to be deposed!'

As the words left his head, so the noxious fumes began to withdraw and take the shape of an immense black dragon, belching poisonous fumes through its wide flaring nostrils. The fumes continued to surround Wigapom as he stood rooted to the spot, barely flinching. He was impervious to their poison. This angered Darqu'on more than ever as the dragon prowled and snorted around Wigapom, its powerful tail swishing menacingly, its enormous wings erect in a malevolent display of rage. Wigapom remained unbowed.

'You do not founder?' said Darqu'on, once more dissolving into the black fumes and swirling around Wigapom. 'You show no fear? I feed on fear and I will have my sustenance. The foolhardiness of your youth will not protect you. See how you fare with this!' And the black fumes turned to red, orange and white-hot flames that leapt, crackled, licked and spat around Wigapom's body. He felt their presence, if not their heat, but there was no escape now. The voice grew to screeching pitch.

'INCENDI MORATORI! Let the fire of your youthful enthusiasm consume you completely until all your energy is burnt out!'

Suddenly there was intense, unbearable pain around Wigapom's whole body as he began to burn in the now white-hot heat. The flames seared his skin with their orange and yellow tongues, licking round his limbs and torso as if hungry to savour his flesh. He smelt his flesh slowly burning, crackling like roasting pork. His eyes burned, as though immersed in some acidic substance and the blood began to hiss and boil under his skin. He shook and twisted with the pain and strength of the heat from which there seemed no escape. This was pain as he had never felt pain before and he did not know how he could ever withstand it. Yet he knew he had to even though his body wanted to cry out for release, to beg for it to finish, but he knew that fear would intensify the whole experience and that he must not succumb to it. That was not the way. It would have been so easy to do so. To beg Darqu'on for mercy, but then the Dark One would have won the battle and the pain would never stop. Ever. Fear and force would have triumphed yet again and Arcanum, his Kingdom, and all its people and races, would be forever enslaved to all that was bad, brutal and destructive. Wigapom knew he had to be different, to change the pattern of response to terror if he was ever to restore the True Magic again. He just needed help to withstand it.

He kept hearing the words '... *is given as... is given as*' sounding in his head and he recited them over and over again, like a mantra, using them to override the pain and go beyond it into a healing space of calm and peace.

He could do this, he would. He must.

'… *is given as… is given as*' he chanted as the flames continued to embrace him like macabre torturers preparing their final sacrifice. Yet it was his sacrifice, his gift, to save others from torment and pain, and from the feeling of separation from all that was good and of the light and he was willing to offer it freely. He would be upheld. Yet all the evil that was, and ever could be, was searing into his being at this interminable moment, as though he was taking the suffering of all the world onto himself and endeavouring to transform it into a state of bliss, which would make all the pain and agony worthwhile. He could not see, he could barely breathe, and his flesh was splitting, his body melting…

'… *is given as… is given as*' he continued to chant in his head, or did he say it out loud? It didn't matter. Repeating it helped him move through the savage pain and into the triumph that he believed awaited him at the other end.

'You are loved and will be upheld,' the image of his father had declared, and he trusted those words. He really did. He trusted the process and knew that it would see him through. Just hold on, hold on, and move through it ….

'… *is given as… is given as* …' The mantra continued and from somewhere came a completion of the sentence. '*Love is given as a channel to take away the pain – you are one with all. The All is love. You are love. You are loved and upheld.*' Wigapom heard himself repeating this 'I am loved and upheld… I am love… I am…'

There was a brilliant flash of light and, in contrast, a darkness so dense that it engulfed him. A complete blackness so deep, so intense that he felt it swallow him whole, yet in the blackness there was a softness that he had not expected, a tenderness that he had not imagined, and then there was light again… a cool calming light so pure, so peaceful that he let it embrace him as the blackness had done and it lifted him, lifted him, lifted him… He was floating far above himself in this radiance… He could look down on a body he recognised as once being his. Yet he did not miss it. He saw the agony that racked this body, yet felt only the ecstasy of the light.

Everything instantly made sense – all questions answered before they needed to be asked, all details crystal clear and in high definition: he knew who he really was, and why, and he touched the triumph of this moment with a compassion and tenderness that knew no bounds.

From the light appeared another figure before him. Not his father this time but an ageless, beautiful ethereal figure surrounded in pure illumination. He sighed with relief at the sight: he was free.

'Come,' said the figure gently, extending a hand towards him, 'we have things to discuss.'

He was drifting through space, guided not only by the light and the figure but also by the unseen hands of many. Together they entered a cave, luminous with shining crystals of every imaginable colour and hue and many that he had never contemplated before.

He felt light. He was Light. And the Light was pure love. Yet he had a form that he could recognise as his. The figure before him invited him to sit on a rose quartz bench that circled the crystal cavern. He did so and looked up at the vaulted ceiling above, staring in wonder and amazement and with the deepest peace, at all that was around him.

The cave seemed endless: like a dream he had once had. Yet this seemed so much more real. The cave contained spaces within spaces and those spaces had no end, or beginning. There were pictures, beautiful images ever changing and forming around him, memories of times gone by, times long forgotten and now newly remembered in such clarity of the moment. There were books, scrolls, illuminated script in his vision that filled him instantaneously with their knowledge and wisdom. There were runes and symbols that he instantly understood, all weaving in and out of his mind like a magnificent tapestry. It was all so effortless, wonderful and truly magical, and the more that filled his being the more rested he felt, the more he experienced the more he understood, the more he saw, the more he knew.

'This is heaven,' he sighed in wonder.

'Almost,' said the figure, 'but not quite. It is a place for rest and assimilation: for understanding the opportunities to turn knowledge into wisdom and thus True Magic.'

He was about to ask, 'What happened to Wigapom?' but felt he already knew the answer, so instead he asked another question.

'What must I do now?' he said. Yet even as he said it he felt he was already doing and being exactly what was meant. The figure looked at him with deep, kind eyes that penetrated his very soul and he read the answer clearly in them.

'I have to go back, don't I?' he said, after what could have been an eternity or a nanosecond, and again knew before the question was out that he did indeed have to return to that place called Dragonmound. To return to the physical pain once more. Yet he was not frightened. Somehow, to return was the most important thing. He had to return. He was not yet ready to remain in this crystal cave forever. Or even to find Heaven, however beautiful. There was more learning, more growing to undertake and there would be another opportunity. He wanted to return. He needed to return. His purpose there was not yet complete.

'You have made your choice,' said the figure, 'go back with love and the power to communicate that love and speak your truth to all who need to hear it.'

And then the cave was disappearing in a stream of pure colour and consciousness and he was swirling amongst it, coming out of the white light and bathing first in the deep violet, then mysterious indigo, before shimmering into the pure blue light, and swimming in the clear green, floating down in the golden yellow, drifting into the joyful orange and finally landing gently into the rose red.

As he entered the red, the pain immediately returned, but less than he remembered. He felt the pull of the earth bring him back and opened stinging eyelids to see the human outline of Darqu'on once more towering over him. The flames and fumes had gone and as he focused on Darqu'on the pain began to recede even more.

'You did not kill me, Darqu'on,' he said.

'You are not dead because I chose not to kill you,' said the by-now familiar voice. 'But you suffer.'

Suddenly Wigapom could feel the silver dragon at his side. He felt the cooling breath of the dragon waft over his body and watched as it instantly healed.

Soon there were no signs of burns. His flesh was whole. The silver dragon retreated and Wigapom pulled himself to his feet, wobbling slightly at first, as he fully returned to his body, and he was smiling at Darqu'on's words.

'You could not hurt or kill me, Darqu'on,' he said, 'whatever you do. I know that now. I do not fear death, because death does not exist. It is an illusion, as were the flames with which you tried to destroy me, as indeed is all this,' and he swept his arm round the scene. 'All is illusion. There is only one reality and that is the reality of love. Love that I have in abundance from my friends, and for myself. Love that, having transcended pain, I can now extend to you, if you will only accept it. Love that you have never allowed yourself to experience, choosing instead to create a place of fear and hatred, pain, greed and separation. That way leads to the illusion of death and an excuse for life. It is not my way and it needn't be yours. You have a choice. Choose the light over the dark and you will no longer walk in shadow.'

Wigapom hardly knew where these words were coming from, yet they spoke such truth to him in that moment, soothing his whole being with their honesty and wisdom. His pain had ceased; his wounds had healed; he was whole once more.

Darqu'on glared at Wigapom as though these words had reached parts of him long since hidden away in dusty, forgotten corners.

'Love?' he spat out. 'You wish to show me love?' He looked around his assembled army as he asked, 'What fool is this I have before me? What strange excuse for a being!' The Living Dead merely stared. He turned to face Wigapom again with such coldness in his eyes that Wigapom felt their chill seek to penetrate him.

'Love is nothing but betrayal. I learned that long ago. I need nothing from you but your subjugation to my will. You are nothing, you are as dirt under my heel. I, and the fear I create, are all that matter.'

'Darqu'on, you are truly misguided and lost,' replied Wigapom, as another wave of compassion coursed through him for this tortured soul, who no longer seemed so big or so powerful any more. 'You use hatred and fear as a protection around you, but they are cold and hard and are destroying you and all that you have sought to conquer. Love is protective too; yet soft and yielding. It gives so much more than it takes. Love is more powerful than fear and hate can ever be.'

But Darqu'on was scathing in his response.

'What can you know of power? Can you kill me with this power of love of yours? No. Yet *my* power will kill. Take the opportunity to fight me, now, and see who is the stronger! Then we may see who has the most power!'

'Have you not heard me even now?' said Wigapom, 'You cannot kill me and I would not kill you, even if I could. True strength is not physical strength but mental and emotional. I will not allow myself to be dragged into the illusion of physical strength, or of death or separation. I offer you instead the opportunity to change your ways; to use your power for good not evil, as you once were born to do; to embrace love not hatred; to help me return this land to all that is pure, honourable and loving; to allow the restoration of the True Magic of wisdom for the benefit of all once more. This would be the greatest act of power that you could ever envisage.'

'True Magic!' snorted Darqu'on, 'What is True Magic but a string of meaningless words and thoughts? Where is the power in this? I have power here. With my army at my command, with sorcery at my fingertips, with the power of darkness and fear to exert control over people's minds – with this I am all powerful, not with your pathetic love!'

Wigapom did not want to give up quite yet. He wanted to have one more try.

'Can't you see you have nothing in reality,' said Wigapom, 'nothing except an empty heart and an impoverished soul. You think you have wealth and power, yet you are poor in spirit. I feel for you, Darqu'on, with all my heart.'

Darqu'on's face darkened even more, his coal-black eyes darker than pitch and colder than a cavern of ice. His hollow voice echoed around the mound for all to hear.

'I do not need or want your sympathy! Look instead to yourself for one to pity! Your existence hangs by a thread: yours, and that of your so-called friends. You think your friends are so wonderful, but you have yet to experience what it is like when they turn away from you, when they stab you in the back, taking what is rightfully yours. And you will feel this and it will hurt like a sword in the heart. Then you will know that the only power is fear and hate. What good is your precious love then? And as for now, I could run you and your so called friends down this instant and have you all begging for mercy.'

'Your threats are as empty as your life, Darqu'on; the only power you have is given to you by token of other people's fear, and yes, people have suffered as a consequence, but that is not winning. It is illusion. Dark cannot overtake light as long as light keeps shining. Inside you surely know this. There is nothing you can do to them or me if we choose not to allow it to affect us. My friends saw me seemingly suffer physically; they saw the burns and the blood. But look: I don't have a mark on me. They can see that I have come through it – and they will too. From today, there is no place for fear or hatred, no place for your sorcery. You have no power unless others give it to you, and today is the first day of the rest of time when you can truly understand this.'

'GET OUT!' screamed Darqu'on. 'Get out, before I cut you all down!'

But Wigapom was rolling now, impassioned, vibrant.

'No one can have power over another unless they give them that power. You can do nothing to me that I do not choose to happen,' he said. 'There is no death. No end. Just new beginnings! With the protection of the True Magic this will be evident. I feel it in me today and I extend it to my friends and to all those who refuse to succumb to fear and hate, including you! The True Magic, the real hidden wisdom, is more powerful than your sorcery can ever be. You cannot change that, but you can change yourself, if you choose. I hope you do choose this way,' entreated Wigapom, making one more attempt to get Darqu'on to see the reality and not the illusion.

For a fleeting moment he thought he saw some change in Darqu'on's eyes: a yearning for something different? A belief that things could change? It was a brief moment when the future hovered between two possibilities. Would Darqu'on choose Wigapom's invitation to be part of the light? Would he have the courage to do this? Or would he continue to abhor the light and get sucked further into the bottomless pit of the dark?

Wigapom had caught a glimpse under Darqu'on's mask of evil and hatred to the pain and fear that lay beneath. The reasons behind this did not matter now; it was enough to witness the dehumanisation that resulted as he struggled to control his hurt by inflicting it upon others. It was an act which had destroyed his very soul.

Darqu'on remained momentarily suspended between these two opposing paths, but the moment of hesitation passed and his eyes grew cold, black and hard again as he retreated from the challenge.

'I WILL NOT CHANGE!' he screamed.

Wigapom knew then that he had lost him. He had to accept it. He sighed.

'Then there is nothing more that I can do,' replied Wigapom gently, 'but go home with my loving friends,' and he turned away, preparing to walk back through the columns of the Living Dead army. This was one challenge too far for Darqu'on who, already incandescent with rage, took this rejection as the worst possible affront to his power.

'No one turns their back on me!' he roared, he and his horse effortlessly shape-shifting back into the fire-breathing black dragon, exuding a stink of rotting vegetation and stagnant water.

The black dragon spread its massive wings, blocking Wigapom's return whilst raising its powerful tail as if to strike. Immediately the silver dragon appeared facing him, protecting Wigapom with its own body. Wigapom heard the command in his head to return to Will in the valley. He needed no second bidding, realising that he had done and said all he could to Darqu'on and he now had to let other forces aid him. Wigapom just caught sight of the black and the silver dragon circling each other – the black dragon breathing fire and the silver dragon dousing it with clear crystal water spraying from its mouth like a waterfall.

Wigapom sped back through the columns of Darqu'on's army as he heard the command of 'ATTACK!' to his troops roar out across the valley. The army of the Living Dead moved as one, but to Wigapom's amazement, rather than attacking him, they began instead to attack each other, as though each separate battalion were the perceived enemy, not Wigapom and his friends. Ghouls fought Skeletons and Zombies, whilst the Haideez and Shadim fought each other with wanton savagery.

Pandemonium raged as Wigapom ducked and dived between the fighters in his attempts to reach the safety of his friends. The mound was thick with swarming bodies, savage blows and blood-curdling cries. Darqu'on's army sliced and hacked itself to pieces before his eyes.

'What will happen?' asked Fynn, unable to tear his gaze away.

'We must wait and see,' said Aldebaran, in that infuriating way he had when Fynn wanted answers.

As Fynn watched he could hardly believe his eyes. The mound, covered by self-attacking creatures, began to shake violently. Large clods of earth erupted from it, shooting into the air like cannon balls fired from below ground. From the depths of the earth came a deafening rumbling and a cavernous hole opened out, like huge arms, towards the army as Mother Earth embraced the Living Dead in physical burial, allowing their souls to be free a last.

Fynn, from his vantage point on the ridge, and Wigapom, from the valley, watched as sparkling rainbow lights drifted down to where the army now lay buried, transforming into a single pure white light that began to lift the released souls upwards. Some souls seemed at first confused.

'Follow the light,' whispered Wigapom and Will together, 'follow the light.' All souls began to ascend, some who were keen and ready helping those who were still unsure. The light drew them upwards before dissolving softly into the atmosphere. A sense of peace spread out across the valley like a soft, silk counterpane, renewing the greenness of the landscape and settling the energy above and below it.

All that was left on Dragonmound were the two dragons, but fire can never conquer water and as Darqu'on saw his army transformed before him, he gave up the fight, shape-shifting back into black vapour, his murderous voice resounding over the entire ground.

'Don't think this is the end! It is just the beginning of a new reign of terror for you and all who support you. You will rue the day you set out to challenge Darqu'on!' And with that he imploded, into what could only be described as a gaping black hole that appeared in the air, swallowing him with a greedy gulp, leaving nothing behind except a waterfall cascading down the mound from the mouth of the silver dragon. With a gracious bow to Wigapom and the others in the valley the silver dragon then disappeared into the now crystal clear air, leaving the waterfall as a reminder of this day.

A deep peace settled upon Wigapom and drew his eyes to the ground. Something glistened by his feet; a flash of brilliant blue. He bent down to pick it up, knowing, even before he felt the etched markings under his curled fingers that it was another rune stone, lying quietly amongst the grass, ready to reveal its message.

As he scooped it up into his hands, he felt the familiar comforting warmth and even stronger, yet finer vibration from the stone in his palm. The retrieval was so swift it went unnoticed by all except Will, who had barely taken his eyes off his Adult self since Wigapom left him to approach Darqu'on, but suddenly the valley erupted into noise again. This time it was one of jubilation and exhilaration as excited figures, in a flurry of limbs, began running down the hill towards them, arms swamping them both with enthusiasm, barely able to believe what they had just witnessed, which was nothing short of the vanquishing of Darqu'on and his dark forces and the return not only of Wigapom and Will, but also of hope, all in one amazing moment!

They crowded round Wigapom, striving to shake his hand, to be close to this person who had shown such strength and presence, even if they had not seen or understood all that had just taken place.

Fynn was the first one at his friend's side, leaping down towards him with long loping legs.

'Wiggy! Wiggy!' he cried, relief, pride and amazement struggling for space to express themselves across his face as he hugged his dear friend, all past problems forgotten and forgiven.

'We did it, we did it!' shouted a jubilant Will, punching the air in triumph and fully sharing in all that he had seen and experienced.

'Well done, Master Wigapom,' came the booming voice of Aldebaran.

'I would never have believed it if I hadn't seen it with my own eyes,' said Skye to anyone who was listening.

'The answer to a prayer!' beamed Lucas.

They couldn't possibly understand all that had happened, especially what had happened to Wigapom during his time in the crystal cave, although Will knew, of course, but they had seen how they too could resist the dark forces and win, without resorting to aggression stimulated by fear. They had that power to stop the evil and terror.

What was it Wigapom had said? 'No-one can have power over another unless they give them that power?' Well, they now saw they often unknowingly had given the Dark One power by allowing themselves to feel fear and terror, even in their resistance. This fear, as well as their antagonism towards Darqu'on, had fuelled his darkness, but they did not have to do this, they could be stronger than the Dark One if they believed in themselves. If they kept this inner strength and belief they could continue to defeat him, until, weakened, he disappeared entirely. It was not the end, not yet, but it could surely be the beginning of a new way of being. This revelation inspired them all and in the euphoria of the moment it was one they believed would stay with them forever.

CHAPTER 26

The Stone Circle

"A fool may talk, but a wise man speaks."
Ben Jonson

Oakendale was a neat village nestled in a wide valley, which had sustained for many years a bustling community of both farmers, and artisans. It had withstood its fair share of troubles since Darqu'on had first cast his Shadow across Arcanum and was thus scarred, yet amazingly resilient. There had been deaths and disappearances, destruction and despair, yet somehow the adversity the villagers had shared had brought their community even closer together and it had become one of the hubs of the underground resistance movement. This was often attributed to the positive energy believed to spring from the majestic circle of blue standing stones that overlooked the village. In fact, there were two circles, one inside the other, with a tall heel stone placed just outside the larger circle. They had been built by unknown ancestors in ancient times and subsequently tended by the ancestral race of dwarves who had mined the area for millennia. The dwarves created beautiful silver and gold jewellery as well as practical artefacts, and they and the stone circle became justly famous. Other races, such as gnomes and faeries had integrated successfully with the dwarves over the years, bringing their individual talents for farming, animal husbandry and healing to the village, and the land continued to be well farmed and well cared for, as well as expertly mined by their descendants.

No one really knew why the stone circle had been built here, although the symbol of the circle had long been synonymous with the cycle of life and death. It had also long been noticed that the smaller circle charted the course of the lunar year and the larger the course of the solar year, whilst the sun rose immediately behind the heel stone, at dawn at the summer solstice, and that directly opposite the heel stone, on the outer circle, where two of the stones were joined by a lintel slab, the sun could be observed in its descent at sunset at the winter solstice. Thus the stone circle charted the movement of the two most important celestial bodies as well as the arrival of summer abundance, or the birth of 'the new king', and the arrival of the dark days of winter, or the death of 'the old king' as they were poetically termed, and it had long provided, before Darqu'on's emergence, a meaningful, as well as magnificent, focal point for villagers to assemble at these times.

Many of these villagers now followed Wigapom as he was carried back triumphantly on their shoulders, to Oakendale, their singing and joyous laughter echoing through the valley as they went. For the first time in years they felt free of Darqu'on's vice-like grip and their euphoria knew no bounds, spreading faster than lightning to the other inhabitants of the village, who quickly made preparations to greet the returning hero. Vast vats of sweet wine were brought from the tunnels, where many of the inhabitants had taken to living; piles of delicious food appeared, spread out on long tables, lanterns strung themselves out along the pathway to the village, and huge bonfires were lit in a double celebration, for not only was Wigapom their conquering hero, but, as synchronicity would have it, today was also the eve of the midsummer solstice.

This particular celebration, like many others in the astrological year, had been forbidden since Darqu'on's Shadow descended, although he did allow the celebration of Samhain, at the end of October, as it was a constant reminder to the people of the coming of dark days and the time when the dead traditionally walked again, which appealed to his sense of the macabre. However, today's events had lifted the restrictions and by the time they reached the hill where the ancient circle of blue stones stood, the villagers had already gathered, not only in welcome, but also thanksgiving, singing and dancing around the outer rim of the stone circle as the sun gradually began its western descent.

Today was important in so many ways, not least that it allowed everyone to celebrate freely for the first time in many years: the wine flowed freely and music from a dozen or more instruments played jolly tunes. People sang, laughed and danced as they had not done for many years and the light of hope strung itself across the whole community like the bright paper lanterns strung from gaily painted posts that glowed like fire-flies in the slowly gathering dusk.

Wigapom bathed in the joy of it all. The memory of the pain he had undergone was already fading, as the scars already had. This miracle was evidence to everyone that the True Magic was returning. If anyone was concerned this might just be a temporary victory and that Darqu'on would return in force again, it was never voiced – there was time enough to think of that if need be in the cold light of day – now was celebration time and they made sure that every minute counted.

Fynn was ecstatic to see Wigapom again, relieved that no permanent damage, either to Wigapom or their friendship, had been done as a result of his rage.

'I thought we'd lost you,' he said when at last he and Wigapom had a chance to really talk, 'I thought it was all my fault. I should never have got so angry.'

'It was never your fault, Fynn,' countered Wigapom, 'I behaved abysmally to you, and everyone in the Temple. Will and I were selfish and foolish. I allowed myself to get carried away by the moment; it was wonderful finding a part of myself that I had rejected for so long, I just didn't think through my behaviour properly, and I now know Darqu'on played his part in bewitching us, which I could have resisted, but didn't. I've learnt a lot and it won't happen again – I don't need to be a needy child anymore, I've grown out of that. Will has grown up too, have you noticed? It happened after we left the Master's house.'

'I had noticed, yes – how has that happened in just nine weeks? He seems quite the adolescent now.'

'Now that's another strange thing,' puzzled Wigapom. 'You seem to think we've been away nine weeks, but we feel we have only been gone a day or two at the most. I don't understand that at all.'

'You mean you seem to have been in one time frame and us in another?' said Fynn with a puzzled look on his face.

'Exactly,' replied Wigapom, 'it seems hardly any time ago that we were being saved by Castor and Pollux from the ghost ship, or helping the people wake up their Master in the house.'

'We didn't see much of that,' said Fynn. 'The Astrolabius kept losing power but Aldebaran said that the Sea of Emotion was your own making and so I guess that was out of our time and space and, well, didn't you say the house and people just vanished when they woke the Master up? So that wasn't in real time and space either. It's all rather strange isn't it. But wonderful too!'

'I reckon it just proves that our thoughts do create reality, but reality is sometimes not real, even though we think it is!'

Fynn pulled a quizzical face before slapping Wigapom affectionately on the back, full friendship restored.

'Now there, Wigapom, you are at risk of confusing me again,' he laughed, 'However, I think my thoughts did a pretty good job in creating Castor and Pollux to save you, as well as the soft landing in the farmyard!'

'Well, thanks for the star twins, but I'm not so sure about the soft landing – you didn't get to smell it!' laughed Wigapom in reply.

Will ran up to them at that point, long adolescent limbs moving in all directions, brown hair flopping across his excited face. Wigapom remembered looking like that and smiled to himself as Will spoke with enthusiasm.

'Come on you two – stop nattering like old women! It's party time, with loads of food and all you're doing is talking!'

Wigapom and Fynn laughed at him affectionately and followed him into the thick of the festivities. Wigapom enjoyed the energy and zest that infused them all, but as the sunset passed and the moon began to rise full and silent in the sky, he felt the need to withdraw from the hubbub of it all, and reflect. For a time he sat at the edge of their revelry, watching as if from a distance, as Fynn became unusually garrulous, telling stories and singing songs from the Brakendor days to his new found friends around the warmth of the bonfires. Will, too, seemed relaxed and happy, now he was older, almost entire in himself. How wonderful to feel so at ease with both lives, thought Wigapom; to him, those Brakendor days were another lifetime away, like a dream that he occasionally caught but wished he hadn't, as it more often than not sent a dull ache to the depth of his belly. Will was lucky; He didn't seem to share Wigapom's memories of adolescence – their joint memories had begun to separate with the Shivastrom. Will was now creating memories of his own out of the happenings of today. He and Wigapom were still mentally connected and thus he had witnessed all that Wigapom had experienced in the crystal cave, but on a different emotional level. Will found he was becoming more and more of his own person, confident and purposeful in ways that Wigapom, at that age, had never been. It was a complex relationship that neither fully understood, but it seemed to work.

There were no such complexities with Fynn it seemed. He had no regrets about his past and was as in touch with his farming days as with these times of nomadic adventure. Wigapom envied that ability in Fynn – to be able to embrace both parts of himself as one. Despite Will's arrival and his own deeper experiences, there were still bits of Wigapom that felt not yet fully formed. There were still things he had to resolve, discover or work through. He was coming to see this was what being on a Quest really meant. He saw the word QUEST as an acronym for Question, Understand, Explore, Sustain and Transcend. Perhaps this was how the word had originated, he thought. He was certainly doing all these things.

He suddenly felt the need to be even more alone and quiet, so softly slipped away from the noise of the merrymaking into the enveloping peace of the night. He didn't actually plan where he was walking, but somehow his feet took him towards the towering blue heel stone, now deserted and glowing effervescently in the moonlight.

As he left the revellers behind him, he could feel the ancient energy of the blue heel stone pulling him towards it, as it no doubt had done for countless others over time. It was bathed in soft moonlight now and reminded him of the blue stone clunking comfortingly against the others in his pocket. Two new stones in as many days! Well, that's what it seemed like to Wigapom. Would the others be so quick to come by?

He sat with his back to the heel stone, feeling its secluded support and strength against his spine, and looked up in wonder at the starry night sky. He had forgotten how beautiful it was. There were so many stars up there: each one an entirety in itself, twinkling light years away from him, yet all were part of his world and each other. His spirits soared at the wonder of it all, as he rested his palms either side of him on the grass.

'Ouch!' he cried, as a sharp pain stabbed his left hand, bringing him back to earth – a small piece of blue stone had been chipped away and had imbedded itself into his hand. It hurt! He picked it off his palm and flicked it away from him; no damage done, just an imprint on his flesh. With the other hand he extracted his new blue stone from his pocket and held it up to the moonlight.

He noticed with shock that it was chipped too, and part of the rune symbol had disappeared. He was sure it had been whole when he found it, but somehow it had become damaged and now he could not read its message. There was a moment when he almost panicked, but that did not last; somehow Wigapom knew he would find the answer, and limited though his knowledge of the elven runes still was, despite all the time he had spent at the grimoire, he was sure that he would not have to struggle to decipher the meaning for long, complete or not. Something had happened to him in his meeting with the ethereal figure in the crystal cave: Knowledge had poured into him and, with the right stimulus could pour out of him. But what could the right stimulus be? He tried to think, but this just seemed to cloud his mind more, so he stilled his thoughts and cleared his mind completely and waited for inspiration to come, as the starry night subtly gave way to streaks of dawn that would soon illuminate the top of the stone.

His own illumination came first: how had he not connected before that his stone and the heel stone were made from the same type of stone – the same type of stone that had sunk into his palm a while ago? Suddenly he knew, with no shadow of doubt that he had to find that piece again – that it was synchronicity that had stuck it to his hand and it was the missing part. He opened his eyes from his meditative state and turned to look amongst the grass close by. Almost as though it was waiting for re-discovery, he saw it lying glistening in the growing light. He held his own blue stone

272

with excited fingers and pieced the parts together – they fitted perfectly and the rune was whole again.

As he absorbed the intricate pattern of the rune without trying to decipher it, he kept hearing a word repeating itself in his head; *Part*. Well, he knew that one piece of stone was a part of the other, he had just discovered that, but what did the rune stand for? He felt the question got in the way of the answer, so endeavoured to clear his mind again from all chattering thought, but kept hearing the word *part*, droning away in his head like an annoying bee against a closed window. He became quite frustrated, trying to dismiss it so that he could just concentrate on letting the meaning of the rune in, but the word in his head kept interrupting him: *part*, it said, *part, part*… and at last he knew. The word he had tried to ignore was the very word he wanted. The rune on the stone meant *part*, that was what his intuition had been telling him and which he so nearly ignored! The words now read …*is given as part*. Wigapom was still baffled; no matter what intuitive knowledge had flowed through him during his time in the crystal cave, or his meditation on the stone, it was obviously still not enough to make complete sense of these words. What was given? And what was it part of? He knew there should be a word at the beginning, which would leave just two words at the end to find; but he was no closer to understanding the meaning. The wisdom of the True Magic was returning; that was obvious by what had happened at Dragonmound, but it was not complete and thus not fully powerful. Maybe nothing was certain until he had all the stones and had placed them in the spine of *The Book of True Magic*, wherever he might find that! It all still seemed so far off. Things could founder again before then and he did not know what his next step was to be. He kept feeling he must just trust that things would happen when they were meant to, that was synchronicity, like the piece of chipped stone. It was predestined. If something were predetermined then nothing would stop it happening, whatever Wigapom did. Did this mean he wasn't really important in this after all? A jab of disillusion stabbed him suddenly, as painful as the chipped stone had been. Then he remembered Aldebaran's other words, about freedom of choice. He'd had freedom of choice as to whether to find the chipped stone or not – nothing was pre-destined, but pure potential. He now had freedom of choice whether to be disillusioned or to rise to the challenge. He chose the latter. To help him get back 'on top' again he laid out the collection of rune stones in the order he had received them; the orange one first, which had arrived when he first heard the name Wigapom and claimed his new identity; then the yellow stone had shown itself when he seemed really ready to make change in his life and go out into the big wide world; then the green stone, after a very long wait, had arrived when he had demonstrated his compassion and love for others, and also himself; and the blue stone came after he proved his ability to listen to his inner voice and communicate passionately and powerfully. He looked at the blue stone again; he had all the pieces but it was still broken; how would a broken stone ever fit properly into the spine of *The Book of True Magic*? Then he realised he was worrying again. Let events take their course, he told himself and let go of any worries. He felt this might be easier said than done, but he had just three stones left to find, or rather, earn. What did he have to discover about himself to gain them?

Wigapom read the runes out loud again – *is given as part* – what on earth did this mean? Things were certainly happening in parts; parts that did not seem connected on the surface, but surely had to have a connecting point somewhere; and what part did he really play in this huge, confusing tapestry of events being woven, or maybe tangled, together, bit by amazing bit? He might be the King designate, but this still didn't seem real to him; he had spent too any years as the awkward son of Samuel and Sarah for that to just disappear. If only he could understand more, and see the whole pattern! He just had to believe that one day he would, but patience was not something that came naturally to Wigapom.

He heard approaching footsteps behind him and glanced up to see the strong-faced, attractive young woman he had first seen with Fynn, and who he now knew was Aldebarans's daughter, Skye. She was standing behind him, her slim outline silhouetted by the gathering dawn-light. His heart lurched.

'I thought I'd find you here,' she said, in a soft voice, with a sort of half smile dancing lightly about her lips.

'Did you?' said Wigapom, wondering why she should think this when he himself had had no idea. He was still rather shy around females, but she was nice; confident and self-assured, which he found appealing, yet also feminine and intuitive; but he was confused by his own feelings about being with her; she was different to Sophie. Skye was a woman, whereas Sophie had been just a girl, but both set Wigapom's heart racing in a very pleasant, tingling way. He hoped he would see more of Skye; hoped she could be part of his life, part of the Quest. Part: there was that word again. His head started to spin and he almost didn't hear her reply.

'Yes, I did,' she said softly, 'I left you for a while as it just seemed to be the place where you needed to be; away from everyone, with the strength of these huge, ancient stones around you. They're wonderful aren't they?'

She sat down beside him, hugging her knees, and the sense of her physical presence so close to him now made him tingle more than the stones. He did his best to gather his thoughts, and not let his feelings show.

'Mmm. The place does feel full of strength,' he mused, trying to cover his confusion, 'but perhaps they aren't as strong as you think; look,' and he held out the two pieces of blue stone towards her. He had shown no one else this stone so far, not even Will or Fynn. It seemed important that she was the first.

'Another rune!' said Skye, appreciatively. 'Oh, I see what you mean – it's broken. Do you know what it says?'

'Not really.'

'Not even a feeling?' pressed Skye, gently.

It was as if she knew, thought Wigapom.

'Well, maybe I feel that it says *part,* as this word won't leave my head alone.'

'That happens to me sometimes. I feel the answer before I know it. I usually know then that I can trust what it's saying,' she said, looking intently at Wigapom in a way he found both pleasurable and uncomfortable at the same time. He felt he might be blushing – thank goodness the sun had yet to rise and his face was in shadow!

'I'm coming to know that myself,' he replied, hoping she hadn't noticed the tremor in his voice, 'In fact I'm coming to realise rather a lot these days!' and he smiled somewhat ruefully. 'But then for everything I think I understand, something else happens to confuse me again!'

Skye smiled back and lightly touched his arm in compassionate understanding: a quietly affectionate gesture that brought an even hotter flush to Wigapom's face, and set his heart racing.

'You were amazing at Dragonmound, never forget that,' she said encouragingly.

'Was I?' began Wigapom.

'Yes you were,' she replied, looking deep into his eyes before lowering her gaze and studying the stone again.

'Can you fix the stone do you think?' she asked, putting the two pieces together in his hand.

'I don't know; although, in a way, being broken helped me understand the meaning of the rune.'

Skye nodded as though she understood. There was a silence filled with a dozen unspoken thoughts.

'Skye...' Wigapom began, unsure quite how he would finish the sentence. He had no need to wonder because Skye was looking at the stone again in astonishment.

'Look!' she said, 'It's mended!'

They both looked at the stone: it was true, it was now completely whole, as though it had never been broken; almost as though everything

275

was coming together, like Skye and Wigapom sitting together, just as it was meant to be; no separation, just wholeness! Magic! Especially as Skye leaned closer to him to share the transformation of the stone, her hair falling forward and caressing his cheek. Then the moment was broken by a loud shout behind them and Will tumbled between them, legs waving in the air.

'Ouch!' was his cry as he knocked a knee against the heel stone, 'That hurt.'

'Be careful, Will!' cried Wigapom, flustered by the unexpected disturbance, 'I nearly lost the rune stone.'

'I knew you'd found another one. Let me see. What does it say? No don't tell me. Let me guess.' Will screwed up his face thoughtfully for a moment, then said, *part*.

'How did you know?' said Skye, amazed.

'He does that sometimes,' explained Wigapom, unsure how to explain his strange connection with Will. 'It's a thing we have between us.'

'It's true,' agreed Will, 'but this time it probably helped that I was just behind you when you told Skye!' and he let out a throaty chuckle as he settled himself between them. The stone may have been mended but the magic of the moment between Wigapom and Skye was broken, although it lingered in Wigapom's memory even as he joked with Will.

'The older you get, the worse you get,' he teased. Will laughed, and retaliated, 'It takes one to know one. Anyway, I came to tell you that the sunrise ceremony is about to start – you won't see the sun rise properly if you stay here.'

'OK Will, we're coming – don't want to miss the sunrise on Midsummer's day do we!' joked Wigapom, smiling at Skye and beginning to gather up the other stones.

'What do you think the rune message means Wiggy?' asked Will, gently taking the blue stone from Wigapom and turning it over in his palm.

'I wish I knew, Will, but no doubt we'll find out soon enough,' said Wigapom, returning it safely to his pocket. There was no point in commenting on the stone mending itself: Will probably knew that anyway and, besides, Fynn was bounding towards them now, colour heightened on his cheeks.

'There you all are – where have you been? What a wonderful night! They're starting the ceremony of the sunrise now.'

'Will's just told us, we're coming,' said Skye, walking with easy familiarity towards Fynn as they all moved away from the heel stone and towards the outer stone circle.

Here villagers, many with oak leaves and the sun-coloured hypericum flowers now woven into their hair, were massing, led by the central figure impressively crowned with tree branches, and all were singing or beating out a rhythm on various instruments, which sounded like the heartbeat of the earth itself. This was accompanied by the evocative sound of horns rising on the wind as though welcoming and inviting the sun to rise on this new and exciting day. The crowned figure, who Wigapom now recognised as Merric, the chief village elder, led the massing throng in a weaving motion, all around the stone circle, where they remained, whilst he approached and faced the heel stone. In a strong commanding voice he called on the four corners of the earth to witness the ceremony, and invited the four elements of wind, fire, water and earth to support the gathered community in the coming months, asking that their courage, love, creativity and sense of responsibility be awakened. He asked for the first three rays of the rising sun to bring peace, knowledge and wisdom to the land. The drums increased in their intensity and then suddenly ceased.

An expectant hush fell over the gathering as the soft golden rays of the morning sun began to edge up behind the blue heel stone, and for a sparkling, shining moment the stone seemed to cradle the sun. The reverential silence was then broken by loud exultant cheers, chanting and clapping, as well as the sound of horns and even more banging of drums as the bright shimmering orb levitated slowly upwards, floating in the soft pinky-blue of the morning sky; a cacophony of noise and exuberance to complete the celebration that was quite thrilling. Wigapom, Will and Fynn had never experienced anything like it before. Hugs, shouts, and smiles were exchanged, which held such a deep meaning for the Oakendale residents.

The Mid-summer Solstice, representing the arrival of the new king, seemed appropriately apt and meaningful this year, in the presence of Wigapom, their new King designate. All believed that Darqu'on and his Shadow of sorcery had been vanquished and a time of peace and abundance heralded in. Wigapom shared their hope, feeling it rise like the morning sun into his own heart. In the glow of the moment he felt the positive forces aiding him and the individual parts of this amazing tapestry of events coming together; being given as part of the whole; slowly but surely he thought he was making sense of the message of the runes. The four stones vibrated gently against his leg, as if in encouragement, and he relaxed at last into the moment.

CHAPTER 27

Dog Days in Oakendale

"Dog days: a period of stagnation and inactivity."
Webster's Dictionary

Wigapom had been more mentally and physically exhausted by his encounter with Darqu'on at Dragonmound than any had first realised and as Darqu'on's presence in their lives was seemingly removed by that encounter it was agreed that all had earned a time of rest and recuperation.

As Darqu'on went into hiding to lick his wounds, they entered a time of comparative inactivity, peace and quiet in the village as the 'dog days' of summer rolled on and energies were restored.

Wigapom, Fynn, Will and Skye had been invited to stay on in the village to recuperate and they had readily agreed; there was something especially energising about being out in the beautiful open countryside and in a warm and embracing community, rather than the volatile atmosphere of Lampadia town, despite the beauty of the underground temple and Aldebaran's hospitality. Aldebaran understood their feelings and knew also that his part in the Quest had come to a natural pause; Wigapom and the others needed to be in Oakendale for the next phase to unfold. He did not mention the tense feeling that twisted his gut whenever he thought of this; what would be would be and it was not for him to interfere. There would be times a-plenty when they would need to call on the positive energy being stored here now in Oakendale, and perhaps he was worrying over nothing.

Wigapom and the others were not worrying at all. In the euphoria after Dragonmound all was right with their world, a new beginning had started and life was good – full of hope and promise. Fynn, Wigapom and Will lived under the welcoming hospitality of Gobann, the dwarf they had first met in Lampadia, in his house cut into the hillside just outside the village centre. Skye stayed with her father's old friend Tamsan in his cottage in the centre of the village, which he had decided to return to in the light of recent events.

Gobann was a benevolent and generous host. Short and squat, with the dark hair and pale face that characterised his race, he was, like his predecessors, a master smith who not only made useful and functional iron and copper artefacts for the village and local community but also worked his own special miracle on precious metals found locally, such as dwarven gold and silver. It was said that the metals found here all carried special magical qualities, which only the dwarves who fashioned them could release.

Gobann's work was much valued and admired by all. He was highly knowledgeable about the metals with which he worked, regarding them as living beings in their own right, with individual characteristics and personalities.

'I have been told by the earth Elementals,' he explained to Wigapom and the others one sunny afternoon after they had been in Oakendale for awhile, 'that the energy emitted by the metals above the ground and previously sullied by Darqu'on's influence is being re-stabilised and balanced, helping to restore the True Magic as well as strengthen our normal magic.'

'But I only have a few of the stones so far,' said Wigapom. 'How can that be?'

'Because it is a gradual process of change. A cumulative effect. The more stones you earn the more the energy increases and becomes positive.'

'So it's happening now, without me having to do anything?' said Wigapom.

'It has happened because of what you have already done. If you do no more, then no more will happen in a positive way. Until all the stones are gained and placed in *The Book of True Magic* any energy gained will gradually revert back to negative again through the power of Darqu'on's sorcery.'

'But I thought he lost the battle at Dragonmound,' said Wigapom.

'Only temporarily. Until *The Book of True Magic* is reinstated, nothing is finished,' answered Gobann.

'But I have a little more time to rest, don't I?' said Wigapom who, as the days went by, was enjoying his time here in Oakendale more and more: especially being in the company of Skye, to whom he was increasingly attracted.

'The choice has always been yours Wigapom – to complete the Quest, or not.' said Gobann. Wigapom took that as a 'yes'.

Wigapom, Fynn, Will and Skye spent many fascinating hours listening to Gobann talk in his deep rich voice, every word as valuable as the metals with which he worked. They learned the concept of *as above, so below* in relation to the seven metals of the earth, learning of their connection to the seven planets, as well as inherent healing properties. With the gentle dwarf as their teacher they began to fully appreciate the wonders and complexities of this mostly unseen natural world and to understand how Darqu'on, despite his power of sorcery, had been unable to cast his wicked gaze into Mother Earth's underground treasure store. Gobann advised them that no one could be complacent, however, until the True Magic was restored, and once the metals were exposed to the cruel light of Darqu'on's days they could be used by Darqu'on to emit their negative qualities instead of the positive ones, and thus all who used them had to be vigilant.

'Gold is the king of all metals,' Gobann told them, 'like the sun, it is masculine, protective and strong and can be used to heal the spine and the heart, but can also corrupt the soul. Silver eases the troubled brain and is the goddess of the moon and night. She shows our unconditional love and appreciation of all things feminine, but can reflect our negativity too.'

'So giving silver would show love for the feminine,' repeated Fynn. 'That's really interesting.' Gobann nodded assent, as thoughtful as ever.

'Copper too,' added Wigapom, keen to show his knowledge, 'That is supposed to attract love – as the Venus of metals.'

'So silver and copper together would be quite a love charm then?' said Fynn.

'A very powerful one' replied Gobann, knowingly.

'I know the planet connected with quicksilver,' said Will, showing an equally quick brain, 'It's easy – because both are called Mercury!'

'Well done, Will,' replied Gobann, 'Mercury is the communicator, and energizer of the nervous system,' and he smiled into Will's bright eyes, noticing more and more how quickly he was growing and how alike Wigapom he was becoming; the same hair and shape of face of course, but mannerisms too. Soon it would be difficult to tell them apart.

'Is there a metal to help me lose weight?' sighed Fynn patting his stomach, 'I'm enjoying the food too much round here.' Skye giggled.

'You're just fine as you are!' she said affectionately, 'You work it all off in the fields anyway,' and she patted his stomach too. Wigapom felt his own stomach lurch and tried to ignore this familiarity between them, but it was becoming more and more noticeable. He replied with a veneer of humour hiding a growing jealousy.

'Looks like flab setting in to me,' he criticised, 'you need the strength of iron in you – from Mars the warrior planet, isn't that right Gobann? It's masculine, active and strengthens the blood as well as the muscles,' and he endeavoured to flex his own. Skye smiled.

'I think Fynn is masculine enough already,' she said, touching his strong shoulders. Wigapom wondered why he felt so puny in comparison, and why a niggle of resentment was pulling at him. Fynn, put his arms lightly on Skye's shoulders as he smiled back at her.

'It's nice to know I'm appreciated, Skye,' he said, 'but I think I'm almost as bad as Wigapom. You have to admit it, Wiggy, our days here are pretty lazy much of the time; we haven't thought or done much about the Quest for ages.'

'We've earned the rest,' said Wigapom in defence. 'A time to think and be calm for a change, like the properties of tin!' He couldn't resist showing off his knowledge even more by adding that.

'Well remembered!' said Gobann, who was, nevertheless, not blind to the fact that Wigapom was trying to score points over Fynn.

'Ah, tin – that's jovial Jupiter stopping us from being liverish and helping us have fun,' piped up Will again, which made Wigapom beam with pride – any cleverness in Will reflected well on Wigapom.

'Well said Will, you and me have good memories,' Wigapom said, hoping that Skye had noticed their cleverness, but she was instead laughing at Fynn as he deepened his voice to comic proportions and pulled a long face to announce,

'I am Saturn, the leaden lord of death, my bones buckle under my weight, my skin sags, and even my hair falls out! Help me pretty lady, please... Aaagh!' and he slumped to the floor by Skye's feet in an exaggerated heap, which made her laugh out loud.

'You're a natural jester, Fynn,' laughed Gobann too, 'but do you remember how to mix molten metals to make tinctures and potions? Or how to use the hard metals to energise the water from the river into magical essences for healing, I wonder?'

'Well, perhaps not!' admitted Fynn, scrambling to his feet. 'But I expect clever clogs Wiggy does!'

Wigapom felt a ripple of annoyance, although he tried not to show it: Fynn was making fun of him and he felt he had failed by not making Skye laugh like Fynn did. He pushed these feelings to the back of his mind and showed exaggerated interest instead in all the fine artefacts Gobann made and imbued with special magical qualities. He thought he covered things up well, but Gobann missed nothing.

As things stabilised in the village more, the villagers began to return permanently to their cottages rather than stay in their underground tunnel hideouts.

Wigapom associated the tunnels with his experience of the Shivastrom and had been deeply apologetic to Aldebaran before he returned to Lampadia through them, for the problems he had caused, and had been encouraged to hear that all problems were really opportunities for personal growth.

'If you had not experienced the Shivastrom or created the Sea of Emotion, you would not have found yourself at the Master's house and thus not had the opportunity to gain the green rune stone, nor indeed the blue, and none of what has just happened would have had a chance to exist. Trust the process, Wigapom. All is perfect.'

Wigapom thus viewed the peace and calmness and general inactivity of his time in Oakendale as part of the unfolding plan and found himself relaxing more into hedonistic pleasures and enjoying them thoroughly.

Whether it was the strengthened energy of the stones protecting the village or whether Darqu'on was just giving Wigapom a wide berth was unknown, but in Oakendale it became too easy to forget, or ignore, that the Shadow still existed.

The four of them continued to get involved in village life, learning, helping, growing, and developing, and the stones and Quest were mentioned less and less. Wigapom had pushed them to the back of his mind, where they nagged a bit but were easily ignored; it had become too easy to slip into a state of denial about them. Oakendale, unlike Brakendor, was unrestricting on Wigapom's life, and seemed to expand it; he loved everything about his life here and wanted nothing to change. As the days moved on, even the events at Dragonmound became a hazy memory and he barely noticed he no longer felt the stones vibrating against his leg anymore, even forgetting, on some days, to take them with him at all. This began to concern Gobann and others close to him, who wondered whether Darqu'on's influence was working insidiously, but when days are long and trouble-free, memories can be very short indeed and as summer stretched towards autumn, the weather became hotter, the corn ripened in the sun's bright beams, and a bumper early harvest resulted, subtle changes once again affected the dynamics of the group.

One of these involved Skye. She stirred feelings in Wigapom he had never felt before. When he was with her he felt energised and powerful. The awkwardness and confusion he had felt around her had gone as he got to know her better, and he found himself wanting to impress her and spend more and more time in her company.

He thrived on talking to her at first, about the merits of the True Magic, the importance of self-esteem and confidence, how to awaken the Master within and create meaningful relationships, as well as the ability to love compassionately and unconditionally. He even shared his experiences in the crystal cave with her, as well as his expanded knowledge of himself, even his thoughts on life and death. But increasingly it was not always philosophical issues that he wanted to share but more sensual earthly pleasures which would allow him to fully blossom as a man.

The only problem to this idyllic plan was Fynn.

CHAPTER 28

The Green Eyed Monster

"In jealousy there is more of self-love than love."
François de La Rochefoucauld

Fynn felt the same about Skye as Wigapom did, and Wigapom was increasingly jealous.

When Fynn had finally realised his true feelings for Skye, during the time Wigapom was 'missing', he was thrilled to find out that she felt the same. They were able to fully relax in each other's company and allow their burgeoning relationship to develop naturally. Fynn got used to Skye being around him and sharing things with her exclusively. All was fine until Wigapom met Skye too.

At first it had been just four friends together, sharing time and companionship, all generally amicable and happy, but feelings began to subtly change as the summer heightened its intensity, and jealousy and resentment began to push their way between Wigapom and Fynn once again, as they unconsciously vied for first place in Skye's affections, as with the incident over the metals. This threatened both their friendship and the peace.

Wigapom continued to notice how Fynn did all he could to spend time with Skye, often edging Wigapom from her side. Wigapom found himself doing the same, so that it became an unspoken battle of supremacy between them. He noticed, too, the increasing familiarity that Fynn showed Skye, not only with an arm around her shoulder, but brushing her cheek with a finger, or holding her hand. Then there were his bright and lively conversations with her, full of easy banter and knowing looks. Wigapom sullenly called it showing off.

Fynn, on the other hand, watched enviously when Wigapom seemed to have Skye's rapt attention over some philosophical or intellectual point they were discussing, as this did not come naturally to Fynn, who felt uneducated and dull by comparison.

Wigapom, in turn, ached when he heard Skye laughing at the frequent jokes Fynn told; Wigapom had always been too self-conscious to be that humorous. Fynn, on the other hand, began to envy Wigapom's royal status as the King's son, heir to Arcanum, and a folk hero, after what had happened at Dragonmound: Fynn felt his own humble roots acutely and felt he had done nothing, in his own eyes at least, that remarkable.

The divide, of their own making, was widening; both were so wrapped up in vying for Skye's attentions they lost sight of her responses. If they hadn't, they may have noticed that whilst she enjoyed discussing things with Wigapom, it was still Fynn she had true affection for. For Fynn and Wigapom, blinkered by their own irrational jealousies, the two once great friends began again to avoid each other's company, or to react suspiciously to each other's actions and supposed intentions. They increasingly made snide comments and judged each other unfavourably. Skye often found she had to smooth the troubled waters created between them.

Will, growing up and away from Wigapom in leaps and bounds, although more and more identical to him in looks, noticed this too and was torn between leaping to defend his other self or feeling a desire to throttle him in frustration.

None of this went unnoticed by the close-knit community of Oakendale, who had taken each one of them under their affectionate and generous wing. Merric, as Elder, was concerned enough about the situation to discuss it with Gobann.

'No good will come of this, Gobann,' he said to the dwarf one day, 'it's creating a further foothold for Darqu'on to rise again, you mark my words.'

'I believe much of this is Darqu'on's work already,' said Gobann, 'I suspect he is working his evil through both Wigapom and Fynn, and he already knows, from personal experience, how strong and overpowering jealousy can be.'

'Wanting history to repeat itself, perhaps?' said Merric.

'We will have to wait and see,' said Gobann diplomatically.

They did not have to wait long. Gobann knew, when Fynn asked him to make a special gift for Skye, that the gathering storm clouds would soon break, just like the hot and humid weather was threatening to do. Both came to a head one sultry afternoon in late August when, after a morning spent working to get the harvest in, it was just too hot to do anything else but laze in whatever shade they could find. They had been talking of nothing in particular as usual when Will casually asked Wigapom if he could see the stones again, as he had forgotten what the runes were like. An innocent enough request, one would suppose.

'Later, Will,' said Wigapom, who had been trying to sleep under the shade of an old tree, 'I'm too tired at the moment. Any way I don't even know if I have them on me, they may be in my other trouser pocket.'

This casualness was a chance for Fynn to be critical: he took it with relish.

'Isn't that rather dangerous? I would have thought they would be your prime concern. To not know whether you have them or not is risking their safety and that of us all, wouldn't you say?' he said curtly.

'Not really,' said Wigapom, covering his guilt with antagonistic defence. He felt in his pocket and, thankfully, his hand closed around them. He didn't show the relief he felt, just arrogance.

'They're in my pocket, quite safe, after all,' he said condescendingly.

'Oh, go on Wiggy, show them to us,' pleaded Skye, who had been lazily pulling at tufts of grass close by. 'Things are so peaceful here it's easy to forget about the troubles, and I'd like to look at the stones again: It's been ages, maybe we will be able to understand what they mean after all this time,' and she reached over to lightly touch his arm. Wigapom brightened visibly.

'All right, just for you,' he said, sitting up and bringing out the stones.

Skye smiled and held out her hand in readiness for them. It was then that Wigapom noticed a ring of fine filigree copper and silver on her finger that he hadn't seen before. Silver, the metal of unconditional love and affection for all things female, entwined with copper, the declaration of love!

'Who gave you that?' he said indicating the jewellery and wondering why his stomach sickened as he saw it, almost as though he knew without asking who had given it to her.

It had Gobann's skill written all over it, but Wigapom knew he was not the giver. Skye blushed, uncharacteristically, and gave Fynn a sweet smile. Wigapom's heart sank even lower and his stomach churned again as his fears were finally confirmed.

'Fynn asked Gobann to make it for me,' she said lightly.

'Oh,' said Wigapom, barely disguising his jealousy.

Fynn, who had been lying brooding on his front, drumming his fingers on the ground pushed himself up onto his knees.

'That's right Wiggy, I gave it to her yesterday,' and challenge ran through his voice like words in a seaside stick of rock. 'I thought it would suit her. Do you want to make something of that?'

Skye felt the atmosphere tightening between them; Will sat bolt upright knowing what was likely to come.

'Why would you want to give her a ring?' asked Wigapom, hackles rising.

'Why not?' replied Fynn, his own emotional dagger drawn, 'I can do anything I want to, can't I?'

Wigapom's jealousy burst from him in a volley of vituperation. He hardly knew what had come over him.

'Seems to me you always do lately – especially where Skye's concerned, fawning over every word, always hanging around her,' retorted Wigapom.

'Wigapom!' said Skye, shocked at his tone. Fynn, however, was ready to give as good as he got.

'Well,' he shot back, 'if we're talking about Skye – perhaps you'd better look at your own habits – you've done nothing but make eyes at her since you met her.'

'I have not!' lied Wigapom, self-righteously.

'What rubbish!' scoffed Fynn. 'She's the focus of everything for you these days Wiggy. It's like Lampadia all over again; first Will, and look what happened there, and now Skye. Perhaps you should look more closely at yourself, if only to remind yourself of why you're here. This is not supposed to be some summer jaunt you know. You came for a purpose. *We* came for a purpose – one that you seem only too eager to forget these days. You might occasionally talk about the stones, when you remember to have them on you, of course, like some bookish philosopher, but you don't seem to have *earned* many lately, do you? Or understood their meaning? Or even remembered their importance! Darqu'on is still out there, you know, even though we haven't heard that much of him lately, but what's a few dead or missing villagers when you're having so much fun in the sun! And do you seem to care a jot? Not a bit! Too busy trying to muscle in on my girl than saving your Kingdom!'

Well it was out in the ether now! To say that Fynn regretted a lot of what he said the second he said it was true enough, but it was too late. The unspeakable had been spoken, pointed and sharp, like a jagged shard of glass sticking out of the ground, just waiting for someone to cut themselves badly upon it: and Wigapom did.

'How dare you accuse me of doing nothing! And what do you mean, *your* girl! What makes you think you have the right to her and I don't? And who says I have feelings for her?' said Wigapom, using attack and bluff as his best forms of defence.

Weeks of building frustration were already boiling over in Fynn; he couldn't stop now even if he wanted to.

'It's obvious you do, all the time; trying to impress her with who you are and what you know and your importance here. If you don't see that then you're more blinkered and stupid than I thought. But it's all a sham, isn't it? You're a sham. You're supposed to be here to save this place from

Darqu'on; supposed to earn these stones, which apparently no one else can, and remember, Mr High-and-Mighty Wigapom, even then it's not finished, you still have to find *The Book of True Magic* so that you can fit them down its spine. How can you do that when you're so spineless yourself? But you want us to think you're so wonderful – a real hero, a saviour! Huh! Some hero; being lazy and eyeing up my girl! What about the Quest? What about your destiny? What about getting rid of Darqu'on? What are you honestly doing about any of it? How many stones have you actively sought to earn lately? I'll tell you, absolutely none. All you've been doing is having a holiday and ogling Skye! The rest of us can go hang as far as you're concerned. Do you know what? You're pathetic! I don't know how I ever got involved with you as a friend; how I ever believed in you. You bore me! But more than that you disappoint me! You disappoint everyone, even Skye I suspect. She's worth more than you any day. She's got spark, she has. She deserves better than you!'

This tirade of long-suppressed venom spurted like arterial blood from Fynn, leaving him red-faced and panting in the heat, not only of the weather, but his emotions. The nerves on his temples twitched erratically. It was almost possible to see steam rising from him.

Wigapom's jaw dropped momentarily then clamped together like a snare around a rabbit and he spat back his reply. Weeks of similarly hidden resentment and jealousy spewed out like rancid bile.

'And you think you're better? How dare you criticise me, Fynn! You wouldn't be able to enjoy these days in Oakendale if it wasn't for me. Who suffered Darqu'on's power at Dragonmound? Me. Who stood up to Darqu'on and deflected that power? Me. Who has had to grow in understanding before the stones have been able to be found? Me. Always me! And why shouldn't I enjoy a bit of rest and recuperation amongst those who appreciate what I've done. Why shouldn't I want to be with Skye? She's better company than you are these days... And much better looking! If you don't like the way things are going then go home to where you belong, to safe sleepy Brakendor and leave Skye and me in peace.'

Will looked from one to the other, alarmed at what was happening.

'Just a moment, Wigapom, I hope you're not including me in this?' he said, not wanting to be involved in any way in his other self's behaviour even though it was his request that had started all this vitriol.

'Keep out of this, Will,' snapped back Fynn and Wigapom together. 'This has nothing to do with you.'

'But...' interjected Will, annoyed and hurt himself now, but no one was taking any notice of him and he sank back into the shade again, quietly fuming and troubled by what he was hearing; angry at Fynn and at

Wigapom and sorry for Skye, who seemed to be such a source of trouble through no fault of her own. But she was not the type to keep silent and spoke out forcefully.

'Wigapom! Fynn! For goodness sake!' she said, upset and angry at what was happening, 'I'm not a toy you can pass around! I have my own mind and my own feelings!' but neither Fynn nor Wigapom heard anything she said, wrapped up completely in their hatred of each other at that moment.

'Leave you with Skye? Over my dead body! yelled Fynn, continuing their argument as he leapt to his feet, sending a dust cloud into the air as he straddled the ground in his fury.

'That can be arranged!' retorted Wigapom in swift menacing response, as he too jumped to his feet, ready to do bloody murder to his one-time friend.

They leapt at each other then, rolling around in the scratchy parched grass, like warring lions on the veldt.

'STOP IT, THE TWO OF YOU! STOP IT!' cried Skye, shocked and really angry now and also leaping to her feet, trying to part the wrangling pair. Even then they did not hear her, until she threw a handy bucket of water at them both in disgust. The combatants spluttered in surprise as the water drenched them and the fight stopped.

'Let's hope that cools your tempers down,' said Skye. 'Look at yourselves and be ashamed. Be very ashamed!'

Wigapom noticed his cut lip and Fynn felt the beginning of a bruise on his forehead, yet still they looked murderously at each other, even though Skye's condemning remonstration had brought some guilt into their heads, if not sense.

Skye looked from one to the other in disbelief.

'Whatever has got into both of you? What makes you think I'd want to be anywhere near *either* of you acting like this? I don't even *like* either of you at the moment, let alone love, and I certainly don't want to spend any time with you. And remember, both of you, that it's *my* choice who I love or not, not yours. Sort your petty jealousies out between you and come back when you're civilised! And you can keep your ring, if this is what it causes,' and she twisted it from her finger and threw it into the grass. 'Come on, Will, we have better things to do with our time!' and she tossed her thick, dark hair behind her as she grabbed Will's hand and pulled him away from the angry pair.

The air around them was very hot still, but heavy grey clouds had blotted out the sun and huge globules of spiteful rain began to descend, spattering them and the ground like tin tacks as a jagged streak of lightning lit the sky and rolls of thunder erupted into a crescendo of noise above them. Despite the storm breaking, however, the temperature remained sticky and was heady with tension.

'I'm going for a walk,' growled Fynn, plucking the discarded ring from the ground as he turned on his heel, and stormed away from Wigapom and the village.

'I'd think twice about coming back!' yelled Wigapom after him, and then found himself shaking like a jelly as the full force of the moment took hold of him.

His hand went gingerly to his lip, already swelling and streaked with warm blood, but he still refused to accept any responsibility for what happened. In is mind he was the innocent party, incredulous at Fynn's behaviour, and he used martyrdom to cover the shame of his own. He wouldn't let himself see the real truth in all that Fynn had said; wouldn't even acknowledge that he didn't want Fynn to go away, or that he didn't want to fight either, especially not over Skye, who had been nothing but wonderful to both of them; wouldn't admit that what Fynn had said was true, however much they hammered at his brain to be acknowledged. Instead, a wave of self-pity swept over him; he wasn't even responsible for the Quest – none of it had been his choice really, despite what Aldebaran said; this was part of some great master plan somewhere, with him just a pawn in the game; he was innocent and being led like a lamb to the slaughter! He hadn't chosen to be the designated Prince of Light, whose destiny was to save Arcanum – someone else had! He took to the role of victim with gusto, blaming everyone but himself for his situation, and stewed like this for some time, just letting the rain fall onto him, searching for a means of retaliation.

He thought of the ring that Fynn had given Skye, a gift to show love. If he asked Gobann to make something gold and precious for her that would show her how he felt! He'd get her back! His mind was in such an irrational state that it never occurred to him that Skye might really love Fynn.

As the rain fell, pock-marking the ground in its ferocity, he marched off towards the forge in the hillside to find Gobann. He would get him to make the most beautiful ring in the world, using the finest gold and precious jewels. Wigapom was, after all, the rightful King – he could command the making of anything! Skye would be so grateful she would love him instead!

Wigapom entered the forge, puffed up with wounded pride and indignation, to find Gobann, who was busy making a pitchfork with as much loving care and craftsmanship as he dedicated to the finest jewellery. He sensed the tension that accompanied Wigapom, but kept on working, and kept his counsel, as was typical of him, as the sparks from the forge spat and fizzled around the pitchfork, while he waited for Wigapom to speak.

'Gobann,' said Wigapom, imperiously, 'I command you to make me the finest ring you know how!' Gobann chose to ignore the word 'command'.

'For Skye, no doubt,' came his slow but perceptive reply.

Wigapom stopped abruptly in his tracks.

'Yes! How did you know?' he asked defensively.

'Because you think you are in love with her and do not want Fynn to have her,' said Gobann, putting the finishing touches to the pitchfork and plunging it into the vat of cold water at his side, where it steamed, hissed, sputtered and finally settled into its completed, perfected shape.

Gobann's calm perception acted like a pin to Wigapom's bubble of self-inflation.

'Is it so obvious?' he replied. He had really thought that no one else had noticed how he felt about Skye, except Fynn, but as he didn't count, he didn't matter!

'Obvious to all those with eyes to see, of course,' said Gobann, and lifted his visor to expose his pale face and sapphire-coloured eyes gazing into Wigapom's with kindness and non-judgement. Wigapom felt less defensive already, affected by Gobann's calmness. Yet he was still feeling somewhat petulant and sorry for himself.

'I want her to be with ME, Gobann, I don't want Fynn to have her. If I give her a beautiful, precious ring, then she will see how much I care for her and love me instead of Fynn.'

'You think love can be bought with gold or jewels, Wigapom?' asked Gobann, moving towards Wigapom and laying a work-stained hand on his shoulder. 'Love is not for sale. The heart can only give it. If Skye loves you, she will want only your heart and nothing else.'

'And if she doesn't want me?' said Wigapom, almost afraid to receive the answer he could already feel was on Gobann's lips.

'Then she will give her heart to the one she loves instead, and no amount of money or possessions or power will make any difference to her.'

'But she has to love me! I love her! I need her! I'm royalty; that must mean something,' cried Wigapom, desperate now to give any reason he could to hold onto his dream, which even now he could feel evaporating before him.

'Love cannot be commanded. Skye is not obliged to do anything she does not want or cannot feel; she is her own person and has her own feelings. You cannot command a person to love you because of your position, or because you feel she should. To try to trap another into that sort of relationship only leads to pain and anger.'

Wigapom made a last-ditch attempt to hold onto his dwindling viewpoint.

'If I can't have her then I won't let Fynn have her either!'

'It is not your choice, Wigapom. But how would you stop him? Would you wish him dead?'

Before he knew he had done it Wigapom had pictured Fynn dead at his feet and the arrival of the image shocked him to the core of his being.

What had he said? What had he done? Had he really just imagined with relish the death of his dearest, oldest friend? Had they already drawn blood and hurt each other – over a girl they both purported to love? He was stung with guilt and knew he had failed again.

'No, of course not,' he said, blocking the image, horrified at how easily it had got there.

'Be careful of what you desire, Wigapom, as it may come true; and realise that, if her heart is given to Fynn, his death may cause her own.'

Wigapom sighed a mighty sigh. He knew this; he'd known it all along. Yet he didn't know how to deal with the situation.

'What do I do?' cried Wigapom, 'Tell me, Gobann, what do I do?'

'I cannot answer for you. You must listen to your own heart. Speak your own truth. Isn't that what the last two stones were trying to tell you?'

'Oh, you and Aldebaran are just the same!' exploded Wigapom in frustration. 'Neither of you will ever give me a straight answer! I don't understand the stones' message. I thought I did, but now I'm confused. And I don't want to have to keep relying on myself for answers all the time. I need someone else to do it for me. It's much too much hard work otherwise!' And Wigapom turned his back childishly on Gobann. Gobann remained calm and logical.

'To be dependent on another for your happiness or your aid is creating a state of powerlessness for yourself. If you look to someone else for the answers, how will you ever find things out for yourself, how will you ever learn to believe in yourself?'

Frustration boiled over at this point in Wigapom, who spun back to face Gobann with deeply troubled eyes.

'Oh, why does everything you say make so much sense, Gobann, even if I don't want it to! I thought I did believe in myself, but I don't know this part of me. I've never loved anyone like Skye before, not like this, and I don't know how to deal with it!' His voice was shrill and desperate.

Gobann looked kindly on him in silence for a while, his blue eyes bright, even in the gloom of the forge.

'Do you know about your parents Wigapom, and what happened to them?' he asked unexpectedly.

Wigapom was surprised at the question, for in truth he knew very little of their earthly lives other than what Aldebaran had told him about their deaths.

'No, not really, not as much as I would like,' he replied.

'You'd best sit down while I tell you. It is time you knew,' said Gobann as Wigapom sat beside him. 'Your mother and father loved each other very much, and were much loved by us all. Even though your mother gave up her immortality to marry your father, she was willing to do this, for eternal earthly life without the man she loved would have been unthinkable for her. It had nothing to do with him being King, but everything to do with her feelings for him as a person. But there was a third party involved, who could not, or would not understand this. He was a good friend of the King, and a talented and increasingly powerful magician, yet he wanted your mother for himself and became increasingly jealous of her relationship with the King. She was always kind to him, but he wanted her to love him, and only him. He began to abuse the magic by casting spells to make her love him and set her against your father – he even used magic in an attempt to turn your father against her. He did not succeed, but a time of great discord and uncertainty was created in the Court and the country, which began to weaken all that was good within it. Your mother resisted all attempts to sway her, and with her elven strength, which the stones you seek are imbued with, was able to do this. She could never stop loving your father; no amount of sorcery would ever change that.'

Wigapom began to recall some things Darqu'on had said at their encounter on Dragonmound, but he had not really taken them to heart until now. Now things were clearer.

'This other party as you call him, it's Darqu'on isn't it?' he said.

Gobann nodded and continued.

'Darqu'on used every means at his disposal to turn them against each other, but instead it made their love stronger. When they married, Darqu'on's jealousy turned to hatred for them both; if he couldn't take your mother from your father then he would take his Kingdom instead. More than that, he wanted total domination over everything and everyone, and you can see now the results of this. When you were conceived, Darqu'on's hatred intensified beyond imagining. He vowed he would not rest until your father and you were dead. You have to understand that through his jealousy Darqu'on had lost all sense of compassion by this time and turned completely to the dark arts of sorcery and necromancy, which ate his heart and his soul and spat them out as dark matter. You know, of course, that he killed your father at Dragonmound soon after you were born, and imprisoned your mother, as he still believed he could turn her mind to love him.'

'My mother killed herself, didn't she?' said Wigapom, soberly recalling what Aldebaran had told him all those months ago.

'She had lost everything she valued – you had been taken away at birth to save you and now she had lost her beloved husband. She chose not to live any more without you both and threw herself from a window in the high tower in the Citadel, in full knowledge that she would suffer earthly death but be reunited with her husband through that act.'

Wigapom now knew why Darqu'on had kept referring to 'her'. How much he must have hated her for not loving him, how much hatred he must have felt for her husband, the King, once his best friend; no wonder he had so much hatred for Wigapom himself, being the constant reminder of his parents' love for each other; no wonder he wanted to make Wigapom suffer in the way he felt he had suffered because of them. He had projected that revenge onto every person in Arcanum, condemning them all to a life of fear, torment, and a living death, turning lives upside down in his insatiable lust for revenge. Wigapom recalled his image of Darqu'on as a frightened young boy and wondered what traumas had occurred in his early life to create such a monster.

'So you see, Wigapom,' Gobann continued, 'trying to make someone love you when they have given their heart to another can lead to greater hatred and destruction than you could ever want to see. Is that what you want to happen with Fynn and Skye and with all those you care about?'

Wigapom saw the parallel Gobann had drawn between his parents and Darqu'on, and himself, Fynn and Skye: it shook him to think of the thoughts of hatred he had expressed just a few moments ago!

'No Gobann, of course I don't want that, I'm not a monster like Darqu'on. I have feelings.'

'He had feelings too, Wigapom, but they over-ran him and he chose to use them for evil ends. What will you choose to do with yours?'

Wigapom was in turmoil, torn by his head and his heart; he knew what he had to do but he also ached for Skye – whatever decision he made would mean a sacrifice. If he chose to pursue Skye he could risk losing her and Fynn, not to mention ruining the lives of all those in Arcanum; how could he betray his heritage and birth for that? Yet could he really give up the woman he felt he loved?

Then he asked himself a more honest question: did he really love her or just want to possess her because she helped him feel good about himself? It was hard to admit, but he knew this was the reality. If he wanted to be able to live with himself he would have to relinquish any feelings for

Skye other than friendship. He would not risk ending up as bitter and twisted as Darqu'on. Besides he could see the truth now: despite Skye throwing back the ring, she really loved Fynn; he had always known from the softness of her gaze and tenderness in her voice. He gave Gobann his decision.

'There is only one choice that I can make if I'm to live with myself in peace. I must leave all thoughts of Skye behind and continue with my Quest. We both know that. In fact I *want* to complete my Quest – I have ignored my real purpose again, and I really thought I'd learned my lesson, but I swear nothing will stop me from seeing it through. I dedicate my life for the benefit of the All in the One, and will not rest until my part in the Quest is complete. I finally accept my destiny.'

Gobann smiled and nodded, content that the right decision had been made and that the magic he had crafted into the ring had done its job well.

Wigapom knew that the decision he had just made would take his life on a very different path from Fynn's, but he wanted to take it. By finally accepting his responsibility to Arcanum, he felt a weight fall from him, and there was the promise of contentment in that. He left Gobann's forge a different person.

He wasn't sure he could face Skye quite at that moment, but he wanted to tell Fynn of his decision to make up for the pain and bad feelings he had caused. But where was Fynn? He had to find him and make his peace. He set out with a determined heart to seek him out.

Fynn didn't know where he was going. He just kept walking and walking: going over and over in his mind all the injustices he felt Wigapom had dealt him since starting the Quest. Any regret at what he had first said was now long buried under a mound of smouldering resentment that spat and rolled, lava-like, from the inner volcano of his being. If there had been a part of him that felt concerned over the vitriol that he'd spewed forth, then the rest of him was totally ignoring it. He wanted to play the victim and he was doing it with style and self-righteous indignation.

'Damn him! Damn him for dragging me out here away from my home; for ignoring me; for putting me through such anger and guilt, and now trying to take Skye away from me! Just because I'm ordinary, and he's not! How dare he! I hope the Shadow gets him! I want him to suffer. I want him to suffer badly!'

The thoughts continued, as if on a loop, round and round in his head: he became more incensed and angry than ever. Had he been able to see himself, he would have noticed a black cloud of negative energy hanging heavy and thick around his shoulders, obliterating his presence, pressing down on him harder and harder the more his acrimonious thoughts continued.

Dark green reptilian eyes followed him, gleefully rejoicing in the creation of such negative energy helping to restore his Master's power – and this had all been Scabtail's idea! Darqu'on had been left reeling after Dragonmound and sunk into a darker place than normal. Scabtail feared this Master more than the other and wanted to do what he could to restore him to his former terrible self, so he had suggested the love triangle as a means of creating discord and destabilising the situation once more. Scabtail grinned at the thought of his success with 'The Other', as he called Fynn. Pity it hadn't worked with The Brat, thanks to that wretched dwarf, although Scabtail had done his best: he wouldn't let that upset his moment of triumph however!

He grinned to himself again, determined to keep the momentum of success at the forefront: The Master would be pleased when he reported back that his idea had worked – maybe Darqu'on would reward him. At the very least he hoped that he would not be punished!

CHAPTER 29

Reconciliation and Retribution

*"Reconciliation should be accompanied by justice, otherwise it will not last.
While we all hope for peace it shouldn't be peace at any cost
but peace based on principle, on justice."*
Corazon Aquino

Wigapom looked for Fynn for hours, but there was no sign of him; it was as though he had dropped off the face of the earth. He thought at one point he had seen him in the distance, but it turned out to be just a black cloud.

He returned to Oakendale with heavy steps to find Skye and Will talking with Merric and Tamsan about Fynn's whereabouts. Skye was worried at his continued disappearance, her usual welcoming eyes clouded now with concern, and disappointment. Wigapom knew without doubt what Fynn meant to her and that he could never have hoped to win her from him.

Will looked as uncomfortable as Wigapom felt. Even Merric and Tamsan did not give their usual friendly greetings, but looked sternly at him as he approached. Wigapom sensed their judgement and squirmed with guilt yet again, missing Gobann's compassion and unconditional acceptance, and disturbed by his own lack of success in locating Fynn.

'I can't find him!' he said, stating the obvious in some despair. 'He's just disappeared. I did try. I did try to resolve this. I'm so sorry Skye, will you ever forgive me? I don't know what got into me.' His voice was pleading but he received no sympathy, just a pained look that tore at his already ripped heart.

'There will be no further peace until this is resolved,' said Merric sternly. 'You and Fynn have created discord and anger again, which is fuel for Darqu'on's fire. You have given him power, when it was your duty to vanquish it.'

'I never meant to give him power!' wailed Wigapom, quite desperate now in his realisation of the harm he had done. 'It just happened.'

'You have to find him, Wigapom,' said Skye, looking at him with pain and accusation in her eyes, which cut him like a knife.

'I can't if he doesn't want to be found! I've let you down by my stupidity – once again! Will I never learn? And my feelings for you… Well, I do care, but I have no right to demand that you feel the same. I'm so sorry. I didn't understand what was happening, but it should never have happened like this. The hardest thing to admit is he was right and now I've lost you all,' said Wigapom trying not to look at Skye. 'But I'll do what I can to make up for it: if I can't resolve this directly with Fynn, at least I can do what I came here for and continue the Quest.' He felt Will's questioning eyes on him, wondering what part he now played.

'I have to do this alone.' he said looking directly at Will, 'You might look more like me every day, Will, but you're growing away as well as up, becoming a person in your own right. Look at you, almost as tall as me now and more of an Adult than I've ever been. My mistakes are not yours. You have earned the right to be an individual, but I have to work on myself much more, to find that Adult in me, and be at peace with myself. I need you to stay here and continue to grow up safely and happily into the person you're meant to be. There's a bigger picture here which none of us can see clearly yet, but we will, believe me, we will.'

Will knew exactly what Wigapom meant; he'd felt it once they'd left the Master's house and found themselves on the path leading to Dragonmound. Somehow he *was* becoming a person in his own right, no longer just Wigapom's inner child. He had his own feelings and opinions that didn't always tally with Wigapom. He'd felt since coming to Oakendale that he had a different role to play in this story and would have to return, in time, to Brakendor. He could still connect with Wigapom's emotions, and wanted to hug him to show his support and compassion, but Wigapom held him back.

'I don't deserve hugs at the moment,' he said. 'Not until I've done what I'm destined to do. I'm a Prince, true born, but what's the point of being one when I have yet to accept the responsibility that goes with it? I'm meant to be a hero but I feel more a villain at the moment; I have to change my colours from black to white. Time for affection when I've done that and finally fulfilled my Quest.'

'Words are cheap unless backed up by action, Wigapom,' said Tamsan sternly, with Merric nodding in agreement.

'I know,' said Wigapom with quiet reflection and sadness in his voice, 'It's strange but what seems a life time ago now, I set out alone from a village much like this one with just a small bag of belongings and a heart full of hope. So much has happened since then. The only thing that's now missing is the friend that loved me enough to follow me. I will do my best to find him and I will do my best to gain the other stones. I'll not let you, or him, or Arcanum down anymore. It's time I stopped letting my lower emotions rule me and let my higher intuition guide me instead, or I will forever be in Darqu'on's grip,' and Wigapom turned to leave with a last, soft glance at Skye. As he did so he saw a tear graze her cheek.

Wigapom went to say goodbye to Gobann, who was sorting through some items when he arrived, having anticipated Wigapom's parting visit.

'These are for you,' said Gobann, 'for your journey. They may come in useful in time.'

'What are they?' asked Wigapom

'Tools to help you, use them well,' encouraged Gobann, proceeding to lay out the items he had prepared: a silver dagger, a mercury lamp, a copper coin embossed with a phoenix and a crown on alternate sides, a tin whistle, an iron key, and a lead weight. Six of the seven main metals. A strange collection, Wigapom thought.

'Use the silver dagger when healing or protection is required,' began Gobann. 'It will always stay sharp and true as long as it is never used in anger. The Mercury lamp will light your way and bring you comfort in the dark times.'

Wigapom was grateful for this; he remembered only too well his wish for a lamp during his first fearful night in the Forbidden Forest.

'The coin will pay your way when you need it, but use your eyes carefully and remember not to accept everything at face value. The key will release possibilities as well as locks, so keep your wits about you, whilst the whistle will make its presence felt in ways that may take you by surprise, but will help. Lastly, take this nugget of lead – the lord of death – and use it when your need is greatest. Remember, Wigapom, that all metals have negative and positive aspects, so use them well.'

Wigapom thanked him, placing the dagger in its sheath in his belt, the mercury lamp in his bag, the lead weight in the pocket with the stones and the coin in the other, along with the key and whistle.

'Do you have your mother's gold ring, Wigapom?' asked Gobann, referring to the ring Wigapom had been given in the Wheel of Life ceremony.

'Yes,' said Wigapom, wondering why Gobann should ask. 'It's on a chain around my neck, where it's always been.'

'It's time for you to wear it on your hand,' explained Gobann, 'it will protect you when you read the inscriptions.'

Wigapom took the strangely shaped ring out from inside his jerkin and looked at it closely for the first time in ages; it was shaped like a snake eating its own tail. It fascinated him, but he had never noticed words on it.

'I can't see any words,' he said, straining his eyes to no avail.

'When you have faith you will see them. When you trust in their presence then they will show themselves to you,' said Gobann.

Wigapom looked confused, not understanding how words could appear or disappear depending on whether you believed in their presence or not. Gobann did his best to explain.

'This is your mother's ring, Wigapom, made from elven gold. It has different magical properties to those found in the mines here. When you have faith and trust in its power, words will appear and disappear depending on the situation you find yourself in, so remember to check them when you need special protection and help. If you have no faith, then no words will be revealed.'

Wigapom was unsure, and said as much to Gobann, who answered him with questions.

'Do you believe in the power of the stones?

Well, of course he did, otherwise he would not be on this Quest.

'Do you believe that your mother and father are helping you in your Quest?'

Wigapom remembered the occasions his mother had appeared to him in dreams, and at the brook, and how his father had offered such wise words under the tree at Dragonmound, so how could he doubt that they were helping him?

'Do you believe it is your destiny to complete this Quest?'

Yes, he did: although he had not always acted in the best ways, he really did believe that this was what he had been put on earth to achieve.

'Then you have faith and trust in the process. Extend that faith and trust into believing that words will reveal themselves to you when you look at the ring, and believe they are there to help your progress.'

Wigapom looked at Gobann and knew he was right. He knew when he looked at the ring words would appear and, sure enough, words were forming, in tiny, neatly engraved letters.

'Jumping Jeepers! It really works!' he said, 'So every time I really look for them, as long as I believe, they will be there, different words will be there to help me?' he said.

'That's right. Read the message now.'

Wigapom looked closer and read out loud.

This golden ring will encircle you with all the protection you need.
Just have faith in your heart to make them appear and all the words you will read.

'You will do well to take heed of the messages, Wigapom. The protection is only there when you do.'

'Why didn't I know about this before, when I needed help and protection?'

'You had to prove yourself worthy of using the elven magic,' said Gobann, 'to be able to lift the magic from the confines of the ring to reality: Every positive act you have done since being on the Quest has allowed this to happen.'

'What about all the not-so-positive acts I have done?' said Wigapom ruefully. 'I don't suppose they have helped much.'

'Even supposed wrong actions, if lessons are learned from them, can be positive,' said Gobann wisely.

'So I can make good out of bad?' said Wigapom, 'That's encouraging.'

Gobann smiled again

'Place the ring now on the middle finger of your left hand. This is the finger that denotes your life's purpose and will be activated by your intuition, allowing you to create the protection you need.'

Wigapom found the ring a perfect fit. His mother's ring, now on his finger: there was something very comforting about that. He threaded the key and whistle onto the chain in its place, replacing it around his neck, and realised that, apart from Gobann's gifts, he was setting out with almost exactly the same things as he had done when he began his Quest in the early Spring. Now it was almost Autumn. So much had happened in that time. How different this departure would be. Now he was leaving a place where he had found happiness, but leaving alone and under a cloud.

When he finally left the village of Oakendale the daylight was already fading. No one bade him farewell, for he had asked to leave alone, and his heart was heavy as he walked away, not knowing where to go or whether he would find Fynn, but trusting enough in the higher power that he had come to recognise was around and within him at times to take him where he needed to be. He now had to pay attention to this higher power and relinquish his reliance on his ego self, which had only seemed to get him into more trouble and take him further away from his real purpose. He saw now that Darqu'on needed him, and every citizen, to function only from their lower self to keep them in thrall to him. If only he had realised this before by listening to his intuition more frequently.

As he walked, he focused constantly on seeing an image of Fynn before him, as though willing him to appear.

'Forgive me Fynn, forgive me Fynn,' he repeated. It became like a mantra and one he found strangely comforting. If only he could say this in person he could go forward with a settled heart.

He had walked some way before he saw, in the gathering dusk, a shape sitting on a rock, which he recognised immediately as Fynn. He stopped in his tracks, offering thanks for the answer to his prayer whilst stilling all movement and sound, as though not sure whether Fynn would want to be disturbed. However, Fynn sensed he was there and turned to face him. Even in the gloom of the evening, Wigapom could clearly sense the expression in Fynn's eyes, and his heart sank again, for they were heavy, dark and troubled. Fynn did not acknowledge Wigapom, but Wigapom gathered his courage and spoke to him.

'I'm sorry Fynn, forgive me, I've been an absolute fool and you have every right to hate me. You've always been a good friend to me, despite everything, and I know that I've hurt you badly. I don't know whether you can ever forgive me, but I hope you will, at least in time. I need you to know that I'm finishing the Quest on my own. I have no right to expect you to give up any more of your life for me – Skye is waiting back in Oakendale for you – please go back to her, and Will too, who's his own person these days, with little need for me, and thank you for shaking me into changing. I will always value our friendship.'

Silence hung in the air, as heavy as the lead in Wigapom's pocket, so thick and heavy, Wigapom thought, it could be cut with a knife! Wigapom turned to walk away, when he suddenly remembered the dagger that Gobann had crafted for him. He had told him to only use it for healing and never in anger. Well, he needed to heal this situation with Fynn: could he use the dagger to cut the air to release the poison held within it? Silver was known to heal wounds, Gobann had said. Well, this was an emotional wound between them. It was worth trying, and something had to break the atmosphere if he was to stand any chance of raising the energy between them and finding reconciliation.

He lifted the dagger from its sheath and held it in the palms of both hands, watching as it glinted with a sparkling sheen. Time hung suspended. He shifted its weight from one hand to the other, noting its sharpness, its fine craftsmanship and beauty, but he also saw how deadly it could still be if he used it with a cold-bloodied heart, keeping anger at bay. Suddenly he became aware that he *was* cold and without feeling of any kind, robotic almost, with the potential to be a killing machine. He was poised on the brink of two possibilities; one of healing; the other, cold-blooded revenge. He paused with the dagger clutched in his hand for what was only a second, but which seemed like an eternity. Every movement happened as if in slow motion. He felt Fynn turn to look at him questioningly, his face harder now and defensive. Wigapom met his gaze, their eyes locking, unblinking, on each other. Wigapom felt an unbidden feeling wash over him like a rushing wave: He watched himself raise the dagger in his right hand. For a moment he struggled between two possibilities: as though the opposing forces of light and dark were both demanding his allegiance. It was a disturbingly powerful feeling and his head swam, his heart pounded, and his vision blurred, as a cacophony of conflicting ideas rang in his ears. An image of Darqu'on's face appeared fleetingly in front of him, urging him to strike out at Fynn.

The stones began vibrating in his pocket and he saw himself sweeping the knife down in front of him, closer and closer to Fynn's questioning face, and he knew immediately what way to take. *Slash*! The dagger sliced through the heavy space between them, splitting Darqu'on's image in two, and something lifted. Wigapom felt connected again, lighter, as his swift action restored his equilibrium. The sensation of normal time and space returned and the air sang with sweet sounds as the dagger's healing magic began to work. Wigapom, however, was shaking; he knew how close he had come in that time to wanting to use the dagger in cold-blooded revenge. Despite Gobann's assurances, Wigapom was sure that he could have accessed the negative power in the dagger. He felt, yet again, Darqu'on's insidious presence, which slithered its way through every thought, feeling, action, and even object, against which he must constantly be on his guard. He was sure it was only the power of the stones that kept him from making the wrong decisions at times like this. He breathed deeply and saw the expression on Fynn's face had begun to change from dark to light; defensiveness and hurt fell away, like ice on a warm wall, as life came back into his face and frame, which had seemed dead just moments before. It surged through Wigapom too and he relaxed again. Knowing he had done all he could, Wigapom sheathed the dagger and stood waiting for Fynn to respond. He did not have to wait long before Fynn spoke in a measured tone, with just a hint of the old sense of humour nudging at the edges of his words.

'Now I know what they mean by cutting the atmosphere with a knife!' he said, eyes bright as he levelled them to meet Wigapom's gaze. Wigapom smiled ruefully at their similar thoughts, but stayed silent; it was not finished yet.

'I promised myself I would never speak to you again,' continued Fynn, not moving from the rock and with eyes fixed on Wigapom. Wigapom nodded; he had expected as much. But at least they were talking now, and the atmosphere between them was warmer and mending.

'I know I hurt you, again. It seems to be a habit of mine,' Wigapom replied, with regret etched in his voice.

'I was hurt, yes,' said Fynn, 'but not by you this time, Wigapom, I see that now. I hurt myself, yet I blamed you for it. It was how I chose to see things that created my pain, not what you did or didn't do. I won't make you responsible for my feelings again – you've taught me that much.'

'I haven't been a very good teacher,' replied Wigapom.

'I've been sitting here stewing in my hatred of you for hours,' continued Fynn, 'calling you every unpleasant thing under the sun and plotting terrible things, but all the time, even though I tried to shut it out and ignore it, there was a little voice inside that kept telling me to look at *my* behaviour, *my* jealousies. I didn't want to for a long time; I wanted to suffer and feel hatred and hurt, yet now I've allowed myself to listen to that voice and I've realised I'm not without blame in any of this. I wanted to kill you at one point, Wigapom, and I realise that this is exactly what Darqu'on has set out to do – to keep people stuck in these lower emotions, to breed fear and negativity and hatred. Divide and rule, I think you might call it, but I've decided I will have none of it. It's not easy; the feelings were so strong they completely overtook me at first, but then, suddenly when you cut through the air just now, I saw that I could change, if I chose to, that I didn't need to live with past hurts – a bit like you, it would seem, and if *we* can change then perhaps others will see that it's possible for them to change as well? I might only be one insignificant person in the scheme of things, but if my decision can help someone put their fear and hate behind them, then that's enough for me.'

Wigapom's heart went out to Fynn: he knew only too well how true those words were. Brave, wonderful, dear, compassionate, thoughtful Fynn. How could he ever have doubted him. He wanted to hug him!

'Oh Fynn!' he beamed, 'You could never be insignificant – you are an inspiration to me and always have been!'

'Me? An inspiration? To you? Really? Well fancy that, and I thought I was just plain old Fynn, the hired hand! But then you've been an inspiration to me too, Wiggy; I would never have left Brakendor without you and would never have got to understand myself as I am beginning to now.'

'You and me both. No hard feelings then?' said Wigapom.

'None,' said Fynn and they hugged, all bitterness forgiven.

'I'm so relieved we're friends again,' said Wigapom, 'but I feel guilty for wasting so much time. I became too complacent after Dragonmound. I know I needed rest after what happened, but it became sloth. Now I have to make up for lost time and move on alone, much as I'd like your company. I have to connect with who I am, where I've really come from, before I can do anymore. I'm sure that I'll never attain the other stones, or find *The Book of True Magic* unless I do.'

'I know you are right,' agreed Fynn. 'I feel I've a different part to play in this too, even though I don't know what it is yet. I'm always there as and when you need me,' promised Fynn. 'Remember all those plans we made as children, Wiggy? Funny the way things never quite turn out the way we expect.'

'But they always turn out for the best, Fynn, everything is perfect, even in its imperfections.'

'That sounds like good philosophy to me!' smiled Fynn. They hugged again as the real friends they were and always would be. Then they parted; Fynn going back to Skye and Will, and Wigapom going back to find his past. Only once did they turn and wave a final farewell before the dusk enfolded each from view, but that image remained with them both, as a special sign of friendship and recognition of the different paths they now had to follow. Paths that would rejoin eventually, as the two parts of the blue stone had done.

High in the dark tower of the Citadel, emotions were very different to those just witnessed on the ground. Darqu'on was incandescent with rage, and intent on blaming Scabtail for all that had just happened, choosing to ignore the fact that his own power had not been strong enough.

'You imbecile!' yelled his shrill voice at a quivering Scabtail, 'I should never have listened to you! Your plan was useless. Can't I trust you to get anything right?'

'Master, forgive me,' cowered Scabtail, 'I was so sure that his hatred was fixed. How was I to know that he would change?'

'You blockheaded, slimy, pathetic excuse for a servant! Get out of my sight!' came the explosive reply, and Scabtail fled as a fender, hot from the fire, flew across the room at him, which not only caught him a painful blow on his long-suffering tail, but morphed, on impact, into a red flash of molten fire that singed his scales. He slithered off into the shadows once more to nurse his smouldering body, as well as his damaged ego.

Alone again, Darqu'on paced the floor, mad and angered yet again by the infuriating ability of his adversaries to rise above the fear, jealousy and hatred he had been pumping into them since they first came through the Forbidden Forest. To have been thwarted, indeed trounced, by The Brat at Dragonmound had been bad enough, and he was still suffering from this, but to have this happen now, after he felt he was clawing his power back, was too much and made him more full of rage and desire for revenge than ever. Someone, somewhere would suffer for this; he had been too soft for too long; kept too low a profile; relying only on his fearsome reputation and not enough on actions, but he realised something else, something he had thought of before, but perhaps not given as much notice to in the past as he should, believing his own power was more than enough to win: The Brat was winning power back with something else, how else would the dwarf's silver dagger have worked its positive magic against his own negative power?

'Those stones are behind all this,' he muttered. 'I knew I should have them – they have more power than I thought, even though they're not all yet revealed. The stones are helping him take the power back, but I WILL NOT ALLOW IT!' he shrieked, the dark veins in his pale neck pulsing with rage. 'Those wretched stones of Magus, may his bones rot in hell, must be mine, and I will have them before I lose more power back to the light – power that is mine by right! I *must* have the stones; I *will* have them, and when I do I will toss them and The Brat into the very pit of hell and be rid of them once and for all. No more playing! Time for swift and final revenge! No one defies Darqu'on and survives!' And with that, he swept into his secret room in the Citadel to plot and execute his final solution.

CHAPTER 30

Hell Fire!

"The fire you kindle for your enemy often burns yourself more than him."
Chinese Proverb

'What was that?' cried Will, returning to Oakendale with Gobann after fixing some damaged ironwork on the lookout tower on the hill. The dusk had already settled around them like a grey blanket when there was an almighty crack, followed instantly by a torrent of colour, bruising the sky with violent red and purple streaks.

'That was trouble!' answered Gobann as the air shook around them, knocking them both off-balance with its deafening noise and heavy vibrational surge.

'Look in the sky!' yelled Will above the ear-splitting sound. As their eyes shot skywards once more they watched in fixated horror as Darqu'on's face emerged from the discoloured sky, spreading itself out above them, while his thundering voice filled the dale.

'YOU THOUGHT YOU HAD SEEN THE LAST OF ME BUT HOW WRONG YOU ARE! FROM TODAY YOU WILL ALL FEEL THE POWER OF MY SHADOW UNLEASHED UPON YOU AS YOU HAVE NEVER KNOWN BEFORE. THIS IS JUST THE BEGINNING OF MY REVENGE ON YOU ALL! BE AFRAID! BE VERY AFRAID!'

Gobann stared at Darqu'on's image smeared across the torrid sky and felt the grip of real fear twist deep into his heart. There had never been as awesome an appearance from him before, never so much venom spewing out in such a dramatic way. Something had changed for the worse, but even this was not what took his or Will's main point of attention, for below them, towards the village they could now see a halo of purple-grey smoke infused with red and orange tongues of flame that spread out along the horizon, reminiscent of the breath of the black dragon at Dragonmound but even worse in its heat and intensity.

'He's burning the village!' Gobann cried in horror as he began to run forward, but Will was already running down the hill, his agile legs easily overtaking the shorter, stiffer ones of the dwarf as both headed towards the inferno ahead.

As they ran, countless leering spectres morphed out of the purple-grey clouds, blocking their path with suffocating tendrils of smoke, clawing at their faces and filling their nostrils with the acrid smell, whilst a violent wind fanned the flames to make them even stronger, yet Will and Gobann continued to push forward. They could feel the searing heat now from the blazing village, hear the crackle of the flames like maniacal laughter all around them, smell the wood and thatch of the cottages as they were consumed by the flames and, even worse, the repugnant smell of flesh burning as if on a giant barbecue.

Will, with his arms vainly trying to protect his face from the smoke and flames, struggled to make his way to Merric's cottage, in the centre of the village, where they had left Skye just a short time before, but both he and Gobann were driven back by the crackling furnace of flames and the choking acridity of smoke. They heard heart-wrenching screams coming from the flaming buildings and could just make out human shapes, some with clothes or flesh on fire, fleeing in every direction from what was left of their homes, desperately trying to avoid burning timbers crashing around them, but it was impossible to identify anyone. Gobann and Will's eyebrows and lashes singed in the heat and smoke as they searched without success for Skye. They could go no further into the village or else they too would perish, as no doubt many already had.

'The river,' panted Gobann, 'head for the river!'

There they would be safer, but Gobann was struggling. Will helped him as best he could, knowing the danger they were in, and together they staggered from the stifling, choking heat, heading towards the only natural source that might protect them from the roaring flames. Other survivors, some barely hanging onto life, had the same idea it seemed; the place was teeming with distraught, panicked, and burned people.

Will recognised Tetric, a village watchman, his arms and hands severely blistered from the flames; he was plunging them into the water, where they sizzled and steamed as he cried out in agony from the pain. Gobann stooped down to help him, ripping the bottom of his coat to wrap round the scarred hands as he encouraged Tetric to tell him in shocked, halting, pain-fuelled bursts what had happened.

'No warning. Nothing. Merric... He died... I saw it... Body just went up in flames... Like a torch he was... And the houses... Like tinder boxes ... Just exploding all around... So many dead... So many burned... So many lost souls… It was like Hell had come to take Oakendale for its own!'

'And Skye? What about Skye?' said Will, his face creased with anxiety, 'And have you see Fynn?'

'I haven't see either of them, and I don't ever want to see anything like that ever again!' Tetric broke down into shaking sobs over the horrors he had just witnessed.

Gobann was as practical and as compassionate as ever.

'I'll do what I can for him Will, and the other survivors,' he said. 'You keep looking for Skye and Fynn, your legs are younger than mine.'

'But I…' began Will, not wanting to leave Gobann unassisted.

'No time for buts – you must find them, for the good of all!'

Will needed no second bidding. He ran, scouring each shape and face, searching for his friends, feeling he was trapped in a terrible nightmare from which he would never wake.

By the time Fynn made his way back towards Oakendale, the sky was as black as pitch, so he was surprised to see an orange glow in the sky as he neared the village, like an early sunrise spread out in a huge halo. Then he smelled the pungent smoke and saw the flames leaping skyward and knew something terrible had happened.

He broke into a run, although he was unsure of exactly what to do. He could already feel the heat from the flames and see that everywhere was burning. Nothing had been left unscathed. In panic his thoughts turned to Skye and Will, Gobann and the others and he ran faster still, praying they had not perished in the flames.

He was close to the river now, where straggling survivors lay exhausted, homeless and bewildered. Around them were charred bodies of those who had not been so lucky in their escape. It was a vision of Hell that ripped into Fynn's anguished heart, yet in the midst of it all there sounded a clarion call of hope.

'Fynn!' came a familiar voice.

He turned and relief flooded over him as he saw Will running towards him. He seemed untouched by the fire, although he was dishevelled and distraught. Perhaps there was hope for Skye!

'Will! Thank goodness you're safe! What happened? Where's Skye?'

'I don't know about Skye. I've been looking for her. This was Darqu'on's doing, Fynn. He set the village ablaze. We saw him. It was terrible. He just appeared in the sky and then there were flames everywhere!

Gobann and I weren't in the village, so we escaped, but so many didn't. Gobann is helping to look after those that are left.'

'Darqu'on did this? If he has hurt Skye, I'll kill him myself!'

'No Fynn! That won't stop him. It won't stop anything! Don't you see? He'll just get stronger through our hatred. We must not retaliate in that way, but build our defences from inner strength, not outer might.'

'You're right' said a more rational Fynn. 'I've just told Wigapom that myself.'

'I knew you'd found him,' said Will, relieved.

'He found me. He has gone on alone, but then you must know that already too. Everything's fine between us now, if you don't count the guilt for what we allowed to happen,' he swept his arm around the scene before him, 'and this wouldn't have happened if we had remained steadfast!'

'There's no point in regretting the past, Fynn, or even concerning ourselves over the future too much. We only ever have now: Now is what we must focus on!'

'You sound just like Wigapom.'

'I *am* Wigapom, but I'm also growing into me, as Will. It's complicated I know, but it's happening. I'm both Wigapom and Will to some degree. I don't understand it, but that doesn't matter at the moment.'

'You're right; Skye is important now, we must focus on searching for her. I won't rest until I know she's safe.'

'Perhaps she managed to escape back to Lampadia through the tunnels, back to her father. She certainly isn't here, and I won't let myself believe she's dead!'

'Neither will I. We must go back to Lampadia too. Now.' said Fynn, and he sprinted towards the tunnels, followed by a new Adult Will.

As they followed the river towards the tunnels they found Gobann again amidst the carnage. He was doing all he could to bring relief to the wounded, but he had some more unpleasant news for them.

'Other villages and towns have been targeted too. We don't know yet about Lampadia, but I fear the worst and Darqu'on is already creating a new army from the dead!'

'We're going to Lampadia to look for Skye! Will you come with us?' asked Fynn.

'No,' said Gobann, shaking his head firmly, 'my place is here, with the injured of my village, but you must go, and go quickly, your help is needed elsewhere.'

'I never expected it to end like this,' said Fynn.

'This is not the end,' replied Gobann darkly, 'but just the beginning of Darqu'on's final revenge. We have seen nothing yet, believe me.'

Will and Fynn found many survivors had escaped to the tunnels cut into the hills, not only from Oakendale, but from other affected villages close by and the tunnels were packed with desperate escapees making their way to the Temple in Lampadia – hoping for safety and sanctuary there. The dank darkness of the tunnels contrasted with the heat and vivid light of the burning villages, but they offered little comfort, echoing instead to the anguish of so many. Distress was written upon every face, held in every hunched, bruised and burned body, each one constantly reliving the moment when their world and community was erased by Darqu'on's revenge. Their pain, rage and hatred, as well as fear, was tangible and filling the tunnels with emotionally jagged vibrational energy.

Will and Fynn understood the emotions only too well, but also knew that this was just what Darqu'on wanted; negativity to breed more negativity, hatred to breed more hatred, fear to breed more fear. They were playing into his hands and these feelings of vengeance and terror were just making vengeance and terror more of a reality for Darqu'on to spread his Shadow wider. Very soon, nowhere would be safe. Not even the tunnels.

'It is working, my obnoxious friend! Let them suffer, let them burn, let them create their own destruction, I have them now,' said Darqu'on triumphantly to the mirrors, as he spied the apocalyptic destruction he had caused. Scabtail preened his scales and rolled his eyes in devilish delight, revelling not only in his master's work but also at his master's recognition of him – obnoxious friend he had been called! Such praise – things were looking up again for him! All memories of singed tails and damaged ego swept away in the presence of such praise. He would do anything for his master now, anything at all!

'Your actions have been truly inspired Master – it can only be a matter of time now before you have all the control you have ever dreamed of!'

'Yes Scabtail, I had not realised how much The Brat's intervention in events could help me gain what I desired. I could almost thank him, if I didn't still hate him so much. Look! Look at these mirrors, the ones that should reflect the underground, the final frontier to my domination: they are gradually clearing and will soon give me visible access to its secrets. Then I will have everything: total power and dominion over all, Scabtail. There will be no escape, no hiding place, and no peace for anyone. I will have it all. And the pinnacle of my pleasure, Scabtail? What do you suppose that will be?' said Darqu'on, positively slavering over the thought.

'Why, Master, it will be his death of course,' said Scabtail in a voice so shrill with excitement that it almost shot off the scale.

'Exactly!' said Darqu'on, wide-eyed with the thought, his own deathly-pale face with its sunken hollow cheeks and bloodless lips splitting into what passed for a smile. Had he but had a mirror to reflect his own image at that time he may not have felt so exultant over what his pursuit of evil and revenge had brought him to, but he had no such mirror to give him awareness of himself, and he continued to plot the destruction of all he could see on the outside, unable to recognise the destruction going on within.

'Fire and destruction will continue around Lampadia, Scabtail. Any escapees will fall to the Roth Riders and Wulverines, as my army expands again. The whole population is so filled with fear and hatred that it is helping me manifest all I could possibly desire! What power I exercise, Scabtail, through doing very little; more opportunity for me to move my energies elsewhere. Soon not a single area will remain untouched by my sorcery or necromancy. Nowhere will escape, but first I will personally deal with The Brat, *and* I will have those stones.'

Part *6*

Self-Responsibility

"Be the change you want to see in the world."
Mahatma Gandhi

CHAPTER 31

Returning To Roots

*"There is nothing like returning to a place that remains unchanged
to find the ways in which you yourself have altered."*
Nelson Mandela

The terrain became more barren as Wigapom went further north. Gone were the fields of harvested wheat. Gone were the cosy comfortable dwellings of Oakendale that offered warmth, companionship and security. Instead were rocks, dust, and acre upon acre of barren heath land, austere and harsh. The stones underfoot hurt his feet; the dust, swept up by sudden squalling autumn winds, filled his eyes, nose and mouth, and the mild September days turned into surprisingly cold nights, to herald the start of a season that ate into his bones with an appetite that threatened to devour him. Yet still he walked, oblivious to the discomfort, keen only to make up for lost time; to get back to his roots and thus reconnect with who he really was.

He had not known which way to go at first, whether further south, north, east or west. He had thought about flipping the copper coin that Gobann had given him, but how could that help when he had four directions, not two, to choose from? In the end he decided to use his intuition to show him the way; he kept recalling the Wheel of Life ceremony and the meaning of each point of the compass, and he remembered north was for his ancestors, who had made him who he was. Wigapom was keen to locate his past since Gobann had told him the full story of his birth and the terrible part that Darqu'on had played in their lives and deaths and, combined with the presence of his mother's ring on his finger, he knew this was where he must go. He felt he would not be able to progress emotionally or mentally until he did. So north he had gone.

As he walked, he kept seeing in his mind's eye the image of his father under the tree at Dragonmound, calling him 'son'. It brought a feeling to his heart of belonging, that he had never had before. The only father figure he had known had been Samuel, who was kind enough but distant, and now he yearned for a closeness he had never known. He had spent too many of his early years feeling separate, now he wanted to be part of something – there was that word again, the word on the fourth stone, *part*. He knew he was right to go north, in the direction of his unknown past.

He walked on in healing silence until the stars of yet another night shone through the darkness, finally allowing himself to find some comfort in their gentle guiding light. It was as though they were inviting him to heal his past and thus join with that of the divine. Through his confusion, doubt and sadness he began to see that all things were possible if he had faith. Now he had to let go of his known past, embrace the present moment and let this higher force of light take him, unresisting, to where he had begun, and thus into a new future. What that future would hold, or where he would be led, was unimportant because he knew it was already perfect; it was time to really trust the process of life.

He gazed into the starlit sky once more, and as if on some celestial cue, saw the streaking tail of a dazzling comet arc majestically over him. It was as if this was a message to him that he had made the correct choice; that the suffering caused by the needs of his physical self had now been won by the higher self and hope rekindled again within him.

He was physically alone in a strange and barren landscape, yet he felt surrounded by unseen support and was supremely tranquil. He was coping with the hardships of the journey, paying penance for his lack of activity in Oakendale, and he would now do whatever was expected of the son of the King. He would bear witness to his true parentage and embrace his birthright; his destiny.

His eyes closed momentarily, the streak of the comet's tail still imprinted on his mind. There was strange comfort in that, although guilt had not completely gone, but he knew he would be able to sleep now, for the first time in days. Here on the flat, featureless ground, with just stones and dust as his bed, he could begin the process of letting go. With his blanket wrapped around him and the mercury light casting its soft blue misty glow, he slept.

'I see him, Master!' cried Scabtail excitedly, pointing a scaly finger at the mirror showing the blanket clad outline curled up on the ground.

Darqu'on pushed Scabtail dismissively out of the way and looked closely at the scene.

'Mmm. He has gone north. Drawn, no doubt, by a desire to connect with his past. Scurvy son of a dog! I will show him his past and his future, if that is what he wants. He will wish, when I have finished with him, Scabtail, that he had never been conceived, let alone born!'

'He will get his just desserts, Master,' agreed Scabtail, rubbing his scaly hands together in glee.

'Then move, cretin, and arrange it!' snapped Darqu'on, fiddling as usual with the black ring on his index finger. Scabtail shuffled to the door. 'Faster, fool! There is no time for delay!' spat Darqu'on as he aimed a kick in Scabtail's direction. The lightning bolt that shot from his foot just missed Scabtail as he slithered away to do his Master's bidding. He had escaped a burnt tail for the first time, ever! This must be an important sign!

Wigapom awoke as the full colour of the sunrise lit the sky before him. It seemed redder and more brilliant than he ever remembered, as though the whole sky was aflame! It looked stunning and Wigapom gazed at it in wonder for some time. If he didn't know better, he would think it really was on fire.

After a frugal breakfast of bread and water and some autumnal berries he found growing by the track, he continued his journey northwards, noting how the hills were fast becoming mountains, towering higher towards the sky. He could taste a tang on the air too and knew from past experience that it was the sea! This time Wigapom knew it was the real thing, not something created by his emotions, and his heart leapt at the thought of actually seeing it for real this time. A boyhood dream realised! He hurried to round the bend ahead of him, but stopped short when he saw the bent figure of an old woman carrying a yoke around her neck, from which were suspended two wooden buckets. She was walking very slowly and obviously struggling with the yoke and its contents. Any concerns for his own safety were swept aside by a rush of compassion for her. He wanted to help. She didn't look as though she posed any threat to him and after a good night's rest Wigapom was eager to be helpful and assuage some of his guilt. He soon caught up with her.

'Good morning!' he said, 'Can I help you carry that? It looks very heavy.'

Very old, pale blue eyes looked at him with a distrust borne of years of needing to be wary about everyone and everything.

'Who are you? What do you want?' came her suspicious reply.

'I mean you no harm, truthfully,' said Wigapom, realising rather late, that his forthright, helpful manner could be regarded as strange in a place where trust was difficult to come by. 'It's just that what you are carrying looks very heavy and I thought I might be able to take the load from you for a while. That's all. I'm new in these parts and I don't know my way around yet. Perhaps you could direct me to the nearest town or village, then we could help each other.'

'Help yourself to my goods more like,' continued the woman, still struggling with her burden. Wigapom kept walking alongside her.

'Really, I only wanted to help. But I understand if you don't want to trust me. I'm a stranger to you and you have every right to be suspicious, especially in these times. I'll bid you good day and be on my way,' said Wigapom, smiling in a friendly manner. He went to overtake her, but as he did so the woman noticed the distinctive ring on his left hand and drew in her breath sharply. Her attitude changed immediately towards him, although Wigapom was unaware of this at first.

'Just a minute,' she said, 'not so fast. I didn't say I didn't want your help, just that you would want to help yourself to what I have.'

'I promise I won't, really,' explained Wigapom again, wishing he had not struck up any conversation and just walked on by. She seemed a bit of a strange old soul.

'Well, you can carry my burden for a while. But I'll have my eye on you, so no funny business,' said the old woman, putting down the yoke with a heavy sigh of relief.

Wigapom now felt obliged to pick the yoke up, although he was now wishing he hadn't offered help in the first place, although knowing he had to honour his word. As he placed it around his own neck he was amazed at its weight – he could barely lift it, let alone carry it. He didn't know how the old woman had managed to walk so far with it.

'Jeepers, this *is* heavy,' he said as the two buckets either side of the yoke arm swayed precariously from side to side, threatening to topple over, and take him with it.

'You have to get the balance right,' said the old woman, 'then it's no problem.'

Wigapom fleetingly wondered why she had struggled if it was no problem, but he chastised himself for such ungallant thoughts; she was very old after all. He still seemed to struggle – one side kept dipping down more than the other. He thought he should be able to balance them – a thought came that perhaps *he* wasn't as balanced himself as he could be and this was causing the problem. He tried to shrug it off, but the feeling persisted and he knew he had to do something about it.

'Perhaps I can even out what's in the buckets,' he said, 'maybe they will balance better then.' He went to set the burden down and undo the string holding the covering cloths in place.

'I said you were after my goods! Keep your hands off them!' admonished the old woman, wagging a wrinkled finger at him.

'I don't want your goods, I told you, I just thought I might be able to balance things up better by moving things around, that's all,' said Wigapom.

'Maybe *you* need to let go of a few things first,' said the woman. Let things go? Perhaps she was right; perhaps *he* needed to do this with things in his own life – now there's a thought! Wigapom had an instant flash of releasing some of his own burdens of guilt that had been weighing him down since leaving Oakendale; he saw them fly away into the past as he jiggled the yoke into place. Suddenly the weight evened out and sat really comfortably across his neck. It felt lighter – and so did he! Whatever was in the buckets, and his mind, had balanced themselves!

'That's more like it!' said the old woman, with a triumphant smile. 'All it needs is a bit of effort! Now we can get going,' and she began to stride along like a woman half her age. Wigapom almost had to run to keep up with her! Suddenly she became cheerful, light-hearted and talkative. Wigapom could hardly believe the change that had come over her in such a short time. She had lots of questions for him, which he did his best to respond to, without giving too much information away, and was relieved when she finally started talking about herself.

She told him her name was Maya and that she was going to stay with her niece, Aimee, who had moved back to the village of Nepton-by-Sea after several years living away. He heard that Aimee, despite being a 'lovely woman and perfect mother' had always 'suffered from her nerves' and had been unwell again recently, with bad dreams and terrible stomach cramps, brought on, so Maya said, by a narrow escape from the Dark One's clutches many years ago. 'She has her daughter, lovely girl, but she needs her aunt's tender care at the moment.' Maya, it seemed, was adept in potions for just this sort of thing!

'I know how to help with women's problems,' she said. 'A sprig of bee balm, a dash of valerian and some camomile flowers three times a day before meals usually does the trick. But those memories trouble her and she will never talk about them, although sometimes she does ramble on in her sleep. Says some strange things that don't make much sense, but sometimes I put two and two together! She's not had it easy! None of us have, but she more than most, poor soul.'

Wigapom offered sympathy over Maya's family situation, warming to his travelling companion.

'I'm sorry about your niece, she's lucky she has you to look after her. I met a lovely lady once who made potions just like you, her name was Cassie,' he said.

'There are a lot of us about! We need to keep the old ways going in these times, and not let the knowledge die out.'

'I'm sure that's important,' agreed Wigapom.

The smell of the sea was so strong now that Wigapom could almost taste it. As they turned the corner he could see it, deep green and sparkling in the fading autumnal light. Wigapom had an instant image of Marvo the magician, who had come to his birthday party all those years ago, resplendent in his deep green coat sparkling with stars and moons. He had brought the first stone. Everything had started with him in many ways. He must have been one of the Magi, a real magician, yet he couldn't remember his real name; if only he had listened more to Aldebaran when he had the opportunity, instead of playing foolish games with Will!

Will – how was Will? Wigapom had barely thought of him since he'd left Oakendale. He still felt their connection and realised he always would, but since Will had begun to grow up and take on a persona of his own they had moved apart. Both still got a sense of what the other was doing, but it was often not a conscious thought, just a feeling or sensation. Wigapom tried to make a conscious connection to Will now, but it was difficult to concentrate with Maya chattering on. He would do it later. Instead he took notice of his location, spotting a grey stone village nestling higgledy-piggledy on the rugged cliff overlooking the natural harbour of the bay. There was a walkway stretching out like a tapering finger from the mainland towards a rocky island dominated by a fortified grey stone castle, slowly sliding into ruin, but with a strangely majestic familiarity that caused Wigapom to draw in his breath in surprise.

Maya noticed his reaction.

'That's the Castle on the Crag, where the King and Queen lived towards the end, bless their memory.'

Wigapom's stomach lurched. The King and Queen! His parents? He caught a questioning look on Maya's face that matched his own.

'Really?' he said, as casually as he could. 'What do you know about the place?'

The old woman looked at him keenly.

'More than I will say,' she replied, mysteriously. 'Some might say the Prince was born there, but that could be just rumour, say others. Some say he was hidden away from the Dark One for protection, but some also say there never was a Prince in the first place, or that he went away, or died. Speculation like that is what keeps rumour going and hides the truth. There can be safety in not knowing, or in not wanting to know. Some say if he were alive he would have returned by now, to claim his heritage, and others say he has returned, and challenged the Dark One, at the place where the old King died. Rumour is a funny thing – spreads like wild fire when no match has been lit at times, but we are all still waiting here for his return. The rumours affected my niece though. I think it was that that made her sick this time. She's always takes it hard when anyone mentions the Prince.'

Maya's scrutiny of Wigapom's face throughout this narrative was unnerving, although her voice and chattiness was never anything but pleasant. He had not realised till now that his very existence was in doubt in some parts and that news of what happened at Dragonmound was so sketchy. He had taken it for granted that everyone had been expecting him, as they had when he first arrived in Lampadia. It would be easy to blurt out to Maya who he was, but something told him to keep his counsel a little longer.

'I heard that the rumours were true,' he said cagily, watching Maya's reaction.

'Maybe, maybe not, but I say if the Prince were really around he would surely have fulfilled the prophecies by now and we would have permanent peace back again.' The statement felt accusatory to Wigapom, but he let it go. He couldn't change the past, just accept it and create a new future, but he wouldn't tell her who he was just yet, he had to find that out himself first. The news of the castle, so close, had filled him with a buzz of excited energy! This was likely where he was born, where his life had begun, with his mother and father. The stones in his pocket pulsed again strongly as they had not for some time, as though they had woken again, refreshed, invigorated and ready for action!

Wigapom knew this place was what he had come to find; he had to visit it at all costs to see for himself where it all started. He felt sure he had been drawn here for a special reason – maybe another stone was just waiting there to be discovered. The castle was all he had to connect him to his family and his Quest and was more important to him than anything at that moment.

'Does anyone live in the castle now?' he asked.

Maya clucked her tongue against her cheeks, like a warning.

'Not as far as I know, although folks do say that strange apparitions have been seen around it late at night. Most folk keep away – too many memories for some and too many prying eyes for others. It's not safe there, for lots of reasons. You're not thinking of going there are you?'

This time Wigapom lied without having to think about it!

'No, of course not, just curious that's all, it's a stunning sort of place.'

'Indeed it is. Well young man. I'll be leaving you now. Here is the path to Nepton and I'm off to find my niece and her daughter. Thank you for carrying my things,' she said as Wigapom helped her place the yoke over her own shoulders again.

'I hope you find what you are looking for,' she added. 'It's funny how you can travel all over the place looking for something only to find it was at home all the time!' And with a short laugh at her comment she set off down the path towards her niece's house, leaving Wigapom wondering why she had said that about home. It was almost as though she knew something. He stood looking towards the footpath that led to his first home and ached to be there. He began to walk towards the Castle on the Crag.

Darqu'on turned to the mirror reflecting the scene before him once more.

'Just as I thought, there he is, back in the hole his father ran to, like a fox to earth! His time has come Scabtail. Make sure everything is in place. The wait is over!'

CHAPTER 32

Lasting Lament

"We often give our enemies the means for our own destruction."
Aesop

Wigapom made the rather precarious journey towards the walkway, which he hoped would lead him to the Castle on the Crag. Halfway down the steep and narrow pathway he was disappointed to discover that the walkway was impassable, much of it having crumbled into the sea. Wigapom wondered if it had fallen into disrepair naturally or whether access to the castle had been destroyed on purpose. Whatever the reason, there would be no access to the castle that way. He was not defeated, noticing that below him, at the bottom of the cliff, a small boat lay anchored in the bay below, with whom, he assumed, was its owner inside it. This might afford him access to the castle.

Slipping and sliding on the sharp shale, he continued to make his way somewhat tortuously down the bank, carving out a path where none had existed before. He fell the last few feet and slithered to a stop, bruised but not too battered. As he fell, he thought he heard Will's voice shouting something in his head but he couldn't quite make out the words. He would normally have stopped to make a full telepathic link, but was reluctant to make contact – memories of his departure still strong in his mind, and he was also impatient to get to the castle, so he delayed linking in with Will and instead struggled to his feet, ignoring the voice for now. He really did hope one day to return to see those he had left behind: to return in triumph having defeated Darqu'on, reinstated the stones in *The Book of True Magic* and released the hidden wisdom – but he was not ready yet, needing time on his own to sort himself out. How long would that day take to happen, he wondered?

Now he was stumbling with some difficulty along the pebbled beach, getting closer to the boat bobbing against a small jetty. There was the boat owner, now tethering it carefully to a capstan. Wigapom would ask him to ferry him over. It was some distance to the rock island on which sat the imposing castle. Wigapom seemed to have thrown all caution to the wind again in approaching a stranger, as he had with Maya. Maya had been friendly enough and Wigapom hoped this man would be no different.

As he approached the boat the man eyed him with a suspicious gaze, but continued winding the rope carefully around the capstan.

'That's a fine boat,' said Wigapom, striking up a conversation whilst trying not to seem too eager. 'And an impressive castle!' The man eyed him up and down, as if wondering what to make of him as he finished winding the rope.

'Aye... the boat's sound,' he said at last, 'but the castle's a ruin now. No one goes there anymore.'

'Really? That's a shame!' Wigapom said, pausing a moment, before plucking up courage to ask his all-important question as casually as he could. 'If I wanted to go there, just out of curiosity, you understand, would you take me across?'

The man looked up again, his eyes boring into Wigapom as though trying to see right through him. Wigapom felt distinctly vulnerable under such a piercing gaze, but did his best not to reflect this on his face. This old sea dog was harmless enough, surely, and he really did want to get to the castle.

'How much would you pay?' said the man, with a quizzical look on his face.

Wigapom remembered the copper coin that Gobann had given him. It was the only money he had left now. Would it be enough?

He reached into his pocket and drew it out: the carving of the Phoenix shone and glistened as he held it out towards the man.

'Will this be enough? It's all I have,' he said hopefully.

The man looked at the coin in disbelief before drilling his gaze back into Wigapom. Wigapom thought he was going to turn it down, because it was only a copper coin and not gold or silver, but the man took the coin in his hand, almost reverentially, staring at the Phoenix as though he had seen a lost friend.

'The Phoenix rises in my hand again,' he murmured, before looking back at Wigapom once more. 'How did you come by this?' he asked.

'It was given to me... By a friend,' said Wigapom, not understanding the man's interest in the coin. 'The Phoenix is a wonderful creature isn't it?' he added, by way of keeping the conversation as light as possible.

'Indeed it was,' nodded the man, turning the full force of his piercing gaze on Wigapom, as before. Wigapom felt totally exposed under his gaze; if he hadn't been desperate to get to the castle he would have taken his coin and walked away, but he stood his ground.

'Why do you use the past tense? I thought the Phoenix lived forever, continually being reborn from the flames?' he said speaking lightly, almost in jest, but the boatman did not smile.

'That's the way it was, but times changed and the Phoenix disappeared, along with the old ways of life. Either you're too young to remember, or not from these parts, else you'd know that. There's been no sign of him now for nearly twenty years.'

Wigapom felt an unbidden thrill shoot through his body as he registered the now unassailable fact that the Phoenix was not a mythical bird at all, but real. He didn't want to draw attention to his ignorance but there was still so much he didn't know about this land, his land; so much he had to find out about, that he was bursting with questions, but now was not the time. He decided not to arouse any more suspicion.

'I'm too young to remember what happened,' he said, by way of explanation 'but I would like to visit the castle – will you accept the coin in payment for a return journey?'

'You have your reasons for going?' the man asked.

'Just interested, that's all,' said Wigapom, being somewhat economical with the truth, but not prepared to explain himself further.

The man looked at Wigapom with what might have been a smile hovering over his otherwise impassive face, and began turning the coin over and over in his sea-worn hand, revealing the crown on one side and the Phoenix on the other: crown, Phoenix, crown, Phoenix. Then he stopped, with the crown uppermost, before wrapping weathered fingers into a tight fist around the coin and looking back at Wigapom with a face now hard to read.

'I'll take you now, but you must be ready to return with me before dark. I won't take the boat out to the castle at night.'

'That's fine by me. There're still hours of daylight before then,' agreed Wigapom.

The man shook his scraggy head.

'You'd be surprised how quickly the daylight can disappear around here at this time of year; catches you unawares. Then you'd have to spend the night there, in the castle. You wouldn't want that.' Wigapom shuddered as though a cold shadow had moved over him. He pushed the sensation away and said more brightly.

'I'll be fine. I've slept in rougher places.'

'Waiting there till morning could turn your head. There're ghosts in that castle. Strange beings and noises; you wouldn't want to stay there long. Men have gone mad for less.'

Wigapom said nothing. He felt the man wanted to unsettle him, but he didn't believe he could be scared of anything in the castle; after all, he was born there. It was his true home – how could that possibly be threatening to him?

'I'll be ready to return before it gets dark,' he said, meeting the man's gaze boldly, 'or I'll take my chances until you can pick me up in the morning. The coin is still yours for a return journey.'

The man gave a hollow laugh that rose deep from his throat.

'Get in the boat then,' he said, pocketing the coin and untying the rope from the capstan.

Wigapom jumped lightly on board, in contrast to the more lumbering motion of the ferryman, who fixed the oars into the rollocks and pushed the boat out before heaving himself in, and rowing steadily away from the shore towards the Castle on the Crag.

The news of the fires had already reached the Temple and the tunnel doors were wide open to the survivors. Lucas and other willing helpers were bustling about, tending wounds, giving healing, finding beds for the needy and generally doing the best they could for all. Aldebaran was studying the Astrolabius, which had flickered into life again to show the full extent of the destruction. Darqu'on, it seemed, was out to create the most devastation he could in the shortest possible time and claim new recruits for his army of the Living Dead.

Will and Fynn were shocked to find how the peace and beauty of the Temple had been so dramatically transformed. People milled everywhere, wounded, fearful, angry, and tearful; there had not been enough bandages to deal with their wounds so the beautiful silk covers and furnishings had been hastily ripped up for this purpose. The wounded lay everywhere, their groans and screams filling the chambers, rest rooms, even the corridors. In some corners angry voices plotted futile revenge on Darqu'on, in others there were arguments over space to lie in, or their entitlement to medicine or bandages. Many were weeping in despair at the loss of loved ones – wherever Will or Fynn turned anger, despair, rage and fear leapt out at them, like rampaging beasts. Such negative emotions had never been expressed before in the safe and peaceful environment of the underground Temple, and the negativity generated was beginning to subtly affect the structure of the building. Small cracks already present in the walls were now widening and zig-zagging alarmingly across ceilings; slivers of plaster, flecks of paint, splinters of wood, were beginning to crack, fall or shatter. Yet it went largely unnoticed in the chaos and confusion.

As Will and Fynn rounded a corner they walked headlong into a familiar and very distraught face, struggling to pass them.

'Cassie!' said Fynn, 'I didn't expect to find you here. What happened to your cottage?'

'Oh, Mister Fynn!' exclaimed Cassie. 'It's terrible – I had to leave my home. If the flames didn't get me the Roth Riders surely would, or the Wulverines – they're all over the Forest! I was so frightened and yet I promised myself I wouldn't be, but it was all just too much. I had to come here. Forced out of my home that I've lived in for years! And now Aldebaran tells me that it has been destroyed! Burnt to the ground! So I have nowhere to go but here. But there are others far worse off than me, folks have lost their families, children, husbands, wives, many have lost their lives! And up above us, there is total anarchy in Lampadia. It's always been a troublesome town since the Shadow fell over it but now there is no rule but mob rule. Everyone is so afraid and grabbing what they can! We even have to keep them out of here! Imagine not being able to help those in need! I thought it was bad before you and Master Wigapom came, but I never in my wildest dreams ever thought it would get like this!'

She looked closely at Will, thinking he was Wigapom, 'And what happened to the young boy, Will?'

'I *am* Will,' Will replied. 'I've grown a lot,' he said by way of explanation.

'You most certainly have,' replied Cassie, amazed, 'and you're the spitting image of Master Wigapom, I couldn't tell you apart if you were side by side.' She looked around, as if expecting to see Wigapom coming round the corner, 'Where is Master Wigapom?'

'Travelling alone. It's a long story,' said Fynn, 'Cassie, I'm so sorry for all that has happened to you and everyone here. I feel partly responsible for it. Wigapom left us to go it alone. I have no idea where he went or how he is, and Will can't get hold of him, although Will feels that he must be all right or otherwise he would have sensed something, but we too have lost someone, someone dear to us – at least, we don't know where she is or whether she escaped the fire. Have you seen Skye, Aldebaran's daughter?'

'No, Mister Fynn, I haven't, but I have only just arrived myself and the journey here was so perilous that I often doubted if I would make it; there are so many souls here. I am sure that if she's meant to be here and for you to find her, then she will be.'

'I hope you're right, Cassie, I really do,' said Fynn, worry furrowing his brow.

'Can we do anything for you?' asked Will, full of concern for Cassie, who had shown him so much acceptance when he had first appeared on the scene.

'Love your generous soul, no!' said Cassie, smiling despite her anguish. 'You go and look for Skye. Aldebaran would want that. I won't be going far anyway!' and she patted Will and Fynn on their arms in a kindly gesture.

With parting smiles of encouragement Will and Fynn manoeuvred their way into the Story Chamber, where Aldebaran was peering into the Astrolabius. When he saw them he visibly brightened and opened his arms to embrace them, but there was no disguising the concern in his eyes.

'Fynn! Young Will! Or should I say not-so-young Will! My, how you have changed since I saw you last; the spitting image of Wigapom, if ever I saw one. Thank goodness you're safe. When Skye told me what had happened in Oakendale and that she didn't know what had happened to you, we feared the worst.'

'Skye! Skye is here?' said Fynn, relief colouring his voice, 'Where is she? Is she alright?'

'She's fine. Shocked, after a lucky escape, but safe. She's tending to those worse off than her in the healing room. There are so many in need at the moment, it's difficult to know where to start.'

'I must see her!' said Fynn impatiently.

'She will be here shortly,' said Aldebaran, calming Fynn's impetuosity, 'but first give me news of Wigapom. The Astrolabius functions even more sporadically since the fires and the information Skye gave me was sketchy, although I know about the argument and that he left to go on alone.'

'Yes, he did,' said Will. 'He wouldn't let me go with him. I've no sense of any harm coming to him, although I did try to transmit a thought message earlier but received no reply. I'm hoping that means nothing bad and that he's all right. We're more like twins these days – we can still connect with each other's thoughts, if we want, and I'm sure that if he or I were in trouble we would sense it,' said Will, keen to talk about the strange things happening to his relationship with Wigapom, as well as himself.

'So, you are becoming your own person,' mused Aldebaran. 'I was not sure how it would work, yet you are growing more like him in many ways; everything about you, Will, was an unknown right from the start. It would seem the more Wigapom develops his own understanding of himself, so do you, and this seems to be helping to create two autonomous individuals, rather than keeping you dependant on each other for your existence. I'm sure this is a positive thing, but it is not something I have ever encountered before. What do you feel is your own way forward now?'

'Well… I keep getting the feeling I have to go to Brakendor,' said Will, hesitant at first, 'something is pulling me there, I'm even dreaming about it, and Fynn needs to go with me too, but I don't know why.'

'Intuition such as this must never be ignored,' counselled Aldebaran.

'There *is* a reason, beyond your everyday understanding; that's what intuition is, the inner teacher – we ignore it at our peril.'

'And what is your intuition telling you, Aldebaran?' asked Fynn, softly, sensing that Aldebaran felt more than he was expressing.

Aldebaran looked at Fynn knowingly.

'Things that I hoped never to sense… but you are using your intuition, also, Fynn, I see,' he said. 'It seems to be developing amongst many of us quite suddenly and forcefully, connected, I am sure, to the next stone that Wigapom is now in the process of earning.'

'What do you mean, Aldebaran? How do you know what the next one will be?' asked Fynn.

'Have you not noticed how the colours of the stones are representing the colours of the rainbow?' replied Aldebaran. 'The last was blue so the next will be indigo. Indigo is the colour connected to our brow, or third eye centre, which indicates our ability to see the bigger picture more clearly, to be intuitive, even clairvoyant.'

'Is this what the indigo stone will mean when it's found? Do you know what all the stones mean?' said Fynn, 'Why didn't you tell us beforehand?'

Aldebaran spoke softly.

'Information is best not given until it is ready to be received.'

'And we weren't ready at the time? said Fynn.

Aldebaran let the shake of his head speak for him.

'Can you tell us now, though?' said Will.

'Yes, it is important that you now understand – yet we are in the midst of such danger and distress and that must take precedence if need be.' The others agreed and Aldebaran continued. 'The orange stone, as you may remember, was the first one Wigapom received, which allowed him to connect to his inner self – you Will – in his sacral centre, and helped him and those here who were open to the magic, to develop their self-esteem; the yellow stone created an opening for developing self-confidence – located in the solar plexus of the body; the green opened the connection in the heart – the bridge I spoke of many moons ago, as you remember, and the blue, is the opening of the throat centre – allowing true spiritual communication, as well as the ability to express our deepest truth.'

'Well, we certainly did a lot of the latter – that's the reason we are in this mess now,' said Fynn, ruefully.

'Every stone has its negative and positive aspects, as do all things – but we *can* turn the negatives to positives and this is what Wigapom, and indeed all of us, must do now,' explained Aldebaran.

'You said they matched with the colours of the rainbow, but orange isn't the first colour – red is,' observed Will. 'Perhaps that means that the first stone is still in Brakendor'.

'You are correct, Will,' affirmed Aldebaran, 'the red stone is the foundation of them all, making our connection to the earth, and thus creating our stability and security. The discovery of this stone is more important now than ever and must be found or everything we have will collapse.'

'But things are collapsing already,' exclaimed Will, 'I was noticing the cracks in the walls here as we arrived!'

'They have worsened since the fires outside. I am sure that until all the stones are located this will continue. This is why you must listen to your intuition, Will – and your dreams – and return to Brakendor. I too have been having dreams lately; about Magus, the wizard who brought Wigapom, and you Will, to Brakendor. He has appeared, holding a package in his hand.'

'A package?' said Fynn, suddenly alive with interest.

'It's connected with the first stone, I am sure.'

'Which we think is in Brakendor?' said Will.

'Yes,' agreed Aldebaran. 'And you and Fynn have earned the right to gain it.'

'Wigapom said I might earn one of the stones ages ago,' said Will, thrilled to think he had an important part to play in the Quest after all.

'This is the strangest thing,' said Fynn intently. 'I've never told anyone this before, but *I've* had a recurring dream since I was a child about someone trying to give me a package, but every time I reached for it, it disappeared. I always wondered what it meant.'

'Ooh! My spine went all tingly when you said that, Fynn,' replied Will. 'Your dream is important – I can feel it!'

'Dreams are valuable tools to understanding our lives, Fynn,' said Aldebaran. 'They are the language of our soul and we learn a lot from them if we give them the attention they deserve. When was the last time you had this dream?'

'Funnily enough, just before Wigapom and I had the argument about Skye, and everything began to go wrong.'

'Was there anything different about the dream this time?'

'I don't know… Maybe…' said Fynn digging deep into his memory, 'Yes…there was … This time, even though I didn't take the package, it didn't disappear, but fell at my feet, as though waiting for me to pick it up when I was ready.'

'Ooh, I've gone even more tingly!' cried Will, excitedly, 'I had a similar dream just last night! Although I was picking up a stone!'

Even Aldebaran looked excited.

'That is the sign that now is the time to collect it! You must both go to Brakendor!' he said with force.

'But where do I fit in? I thought only Wigapom could earn the stones,' said Fynn, who had not heard Will's comment earlier.

'But I am *part* of Wigapom, Fynn,' explained Will, 'the part of him that experienced those early years with *you* in Brakendor. It seems right that you and I should be able to earn one too – you are Wigapom's dearest friend, that's why you are on this Quest in the first place!'

Suddenly, the light dawned completely in Fynn's head and he knew without a shadow of a doubt his role in the Quest.

'I'm the hired man!' he shouted, 'Wigapom and I talked about it when we first got to the Forbidden Forest, but I didn't believe it could be me. But it is! You and me, Will, have to get the stone back from Brakendor!'

Before any more could be said, there was a sound of a door banging behind them and they turned to see Skye burst into the room, eyes shining with delight.

'Fynn! Will! I heard you were here! Thank goodness you're safe! I thought you were lost forever!'

Fynn hugged her as though he would never let her go. 'We thought the same about you! How did you escape the inferno?' he asked.

'Luck, good fortune, synchronicity, fate, who knows? I left Merric's house to see if I could find you, and the flames struck. I just ran to the tunnel as fast as I could to escape the burning timbers. Had I been in the house I would have suffered the same fate as Merric and be amongst the dead or badly wounded. As it was I burnt my arm on a falling beam, look,' and she showed them the raw, red mark down her left arm. 'Once in the tunnel, I couldn't get back out because of the flames – there was nothing else I could do but come straight here and I've been helping out as best as I can. But I'm really concerned about the increasing negative energy in the Temple at the moment, not only with the wounded but also from the fear and anger being generated by what has happened. It's threatening to destabilise everything here and I truly fear for our safety. Mother Earth is no longer able to protect us from Darqu'on's power!'

'We've just been talking about this,' said Fynn, 'something is going to break soon and I don't think there is anything we can do to stop it.'

'I saw as much in my own dreams over these past days,' said Aldebaran, 'A climax of terror is building, much of our own making! Destruction is coming. Fate is stepping in.'

'But Aldebaran, we create our own future – if we believe it will be destruction then that is what we will attract, so we must believe the opposite!' said Will, wondering quite where these philosophical thoughts were coming from.

'For one so young, you show increasing wisdom Will; truly you are already wiser than I,' began Aldebaran, but as if to reinforce what he had previously said a heavy shower of plaster and dust crashed from the ceiling, missing them by a fraction. As they looked up there was a cracking, splintering sound, and they saw the central column supporting the ceiling splitting asunder, like a tree split by an axe.

'Too late!' cried Aldebaran, 'We have no more time! The Temple is dying, we must evacuate immediately or there will be many more deaths, more fodder for Darqu'on's army! Follow me.'

He seized the Astrolabius and pushed it and the others urgently out of the chamber as the sumptuous ceiling began to vomit its decorative plaster onto the ground like yesterday's undigested meal.

They ran for their lives, choking dust filling their throats and lungs as it billowed into the room and corridors, clouding vision, clogging every orifice and covering everything with a thick, grey mantle like cremated flesh. People gave in to panic as they struggled to escape death, their cries of horror and fear echoing around the Temple, along with the unnecessary injunction to 'evacuate, evacuate!'

Some ran only to save themselves, others did their best to help those less able than themselves, but the destruction enveloped them all, many succumbing to its power as they sought escape from the place that had once been their refuge, but was now turning into their tomb.

CHAPTER 33

The Castle on the Crag

"So we beat on, boats against the current, borne back ceaselessly into the past."
F. Scott Fitzgerald

The boat docked at a decrepit jetty on the crag and Wigapom clambered out onto its precarious salt-stained boards, the sea lapping below him through the cracks. The boatman barely stopped before straining on the oars once more, turning the boat around towards the shore. He called out to Wigapom:

'I'll be back before nightfall. But if you're not there, I won't wait. Make sure you're ready!'

Wigapom nodded in agreement and watched him depart before approaching the pathway leading to the castle gates.

Apart from the sea lapping exhaustedly against the rocks, and the wind sighing morosely around the walls, it was incredibly quiet, as if life had given up on this place long ago. Wigapom sensed the desolation and unhappiness that seeped through the stone walls of the castle towards him, wrapping despairing fingers around his heart, and seeking to suck the life-force from his body, like parasites. He unconsciously fingered his mother's ring and, remembering Gobann's words, glanced down to read what might be written there.

Home is where the heart is, or so the saying goes,
But here the heart is ripped right out and scattered where no one knows.

His own heart skipped a beat at that message and he wondered what horrors he would find inside the castle walls. He was facing the remains of the wide wooden walkway that led towards a broken drawbridge. Beyond that, set into the grey stone walls, were the thick wooden gates of a stone gatehouse, which formed part of the lower curtain wall, still mainly intact. The gates were wide open, like a mouth frozen in horror at the sight of some past hell that had once rampaged through them. Thick tufts of stumpy grass wedged them open, trapping them in place. Through the gates, across a cobbled courtyard, were stables and storerooms, now abandoned and wretched, like beggars pleading for sustenance that would never come. Beyond these were the cadaverous grey walls of the inner castle, as if pecked by vultures and now awaiting final decomposition. Everywhere was choked with weeds; they pushed their way through broken cobbles, climbed ancient walls, and attacked fallen timbers, which once formed integral parts of the castle structure. Broken remains of once-gracious furniture lay discarded, as though violently tossed aside; curtains that once graced elegant windows lay mouldy, tattered and torn in forlorn heaps on the ground, both sodden and bleached by the trials of varying seasons; broken pots, bowls, a picture frame, a single shoe, all lay abandoned to the elements, whilst jagged glass waited silently to tear into unsuspecting feet or fingers. The flotsam and jetsam of a violent and turbulent past were all around him.

Along the inside of the lower curtain wall a wide ledge barely remained, where once keen-eyed soldiers scanned the horizon for the enemy, or maybe in more peaceful times, ladies in their finery took the air and enjoyed the sea views. Some parts were still supported by arches which had provided a covered area to walk in, or store goods in better times; now mouldy hay, with the stench of old rat droppings, lay solidified in shabby stacks, next to carcases of rodents who had long since given up trying to exist here, and never got the chance to leave.

The main castle walls had fared little better than their protective outer ones and just two of the original four towers remained, along with the central keep. Long narrow windows, high up in the towers, overlooked the sea, the mainland and the courtyard and captured Wigapom's imagination. Who had looked from those windows in the past? His mother? His father? Had they lifted him as a baby to the morning light from one of them? Now the windows were blind to the world, gouged out and sightless, like something from a Greek tragedy. A wave of horror mixed with sadness swept over Wigapom as his own eyes began to sting with tears. He let the tears fall, grieving, as he did so, for the loss of everything he would never know and for all that could have been. He had never known his home and true family, and now he never would; the loss seemed unbearable, yet the walls absorbed his sadness and echoed with sighs of their own; voices from the past calling across the years in both love and sorrow. He knew instinctively why outsiders were afraid of this place. It emitted an atmosphere of such deep gloom, as if, like Atlas, it carried all the weight of all the pain of the world on its back. It threatened to drag down any spectator, but the more Wigapom connected with this grief and released it, the lighter he felt, as though unseen arms were reaching out to support him in this place of his birth. Despite, or maybe because of all that had taken place here in the past, he knew he was being welcomed home and the tears dried on his face and did not return as he walked across the courtyard and through the huge open door of the castle keep.

Here there were corridors running off in all directions from a central hallway. A wide stone staircase in the centre led to the various floors above and smaller, circular stone steps wound their way up to what remained of the two still intact towers. Wigapom gave his imagination free rein as he visualised the castle in his parents' time, before Darqu'on destroyed their happiness. This would surely have been one of several castles they could have inhabited. It had certainly known fear and despair. Perhaps it had been chosen for its isolation and protective qualities, but Wigapom liked to think that once it had also been a much-loved family home that had known laughter and happiness too, and had once rung to the sound of joy. Now it breathed only sadness from its walls, yet the deeper into the castle he went the more he detected other sensations imprinted on the fabric of the building. Most of all he sensed an atmosphere of secrecy and concealment, a clandestinity that would perhaps only reveal itself to him.

He began by exploring the ground floor – first, a large, square kitchen, with battered pots and pans hurriedly discarded on the floor, a half-empty rack of plates, some broken, with the dust of years shrouding them. Then the great hall, with its huge arched fireplace at its furthest end, and cold and lifeless ash the only indicator of once warm and welcoming fires. An iron fender lay prone by the grate, as though caught asleep on duty. Next came an anteroom, stripped bare, apart from a faded ripped cushion, its chewed stuffing scattered about the floor, abandoned even by the rats. Everywhere, the same desolate air and hastily discarded elements of everyday life spoke eloquently of what had gone before. He knew violent death had visited this place – the stench of it permeated every stone and still lingered on the air, and a handful of scattered bones lay, pecked clean now, as grim testimony to this fact. Inhabitants had not suffered the legacy of a living death it seemed, but their souls still lived here, unable to leave this place, trapped by their overwhelming sadness until the restoration of *The Book of True Magic* could release them. Wigapom sensed his responsibility deeply here.

He climbed the main stone stairs, the click-clack of his steps echoing loudly in the forlorn building. The room on his right drew him in through its partially open door into a large space with a west-facing window, where late afternoon daylight cascaded through broken glass. Here there was more furniture – against the opposite wall, a canopied bed, indicating perhaps a royal bedroom. The once magnificent canopies were faded and

335

slowly rotting away with exposure to the damp, salty air and hung limply, like exhausted arms cradling the bed as though grieving for their lost occupant.

'I could have been born in this bed,' thought Wigapom. He put out his hand to touch the once fine silk and shuddered as it collapsed with exhaustion under his fingertips, as though unable to hold onto life any more. The sudden, sad movement let a chill sweep through the room. He sensed so many emotions here he hardly knew what to do with them; they were reaching out across the years, desperately trying to get him to understand, yet they confused him. He wanted to feel a sense of completeness here but he was feeling more fragmented than ever. He yearned for the family he never knew, yet felt the depth of responsibility of being their son and heir. He sensed young Will in him then, with all the old frustrations, loneliness and despair his early life had caused. He was gratified that the newfound Adult within him helped carry that burden and gave him strength, but it couldn't stop the feelings entirely. He tried to make a conscious connection with Will, but the pain and sadness inside him bit too deeply and he had to withdraw his connection temporarily. There was another, as yet undiscovered part of himself he had barely been conscious of which now tugged at him for recognition, and loomed out from the shadows cast by the fading sunlight in the room. He usually welcomed shadows such as these, for not only did they provide cool refuge from the heat of the day, but meant that light was present, but these slunk back like wolves into the dark. A shudder rippled through him, which he explained away as the emotion of returning to his past. He told himself that despite everything, or maybe even because of it, he was attaining a state of balance, even wisdom, and his thoughts went back briefly to Maya and the yoke he had carried earlier. She had been right. When you get the balance right the burdens don't seem so heavy. Life was all about balance and distributing everything evenly. This was where Darqu'on had lost his way and embraced instead the sorcery of the Shadow, rather than the magic of the light in his greed of wanting what was not his to have. That Shadow now cast darkness over his soul, which he refused to see. Yet Wigapom, as he stood in a room that oozed a bittersweet mixture of love and loss, recognised that his own family, and likely all the inhabitants of Arcanum, were as responsible for Darqu'on's emergence as Darqu'on himself. They had been so intent on showing their light and ignoring the Shadow cast by it that they had encouraged it to make its presence really felt by growing into the monster it became, casting a legacy of fear. The more they had tried to ignore it the more it grew in size, power and darkness. Wigapom realised then with great clarity that situations have to be faced, not run away from, only then can they be transformed. As this thought floated through his mind he fancied he saw and felt a wispy shape, like a vapour trail, brush by him and he heard a voice behind him.

'Everyone is a balance of both the light and the dark,' it said.

Wigapom spun round immediately, expecting to see someone there, but there was no one; yet the voice continued, this time clearly inside his own head. 'The good and the evil; negative and positive; Yin and Yang. It is false perception to think we have one without the other, and the false perception creates fear. The more we refuse to face the reality the more the reality will make itself known. And what is fear? Nothing but false evidence appearing real.'

False evidence appearing real – Wigapom had read that somewhere once. Or had it come to him in a dream? It didn't matter, because it made sense. He lost his concern at the voice and began to listen carefully.

'Everyone is a mixture of both light and shadow, a duality, and whilst it is important to acknowledge the light of our souls it is also important to acknowledge the shadow side of our personalities, so we may integrate and accept them both as the whole of us.'

'YES!' said Wigapom, out loud, 'I had to do this when Will came into my life; I had to accept and integrate him within me, even though I hated and feared him at first and did my best to deny him, yet by accepting him I've gradually found the balance inside me, and I'm not afraid any more.'

Wigapom felt his spine tingling with inspirational energy; it was pouring into the centre of his forehead and cascading down each vertebra, making everything seem crystal clear, brighter and bigger somehow. His eyes brimmed with emotion, yet he felt euphoric! A wide grin spread across his face as he revelled in the amazing bliss that these insights were giving him, wanting to pass them onto others.

'I don't know whether to laugh or cry!' he said out loud, 'If my own family had understood what I now understand they would still be here with me now!'

It was this last awareness that popped the euphoria in his head like a pin in a balloon and swaddled him again inside the castle's sad atmosphere; tears of sadness pricked his eyes once more. He wiped them away with the back of his hand; how close the emotions of bliss and despair were. He looked around the rest of the room in an attempt to bring himself back into the moment.

On the other side of the bed, on a small table, was an elaborately painted, broken bowl and wash jug, along with a discarded piece of cloth that may once have served as a towel or soothing compress. He picked it up, and held it to his face wanting it to soothe him, to soothe the world; if only it could, but all that came from it was the mustiness of the years laced with a hint of something that might, once, have been lavender. He thought he heard a sigh behind him and turned expectantly towards it, half expecting, or hoping, to see his mother standing there waiting for him with her arms outstretched, but there was nothing: just the wind whispering through the broken casement.

He turned the cloth over in his hands and without really knowing why, stuffed it into his pocket, like a child would a comforter. As he made this small gesture a wisp of something delicate drifted in front of him, mixed again with the perfume of lavender: an apparition of tenderness and love breathed into his soul, filling his head once more with words and emotions.

'My dear son, you believe that you lost so much as a child, yet it has enabled you to find so much more. Keep opening your eyes to the truth, as you are doing and the magic of hidden wisdom will be yours.'

A mere whisper of a soft caress skimmed lightly across his forehead, like a soft, cool hand stroking his brow and then the perfume, the apparition and the sensation melted into nothingness, yet the memory lingered, growing stronger, as did Wigapom's resolve. With one last look around him he left the room, to explore the others on this floor.

Not one room, corridor, nook or cranny was ignored, but nothing gave him the feelings he experienced in the first room. Mindful of the gradually departing day and his desire to visit both towers before he returned to shore, he made his way back down the staircase and towards the east tower.

It was dark inside, with several narrow stone steps to negotiate, circling up and round. He stopped halfway to rest, looking through one of the narrow window slits and out across the water towards the shore. The afternoon light was mellow but still bright enough; he had plenty of time left before he had to leave. As he turned away from the narrow slit he thought he saw a young woman standing on the beach facing the castle. She seemed familiar, but how could she be? When he looked again she had gone. Wigapom dismissed it as unimportant – perhaps the boatman had said something and idle curiosity had brought her there. No matter. He continued his climb, endeavouring to put it from his mind, but the figure had had a familiarity about it that Wigapom struggled, yet failed to place.

The steps at last reached a solid, wooden door, standing half open. At first glance Wigapom thought it might have once been a study; there was an overturned chair, richly carved, laying, as if quickly abandoned, against one wall and a heavy wooden table in the centre, now split in two, as if by some great and angry force in its past. The sharp-edged pieces of a broken black dish lay strewn haphazardly on the floor, but there was little else in the room of any note that Wigapom could see and, mindful of the time, he was about to turn away towards the south tower when something small and round caught his eye, just underneath the arm of the chair. It was blinking at him, like a dark blue eye. As Wigapom looked, whatever it was moved suddenly upwards, as though pulled by an invisible thread, until it hovered, parallel with his forehead. He saw clearly then it was not an eye at all, but an indigo stone, with its runic message etched tantalisingly on one side. It was so beautiful and unexpected, just suspended there, that he stood totally mesmerised by it as the colour filled the space with the infinity of a midnight sky, drawing him with it into its unfathomable depths.

The stone began to drift towards him, gently touching his forehead. Instantly an explosion of colour flashed inside his brain and what felt like a river of pure light flowed through his body in a timeless outpouring, whilst stars burst into life around him, emitting a sound sweeter than a nightingale's song. How long this experience lasted he never knew, but he eventually became aware that he was holding the stone in his open palm; it vibrated like the others, although Wigapom felt that this was the finest vibration yet. He could feel the pulse of it still in his forehead as well as his hand and it created what he could only describe as a window in his mind, through which he could see and understand everything he could ever want to see and understand, including the meaning of the rune etched upon it. It was another small word; *of*. He could see its connection with the word on the blue stone, as together they read *part of* and in that instant *he* felt part of everything; the stone, the chair, the floor, the castle, even the space around him, there was no division, no separation, just Oneness. He was part of all that was, is and all that ever would be and, in that fleeting instant, he tapped into the meaning of life. Yet as quickly as it came, it receded, like a wave washing away etched imprints on the sand, and, instead, came an image of a phoenix rising from huge flames. He heard its glorious song, smelt the pungency of the smoke, felt the heat of the fire, and saw the leap of the flames, from which came the clear image of Will, looking exactly like Wigapom. This too faded to be replaced by beautifully sculpted, painted walls and ceilings falling silently around him, along with flashes of faces he knew: Cassie, Lucas, Skye, Aldebaran and Fynn and all the time he sensed a message, although he didn't know who was sending it.

'Out of destruction comes construction. All is well.'

Almost imperceptibly the vision was changing to a high mountain spouting thick bursts of molten lava. On top there was an outline he struggled to recognise before the mountain morphed into a tall, gaunt–looking tower with someone he did recognise at a window; it was Sophie, the girl who had shared so much with him in his boyhood. Her eyes seemed to plead with him as she stretched out her arms towards him. He reached out to her, but her arms went right through him towards Will, who now stood behind him, still framed against the flames. Wigapom felt he was floating in a nothingness that seemed to belong to everything, and found himself looking down on the familiar cobbled streets of Brakendor where Fynn and Will were striding towards the bakery. He stared at the vision of his adopted home and then at the place of his birth and the two points of his life came together in partnership, whilst both reached up towards the point of floating consciousness, to form a perfect triangle. He saw immediately how he was part of both sets of parents and how both were important in his life. He also knew that he was part of everything and, thus, everywhere was truly home. He felt grounded and complete, as though he was a tree with strong roots firmly in the earth, whilst the branches reached up and spread out to the sky. At this awareness his consciousness once more returned to his earthly body; he was back in the room in the castle, holding the indigo stone, the buzzing fading from his forehead until all was quiet and peaceful again, but the memory of all that had occurred was forever with him.

Placing the new stone in his pocket, he left the east tower and made his way to the south tower, climbing up another set of worn spiral stairs to the room at the top. A similar heavy wooden door greeted him, but as he pushed it open a very different room faced him and he knew immediately this had once been a wizard's work place, for painted in gold on the dark walls was a six-pointed star with twelve other strange symbols painted in silver around it. Wigapom recognised these as astrological symbols he had seen in the Temple at Lampadia. Underneath these was a long wooden chest of drawers, pushed tight against the wall, with names of plants and potions written on each drawer. The top of the chest was still strewn with pewter ink pots, old parchment pieces, now crackling with age, and the odd quill or two, encrusted with flaking dried ink. There were several dark blue potion bottles, spread over the top, some broken, their contents permanently staining the chest. Shelves with a few dusty books scattered on them were on the opposite wall, but they were not books of spells, but of herbs and their medicinal uses. Wigapom picked one up at random; 'The magical healing properties of Lavender,' and opened it at random to read 'Lavender: a natural relaxant, also aids the healing of burns and other wounds and can be applied direct to the skin...' Practical, matter-of-fact information. Where was the wizard who had once made healing potions here ? Was it Magus, whom Aldebaran talked of? The one who gave his life to save Wigapom's? It seemed likely that this was his room. Could it have been *his* voice that Wigapom had heard in the east tower? To think that he owed his life to the one who perhaps worked in this very room and who had given his life for his protection. Wigapom felt humbled and grateful. He mouthed 'thank you' and the words were received silently. Wigapom wondered where the magic books had gone – removed to safety perhaps, or destroyed by Darqu'on? There were several loose, crumpled pages littering the floor, as though ripped out in anger. Wigapom picked one up that caught his eye. On it was another six pointed star, which he recalled as the symbol for harmony and balance, and several other geometric symbols; triangles, circles inside triangles, and circles interlinking, and a very complex pattern of lines and angles and squares, which he didn't fully understand. There were also the numbers 3, 4, and 5 written, as if in a triangle, with the number 3 at the top. He did remember Aldebaran telling him the significance of these: the number 3 represented the All, or the completion of birth, life and death. The 4, set here in the left hand position of the triangle, represented wholeness, but also the illusion of time, and the 5, set here in the right hand position of the triangle, represented the perfection found in meditation and spiritual aspiration. He was strangely comforted by these numbers and put the page into his pocket, as a talisman. As there was little else left in the room, and he was mindful of time passing and a need to return to the walkway, he turned to leave, but the new stone in his hand pulsed strongly and his gaze was caught by a small indentation in the wall, behind the door. It drew him towards it until it became the only thing he saw, and without really knowing why he did so, he placed his finger in the indentation and pushed.

From deep inside the wall came a grinding sound, as though some ancient creature was being awoken from a long, deep slumber and forced into reluctant action. As he watched and listened part of the wall began to fold back on itself, revealing, slowly, creakily, but surely, an aperture. It stood open patiently as though waiting for Wigapom to reach inside, but he hesitated for a moment, suddenly cautious to discover what was inside.

'What are you afraid of?' came a voice from behind him. Wigapom spun round. He saw no one but felt a piercing chill ripple along his spine as the temperature plummeted suddenly. The other voices he had heard had been inside his head and he had been unafraid, but this one was outside, and filled him with concern.

'Who are you?' said Wigapom, in a hushed, tremulous whisper, spinning back to the aperture and automatically clutching the stones in his pocket for protection, conscious too of the ring on his finger and wishing he had remembered to read its inscription before entering the room.

There was a hiss, like a long, drawn-out breath, then nothing but silence that seemed so heavy it rooted Wigapom to the spot. Yet still the aperture beckoned. He knew he had to reach inside, but he wanted to check the ring first: something did not feel right about this. The words on the ring began to form.

Too late, too late, to turn back time, too late to be protected.
Too soon to know if the outcome will be as you suspected.

Well, that was ominous. Too late to be protected, that's what the words said, too soon to know what would happen. No help at all – it was his fault for not looking sooner, but he couldn't ignore the aperture: he had to take a chance and reach inside. The black space seemed to swallow his arm up to the elbow until his tentative, probing fingers touched something reliably solid and heavy. A rectangular box, with what felt like carving and ornate hinges. Relieved, he gently pulled it out into the room. He was not surprised to find the box was locked, but he was surprised at how his body began to tremble violently when he held it. And how the stones in his pocket began to vibrate madly against his leg! The feeling of being watched was pushed to the back of his mind: instead he sensed the importance of this find and knew he had to open it. He needed a key! Wigapom felt inside the aperture again but came away empty handed, then he remembered the key Gobann had given him. It was a long shot, but he drew it out from around his neck and knew even before he put it in the lock that it was going to fit, although how or why remained a mystery. As he lifted the lid, he knew already what he would find. It was a book, bound in dark, green leather with seven holes surrounded in gold running up its spine.

'*The Book of True Magic!*' Wigapom whispered, under his breath. It had to be. A chill breath grazed his neck, momentarily taking his attention and he held the book close to him as the stones pulsed stronger in his pocket.

There was no writing on the cover to confirm it as the stolen book, but why else were there seven holes along the spine if not just waiting to take the stones? He took the book over to the long chest, to look at it closer.

It was not overly thick, with creamy pages that Wigapom carefully and reverentially turned one at a time. To his disappointment and surprise he found that each one of the pages was completely blank.

'It needs the stones to reveal itself fully,' came the voice behind him. Wigapom turned again, this time catching a hazy glimpse of a robed figure outlined against the bookshelves. The figure came more into focus as Wigapom looked. A learned face with a long beard and white hair under a conical hat brimming with stars. No one to be frightened of, surely, but someone who had saved his life as a child.

'Magus?' said Wigapom, surprised and honoured to be in his presence, whilst wondering why he still felt so cold.

'The same,' came the reply. 'You need the stones to reveal the contents of the book.'

The stones! Yes, of course. He took out the five stones he had from his pocket, orange, yellow, green, blue and now indigo, and tried to slip them into the first five holes up the spine; they didn't fit. It was only when he moved each of the stones up a hole that they slotted in perfectly. Of course, he remembered there had to be a stone at the beginning, otherwise the words just didn't make sense! It was obvious that he had to find the first as well as last stone. Did that mean he had missed out on receiving one or was there a reason why the first stone had not yet revealed itself ? Would he find the reason in the words? *'Is given as part of,'* he read silently, ignoring again the sensation of cold seeping through to his bones. Nothing helped him there. He then looked at the initial letters of the words, I.G.A.P.O. Just random letters; he would have to think again. A sudden flash of Fynn and Will's faces came to him, and a fleeting glimpse of a package, but he could no longer ignore the change in temperature – he was freezing! His jaw was beginning to lock, his fingers turning white with the numbing cold. It was so cold it was hard to hold the book. He could feel it slipping from his grasp, along with the five stones lodged within it. No, not slipping – it was being taken! Invisible hands were prizing it from his frozen fingers! He had been duped! Wigapom tried to resist the book being ripped from his hands but he was weak now and the invisible hands were strong! He began to panic. He was losing the book and the stones to an invisible force that could only be Darqu'on! He had to stop him!

The coldness intensified even more. Wigapom's whole body began to solidify as though coated with thick frost. He looked down at the book, with staring eyes, as he struggled to hold on to it and as he did so the ring on his hand momentarily took his attention – he could see words forming clearly on it again.

Keep the stones out of sight, in case they vanish in the night.
There are those who would discard all you have come to closely guard.

He should never have taken the stones from his pocket in the first place, but it was too late to think about that now; now he had to save them. He couldn't let Darqu'on take them. He shivered again, body locked into position with the cold, and recited the message through chattering teeth, while he forced one hand to shake the stones from the book into the other hand. Instinctively he knew that once he had the stones about his person again he, and they, would be safe, but he had no strength of grip left in his frozen fingers and instead they scattered in all directions around the room, which itself seemed to erupt into turmoil as the biting cold of the unseen fingers penetrated every particle of the air, as if grasping for the stones. They whizzed around Wigapom's head, darting here and there as though under some rocket-powered propulsion and then, as if remotely controlled, zoomed back towards his trouser pocket and disappeared inside. He felt the claw of those icy hands grappling over his body, but Wigapom knew nothing could reach the stones now and was grateful to whatever power the ring and the castle had been able to generate to return them to safety. With the stones back in his pocket his body began to slowly thaw, but it was not over yet; another icy breath spread across the back of his neck and he felt the presence of something by his left shoulder. He involuntarily backed towards the wall. The shivering returned all the way up his spine, this time with a loud and painful humming in his ears. He found himself once more facing the bench and the window, looking out onto the gathering dusk at the jetty. He could see the boatman waiting. He had to get out of this room, away from this evil presence trying to steal the stones! He had to get out of the castle and back to the mainland! But to the left of the long chest the icy presence was solidifying. He watched transfixed as it expanded out into the exaggerated shape of a person. Two dark eyes hovered in midair before all the features of a face became clear, yet the face alternated between friendly and frightening, as though both good and evil were battling for supremacy within it! And filling the room were two male voices struggling to be heard above each other.

'Do not be afraid,' said one, 'all is well. The hardest challenge is yet to come.'

'You are mine now and will never win!' the other gloated.

Wigapom held up his hand, as if to block the second voice, but a severe pain hit the centre of his head, making him reel. It was as if his head was exploding and imploding at the same time, and filling with horrific, leering images that were dragging him down with them. He was losing all control of his body, spinning and spiralling down, helplessly swallowed into a blackness that had no end. As he hit the ground, unconscious, the indigo stone bounced out from the safety of his pocket and, like the book that he had dropped when he fell, was swallowed up into the lengthening shadows.

CHAPTER 34

The Ferryman

"Don't pay the ferryman before he gets you to the other side."
Proverb

'Foolish reptile!' fumed Darqu'on. 'To have the stones within our grasp and then to lose all but one! They are not attainable whilst on The Brat's person. Magus still works his charms from beyond the grave.'

'Master, it was not my fault. I was not present at the time,' complained Scabtail, who felt he had carried out his part of the plan very well.

'It is always your fault when things go wrong, you scaly imbecile!' rounded Darqu'on, 'for it can never be mine. I am all-powerful!' and, with hand poised, he was about to inflict more pain on his hapless lackey. Scabtail jumped in with placating words, determined not to suffer a further damaged tail if he could help it.

'Powerful indeed, Master, by using the book as bait you gained one of the stones, *and* retained the book, and you have him now, to continue to deliver pain. He never felt that coming until it was too late!' he said.

The words did the job. Darqu'on was convinced he still had the upper hand. He *had* kept the book *and* gained a stone, and had The Brat at his fingertips. It would not be long before he had retrieved all the stones and could dispatch The Brat accordingly! He focused on that, gloating now with self-deluded pleasure.

'Yes indeed, it will be easy enough to prise the stones from him now I have him. With only four stones, rather than five in his possession, his power is already diminished. The final plan is good. You have done well, after all, my saurian friend.'

'It was a pleasure to serve you, Master, as always,' sighed Scabtail, relieved he had saved himself from further agony and rather taken with Darqu'on's new epithet for him – 'saurian friend' had a certain ring to it!

'When he has forfeited all the stones he will no longer be able to utilise their energy. I was right to seek them out. It has been worthwhile biding

345

my time. The stones are useless to him without the book, but invaluable to me. He is providing the tools of his own destruction, Scabtail. There is a strange irony in that which I find very satisfying.'

'He has always been the instrument of his own destruction my Lord, by virtue of his birth,' said Scabtail, flicking his mangled tail with excitement at the prospect of what was to come, and relishing his own part in it.

'True, Scabtail, your words, like the scorpion, have a sting in them! Is all now established in the Citadel tower?'

'Yes Master, all is in place.'

'So, are you ready for the final solution?'

'I am ready, Master.'

'Then let it begin.'

Aldebaran sought to save the others from the falling masonry crashing around them, but did not escape injury himself. A decorative cornice smashed down onto his skull, felling him like an axe does a tree. He let out a short, surprised cry and a lingering groan, loosed his grip on the Astrolabius and lost consciousness before crumpling to the floor. Skye let out a cry of anguish of her own as Fynn, Will and Lucas struggled to drag him and themselves away from the rest of the collapsing Temple walls.

'We must get him outside,' cried Skye, as they carried him along the winding corridors, into the tunnels, blinded and choked as they were, by the thick, consuming debris and dust, 'or I fear he will die.'

'We will all die if we don't get out of here soon,' grimaced Fynn.

'We'll take him with us to Brakendor,' shouted Will above the noise of collapsing walls and falling earth. They continued to stumble and fall on their tortuous journey, but refused to give up. A faint glimmer of daylight lay ahead and they made a final surge towards it as Aldebaran began to rouse. 'Stop!' he whispered, his voice weak and his face grey with ash and pain; it was streaked with blood, flowing from a deep gash on his temple.

'Father, we are taking you to safety,' reassured Skye, as she attempted to stem the bleeding with a strip of torn silk curtain. 'We must keep going.'

'I am dying,' he whispered, 'Leave me… to the ferryman.'

'No Father, don't say that!' said Skye, panic choking her voice and tears washing rivulets through her dust-coloured face, knowing full well her father was alluding to the mythical boatman, Charon, who ferried the dying souls to the place of the dead in the Underworld.

'It is… the truth,' Aldebaran said, his breathing laboured, 'Charon is… waiting… for me. My time… has come. Leave me… Go… alone.'

'We can't leave you!' said Fynn, his heart going out to this brave soul, whose hold on life was tenuous. 'Look, daylight is just ahead.'

'Not see… daylight again… in this… life,' whispered Aldebaran, as his eyes closed on the world for the last time and his life finally slipped away.

'He's gone!' said Fynn, unable to believe they had lost him so quickly – that life could be there one moment and gone in the next. Skye screamed as she tried to rouse her father, refusing to accept that his life had departed, but it was useless; Fynn had to gently pull her away. They all knew they could not remain with his body, unless they too wanted to risk the same fate.

'We have to leave him. I'm sorry, Skye,' said Fynn, as more of the tunnel collapsed onto Aldebaran's lifeless body and threatened them. He pushed her in front of him towards the daylight and safety and they ran until they could run no more.

When exhaustion forced them to stop, Skye yelled in her despair.

'My father's soul will not rest until Darqu'on is defeated, and neither will mine. His death will not be in vain. That I swear!' And she sobbed into Fynn's arms

'We also swear that,' vowed Fynn. 'You can be sure of that.'

'Then we must go now to Brakendor and find the stone,' urged Will.

'Yes!' agreed Skye, passion in her voice. 'Do whatever you can to bring an end to this nightmare. Lucas and I will get word to the resistance that hope must be kept alive.'

'But I've only just found you,' cried Fynn, I don't want to lose you again,'

'You must,' Skye insisted, sweeping away her tears with the back of her hand, 'there is nothing you can do here that we can't achieve without you, but only you and Will can find the stone. If it is meant to be then we will meet again. Go now. Don't worry.'

'She's right, Fynn. We can't do anything if we stay here, and I can feel the urge inside me, pulling us back to Brakendor. We have to find the package there, as Aldebaran said, you and I together, for the good of all!'

Fynn knew this made sense, but he was torn between his heart and his head. Lucas took charge, stepping in, urging them in his falsetto voice.

'Go! Do not betray Aldebaran's trust and hope in you. Darqu'on must be stopped. You must go! Now!'

The urgency in the wizened dwarf's voice and the look in Skye's eyes made up Fynn's mind. With a last farewell he and Will ran down the mountainside towards the road that would lead them back to the Forbidden Forest and a return journey that would be very different to the outward.

Wigapom battled to open his eyes against a pressure determined to keep them closed. He struggled to move his arms and legs, but he had no control over them, as if they did not belong to him. Everything was at odds with how it should be and he was having to pull himself back from a place he hadn't recognised to one that wasn't real; he had to focus his energy and thoughts, had to open his eyes. It was a shock to find that his eyes *were* open, but not seeing clearly at all. His head swam, he felt sick and so cold, lying on a damp wooden floor that was swaying from side to side. He could smell the sea, hear the lap of waves against the prow and the splash of the oars as they moved through the water, but everything seemed unreal. He remembered losing the book, and the stone rolling from his pocket, but then he had been in the castle. Now it seemed he was in a boat. Had the boatman come back for him after all, and how long had he been in it? Judging by his stiffness it must have been a long time and he struggled to sit up. His head hurt and a wave of nausea washed over him. His vision blurred a moment then gradually cleared. He saw the outline of a hooded shape wielding the oars. Backwards, forwards, backwards, forwards, they went, slicing steadily through the water, and it took a while for Wigapom to realise that he was not being rowed towards the shore but away from it and out to sea.

'Hey!' said Wigapom, feeling really sick now, 'What's going on? where are we going?'

'To the Master,' said a triumphant voice from under the cape, and for the first time Wigapom noticed the reptilian tail slipping out from under it and the scaly fingers gripping the oars. It wasn't the boatman but the odious Scabtail!

The moon had now slunk back behind a cloud and it was too dark to see, half submerged in the water, face down and spread-eagled, the bloated, bloodied corpse of the real ferryman.

Wigapom made to lunge forward but sinuous rope-snakes rose, hissing from the bottom of the boat. They coiled themselves around his limbs and body, gripping him tightly, rendering him unable to move. It was too late then to admonish himself for not using the protective message of the ring, nor taking heed of what the nausea had been trying to tell him. Now he was trapped by slithering rope-snakes in a boat manned by Darqu'on's reptilian henchman, going who knew where into the darkness! All too late he remembered the words he had heard in his head earlier: 'the hardest challenge is yet to come' and, 'you will never win.' He was sure that those voices belonged firstly to Magus, and then Darqu'on as they battled for him. It appeared Magus had lost. Wigapom was angry at his own stupidity, as well as at a complete loss to know what to do – but what about the ring? Maybe that would still offer him protection of a sort, better late than never he supposed. It had told him already to hide the stones. If only one had not fallen out somehow. No point in looking back. He glanced at his hands bound in front of him. If he could just twist his hand very slightly he would be able to see the ring, but the snakes were not only tightening their grip but also spitting venom at him, which he was doing his best to avoid. They spat again and without thinking Wigapom spat back in anger. His spittle landed, *plop,* in the snake's gleaming eye and it hissed, releasing its hold enough for Wigapom to twist his hand to see the ring, but how could he read the words in the darkness? It seemed an impossible task, yet something he had unconsciously absorbed in the wizard's room at the castle was telling him there *was* a way. Not only did he have to believe that the words would appear but he had to believe he could *see* the words in the darkness, and he would. What a test of trust and faith!

Holding his bound hands in front he looked hard at the ring and began to believe the words were perfectly clear. At first there was nothing but darkness, but he persisted, constantly affirming to himself he was reading the words by the clear bright light of a full moon, 'I am reading the words perfectly well, I am reading the words perfectly well,' he intoned to himself.

Deep inside his pocket, vibrating against his leg, he felt the remaining stones tingle as he repeated the mantra again and again. Sure enough, as he continued to focus on his ability to read the words, despite the darkness, they did indeed become perfectly clear! Yet he was surprised at their content.

Let night's cloak wrap its arms around you, but embrace the dark with care.
Sometimes who you think is present, is found to not be there.

Well, that wasn't telling him anything he didn't know already. Scabtail wasn't the boatman: that was clear. It didn't seem like a protective sentence at all! But he said the words to himself silently nevertheless. If he expected something magical to happen, then he was disappointed. There was no disappearance of the reptilian creature, no further loosening of the snakes, no protective intervention of any kind. Just the same splish and splash of the oars as they cut slowly and steadily through the water, going further and further out into the all-enveloping blackness of the silent sea and endless night. It seemed that, ring or no ring, he was still very much on his own.

Darqu'on watched every moment. It was all laid out before him in the mirrors, every one depicting a different story, but with the common theme of chaos – chaos that he had instigated. He thrilled to what he saw and the sense of power surged through his pale body, energising him without the need of blood. He felt drunk on the experience. First, the fires raging in this mirror, figures running to escape the flames in another; here, Roth Riders hunting down escaping stragglers in the forest, whilst Wulverines salivated at the prospect of gorging on their flesh, all the time creating more of their kind; there, the collapse of tunnels falling onto screaming victims; here buildings demolishing before his eyes, and in all the mirrors the sight of pillage, fear and death, and to cap it all, his first ever sight of the underground, although still hazy, to which he could now finally begin to lay claim. He had never felt so powerful! But best of all was the sight of the small boat and its trussed occupant being rowed into the night. Only the best for her son, and an opportunity to draw out The Brat's pain and inevitable demise for as long as he chose: such perfect rapture! He positively shook with vindictive pleasure. They would be there soon and the process could begin in earnest. As soon as he had his hands on the remaining stones The Brat would have no power and no escape. Could success taste any better than this?

But what of the two in the forest? Darqu'on had at first been intrigued by the young self The Brat had created, thinking it might work to his advantage, but this had not been sustained, despite his best efforts, and he had begun to lose interest in him. Despite the similarity in looks, this one, now running towards the forest, was not the real one. He did not have the stones, thus would never be as important as The Brat. She had, after all, only given birth to one son, not two! One was just a product of enchantment, a mirage without real foundation, not a real person; Darqu'on was sure when The Brat died the other would die also, or he could let the forest take care of him and his light-haired companion. He had created enough there to provide them with sufficient trouble and keep them out of Brakendor! He grinned in pleasure, then dismissed them to return to his primary mission. He needed to focus all his efforts on The Brat. He could forget the other two.

CHAPTER 35

Return to the Forest

"The important thing about a problem is not its solution,
but the strength we gain in finding the solution."
Unknown

The decision made high in the tower at the Citadel to dismiss Fynn and Will's activities was more help to them than they would ever realise as they made their way back to Brakendor. There had been a slight set back when Will, for no apparent reason, keeled over and hit the ground hard with his head, leaving him woozy for a while, whilst babbling about losing something. Fynn was concerned, but Will was soon himself again and they were able to focus once more on the job in hand.

The compulsion to get to Brakendor as quickly as they could was strong, but the road to the forest was by no means empty, and their progress was slow and traumatic. The terrible sight of refugees fleeing from their burning homes or escaping from the collapse of Lampadia were all around them, and there was always the danger of attack, whether from Darqu'on's forces or opportunistic vagabonds, but there was no choice but to walk. Many around them were wounded and all knew that by heading towards the forest they were likely heading towards attacks from Roth Riders and Wulverines, but when desperation strikes, the desperate will do anything to survive. With no homes to shelter them the hope of finding refuge amongst the trees was all they had, however fragile the chance may be.

Fynn and Will knew the dangers too, but there was safety in numbers and here they had plenty of companions amongst which to lose themselves, bringing a strange anonymity to their progress, but with so many on the road, the going was tortuously slow and it soon became clear to both Will and Fynn that they would need to separate from this straggling, fleeing crowd if they were to make any headway at all. Taking their own chances with any Shadow-motivated forces they might find en route, they made a decision to split from the crowd.

'This way,' beckoned Will, taking charge more than ever as he slipped down an almost forgotten pathway that looked as though it might head towards the forest.

Fynn followed and they found themselves struggling through nettles and brambles, that made the going tough and painful, but at least they were moving. Despite the smell of burning still contaminating the atmosphere, the air was crisper here, with a distinct autumnal feel. As they stopped to drink and refresh themselves from a small stream gurgling its way through the trees, the leaves were already turning golden brown and orange, some already laying a thin carpet over the forest floor. Despite all they had experienced, this place still held the enchanted magic of Mother Nature within it, as though she was proving to them she would continue to do what she had always done and survive to see another day. Fynn and Will had taken Aldebaran's death very hard, but knew they could not let it affect their progress, so they instinctively decided not to talk about it, but did what many do when emotions cannot be voiced – they spoke about the weather.

'It's getting colder already,' Fynn said, 'more like October – the seasons seem to be speeding up.'

'Maybe that's why I'm growing up so fast,' said Will, looking every inch the mature young man now.

'Perhaps Darqu'on wants to take us to eternal winter as part of his master plan!' replied Fynn, with more than a touch of irony in his voice. 'With so many folk now homeless that would make life very hard, even without the threat of Roth Riders, Wulverines and the like.'

'You're right, Fynn. All the more reason to get back to Brakendor, find this stone and get it to Wigapom to restore peace and harmony again.'

'We're still some way from that, I think,' said Fynn, ruefully. 'How many other friends will we lose before then?'

Will suddenly looked rather nauseous. Fynn wondered if it was being reminded of Aldebaran and Merric's death.

'Sorry Will, I shouldn't have said anything. Are you all right ?' he asked, putting a caring arm around Will's shoulder.

'Yes, I just felt a bit seasick all of a sudden,' said Will.

'Seasick? We're only by a stream, Will, not on the sea!'

'I know that, I think it's to do with Wigapom. I'm picking up on his feelings, like the head bang earlier. I felt as though I was on a boat for a moment just then. I'm all right now. I hope Wigapom is,' said Will, brushing off his strange feeling. He had not managed much direct communication with Wigapom since Wigapom had left, apart from a time when he felt he was in a dark tower surrounded by water with the beautiful image of Sophie opening her arms out to him. He had liked this image. He remembered her well.

'I think this stream could run into the brook that flows through Brakendor,' said Fynn, doing quick directional checks in his head, 'it seems to be flowing in the right direction anyway.'

'I think we should follow it,' said Will, coming back from his reverie, 'Then we will have to hope that the entry to Brakendor is revealed to us. It's still hidden, after all.'

'Yes,' said Fynn, 'we'll find it if we are meant to.'

The stream took them along the forest edge, before turning towards the thickly foliaged centre, mercifully untouched by Darqu'on's flames, and they ran lightly, jumping brambles and nettles where they could, all the time going deeper and deeper into the forest. They heard Wulverines in the distance, howling and baying, and their hearts went out to any victims, but they were thankful they were so far lucky to escape them. The dusk came suddenly upon them and the unexpected chill of the air bit into their fingers and toes, and seeped through their bodies. They were a long way from the fires now and the need for food and warmth filled their thoughts. When the unexpected but welcome smell of potatoes baking drifted towards them, their mouths watered at the thought, yet they could not let their need for warmth and sustenance take away their need for caution. They both crept closer to see where the delicious smell was originating from.

Squatting around a small fire were three trolls, one poking the potatoes in the fire, one whittling a wooden skewer, the other sharpening a knife. A young doe was tethered to a tree; the whites of her frightened eyes shining like beacons in the glow from the fire. Despite her infancy, she knew only too well what fate awaited her at the hands of the trolls. The times were long gone when trolls would look after animals with care and tenderness. Now anything that moved was deemed fair prey for their deadly knives and bottomless stomachs.

They were talking in low, gruff tones, constantly casting furtive looks around them into the deepening dusk, anxious to stay alive, no matter who or what suffered in the process. Fynn, being tolerant of many things and aware that the odds of three trolls against the two of them were not good, would normally have left them alone, but Will became totally impassioned by the plight of the female deer tied to the tree and knew in his heart he had to save her from her fate.

'Don't worry! I won't let them kill you,' he said in a whisper under his breath, and then, a little louder so that Fynn could hear. 'We can't let them kill that poor creature. We have to save her, Fynn!'

'What?' said Fynn, horrified. 'Are you mad? Those trolls would eat us too, given half a chance. Best to move on and leave them alone. Goodness knows what else might come out of the forest if we make a commotion!'

'No, Fynn, I won't leave it. That's a living creature out there that has as much right to life as we do. I won't stand by and watch her butchered by those hulks of flesh! There's been too much of that lately.'

'Will! Even trolls need to eat!'

'But they don't have to eat animals, Fynn. They never used to before the Shadow overtook them, and they don't need to now. Mother Nature provides many other foods.'

Fynn was aghast. 'What about the package, and Brakendor?'

'I haven't forgotten them, but this is a life, Fynn. Wigapom would understand. I know he would. He'd want to help save the deer too.'

Fynn could see the familiar stubbornness in Will's eyes. He had seen it many times in Wigapom. He knew there would be no denying him. He just hoped that saving the life of a deer did not cost them their own.

'Well, what do you propose, animal saviour?' he said as he capitulated to this unexpected change of events.

'There's a story we read once about a deer who was on her way to the Great Mountain, don't you remember? When a terrible monster met her, yet she did not show any fear, just asked to be allowed to go on her way. The monster did all he could to scare her, but she just treated him kindly and compassionately and the monster's hard heart began to melt and he let her go on her way.'

'And you propose to ask the trolls nicely to let the deer go on her way? Is that it?' said Fynn, more incredulous than ever.

'No, but you will,' said Will.

'You're mad!' spluttered Fynn, through his teeth, really thinking that all the stress and trauma of the past few days had finally caught up with Will and he had flipped completely!

'Not really, you create a diversion, I release the deer, simple as that,' explained Will, as though it was the most logical thing in the world.

'What! You mean I just walk in there and strike up a conversation with them?' said Fynn, aghast.

'Well, I guess you can be inventive. Maybe if you ran in and said you had seen the Wulverines heading this way that might unsettle them enough to give me time to release the deer. Come on Fynn. She'll be on that skewer if we don't get a move on!' And with that Will darted as light as a deer himself around the clearing to position himself close enough to release the deer when Fynn had gained the trolls' attention.

Fynn's jaw dropped in disbelief, but now he had to act, if only to protect Will.

He took a deep breath, asked for protection from harm and to be given courage, and then charged into the clearing. The trolls, by now eating their baked potato aperitif, staggered unsteadily to their feet and turned to face him, daggers drawn.

'Save yourselves! Save yourselves!' cried Fynn, dramatically, 'The Wulverines are coming!'

The trolls looked fearful but confused – no one had ever tried to save them from anything before. They were usually feared and run from and had to fight the best they could for their survival. Yet here was this wild-eyed, slight figure of a man trying to save them from the dreaded Wulverines! Never particularly quick on the uptake, they believed him.

'Where?' they grunted, the whites of their eyes showing clearly in the gathering darkness

'Just back over there,' said Fynn, pointing wildly behind him. 'I saw them. Run if you don't want to be swallowed whole by them, and live forever as a lost soul!'

Will had reached the deer and was untying the rope that tethered her.

'The Wulverines!' roared the trolls, as fearful of these hideous unworldly creatures as anyone, 'Run! Run!' and to Fynn's utter amazement they ran, without a second thought, lumbering away from him and Will and the now un-tethered deer, as though a whole pack of Wulverines were already chasing them. Their cries and pounding footsteps could be heard disappearing into the trees away from the stream and, more importantly, away from Fynn and Will.

'There, I told you it would work!' said Will triumphantly, appearing from the thicket with the deer, now free of the rope around her neck.

'I would never have believed it if I hadn't seen it with my own eyes!' said Fynn, amazed not only at his own courage, but also Will's brazen cheek, not to mention the result achieved. 'Just don't ask me to ever do it again!' he added, heart still pounding from the surge of adrenalin that had shot round his body.

The deer, on gaining her freedom, did not run away as Will expected, but looked at them both with kindness and gratitude marked in her huge beautiful eyes.

'You risked your life to save mine,' she said. 'For that act of kindness there must be something I can do in return.'

They had both lived long enough in this part of Arcanum not to be surprised any longer by talking animals, so they answered her.

'We need nothing in return,' replied Will, 'unless you can show us the way to Brakendor.'

'The hidden village? I can take you close enough,' said the deer, 'if you can run with me.'

'What are we waiting for! Let's go!' said Fynn and Will together and the four feet of the two of them followed the four feet of the deer down another path as night's cloak continued to wrap herself around them.

CHAPTER 36

The Hybrid

"...this idea of spirit-matter is regarded as a hybrid monster..."
Teilhard de Chardin

A cloud had again swallowed the sliver of moon, but the boat seemed to be approaching land. Something solid was looming ahead of them and the odious Scabtail was straining less on the oars.

'Where are we?' said Wigapom, increasingly annoyed at being trussed by the hissing rope-snakes that were squeezing him tighter than ever, 'Where are you taking me?'

'To the Master! To the Master!' repeated Scabtail's triumphant voice. 'There is nothing more to say. You will know soon enough.'

The scaly creature was already pulling the boat up onto the shore before Wigapom knew what was happening.

'Out! Out!' Scabtail said impatiently to Wigapom who, constricted by the rope snakes, was struggling to stand, let alone get out of the boat. Scabtail yanked at him, impervious to the rope snakes, which slithered and slimed their way tighter around Wigapom, causing him to fall awkwardly onto the shore.

'Where is your Master?' he demanded, catching his breath. He had expected to be taken to the Citadel, not to some deserted shoreline, on the edge of who knew where.

'He is everywhere you are,' said Scabtail, his scales rattling with pure venom. 'Oh, he is so pleased with me! I am his special one! His obnoxious and saurian friend! We will both enjoy what is to come, before your final demise!'

'I have no intention of demising at all, you can be sure of that,' retorted Wigapom, trying but failing to right himself on the shingle, much to Scabtail's amusement.

'You are weak! Yet you still think you have a choice? You have nothing and the Master has everything – total power. Your friends are dead, and you are in his control. There is no escape for you this time. You can be sure.'

'What do you mean, my friends are dead?' said Wigapom, disturbed by this statement. Were they really dead, even though he had seen their faces in the vision at the castle? Or was Scabtail just trying to make him think the worst to demoralise him? Well he wouldn't succeed, he knew Will wasn't dead – he would have felt it, but Fynn, and the others? He had no way of knowing about them and a tremor of concern shivered through him: he didn't want to lose them before their time, especially not to a living death at the hands of Darqu'on! He did his best to brush the thought away. There was no point in giving up hope; he would just be playing into Darqu'on's hands.

Scabtail had not answered, but turned to look into the pitch-blackness of the night sky as though searching for something. He gave a hefty flick of his battered tail and began to shout exultantly, as if seeing something that Wigapom could not.

'He is here! He is here! Now it begins!' He turned sharply to Wigapom and uttered the command 'RETURN', to the snakes. To Wigapom's surprise and relief they released him, hissing and slithering away into the darkness of the night, along with Scabtail and the boat.

Wigapom did not know what to make of this – it made no sense at all. Why had he been released? Where had Scabtail gone and where was Darqu'on?

The feeling that this was all some strange dream kept washing over him, but the sound he heard in the darkness was real enough; a squalling, screeching noise, sometimes seeming a long way off, sometimes close, mixed with an occasional soft pattering and a harsh whoosh. Then he felt a sharp painful jab at his arm and he knew it was real! It was so dark he could barely see in front of his nose, but his eyes shot wide open, in pain and shock, staring at the black sky as if just by peering hard he could make the image of whatever had attacked him appear. But all that filled his vision was a blackness that seemed to envelop him like a cloak. Yet this was not night, but the wings of an enormous creature, the like of which Wigapom could never have imagined even in his wildest dreams. As the creature drew back, before attacking again, Wigapom saw a wide open razor-like beak, enormous flat head and huge, yellow, hooded eyes coming towards him. A thick long neck swooped towards him, whilst gigantic talons, like some mechanical gripper, hovered over him. The flick of an enormous sinewy tail, topped by a double-headed serpent appeared. It flicked out both forked tongues, exposing sharp teeth coated with venom! He couldn't see the full enormity of the creature, just those parts that swooped closest to him, but he knew it must be the Hybrid; vicious, deadly and just inches from his face. Wigapom instinctively rolled away into a ball to protect himself, but the Hybrid had perfect nighttime vision and there was no way he could avoid being attacked by the creature. First came the sharp beak, slicing through Wigapom's sleeve, then the strong teeth and forked tongues of the serpent heads, whose bites punctured his trouser leg, and all the time the shrieking, like maniacal laughter, filled the air. The shock of the attacks seared into Wigapom like hot knives, but no blood had yet been drawn and adrenalin fended off pain. Perhaps the protection of the gold ring was working after all! There was no time for relief, however, as the Hybrid struck again. Wigapom rolled away as far as he could, over and over, trying to keep within the protective darkness of the night. The double-headed tail lashed from side to side, seeking him out with radar-like vision as the creature soared up on its strong wings, preparing for another nosedive attack.

Wigapom jumped to his feet, arms raised already in defence, preparing to fight or flee. But where could he run? With what could he fight? How could he protect himself? The image of the tin whistle came to mind. Well, when a man is drowning he will grab at anything. Wigapom fumbled for the whistle from around his neck and blew it for all he was worth. It emitted a high-pitched sound barely audible to Wigapom but which obviously affected the Hybrid, whose flight became more erratic as Wigapom blew. The sound was confusing the Hybrid's homing sense, which was now way off-target when it plummeted towards him again. Wigapom continued to blow the whistle as hard as he could, but it did not stop him from being hit on the back of the head by the double headed serpent's tail, which knocked him off balance and the whistle flew from his mouth.

Before he had time to stabilise himself and replace the whistle between his lips, the Hybrid had struck again, this time with perfect precision, picking Wigapom up in his sharp talons. The long sinewy tail-head wrapped itself around Wigapom's legs and squeezed like a tourniquet. Wigapom was lifted helplessly into the blackness. Thankfully he had chosen to wear his bag across his body or that would have been lost; it swung heavily against his chest before he was carried away, bouncing across the harsh stones as the fearsome creature adjusted its flight to accommodate the weight of its prey, the enormous wings accessing the air currents and soaring up into the blackness.

Wigapom struggled to put the tin whistle back in his mouth with his free hand but the speed at which the creature flew made this impossible; instead it clunked uselessly against his chest, along with the iron key. He could still detect gleeful laughter riding on the air currents and Wigapom was sure that somewhere Darqu'on, along with the reprehensible Scabtail, was revelling in this, like an ancient Emperor might at a gladiator fight. He

358

felt angry that this should have happened before he'd had time to prepare himself mentally, but he was scared too; he had no opportunity to go into that peaceful inner state of calm he had managed to source when last under attack from Darqu'on at Dragonmound. Instead he grappled for the whistle, which clanged on the key and banged uselessly against him as he swung dangerously far above the ground.

On and on they flew, until a malevolent dawn light streaked the sky with gashes of blood red and putrid yellow. It was not a dawn that Wigapom wanted to see and he wondered how long he would be clutched in the talons of this creature. An answer came sooner than he thought. Around him was a range of mountains, some tall enough to be snow-capped, and the Hybrid rose to reach the peaks. The air was bitterly cold here and, despite the sky colours, there was no sun to warm and soothe – just a biting wind that pierced Wigapom's body as much as the Hybrid had pierced his clothes.

The Hybrid was now circling one of the mountain peaks and Wigapom's heart leapt into his mouth as the creature dived vertically down towards it. The sensation of the mountains hurtling towards him at such speed left Wigapom reeling. He was barely aware that the claw-like talons of the Hybrid were releasing their grip and dropping him, expertly towards the summit below. He hit the snow-covered rocks and rolled a short way, gathering snow on his clothes like a living snowball, but apart from some bruising and a small gash on his leg he was unharmed. He thanked the ring again for its protection as he looked up for any sign of the Hybrid – fully expecting it to dive at him again – but the sky was clear. The Hybrid had disappeared.

Wigapom lay exhausted as the cold crept deeper into his bones. The snow was deep and the air thin and he was finding it difficult to breath at such a high altitude. Already a warning, dull ache throbbed threateningly in his head, yet the question why Darqu'on had not let the Hybrid just kill him filled his mind more than the pain in his head. What was going on? What game was Darqu'on playing? Perhaps that was it – he was playing with Wigapom, as a cat would a mouse – before coming in for the final kill.

Wigapom could not focus on reasons or logic for long in the mind-numbing cold and biting wind that whipped up the powdery snow in a snowstorm. He felt his ravaged body shutting down bit by frozen bit. Wigapom knew if he were to stand any chance of survival at all he would have to seek refuge from the freezing temperatures and wind, but he could barely move his body. Each effort he made managed to rack his breathing, tighten his chest and leave his head and body throbbing as if his brain was pushing out of his skull. Yet he had to move if he was to survive. He slowly and painfully dragged himself over the unforgiving rock, the urge for survival, oxygen, and warmth giving him a new strength. He looked over the edge of the rock. It was a very long way down! There was a protected ledge below him, which might offer him some temporary respite from the biting wind, but what then? Even if he managed to get down the mountain he was still in Darqu'on's control – a pawn in a dangerous game. This was definitely his hardest challenge yet, as the voice of Magus has said back in the castle. Yet he had to see it through and show Darqu'on what he was made of. He still had to find the missing stone and earn another, as well as retrieve *The Book of True Magic* again.

He took the blanket from inside the bag with freezing fingers and tied it as best he could around his shoulders for some warmth, and began to edge closer to the rock just below him. He had reached the overhang now and, resting on his knees, gripped it with his frozen fingers and looked down. Yes, there was a flatter part, with rocks jutting out, which could be used as a temporary shelter against the wind. There were even rocks he could use as handgrips and foot rests. Gingerly he eased himself over the ledge, not daring to look at the distance below him or how far he could fall if he let go. His head was swimming enough already as he reached into the furthest depths of his lungs for breath. Plucking up every ounce of courage and resolve he dropped as smoothly as possible, over the ledge and onto the rock below. He landed awkwardly and felt himself slipping on the icy shale towards the edge of the ledge. His stomach lurched into his mouth but somehow he managed to cling to a rock jutting out at the side and stabilise himself. He lay exhausted for a few moments, trying to re-establish the lining of his stomach in its proper position in his body. He was gasping for breath again due to the extra exertion and thin air. He made sure he had as firm a grip as possible on the rock and, with a determined pull, hauled himself away from the edge into the more protected space. So far so good, but what now? This action had not got him very far and his fingers were still blue from the cold, making holding on to anything near impossible. There was no feeling in his toes either, making walking even more impossible. His eyelashes were even frosting up as he looked down at the ring, teeth chattering, to read any message of protection.

When the mountain tumbles inward, then the challenge will begin.
Keep your wits about you, don't let the dark side win.

He hardly had time to digest these words before he heard the sound he had dreaded ever hearing again – the sudden swoop of wings as the Hybrid predator returned. Wigapom pushed himself against the side of the mountain, trying to remember the protective words of the gold ring as he again saw above him the sharp talons and hooked beak. He didn't want to be gripped by those again. The long neck stretched towards him, beady eyes searching everywhere; the double-headed tail scanned and sensed with its sensitive tongues but it was as if neither could see him! He thanked the ring again for protection, yet pressed his body close into the rock, just in case. Without warning, the mountainside began to swallow him whole, opening out in response to his body's pressure. He was tumbling backwards into the inside of the mountain and the words on the ring seemed instantly prophetic! The Hybrid and the daylight disappeared as Wigapom fell through the blackness again, banging against the hard interior rock face, sucked into the stone gullet of the mountain as though being swallowed alive.

CHAPTER 37

The Questioner and the Phoenix

"It's best to have failure happen early in life.
It wakes up the Phoenix bird in you so you rise from the ashes."
Anne Baxter

He landed with a painful thud on hard ground. He had plunged back into darkness again and could not see his surroundings, but felt a presence close to him and knew he was not alone. It was unsettling, feeling watched, when he could see nothing himself and he considered searching for the mercury lamp, still in the bag over his shoulder, but before he could do anything a deep, hollow voice reverberated across this unknown, unseen place like a vibrating wall of sound, and he held only what was left of his breath.

'Who enters here, friend or foe?' the voice questioned, seeming to come from everywhere at once. The vibrations had barely ceased before the voice repeated again.

'Who enters here? Friend or foe?'

Wigapom staggered to his feet. His body was pockmarked and stinging from the fall. He was aware he was bleeding, from the sticky sensations beginning to ooze on his body, although he was still too cold to feel any pain. Had the ring's protection begun to fade? He swung his unseeing gaze around, trying to detect the source of the voice. He could see nothing but the deepest, darkest black. It reminded him of the time he walked, unseeing, along the shifting sands by the Sea of Emotion. He remembered how that place had seemed so real, with its evocative sounds and aromas, but had only been in his imagination. This place smelt musty and dank but was it also a figment of the same imagination? This thought dispelled any fear he might otherwise have had and encouraged him to go with the flow of events – to trust the process.

The voice came again, more insistent this time.

'Who enters here? Friend or foe?' Whoever, or whatever it was wanted an answer.

Wigapom raised his voice and spoke, hearing the words echo back at him from all angles.

'To whom must I address my reply?' he replied, cagily.

'To the one that asks the questions,' came back the elusive response.

'I, too, need to ask questions,' said Wigapom, determined not to give too much away. 'Who are you and where am I?'

'The two big questions of the universe and both in the same sentence! Do any of us know who we are truly, or our rightful place? Sages and philosophers have puzzled over these questions for millennia and are no further forward in finding answers. What makes you think you are different from them?'

'You're playing with my words,' said Wigapom. 'I merely wish to know who I'm talking to and my immediate location.'

'That is simple then. You are talking to me and you are located here!'

Wigapom could feel disquiet bubbling in his veins at the sidestepping of these simple questions. The questioner *was* playing with him. If it was mind games this unseen being was looking for, then Wigapom would need to give as good as he got.

'It is said that a wit so sharp is in danger of cutting itself,' he retorted.

There was a sound that could perhaps have been laughter before it disappeared into a low rumble.

'Your own wit could lead to the same end,' came back the reply.

'Then we would both lie wounded, and still be no further forward,' responded Wigapom, pleased at his own quick retorts.

'Then introduce yourself and the matter will be closed.'

Back to square one it seemed.

Wigapom thought for a moment. This bantering and exchange of dialogue could go on without resolution forever at this rate and would lead nowhere. Something had to shift, to break this impasse and move them on. He remembered the words on the ring when he had read them in the boat: '*Sometimes who you think is present is found to not be there.*' Maybe the questioner was not really there. Maybe it really all was an illusion, but then the words had also said that the challenge would begin once the mountain tumbled inward, so maybe this was very real after all and going to be tough. The sooner he found out the better. He would do the only thing he could to stop the games, and that meant being honest. He took a deep breath and began.

'I am Wigapom, son of the deposed King and Queen, and heir to the Kingdom of Arcanum. I claim protection from harm by the power of my mother's golden ring and by the power of the stones that I carry. I am here to put right a terrible wrong but have so far not lived up to expectations, neither my own nor others and for that I have suffered. I am not beaten and will rise again, like the Phoenix from the ashes, in order to fulfil my destiny.' It was the first time he had really acknowledged his birthright, and his confidence grew even more.

'So you wear your mother's ring?' said the voice.

'Yes,' said Wigapom, surprised that out of all he had said this should be the one thing that the questioner had picked up on. He thought the questioner might have focused on Wigapom himself but it was as if the questioner already knew who he was. Why, then, did he make a point of pretending he didn't? Wigapom continued. 'Now that you know about me, perhaps you will introduce yourself?'

'You must be cold and tired,' said the questioner instead. This did not seem a compassionate statement to Wigapom, but rather one to deflect more questions. Wigapom was not deterred and tried again.

'I *am* tired and cold, but that's not surprising considering what I've just been through. I still want to know your name, and whether I can trust you,' he said.

'Trust? What is trust? Do you need to trust me?' came back yet another loaded question.

'I don't know if I *need* to trust you but I would like to know I could. Until I know who you are, how can I give that trust? I have been honest with you and you haven't been with me so far. It is hard to trust someone when they're so evasive,' said Wigapom, becoming more exasperated and unsettled by the questioner's avoidance at identification. 'It would be easier to trust you perhaps, if I knew your name.'

'Ah, so trust comes when you have a name to hang onto. That is easy to secure. I can give you a name but… Let me riddle you with it first,' said the questioner.

'What?' said Wigapom, 'What do you mean riddle? I don't want riddles, I want answers.' He was tired and hungry, his head and body ached and this dialogue was becoming unsettling and confusing, if not to say annoying.

'I am alive when I am dead,' added the questioner, again giving no straight answer, but Wigapom was beginning to understand – he was meant to guess the clues being given him. It *was* a game, and Wigapom was unwittingly becoming a defenceless player.

Another riddle came before he had time to absorb the first.

'From an element of destruction I am created.'

'Wait… I don't understand…' began Wigapom, his head suddenly swimming with confusing images.

'I am born from flame,' the questioner continued, ignoring Wigapom as before.

Despite himself Wigapom was being skilfully hooked in to the game. His unseeing eyes grew larger – as he thought he recognised a clue, which seemed to bring sense to the questioner's other statements 'born from flame' – could that be the Phoenix. He could hardly believe it. Was he really in the presence of the fabled magical creature that he had read, dreamt and fantasised about since he was a child and whose picture was in pride of place on the wall back in the Brakendor bakery? The creature that the ferryman had said was real yet had been missing for many years? Had he really found the Phoenix? Wigapom's confused brain began to clear at the thought and his imagination was truly caught; despite his better sense he became the innocent, impressionable child again, faced with the promised reality of a dream.

'Born from flame? Alive when dead? Created from destruction?' he said excitedly. 'That's the Phoenix! Are you really the Phoenix?'

'Would you like me to be?' asked the silky-smooth voice, hypnotic in its quality. Wigapom was hooked, like a minnow on a line.

'Oh yes! I loved the stories as a child,' he replied, already back in the enchantment of those stories, and with common sense suspended. 'The miracle of rebirth! I always wanted the Phoenix to be real but never thought he could be until the ferryman told me he was, and now you are telling me *you* are the Phoenix! The ferryman said you had disappeared. But now you're here: you are found, even though I can't see you yet. How did you come to be in the centre of a mountain, shouldn't you be on top of it in the sun, being reborn?'

There was that strange laugh again, like stones rumbling down a hill.

'Can you guess how I came to be here yourself?' came another question. Wigapom was so swept up by childish excitement at his discovery he did not stop to question why the Phoenix, if that was who he really was, was still not giving straight answers, nor did he recall the advice offered on the ring: '*someone who you think is present is found to not be there.*' Instead he created and believed his own story.

'I expect you fell, like I did. Then you were unable to rise again, unable to reach your nest and burn yourself in the fire ignited by the rays of the sun and instead remained plunged in darkness.'

'Can you help release me?' came the final question.

'Oh yes, I'll do anything, anything you ask!' cried Wigapom, totally bewitched now into childlike gullibility.

'Anything?' affirmed the Phoenix.

'Anything,' replied Wigapom, fumbling for the mercury lamp to prove it all to himself. 'If there was one creature that I hoped would be real it was always you. You gave me hope when I was younger that I could one day start *my* life anew.'

He found the lamp and lit it with fumbling fingers, keen to see this magical creature for the first time. As the soft blue glow gradually spread out from the lamp it caught the gloss of feathers around the neck of an immense bird, which shone strangely in the pale light. There was no colour, just shades of black and grey but Wigapom put this down to the poor quality of the light, for the Phoenix was otherwise the most majestic creature Wigapom could imagine: large and powerful, with a ruff of feathers around his neck, a crest framing his head, and a tuft of feathers on top and the deepest, darkest, blackest eyes Wigapom had ever seen. Wigapom could see that one wing hung down at his side in an awkward way. He glided over his knowledge of the fabled self-healing powers long attributed to the magical bird and focused purely on what he saw.

'You are hurt!' said Wigapom, immediate concern in his voice. 'Something is wrong with your wing.'

'It was damaged when I fell. I fear it may be broken,' came the Phoenix's reply, in a voice designed to elicit sympathy. At least the questions had stopped. Instead the Phoenix's eyes flashed like jet. Wigapom was surprised to feel an involuntary shudder move suddenly up his spine as though the Phoenix had penetrated his very being. It was an uncomfortable, frightening feeling, which he did his best to ignore – after all, this was the Phoenix – he could never be scared of the Phoenix!

'So that's why you disappeared! Is there anything I can do to help?' said Wigapom totally enrapt and hypnotised by everything he saw before him.

'Unless you have the gift of alchemy, then the answer is no,' came the sombre reply.

'What do you mean the gift of alchemy?' asked Wigapom.

'You do not know of alchemy? The ability to transform one thing into another?' Wigapom shook his head and the Phoenix continued. 'Philosophers have sought for millennia for the stone to turn base metal into gold but I do not need gold. I need to transform my broken wing into a new one as it is impossible for this wing to mend – I have to grow a new one, or I cannot fly to the top of the mountain and be reborn, so I will die,' explained the Phoenix, his eyes increasingly black and unblinking and more focused than ever upon Wigapom.

Wigapom was by now totally submerged into the drama playing out before him and horrified to think that the Phoenix might die if he couldn't help him. He had to rescue him!

'Oh, jeepers! I'll do what I can. I don't want you to die, now I've just found you.'

'You are my only hope,' said the Phoenix, pathos running through the creature's voice like too much honey on bread. 'Do you have the alchemical

366

philosopher's stone about your person, perhaps?' Wigapom could not detect the hard edge that came to the voice at that point, instead he asked, wide-eyed and entranced like a child desperately wanting to help his hero.

'What is the philosopher's stone?'

'Some say it is the elixir of life, others that it brings immortality or even enlightenment. Others say that it has transformative powers to change one state of being into another. This is what I need,' said the Phoenix, eyes glinting more intently by the blue light of the mercury lamp.

Wigapom would have given him anything at that moment, if it would help. He ignored again the shiver that ran up and down his spine, chilling him to the marrow. He thought instead only of the four stones now vibrating alarmingly in his trouser pocket; could one of these be the philosopher's stone? Maybe they all were!

'I do have some stones although I lost one,' he admitted to the Phoenix, 'and they set me thinking quite philosophically at times, perhaps they are what you mean?'

If Wigapom detected a sharp intake of breath in the Phoenix at that statement he paid no attention to it, nor the change of tone in the Phoenix' voice as it commanded, urgently and abrasively, 'Show them to me.'

'Of course,' replied Wigapom, virtually falling over himself now to comply with the request from his childhood hero.

Without any rational or intuitive thought as to what he was doing, he reached into his pocket and drew out the four remaining stones. He ignored the desperate clamouring of their vibrations on his palm, and laid them out on the ground close to the Phoenix, like a sacrificial offering to a god. In the blue light of the mercury lamp it made them all appear a strangely uniform grey colour. 'Here they are!' he said.

The Phoenix looked at the stones with the blackest gleam in his eye. He could barely contain his voice rising in excitement at the sight of them.

'What wonderful stones and with ancient writing too! Do you know what they say?'

Wigapom would have been more than ready to translate what was on the stones if it could have helped the Phoenix mend its broken wing and ensure the continuation of this wonderful creature, but there was something about the way that the Phoenix was edging closer to the stones, with the damaged wing not seeming quite so damaged after all, that stopped him, especially as he'd had the strangest sensation the moment he'd let go of the stones; that the protection they had given him, and that of the gold ring, had been broken. Something was not right. His intuition was back on track, having taken a massive detour in child-land, and was now screaming at him to take back the stones and get away from here as fast as he could.

But it was too late. He temporarily lost the use of his arms and legs and could do nothing but watch, as though in slow motion, as the Phoenix morphed into the Hybrid and, stretching out its neck, swallowed the stones with a triumphant gulp!

'No!' cried Wigapom 'No!' The stones were gone! His stones! The vital stones! The future of Arcanum, swallowed by this creature that, even as Wigapom stared, shivered out of vision, to be replaced by the leering face of Darqu'on.

'Too late, Brat!,' he mocked. 'Learn, as I did, to trust no one and nothing. Then you will never be disappointed.'

Wigapom had been tricked. He couldn't believe how gullible he had been.

'Darqu'on!' cried Wigapom, straining to move his limbs, 'what have you done? What have *I* done?'

His throat was dry, his forehead clammy and his stomach heavy like lead. 'I should have known that you couldn't be the real Phoenix. Your voice was not beautiful enough and you could not heal yourself as the Phoenix would be able to do! You have betrayed my trust, as you betrayed my father's, but I take responsibility, as my father also did. I was wrong to let myself be so trusting when all the indicators told me not to.'

Darqu'on laughed.

'But you did, you trusting fool! Did you really think that you could win! I, Darqu'on, have total power. I have you and your precious stones, along with the magic book, you have no chance of restoring the pathetic magic you seek. You are trapped in this place forever to die a slow and lingering death if I choose, or shall I make it quicker but equally painful in the hellfire of the Volcanister! Oh, yes, I have increasing dominion, at last, of the underground, so nowhere is safe any more. Oh the wonderful choices open to me now. You talk of trust betrayed and you have betrayed the trust invested in you – you will feel the pain of it, as I felt the pain when your mother and her paramour betrayed me. Revenge is sweet. It's payback time.'

The full realisation of what Wigapom had let happen hit him like a hammer blow. He had allowed Darqu'on's sorcery to take hold again! How could he have been so foolish? But there was no time for recriminations as he found himself sucked into a forceful swirl of dark energy spinning him and everything around him into a violent vortex, in which time was the only thing not moving.

When the energy stabilised again, to his horror he found himself in the Hybrid's beak, close to the edge of a bottomless chasm, which bubbled and spat with molten lava – heat so intense that it singed his hair and eyebrows

– an experience of hell from which it seemed there was no escape.

Wigapom was thinking very hard and very fast now. He had to avoid falling into the erupting Volcanister, get the stones back, and kill the Hybrid before it killed him. Somehow the intensity of his situation brought great clarity to his mind.

He had already discounted using the dagger tucked close in his belt as that could not be used in anger against another creature, or it would lose its sharpness: and Wigapom was angry, very angry, especially with himself, but he *had* remembered the lead weight Gobann had given him: the lord of death, he had called it. Lead was poisonous and would bring instant death if the Hybrid ingested it. Only then would he be able to use the dagger to remove the stones from the Hybrid's throat. He was swinging precariously from the Hybrid's beak, moving closer to the bubbling lava of the Volcanister. There was no time to lose if he was to kill the bird before it killed him. Struggling against the motion, he grappled in his pocket and found the lead weight. Gripping it tightly in his fingers he took it from his pocket and threw it down the gullet of the creature, preparing himself for the fall he knew would come and praying that it would not be into the Volcanister.

The effect was immediate. The Hybrid's face contorted, eyes bursting. Spluttering, choking and retching sounds rose like bile from his throat and his beak opened wide in agony, dropping Wigapom, who landed heavily at the very edge of the Volcanister. Wigapom drew in his breath, feeling the heat singe his lungs, and prayed the Hybrid wouldn't fall into the Volcanister before he had a chance to remove the stones.

The Hybrid made a dying lunge at Wigapom, its huge wings flapping weakly as the lead leeched its deadly dose. Wigapom turned to the ring for protection again, reciting the words he saw illuminated now by the boiling lava.

Let all that's good and honourable avoid the heat of Hell,
And let them find their path again and prove that all is well.

It was an encouraging message, yet still the Hybrid did not die, but lashed out with his huge talons. He was heavy and unstable, nearly overbalancing on his legs. Wigapom had to duck and avoid the Hybrid's flailing body, as well as being knocked over the edge of the Volcanister. The Hybrid's eyes were rolling in his face, he was moments from death, yet he could still crush Wigapom with the sheer weight of his body and topple them both into the hellish chasm. The end came. With one last gasp the Hybrid dropped motionless, all life spent, its grotesque face fixed in an expression of stupefied agony, burying Wigapom under its dead weight, its wings hanging lifeless over the edge of the Volcanister, where they began to sizzle and burn.

Wigapom spluttered with feathers in his mouth as the forked tongues of the serpent heads on the tail flicked momentarily in muscle spasm before falling, grey, stiff and lifeless, out of the side of the huge mouths. Wigapom was trapped so close to the edge of the Volcanister that, even had he been able to escape from under the creature, one false move would have toppled him over the edge. He had to move or risk being burned alive, but as he looked into the furnace more horror gripped him as he watched the Phoenix rise from its centre. Had he worked so hard to escape from one creature only to be brought down by another?

Then there was movement above him, as though the Hybrid was shifting position – no – it was being lifted from his body by the strong claws of the Phoenix. He heard the thud as the Hybrid fell to the side of him. No doubt he was next. Wigapom lay exhausted, awaiting his fate, but instead heard the most beautiful singing voice he could ever imagine. It conjured images of peaceful places; a tranquil lake, cool and refreshing, soothing his hot body. It was pure magic. He closed his eyes, sinking into the still coolness of the sound, and floated effortlessly on its waves. When he opened his eyes he was at a safe distance from the Volcanister and looking into the emerald green eyes of the Phoenix – the real one. Wigapom sighed in relief and sank into this feeling of blissful relaxation.

'I know who you are by your song – you are the real Phoenix,' he said, dreamily, 'I always wondered what it was like. Now I know. It's just the most beautiful sound I have ever heard, but I don't understand how you got here?'

The Phoenix bowed his noble head in acceptance of the compliment and then answered.

'I was here all the time,' he said in his melodic voice, 'but unable to move until that creature breathed its last. You broke the spell when you killed it. Saving you is my way of repaying you – a fair deal I would say, wouldn't you?'

Wigapom couldn't stop a smile spreading over his face, even though questions were jumping to attention inside his head like soldiers on parade.

'Absolutely! But I must get the stones from the Hybrid first, before I lose them completely.' Taking the dagger and gritting his teeth at the task he had to face, he returned to the dead creature and, even as the lava from the Volcanister continued to cook the flesh, he slit open the gullet of the Hybrid to remove the four stones. To his amazement, he found five, not four! It was not the stolen indigo stone, nor the lead weight, but a beautiful purple stone with another runic message carved across it.

'I have another stone!' he gasped, removing them all, 'and I think I've killed Darqu'on!'

The Phoenix was flapping its wings in warning.

'Darqu'on was not part of the Hybrid when it ingested the lead – but we have to get out of here before he comes back and shape-shifts into something else,' and the Phoenix spread his wings for Wigapom to climb on his back. Wigapom needed no second bidding, and with five stones now happily vibrating in his pocket, they flew towards the rising sun.

Part 7

Self-Realisation

"Knowing others is intelligence; knowing yourself is true wisdom."
Lao-Tzu

CHAPTER 38

Home Sweet Home

"Home is a place you grow up wanting to leave, and grow old wanting to get back to."
John Ed Pearce

Fynn and Will were exhausted. They seemed to have been running forever, struggling to keep up with the stamina of the little deer.

'Need to rest,' gasped Fynn.

'So hot!' panted Will, 'I feel as though I'm in a furnace, or something!'

The deer stopped in her tracks.

'Refresh yourselves from the brook if you need,' she said gently. 'You're nearly there. I've brought you as far as I can. You must travel without me the rest of the way, as I cannot go beyond this point: Only those who have come from the hidden village are allowed to return.'

Fynn and Will drank gratefully from the brook, relishing the cool water that trickled down their parched throats. The deer became rather nervous, her ears flicking back and forth, her nose repeatedly twitching in the night air as though picking up a million different unnerving scents.

'Is anything the matter?' asked Will, aware of her nervousness. The reply came in the form of an unearthly howl, very close by that set the whole forest, and them, trembling.

'Wulverines!' said Fynn, water still dripping from his chin as he froze mid-gulp.

'Quickly,' said the deer, leading them deep into a thicket that gave more cover, but both Fynn and Will were aware that it would not be enough to protect them from the Wulverines. Fynn was sure that he had attracted their attention when shouting their presence to the trolls earlier and wondered if this was why the deer had been running them so hard through the forest. Now they hid as best they could, knowing that any movement would draw the Wulverines to them. They watched, and prayed.

Through the trees they came, a pack of perhaps twenty or thirty, hungry for victims to devour, loping with long loose strides, red eyes shining like hot coals in the darkness, scanning for life to destroy. Fynn and

Will reminded themselves that the Wulverines were what remained of those killed by the Roth Riders; they needed a constant supply of lives to survive in their new form. Fynn and Will had only ever seen the damage they had done before, at Cassie's cottage, but now so close, they saw the real beasts and felt real fear. Although they knew that the Wulverines would rather catch their prey unawares than chase it, neither Fynn nor Will wanted to have to try to outrun them if they could help it. Fynn began smearing himself with soil in an effort to disguise his own scent and Will swiftly followed. They looked at the dagger-sharp teeth in the creatures' cavernous jaws, the wet, red tongues hanging from the sides, and the all-seeing red eyes with their perfect night vision and wondered how they would escape from this.

Then some totally unexpected and seemingly unrelated things happened. The deer decided to lay her life down for her previous rescuers by running across the Wulverines' path, and at the same time, the three trolls, which Fynn and Will had encountered earlier, lumbered out of the trees, a little the worse for drink, and ran into the direct path of the pack.

The effect was similar to splashing water onto hot fat; the place erupted into violent pandemonium. Wulverines howled, snapped, fought, and charged together, while panicked, intoxicated trolls yelled, fell over each other and tried unsuccessfully to run whilst barely knowing what had hit them. Between them streaked the graceful, brave flash of the dappled deer. It was a melee of tangled bodies, howls and screaming cries and horrific to see – and then the ground gave way beneath Fynn and Will's feet.

Down they tumbled, earth filling their mouths and eyes, landing with a heavy thump on smoothed, damp soil.

'Thanks for dropping in,' said a slow voice they both recognised, and they found themselves staring into the male end of the Megadrill.

'Ollie!' they cried in unison, amazed and delighted to see their old friend.

'Don't forget me!' came Annalid's voice from far down the other end of the tunnel they found themselves in.

'Are we pleased to see you!' said Fynn, as more of a statement of fact than a question.

'But it's too late for the deer,' said Will, tears filling his eyes as he thought of the brave and wonderful deer sacrificing her life for them. If it hadn't been for her and the trolls bumbling in at the right time this could have had a very different outcome.

'There is no greater expression of love than that – it is an honourable death' said Ollie. Will knew he was right.

'Ollie, we need to get to Brakendor quickly, you know, the hidden village? Can you help us?' said Fynn.

'We thought you would need us again; we have been preparing this tunnel for this purpose. It goes just to the boundary – we can tunnel no further,' said Annalid's voice.

'Thank you!' said Will, 'you are just wonderful!' and he and Fynn followed the Megadrill, who moved amazingly fast, to the end of the tunnel.

As Will and Fynn finally erupted through the mound of earth on the surface they could see they were out of the forest now. All they had to do was head across the no-mans-land that they remembered from almost another lifetime away. If the protection around Brakendor was still intact then it would block the village from view, as it had done for all these years – but there was the tree that provided both the access and exit point. By breaking back in they could destroy any protection, but they had no other choice. They sprinted across the grass, running so fast towards the tree that they hit the protective field it created, which shattered it immediately with a sound like breaking glass. They crashed straight through the trunk, flew through the air and landed right by the brook, now basking in the autumnal sunlight of a day that would be like no other in Brakendor's history. They were home!

The Phoenix landed in a valley some way out of the gates of Sapientia, the capital city, and Wigapom slid from its back, still hardly able to believe all that had just happened.

'How can I ever thank you?' he said to the magical bird. 'You have helped me in so many ways. Not least in allowing me to see that true rebirth is possible! You've been an inspiration to me all my life and when I find the hidden wisdom and restore this land to peace and prosperity once more, I will make sure that you will be on my coat of arms.'

The Phoenix looked at him with a gentle expression.

'Prince of Light,' he said, 'have you not yet been made aware that I have always been in just that place? Your father, and his father before him always used me as their emblem. This was then joined with the Unicorn emblem of your mother. This will continue when the magic returns, of that you can be sure. But I also owe you a debt of gratitude, for freeing me from Darqu'on's clutches. You have allowed me to continue to be reborn.'

'Perhaps that explains why I have always felt such an affinity with you. We are both in each other's debt it seems,' said Wigapom.

'Let us owe each other nothing but give all we have freely,' replied the Phoenix.

'I couldn't have said it better myself.'

'If you should need my help again then release this feather to the wind and I will come,' said the Phoenix plucking from the underside of his wing a most beautiful electric blue feather tipped with gold, and giving it to Wigapom.

Wigapom looked as though he had been given the moon and he beamed widely from ear to ear.

'Thank you, I will,' he said and watched as the amazing bird soared vertically up into the morning sky and flew back to his eyrie on the mountaintop.

Wigapom then carefully placed the feather in the lining of his coat and assessed his situation. He had five of the seven stones, having lost one to Darqu'on, which he would have to retrieve, but at least he knew what it said. He still didn't know what the newest, purple stone said, so that would have to be his next task. He knew the first stone had yet to be found, but had a feeling that Fynn and Will were already on its trail. He had found but lost *The Book of True Magic* to Darqu'on, but was sure that it, along with the lost stone, would both be in Darqu'on's stronghold, the Citadel, by now. This would have to be breeched, no matter what dangers he had to face. He would not let himself be duped again by Darqu'on and he also sensed that after what happened at the Volcanister, Darqu'on would not want to play games any more.

But first he must decipher the purple stone.

He sat with his back against a boulder, out of sight of prying eyes, and studied it. He was disappointed that no intuition as to its meaning came to him. He really thought that this one would be as easy as the others. He recalled their words, to see if he could get any help from them. *Is... Given ... As... Part... Of...* Part of what? Time? Yesterday? Everything? Anything? Nothing made sense without the first word, so any word could be right.

No, nothing was coming to inspire him. He looked at the rune, but despite his studies of the grimoire he experienced a total memory block. Why? After the first one the others had all come so easily. Why should this one be proving so difficult?

'What's wrong with me?' he said, frustrated at his lack of inspiration, 'Why can't I read it? It's not been this difficult before,' but his mind stayed as blank as the pages of *The Book of True Magic*. Perhaps if he read the ring it might help him. He looked intently at the gold band on his finger, totally believing in his ability to attract the words to the surface, and sure enough, there they were. They seemed as confusing as his inability to intuit the meaning on the stone.

The city hides so many things, all waiting to be discovered,
But what seems to be a threat at first, may turn out to be a brother.

He shrugged, confused; he would have to leave it all for now, there were more practical things to consider, such as finding a place to stay and something to eat! Re-wrapping the blanket around him as a cloak, and with a strong sense of the heroic traveller about him, he set out to find lodgings in the city.

Although Fynn was reluctant to admit it, it was really good to be home amongst the people and streets that he knew so well. It was good too not to be looking over his shoulder every few seconds in case some new terror was being unleashed. Maybe they had smashed the protection, maybe Brakendor was no longer hidden, but it still seemed an untouched backwater and he could be who he always had been; farm labourer and hired hand. At least that was his fantasy, but he had been gone for too long and a lot of water had passed through the brook since then! He had seen so much and still had so much to do, not least explaining where he had been all this time. This was doubly complicated by the presence of Will who, although looking exactly like Wigapom, and having begun his life as his inner self here, was now very much a real person in his own right; mature and with new memories, as well as the old. A very different person from the one that had walked out inside Wigapom in the early spring.

The first person they saw as they made to cross the brook was Martha Channelling, on the village side of it. She gasped, hand flying to her mouth, as though she had seen a ghost. Without stopping she hurried off as fast as her arthritic legs and walking stick would allow her, to spread the news of their return. She did a good job, for in the time it took them to walk across the brook to the bakery much of the village seemed to be descending on them. All had questions or comments; some curious, some angry, some amazed, some resentful, but most just pleased to see them again.

'Well, I never did, if it ain't old Fynn Barrowman and Willerby Sawyer, back from the dead!'

'My word Fynn, you look a little peaky, my lad. A bit of home cooking will soon sort that out.'

'Where did you go to Wiggy? When you went beyond the brook?'

'Has anyone told Sarah that her boy's home?'

'How could you leave your poor Ma distraught like that? She was in bed for weeks, gabbling on about her boy, and that she had failed him, and where was the hired man?'

'Well the hired man was with him, look!' Seb Harsen pointed out, waggling his shepherd's crook at Fynn. Fynn knew then that his inspiration in the Temple had been proved correct; he *was* the hired man. Was it connected to the location of the stone? He must speak to Sarah Sawyer, and quickly. The villagers had other ideas.

'The return of two of our own demands a celebration, I believe!' said Thomas Spinnaker, as ready as always to sup a pint for any reason that presented itself and, without taking no for an answer from Fynn or Will, they were paraded in triumph along the high street and into the Ram & Ewe along with half the village, to toast the return of Brakendor's prodigal sons.

It was there, surrounded by a mass of agog residents, that Wigapom's mother first caught sight of her wayward son for the first time for many months, hardly able to believe what she'd been told about his return and hurrying to the inn to find out for herself.

'Willerby!' she cried, her arms waving in the air and all rheumatic knees forgotten as she pushed her emotional way through the crowd. They parted like the biblical sea for her. 'My son! You've come home! You've come home! Praise be for your safe return!' she cried as she flung her arms around Will's neck and wept tears of uncontrollable joy.

Will duly beamed with embarrassed pleasure and hugged her back, but neither he nor Fynn had forgotten the reason for their return, and Fynn had a question for her.

'Mrs Sawyer, Seb here mentioned just a moment ago that when Wiggy – Willerby – left, you asked where the hired man was? Could I ask why you did that?'

The change that came over Sarah Sawyer was profound. She looked as though she had been hit in the mouth! Her lips clammed tight shut, her eyes stared in fear and she shook her head wildly as she flustered her way through denial.

'I... I... I don't know what you mean. I... I... I said no such thing. I... I... I must have been misunderstood. I'd just lost my son. I probably said all manner of silly things in my grief.'

'Aw, come on Sarah,' said Seb, 'I remember you going on and on about it; that you'd let Willerby down and where was the hired man? I remember it very well.'

'So do I,' piped up Martha Channelling, and several others nodded sagely in agreement, but Sarah refused to be drawn on it and consistently denied saying anything of the kind. Fynn was more and more certain that he and Will would have to get her on her own to find out more. Sarah also wanted to have Willerby on her own, although that did not necessarily include Fynn, in her mind.

'It's lovely to have you all pleased to see Willerby home again, and Fynn of course,' she said in a voice that held the promise of a soon to be delivered and very large 'but'…'But I'd like to have my son to myself, if you don't mind,' she said firmly, the tone in her voice telling everyone who knew her well that they had to leave her and Willerby well and truly alone. So, with affectionate parting words, the crowd drifted away and left Sarah, Will and Fynn alone.

'I said I'd like my son to myself Fynn, if you please. I'm sure your family will want to see you, too,' she said, dismissing Fynn, but Fynn was not to be so easily ejected. He had not returned to Brakendor on a family visit, but to locate the all-important package.

'Mrs Sawyer, forgive me, but we are here for a very special reason. Not only for Will here but Wiga… well… everybody in Arcanum. I think you know more about this hired man than you're letting on. You have to tell us what you know, it's really important.'

Sarah looked frightened and indignant at the same time, so Will came to Fynn's rescue.

'Listen to him, Mother,' (oh, that sounded strange and yet quite nice!) 'He knows what he's talking about. There are a lot of lives at stake here. Tell him anything you know. This is important. Perhaps it will help if I tell you that I know you adopted me and that I know who my real parents were.'

Sarah looked shocked at this disclosure, memories flooding back of that strange night in late February twenty years ago, yet Will's face was so earnest and he looked at her so kindly, which made such a change from their previous argumentative relationship, that Sarah accepted what he said immediately. She took a deep breath and looked furtively around her to check that they really were alone before saying quietly,

'Best come back to the bakery then,' and she hobbled and puffed and panted her way up the hill towards Sawyer's Bakery, with Fynn and Will following behind.

When they were inside the small front room that led off the bakery itself she spoke again, even then in a whisper, as though the walls might have ears.

'I did talk about a hired man and I have regretted it for all this time. I promised that gentlemen who came that I would take care of you and never breath a word, and I never did until you left, Willerby. I was distraught, so guilty, thinking I had let the gentlemen and you down and been so selfish to want you to stay here with me and not fulfil your destiny. I did it through love and fear for your safety, but I also wanted to keep you for myself and I know that was wrong. Don't you think I've suffered for it every day since you went?'

'There's no need to feel guilt for anything, Mother,' said Will, touched by her distress.

'But what about the hired man, Mrs Sawyer?' prompted Fynn, gently but firmly.

Sarah looked at Fynn as though she had momentarily forgotten he was there and the sight of him in her living room was a surprise!

'Oh my! Yes, the hired man. Well, when the important gentleman brought you here as a baby, Willerby, and left me and your father to raise you as our own on that night I will never forget, he told your father and me to keep you safe, which we did. He gave us a package to give to the hired man when he called. Neither your father nor I ever looked in the package and no hired man ever came, and you grew up and we loved you and wanted to keep you from what you were meant to do. Then when you did it anyway and still no hired man had come, I thought I'd let you down and that you would die and I would never see you again! Oh, forgive me, Willerby. Please forgive me!' Sarah burst into tears again, sobbing into her apron.

'There is nothing to forgive,' said Will, tenderly removing her hands from her eyes, 'you always did the best you could. No one can do more than that.'

'Where is the package that the gentleman gave you, Mrs Sawyer? It's really important,' prompted Fynn again.

'I don't know if I should…' said Sarah, looking at both of them in turn.

'Not even if I am the hired man?' finished Fynn, 'Because I think I am. That's why we had to return here, and we really need that package, Mrs Sawyer. Really badly.'

Sarah looked from Fynn to Will and back again, not sure of what to do. It was still hard for her to see these two as any more than the young boys she had always known and often chastised. It was difficult to believe that Will was more than her own son and that Fynn was the hired man. Yet the kind, but firm urgency in both their faces was enough to convince her of the truth, and what she had to do.

'I'll get it for you,' she said. 'Follow me.'

She took them into the bakery, as scrubbed as ever, and pointed to the picture of the Phoenix on the wall.

'Remember, Willerby, you put that picture there, after your father died!' she said. 'You insisted on bringing it out on show, even though we'd kept it hidden for all those years. Get the picture down now, will you, Willerby?' she asked. Will did so, remembering his childhood feelings about the fabled bird.

'Now lift it out of the frame, if you please.'

Will did so. As he lifted the back off the frame, there underneath, somewhat faded now was the red cloth package that Magus had left all those years ago.

'I think that is meant for you, Fynn,' she said.

Will and Fynn exchanged glances as Fynn carefully picked up the package and unwrapped it. Inside was a beautiful red stone with another runic symbol etched upon it. Fynn and Will drew breath in unison and looked at each other again,

'We have the stone!' they said together. 'We have the stone!'

CHAPTER 39

Gone To Earth

"And hermits are contented with their cells."
William Wordsworth

The Citadel, Wigapom soon discovered, was a fortress, which sat like a fat spider on its web in the centre of the city. It was a huge walled building with four gates, one to each main compass point, surrounding a large tower in the centre, which overlooked the city below, where radial roads met smaller concentric roads and spread out, like the patterning of a web. He could sense the Citadel poised, ready to pounce on any unsuspecting prey that came along.

In the city itself, life went on as in any large metropolis; throbbing with hustle and bustle, its citizens living life as best they could under difficult circumstances, ever mindful of the potential threat in their centre, but wily as well as wary. Wigapom did his best to look as though he belonged here as he made his way discreetly through its maze of roads and alleyways, which spread out around the outside of the Citadel itself.

The Citadel was Darqu'on's centre of command. Here he planned and directed activities, watching everything that unfolded in every corner of Arcanum through the myriad of mirrors that lined the walls of the room in the tower. The Citadel, in gentler times, had once been the ancient Temple of Wisdom, before Darqu'on's sorcery turned it into a fortress. It was now guarded by the latest addition to his fighting and defensive force, automotive robots cloned from his own DNA and totally in his command. The devastating experience at Dragonmound had taught him to put his immediate safety in no one's hands but his own. The clone guards were his toughest fighting force yet and his greatest defenders. They were also in unlimited supply, programmed to do his bidding. Since their inception, Darqu'on had felt more powerful and protected, but also more isolated than ever. He could trust no one (not even Scabtail at times) but himself. It was a double-edged sword, but one which he chose to wield.

Wigapom mingled with the crowds by the Citadel walls where, perched on the battlements like the vultures at Lampadia, the black-clad clone guards stood impassive: eyes programmed to notice the slightest trouble and bodies programmed to kill. Wigapom wondered how he would ever penetrate the seemingly impenetrable. No wonder many of the citizens spilling in and out of the city looked nervous, their downcast eyes refusing to make eye contact, anxiety etched into the lines of their faces, whilst others looked angry and tense; far worse than Wigapom had experienced in Lampadia. Wigapom wondered how they managed to live like this day after day. He also wondered how easy it would be to find a place to stay without attracting too much attention. He needn't have worried on this score as synchronicity stepped once more into his life.

He left the Citadel and passed what seemed to serve as a hostelry, at the junction of a radial road and a circular one, some way from the Citadel's South Gate, when a youth skidded across his path, knocking him sideways before ending up sprawled on the cobbles just beyond Wigapom's feet. As both of them righted themselves, an angry voice bellowed from the doorway.

'And you can stay out too, you double crossing, low life! Don't think I'll ever take you back either. Think yourself lucky that I haven't handed you over to the clones! Now beat it, before I beat you black and blue!'

The bear-like body and florid face of the landlord accompanied the authoritative voice through the door, revealing a mop of hair straggling across broad shoulders and work-stained hands being smacked together in dismissive contempt.

The youth cursed under his breath, but took him at his word and hotfooted it down the alleyway to disappear into the shadows. Wigapom couldn't help but stare at this unexpected slice of city life. Although at first sight the man had looked a bit of a bully, it now seemed that, despite the corpulent man's appearance, here was someone who might still have principles to uphold! Yet another illustration of not making snap judgements, he reminded himself, recalling the latest words on the ring.

Wigapom's staring did not find favour with the landlord, however, who rounded on him with a temper sharp enough to cut paper.

'What are you looking at, nosey parker? Trouble comes to those who don't mind their own business here. Get lost! Haven't you got any work to be doing, rather than gawping at me like some fish out of water? Answer me now!'

Intuition told Wigapom to be candid with this man, so he replied truthfully.

'I don't have a job yet. Nor a place to stay.'

'So you're a lazy skiver, as well as a nosey parker, eh? Another dosser! I could have the guards on you for less!' The man glared at Wigapom ferociously, burly arms folded across his corpulent belly.

Wigapom was momentarily concerned by the threat. It was like being back in Lampadia. He had only just arrived and was already creating a scene around him! Why did he seem to attract them? Perhaps he should do as the landlord said and leave, quickly. Yet he recalled the last words on the ring again, about a threat turning out to be a brother, and there was something about the man he liked – something in his eyes that didn't tally with his brusqueness of manner. Wigapom looked back squarely into them, decided to trust his instincts and declared.

'I'm not a skiver or a dosser. I'm willing to work for my keep. I could even work for you, perhaps,' he suggested, the words flying out of his mouth like an arrow and landing the proposition squarely at the landlord's straddled feet. 'I see you've had to fire your potboy. Maybe I could do the job instead?'

The man's eyes narrowed slightly at Wigapom and he scratched his unshaven chin as if not knowing what to make of this bold youth before him. Then he snorted with something that might have been amusement.

'You're a cheeky one and no mistake. Sharp enough to cut yourself too, I shouldn't wonder, but you can look me in the eye. There's not many can do that these days around here. Best come inside, away from prying eyes,' and he turned back through the doorway with Wigapom following him. It seemed the right thing to do somehow. The man was brusque, but Wigapom believed in the words of the ring: he could trust him.

When the door shut behind them, Wigapom found himself in a chaotic kitchen, piled high with unwashed tankards and un-scrubbed tables. He could tell that the lad who had just left this man's employ deserved the sack! The landlord perched his rotund behind on the one uncluttered corner of the table in the centre of the kitchen and said, 'What's your name?'

'Will,' said Wigapom without hesitation.

'Will, eh? Well, you're right, I will need a potboy, and you'll do as well as anyone. Six days a week, mind, seventh off, three-penneth a day, paid in arrears, lodgings thrown in and food too, if you please me. Want it or not?'

Wigapom scanned the kitchen, and the man's face. He would have to work hard, he could tell, but he saw how fate was working another one of her mysteries and nodded his head – besides, the kitchen might be untidy, but the smell of food coming from it was delicious!

'I'll take it,' he said before the man could change his mind.

The landlord threw Wigapom a crumpled apron. 'You best start now then,' he said, 'and I'll see what you're made of.'

So began Wigapom's undercover life as potboy at The Hermit Inn. Hard though it was, it allowed him to blend into the background of the place and thus discover a great deal about the workings of the city, its inhabitants and, equally importantly, the Citadel.

The Hermit was a busy place, always thronged with people, exchanging ribaldry if the beer was particularly potent, but mainly mutterings in dark smoky corners about their grievances and problems. Wigapom became very adept at listening to what was said and watching what went on, whilst keeping well out of trouble. He discovered there were more folk than he suspected who did not follow the dark ways of Darqu'on and actively worked for the old days of peace and prosperity. The Hermit was a centre for their discontent and resistance, due in no small way to the strength of character of the landlord, Arcturus, a great bear of a man, who, as well as championing the cause of freedom from oppression, shepherded his flock of customers as though they were the most valuable people in the world, giving short shrift to anyone he suspected of giving them poor service. Wigapom reminded himself yet again that he had been wrong to make a snap judgement about him.

Arcturus took to Wigapom quickly, as did his wife, the quietly spoken but practical Bethulah, and Wigapom discretely heard many plans for Darqu'on's overthrow expressed over warm beer in musty corners. He said little himself, but soaked everything up like the sponge he used for washing up the pots in the huge kitchen. The whole experience allowed him considerable reflection time, even though he was constantly active and usually flopped exhausted into his small bunk under the stairs at night. The only day of rest for him was at the end of a busy week and he took these opportunities to wander at will around the city, where he would stake out the Citadel, watch its comings and goings and work out the best means to enter it when the time came. He often mulled over whether to come clean about who he was to Arcturus and his friends, and involve them in his plans, but had not felt the time was right. He lived this life for longer than he planned but shorter than he thought he might have to.

October was nearing its end. The short days and long nights were established again and there was much talk about the up-coming festival – the only one that Darqu'on allowed – that of Samhain. Darqu'on liked the imagery of the day as the day of the dead. He wanted to reinforce his own deadly power and stress the return of the dark days of the coming winter. What he did not understand was that for the Arcanese with long memories this time had always been celebrated as the start of a new cycle, where in the silence of the long darkness could come the subtle whisper of a new beginning. Every year, since the death of the King, they had celebrated Samhain with this as their secret focus. This feeling seemed intensified this year.

Wigapom was unaware of all the deeper subtleties of the festival's message but had been thoroughly involved in preparing for it at The Hermit, and now breathed a sigh of relief after finishing an even more exhausting week's work as their potboy. Today he could be his own person again and at no one else's beck and call. Arcturus was fair, but worked him hard. Wigapom had developed a real physical strength by dragging barrels of beer from the cellar, as well as clearing and washing up endless glasses and dishes until his fingers began to wrinkle from the suds. But for twenty-four hours each week he was free. He spent much of them outside the Citadel walls.

Today was business as usual – citizens were still going about their daily tasks, trying to scrape an existence together whilst having one watchful eye always on the activities in the Citadel. For the Lampadians, it had been hard to relax and live a comfortable life; for the citizens outside the Citadel it was almost impossible. Suspicion, aggression, despair, fear; all were here, in every corner, in every crevice, in everyone. Yet life had to go on. Food needed to be bought and sold, artefacts made and distributed, lives lived. Even then, few of the stallholders and shops that outlined the Citadel walls ever went inside the Citadel itself and if they did they did not linger. Darqu'on, when not shape-shifting into some creature or another, kept himself separate from those he controlled, even his clone guards, who were abundantly evident, positioned around the walls, emotionless in their scrutiny of everyone and everything, but not allowed too close to their controller.

Wigapom watched them on the battlements, at each of the four gates, and ranged along all the levels of the Tower. They marched, they watched, they stood to attention, they challenged, they fought; automatic reactions built in to deter intruders, and few would choose to thwart them, yet Wigapom knew he would have to.

In his frequent forays to the Citadel he had got to know the outer layout of the fortress very well, including the market stalls that somehow managed to survive around its walls. Wigapom had studied each of the Citadel's four gates. He knew the North Gate was likely to be his best point of eventual entry, as it was the least active of them all. He knew that the guards on each gate were changed once a day at dusk and that the Citadel was filled with them, all programmed by Darqu'on to respond to his bidding. Wigapom assumed that after Dragonmound, Darqu'on would have programmed out any self-destruct tendency, although Wigapom mused, if they were clones of Darqu'on they must still have that trait inside them somewhere! Wigapom was increasingly sure that Darqu'on was his own greatest enemy, and despite all that had happened Wigapom couldn't help but feel compassion for him as a lost soul. But compassion aside, he had to outwit him if the destructive and brutalising grip of his sorcery was ever to be replaced.

He had thought about using the feather the Phoenix gave him to summon the magical bird to fly him to the Tower in the Citadel, which was built on five increasingly narrowing levels, but this would obviously attract too much attention. He would have to enter unseen, and arriving on a blue, gold and purple bird might not quite fit that bill! He still had the gold ring, and the artefacts Gobann had given him – apart from the copper coin and the lead weight – and of course he had most of the stones, which had progressively imbued him with attributes such as courage, self worth, confidence, a compassionate heart, the ability to speak his truth, and clarity of vision. It was unfortunate he had lost the stone that aided his intuition – he needed that to help him decipher the purple stone, whose message still eluded him. What of these could he use to gain entry into Darqu'on's stronghold and, indeed, gain entry into Darqu'on's mind? No doubt he would need each one of them at varying times. He would have liked the help of Will and Fynn too. He was thinking this today, letting his mind drift for a moment to see if he could connect with Will. He had experienced some strange images lately when he had done this, such as trolls and deer and even Sarah, his adoptive mother, along with the picture of the Phoenix in the bakery! Funny he should recall that; it reminded him of his own encounter with the real Phoenix and he constantly visualised the bird bringing Will and Fynn to him – but this all seemed like wishful thinking. He had no idea when he would ever see them again.

Wigapom sighed. This was getting him nowhere. Enough with planning, he would trust that things would work out in the way they needed. He would walk around the Citadel perimeter once more and then head back to The Hermit for an early bed. If he was meant to put these stones in *The Book of True Magic* then it would happen, even though he didn't have access to the book, or even all of the stones yet.

'Trust the process, Wigapom,' he told himself again.

Fynn and Will were preparing to leave Brakendor again, this time with the package containing the red stone safely in Will's pocket. Sarah was churning with emotion. Having been so overcome with their arrival, she was now having to face losing them all over again, yet this time she knew she had to let them go. They hadn't told her all that had happened outside Brakendor; there hadn't been time, and some things were probably best left unsaid, but she accepted that there was more to understand than she ever would, and was prepared to let it be.

One thing that had changed was that Brakendor was no longer the hidden village. Although some protection still remained, it had not re-formed completely after Fynn and Will had crashed back through the barrier with such force, and now a vulnerable gateway existed which had not been present before. What this meant for the village was as yet unknown and both Fynn and Will hoped that nothing terrible would overtake Brakendor as had happened in Oakendale. Sarah was surprisingly philosophical about it.

'We've been stuck in a time warp for too long,' she said. 'Change is natural and I've come to realise that we can't stay still and be cosseted all our lives. We need to live in the real world and take our chances like everyone else!'

'With any luck, you giving us this stone will speed up proceedings and help to bring a sense of security and stability back, so that we can all live in peace and harmony together, at last,' said Fynn as they prepared to take their leave.

'That's what I'll be hoping and wishing for,' said Sarah, hugging them both.

'Something's been on my mind,' said Will, 'What happened to Sophie, the girl that lived here? I haven't seen her since we've been back and I'd hoped to.'

Sarah's face took on an air of mystery and her voice lowered again.

'That was a strange case,' she said. 'She and her mother just upped and left one day, not long after you did, Willerby. No one saw them go. We don't know what happened to either of them, although gossip was that they went back to where the mother used to live, by the sea. To be honest, we were so astonished that you had left, that when they disappeared we hardly paid it any attention! They kept themselves to themselves anyway. Rather a sad woman, I always thought, very quiet and reserved, though her daughter was a sweet thing.'

'Yes, she was,' said Will, with a dreamy, far-away look in his eyes. 'I've been thinking about her a lot lately for some reason.'

'No time for that, Wiggy,' teased Fynn with a smile, 'We've got your Kingdom to save!'

'You've just called me Wiggy,' said Will.

'So I have,' remarked Fynn thoughtfully.

Darqu'on rubbed his thin pale hands together, feeling the shape of the stone he was holding between them. His hands were cold and the stone felt colder still; all Darqu'on's energy was focused on his plans for The Brat. He had been so sure he'd had him trapped last time and had relished his suffering, especially at such close quarters! Yet he had still lost him, and the stones, apart from this one. He turned the indigo stone over and over in his hand. It was just a matter of time before he had them all and thus removed all of The Brat's power! Then he would remove his life! He had thought his final solution had been foolproof, but The Brat was not a fool. He could see that. He had grown from that immature, rash lad who had tumbled out of nowhere into the mirror's reflection into an astute, mentally and emotionally strong young man – a real challenge for Darqu'on. When the kill came it would be all the sweeter, especially with the back-up plan Darqu'on had now set into operation. The Brat would be like a lamb to the slaughter. Darqu'on's thin lips spread wide as he thought of his new plan: it relied on manipulating The Brat's strengths of kindness and compassion and turning them into weaknesses. One of those weaknesses was even now in safe keeping in the Tower; the bait – the damsel in distress waiting for her knight to rescue her and thus bring about his own downfall! Oh how Darqu'on revelled in his own audacity and the thought of what would ensue.

He had it all worked out – he would even make it easy for The Brat to enter his lair – and when he came to the Tower to find the book and the stone, bringing the other stones with him, imagine The Brat's surprise to find her imprisoned here. He would have to rescue her, he would have no choice, and then Darqu'on would strike. If it meant sacrificing her also, then so be it. What was she to him anyway?

As Wigapom returned to The Hermit he knew something was different. There was an intensity that was tangible as he walked into the taproom. It was full of people he recognised as friends of Arcturus and Bethulah, who were both busy topping up tankards of beer while the assembled crowd gave their attention to the person speaking earnestly in their midst.

'… Everything was collapsing…' the female voice said.

Wigapom knew that voice! It was Skye! He could hardly stop his heart from leaping at the familiar sound. Uncharacteristically, he pushed his way to the centre of the group. It *was* Skye, her lovely face looking tired but as determined as ever.

'... By then it was too late,' she continued, 'but we tried...' Then she caught sight of Wigapom and stared in amazement.

'Wiggy? Is it really you?' she cried in delight, all memory of their last unhappy meeting long forgiven and forgotten. All faces turned to see whom she was addressing and were more than surprised when it turned out to be their potboy.

'The last time I looked!' joked Wigapom, opening his arms out expressively as she launched herself into them, delighted to see him.

Arcturus, in the middle of pouring ale into a tankard, spilled a quart of it onto the floor in his surprise.

'You know each other?' he asked.

'We certainly do,' said Skye, 'but none of you obviously realise who you have in your midst! Ladies and gentlemen of the resistance, may I introduce you to Wigapom, the Prince of Light!'

There were jaw-dropping gasps from the crowd, looks of disbelief, amazement, relief even, and Wigapom felt himself flushing an embarrassing red at all the attention, especially as he had so purposefully spent his time here as quietly and unobtrusively as he could. That would now be a thing of the past, but already he sensed a real time of change, of things coming together just as they needed to, and was encouraged by this.

'I always sensed there was more to you than just Will, the potboy,' said Bethulah, breaking the astonished silence with her quiet and gentle voice, whilst placing an affectionate hand on Wigapom's shoulder. Wigapom was grateful for her comment and the feeling behind it.

'I think there is some explaining to do here,' added Arcturus. 'This puts a whole new light on our plans.'

'Indeed it does,' said another vaguely familiar voice. Wigapom looked at him closely; he was tall, with greying hair, hypnotic eyes and long tapering fingers.

'Oh Wiggy, I almost forgot, this is Asgar,' said Skye, as the figure by her side bowed graciously.

'Asgar!' said Wigapom, 'I know you! You were Marvo at my party. You gave me the orange stone, and did magic.'

'I had that honour, indeed,' Asgar acknowledged, 'and now you are set to bring the magic back again. All is well!'

That phrase! The one he had heard in the castle! And in his dreams. All was coming to pass. All was well indeed.

And so the full story of everything that had happened came out. Wigapom told his amazed audience everything he had experienced since leaving Oakendale and a little of his back history too in Brakendor, especially his meeting with Asgar, and learnt in turn of what had happened in Lampadia. He was shocked to hear of Aldebaran's death, but gratified to hear how Asgar had stepped into Skye's darkest hour.

'He saved me,' said Skye. 'As simple as that, physically and emotionally. Apart from the trauma of watching my father die, escaping from Lampadia was horrendous. Lucas and I got separated and if I hadn't come across Asgar I don't think I would have made it – Ghouls were everywhere. If I do nothing else in my life I swear that I will work tirelessly to release all the Living Dead from the hell they are trapped in and programmed to inflict on others!'

'Aye to that,' added Arcturus and the agreement of the resistance workers sounded emphatically around the room.

Wigapom looked around at the assembled crowd.

'We must work together in this,' he said. 'You call me the Prince of Light, yet we are all Light workers here. If we work as one we will free Arcanum from repression and bring back peace, harmony and the True Magic again. I have nearly all of the stones and even though I lost one to Darqu'on, I know he has it in his possession, as well as *The Book of True Magic*. The last stone is surely being retrieved from Brakendor by Will and Fynn as we speak, and with your help and the grace of all that is good, true and honourable we will breach the Citadel and return the stones to the book. All we need is for Fynn and Will to return to us.'

'I wish for that too,' said Skye. 'Have you heard from them, Wiggy?'

'Only indirectly, yet I feel they're close. But we must wait a little longer and continue to make our plans to penetrate the Citadel.'

'There are many of us now!' said Arcturus. 'We had hoped to storm the gates.'

'And find ourselves surrounded and outnumbered by the clone guards?' said Wigapom, 'No; our approach must be more subtle than that. I must enter without anyone being aware that I have done so. Your job must be to create a diversion outside the Citadel, to draw attention away from me. Once in the Citadel I have more chance of finding what is needed, but there's no point in entering until I receive the final stone, so we must continue as before and wait for Will and Fynn.'

'You cannot go into the Citadel alone, Wiggy – you are too important – you will need help,' said Skye.

'Maybe, but entry must be as quiet as possible. I know Darqu'on has eyes everywhere, but let's make sure he has something else to focus on, and hope he misses me.'

'We will plan the diversion,' said Arcturus. 'It will be easy enough to create a brawl when the time comes.'

'It may need to be something more than that,' said Asgar. 'I will work on it with Arcturus.'

'Entry is best at the North Gate,' said Wigapom. 'If you cause a disturbance at the South Gate it will draw the guards' attention away.'

'Consider it done.' pledged Arcturus, extending his hand to Wigapom to seal the deal.'

CHAPTER 40

The Way In

"The Buddhas do but tell the way; it is for you to swelter at the task."
Siddhārtha Gautama Buddha

The last day of October – the day of Samhain – dawned crisp and bright and the streets around the Citadel walls were full of hustle and bustle, as folk did their best to ignore the ever-present clone guards around the battlements, and enjoy the festivities. The citizens were making the most of this opportunity to release pent-up feelings of repression with a pageant of mummers, acrobats and jugglers, as well as a lively market and, as the evening came, huge bonfires and feasting. They jostled to watch the jugglers and even smile at the mummers in their finery, and Wigapom mingled good-naturedly with the crowds at the South Gate. He had become familiar with their ways by now, as well as with many of the people who lived here, having spent time listening to their conversations, and dreams as well as their shouts and curses. There was usually little joy here and today it was good to see the usual aggression, pain, and fear replaced by a veneer of joviality, however thin. However, the tinderbox of repressed emotions felt heightened, as though straining at the leash for freedom, and he felt more than ever the importance of fulfilling his Quest and releasing these people from their negative burden. He couldn't help but think that today would be a perfect day for the planned diversion that those from The Hermit had been preparing. Everything depended on the return of Will, Fynn and the last stone. Where were they?

Darqu'on had been looking at the mirror, watching The Brat walk the walls for some time. He knew what a regular occurrence this was and it amused him. If only The Brat had known that he was being enticed into a trap, as a hungry spider sets one for his prey! He had already instructed the guards about the North Gate. He was sure The Brat would use this entrance. He had done what he needed to make it the most obvious access point. It did mean that the activity would not show up so well in the mirror – there were times when darkness could be a curse even to the Dark One – but he would see him easily enough once inside the Citadel. Then came an unexpected and unwanted disturbance.

'Begging your pardon, Master,' said the familiar cringe-worthy voice, 'but she has come round now and is proving more troublesome than we thought. Where do you want me to put her?'

Darqu'on turned away from the mirror to see an obsequious Scabtail cowering before him. He was annoyed at having his vigil at the mirrors disrupted and looked at Scabtail with eyes like molten lead.

'Where I told you, imbecile, in the inner room, of course. Are you incapable of listening to orders?'

'No Master, but I was unsure and wanted only to serve!' replied Scabtail, realising that his relationship with his master had plummeted again and that he would, surely, always be in the wrong with Darqu'on.

'Then serve me by getting out of here,' shouted Darqu'on, throwing a small lightning bolt in Scabtail's direction, which singed his tail yet again. Scabtail fled through the door, his tail smoking painfully and with not only fear but resentment written all over his face.

Darqu'on turned to the mirror again, and cursed. The Brat had gone. He searched the other mirrors but there was no sign of him. He had lost him again, all because of that pathetic reptile servant of his. He would make him suffer for this!

Wigapom had been trying to communicate telepathically with Will since coming to the city; he'd been hoping to find news of him and Fynn and the whereabouts of the final stone. Apart from a jumbled dream a couple of nights ago that consisted of Will waving at him with something red in his hands before it changed into Sophie playing a balancing game with seven stones in her palm, and then the Phoenix riding a Unicorn in a silver forest, he had not received any meaningful communication! He knew that dreams were supposed to be important, but this was so peculiar that, other than the fact it had something to do with the stones, he didn't hold out much hope that he would be able to make sense of it. Instead he just kept visualising Will and Fynn arriving today so that the plan to enter the Citadel could be put into operation. But when he turned the corner, just past the South Gate, and saw walking towards him none other than

Fynn and Will, he was still as surprised as both of them were to see him. All had to keep their feelings in check so as not to draw attention to themselves, so Wigapom, stilling his thumping heart and the desire to jump up and down with joy, turned and walked as casually away as his emotions would let him, knowing they would follow. He led them to a secluded place in a nearby alley, where market stallholders threw their rotten rubbish but avoided staying at all costs! As he turned the corner and pulled Fynn and Will into a dark doorway, their noses recoiled in disgust at the putrid smell, but the doorway was as close as they could get to being completely hidden. Wigapom whispered out of the corner of his mouth.

'At last! I've been trying to connect with you for ages.'

Will replied in a similar fashion.

'Us too – I've been sending you dreams! Everything else seemed blocked. How long have you been here?'

'Oh, ages, I've been staking out the Citadel, and working out a plan of entry with the friends I've made here, and today is a *perfect* day for it. It's all planned; Darqu'on has the Book and a stone and ...'

'That's not the only thing he has,' interrupted Fynn talking through motionless lips and in a low whisper.

'What do you mean?' asked Wigapom.

'He has Sophie too,' said Will.

Wigapom's smile dissolved from his face into a look of shocked horror at this revelation. Darqu'on had Sophie? So that's why he'd dreamt about her – Will had been trying to tell him. She'd featured a lot in his own thoughts lately, but why would Darqu'on want to capture her? What had she got to do with all this? If Darqu'on had hurt her then he wasn't sure he could be responsible for his actions! He demanded to know more about Sophie from Fynn and Will.

'She and her mother left Brakendor not long after we did,' explained Fynn. 'They went back to where her mother had lived before, somewhere by the sea.'

'Nepton,' added Will, pointedly to Wigapom, 'where the castle is.'

'The Castle on the Crag? I've been there!' replied Wigapom.

'I know,' said Will, 'I sent a message to you there, remember?'

Wigapom did indeed remember the image of Will coming out of the flames. He recalled Sophie being part of that vision too – of slipping through him to reach Will.

Fynn continued, 'Sophie's mother is in delicate health, a troubled soul apparently. Sophie was looking after her, with an old aunt... Can't remember her name...'

'Maya!' Wigapom interrupted, as suddenly things began to fall into place. 'I met her – the aunt – her name was Maya. She told me about her niece! She was attacked by Darqu'on once but escaped. Do you mean that Sophie is there too?'

'*Was* there, Wigapom,' corrected Will. 'Apparently her aunt suspected who you were and told Sophie, who went to the beach to find you. But she was kidnapped by that odious Scabtail and brought here to the Citadel.'

'I saw her...' Wigapom remembered. 'I knew she looked familiar... But why... How do you know all this?' he said.

'The Phoenix told us – he told us lots of things,' said Will.

'The Phoenix? But...? How did you meet... ? Oh never mind, that'll have to wait! So Sophie's in danger?' said Wigapom, needing to focus on one thing at a time.

'Yes, she is. He has her in the Citadel Tower,' replied Fynn.

'We have to save her,' said Will and Wigapom in unison.

'I knew you would both say that,' said Fynn, remembering the incident of the young deer and wondering what hair-brained scheme they might think up between the two of them.

Will's brain was working overtime.

'And you say Darqu'on has *The Book of True Magic* too?'

'And the indigo stone, which says *of*, by the way,' added Wigapom.

'How did he get the stone?' said Fynn.

'It's a long story. I expect Will experienced something of what happened, but how do you know all this about Sophie?'

'We told you, the Phoenix,' said Will, animated as he thought of what had happened to get them here. 'We were just leaving Brakendor, and I was thinking about the Phoenix's picture in the bakery and the next minute the Phoenix landed in the high street and said he was asked to bring us both here, to the Citadel! You should have seen the faces of everyone in Brakendor when he landed right in front of them on the high street! I've never seen so many jaws drop all in one go! Made everyone's day! He flew us over the forest and dropped us in a valley near here, saying he couldn't come too close as he didn't want to attract too much attention... He is pretty attention-grabbing, isn't he?'

'I might have guessed that my thoughts would be heard by him,' said Wigapom, amazed at how things were all falling into place.

'And mine,' said Will.

'It was lucky he did,' said Fynn, 'because at least we were able to get the stone here quickly, without it falling into the wrong hands.'

'The stone? You really have the last stone?' said Wigapom, almost jumping for joy.

'Well, it's the first one really, but yes, didn't you understand the dream I sent you?' said Will.

'No, I didn't! You could have made it clearer!... Oh, never mind.'

'Do you want to see it?' said Will.

'Yes, but not here, its too dangerous. Follow me, at a distance. We'll go where it's safer.'

He led them through the crowds back to The Hermit, where Arcturus and Bethulah were amongst those delighted to see them. Wigapom told them about Sophie and the stone.

'Poor girl,' said Bethulah, full of compassion as always.

'All the more reason to act now,' said Arcturus, 'It's the perfect opportunity for the diversion, and we've been waiting a long time for this day.'

'Indeed, we have a double reason to stop Darqu'on now, eh, husband?' said Bethulah, with determination in her voice.

'And what better day for action than the ancient festival of Samhain, when the veil between the living and the dead is truly pulled aside: the souls of our ancestors will be there to help our fight,' Arcturus replied, his eyes bright with passion and enthusiasm 'This is meant to be. I feel it. The time has come at last,' and he swung into action, leaving The Hermit immediately to prepare for the planned disruption. Wigapom was curious about the stone.

'Can I see it now?' he said. 'Do you know what it says?'

'No, we really haven't had time to look,' said Will, carefully getting the cloth package in which the stone was still wrapped out of his pocket. He opened the cloth to show Wigapom the stone resting tantalisingly in his palm, waiting to be deciphered. The image was of a snake eating its tail.

'This is like the shape of my mother's ring, it's not a rune!' said Wigapom.

'It's the Ouroborus – creation out of destruction. A positive sign,' said Bethulah, knowledgeably.

'There's something on the cloth. Look!' urged Will, opening it out fully, for woven into the fabric was a complicated pattern, like a mandala, containing eight gradually decreasing circles, cut equally by eight straight lines, and in the centre an endless knot of lines, which formed ten squares.

'That wasn't there before, I'm sure,' said Fynn, puzzled at the appearance.

'Perhaps it's like the words on my mother's ring, which appear when we are ready to believe in them,' mused Wigapom.

'The pattern reminds me of a spider on its web,' interjected Bethulah again, looking over their shoulders at the cloth and stone.

'That's what the city has always reminded me of, with the Citadel as the spider in the middle,' added Wigapom.

'Spiders and their webs are evocative emblems too,' commented Bethulah, thoughtfully, 'as are snakes. We often fear them, but a snake has always been the symbol for the continuation of life and wisdom, and before Darqu'on spun his web of entrapment in this land, the Citadel was known as Arachne, which means spider. Spiders were seen as the spinners and weavers of destiny, and their webs showed the interconnectedness of all life. With the negative energy of Darqu'on, snakes turned into serpents; webs became places of entrapment and spiders became cunning killers.'

'Let's hope our destiny doesn't involve being trapped or killed,' replied Wigapom.

'Every negative has a positive, remember,' said Bethulah solemnly.

Something Bethulah said earlier had set Wigapom thinking.

'Bethulah, you're right about the pattern on the cloth. Not that it's a spider and web, but that it's a map – the layout plan of the city, with the Citadel in the centre. Look, these eight outer rings, and the lines crossing them are the roads of the city, these four squares on the outside of the knot are the gates around the walls and then the six smaller squares are rooms or maybe corridors, or both inside the Tower.' Fynn, Will and Bethulah looked again.

'You're right, Fynn. It is!' said Bethulah. 'And I am beginning to understand its meaning.'

'Is it connected to the book?' asked Fynn.

'Or is it to do with Sophie?' asked Wigapom.

'Perhaps it's both,' said Bethulah, 'The book you seek is really the Book of Wisdom, because that's what True Magic really means, and the name Sophie also means wisdom. What's more, Sapientia, the city means wisdom, and the Tower used to be a temple dedicated to wisdom, before Darqu'on contaminated it. It was very beautiful. When Darqu'on took control, wisdom and beauty disappeared, leaving fear and ugliness in their place.'

'So the word on the stone means wisdom?' said Wigapom.

Bethulah nodded. 'What greater wisdom can there be than 'My end is my beginning', which is what the Ouroborus means.'

'That makes sense!' cried Will and Fynn together.

'It does makes sense, but that can't be the only reason Darqu'on has kidnapped Sophie,' said Wigapom, suspicious as always of Darqu'on's motives.

'She's the fly,' cautioned Fynn, 'to trap you, Wigapom. Darqu'on is the negative image of the spider after all – stretching out his web of entrapment, as Bethulah said. He knows you'll try to rescue Sophie. Once he has drawn you in, then he will kill you,' and with this sobering thought he absentmindedly slipped the cloth and stone into the safety of his pocket, as if to protect it somehow.

'I don't believe he will kill me,' said Wigapom. 'He's had lots of opportunities but never taken them. His power is diminishing.'

'That's why he wants the stones,' said Will,' don't underestimate him, whatever you do.'

'Will's right, and what's more, you can't look for Sophie, and the stone and book all by yourself,' reasoned Fynn, 'so we'll have to help you.'

'No Fynn, getting one of us in the Citadel without being seen will be hard enough, all three would be impossible.'

'You have to take *me*,' said Will, 'you and I were once one and the same and we still are in many ways. Who better than me to help you search? We look the same, we think the same, and can communicate silently if we need to. It will be quicker too. You can find the book and missing stone, as you're meant to, whilst I find Sophie. Besides, I want to. It's time we worked together again, as one.'

'He has a point, Wigapom, at least one of us ought to go with you,' said Fynn, still hopeful he might have a role to play.

Wigapom was about to disagree, but Will interrupted with a sudden thought.

'Talking about the stones... Do you have the last one Wiggy? What does it say?'

Wigapom frowned.

'Yes, I do have the last stone, but I don't seem to be able to read it. I don't know why. It's only a little word again I think. The other stones read, *Wisdom is given as part of...* What do you suppose wisdom could be part of?'

'The Temple?' suggested Fynn, 'No, that can't be right, because there's only one word and just having 'Temple' wouldn't make sense'

'Have you realised what I've just realised?' said Will, his face lighting up in delighted surprise at this further flash of brilliance. 'If you take the first letter of every word on the stones, what do you get?'

Fynn and Wigapom looked baffled at first, until they worked it out.

'It spells *Wigapo!*' they said to each other in an excited hushed whisper.

'Exactly. So perhaps the last word begins with M?' suggested Will, 'To complete your name... *Wigapom?*'

'Of course! How did I not see that before!' Wigapom said. 'It's been staring me in the face for so long and I just didn't see it! It's so obvious now!'

'But it doesn't tell us what the M stands for,' said Will.

'Perhaps its magic?' said Fynn. 'Wisdom is given as part of magic. That would sort of make sense. Magic is another meaning for hidden wisdom.'

'Mmm, maybe,' said Wigapom, but neither he nor Will were completely convinced. At that moment Arcturus returned.

'Asgar and I have everything in place. The diversion will start at dusk, as the guards are changing on each gate, and the Samhain bonfires are lit by the South Gate. We have just a short time till then. You, Wigapom, must get to the North Gate and wait for the moment to enter. There is no time to waste.'

'Where's Skye?' asked Wigapom, suddenly.

Fynn looked at Wigapom open-mouthed.

'Did you say Skye?' he said.

'Yes, I forgot to tell you. She's here in the city, has been for weeks. Along with Asgar, or Marvo the Magician, from my party – oh, I forgot, you won't remember him, you thought it was Corrin, the conjurer.'

'*I* remember though,' mused Will, recalling the very special memory of when he and Sophie flew together.

'Why didn't you tell me before!' cried Fynn. 'Thank goodness Skye's safe. Where is she now? I want to see her.'

'She's usually close at hand, watching out for me,' said Wigapom, concerned suddenly that she had not appeared back at The Hermit yet.

'We'd better look for her,' said Fynn, picking up the concern in Wigapom's voice.

'There is no time,' said Arcturus. 'Everything must happen as planned. It cannot stop now. You have to go, Wigapom; we will only have this one perfect opportunity for disruption.'

'I know you're right, Arcturus, but I am concerned about Skye. Will you look for her, Fynn? I know how important she is to you,' said Wigapom, with a sombre tone to his voice as he remembered the last time he and Fynn were together.

'Of course I will,' said Fynn, 'as long as you will be alright.'

'He'll be fine, Fynn, Wigapom's got me to help him,' stated Will forcefully, looking Wigapom straight in the eyes, as if daring him to disagree.

Wigapom stared back, knowing Will had to do this with him, 'Yes, I have got you. And because of the stones, and our growing abilities, we can all tap into the powers of Low Magic – to cast positive spells and maybe even do some astral travelling, which Asgar has been teaching us, although that might still be tricky, and we, Will, can still use the protection of mother's ring,' said Wigapom, holding the ring up to look closely at the new words beginning to form in a tiny, yet shimmering, sparkle of light around the edge,

The search for Wisdom culminates here and may take you by surprise.
Allowing something new to live means another something dies.

'Something dies? That sounds a bit ominous,' said Will, as Wigapom slipped the ring back on his finger, 'but perhaps it just means when we open *The Book of True Magic* then everything that is bad will die. That has got to be a good thing.'

'Who knows what will happen?' shrugged Wigapom, philosophically, 'We must just trust that whatever it is, it's for the highest good of all. Here, let's share out the artefacts Gobann gave me.'

Wigapom offered Will the dagger and tin whistle. 'Take these Will, remember not to use the dagger in anger and you can always scare creatures away with the whistle if you need to. It worked for me! I'll keep the key and the ring. Fynn, you take the mercury lamp, to help you in the dark. Jeepers, the day has flown by, its almost dusk now – we must go,' and he and Will slipped out of The Hermit to get to the North Gate in time, as Fynn set out to find Skye.

Fynn was anxious as to what might have befallen Skye. Firstly, he tried using the Low Magic powers of remote visualising but abandoned it as all he saw was a small, confined and dingy space, which he thought meant he was doing something wrong. Instead, he set about scouring the streets, checking every face, every shape, willing it to belong to the girl he loved – but there was no sign of her. He saw the crowd already gathering around the ready laid bonfire at the South Gate and recognised Arcturus – not long now until it all started. He could feel a tight knot of concern and anticipation in his stomach, and an image of a face from the depths of his unconscious flickered in his mind, like a freshly lit lamp. He felt a light tap on his shoulder and spun round, wishing it to be Skye, but found himself instead staring into the hypnotic eyes of the face he had just seen in his mind.

'Greetings, Fynn.'

'I've just seen you… do I know you?' Fynn blurted out. The tall figure with long tapering fingers smiled at him and Fynn struggled to remember, but trusted him immediately.

'I am Asgar – you don't consciously remember me, but I remember you; you are Wigapom's young friend, now with an important task to fulfil.'

'So *you're* Asgar, or should that be Marvo! Wiggy told me. I wish I did remember you – I half thought I did just then but…' said Fynn, expecting to see Skye close by. 'Is Skye with you? – I've been looking for her – do you know where she is?'

'Skye and I went our separate ways earlier – she told me she had an errand to run. I have not seen her since.'

'I'm worried about her,' replied Fynn.

'Perhaps you should trust your intuition more,' said Asgar, 'rather than doubt your abilities so quickly. No matter. There is something else that you should be more concerned about at the moment. Look in your pocket.'

'My pocket, what about my pocket?' said Fynn, rummaging in it nevertheless. His hand touched something hard, wrapped in a soft cloth, and the colour drained from his face.

'The red stone! I still have the stone! Wigapom can't open the book without it! How did you know it was in my pocket? How did you know we'd even found it?'

'That is of no importance now,' said Asgar, 'but getting the stone to Wigapom is; that must be your priority.'

Fynn was furious with himself for forgetting the stone, and torn between his desire to look for Skye and help Wigapom, but he knew that Asgar was right.

'Find her and keep her safe for me, Asgar, please,' he said.

'I will. Go, Fynn, before it is too late,'

Fynn did as he was bidden, hotfooting it to the North Gate, hoping to reach Wigapom before the gate closed, and praying with all his might that Asgar would find Skye.

The shops and stalls were closing in preparation for the lighting of the bonfires at the South Gate. Once alight, the crowds would be feasting around the flames before eventually returning to their homes, mindful of the possibility of evil spirits and ghosts coming out of the darkness. Wigapom and Will did their best to mingle and look part of the scene, gradually making their way towards the North Gate, ever watchful of the clones stationed there and lined along the battlements. Their hearts pounded at the thought of entering Darqu'on's lair; the Quest and all they had been through would culminate in whatever happened inside the Citadel. So much depended on these next few moments. Time enough to concern themselves about what would happen once they were inside. Getting in was all that mattered now.

'We have the protection of the ring, Will, but we must also create it in our own minds. We must use the magic now available to us and believe we will enter the Citadel unseen,' whispered Wigapom.

'I've already done this for both of us – the power of positive thought is a spell in its own right,' replied Will. 'We will succeed.'

'Put that in the present tense, Will – create what you want as though you already have it –we have *already* succeeded!' Will and Wigapom smiled at each other, feeling connected and whole.

It had grown colder as the light faded, and they shivered in the still air. As they hid out of sight, the street emptied, falling silent and dark. They wondered what was happening at the South Gate and adrenalin surged through them at the thought of what lay ahead. They were grateful for the gathering darkness that fell through the air like a cloak of invisibility – it did have some positive uses after all – and they hid in the camouflage of night's thickening shadow and waited.

CHAPTER 41

The Citadel

*"When all is said and done, the real citadel of strength of any community
is in the hearts and minds and desires of those who dwell there."*
Everett Dirkson

Darqu'on returned to his room of mirrors after checking on his captive.
She had roused briefly, as Scabtail had said, and had made a vain attempt to
escape. Darqu'on was dismissive of her, as he was of all females, and did
not want any unnecessary complications from her, wanting to focus all his
attention on The Brat, so he had drugged her again with a stronger potion
this time. It had taken mere seconds to work.

As he looked down on her stupefied body, slumped and bound to the
chair (he was taking no chances of her escaping again) a distant memory
stirred fleetingly inside him; a road, a cave and a scared young woman; a
quick moment of physical release for him, made more arousing by her
terror. A death. He shivered, despite himself, as though someone had
walked over his grave, and chose not to remember whose death or when. It
was a long time ago, with no relevance to the here and now. But this girl
was attractive in a fey, delicate, way, like a newly opening flower, yet she
had a spirit that belied her seeming fragility. He turned away. He did not
want to be reminded of beauty unless it was to crush it. He left the room
and returned to the life he had chosen – the pursuit of power and
vengeance.

Wigapom and Will, from their dark hiding place, could see the outgoing
clone guards at the gate waiting for their replacements and heard the
approach of the new clone contingent who would lock the gate. The time
of changeover was the cue for the disturbance to happen, which would be
so attention-grabbing that it would draw the guards away from the other

gates to lend assistance. This would provide Will and Wigapom with their window of opportunity to slip in unnoticed. Their hearts pounded as the seconds ticked away. Any moment now!

Suddenly a flurry of crackling, squealing, multi-coloured sparks shot skywards, accompanied by a deafening explosion as the first firework of the disruption was ignited. Fireworks had not been seen in Arcanum since long before the King was killed and were expressly forbidden by Darqu'on, so their suddenness and volume created exactly the element of surprise and disruption that Asgar and Arcturus had planned. As cries from the clones and the citizens were heard, so came more bangs, thuds and crackles as another barrage of fireworks splintered explosively into the atmosphere, illuminating the night sky before cascading down in a spectacle the city had not witnessed for years. It caused shock amongst the clone guards at the North Gate who stopped in their tracks, taken by surprise by the spectacle.

'Disturbance at South Gate,' came a yell. 'All available guards ordered to attend!' The guards responded swiftly, leaving just two to secure the gate for the night. One guard turned away to press the closing mechanism, the other gazed into the sky, distracted by the amazing sound and light show. This gave enough time for Wigapom and Will to slip towards the gate unseen and crouch in the shadow of the wall. More fireworks shot skywards and both guards turned to face them, leaving the gate momentarily unattended. Will and Wigapom slipped inside. They'd done it!.

They split up immediately, recognising it was best if they were not together; they could communicate telepathically when they needed. It had all been easier than they imagined, almost as though they were invited in.

Fynn ran as fast as he could, back through the alleyways to the North Gate, hoping against hope he would get there in time to give Wigapom the stone before he and Will entered the Citadel, or at least manage to get in himself before the gate closed. He heard and saw the fireworks on the other side of the Citadel – well, no one could miss them – and was impressed at the quality and impact of the disturbance, but he daren't stop to look, as he was still not at the North Gate. Were they already inside the Citadel? Would he be too late to reach Wigapom? He groaned inwardly, sure that the gate would be closed. As he rounded the final corner he saw no sign of them, yet was surprised to see the gate still standing open. Two guards, with their backs to him, were trying to close it, but it seemed stuck. Something was wrong with the mechanism – another delaying tactic by Arcturus and his merry band perhaps? The guards were so engrossed in the faulty machinery that they did not see or hear Fynn creeping behind them as he took his chance. With his heart in his mouth, he too slid into the shadows, where Wigapom and Will had been moments before, hiding behind a pillar just as the guards rectified the problem and the gate sealed itself for the night. Fate had stepped into Fynn's life as surely as he had stepped into the Citadel!

Asgar had come a long way from his apprenticeship days with Magus, and had continued to secretly study his magician's craft at every opportunity. It had been hard at first, particularly after the devastating news of Magus' death, and those of the King and Queen. The years between then and his important visit to Brakendor had tested his belief in the power of the light but the knowledge that the child was safe kept it burning inside him, and the desire to retain as much magical knowledge as he could for the future. When the orange stone revealed itself to him, he knew Magus had chosen him to awaken Wigapom to his destiny and was determined to make that experience as magical as possible for the young Prince; he felt he did a good job. As Wigapom gradually earned the stones, Asgar had felt his own magical knowledge and power strengthening in leaps and bounds, and now he was as magically strong as Magus had been before the rise of Darqu'on. Yet he had something more, something Wigapom had also been sensing ever since the indigo stone floated so gracefully into his grasp in the castle; an understanding of the dualism of all things; the balance of good with evil, of light with dark, negative with positive, where two opposites exist in harmony to prove the other's existence; an inner knowing that everything is perfect, even in its seeming imperfection. This was why he knew, even if Skye was in danger, that it would be for the highest good, and thus good would come from it. He was going to help make this happen, and he would use magic to do so.

He found his intuition guiding him towards the East Gate: In ancient times, this was the gate associated with the open qualities of light, truth, and righteousness, but this one was shut and bolted, as he expected. It was also deserted, as all activity was now focused on the South Gate. Undaunted, he pulled his plain woollen cloak around him, hid his face inside the hood and closed his eyes, allowing an image to come to him of a damp, dark tunnel close by. As he concentrated on this, his body began to dissolve until there was no visible trace of him, yet he was still present – although now inside the Citadel, in the visualised underground tunnel. He followed its winding route whilst listening to the sound of soft sighs and groans leading him forward.

'Help me,' the sighs seemed to say, 'help me.'

He was heading towards the underground centre of the Tower now; he could sense his position as surely as if he had been following a map, yet he just followed his senses – and the sounds. It was not only the voice calling for help that he sensed, but felt as though the structure of the whole building was in pain, and needing his help; as though the Citadel was a living breathing entity, hijacked and held against its will by Darqu'on and his guards.

The tunnel led into others, a veritable labyrinth of dank darkness, seemingly without end, yet Asgar knew it would take him where he needed to be. He was still in non-physical form, knowing that even in this forgotten place it was sensible to keep hidden. If only he'd had time to teach the skill of invisibility and astral travel to Wigapom; he had outlined the basics, but it had taken Asgar years, and he had barely had weeks with Wigapom. He had had longer with Skye, and she had been a quick learner, but she was still a novice. Asgar believed Skye had experimented with astral travel, but it had gone wrong. Why she attempted it on her own, he could only guess at, but it had got her into trouble and he had to get her out of it.

The groans and sighs continued, leading him directly underneath the centre of the Tower and, as he expected, there she was, huddled on the ground, exhausted, cold and barely conscious, with a swollen ankle twisted into an awkward position.

'Skye!' he called softly, materialising again and bending by her side, 'Skye! You are safe now, open your eyes, you are safe.'

Skye flickered open her eyes at the sound of his voice. Blurred shapes and dark colours swam before her before gradually stabilising themselves. Her head hurt and she became aware again of the throbbing in her ankle as she remembered where she was, and how she had got there. She felt foolish now, but her intentions had been good. She had felt sure she could put Asgar's teaching on astral travel into positive practice to help her find the book and stolen stone without the need for Wigapom to endanger himself. She had managed the travelling, but not location, and ended up here, in the bowels of the Citadel, concussed and with a damaged ankle. Yet here was Asgar, her saviour again, kneeling compassionately by her side, gently holding her swollen ankle with a hand that radiated healing heat throughout her body. She instantly felt a great wave of peace flow over and through her and closed her eyes in blessed relief, knowing she was safe at last. The pain in her head stopped and she could feel the damaged ankle mending as the swelling subsided. As she opened her eyes again, she even fancied she saw a blue healing light radiating around Asgar's hands.

'Asgar, thank you; I've been such an idiot. I wanted to help Wigapom, I felt so useless doing nothing, but I've only brought trouble to you, and worry to everyone,' she said, slumping back against the damp tunnel walls.

'Fynn has been especially concerned,' said Asgar, smiling at her. Skye sat up again, eyes wide open with excitement.

'Fynn! Is Fynn here? Oh, how is he? Can you take me to him?' she said, unsure whether to laugh or cry. She had missed Fynn more than she thought possible, and this emotion had mingled with the grief of her father's death. When she met Asgar, she asked him to come with her to the city to meet up with her contacts there and inform them of Wigapom's progress. She had been surprised and delighted to find Wigapom already there, but had become increasingly perturbed when there had been no news of Fynn or Will. She had lost her father – she couldn't bear it if Fynn was lost to her as well. Perhaps they had not made it back to Brakendor, she thought in her darkest moments; their deaths would be two of many in these terrible times; so she fixated on Wigapom surviving – Will would have to survive then, surely – and if Will survived, why not Fynn? In her mind, everyone's survival rested on Wigapom. He had the stones, after all, or most of them, and they afforded him increasing protection as well as use of some of the magic again. He was the figurehead on which she and many others hung their hopes. She had thrown herself back into her resistance work, which she had let slip during those months of calm and false hope in Oakendale, and worked secretly on developing the gift of astral travel that Asgar had been teaching her, so that she could enter the Citadel instead of Wigapom, in the hope of keeping him, and those she loved, safe. Being active again had helped her block her grief and gave a purpose to her life. But she had failed in her task. Tears of self-pity rolled down her face.

'I have failed everyone!' she sobbed.

'You have failed no one,' soothed Asgar, 'Wigapom and Will are already inside the Citadel, and so is Fynn – he has the first stone to give to Wigapom, and Will is set to find Sophie, who has been captured by Darqu'on – the final assault has begun and all is well.'

Skye looked up through her tears.

'So, I've missed Fynn again, before I properly found him, and all through my impetuousness,' she cried.

'Emotion is often the enemy to rational thought, but your intention was pure, and at least they are all alive,' Asgar reminded her. 'That is something to be grateful for.'

Skye nodded. Somewhere in that forbidding grey Citadel, now directly above her, all her hopes were encapsulated, firstly in Wigapom for the salvation of Arcanum and the return of the True Magic, and finally in Fynn for her future personal happiness.

'What do we do, Asgar?' she asked, unable to think for a moment.

'Wait for when the time is right to help them,' replied Asgar, giving the reply she least wanted. She wanted instant action, but knew that she had to curb her impatience this time or else jeopardise the safety of those already in the Citadel.

'I know you are right,' she said, 'but it will not be easy.'

'It will not be easy for them either,' added Asgar soberly.

Wigapom found his journey into the innermost aspects of the Tower interesting to say the least. Having come through the North Gate, he had so far managed to avoid encountering any guards, even though he had seen several, either marching or standing to attention. He attributed his ability to blend into the background to the power of his positive thinking and the protection of his mother's ring. The closer he got to the inner sanctum of the Tower, the closer he felt to her; this was, after all, where Darqu'on had incarcerated her and where she had fallen to her chosen death. He felt her personal protection, even from the stone beasts he had encountered on the lower floor, who had still managed, no doubt from a trick of the shadows in this dark place, to seem to flick their tails and paw the air before petrifying again when he looked directly at them. No doubt in times when this was a temple to wisdom, the statues would have depicted gracious and beautiful images, but in a fortress formed by fear they were anything but; a Basilisk, Gryphon, Roc and Peryton. He recognised them from *Mythical Monsters and Fabled Beasts,* one of the books he and Fynn had scared themselves with as children. Nasty creatures, each and every one – he was glad he had left them behind.

As he ascended the floors of the Tower, he found himself between two more statues; a male, holding a sword in his right hand and a book in his left, and a female, holding a staff with a seven-ringed emblem running up it. The stone faces were impassive, but he felt their eyes following him and yet again he thanked the protection of the ring, but when he heard the whoosh of large wings and the heavy pounding of feet behind him he began to wonder how protected he really was.

Will was lost. On leaving Wigapom he had turned left and found himself in a corridor that seemed to slope upwards. Then he had come to some steep stone steps, which he had climbed. These had opened out into a maze of corridors that met other corridors that he thought he recognised, and he turned left, then right, then right, then left but ended up coming back to where he first started. He was confused and frustrated at not getting himself where he felt he needed to go, and wondered if his way was being purposefully blocked by Darqu'on, although there was no sign of him or his minions anywhere. He wondered if Wigapom was having similar problems, although had felt nothing from him.

Will had fully expected to see hordes of guards around every corner, waiting to pounce, yet every corner – indeed every corridor – had so far been deserted and frustratingly just like every other corner or corridor. He was getting nowhere. Then he saw what he hadn't expected and was rooted to the spot.

Fynn had no idea where either Wigapom or Will had gone. They seemed to have been swallowed up by the darkness. He had no time to concern himself about Will. He had to find Wigapom to give him the stone. Surely he couldn't have gone far? Now he was inside the Citadel he was astonished at how huge it was; bigger than it looked from the outside, and apart from a few flaring wall sconces, very dark. Thankfully he had the mercury lamp with him, which he took from the bag and used to see where he was in relation to the map on the cloth. He could see he was in a wide hallway with four scary stone statues in front of him. By looking at the map, if he went between the middle of them he would eventually reach another doorway, which would in turn lead upwards to a higher inner sanctum and further doorway, culminating in the uppermost part of the Tower. He had no idea if this was where he needed to go, but hoped that intuition, which he had been working hard to develop, would see him through.

He re-wrapped the cloth around the stone in his pocket, fancying he felt a slight vibration from it, before returning the lamp to the bag, which he slung silently across his back before moving stealthily across the floor towards the four statues. He shuddered as he approached them: they were so lifelike. In the strange shadows thrown by the flickering torches, Fynn fancied he saw them breathing, but of course they were only stone.

He darted as soundlessly as he could between the Basilisk, with its dragon

412

body and cockerel head, and the Gryphon with its eagle head and lion torso. He kept his spirits high and his head down, remembering from the stories how the glance of the Basilisk could turn the observer to stone. He had to keep reminding himself it was the statues that were stone, especially when he felt a chill breath of air on the back of his neck as he passed between them, but he remained unscathed and thankfully began to climb to the next level. Here he darted behind a pillar as several guards marched into view from nowhere and stood to attention along one wall. How would he get out of this? He paused to think, but the decision was taken from his hands as he heard a heavy thud of feet coming from somewhere to his left and, turning his head, froze as he saw the previously immobile stone statue of the Gryphon now very much alive and hungry for prey!

Fynn flattened himself against the pillar, holding his breath, as the creature padded across the floor, sniffing and snorting in a somewhat disorientated way as though stiff and unsure of its movements.

'Don't let it see me, don't let it see me,' thought Fynn, and his plea was answered; the beast walked right past him, disturbed, instead, by the sight of the guards, who had jumped to active attention at the noise of its approach. The movement was enough to make the Gryphon pounce, knocking the guards to the ground with its huge body, in a clatter of sound, like dominoes collapsing on a table, before he proceeded to eat them. By the look on the Gryphon's face, they were not at all to its taste and the retching sound it made as it spat them out in disgust turned Fynn's stomach almost as much as the sight of the ground strewn with half-chewn body parts.

The remaining guards, programmed to fight, not run, pounced on the Gryphon and quickly succumbed to the same fate. Fynn's stomach heaved as limbs and innards were gorged and tossed around, littering the floor in a gory mess. Fynn did his best to hold in the contents of his own stomach – this was no time for queasiness – but it was a perfect opportunity to dash to the next level. He was grateful not to have fallen foul of the Gryphon, or the guards; he was either very lucky or very assisted!

On hearing the loud thud of feet and swish of wings, Wigapom knew he had to hide, and seeing a door slightly ajar to his left, decided to take a chance on this, rather than face the source of the noise. He found himself in an antechamber with a thick black curtain hanging across the middle, from which a dull yellow light glowed beneath. Closing the door swiftly but quietly behind him, he edged towards the curtain, unsure of what he would find, and very carefully lifted it back a fraction. It was heavy and musty-smelling and his nose wrinkled at the unusual aroma, yet his eyes opened wide as he found himself staring onto a bigger room, with just enough light from a flickering sconce on the wall to show it was full of chests, cupboards, and shelves, the latter filled with rows of books, various sized black glass phials, crucibles for mixing powders, and jars of strange objects that floated like submerged wrecks, in brine, all regimentally lined up like battalions in an army. It reminded him of the wizard's room in the Castle on the Crag, but ordered to the point of obsession. It carried the mark of someone who coveted power and gave nothing away. It could only be Darqu'on's sorcery room.

Wigapom could hardly believe his luck, or misfortune, depending upon how it was regarded. *The Book of True Magic* could be here, amongst all the other books meticulously ordered in rows on the shelves, but Darqu'on could also be close at hand. He quickly scanned the shelves, hoping to recognise the book when he saw it, but to no avail; he would have to look more thoroughly. He was prepared to do that if he had to but the longer he remained in the room, indeed the Tower, the more dangerous it was. He listened again. Whatever had caused the disturbance had moved out of earshot, but now he heard the tramp of many feet marching with precision timing past the room. He ducked down behind a chest and froze, waiting for the sound to pass, ears on full alert and fingers heavily crossed and found himself glancing at a new message appearing on the ring:

Hide, hide, your time to bide, and listen as well as learn.
When all is done, your time will come, the final reward to earn.

That sounded encouraging at least! Although he was not looking for reward – just the ability to bring the True Magic back at last. Nonetheless, he said the words over and over inside his head as the steps grew fainter and the Citadel returned to an unearthly quiet again. Wigapom breathed a sigh of relief and sent a thought communication to Will about the message on the ring. The reply was jumbled and confused. He hoped Will was safe, but knew he had to let things take their course, trusting the process as usual, and he began a more systematic search of the room.

The books were fascinating, in a ghoulish way, with titles like *The Seven Steps to Total Domination, Fear and its uses for Control, Terror Tactics for Tyrants,* and *Using Stone Creatures for Sorcery.* It was evident that Darqu'on authored many, if not all the books. What a tragedy that such a creative brain should be used for such negative ends. Wigapom's mind asked many questions as his eyes scanned the shelves; did Darqu'on know Wigapom and Will were here,

414

inside his lair? Was he just waiting to unleash one or all of those stone creatures on the lower level, as his book suggested, or would he and Will find what they were looking for with minimal struggle? He didn't think the latter was very likely! He also wondered what had happened to Arcturus and the others after the disturbance. Had they managed to get to safety, or had Darqu'on let loose more savagery on them? He admired their bravery and hoped that his own courage would see him through.

As he searched more shelves and cupboards his thoughts turned to Sophie. He would have liked to find her himself, but knew he couldn't do both – but then Will was part of him still, and he would find her. Sophie would understand. Try as he might, he couldn't think how or why she was involved in this at all, yet she did keep turning up in his mind and dreams and visions rather a lot, so she must be important. Was it just because she was special to him? Or something more? His head ached with the unanswered questions.

He focused his attention once more on the moment and kept up the search for the book, well aware he still had to find the stone Darqu'on had stolen from him. Neither was on any of the shelves, of that he was certain. He began to look in the drawers: *Putrefied flesh, Pulverised brain,* stated labels on various boxes. Wigapom was filled with disgust, barely able to continue looking, until he noticed one marked *Unicorn horn,* from which he recoiled even more. Like the Phoenix, the Unicorn had always fascinated Wigapom, its horn reputed to have magical powers, and he had been thrilled to discover both it and the Phoenix were on his family coat of arms, being a blend of his father – the Phoenix – and mother – the Unicorn. It seemed that the Unicorn too, like the Phoenix, was a real creature, and not just a storybook invention as he had always believed. He knew that, according to ancient legend, only a beautiful, innocent girl could tame one, and then only with kindness and compassion, and Wigapom knew Darqu'on would never get a unicorn horn without a girl to lure it. Had he used Sophie to do this? Wigapom opened the box in trepidation and, to his relief, it was empty. The Unicorn was still alive. In his thoughts he urged Will to find Sophie, and quickly.

Suddenly there was a low rumble, like a beast's hungry stomach, and part of the wall began to move. Wigapom's previous thoughts were distracted. He had more immediate things to concern him now.

Will froze as the spectral figure drifted down the corridor towards him. At first glance he feared it was a Ghoul and his heart almost stopped beating with the fear, but it was far too beautiful to be anything so horrendous. What was more, he recognised her from boyhood dreams; a memory from the joint past he shared with Wigapom and a hope for the future. It was Elvira, the elven Queen. Their mother. She spoke softly to him.

'You have come at last, my darling boy. It has been such a long wait roaming these corridors waiting for you. Follow me now, there are things that you must know.'

Will hesitated.

'I'm Will, not Wigapom,' he said, almost by way of apology, in case she didn't realise that he was not actually Wigapom in the flesh.

She smiled at him with those wonderful green eyes.

'Do you think a mother would not recognise her own child? It is you that must come with me now. There are things you must know,' and she floated gracefully down the corridor; the scent of lavender and neroli drifting in her wake.

Will remained rooted to the spot. He was her son, she had said so, and she wanted him – Will, not Wigapom. Not as Wigapom's inner child, but for himself! Somehow all the self-maturing, growing and developing came to fruition at this moment; he was a real person, complete and entire within himself. It was a sensation like nothing else, yet it scared him too, wondering what it might mean. The apparition of his mother looked back at him and beckoned.

'Come, my son, you have things to learn and discover,' and Will did as she asked.

Wigapom stared as the hidden door began to open. Someone was entering the room! He needed a better hiding place than behind the chest and hastily looked around for another. Thrusting the packet back into the dark reaches of the drawer he pulled open the nearest large cupboard and squeezed himself in amongst the artefacts there, pulling the door to. Just in time – the rumbling had stopped and the soft pad of footfall and swish of a tail took over. It was Scabtail, muttering to himself in an agitated fashion.

'Now Master wants the Unicorn horn for his Sorcery! But he doesn't know I don't have it! It's all that girl's fault. If only she hadn't shouted when she did and let the creature escape! What do I do? I'll have to use the horn from the Mantygre instead – lucky I kept it – but if Master ever finds out what I've done there will be a terrible price to pay. Now where did I put that Mantygre horn?'

Wigapom's mind whirred with the information that Scabtail had unwittingly revealed: so the Unicorn had escaped, thanks to Sophie! And Scabtail was deceiving his Master by replacing its magical horn with one from a different creature! Scabtail would be in real trouble if Darqu'on discovered the deception! But it could work to Wigapom and Will's advantage. He would have to wait and see.

It was stuffy and dark in the cupboard, even with the door slightly ajar but at least Wigapom was hidden. He waited with baited breath, hoping that Scabtail would find what he was looking for before he investigated this hidey-hole! He heard the swish of the heavy curtain as it was pulled aside, the rustle of paper, the frantic opening and closing of drawers and cupboards: Scabtail was so close that Wigapom could smell his foul breath seeping through the partially open cupboard door. Wigapom prayed for invisibility! There was the sound of more opening drawers, and the clink of jars hitting each other as Scabtail continued his feverish search, all the time muttering and moaning.

'Where *is* the Mantygre horn? I know I had it here somewhere! I knew it would come in useful one day! And today is the day! Master demands the horn in the inner room with the girl. If I don't bring it quickly then I will suffer again! Where is that horn? Master gives me so much work and no thanks for anything! Yet I do everything for him – didn't I help him get the book and the stone? The Brat will never find them, even if they are right under his nose! Ah! There it is, at last!'

There was more feverish rustling in the drawer, and a wheezy sigh of relief as the vital substitute for the Unicorn horn was retrieved, followed by the sound of Scabtail leaving the room through the rumbling partition. All became quiet once more.

Will followed the apparition to a space, which at first was full of light. He could barely believe it was any part of the Citadel: it was far too peaceful and beautiful. His mother turned and smiled at him again in encouragement and his heart melted towards her as her thoughts filled his head, but he did not understand the thoughts transmitted to him, which told him first that he was the hope of the nation and the future was invested in him. He was told to trust all that happened, knowing it was for the highest good. To not be afraid. He wanted to say again that she had the wrong person; that she should really have been telling Wigapom this, not him, but he could not speak, for now he was afraid: she was telling him things he did not want to hear, showing him things he did not want to see, changing her beautiful shape into something black and monstrous. Legs everywhere, eyes everywhere. He tried to avert his own eyes, both to block out the horrific images before him, and also escape her penetrating gaze, but even with his eyes tightly closed the images invaded his mind like a relentless army. Her long legs trampled over his body, wrapping him in a fine silk thread that streamed from her body and imprisoned his own in a silken cocoon. He could not escape. Could never escape.

In his mind he asked her, 'Why does it have to be like this?' yet he couldn't bear the answer, even from her. Especially from her. His mother. The Spider. He had trusted her to love him, protect him, yet the words and images she wove into his mind and the web she was weaving around him, were destroying him. She was betraying him. No. He could see in her eyes she was not, but he wanted it all to stop, to go away. He had his own destiny, he knew that now, but it was one he hadn't sought and didn't want and now refused to acknowledge; he tried to fight against it, fight her. How could this happen to him, to them? He sobbed, he ranted, he pleaded, he screamed; yet the silk blocked out the sound and no one heard his cries. Finally he succumbed to the inevitable. To her all-encompassing embrace that had wrapped itself around him like a shroud. He felt alone and frightened. Yet he wasn't alone. She was with him. She understood. She soothed him, telling him there was no other way and that this way had always been the way. To trust the process.

He had to believe her, but he wished they all were a million miles away and that he could forget it all. He closed his eyes and felt a tender kiss on his forehead; the kiss of death? Or was it life? Suddenly he was alone again, and free, with sweat pouring from his body and on the fourth floor of the Tower, the images fresh and clear in his mind.

Wigapom had learned several important things from his eavesdropping episode: that Scabtail was having to lie to Darqu'on about the Unicorn horn; that Darqu'on wanted to use the Unicorn horn for some special purpose; that Sophie was in the inner room; that the Unicorn was still alive; that some disguise had been used on the book to hide it from him, and most important of all, that Darqu'on had been expecting Wigapom all along and maybe knew he was already in the Citadel. Suddenly Wigapom began to feel like the fly the spider had trapped! But there was no going back now. He sent a mental image to Will of an inner room to help him in his search for Sophie and once more scanned the books for the disguised *Book of True Magic*: a hopeless task – Darqu'on could have disguised the book as anything – the sconce on the wall, or even the cupboard he was in!

He had no idea how he would ever find it. He became aware of the stones in his pocket pulsing erratically against his leg. He realised they had been doing this for some time, but with so much else going on he'd not taken much notice. Their persistence indicated they were trying to tell him something. He drew them out of his pocket and counted, to his horror, five instead of six! He had lost the red one! A memory of Fynn putting it back in his pocket popped into his mind. That was it! Fynn must still have it! Had Fynn realised this by now? Was he stuck on the outside of the Citadel with it or had he managed to get in? Whatever the answer he couldn't put the stones in the book even if he found the indigo one, until he had the red stone! He felt he had gone right back to square one. What now? He thought long and hard. He knew Darqu'on was planning something that involved Sophie and the supposed Unicorn horn. Perhaps it also involved the book, or the stone? It was a long shot, but he decided his only option was to find Will and together find Sophie in the inner room and just hope that Fynn had somehow realised he had the stone and got into the Citadel in time. He did his best to send these thoughts not only to Will, but Fynn as well, and began to remotely view where Sophie, the book and stone could be. All he kept seeing was his mother, riding a Unicorn towards him with a look of such love and compassion in her eyes that it filled his heart and gave him hope.

CHAPTER 42

Monsters and Magic

"There are very few monsters who warrant the fear we have of them."
André Gide

Will was on the fourth level of the Tower, trying to make sense of the brief encounter with the apparition of his mother. He couldn't begin to make sense of the nightmare that followed it – why she should appear as a spider, or why the images she showed him were so horrible. They couldn't be true. He had to blot them from his mind and focus, for his own sanity, only on the moment. It was not easy.

He was beginning to receive increasingly urgent, if muddled messages from Wigapom. He wasn't sure about the one referring to the inner room, as the image was sketchy and constantly changing, but he definitely received the one about Fynn still having the stone and the one about Wigapom wanting to join forces with… well, he wasn't sure, was it Fynn or him? Somewhere amongst all that mix of information was something about a Unicorn, although this was even less clear. Will was in the middle of sending a message back to Wigapom, concentrating very hard to make his location clear, when he had to jump back out of view from a group of guards marching around the corner. After a moment or two, he risked a peek: there were eight of them and as he had seen none so far, they came as something of a shock, especially when he saw them bearing down on him at speed! He wondered fleetingly why the apparition of his mother had brought him here. Had it really been his mother, or Darqu'on setting a trap? Could they even be working together? He didn't want to believe that, but the images he had seen had been horrific… But there was no time to work this through.

He looked behind him for an escape and saw another group of clone guards approaching from the rear, weapons drawn; he was trapped. It was then he remembered the tin whistle. Wigapom had said it had helped him with the Hybrid. Well now was the time to see if it worked for him – he had nothing to lose. He put it to his lips and, with a deep breath and a fervent prayer, blew hard. No sound that he could hear came from it and he felt sure he was in big trouble, but if he had not heard any sound, the guards most certainly had. They dropped their weapons, which clattered to the ground, and began to dance like whirling dervishes, round and round and round, clutching their hands to their ears as though trying to block out a terrible cacophony of noise. Will kept blowing. Their faces contorted as though in great pain. They staggered on their feet and began to literally fall apart; legs separated from torsos, arms too, as smoke poured from all sockets as the high frequency of the sound incinerated them from the inside out.

Will was forced to take cover behind a pillar from the combusting debris of the guards shooting towards him, whilst above the chaos of this he was sure he heard the sound of chilling laughter, echoing around him. He knew it was Darqu'on, spying on him, although he could see no one, and suddenly he sensed what Wigapom had also sensed, and what Will had dreaded – that Darqu'on knew they were here, and had enticed them, spider-like, inside the Citadel. The thought of the spider again made him shudder and he struggled to focus on Darqu'on: He was playing with them, even now.

Will began to wonder what was really responsible for the guards' demise. Was it the blowing of the tin whistle, or had Darqu'on set his own guards to self-destruct for his own warped amusement? He was just wondering quite how to deal with this new implication when a further ear-splitting commotion came from the floor below him, growing louder as whatever it was came closer.

Chasing each other up the stairs came a pair of rampaging beasts, which he recognised as the Basilisk and Roc; two of the four statues on the ground floor, now very much alive, as well as angry and hungry for blood. Had the sound of the tin whistle, inaudible to his own ears, re-awakened the creatures, or was this yet another example of Darqu'on's work? Will, hiding in the shadows, wondered how he was going to get out of this situation with his life intact.

Skye's ankle was much better. Whatever Asgar had done had worked, and she was ready for action again, but she was told she still had to stay in the tunnel, while Asgar astral-travelled back to help Arcturus.

'I'll be back soon,' he assured her.

'But why can't I come with you?' she asked.

'Because it will be chaos on the streets of the city after the disturbance Arcturus and I set off, and I don't want to risk losing track of you again. Your astral travelling needs refining, Skye, which is why you ended up down here, rather than where you'd hoped, and I need to help Arcturus and the others reach safety, after the disruption they caused. Such a magnificent firework display, if I say so myself! I had always wanted to create one,' Asgar explained, animatedly 'But there will surely be penalties attached. I'll be as quick as I can.'

Skye realised the truth of his words and watched as he dematerialised in front of her, leaving her once more alone in the dingy tunnels. Never one to sit around idly, she decided to explore more of the labyrinth in which she found herself, imprinting in her memory when she turned left or right, so as to find her way back to where she began.

All the tunnels looked the same at first sight, until she turned a corner and noticed an almost hidden hatch in the tunnel roof. It was circular, probably just big enough for a person to squeeze through, and was held in place with bolts around its rim. She wondered about its purpose and where it led, and how to open it. By standing on tiptoe she could just touch the bolts with her fingers, but could never hope to undo them. But then again, if it could perhaps provide a way to get to the others above, she ought to try. She took off her shoe, stretched up and began to bang on the bolts with it, to loosen them. To her utmost surprise, the bolts fell out one by one and they and the hatch lid clattered to the ground, narrowly missing her. The sound echoed throughout the tunnels. Would anyone in the Citadel have heard? Had she messed things up again with her impetuosity?

She knew she should remain where she was, but curiosity overcame her and she tried to pull herself up by holding onto the sides, but was just not tall enough. She slumped to the floor again, disheartened. Yet it seemed she had dislodged more than the bolts, for as she glanced up, she remained transfixed as ethereal images floated down towards her through the hole; long lines of silver-grey figures in hooded gowns gliding softly, arms folded into capacious sleeves, their melodic voices chanting quietly as they approached. She jumped to her feet, unsure of what to make of them, whether to be scared or awed. She pressed back against the wall as they passed her. More of these beings were approaching from the left of the tunnel and as they moved through her, she felt the wispy essence of their energy fill her body. She gasped at the strange feeling, yet a sense of peace and upliftment passed from them to her, creating a meditative space that breathed tranquillity, as well as quiet power.

'Who are you?' she said, her voice catching in her throat. The figures stopped and spoke as one, filling the dank tunnels with images of never-ending peaceful silvery-white light, and Skye's own spirit expanded into it.

'We are Elohim, from the lineage of light, trapped here in the bowels of the Citadel by the darkness that blotted out the light of Wisdom from this once peaceful Temple. You have released us with your determination and we rejoice in walking through the veil that divides our two worlds. This veil will not close again until the light returns – we offer our love and service to you by releasing the etheric template of wisdom in this place, and in the city. We will work with you, and those who also hold light, truth and righteousness in their hearts, so that the darkness is overcome.'

'I am honoured and humbled to meet you,' said Skye, quite overcome, 'Asgar said that the East Gate would let in only the light of truth and righteousness.'

'Did someone call my name?' said a voice at her shoulder, and Asgar materialised again.

'Welcome, brethren!' he said, speaking directly to the Elohim, as though he had been expecting them, 'You come at a most auspicious time!'

Fynn felt he was making progress. He was already on the second floor and the map on the cloth was really aiding his progress. He thought of Skye; had Asgar found her? Was she safe? If only she were with him now, but she wasn't and he convinced himself there was a good reason for this. Wigapom always said, 'Trust the process,' and, so far, so good, so who was he to question it? He carried on his steady ascent, certain he would find Wigapom soon.

Will recognised the eagle face of the Roc, who, with its lionesque body and huge wings, had been the first one to swoop up the staircase. The beating of the wings echoed loudly in the space, whilst its sharp beady eyes, scanned every inch. It was quickly followed by the cockerel-headed Basilisk, fortuitously turned away from Will, its grotesque reptilian tail and body supported on two enormous and viciously-clawed feet. Will instinctively looked down to protect himself, aware that he could so easily turn to stone himself if the creature looked him in the eye. He remembered thinking that Darqu'on must have tremendous power to remain un-petrified, but then perhaps he was never able to maintain eye contact with anyone! As Will turned his gaze, he noticed another corridor leading away from the creatures and, with no alternative in view, ran as fast as he could down it, searching for somewhere to hide. He skidded on the floor, falling forwards, and the dagger Wigapom had given him fell from his pocket. He groped to retrieve it, only to see it dematerialise in the air before him. There was nothing he could do but keep going, as he heard the creatures close behind him. There was a door to his left. He grabbed the handle and turned it, hearing and feeling the hot breath of the beasts close behind him, and pushed himself into the open space, trying to get something solid between him and the creatures. The Roc swooped, wide cavernous beak dripping with saliva. Will just managed to slam the door shut. The Roc's beak speared it with such force that it stuck in the door. He heard the Roc rattling it violently, but the hinges were strong and it stayed firmly closed.

Will now heard the beating of massive wings and clawing of strong talons against the door as the creature struggled to pull itself free, peering through the hole its beak had made. The Basilisk could be heard making equally loud crowing and thudding sounds, as though charging the Roc from behind. Will heard the vicious battle that ensued and thanked his lucky stars that he was not in the middle of it.

Then there was silence. Will froze. Had the Basilisk petrified the Roc? Was it dead? Were they both dead? He heard the triumphant crow of the cockerel-headed Basilisk outside the door, and knew that the Basilisk at least was still very much alive. The crowing was followed by the thud of wood being pummelled, shoved and hacked; it wouldn't be long before the creature broke down the door. Will spun away from the door, unsure what to do next, and found he was in a room full of full-length mirrors. His reflection gazed back at him many times over from around the walls! He suddenly remembered that the Basilisk could only be stopped if it looked at its own reflection and, working on instinct he threw open the door again, hiding behind it as he did so, whilst holding his breath – not daring to look at what took place. He heard the creature lumber through the opening, and Will imagined it catching sight of itself in the mirrors. He prayed that the outcome was as he had hoped, and when there was no more sound, gingerly opened one eye and then the other and peeked out from behind the door. He saw exactly what he wanted to see – the Basilisk had looked at its reflection and turned to stone, immobilised in a pose of grotesque surprise.

Will, shaking but resolute, edged his way past the petrified remains of the Basilisk out into the corridor, where he jumped at the petrified shape of the Roc in front of him! Will was in no danger, but there was still nowhere for him to go, other than back into the mirrored room. Quelling his fear at sharing the same space as the stone Basilisk again, he returned to the room only to notice something he had not seen before. Not only did the mirrors reflect what was in front of them, some of them seemed to be showing what lay behind them, in the Citadel itself. Will noticed one in particular showing a large room opening out in front of him. He walked towards it, drawn by the hazy image in the centre of the mirror, which, as he got closer, became clearer. It was the image of a young woman; head slumped on her chest, legs and arms bound by strong ropes to a chair.

'Sophie!' said Will.

He placed his hands on the mirror, as though trying to reach through the glass and touch her, but the mirror was firm and solid. Yet he was sure that somehow he could get through the mirror to reach her inside this inner room. He couldn't smash the glass as he felt that if he broke the mirror he would lose any possibility of accessing the inner room. Yet he felt sure there had to be a way of moving through it. He touched the glass again, feeling its solidity, unyielding under his fingers, when an idea came to him. Supposing he believed that it *wasn't* solid? Supposing he believed it was liquid, like a sheet of vertical water? Would those thoughts create the reality of this new belief and allow him to move through it safely? He believed they would! Yes, he truly believed he could create his own entry into the room before him, where Sophie was trussed, just by imagining it happening.

He had to believe it could happen. He wanted to believe it. He had to get to her!

He began to actively visualise everything in his head; he saw himself pushing confidently through the glass, as though there was no solid barrier to stop him. In his imaginings he felt the mirror give way under his penetrating fingers, saw himself stepping into the room with her, and as he put out his hand again, was not surprised at all to find that this time it slid through easily, like a hand in water. Nor was he surprised when his whole self was able to step into the room to what lay on the other side, as though he had stepped through a waterfall,

Darqu'on watched with maniacal glee as Will accessed the inner room.

'Now I have him!' he gloated to Scabtail, who stood just behind him, 'I knew he could not resist rescuing the damsel in distress. It is nearly over, Scabtail. The end is in sight. I have enjoyed the chase and will be almost sorry to see it finished, but what a finish it will be!'

'What about the other two, Master? They have both accessed the building.'

'I am aware of their whereabouts, Scabtail. You forget I have seen all their moves.'

'Almost all of them, Master,' corrected Scabtail and then immediately regretted it as a lightning bolt flared from Darqu'on's fingers towards him; a searing pain coursed through his tail and the smell of scalding scales filled the air yet again. Would he never learn to keep his mouth shut? He knew Darqu'on did not want to be reminded of the fact that the more stones Wigapom seemed to acquire, the less effective his mirrors were at tracking his prey.

'And whose fault is that, blockhead?' hissed Darqu'on as he sought to control his temper once more. Nothing, absolutely nothing was going to spoil his enjoyment of this long-awaited victory over The Brat. Certainly not this odorous reptile!

He barked out another order for his minion.

'The guards have orders to seize and bind the other two and throw them in the dungeon. They are of no importance any longer to me. Check on them if you wish, but let them rot there. One of them will die anyway when The Brat dies.'

'Are you sure you know which one *is* The Brat, Master?' asked Scabtail, and could have kicked himself again for the stupidity of his question, as yet another burning hot finger flare shot towards his tail.

'Blockhead! Of course I know which is which! The one who has been looking for the girl is the one that has the stones and I already have him trapped in the inner room with her. The maiden drew the Unicorn to her before and has now drawn The Brat as well! Now he is mine to slay with the bewitched Unicorn horn!'

Scabtail remained silent; not only because he knew that Darqu'on did not have anything belonging to the Unicorn, as he thought, but also because he was sure he did not have the real Wigapom in the room either, but Scabtail did not want to suffer another lighting bolt, or worse, so decided to keep his thoughts to himself from now on.

'You know of the Elohim, then?' asked Skye of Asgar.

'Yes, I knew that we stood more chance of accessing their energy than ever before on this particular day of Samhain,' replied Asgar, 'It is wonderful to see you here at last,' he said to the Elohim again.

'There are many that need our help,' they replied in unison.

'You mean Wigapom, Fynn and Will,' replied Skye, anxious to be with them, 'not to mention Arcturus and the other light workers in the city.'

'That is already in hand,' replied Asgar, 'They will be with us soon.'

The Elohim spoke again, as one.

'We are better used to help those unable to help themselves – the lost souls of the Living Dead come first to mind, but we will aid those you mention, at their point of greatest need.' They drifted freely again through the hole that Skye had opened in the roof of the tunnel.

'Well done, Skye,' said Asgar, 'I knew if I left you alone your determined nature would work a miracle. I'm sure this will lead us to Wigapom. Best get going,' and amazingly Skye found herself levitating through the hatch, with Asgar following closely behind.

Fynn had made it to the next level, but still had no idea where to find Wigapom. If only he could communicate telepathically with him, as Will was able to do. Somewhere in his memory he thought he recalled Aldebaran telling them that telepathic communication was possible between anyone, but if it was it did not come easily to him! The part of his brain that allowed it must be under-developed, as in most people, he thought, through lack of use. Fynn silently cursed this fact now, whilst subconsciously searching for that part in his brain so that he could start to develop it – surely it was never too late, and he needed that ability. Now! Nothing happened. His mind was as blank as before. All he could do was trust that a greater force than his would somehow bring them together. He silently kept asking for this to happen as he crept along the corridors, dodging into shadows to avoid the guards that seemed more evident on this level.

He turned another corner, still asking to be brought together with Wigapom, and did a double take as he came face to face with yet more stone statues, this time of a man holding a sword and a book, and a woman holding a staff with seven rings running up it. These statues were non-threatening, compared to the monsters on the lower floor, but they still caused Fynn to take a sharp intake of breath! An even deeper one occurred when he saw what came out of the room behind the statues. It was none other than Wigapom himself!

Wigapom heard the surprised gasp and spun towards it, ready for fight or flight. Instead, he froze in shock at the sight of Fynn in front of him. Both opened their mouths to speak, but there was no time for words, as in the next instant guards flanked them on every side, seizing them both roughly. They were trussed, gagged and blindfolded before being marched away. It all took less time than it would to say *The Book of True Magic*.

Behind their blindfolds both Wigapom and Fynn thought ruefully that perhaps they should have made their requests to find each other a little more specific; something that did not allow for capture by clone guards!

They wouldn't make that mistake again, if indeed there would be a next time.

The guards roughly pushed and pulled them along, dragging them upright if they stumbled, spinning them round corners and pushing them up and down varying levels, all of which had the effect of disorienting them completely. Apart from the stamp of many pairs of heavily-booted feet around them, they could hear the occasional door swing open and slam shut, as well as smell an increasingly musty smell hanging depressingly in the air, which felt chill and damp. Both let out involuntary shivers that were as much to do with their concern for what was going to happen to them, as they were in response to the cold.

Finally, they were yanked to a halt. Another door creaked open.

'In there,' said a rough voice, and they were pushed through. Stumbling and falling onto a damp, cold stone floor, slimy with foul-smelling mould. They were tightly bound together, back to back, before the door slammed behind them, locks and bolts grinding into place. The sound of retreating feet marched away and an eerie silence fell once more, save for the pounding of their hearts and the constant rhythmical drip, drip of water soaking into their bindings.

They waited for something to happen, anything, but nothing did. They both realised that, apart from each other, they were alone. Neither could speak or see as yet, but they both began to work at freeing the ropes that bound them. Cold fingers do not make it easy to unleash bonds, and with teeth chattering with the increasing chill, it was hard going. They managed to grunt at each other through the gags binding their mouths and this basic communication was strangely comforting as they did their best to release each other.

Wigapom managed to slip his bonds first and, in relief, tore off his blindfold and gag before helping Fynn release himself. Soon both were free to look around their prison.

There was disappointingly little to see; a small square room with a high ceiling and a small window, cobwebbed and grimy, too far out of reach even if they stood on tiptoe, and the heavy, studded, locked, bolted and immoveable door through which they had been pushed. Wigapom knew without trying that his key would *not* fit this lock.

'Well, things could have turned out a little better,' said Fynn, his voice heavy with irony. He looked around, rubbing the friction marks made by the bonds on his wrists as he did so.

'He's made a mistake,' said Wigapom, almost to himself.

'You mean, we should be in a suite of rooms with a bath and a hot dinner?' said Fynn wryly, wondering what Wigapom was meaning, and indeed if he had flipped a little under the strain of everything.

'No. He's made a mistake. He thinks Will is me!'

'What? How do you know?' said Fynn, baffled.

'Because I can feel what's happening with Will as though it's happening to me. Yet it isn't happening to me, because I'm here and Will is in the inner room with Sophie and Darqu'on!'

'With Sophie *and* Darqu'on?' repeated Fynn. 'Does he know he's made a mistake?'

'I don't think so, not yet. But he will when he discovers Will doesn't have the stones.'

'Because you have them.'

'Yes, of course I do. In my pocket. Five of them. And you have the sixth,' said Wigapom, jangling them together as if to prove his words. They vibrated against his leg stronger than ever.

'I know. That's why I'm here,' said Fynn, holding out the red stone he had accidentally put in his pocket in the city. Wigapom took it.

'Good job you noticed it in time. Did you manage to find Skye?' said Wigapom.

'Not exactly – but I found Asgar, and he is finding Skye, I hope,' replied Fynn, doing his best not to contemplate never seeing her again.

'I'm sure you can trust Asgar to find her,' said Wigapom, putting the stone with the others. 'Now all we have to do is find the other stone that Darqu'on took and we have them all!'

Fynn looked bemused. 'You seem to have forgotten one small thing – that we aren't able to go anywhere at the moment,' he said, indicating their stark and dismal prison.

'Trust the process, Fynn! Everything's perfect,' said Wigapom, getting his resolve and optimism back very quickly.

'You and that process! What makes you so sure that everything is perfect!' derided Fynn.

'Because I feel it and believe it, Fynn, and the stones are positively buzzing with energy! It's no accident we're here, Fynn! We've been brought here for a purpose! We just have to find what that purpose is! Let's think creatively for the answer! Maybe I need to look at my mother's ring again. It might help.'

'It hasn't done a very good job so far,' retorted Fynn sarcastically.

'That's not true. It *has* protected me when I have used it properly. It's only when I haven't looked at it or ignored it there have been problems. There was probably a message on it before the guards appeared but I didn't read it.'

'OK, Mr Optimistic, what does it say now?'

Wigapom peered at the ring, willing the words to appear.

The stones have brought you here this time, they can also help you leave.
Now you need to use their gifts and in yourselves believe.

'Well, forgive me for not thinking that very helpful,' said Fynn, unable to understand its meaning and frustrated at Wigapom's unrealistic belief in being able to do so.

'Don't you see, Fynn? The stones brought us here. We're meant to be here, the words on the ring say so, and I can feel them communicating that to me. The ring also says that we can get out of here using the stones' gifts, and to do that we have to believe in ourselves, in the same way that the words appear when I believe they will.'

'Well, fine words don't make things happen – how can six stones and us believing in ourselves get us out of this place?' replied Fynn, in despair.

'They won't if we don't believe they can! This is not a time for negativity, Fynn! We have to think positively!'

'I *am* positive! Positive that we won't get out of this place!' retorted Fynn. 'Look at our situation, Wiggy,' he said as he shot a defeated glance around the room, 'what is it about this place that gives you hope?' and he slumped to the ground, head in hands. Wigapom squatted beside him.

'Come on Fynn! This is not like you! We've done so much, and things have gone well so far. Don't let this defeat you. I need your courage now,' cajoled Wigapom, getting out the stones and spreading them out on the damp ground.

'Look, we know the red stone stands for *Wisdom* and red is a bold, courageous colour, a colour to feel strong and secure in; well, *we* need to feel strong and secure and courageous right now and use *our* wisdom to get us out of this mess. The ring says we can. I believe it. Do you?'

'Well...' began Fynn, but Wigapom continued without waiting for a reply.

'And the orange stone means *is* – I am, you are, he is – it's telling us to have faith in ourselves, in who we are, to value our worth. The stone came to me when I finally knew and accepted my name was Wigapom. It gave me an identity I could value, so I could assert myself at last. Now we have to assert ourselves again – do you see?'

'I...' but there was no stopping Wigapom now.

'And the yellow stone – this is *given*, remember, and the colour for confidence, well it's given *me* confidence in myself just to look at it. If it hadn't been for this stone, Fynn, neither you nor I would have begun this Quest, nor gained so much confidence in our own abilities to face things, isn't that right?'

'Maybe...' Fynn replied cagily. Wigapom was on a roll now.

'And look at the green stone – it says *as* and is the heartfelt, balancing colour of nature and our relationship to it, ourselves and each other, and it's as if I can feel it right in *my* heart, binding you and me together in the love of friendship and companionship with each other. You and me Fynn, always, as brothers. Can you feel it too?'

'Well, sort of…'

'And here is the blue stone, helping us to communicate all this to each other and to others – to show them we are all connected to the same thing, all *part* of each other, because that's the word on it, remember? Surely you can sense our connection to that?'

'I… But…' said Fynn again, although Wigapom was still in full flow.

'Now, I don't have the other stone at the moment, the indigo, but I know what it says, it says *of* and I know how it made me feel when I held it and what it helped me to see. And I still feel that, even though I don't have it in my hand at the moment, it's still *part of* who I am, whether it's here or not, it's part of who you are too Fynn – part of all of us, if we let it. The indigo colour represents our ability to see inside ourselves, to sense things with our intuition, to connect with our inner teacher – what a wonderful gift that is, and we both have that, isn't that right?'

'Yes, I suppose it…' agreed Fynn as Wigapom's voice became even more passionate.

'And here is the purple stone – the pinnacle of them all, and do you know what it means, Fynn? Do you know what it really means?'

'We thought it meant magic.'

'I know, and it *is* magic in a way, because magic means hidden wisdom and this is what we are all searching for, although somehow nothing seems hidden anymore, at least not from *me*, and it won't be hidden from you either when you open your mind to it! Oh Fynn! Don't you see? The missing word is *me*. And that means me, and you, and everyone! We are all *me*, all One; a simple little word, but such an important one – like Wigapom, remember: *Wisdom is given as part of me!* My name has been telling us all along that we already have wisdom inside each and every one of us. We don't have to look elsewhere for it, or search outside for it, we probably don't even need a book about it, because we have it already inside us, just waiting to be discovered and used!'

'Maybe *you* do Wigapom – it's *your* name, remember, not mine.'

'No Fynn, I don't believe Wigapom is just a name. I believe it's an acronym for a belief, an acronym that belongs to everyone, to help us believe in our personal connection to wisdom, to the Divine, and the source of everything. We are all Wigapom inside! We just have to find that part of us. We all seek knowledge, but what good is that without the wisdom to show us how to use it properly? That's the difference between the two words. We can all acquire knowledge, and knowledge is power, but we never become wise until we learn how to use that knowledge for the best possible reasons. Then we can be said to have real wisdom. That's when we become Wigapom! People lost sight of that when they began to ignore the danger signs that Darqu'on was exhibiting. Darqu'on, especially, lost sight of it when his thirst for knowledge and power overtook him: when his lust for my mother was rejected and it turned into vengeance! That's how the wisdom got lost. Now we have to find it again by searching inside each one of us and using that self-knowledge and awareness in the best possible way to be more than we have ever been before! *Wisdom is given as part of me!* Say the sentence to yourself, Fynn and see if it doesn't make sense to you! Go on, Fynn, say it and believe it. Make it your truth!'

Fynn looked into Wigapom's vibrant eyes, as clear and as sparkly as a polished crystal, and saw how much he believed in what he was saying, how much he knew it as the truth. Wigapom's belief was infectious, inspirational even. Fynn did understand everything he had said, it made complete sense, and he saw it clearly, as clearly as he had seen the room they were in when he removed the blindfold. He repeated the phrase himself out loud, the words reverberating around the walls and coming back at him as if in confirmation.

'Wisdom is given as part of me! Wisdom is given as part of me! Wisdom is give as part of *me*!' He stressed the last word and owned the sentence for himself. The more he said it the more he knew it was right. He did have wisdom as part of himself, he always had, but the recognition of it made the world seem a wonderful place, even here in the dark and damp cell.

'It feels good to say it, Wiggy. I really do believe I am talking about me!'

'YES!' said Wigapom passionately, shooting his fist in the air in triumph. 'You are! Nothing's impossible. Now, let's use that wisdom to get us out of here! Let me stand on your shoulders so that I can reach the window.'

Fynn supported Wigapom as he knelt on his broad shoulders. From this height, Wigapom could reach the tiny window looking out just above ground level. Using the red stone held tight in his hand he smashed the grimy glass and felt the crisp, cold air of a new day blow in like probing fingers, anxious to free them. From his jacket pocket he took the Phoenix feather and held it briefly in his fingertips where it pulled to be free in the breeze. He spoke out loud.

'Find the Phoenix – we need his help,' and he let the wind catch the feather and lift it from his hands. The feather, as though pleased to be free again, flew upwards at speed, carrying Wigapom's message as it travelled back to the Phoenix on the mountaintop. Help would soon be at hand.

CHAPTER 43

The Maid and the Unicorn

"She is more precious than jewels, and nothing you desire can compare with her.
Happy is the man who finds wisdom and the man who gets understanding,
for the gain from it is better than silver and its profits better than gold."
Proverbs 3: 13-15

Almost as soon as Will stepped inside the inner room, he knew he had been lured into a trap. Sophie was real enough, there was no denying that, but so was Darqu'on, who Will soon found himself face to face with. Will also realised immediately that Darqu'on had mistaken him for Wigapom – unless someone knew them very well it was impossible to tell them apart. What would happen if and when Darqu'on discovered his mistake, Will could only guess at, but he was determined to keep both himself and Sophie alive in the process. He looked defiantly into Darqu'on's eyes, determined not to flinch under their cold gaze, whilst sending a powerful thought message to Wigapom, telling him of his whereabouts.

Sophie was still slumped, tightly bound, to the chair. Drugged by some fiendish potion, she would be going nowhere for a while, so Will declared to himself, neither would he. He stood his ground.

'So we meet for a final time,' drawled Darqu'on, confidence oozing from every pore as he believed Wigapom and the all-important stones were now in front of him.

'Final for you maybe!' replied Will, with no indication of any of Wigapom's previous compassion towards Darqu'on. This change in attitude did not go unnoticed by Darqu'on.

'Oh, The Brat bites back at last!' was his comment, 'I was wondering when I would stir your hatred for me. I am so much more comfortable with hatred or fear being directed at me. Anything else seems rather tedious.'

Will took heed of this slip-up, yet his response was still biting.

'It didn't seem that tedious to you at our meeting at Dragonmound,' he said. 'You were offered a way out, refused it and lost half your army because of it.'

Darqu'on's smile froze on his pale face. He did not like to be reminded of what had happened at Dragonmound. His eyes hardened even more and he snapped back.

'That was then and this is now. Now you are my captive. Along with her.' And he indicated Sophie in the chair.

'I don't know why she's here, nor why you think she is important to me,' bluffed Will, 'I haven't seen her since I was a child; she means nothing to me now.'

'If she meant nothing to you, you would not be here in this room wanting to rescue her. I know she is important to you and that you will do anything to save her.'

'I told you, she means nothing to me,' insisted Will, hoping that somewhere in her drugged state Sophie was not hearing him say this.

Darqu'on paused for a moment. The silence was heavy with tension.

'Then I will kill her now,' he said, drawing out from inside his black cloak a long, glistening dagger, and with one swift move plunged it towards the sleeping Sophie's heart.

'NO!' cried Will, instinctive emotion overtaking everything else.

The dagger stopped inches from her body. Will gasped, not only because of what had just happened, but because he recognised the dagger as the one that had dematerialised in the corridor earlier – the one that Wigapom had given him – so Darqu'on had been there too, watching and waiting. Will remembered it was this dagger that had removed the stones from the Hybrid's throat, yet he knew that Sophie could not be killed by it if Darqu'on used it in anger, and behind Darqu'on's taunting smile there was deep-seated rage.

'She means nothing to you, eh? Oh, but your actions tell a different story. And so I can continue with mine. If you wish to save her life then you must seriously challenge your own.'

'What do you mean?' said Will, knowing his bluff had been called and fearing what might now happen to both him and Sophie.

'You have a little task to fulfil to secure her freedom and safety. If you fail, in any way, she will be killed. But first I want the remaining stones to go with this one,' and Darqu'on dangled the indigo stone between his fingers.

Will's stomach, which had already dropped to the floor once, rose rapidly again when he saw the missing stone in Darqu'on's hand. At least he knew where it was now!

'When I have the stones, you and I can play our last and deadly game. If you resist in any way then she will die, as indeed will you.'

'What last game?'

'Hunt the Unicorn.'

'Hunt the Unicorn?' echoed Will, 'So that you can kill it, you barbarian? Never!'

'Barbarian he calls me! Such judgement from you! Where is the compassion? Where is the acceptance you offered me before! Ha! A transitory state, as they all are. No matter! It is better this way. It is easier to hate you like this, and hate you I always have and always will.'

'How can I bring you the Unicorn? You know the Unicorn can only be summoned by a Maiden that it trusts. The only Maiden here is drugged up to her eyeballs with goodness knows what sorcery. How am I supposed to find the Unicorn without her?'

'You seem blissfully unaware that she has already attracted the Unicorn, not once, but twice. On the first occasion the horn was sliced from the real Unicorn's head, on the second occasion, she attracted you, like a lamb, or should we say, Unicorn, to the slaughter, for here you are, standing in front of me, ready to do battle for her life, and indeed your own!'

'You want to hunt me like a Unicorn? You have a warped and twisted mind, Darqu'on.'

'Thank you for the compliment,' said Darqu'on with a slithering smile running across his face. 'But first I will take the stones.'

'Why didn't you ask the Phoenix to get us out of here?' said Fynn as Wigapom climbed off his shoulders.

'Haven't you realised even now, Fynn?' said Wigapom, a huge smile streaking across his face as though he was the happiest person in the world. Fynn shook his head. He'd realised a lot of things, although he was beginning to wonder if Wigapom had a complete grip on reality. Wigapom spoke, and seemed to confirm this.

'Everything you see around you, Fynn, is not real. It's all illusion! And that includes the door that you are at present experiencing as barred.'

'What do you mean, 'illusion'? Do you mean it isn't really there? Because it looks very much there to me!' responded Fynn, ever the practical, logical one.

'Only because you are choosing to see it as an obstacle is it appearing as one. If you create a different belief then that becomes your reality. You, me, we all create our own reality and there are many, many other realities, or potentialities out there just waiting to be real-ised, or made real, which is perhaps a clearer way of expressing it.'

'Real-ised? Made real? Was that an intended pun just then?' said Fynn.

'Do you really mean that this door is not there?' and Fynn banged it with his fist, hard and strong. It seemed very real indeed to him.

'Everything is just energy, Fynn, even things that seem solid to us are still made up of trillions of energy particles that are just hanging out together in whatever shape we have formed them into. But it's an illusion that they're solid, or impenetrable, because nothing is, unless we make it so.'

'Are you telling me that you could walk through that door without having to open it first?' said Fynn, his rational mind screaming at him that this was impossible, but his creative mind wide open to any possibility now.

Wigapom was about to speak, but they heard the sound of softly beating wings on the other side of the window and in the next instant the Phoenix appeared in front of them in the dank cell, as though no wall could ever keep him out, or in, anymore.

'I knew you would come!' said Wigapom in greeting.

'I knew you would call,' replied the Phoenix, his gloriously coloured feathers shining in the dark room.

'How did you do that?' said Fynn, baffled at how the Phoenix could seemingly fly through solid walls.

'I believe Wigapom now understands the principle,' said the Phoenix, 'It's thanks to him that this form of magic has again become possible.'

'I do understand,' replied Wigapom, 'and we are going to use it ourselves right now.'

'I am pleased to be of service once more,' said the Phoenix graciously.

'I wish you could help Asgar find Skye,' said Fynn.

'I have already completed this last request,' said the Phoenix, 'I believe they are close by,' and as Wigapom and Fynn listened they heard a familiar voice coming from the other side of the door.

'I think they're in here, Asgar.'

'That's Skye!' exclaimed Fynn in excitement, 'She's OK, but how did she get here so fast? You brought her didn't you, Phoenix? Although I don't know how you did it!'

'We all have worked together, as one, to create this moment, but it may be better to leave full explanations for later,' said the Phoenix in his singsong voice, 'there is much still to do.'

'You're right!' agreed Wigapom. 'We must leave here and find Will and Sophie. I know they're in the inner room with Darqu'on, and Will could be in serious trouble once Darqu'on finds out that he isn't who Darqu'on thinks he is.' He turned to the Phoenix. 'Thank you for being our messenger,' he said, 'and my saviour – I will treasure the memories always.'

'My job is not yet over,' said the Phoenix, rather more sombrely, 'I will be needed again,' and before they could question him further he dissolved into the air in a sparkle of shimmering colours.

'Wigapom? Is that you? Is Fynn with you?' came Skye's voice, louder this time.

'Come on Fynn, follow me!' said Wigapom as he stretched out his hand towards the door. Instead of touching the door, his hand slid right through it. Fynn looked on in amazement as with his other hand Wigapom took hold of Fynn and pulled them both through the seemingly solid door into the tunnel beyond.

Skye, and Asgar were waiting for them. They didn't seem at all surprised to see their entry – it was almost as though they had never seen a door in the first place.

'Skye!' cried Fynn, overcome to see her again. Her smile shone like a ray of sunshine in the gloom.

'This day has been a long time coming!' she said, and hugged him as though never wanting to let him go.

'Save some of that for me, later,' joked Wigapom, all jealousy long gone, and delighted to see two of the people he cared for most so happy in each other's company again, 'but now there's no time to waste. I'll lead the way.'

CHAPTER 44

Revelations

"Revelations come when you're in the thick of it,
pitting yourself up against something larger than yourself."
Frank Langella

Will was stalling. He had no idea how he was going to bluff his way out of not giving the stones to Darqu'on, and as for being hunted like a Unicorn; well, Darqu'on really had lost the plot! It was then that Fate stepped in again. This time in the waking form of Sophie. She stirred in the chair and opened her eyes. Both Darqu'on's attention and Will's were momentarily taken by this action – Darqu'on, because he didn't want any complications from the girl, whom he couldn't yet kill, at least not until he had the stones safely in his possession, and Will because he was genuinely concerned for her well-being and grateful that no real harm had come to her.

Sophie's first words were to Will. He was not sure if she had even seen that Darqu'on was present.

'Is it really you?' she said, struggling to turn towards him, but restricted by the ropes that bound her.

'Yes Sophie, it's me. Everything will be alright.'

Darqu'on slid into her vision, eyes mocking her plight.

'Well, Sleeping Beauty wakens once more! Behold, damsel, your heroic knight has come to save you. A pity he will be unable to save himself when I am done.'

Sophie managed to level her gaze at him. It was strong, yet compassionate. Darqu'on had not expected this. He wanted fear and terror, or at the very least, resistance, as she had given him before. He understood those responses. He did not want to understand anything else.

'I know who you are,' said Sophie quietly.

Darqu'on snorted with derision.

'You would be more than the fool I take you for already if you did not,' he said, ego swelling like a goitre.

'Even now, you do not understand,' replied Sophie, with real depth of emotion lighting her eyes. 'I know who you *really* are. And who I am. Yet it seems you do not. How can you be so unaware of the consequences of your actions?'

Despite himself, Darqu'on was unsettled by her comments, and even more by the look she fixed upon him, which was one of deep sadness, but also longing. He had seen this look before on Her face. He didn't know how to deal with it now, any more than he had then, and brushed it off as though it were an annoying fly around his head.

'What I do is no concern of *yours*,' he spat out, 'and what you think is of no consequence to *me*. You are nothing to me, other than a means to an end.' His tone was derisory and dismissive and he turned his attention to Will once more.

But Sophie had not finished, and her next comment shocked him like the sting of a scorpion.

'Not even if I am your *daughter*?' she said.

Will's eyes went wide with shock, but this was nothing compared to Darqu'on's reaction. His dark eyes almost swivelled in their sockets as he struggled to comprehend what this slip of a girl had just said. He fought and failed to regain composure and, instead, leapt behind his usual defence of scorn .

'My *daughter*? I have no daughter. I am Darqu'on, all powerful ruler of this land and you are a mere pawn in my game!'

'I am the child born to Aimee, nurse to the young Prince of Light, known as Wigapom, conceived on the road out of Brakendor one dark night in early Spring twenty years ago by such an act of horror and lust that I shudder to think of it. I carry your genes and your DNA, if not your name, and how I have fought not to let their cancer overtake me! How I have seen my mother's shame cripple her body and mind as a result of that night, and how I have sought to make amends for your evil actions with compassionate ones of my own! I thought I would hate you, for what you have done, not only to my mother and myself but to all people who have suffered through you! I could have hated you, so many times, but why should I harm myself by hatred? I would not hate you, I chose not to, and I will never hate you, because that would mean you had won and I would be no better than you, and I will *not* allow myself to be so corrupted. I have worked hard all my life to hold my head up high and to understand your actions, to see the spark of goodness that I know must have been there once – is still present somewhere – although flickering to the point of extinction. I have worked hard not to judge you, even though your actions are abhorrent. I have told myself that actions are not the person, just the outer representation of a troubled soul. This has been so hard to do, yet I have done it, because I wanted one day to meet you face to face and be able to forgive you, and for you to recognise that out of your hatred and cruelty something good survived, in the hope it could show you a different path. My mother chose my name – it means wisdom. And here in the Temple once dedicated to wisdom, I have met you. In that there is a strange justice and synchronicity. Yet you have used me, an innocent who shares your own blood, as a pawn in your sad and sick games to lure another innocent, Will here, into your lair. It would be so easy for all that I have worked to achieve to die here, but I will not let it happen. Instead I will use it as a means of redemption, and no matter what you do, to Will or to me, nothing will change that. I hope you understand that, Father.'

The familial word struck Darqu'on like a sword in his side. Will, too, was dumbstruck at what he heard and was struggling to take it in. Darqu'on was rooted to the spot by her words and the look in her eyes. For what seemed a very long time, the silence continued to hang there, like a dewdrop on a spider's web, a delicate balancing act. It could remain intact, as a symbol of strength and beauty, or it could rip the web asunder. All depended on the choice that Darqu'on made. For a brief moment he seemed unsure. Could he relinquish his arrogance, power and hatred and embrace the love and compassion of his daughter? Could he, would he, turn his back on his ways of sorcery and follow the deeply rutted and overgrown, but still just visible path back to his true self? Or would he refuse to face the monster he had become and thus reject redemption?

Darqu'on chose the latter. With his thin, black-clad arms he lunged angrily at Sophie with the dagger, yelling incomprehensible sounds like a wounded animal on the rampage.

Sophie stood her ground as the blade hit her. Darqu'on backed away, angry and surprised, as the blade went limp on impact with her body, yelling for Scabtail to bring the bewitched Unicorn horn. Scabtail appeared in a trice, with the supposed horn in his hand; only he knew it was not the bewitched Unicorn horn but an old Mantygre one instead. Only Will noticed his shaking tail and troubled face.

Darqu'on, his wild eyes more crazed than ever, seized the horn in his right hand, dropping the indigo stone as he did so, which rolled, as if with a mind of its own, underneath Sophie's chair. The fingers of his left hand spurted flame, setting the ropes that bound Sophie alight. Darqu'on swung the horn towards Will, brandishing it as though it too, was a weapon. Will knew enough about Unicorn horns from his childhood stories to know that it had both positive and negative qualities: it could heal flesh in its true state, but when cursed, it could eat the flesh away, leaving nothing but bone. A slow and hideous death, yet still Will thought of Sophie first; he had to free her from her bonds before the flames reached her skin, then he would defend himself. Retrieving the indigo stone would have to come later. Quickly he reached down towards the dagger that Darqu'on had dropped, and with one swoop cut Sophie free from the chair with its now sharp blade. She rolled to the floor, her dress already alight, rolling herself over and over until the flames were out. She had already spotted the stone under the chair and grabbed at it as she sought cover. Will, in the mean time, spun to face Darqu'on, dagger still in his hand. He knew he could not use the dagger in anger, yet hoped that by using it in self-defence it would still retain its sharpness if needed.

Darqu'on lunged at him with the horn, slashing and stabbing as a thing demented. It took all of Will's agility and quickness of mind to avoid what he believed was a deadly instrument. Darqu'on, for all his sickly pallor and shrivelled frame, was surprisingly forceful. Even then he played by his own rules, conjuring all manner of demonic creatures to aid him, all of which Will, showing much courage, fought to deflect with the dagger, which seemed to have a mind and skill of its own. He lost track of Scabtail and Sophie, of the concept of time, even his bearings. Nothing seemed real, other than his struggle with Darqu'on and his desperate attempts to avoid the repeated slash of the horn, thrust with malevolent energy undimmed with time. Yet Will was reaching exhaustion point. He desperately needed a boost to his flagging energy. His prayers were answered as, through the walls of the room seeped the ethereal presence of the Elohim to surround him. He barely saw them but felt their loving strength flow towards him, giving him the energy to continue the battle.

CHAPTER 45

The End of the Beginning

"Miracles do not, in fact, break the laws of nature."
C. S. Lewis

Wigapom led the others through walls and doorways with ease. It was as though they were invisible, or in another time frame altogether from what was around them. It was as though Wigapom was seeing only what he chose to see and create, and this did not include any walls, monsters or guards!

They finally stepped back into the place where they had started before the guards attacked them, coming face to face with the two stone statues of the male and female figures. For a moment even Wigapom, who had seemed driven by a new purpose since his inspiration in the dungeon, wondered why they were here. Yet he trusted in the synchronicity of the moment, knowing there must be a reason. He stopped; the stones in his pocket were going wild.

'Come on Wiggy, no time to stand and stare,' urged Fynn.

'No,' said Wigapom, 'wait, we're here for a reason. We must open our minds as to why,' and he began to look around.

'What are you looking for?' said Fynn, 'There's nothing here that we haven't seen before, and Will and Sophie are in trouble!'

'I can feel something though, can't you? said Skye.

'Yes, Skye. Something we want is right under our noses and yet we aren't seeing it,' said Wigapom, looking around intently.

'Then we must look closer at what is here,' replied Asgar simply.

They looked. It was all as before, just the statues of the man holding the sword and the book, and the woman holding the staff with seven rings. Wigapom thought of the seven stones he had to fit down the spine of the book. This was a clue, but did he understand its message?

'Search the statues!' he said and began to touch the one nearest to him. It stayed solid. He felt the smooth coldness of the stone under his searching fingertips, the shape of the man's arm, his wrist, the book he was holding... Then he knew.

'The book!' cried Wigapom. 'He's holding the book!'

'*The Book of True Magic*?' said Fynn, 'But it's made of stone.'

'No! It's only disguised as stone – another illusion,' said Wigapom, certain now that he had found what he was looking for.

'But how do we change it back?' said Skye, as baffled as Fynn.

'By believing that we can. We have to create our own reality, or illusion, if you like, to disperse that created by Darqu'on,' exclaimed Wigapom. 'That's part of the hidden wisdom.'

'As Magus taught, all those years ago,' said Asgar, finally understanding the truth.

'That's right,' agreed Wigapom, 'this is the True Magic. Come on everybody, use the power of your minds to create the reality we want – the stone book to be made real.'

'If we make that real,' said Fynn, 'how do we know the statue won't come to life and attack us with the sword?'

As he voiced this fear there was a low rumble from the statue. They all looked up. The figure holding the book and the sword began to move. Black, piercing eyes glowing now from previously inoffensive sockets. The sword in his hand smote down towards them, taking on a life of its own, whilst the statue fragmented into hundreds of rock missiles hurling themselves in vengeful spite before rebuilding into the statue again and repeating the process. Everyone dived for cover, pulling Wigapom with them.

'NO,' shouted Wigapom, resisting, 'don't allow yourselves to be deluded! Create the reality WE want, don't feed the one that we fear! We can stop this with the power of our minds, but you must believe you have the ability to do this!'

The others quickly understood what they had to do; it was their doubt and fear creating the illusion before them. If they could create this then they could create anything! All eyes, hearts and minds focused as one on the moving statue, as they used their combined mind power to dissolve the stone. It was hard at first, doubt weakening the act, but gradually they focused and the statue began to crumble, this time into nothing; even the dust did not linger, but began to disappear in the air.

'Remember to save the book!' yelled Wigapom as that too seemed to be disappearing into the ether. Minds focused again. The particles of dust – or was it pure energy – began to re-form, yet this time it was no stone illusion; but the real book, as Wigapom remembered it from the room in the castle. The dark green cover shone, but there were no holes along the spine.

'This can't be it,' said Skye, 'Where are the spaces for the stones?'

'Here before our eyes,' said Wigapom in triumph and touched the staff of the female statue. Immediately it dissolved in a shower of sparkling light, and re-formed in the book as clearly evident holes along the spine. Skye ran to retrieve it, opening the cover.

'But there are no words inside,' she said, disappointed.

'They *are* there, we just need to believe we will see them when the stones go in.' said Wigapom, 'I can put the ones in that I have but I still need the indigo stone that Darqu'on stole before it is complete.' He removed the six he now had from his pocket. They were vibrating so hard that he could feel the tremors coursing through his whole body. He laid them out on the floor. The penultimate act of his Quest was complete – just one more step to take.

As Skye passed the book to him, time seemed to suspend itself for Wigapom as he caught a glimpse of an unexpected future; one he had not even considered before and which took him by surprise. He held the book close to his chest, feeling quite shocked. Momentarily he was unsure how to progress. He thought deeply: Did he really want to complete his Quest? He didn't have to put the stones in if he didn't want to; he had choice. He was young and resourceful, even powerful. He could stop right now and take a different path to this. He looked up at the others, seeing concern mingled with hope etched on their faces, he recalled the look on his mother's face as she appeared to him at the brook and saw, as if in a flash, all the elements that had brought him to this moment and knew without doubt what he had to do, no matter what the consequences. Serenity through surrender. He wouldn't let them down, but continue to trust the process: All was for the highest good. All was well. He smiled to himself, suddenly feeling very calm, as he placed each stone, bar the penultimate one, in the spine; they fitted perfectly. Time sped up, propelling all of them into a new tomorrow. Holding the book as if it were a precious child, Wigapom led the way into yet another reality.

Will did not notice the room dissolve away and become a silent winter forest, sparkling with frost and ice. He was unaware of the ethereal figures drawing back; he neither heard nor saw Wigapom and the other light workers emerge as if from a mist rising through the bare trees, nor did he notice the book in Wigapom's hands, already glistening with six of the seven stones. Instead he was purely focused on avoiding contact with Darqu'on and the horn being wielded with such venom. He barely heard Wigapom shout out his name, but he felt his presence and could not stop himself from shivering momentarily, as though someone had just walked over his grave.

'WILL! WILL!' cried Wigapom, 'The Unicorn is alive! Change your thoughts! The horn is not real! There is nothing to fear!'

Will may not have heard properly, but Darqu'on had and Scabtail clearly knew his barely concealed deception was now fully revealed. He flew at Wigapom, claws outstretched in attack in the vain hope of salvaging something of his credibility in his Master's eyes.

Wigapom dropped the book and found himself knocked off balance by the speed of the reptile's attack. They both fell to the ground, grappling for supremacy.

Darqu'on saw Wigapom and despite the closeness in looks between him and Will, knew instinctively, now they were side by side, that he had been fighting the wrong one. He was furious at this double-deception: he wanted Wigapom, not this figment of imagination made flesh! He twisted away from Will, towards Wigapom, who was still struggling with Scabtail.

'LEAVE HIM!' he ordered, 'HE IS MINE!' and rained down thunderbolts and lightning strikes upon them both. Scabtail took the brunt of these as he was on top of Wigapom and rolled away in fiery, deathly agony and torment, his scabby tail held in his mouth, in a macabre parody of the Ouroboros.

Will ran to Wigapom's aid as Fynn, Skye, Asgar and other resistance workers rescued by the Elohim were suddenly trapped behind a wall of flame that shot up in front of them with such force and power that they were temporarily knocked off their feet. They struggled to rise, believing they would not only have to defend themselves from the flames but also Darqu'on's new army of the Living Dead, and the ranks of clone guards who were even now erupting from the Yuletide forest. Yet behind them came the Elohim again, transforming the flames into a safe, protective barrier, and encircling the Living Dead army in a growing field of pulsating light.

Sophie saw all this, but her only thought was to save those she loved. She had already retrieved the book and, holding it to her chest, stepped between her father, Will and Wigapom.

'STOP FATHER, I BEG YOU, STOP THIS!' she cried. Darqu'on saw her and his eyes filled with hate as he slammed the sharp horn down towards her body. Wigapom pushed Will aside and jumped in front of Sophie, catching the full force of the pointed weapon, which drove itself fiercely right through the centre of Wigapom's chest.

He gasped with shock and pain. His eyes wide and staring. His hands grabbing uselessly at the weapon, before falling to the frozen ground, gasping for life.

'NO!' cried Sophie.

'WIGAPOM!' yelled Will, falling towards him, momentarily doubled over with a similar pain in his own chest, and remembering with horror the images shown to him earlier by his mother.

'I WIN!' gloated Darqu'on triumphantly.

Wigapom, life ebbing from his body, whispered, 'The book'.

'I have it,' said Sophie, who had rushed to Wigapom's aid.

'And I have the stone,' said Will, sliding the last stone into the final space in the book's spine, hoping and praying that this act would restore Wigapom. But destiny plays by her own rules, for as the stone completed the spine, Wigapom closed his eyes and breathed his last.

The stones immediately transformed into sparkling, coloured crystals that shot forth beams of rainbow light to surround him. The colours doused the protective flames and blended as one, illuminating the forest and everything within it with pure white light. The ethereal Elohim swept through the trees, chanting as one voice as the clones desiccated into frost on the forest floor and the Living Dead collapsed lifeless, at last, to the ground. Darqu'on stood immobile. Only his black eyes expressed movement, and questions.

'But I killed him!' he said, unable to comprehend how, even with Wigapom's death, he had still not won ultimate power.

'Death is not the end, but the beginning,' said the Elohim as they surrounded him in dazzling light and pure sound. As the brilliance expanded, so Darqu'on began to diminish in size, as if his inflated self had been punctured. Soon all that remained was a tiny black orb that hovered for a moment in the air, as if uncertain as to what to do or where to go next. The Elohim transformed into a multitude of shining coloured orbs, which formed a deep circle around the black one, which began to glow and change colour, like a bruise beginning to heal – from black to blue, to purple, then pink – until it was gently escorted away by the other orbs of the Elohim into the sky, finally disappearing from sight.

'He's gone,' whispered Skye, but she was referring to Wigapom, not Darqu'on.

For, as other eyes were again transfixed in shock and disbelief on the lifeless body before them; it was very clear that Wigapom was indeed dead. This was reality.

Yet Will was not dead; but how he wished he were. How could he live on with part of his own self dead? He knelt, rigid with trauma, by Wigapom's body, unable to comprehend what had just happened, even though he now fully recalled everything that the apparition of his mother had warned him of earlier.

'But I never thought it would really happen,' he kept repeating to himself, over and over.

Fynn, too, was beside himself with grief at the shocking sight of his beloved childhood friend, his dearest companion, lifeless before him! The Quest seemed to have no point any more.

Skye knelt by the body and tenderly wiped Wigapom's lifeless face with her fingertips as she washed it with her tears. How could this happen, when *The Book of True Magic* had been found and completed?

Sophie picked up the book. The pages were now filled with writing, the contents of which flowed permanently into her mind, even though she did not read them all. She clutched it to her chest.

Arcturus was the first to notice the wispy, transparent forms rising, like mist, from the immobile bodies of the Living Dead. He recognised some as his friends and colleagues, freed now from their physical prison and able to move into the light.

'Look!' he whispered, 'they're being released.'

'There's Merric,' said Fynn, confused at the juxtaposition of Wigapom's death and transfiguration of the lost souls.

'And Lucas,' said Skye. 'And there is my father.' Tears of joy flowed from her eyes as Aldebaran softly brushed against her cheek before rising up with the others. He was free.

They were all floating upwards towards the light that welcomed them into its loving embrace, going home at last. There were thousands upon thousands of them; men, women, children, all ages, all races. So many that they filled the sky, ascending into the light as a deep sense of peace began to descend. Despite the deepening winter weather, light shone through the branches and birds began to sing once more in the silvery trees. The sound created a rainbow, which arched gracefully above the trees and into infinity.

Yet no such wispy shape arose from Wigapom's body; no such spirit ascended. It seemed he had given his life and soul to set others free. Something, however, was appearing through the trees.

'It's the Unicorn,' said Sophie under her breath, as they saw the gracious creature coming out of the silvery morning light, through the bare trees of the winter forest, its white coat as pure as the driven snow that was beginning to fall to the ground like angelic dust. As the Unicorn walked closer, all saw its majestic silver horned head lower in respect to the scene. And despite everything, they marvelled. Its glossy, pure white coat shone as bright as the pure white light coming from the crystals in the book held in Sophie's arms.

The Unicorn first approached Sophie, who instinctively let it nuzzle her hand before they approached Wigapom's body together. The others backed away in awe, unable to assimilate what was happening. The Unicorn nuzzled Wigapom's body with its soft muzzle, the point of its horn first lightly touching the centre of his forehead where the area glowed momentarily with a deep indigo light, suffused with the shimmer of a million stars, and then the Unicorn's horn gently touched the weapon, still imbedded in Wigapom's heart, which vanished in a sparkling haze of silver white light. The Unicorn then touched the wound with the tip of its horn, and this instantly healed with a soft pink glow, whilst somewhere on a far distant tree a fresh green leaf began to unfurl to greet the light. Sophie gently placed the book on Wigapom's chest, lovingly folding his hands across it. It seemed the right thing to do somehow: an intuitive, instinctive act. The Unicorn whinnied gently in approval, and then pawed the ground, as though waiting. It did not have to wait long.

Through the trees, swooping low and shining brilliantly, flew the Phoenix, singing his glorious song. The beautiful sound suffused the air and the Phoenix's green eyes scanned the shocked, disbelieving crowd. It landed softly by Wigapom's side and spoke to them all.

'You believe you see him dead before you, but did you not listen to him? All is illusion, and death is the ultimate illusion. Have faith and trust. All is well,' and with those words Wigapom's limp body was lifted onto the Phoenix's back by sprites and elementals, which appeared from the earth, and was flown, along with *The Book of True Magic*, across the rainbow arc and into the sky, soaring higher and higher towards a white light that shone brighter than any sun, until it too disappeared. The Unicorn whinnied softly, its tender eyes watching until there was nothing left to see, before once more returning to the depths of the forest.

Skye could barely console herself as she clung to a distraught Fynn. They held each other as though the world had ended, rather than just begun. Arcturus and the others stood lamely around, lost and unsure as to how to deal with all they had witnessed. Darqu'on had gone. They should be joyful. The threat and terror had vanished, but at what a price! Only Asgar seemed to understand the meaning behind it all, but he kept his counsel and waited. It was up to Sophie and Will now.

Sophie bent towards Will, who remained crumpled on the ground, and raised him to his knees to look into her eyes. They were glistening with tears of emotion, compassion and love.

'Did you hear what the Phoenix said Will? This is not the end. It is a new beginning,' she said. 'Wigapom's heritage lies with you.'

'I don't want it!' cried Will, his voice shattering the silence of the forest, 'I am NOTHING without him! How can I even EXIST without him! He created me!' His tear-stained eyes scanned hers for some possible explanation of the unexplainable. Sophie spoke calmly, hoping he would be able to really hear her through his grief.

'He may have created you, but you too are a creator, as we all are, and over this Quest you have learned to recreate yourself. You don't have to rely on Wigapom any more for your existence, but can stand alone. You have proved that many times, I know.'

'I'm not sure of anything anymore. I'm in a wilderness,' Will replied, confused, lost and distraught.

'Then we will share that wilderness together until you find your way through. You are not alone.'

'I've never felt more alone in my life,' said Will, but he allowed her to hold him in his grief.

EPILOGUE

After the End

"There will come a time when you believe everything is finished.
That will be the beginning."
Louis L'Amour

Time passed and an existence of sorts went on in Arcanum. The land had been plunged into a deep, enveloping sadness at the tragic and unexpected loss of Wigapom: they had expected to rejoice at the arrival of their new King, not to mourn his death. The weather mirrored this time of grief: the hard winter months holding life dormant under sheets of ice and thick blankets of snow. The atmosphere was as restrictive and heavy as the dark clouds that swaddled the sky. Everyone seemed to hibernate, turning in on themselves, as though shutting off their life force; unsure of how to use it, or if it would ever sustain their growth again. All was sombre and lifeless.

Yet, just as the coldness of winter creates a space for regeneration in nature, so it did amongst those in Arcanum and as the snowdrops began to push their dainty heads through the thawing earth to greet the promise and hope of Spring, so did the citizens of Arcanum begin to welcome the opportunity for new life, new birth, new hope.

With the terror lifted, and the warming sun, the potential for joy was there to fill hearts once more. They began to rebuild the Citadel as the Temple of Wisdom and they began to look for another to take Wigapom's place as King. Who else but Will? They knew he was part of Wigapom – he was identical to him – but more importantly they respected him in his own right. Even Fynn and Skye had begun to suggest he take on the role that seemed to be his by right, but Will, although he listened, still resisted.

Sophie had remained quiet on the subject since that unforgettable day in the frosty forest, but her silent support and love was helping him slowly to heal. They had rediscovered that special feeling that both felt for each other as children and, knowing they were connected so strongly together, not only by the bond of Wigapom, but also the presence of Aimee and their

450

shared history of Darqu'on, it seemed to show completion, a blend of Light and Dark. Wholeness.

Yet Will had not grieved enough. Indeed there were times when he felt that he would never be able to grieve sufficiently for his loss; never be able to move on from what had happened.

But one early Spring day, when new leaves were bursting into life on the bushes and trees, he and Sophie took a walk on the hillside outside the city and two things happened to lift his grief, lighten his heart and help him and the whole of Arcanum truly live again.

Will and Sophie had been noticing the primroses and crocuses pushing their enthusiastic way through the grass and watching the busy birds gathering materials for their nests in anticipation of new life to come, when a young child they recognised from the city skipped joyfully towards them. Will stared at her, enchanted at her innocence and spontaneity, and allowing her joy of life to reach, at last, into his own heart.

'Hello,' said the young girl, 'I have a message from the Megadrill for you.'

'The Megadrill? Do you mean Annalid and Ollie?' asked Will, remembering that amazing creature who had helped them so much when Wigapom was alive. He hadn't seen the worm since it helped them reach Brakendor.

'Yes, it came into our garden and asked me to say 'thank you' to you – it's normal worm-sized now, you know, and has just had lots of babies. It wanted you to know how happy it is to be a parent at last.'

Will's heart skipped a beat. 'Really?' he said. 'Well that's wonderful news. I know how important being a parent was to the Megadrill,' and he looked at Sophie with love and light in his eyes. Sophie smiled as she returned his loving gaze.

'Bye, then,' said the little girl, having run her errand and now keen to play in the spring sunshine. They watched her as she waved at another figure on the horizon, before skipping away without a care in the world.

Will looked at the approaching figure, which became more familiar the closer it came, but he couldn't believe what he saw, although Sophie knew at once who it was.

'It's Wigapom!' she said, delighted surprise in her voice.

Will tried to deny it.

'He's dead,' he said.

'But it really is Wigapom!' cried Sophie. 'Look,' and she waved.

'How can it be?' doubted Will, but he looked, in spite of himself and saw the figure wave back.

'Anything is possible. Wigapom showed us that,' said Sophie, 'and it *is* him.'

'It can't be!' said Will, but Sophie was right.

Striding towards them, looking happy, healthy and whole, was Wigapom, just as they remembered him before the events in the winter forest.

'Hello Will. Hello Sophie,' he said smiling broadly. He was carrying the book.

'I don't understand!' said Will and went to touch him, but his hand went right through Wigapom, and he drew back his arm in shock.

'Sorry about that,' said Wigapom, 'but that's what happens. My energy is vibrating at a much faster rate than it used to when I was here last. But it doesn't make me any less real, or less alive. In fact I feel great! But I had to come back because *you* don't feel great, Will, and I needed to remind you of some things so that you can live out your destiny as I am mine.'

'Your destiny was to find the book and stones and bring back the True Magic,' said Will. 'But you're dead! I saw you die! I felt the pain!' And tears of something – joy or sadness – pricked at his eyes. He didn't know. It was all too confusing.

'And I did find the book and the stones and the True Magic,' replied Wigapom. 'I fulfilled my destiny. Now I have to pass them on to you so that you can fulfil yours. Death is nothing, Will, just a change of state. Nothing to worry about. I'm still here. Actually, I've become a Wizard where I am now, a real Wizard, based on self-awareness and wisdom. My role is to help everyone remember they have the potential to be Wizards too, and I need to remind you that *you* are one – we all are – remember what the stones said in *The Book of True Magic*? *'Wisdom is given as part of me'*? Well you are part of me and we are all part of each other, so we all have wisdom. We just need to access it and use it. Then we can all become Wizards. And you need to use your wisdom, Will, to be who you are meant to be. You need to take up your true place, with Sophie here. This land needs a new King and Queen, a new beginning, and that's you two. Don't you see the perfection in that? The best way to combine the Light and Dark in both of you, because they are One, you know, you can't have one without the other. You have an opportunity here to create a new, better and more holistic world, one grounded in the stability of the earth, whilst reaching to the heights of the spiritual sky of wisdom! Think about that possibility, Will. The Magic of it! What do you say?'

'I didn't see it like that before,' said Will, the dark shades of grief beginning to fall from his eyes to be replaced by the light of true awareness. 'I was too stuck in my sadness over you, but now that I've seen that you are still part of me – albeit a higher self, then I think I can, I know I can, and I will. In fact … *I am* … from this moment!'

Wigapom smiled, 'Attaboy, Will. I knew you would understand.' He passed *The Book of True Magic* into Will's hands, 'This is for you now. Read it, share it, live it and put it where it rightly belongs.'

'I will,' said Will, gazing at the book, now sparkling with the seven crystals.

'You're right, you know,' said Wigapom, 'I *am* your higher self and as such will always be with you. We can talk any time you want. I am always around you and I can be inside you, just as you were once inside me. What a great place to be!'

Will took a really deep breath, as though taking in everything he had just heard and seen and felt. Before anything further could be said, Wigapom transformed into a sparkling mass of rainbow colours, which, almost before he realised what he had done, Will had breathed deep inside him.

He felt his body shiver and shake as Wigapom's energy settled there, reaching every part. It was a wonderful feeling, yet he was also aware that it was all around him too, like a protective bubble of light, reaching into infinite space. It was everywhere – inside and out – with no restriction on its movement. He couldn't see Wigapom any more, but he didn't have to, because he felt him. He knew he was there. Finally, he could be at peace.

He turned to Sophie, light illuminating his face from within.

'We have a life to create between us,' he said, 'and a New Age to bring into being,' and he took her hand in his, 'Will you share it with me?'

'Yes, of course I will,' replied Sophie, her eyes glowing with love, tenderness, and joy.

'There's no time like the present,' said Will.

Indeed, there isn't.